"Isabel! It is I—

Isabel's nightma[...]

awoke. She realize[...]

middle of her dar[...] [...] Carlos Valverde

was kneeling before her. They were face to face.

Shaky from the nightmare, she fell against him. His arms went around her. She wore only a thin chemise, and the sensation of being nearly naked in his embrace made her almost dizzy. The heat of his body enveloped her. It was like a haven.

It was more. It was a surging, living heat and the pressure of his arms was a pulsing strength. She was aware of the hardness of his body, of the scent of leather on his shirt. She pulled away and turned, but the overwhelming power of his presence snared her. . . .

Isabel knew this was dangerously wrong. She was pledged to another man. And other warring loyalties demanded all her courage now—she had to save her father, unjustly condemned to death, and in her hands lay the fate of a bold English rebellion. But to succeed she needed the skill in arms of this ruthless Spanish adventurer. . . .

Suddenly his hands were on her. He groaned and pulled her backward. She sank, unresisting. She was on the floor and he was over her, and now there was nothing but the sound of his breathing, harsh with want, and the feel of him, and the yearning of her body. . . .

A Dangerous Devotion

A ~ Dangerous Devotion

by

Barbara Kyle

AN ONYX BOOK

ONYX
Published by the Penguin Group
Penguin Books USA Inc., 375 Hudson Street,
New York, New York 10014, U.S.A.
Penguin Books Ltd, 27 Wrights Lane,
London W8 5TZ, England
Penguin Books Australia Ltd, Ringwood,
Victoria, Australia
Penguin Books Canada Ltd, 10 Alcorn Avenue,
Toronto, Ontario, Canada M4V 3B2
Penguin Books (N.Z.) Ltd, 182–190 Wairau Road,
Auckland 10, New Zealand

Penguin Books Ltd, Registered Offices:
Harmondsworth, Middlesex, England

First published by Onyx, an imprint of Dutton Signet,
a division of Penguin Books USA Inc.

First Printing, July, 1995
10 9 8 7 6 5 4 3 2 1

Acknowledgments

I would like to thank Peter F. M. Jones for advice on legal points in the book, Dr. K. R. Borland and Dr. Joan Borland for advice on medical points, and Marie Blazic for advice on the Spanish. Any errors that may have crept in despite their help are mine alone.

My gratitude also goes to my agent, Al Zuckerman, for invaluable help in the outlining process; to Nika Rylski for an illuminating critique; to my editor, Audrey LaFehr, for her meticulous work and succinct suggestions; and especially to my husband, Stephen Best, who always reminds me that the whole point in making up stories is to tell the truth.

Mistrust me not, though some there be
That fain would spot my steadfastness.
Believe them not, since that you see
The proof is not as they express.

> —Sir Thomas Wyatt, the Elder
> (father of the rebel),
> from *Songs and Sonnets by the
> Earl of Surrey and Others*

Historical Preface

In 1547 the obese body of Henry VIII gave up its hold on life. During his tumultuous reign, Henry had defied popes, brought the sentence of excommunication on himself, and forged a national Protestant church—all to get a divorce. He had also wiped out a thousand monastic houses and dispersed their rich land holdings to loyal servants of the Crown in an avalanche of sales. Henry had altered forever the face of religion in England.

He left behind three heirs from three different marriages: Mary, age thirty; Elizabeth, age fourteen; and Edward, age nine. As the only son, Edward ascended the throne as King Edward VI.

The boy king was guided by councilors. These included such powerful Protestant men as Henry Grey, Duke of Suffolk, and John Dudley, Duke of Northumberland. Led by Northumberland, the government hardened into a severe Protestant regime that created strangling inflation through debasement of the coinage, siphoned off public moneys and lands to Northumberland's friends, and brought in foreign mercenary troops to ruthlessly put down unrest.

On July 6, 1553, Edward VI, not yet sixteen, died. His half sisters were his heirs, but a young great-niece of Henry VIII also stood in the line of succession: Lady Jane Grey. Jane was the daughter of the Duke of Suffolk and was married to the Duke of Northumberland's son. Northumberland immediately made a grab for power. He gathered a small army, bullied the royal council into acquiescence, and had his daughter-in-law Jane proclaimed Queen on London's main street. The people listened in sullen silence, for they stubbornly believed that a child of old King Henry's loins should inherit the crown.

Meanwhile, in Norfolk, Princess Mary was biding her time. Influential men started going to her side, and soon supporters were flocking to her. Northumberland could not shore up his position. The royal council switched allegiance and publicly proclaimed Mary as Queen. The people of London cheered, the Tower guns boomed, the city bells rang. On August 3, Mary rode into her capital, triumphant. Jane, the nine-day Queen, was imprisoned in the Tower. Her father, Suffolk, oddly, was set free. But Northumberland was beheaded.

The people were satisfied that the rightful heir was now on the throne. Many were anxious about Mary's rigid Catholicism, but England was ready for any change that would deliver the country from the spoliations of Northumberland and his cronies.

The change that came was Queen Mary.

PROLOGUE

>┤◆>─◇─<◆┤<

The Vow

New Year's Eve, 1553

Snow crunched under the feet of three cloaked figures—a queen, her lady, and a gravedigger—as they hurried along a moonlit path in Windsor Castle's lower ward. The gravedigger was pushing a cart that held a slab of marble, his pick and shovel, and some straw. When the trio reached the steps of St. George's Chapel, Queen Mary stopped. She turned her head, pushing aside the fur of her hood, and a gust of wind needled her eyes with crystallized snow. She looked back at her attendants. Was she wrong to trust them with this night's work?

The gravedigger lowered his eyes in deference and nervously tightened his grip on the cart's handles. Queen Mary had sworn him to secrecy. He shivered stoically and waited. The tall lady beside him stood pale-faced under the torch she held. She, too, looked anxious. But she did not turn away from the Queen's scrutiny. Mary smiled. No oath of secrecy had been necessary with Frances. Daughter of a noble family, she and Mary had lived together as girls and women, enduring years of adversity. They were both in their thirties now; both had waited a long time for their happiness. More than a lady-in-waiting, Frances Grenville was Mary's friend.

Satisfied, Mary beckoned the two to follow. She picked her way up the ice-crusted steps. The gravedigger's cart thudded up each stair, grating over ice and stone. At the top Mary pushed open the double wooden doors. Ghosts of snow swirled past her shoulders into the church as though frantic for sanctuary, and then instantly, as if overcome with relief, collapsed in powdery drifts on the stone floor.

Mary led the other two down the dark nave, redolent with incense, toward the altar where two candles burned. The torch behind her swept firelight over the heraldic brass plates on both sides of the choir, each brass—of lions and leopards, swords and crowns—commemorating a Knight of

the Garter, immortalized here for two hundred years. But
Mary did not look at the walls. She was searching the floor.
Her father's tomb was beneath this central aisle. Henry VIII.
Great Harry. Bluff King Hal.

Mary reached the tomb's marker on the floor near the
high altar. She pointed at it for the gravedigger. "Begin," she
said.

The gravedigger's iron tools clanged as he set them down.
Mary walked on toward the altar. When her back was
turned, the gravedigger glanced at the altar and crossed himself. Then he spit on his hands and set to work.

Mary knelt before the gem-studded great cross. She beckoned Frances to do the same. "You are my witness," Mary
whispered. She gazed up at the cross and was soon lost in
communion with it. The gravedigger's pick smashed into the
stone, but Mary's face remained still, as rigid in concentration as the marble saints watching her from their shadowed
niches. This time, the saints would see that she was doing
what was right. Once, she had known what was right but did
not do it. She had tried to withstand her father's torments
and threats, but he had crushed her, just as he had crushed
her mother; crushed all God's faithful here, driving the
realm into heresy and ruin. All to get himself a new wife, to
satisfy his lust. Defeated, Mary had signed his abominable
oath, acknowledging her mother as a harlot, acknowledging
herself as a bastard, betraying God himself. The saints had
watched her surrender. And seventeen years of misery had
followed, for her and for England. Seventeen years of heresy. But five months ago God had given Mary a miraculous
deliverance. He had brought down her enemies and raised
her to the throne. God had not forsaken her. He had made
her Queen of England. And from now on she would do what
was right, no matter the cost.

"I make this vow," Mary began, speaking to God, "to
honor the memory of my mother, Catherine, Princess of
Spain, who—"

A draft rustled the altar cloth. Mary stiffened. A breath
from her father's tomb? Her eyes followed its path as it
warped the altar candle's flame, twisting its thread of smoke
so that it snaked up to an oriel window overlooking the altar.
Her father had built the window for her mother in the first
happy days of their marriage, as a gallery to partake of Mass
in the manner Catherine preferred—privately, silently, de-

voutly. Mary stared at the window. It was dark and empty. Her mother was with God.

And her father's spirit, if it was here, came from the damned.

". . . the memory of my mother, Catherine, Princess of Spain," she went on steadily, speaking again to the cross, "who spent her life in devotion to our Blessed Savior. For my mother's sake, I vow to return this realm to the bosom of the one true Church. For her sake, I vow to take my cousin, Philip, most Catholic Prince of Spain, as husband. And if I fail to keep faith in all of this, may You destroy me utterly."

The Queen and her lady knelt for some time in murmured prayer. Behind them, the gravedigger hacked and shoveled, his labor forcing his breathing into grunts.

A last groan from the gravedigger and a final grating of stone told Mary it was done. She rose and approached the spot. The new marble slab the gravedigger had brought covered the tomb. On the cart, a dingy piece of canvas shrouded its contents. The gravedigger stood wiping his glistening forehead with a rag. Mary lifted a corner of the canvas.

"No!" the gravedigger breathed in shock. But Mary was already reaching out to touch the gray bones. Was she imagining it or did they give off a putrid odor, the very stench of degeneracy? She laid her hand on one. Its coldness sent a thrill of victory spiraling through her veins as if she herself had made the kill.

"Take the cart out to the cloister," she said. She nodded toward an aisle to the left.

The gravedigger pushed the cart out of the chapel. The two women followed. The cart scraped over the flagstones of the dean's arcaded cloister surrounding a snow-filled garth. Mary ordered the gravedigger to turn into a narrow passage close to the outer wall of the castle. Here the dozen canons of the chapel had their two-storied houses. But the priests were asleep. All was dark and quiet.

Beside a kitchen door a cat's eyes glinted in the moonlight. The cat stood still beside a mound of scullery refuse. As the intruders approached, the cat streaked away.

"There," Mary said, pointing to the pile of moldy bread, cabbage leaves, fowl carcasses, and offal—all sheened with an icy slime. "Dump it there."

The gravedigger's jaw dropped. A king's bones to be left out for the dogs? He did not move.

"Never mind," Mary sighed, as if to a child. "You've done enough. Go home to your bed." She motioned to Frances, who took out a purse and gave it to the gravedigger. He jerked a grateful bow at his liberation and hastened away.

"Frances, go in and wake Father Williams," Mary said. "Bring him here. A man of God must do this office."

Frances hurried toward the priest's house. When her torch disappeared, there was only moonlight.

Mary stood alone in the alley, staring at the cart. She grasped the handles and pushed the load toward the rubbish heap. She raised the handles high, then shoved. The contents slid out onto the scullery mess—canvas, straw, and grimy bones. A king's bones. Great Harry. Bluff King Hal. He could do nothing to her now. She was Queen. She would restore the one true faith in the realm, and she would bring the heretics to burn at the stake, as they deserved for their wickedness. She would marry Philip, most Catholic Prince of Spain, and make a holy, new beginning.

The priest roused by Frances arrived confusedly blinking away sleep, then became wide-eyed with even greater confusion when he saw the Queen standing in the kitchen alley.

Mary took the torch from Frances. Without a moment's hesitation she plowed it into the rubbish heap. The straw blazed instantly.

"Say the office, Father," the Queen commanded. "Tonight we are burning a heretic."

CHAPTER ONE

Ludgate

Isabel Thornleigh had treason on her mind. It was hardly the normal preoccupation of a well-brought-up girl of nineteen who planned, within the month, to marry the man she loved. But Isabel's upbringing had hardly been conventional. And these, as she reminded herself, were hardly normal times.

Isabel slapped her palm down on the open book her father was perusing at an outdoor stall beside St. Paul's Cathedral. "Father, we're late," she said. "We were supposed to meet Martin at the Belle Sauvage at noon. I won't wait for you a moment longer!"

Her father peeled her hand from the page. "Why not?" he said. "*He'll* wait. If he won't, he's a fool. And if that's the case, perhaps I shouldn't be letting him have you after all." He casually flipped the volume shut. "No, Martin will wait," he said with a smile of challenge. "Even if *you* can't." He winked at her with his one good eye.

Isabel felt a blush flare. She looked down, letting the furred hood of her cloak hide her cheeks. A stupid reflex, she told herself; no one was watching.

They were standing in the section of the busy churchyard where bookstalls were snugged between the cathedral buttresses and against the precinct's wall. The place hummed with the drone of trade. Men and women strolled and haggled. Sellers coaxed, buyers dithered. It was a clear, bright afternoon in the middle of January, and half of London seemed to be milling through the churchyard, energized by the reprieve of sunshine after ten days of snow, sleet, and fog. A scrawny woman on a donkey harangued the browsers clogging her way, shouting abuse at them with surprising vigor. A yapping spaniel chased a sparrow and almost caught it. But although the people all around them seemed enlivened and purposeful, Isabel was afraid her father would never move on. She watched, exasperated, as his gaze roamed over a set of Chaucer's works as if he had all the time in the world. "Besides," he said, leaning over to finger the spine of an *Herbal* with an exaggerated show of procrastination, "I can't go back to the inn without finding that volume your mother asked for."

"The *Cosmographia*?" Isabel asked slyly. She pulled from her cloak the very book. "I've just bought it for her." She held it up, victorious. "*Now* can we go?"

Thornleigh smiled, acknowledging defeat. And before he could muster another defense, Isabel steered him out of the honeycomb of stalls. But at the last one, a display of religious books and tracts, he dug in his heels with an extravagant "Ah!" of delight. Isabel groaned at the further delay. Thornleigh lifted the book that had caught his eye, a massive volume entitled *The Whole Duty of Woman*.

"A wedding gift, Bel?" he teased. He leafed through the pages, simpering and sighing in a schoolboy's parody of an ecstatic bride. More than six feet tall, looming over Isabel with his sea-weathered skin, storm-gray hair, and a leather patch on his blinded eye, he looked instead like a bridegroom's worst nightmare. Isabel could not help herself—she laughed. Loudly enough to make heads turn. The earnest buyers of religious instruction who glanced around were not amused, and that made Isabel laugh more.

Thornleigh chuckled. "Well, I can see this weighty tome is what you'd really like," he said.

Isabel saw his delight at teasing her glitter in his eye, its color mirroring her own eyes, cobalt-blue. She had inherited that from him; her dark hair from her mother. But there the similarity with her parents ended, Isabel noted with relief. She loved her mother and father, but they lived such quiet lives, so retired, so dull. She wanted far more from life. And with Martin St. Leger she was going to have it.

Thornleigh was pretending to stagger under the book's weight. "Hefty, though," he said. "An awful lot of duty here. We'll have to have it specially carted home for the wedding."

"I won't have time to digest it all before the date," Isabel said, still smiling.

"How's that?" He was setting the book down under the bookseller's frosty glare.

"It's in three weeks," Isabel pointed out.

"What is?"

Isabel rolled her eyes. "The wedding, Father."

Thornleigh looked surprised. "Is it? So soon?"

Isabel watched the mirth drain from his face and uneasiness flood in. She always thought of her father as a hardy, handsome man despite his fifty-five years, but this sudden wash of worry seemed to bring into unkind relief all his age and cares. "Father, what is it?"

"It's just that—" He hesitated, then smiled gently. "That you really *are* in a hurry." But his smile was fleeting. "That makes two of you," he murmured. "They say Queen Mary prays every day for good weather to send the Prince to her."

It was Isabel's turn to hesitate. Should she confide in him about the exciting, secret plans? No; she had promised silence. "Then the weather had better oblige soon," she said, retreating into her customary mild scorn for the Queen, "for she'll refuse to be married in Lent. Besides, she's almost forty, for heaven's sake. At her age, she *mustn't* wait."

Thornleigh laughed, his good humor rushing back. "Oh, yes," he said, "Her Majesty is ancient!" He grasped her arm. "Come on, let's meet Martin."

They pushed their way out of St. Paul's crowded precincts. Under the shadow of its great spire they headed west along Paternoster Row, which was equally crowded with strolling shoppers, gossiping priests, wandering dogs, and pigeons pecking at patches of brown grass in the trampled snow. Isabel and Thornleigh's destination, the Belle Sauvage Tavern, lay next to Ludgate in London wall, only a long stone's throw from the cathedral.

They went down Ave Maria Lane and turned the corner to approach Ludgate.

Isabel heard the mob before she saw it.

"Spanish papists!" a man shouted. "Be gone!"

"Aye, back home with you!" a woman cried. "We'll have no Spanish vultures fouling London!"

Isabel felt her father's hand clutch her elbow and yank her aside. Too late. From behind, a running youth thudded against her side, almost knocking her down. Ignoring Thornleigh's curses, the youth regained his own balance and scrambled on to join the angry crowd, about three houselengths away. There, on a slight rise in the street, fifty or so people had formed a ragged circle and were shouting at someone trapped in their midst. The people were so packed

shoulder to shoulder that Isabel could not see the object of
their insults and threats. "Father," she asked as she winced
at her bruised ribs, "what's happening?"

"I don't know," Thornleigh said. But his face had hardened with mistrust at the mob, and he kept a protective hold
on Isabel's elbow. More people were running to join the
crowd, drawn from nearby Ludgate on one side and from the
western door of St. Paul's on the other, making the scene in
the street even more chaotic. From the crowd's center Isabel
heard the frightened whinnying of horses and saw the steam
of horses' breath roil into the cold air above the people's
heads. Then she glimpsed in the crowd the top of a young
man's head capped with thick brown curls. "Martin!" she
cried. The head bobbed, then disappeared. Isabel broke free
of her father's grasp and ran forward.

"No, Isabel!" Thornleigh shouted. "Stop!"

But Isabel was already pushing her way into the dense
knot of bodies—men, women, and children—trying to reach
the spot where she had glimpsed Martin St. Leger, her
fiancé. She saw his face—was his nose bleeding?—but he
instantly disappeared among the shouting people. Was he
hurt? Isabel shoved her way farther into the mob.

A gaunt man beside her yelled at the trapped victims,
"Get you gone, papist pigs!"

Isabel was now close enough to see the objects of the
crowd's rage. The people had surrounded a half-dozen
horsemen, all nobles. Their style and bearing reminded Isabel of the Spanish overlords in the Netherlands where she
had lived as a child. Their raiment—brilliant silks and velvets, plumed hats, jeweled sword hilts—was a shimmer of
color above the winter-drab Londoners, and their magnificent mounts were caparisoned with silver trappings. But the
lords were in a panic to rein in their horses, which danced
nervously and tossed their manes and snorted as the crowd
hemmed them in. Beyond them, arched Ludgate stood open
beside the Belle Sauvage. Ludgate had clearly been the
lords' destination, Isabel thought. Or rather the route to their
destination; about a mile beyond Ludgate lay Queen Mary's
palace of Whitehall.

Again, she saw Martin. This time he saw her, too. Her
way to him was blocked by a huge woman clutching a child
on each hip and by men crushing in on either side. But Martin was plowing through toward Isabel. "Stay there!" he

shouted to her. But he lurched back as a man hoisted a club in front of his face, crying, "Down with the Spanish vultures!" This brought a cheer from the people, and the man with the club marched forward. Others fell in beside him. But a man flanked by two burly youths suddenly blocked the aggressors' path. "The Spanish lords be Her Majesty's guests!" one of the defenders shouted. "By God, you will not harm them!"

The two factions fell on one another. Other men barreled into the fray. Isabel saw fists swing, heard bones crack and men yelp in pain. She saw Martin watch the skirmish for a moment, his dark eyes glistening with exhilaration. "Down with them!" Martin yelled. Then he pushed on again toward Isabel. But he had barely taken three paces when a fist struck his jaw. Isabel gasped. Martin rocked on his feet, blood trickling from his lower lip. Isabel dropped her mother's book in the snow and clawed around the fat woman, trying to get though to Martin. Martin, recovering, was squaring off to fight his attacker, who had drawn back his fist to hit Martin again. But as the fist shot out, Martin was jerked backward by a hand grabbing the back of his collar. Isabel looked behind Martin. There stood the lanky, sad-faced figure of his older brother, Robert. Father Robert. A man of God, he did not attempt to engage his brother's opponent, but simply yanked Martin farther backward by the collar, away from the mayhem. Isabel could see that Martin, off balance and scuffling, was protesting—though whether to return for her or for the brawl, she could not tell.

"Isabel!" Her father's face, pale with worry, rose above the skirmishing men. "Take my hand!" he called. He was pushing forward, reaching out to her. Isabel stretched her arm toward him through the thicket of bodies. "It's Martin and Robert!" she cried as her father caught up to her. "They're over there!" She pointed to the mouth of an alley beside the Belle Sauvage where Robert had dragged Martin.

Thornleigh scowled. "Come on, then," he said. Together, they hurried toward the alley.

Seeing Isabel approach, Martin finally, violently, shrugged his brother off. "I *told* you she was out there!" He ran toward Isabel. "Are you all right?" he called to her.

"We're fine," she called back, running to meet him. As she reached him she saw the bright blood dripping from his lip down onto the snow. "Oh, Martin!"

He grinned. "It's nothing." But Isabel pulled off her glove and reached inside her cloak for a handkerchief.

Thornleigh was catching his breath. Here at the mouth of the alley the four of them were well beyond the fracas. "What in God's name is this all about?" Thornleigh asked as he watched the skirmishing mob.

"Spanish bluebloods," Martin said with a sneer. "The Emperor sent them to sign the royal marriage treaty. He can't have his son, the high and mighty Prince Philip, arrive before every 'i' is dotted and every 't' is crossed—and, of course, every royal post handed out to Spanish grandees. The arrogant blackguards act like they own the country already!"

"Hold still," Isabel said, dabbing the handkerchief at Martin's cut lip. He grinned at her, and she couldn't resist smiling back, thinking how handsome he looked, his brown eyes sparkling from the excitement, his thick unruly curls as shiny as chestnuts in the sun.

There was a scream. The four of them looked out at the mob. One of the Spanish lords' horses had reared, and coming down, its hoof had smashed a woman's shoulder. She lay writhing on the ground. As the jostled lord clawed to regain his seat, a boy darted forward with a snowball and pitched it at the horse's nose. The horse reared again, hooves pawing the air, eyes flashing white. The lord tumbled from his saddle and thudded on the ground. The crowd let out a loud cheer. As the lord lay thrashing in the snow, slipping as he tried to get up, a dozen hands grabbed his horse's reins. The horse was pulled into the crowd. Its silver-studded harness was stripped. A cry of victory went up.

Heads bobbed everywhere as people ducked to scoop up snow. Volleys of snowballs began pelting the lords. Shielding his head with his arms, the fallen lord hobbled toward one of his brother noblemen who swooped him up onto the back of his own horse as if they were on a battlefield under attack from French cannon. A snowball spiked with a rock smashed the rescued man's right temple. Blood spurted. The man's head slumped onto his rescuer's shoulder.

The horseman nearest Ludgate broke through the crowd. His sword was drawn and he was shouting in Spanish. Sensing escape, the other lords spurred their mounts and bolted after him. The people in their path scattered, several tripping and falling in the crush. As the lords dashed toward Ludgate a hail of snowballs drubbed them from the rear. The lords galloped under the arched gate and out to safety. The few citizens who had been resisting the mob gave up, turned, and scurried back toward the cathedral. The victorious faction, having won the field, crowed insults after the fleeing lords and losers.

Standing at the mouth of the alley, Isabel, her father, Martin, and Robert had watched it all. Thornleigh turned, running a hand through his disheveled hair. "Martin," he said sternly, "did you have anything to do with this?"

"No, Master Thornleigh, he did not," Robert broke in evenly. "We were waiting for you in the Belle Sauvage when we heard the disturbance begin. Martin was anxious that Isabel and you might be caught in it, and he ran out to see. In fact, he's left his hat inside, and—"

"Never mind that, Robert," Martin interrupted. He turned to Thornleigh and offered a sheepish smile. "Sir, I'm afraid you've come for nothing. The business friend I asked you here to meet bolted as soon as the trouble began. Sorry. Especially after I had Isabel lure you with promises that my friend and I would make you rich."

"I *am* rich," Thornleigh reminded him sourly.

Isabel had to hide a smile.

"Yes, sir," Martin said carefully. "But the Muscovy consortium my friend is organizing really is a fine scheme. Particularly for a Colchester clothier like yourself. The vagaries of markets you face, and all that. I mean, the risk you carry in your ships alone—"

"Martin," Thornleigh interrupted, "leave the Colchester cloth trade to me and stick to your family's wine business. Even in lean years vintners never suffer. He added with an anxious glance back at the still-excited crowd, "Now look, the Crane Inn, where we're staying, is not far. You need that lip seen to, Martin, and my wife has some excellent balm. And I'm sure Father Robert here could use a quiet half hour by the fire after this." He wrapped his arm around Isabel. "I know *we* could, eh, Bel?"

"Thank you, sir," Robert said quietly, "but I have another appointment." He gave his brother a severe look. "Stay out of trouble, Martin," he said. He bid good-bye to Thornleigh and leaned over to kiss Isabel's cheek. She whispered in his ear, "Soon, Robert, you won't have to visit Meg and your babes like some thief in the night. We'll make this Queen let priests live like men!"

Robert pressed her hand in thanks and gave her a wan smile. He calmly walked away toward the cathedral, leaving the crowd behind.

Martin shook his head. "Robert always thinks he has to watch out for me," he scoffed, but the affection in his voice was unmistakable.

Thornleigh was scowling as he watched the crowd. Some people were drifting away—women and older men—but most of the young men remained, cockily milling about after their triumph. Someone kicked a Spaniard's tangled horse harness lying in snow that was pink with blood. Not far from it were a citizen's cudgel and a scatter of iridescent blue feathers from a lord's hat. Two boys in tatters were foraging for the spoils. One of the boys whooped at finding a Spanish leather glove. Watching, Thornleigh muttered, "This was a bad day's work."

"Maybe not," Martin said, "if it makes the Queen think twice about the Spanish marriage." He gave the handkerchief back to Isabel. "And about bringing back the Mass."

"The Mass is the law now, Martin," Thornleigh said. He made it sound like a threat.

Isabel stuffed away the handkerchief, hoping to get both men moving toward the Crane before an argument could swell.

"Aye, it's the law," Martin grumbled. "And there'll be full-blown popery next, just as soon as Philip of Spain lands. And dumb dogs set up again in monasteries. And the Inquisition. They'll be burning people in our market squares."

"Don't talk rot, boy," Thornleigh snapped. Then he added, more gently, "The Catholics bought up as much monastic land as we Protestants did. They won't give it back, any more than we will. As for the Inquisition, Englishmen would never stand for it."

"Englishmen may not have a say in it! There'll be Spaniards at court, and Spanish troops here obeying a Spanish King of England."

Thornleigh sighed heavily, apparently unwilling to debate the matter. "All I know," he said steadily, "is that we've got to help Queen Mary find her way toward tolerance. In spite of what happened here, people are ready to support her.

They rallied to her when Northumberland tried to change the succession. We must—"

"Good heavens, sir," Martin cried, "you sound like the papists!"

Thornleigh looked the younger man intensely in the eye. "Some of my very good friends and associates hold to the Catholic ways. They wish me no harm. And I wish none to them. That's the only way to make this country work."

"Sir, I only mean—"

"Just what the hell *do* you mean, Martin?" Thornleigh flared. "You'd better think hard on it, boy. Because you're going to have the responsibility of a family soon. And if you think I'm going to let my daughter—"

"The book!" Isabel cried. She was staring at a man who was unconsciously trampling over the volume she had just bought for her mother. The man moved on and the book lay in the dirty snow, abandoned in the open space between the alley and the crowd. Isabel started toward it.

"No, I'll get it," her father said, stopping her. "And then, Bel," he added sternly, "we're leaving." He moved out to retrieve the book.

Isabel and Martin watched him go. Martin whispered to her, "Does he suspect?"

She shook her head, smiling. "Nothing."

"Good girl." There was no condescension in his voice, only admiration.

"It hasn't been that difficult," Isabel said, her smile turning wry. "My parents see nothing but their own little world. Father with his eye all day on wool fleeces and cloth bales. Mother with her nose forever in a book." She shook her head with disdain, then with vigor to clear such considerations from her mind; it was not about her parents that she wanted to talk. She looked at Martin expectantly. "Well?" she asked. She could barely mask her excitement. She wanted so much to be a part of this great undertaking with him.

"Yes," he said with a grin. "Sir Thomas Wyatt has agreed to meet you at our conference."

Isabel took in a sharp breath of delight and felt the cold air sting her lungs. "When?"

"Tomorrow afternoon. When do you leave London for home?"

"Not till the day after."

"Good. But will you be able to get away from your parents for the meeting?" he asked.

"I'll manage it. When tomorrow?"

"Dinnertime."

"Your house?"

Martin nodded.

"But is that wise?" she asked.

He smiled. "Most of my relatives have stayed on after Christmas, and with so many people coming and going at the house, it's actually the safest place to meet. And tomorrow's Thursday, so the family will all be trooping off to the bear garden."

Isabel smiled, too. She felt a thrill warm her veins. It was part exhilaration, part apprehension. She pressed Martin's arm, wanting to mark their communion in this great risk. Naturally, it was the men who would be facing the real hazards, but she was sure there was something she could do—arrange for horses, deliver a message, *something*. "I want so much to help," she said eagerly.

Martin covered her hand with his own and squeezed it. The look in his eyes was pure love. Isabel lifted her face nearer his, wanting him to kiss her. "You're wonderful," Martin murmured as their lips came close. Suddenly he straightened and laid a warning finger to his mouth. Her father had started to come back, batting snow from the book.

Thornleigh was halfway across the open space when a shout made him turn. There was the sound of horses' hooves galloping up Ave Maria Lane. Isabel and Martin turned, too.

"It's the sergeant and his men!" Martin cried.

Twenty or more horsemen in half armor were bearing down on the remnant of the mob. The young men in the street stood still, gaping. From the opposite direction a matching thunder of hooves echoed as another troop of a dozen horsemen from Whitehall Palace tore in through Ludgate, the pounding hooves reverberating under the stone arch.

"Run!"

The mob broke apart. People dashed in all directions. As Isabel watched, her father was engulfed in the swarm of fleeing bodies and converging horsemen. She saw a horseman's sword swing up and glint in the sun. It came slashing down. There was a scream.

"Father!"

She lurched toward him. But shouting men surged around her, stopping her. She was trapped. She caught a glimpse of her father's face, then heard another cry of pain behind and whipped back to look for Martin. But the swarm of brawny arms and shoulders swamped her vision. She could see nothing. A man's elbow jabbed her breast, and pain shot through her chest. She twisted around and saw a horseman's sword plunge down. She saw a screaming man claw at his torn ear that was dangling and gushing blood. She saw a dagger raised before her face. She dropped to her knees.

She scrambled blindly back toward the tavern alley, past boots and hooves and blood-spattered snow, the cries of men above her. She saw the tavern's brick wall and made it to the mouth of the alley and struggled to her feet. She twisted around to find Martin. But the battling men had pushed closer to the alley, and Martin was nowhere to be seen. Men ran past Isabel, shoving her aside in a frantic bid to get to Ave Maria Lane and escape the sergeant's horsemen. A horseman was pounding straight toward her, his sword raised and murder in his eyes. She bolted into the alley and ran. The high walls darkened the narrow space. A litter of garbage made her stumble and almost fall. Ahead, she saw that a lopsided hay wagon missing one wheel blocked the alley. She stopped and frantically looked back. The horseman had not followed her.

Someone laughed. Her head whipped around. Crouched on the back of the wagon, under a burlap cover tacked across its sides, were the two scavenger boys. The wagon was their hideaway. Isabel looked beneath their perch and gasped. They had hanged a black cat from the back of the wagon and had stuck one of the iridescent blue feathers in its ear. One boy grinned out at Isabel as he gave the limp cat a poke to set it swinging. "See?" he said to her with a leer. "It's the bloody Prince of Spain!"

CHAPTER TWO

>→←◦→←

English Justice

Carlos Valverde, the defendant in the fifth case at the quarter sessions in Colchester, Essex, about to begin, narrowed his gray eyes on the visiting circuit judge and channeled his intensity onto the man, willing his favor. Miraculously it seemed to be working, because the squat, thick-necked judge suddenly glared down from his bench at the opposing lawyer and said sternly, "Master Sydenham, this court has other pressing business. In view of the absence of the plaintiff, I must rule that—"

As though responding to the summons, a man pushed through the rear door and strode forward to his lawyer's table. The lawyer, Sydenham, stood. "Your Honor, here is my client, Lord Anthony Grenville." He added respectfully, "And we do beg pardon for the delay." Grenville and Sydenham sat. Carlos swallowed his deep disappointment. He was not surprised, though; miraculous things, he'd always found, were too good to be true. This was going to be war.

"Quiet in the court!" the bailiff barked. Grenville's entrance had caused a stir at the back of the room among the small crowd of observers, including a knot of family well-wishers who had been quietly congratulating a lady who had just won the previous case. The victorious family scuttled out. The remaining dozen or so people hushed.

Carlos was studying his opponent, Lord Grenville, a solid, florid man of about seventy, dressed richly but not fussily, with a thick mass of white hair and an impatient air of authority. Without speaking a word to his lawyer, Grenville sat back and laced his fingers over his stomach as if to say, *Let's get this over with.* It was the first time Carlos had seen Grenville, though the harassment had been going on for months through Grenville's agents. Carlos had had to sell his warhorse and all his battle gear to pay the legal costs; there was nothing left except the land. He had even been considering taking a wife, some wealthy citizen's plain-faced daughter; the plainer the woman, the bigger the dowry. Carlos had taken possession of the manor only four months ago, so his tenants' rents weren't due for another month, and God knew he'd needed cash these last weeks to pay Powys, the bloodsucking lawyer seated beside him. *And to buy this fancy cloak*, he thought wryly, looking down at the fox-lined, black velvet folds that draped from his shoulders. The extravagant purchase of the cloak had been a bid to appear the fine gentleman in court, as his new status as a landowner demanded. But he wore his battered, quilted-leather jerkin underneath and, as always, his scuffed riding boots. He could do very well without fancy clothes, but not without the land. The land was everything.

He shuffled his feet in the cold draft, pernicious as ground fog, and felt a familiar jab of pain in his right knee—the legacy of too many of his thirty years spent in the Emperor's soggy bivouacs. English winters afflicted his knee the worst. *Madre de Dios*, he thought, *how could a country be so cold and so wet at the same time?*

"Thank you, Master Sydenham, we now have a plaintiff," the judge said witheringly. "However, the question remains, do we have a defendant?" He looked hard at Carlos, then at Powys, the lawyer beside Carlos. Powys was a reedy man with wispy gray hair, parchment-colored skin, and sour breath. "After all, Master Powys," the judge went on, "I understand your client is an alien. Is that correct?"

Carlos stiffened. After six years in England he spoke the language well enough, but he feared a barrage of bewildering English common-law terms was coming. The law was terrain he had no experience in, and his ignorance made him feel awkward, exposed. He hated that.

Powys stood. "With respect, Your Honor, my client was awarded denization five months ago along with the grant of the lordship of this manor, a deferred reward for his exemplary service in the King's wars against the Scots. The affidavit from Chancery is before you."

"Denization? Of a Spanish mercenary?" The judge was searching for the affidavit among his papers. "Most unusual."

"Yes, Your Honor, but not without precedent," Powys said. "One Alfonso Gamboa, colonel, received denization with his grant of the lordship, manor, and advowson of the rectory of Stanmer in Middlesex, in the year—"

"Quite, Master Powys," the judge interrupted, holding up his hands, having found the document. "I said it was unusual, not impossible. I have no trouble accepting the veracity of this affidavit. And therefore the legitimacy of the defendant."

"Thank you, Your Honor." Powys sat.

The judge cast a look of skeptical appraisal at Carlos. "And how do you like it here, Master"—he glanced at his notes—"Master Valverde?"

Carlos felt a prick of caution. But he offered a crooked smile. "It is cold, sir."

The judge barked a laugh. "Well, I trust you will not find our justice cold!" He looked at his clerk for some appreciation of his wit and received the clerk's insincere smile. Both lawyers also chuckled politely.

Carlos swiped a hand uneasily over his head, the hair close-cropped like boar bristles, then scratched his stubbled jaw. He had no envy for these soft, book-wise men, but he knew it was they who wielded the real command in this arena. He glanced at the two bailiff's men who lounged, bored, against the wall near Sydenham, and he knew, with an uncomfortable conviction, that he had more in common with them. They were the brawn here, but not the power. The knot in his stomach tightened, a mixture of desperation and hope that had tormented him for weeks. He tried to scoff at himself; he had faced far greater dangers on the battlefield and survived. But that was just it. He'd had enough of battlefields. And the tantalizing taste of luxury and status he'd been given—and, even more intoxicating, the power of building something permanent—had sharpened his hunger to hang on to what he had, no matter the cost.

"Now," the judge said, suddenly all business. "The manor in question," he began pedantically, "is known as—" He scanned his notes. "What's its name, Master Powys?"

Powys jerked halfway to standing. "Prittlewell, Your Honor." He sat and glanced at Carlos with a tight little smile that said: *Our title deed is good. We'll win.*

"Prittlewell, yes," the judge said. "In the borough of—"

Powys jerked up again. "Rochford, Your Honor. By the sea." And sat.

"And the manor is comprised of ... ah, yes." This time

the judge had found the information in his notes. "Comprised of two hundred and ten acres of arable land and meadow," he read aloud, "and one hundred and twenty of heath. A windmill and a horse mill. Twenty-one farming tenants, of which eight have freehold tenure and thirteen have leasehold tenure. The demesne, I see, is chiefly marshland." He peered down at Carlos. "Good for livestock farming, that," he said informally. He smiled. "And horses."

Carlos liked this judge. They saw things the same way. After studying the good horseflesh bred and raised on the marshes, Carlos had already planned to expand in that area. Horses he knew.

"Well, then," the judge said, "on to the matter of the plaintiff's claim to the manor." He looked hard at the opposing lawyer, Sydenham. So did Carlos. There was something in Sydenham's bearing that put Carlos on his guard. The man was past the vigor of youth, not strong-looking, not particularly fiery in aspect despite his red hair. In fact, the languid ease with which he sat, absently flicking a trace of dirt from his green satin sleeve, gave him a sheen of effeminacy. But Carlos sensed that it was, indeed, only a sheen.

The judge went on addressing Sydenham. His stern look deepened into something resembling contempt. "The plaintiff claims title to Prittlewell by authority of a writ from the Court of Augmentations. Is that correct?"

"The manor was part of the estate of the late Duke of Somerset, Your Honor," Sydenham said in apparent acknowledgment. "Forfeited to the Crown at Somerset's attainder, the manor was deeded to my client in socage tenure."

"Quite," the judge sniffed. "Indeed, I note before me a paper drawn up by a clerk of that august body. However, this . . . document"—he sneered the word as if he were dignifying a notorious whore with the title of "lady"—"bears no date, Master Sydenham." He lifted the paper by a corner as if it gave off a foul odor. "It bears no witnesses' signatures. It bears no description of the manor. It bears no description of the manor's whereabouts. Can it, in all conscience, be called fit to bear this court's scrutiny?"

Sydenham opened his mouth to speak.

"Or even," the judge boomed suddenly, frighteningly, "to bear our *interest*?"

The court hushed.

"I can only reiterate, Your Honor," Sydenham said, "that the document does issue from Her Majesty's Court of Augmentations at Westminster which—"

"Master Sydenham, farts and belches also issue from the Court of Augmentations at Westminster, but I do not acknowledge them as jurisprudence!"

Sydenham looked down.

"Therefore . . ." the judge said expansively, shoving aside the papers.

Carlos felt a ripple of hope. Was this victory? He stifled it. *Wait,* he told himself.

". . . as I can find no claims outstanding against the defendant's lordship of this manor . . ."

Madre de Dios, it is true. The judge is ruling in my favor!

". . . and as I can see no other impediments to the defendant's lordship of the manor—"

"I beg pardon, Your Honor," Sydenham broke in. "But if it please the court, there is a witness I should like to call."

"A witness?" the judge asked, annoyed.

"I heartily concur with Your Honor's astute appraisal of the writ," Sydenham said. "It was presented by my predecessor, Lord Grenville's former solicitor. However, new evidence has come to my attention that warrants this court's notice."

Carlos watched Sydenham through eyes narrowed in suspicion. What he was saying about a change of solicitors was true enough. Lord Grenville had got rid of the last one a few weeks ago, and this man Sydenham had stepped into the breach. But Carlos now had the uncomfortable feeling that Sydenham had been merely waiting for his predecessor's tactic to be played out before launching his own fresh assault.

Powys leapt to his feet. "Your Honor, I must protest! What need is there to drag in a witness when the plaintiff's claim to the manor has been dismissed outright?"

Before the judge could respond, Sydenham spoke, fixing his pale blue eyes almost threateningly on the judge. "I humbly request that you allow me to proceed, Your Honor. Her Majesty Queen Mary, whose interest in seeing justice done throughout her realm has extended to Your Honor's own exemplary appointment, would surely wish it."

The judge cast a baleful eye on Sydenham. "Very well, sir," he said. "In the interest of the Queen's justice." He sat back with a sigh that showed he was exasperated but willing. "Call your witness."

Powys sat down huffily.

The witness was a thin, stooped, bald man. He was sworn in. George Hoby, farmer, leasehold tenant on the manor of Dindale. Sydenham pointed out to the court that Dindale was adjacent to Prittlewell.

Powys frowned at Carlos and whispered, "What's he here for?"

Carlos shrugged his ignorance.

Sydenham smiled at the witness. Hoby responded with a deferential nod. He did not look comfortable, but neither did he seem intimidated. "Master Hoby," Sydenham began, "will you tell this court of your actions on the afternoon of October second of this year?"

Hoby cleared his throat. "Took a pig to market. Came home for dinner. Went to the beach with Susan."

"And Susan is . . . ?"

"My granddaughter. She'll be six come Lamas Day."

"And what occurred on your way to the beach?"

"Came upon the new lord of Prittlewell. The Spanish lord, yonder," Hoby said, pointing at Carlos.

"Master Valverde," Sydenham clarified for the court. "And what did Master Valverde say to you?"

"Not much. He were busy putting up a hedge fence. It cut off the path to the beach. He said Susan and me should take the other path, the one round Pollard's hazel grove."

"So the path he told you to take passes through Dindale, not through Prittlewell?" Sydenham emphasized.

"Aye. Past Pollard's marsh. Path used to be all bog, but the Spanish lord's drained it all thereabouts for horse pasture. He said the path through Pollard's were a fair route now. Quicker, too, he said. So Susan and me, we went round that way."

"Now, Master Hoby, how long have you been accustomed to using the first path, the path through Prittlewell, to get to the beach?"

"Oh, time out of mind." Hoby pulled his ear, thinking. "At Susan's age I stumped along it with my grandfar's pa."

Sydenham turned to the judge. "In point of fact, Your Honor, Master Hoby's family has enjoyed ancient, customary rights of access to the beach via the path through Prittlewell. Master Hoby's ancestor, one Cuthbert Hoby, was

verderer of the Dindale and Prittlewell forests during the
reign of King Henry IV. In recognition of Cuthbert Hoby's
service in saving the King's life, the King granted the post
of verderer to Hoby's direct descendants in perpetuity."

"Saving the King's life?" the judge asked, intrigued.

"I believe the circumstance was an attack from a boar,
Your Honor," Sydenham explained. "I have here an
affidavit"—he glanced up—"dated and witnessed," he added
smoothly. "It sets forth the particulars."

The judge perused the affidavit and appeared satisfied.
"But, Master Sydenham," he asked, "what has this event of
some hundred and fifty years ago to do with the case before
this court?"

"Your Honor, for many generations the residents of
Dindale have taken the path through Prittlewell to collect
sand."

"Sand?" The judge turned to Hoby. "Is that what you
were after that day? Sand?"

"Oh, aye, Your Worship."

"For what purpose?"

"Susan's rabbit hutch. She's a good girl with rabbits, our
Susan is," Hoby added proudly.

"But Master Valverde stopped you, did he not?"
Sydenham said, bringing Hoby's attention back to the important fact.

"Aye. Pointed out the other path. 'Twere quicker, too, just
like he said."

"But he *did* impede you from taking the customary path,"
Sydenham emphasized sternly.

Hoby shrugged. "Aye."

Carlos threw Powys a look of concern and confusion.
What was all this about? But Powys ignored him, frowning
in concentration as he followed Sydenham's line of questioning.

"Now, Master Hoby," Sydenham went on. "Yesterday you
made a formal complaint to Master Valverde about this matter, did you not?"

"Aye."

"Would you tell the court."

"He were in the alehouse. I told him he should not
have"—he paused to find the word—"impeded me from taking the path."

Powys's head jerked toward Carlos. "You didn't tell me

this," he hissed in a whisper. Carlos bristled. Was he supposed to run to a lawyer every time a daft old man spoke nonsense in an alehouse? "Well," Powys growled, "Sydenham sent him to complain. I can smell it."

Sydenham continued his questioning. "And was there a witness when you made your complaint?"

"Aye. My neighbor, Roger Pollard."

"And what answer did Master Valverde give?"

"He said 'twere easier both for his pasture and for my Susan if we used the other path."

"So he refused to redress the wrong he had done you?"

Hoby appeared reluctant to go so far. But he eventually grunted, "Aye."

Sydenham told Hoby he was excused. Hoby walked past Sydenham, touching his cap to Lord Anthony Grenville. Sydenham, ignoring Hoby's exit, lifted a heavy volume. He began to read. The language was Norman French. Carlos could follow none of it. "What's he saying?" he whispered.

"An ancient statute," Powys murmured. "Basically, if a landlord impedes the progress of a verderer of the Crown's forest through a customary right of way while the verderer is acting on the commission of his duties, and if, after receiving complaint by the offended party, the landlord willfully continues to impede, the landlord shall forfeit his property to the Crown."

Powys had spoken quickly, and Carlos understood imperfectly the rush of English words against Sydenham's droning of the French. But one word hit him like a canon shot. *Forfeit.*

"But Master Sydenham," the judge said with a frown, "there has not been forest in Dindale for over fifty years. And the witness has just told us the child only wanted sand for a rabbit hutch."

Sydenham put down the volume. "Your Honor, Master Hoby and his family, as direct descendants of Cuthbert Hoby, hold the rights of verderers of the Crown. And a verderer, as you know, is responsible for maintaining order in all manner of trespasses of the forest, of vert and venison."

Sydenham's point dawned on the judge. "And rabbits," he acknowledged grudgingly.

"Brilliant," Powys breathed in spite of himself.

Carlos glared at his lawyer. "Do something!" he whispered fiercely.

The admonition seemed to rouse Powys. He stood suddenly. "Your Honor, I must vehemently protest this abuse of court procedure! Earlier, the plaintiff was claiming with his writ that my client did not legally own the manor. Now, suddenly, he claims that my client *does* own the manor but must forfeit it. This shift in the parameters of the case is insupportable!"

"But," Sydenham quickly spoke up, "Your Honor wisely saw fit to discredit the former parameters because of the flawed writ."

The judge frowned. "Still, Master Powys's point that—"

"Your Honor," Sydenham interrupted smoothly. He lifted a paper. "I have a writ of mandamus to present . . ."

"Good God," Powys whispered in amazement.

"What's mandamus?" Carlos demanded.

"From the Queen's own hand!" Powys shot back, wide-eyed.

". . . which I trust Your Honor will find satisfactory in execution," Sydenham finished. He gave the Queen's writ, along with the legal volume whose statute he had cited, to the clerk. The clerk carried them to the judge. The judge took the paper and looked at the Queen's handwriting with unabashed awe. "This writ," Sydenham went on, "gives title to my client, Lord Anthony Grenville, of all land forfeited to the Crown in this shire. By the events you have just heard related, the manor of Prittlewell is forfeit. It must therefore become the property of my client."

The judge stared at the evidence, clearly daunted. The court waited. Carlos's heart thudded in his chest. Something terrible had occurred, but what? The sick feeling of panic was alien to him, disorienting. He sensed only that he had taken a fatal blow. And that the lawyer, Sydenham, had delivered it.

The judge sighed deeply. His shoulders sagged. He put down the Queen's writ and sat back, a man rendered powerless. Carlos knew his land was lost.

When the verdict finally came from the judge's mouth Carlos barely listened. His eyes were fixed on Sydenham. Sydenham glanced over at him, then turned back to the judge. But Carlos had recognized something in the look. He had seen the same nonchalance in the eyes of a German Prince-Bishop he had once fought for. Following a murderous skirmish before a fortified town, the Prince had sat his horse on a safe mound, gazing over the strewn corpses of his own troops. "Eighty," the Prince had said. But it was not the dead men he was counting, only yards of terrain gained in the brutal advance. Sydenham's glance at Carlos had made the same cold-blooded reckoning.

The judge rose. The court rose. The judge left through a side door. The clerk rustled papers together. Grenville got to his feet, bestowed a smile on Sydenham that said he had expected no less, and strode out of the court. Sydenham moved toward the clerk to retrieve his legal volume. Carlos heard Powys's voice at his shoulder, a drone of apology—the words, to Carlos, a senseless mumble. Then Powys, too, walked out.

Carlos rose, his eyes still locked on Sydenham. Sydenham had killed him. Despite his haze of disorientation, Carlos knew that much: he was still standing, but Sydenham had killed him. And now Sydenham was bantering with the clerk and laughing. A self-aware, polished laugh, like a woman's. Something snapped inside Carlos's head, like a longbow too tightly strung. He started walking toward Sydenham.

Sydenham turned and saw Carlos coming, and the mirth drained from his face. He stepped backward toward his table, the backs of his thighs hitting the tabletop. Carlos kept on walking, stalking. The bailiff at the back of the room shouted, "Hoy!" at Carlos. Then, to his two men, "Stop him!"

One of the bailiff's men thrust himself between Carlos and Sydenham as a shield. All that registered in Carlos's mind was that the man was smaller and afraid. Carlos grabbed two fistfuls of the man's jerkin at his chest and shoved him aside like a scarecrow. The man fell, then scrambled away. Carlos was now only an arm's length from Sydenham's neck. Sydenham, trapped by the table, groped behind him for balance, knocking books and papers off the table.

Carlos reached for Sydenham's throat. But before his fingers could make contact, two hands from behind clawed at his ears and jerked back his head. Carlos knew it was the bailiff's other man. The man's knee rammed the small of Carlos's back, sharp as an ax. His arm whipped around Carlos's throat, clamping his neck in the crook of his elbow. With his windpipe on fire, Carlos leaned forward to break the stranglehold, but the bailiff's man hung on so that he was practically on top of Carlos's back. Carlos absorbed the

pain, knowing that to get to Sydenham he must shake off
this pest. But he saw Sydenham inching away along the edge
of the table—slithering toward safety. Rage exploded in his
brain. With a sudden savage burst of power, Carlos ran backward and rammed the man on his back against the wall. The
man's head thudded against the wall, then he slid off
Carlos's back and collapsed on the floor, moaning in pain.

Sydenham straightened and hurried for the end of the table. Carlos saw it. He was about to lunge for Sydenham, but
from the corner of his eye he saw that the bailiff himself was
now running toward him from the end of the wall, and he
had his dagger raised. Carlos responded instinctively, reaching for the hilt of his sword. He stepped out from the wall
to give himself a broader field of play for his weapon, and
the people watching lurched backward from the blade's
deadly arc. As the bailiff reached him with dagger lifted,
Carlos swung around, raising his sword and bringing it down
sideways, all his weight thrown into the movement, giving it
ferocious momentum.

The sword hacked diagonally into the bailiff's face. The
blade carved off half his chin. The tip sliced the artery in
that side of his neck, then ripped a gash through the cloth
and muscle of his opposite shoulder. Horror flooded his
eyes. His hand dropped the dagger and clutched the scarlet
pulp where his jaw had been. Blood gushed from the severed
artery. He thudded to his knees and looked at his dripping
red hands with amazement. Then he toppled. He was dead.

Carlos heard the commotion around him—shouting, scuffling, sounds of panic. But he was calm now, no longer disoriented. No man in this room could have killed so swiftly.

He swung around to locate Sydenham. But other men had
moved in around Carlos in a wide circle, and Sydenham was
not among them. The men's eyes were full of fear and aversion, as though they had surrounded a maddened wolf.

Carlos heard an icy voice inside his head telling him that
he had made the biggest mistake of his life.

CHAPTER THREE

>━◆━◇━◆━<

The Agreement

"Christ, Honor, don't you see that we've *got* to leave? You're not safe in England!"

Richard Thornleigh angrily slapped down his gloves on the table in his room at London's Crane Inn. It was the day after the mob's attack on the Spanish envoys, and despite the fact that he and Isabel and Martin had got clear of the scene unscathed, Thornleigh's anxiety over the incident had not left him. He and his wife had been arguing about it, and its consequences, as they returned to the inn after a morning at the Blackwell Hall wool market. In Cheapside they had passed a gallows where the body of the mob ringleader, executed that morning, was still hanging.

"You don't know that," Honor answered. "It was all so long ago, no one remembers." She whirled off her cloak, making snowflakes flurry around her. "In any case, I won't let them run us off, Richard. They have no right."

"They have the *power*! And, by God, this Queen will use it. She's dead set on bringing back all the terrors of the old Church. The Protestant priests here know it. That's why they're fleeing to the German cities, getting out before she strikes."

"Priests are conspicuous. I'm not a priest."

"You're a perfect target nonetheless."

"Not if I'm careful. I've already given Father Gilbert a generous contribution for the new parish cross and a pyx for Mass. He's singing my praises. He doesn't suspect I am, or ever was, anything but one of the faithful flock."

"And Anthony Grenville? Do you think you can buy him off with such baubles?"

"Lord Grenville knows nothing about my past," she said, loosening her hair to shake off some snow.

"Not yet. But we've only been his neighbors for a few months and he's already gathered that we're hardly the ideal Catholic family. That's grist for his mill. And now that the

Queen's made it the law to restore the Mass, how long do you think you'll be able to avoid attending? How long until Lord Grenville publicly scorns you for that in the parish and begins investigating?"

She shrugged. "I won't be alone. Half the parish won't attend. *You* won't attend."

"Good God, woman, it's not me they'll come after!" Their eyes locked. Thornleigh saw that she was not backing down.

There was a knock on the door. It opened, and a boy of about fourteen poked his head in. He held a lit taper. "Light your fire, sir?"

"No," Thornleigh said irritably, "go away."

"Oh, yes, please, Peter," Honor said to the boy. "It's cold in here, Richard." She moved away from him and beckoned the boy in. Thornleigh threw up his hands in exasperation.

The boy clattered with logs at the fireplace. Thornleigh walked to the window and looked out. The falling snow had almost stopped, but although a pale sun was struggling out from behind the cloud cover, some stubborn flakes still drifted down. In the street below, children squealed in a snowball war. On the church steps across the street an official had stopped a palsied pauper to inspect his hand for the brand that was his license to beg. Thornleigh turned back to the room. Honor was moving about, folding clothing for their journey home to Colchester tomorrow, and chatting with the boy. Was his mother's cough better? she asked. And had he enjoyed the city's Twelfth Night revels? Thornleigh watched her. Why was she willfully blinding herself to the dangers? Had the past taught her nothing?

The boy finished his task and stood, a robust fire crackling behind him. Honor thanked him and asked him to have Master Legge prepare dinner for three. Leonard Legge, the landlord, was an old friend of the Thornleighs.

"Oh, Mistress Isabel's not in her room, my lady. She said to tell you she was going out."

"Did she? Where to, did she say?"

"The apothecary's, my lady. Said she wanted sweetmeats for her nephews. I told her Sandler's makes the best."

"Well, in that case, dinner for two." Honor moved toward him with a coin, tossing back her dark hair as she held out her hand to him. The boy flushed. Thornleigh almost smiled, appreciating the boy's discomfort; at forty-four his wife was still a beautiful woman. The boy took the coin, mumbled his thanks, and hurried out.

Honor sat on the edge of the bed and looked at Thornleigh as if their earlier conversation had not been interrupted. *Good,* he thought. *At least she's not going to pretend.*

"Richard, you know how I feel about this. We've been through it, and—"

"And you refused to leave. I know." He yanked a chair over to the bed and sat, leaning forward in the chair so they were almost knee to knee. "But that was before Christmas. Things have changed. For the worse."

"Perhaps for the better," she said cryptically. Her dark eyes seemed to be testing him.

"No, Honor," he said harshly, "for the worse. The Queen will bring back the heresy laws. Burning at the stake for all who defy Catholic authority. It's only a matter of time."

"Last month you said she might not."

"Last month I still hoped she might keep to a course of restraint. And God knows I've tried to convince myself of her goodwill." He shook his head. "You should have heard me yesterday lecturing Isabel and Martin. Give the Queen a chance, I told them. She's showing tolerance, I told them. But the fact is, she's doing no such thing. We must leave England, now. Isabel and Adam, too."

Honor was looking at the floor. "And go to Antwerp?"

"Yes."

"Again." She said it like a declaration of defeat. "And start all over?" she asked.

"Yes."

"Again."

She raised her eyes to him. The sadness in them stung him like a rebuke. "You don't think I could?" he challenged. He was eleven years older than she. An old man, some would say, though he did not feel it.

She leaned forward and rested her hand on his knee. "You could, my love, and you would," she said softly. "Of that I have no doubt. But that is not the question here." Her eyes hardened. "I won't let them chase us out. Not this time."

So obstinate, Thornleigh thought. He looked at her tumbled hair, and imagined he caught the scent of lavender from it. He recalled the many different ways he'd seen it. Piled up like a milkmaid's as she hoed her herb garden. Glossy as ebony that night a few summers past when they swam in the moonlit pond after making love on the grass. Caked with filth that dreadful moment twenty-odd years ago when he had pulled her body from the hold of his ship. His heart had shrieked in his ears then at the certainty that she was dead. What courage she had shown in those dangerous days. Courage, he thought, and obstinacy. Honor did not change.

"So," he said, "we just sit and wait for the burnings to begin, is that it? Wait for them to come for you and strap you onto the hurdle and haul you to the stake?" Damn it, he would *bully* her into acting rationally if he must.

Honor sat up. "There may be another course," she said. There was controlled excitement in her voice. She went to the door to make sure it was tightly shut, then came back and stood before him. "Richard, you know we've been hearing the rumors for weeks. The city is crackling with them. But now I believe they are true. There *is* going to be an uprising."

Thornleigh straightened. "What have you heard?"

"At Gresham's goldsmith shop yesterday morning two apprentices were whispering that a dozen pistols were delivered the night before to a house on the Strand."

Thornleigh was unimpressed. "I know. To the Duke of Suffolk's townhouse. Calthrop was buzzing about it at the wool market."

"Really?" Honor went on with growing excitement. "And when I played cards yesterday at the old Marchioness of Exeter's, someone said the Queen should be careful the country does not rise up in anger, and the Marchioness went white and hushed her friend and said, 'Not a word of that!' And then, here this morning, a gentleman at breakfast said Lord Courtenay, the Earl of Devon, has placed an order with his tailor for the trimming of a new suit of mail."

Thornleigh waited for more. "That's all? That's your evidence of rebellion?"

"All?" Her eyes flashed irritation. "Richard, the Earl of Devon is planning an insurrection, and his mother, the Marchioness, knows it!"

Thornleigh shook his head. "Courtenay's just an addle-brained young fop. He spent too many years in that comfortable Tower cell. Not his fault. Old King Henry never could abide a kinsman to be out loose—not one with as much royal blood as Courtenay has. But since he grew up in that pampered prison, the poor dolt can barely even sit a horse. He never learned. A fearless commander of rebels? I think not."

"But he was the royal council's choice to marry the Queen—probably the whole country's choice. *Because* of that royal blood, and because he's English. And the Queen must have insulted him terribly by refusing his suit and choosing the Spanish Prince instead. Courtenay's a perfect candidate for conspiring against her, whether he fits your image of the manly soldier or not. And the country would rally behind him."

"Not necessarily."

"Richard, people don't want this Spanish alliance. The country won't stand for it."

"Talk is cheap. The country may not like what's happening, but the Queen is the Queen and the law is the law. People will grumble, then they'll accept. It's what people do."

"But what if, this time, they *don't* accept. What if they fight?"

"Then they'll become gallows fruit," he said severely.

"Not if they're at the forefront of a massive revolt—if enough people support them. *We* could. Perhaps by giving them money."

"Absolutely not! Christ, Honor, face the facts that concern us, will you? A harebrained uprising has nothing to do with us."

"It has *everything* to do with us! A rebellion could sweep the Queen from the throne. Princess Elizabeth is next in the line of succession, and she is no religious zealot. Don't you see? Rebellion will bring real hope!"

"And if the rebellion is crushed? Then there'll be *no* hope."

Honor answered quickly; it was clear she had given this serious thought. "Even if an uprising is put down, Queen Mary will at least have seen the extent of the anger at her policies. She'll have to temper her actions. She might *never* bring back the heresy laws."

"And pigs might fly."

"Stop it, Richard! Look past your cynicism for once. It's not just us involved here. Look at how many *others* will suffer unless the Queen is stopped. Can't you see how important this is?" Her voice had risen with emotion.

"With only one good eye," he said wryly, "I get a different view."

She shook her head, then looked away, struggling to compose herself.

Thornleigh came to her and took her by the shoulders. "I do not see this much, Honor. You're hoping that a gang of hotheads will solve our problem. But I won't put my trust in such a chancy prospect. The Queen is going to marry a ruler who believes with all his heart in the sanctity of the Inquisition, and in using the most hardened Spanish troops to pacify resistance. Once Philip of Spain lands in England, there will be no turning back."

"Turning back?" she murmured, her eyes misting. She smiled sadly. "Lord, Richard, how many times in Antwerp I wished we could turn back and come home! A pampered prison, you just said about Courtenay in the Tower. That's what our exile was. I'll never forget finally sailing back into Great Yarmouth after all those years abroad, and standing on the deck and pointing out to Isabel the native country she'd never seen. She was only eleven and she didn't really understand, but it was one of the happiest days of my life." She looked deeply into Thornleigh's eyes. "Richard, this is our home. It's Isabel's home, and Adam's, and Adam's children's. What we've built here belongs to them. This *country* belongs to them, as much as to Lord Anthony Grenville or even the Queen. I want to live here and die here."

For the first time, he saw how much it meant to her.

"Consider how much we stand to gain by this rebellion," she went on eagerly. If it succeeds and Princess Elizabeth takes the throne, it will usher in a new age of tolerance and we'll never have to fear again. And if it fails, the Queen will be busy dealing with the known rebels. As long as I stay quiet, no one will even look my way. There could hardly be less risk to us."

Thornleigh sighed heavily. He was far from convinced, but her arguments were beginning to make sense.

"Look, Richard," she said, as if pressing her advantage, "we can send Isabel and Adam to Antwerp now. That way, if you're right and we do see danger coming, they'll be safe on the other side, and the two of us can slip onto a ship at the last moment and join them. If, on the other hand, everything turns out well here, as I think it will, we'll bring them home—to a new, moderate regime. All right?"

Did she really not understand? "Honor, it's *you* who will be in danger, not Adam and Isabel."

"But in troubled times, innocents often pay for the acts of others. And Bel is a true innocent in this."

Thornleigh knew what she meant. They had always kept their daughter ignorant of their former life, for her own safety.

"So let's send them off immediately," Honor said.

"Agreed," Thornleigh said. This was a start, after all. "In

fact, I have the *Curlew* set to sail for Antwerp with a cargo next week, so they can take passage on her." Besides, he thought, Adam could begin scouting business prospects there right away. Thornleigh wasn't worried about that end of things. He kept a small residence and warehouse in Antwerp for the twice-yearly international cloth fairs, and he could sell the Colchester property through an agent. They'd be starting over, yes, but hardly poor.

"But *we* will stay," Honor said.

Thornleigh turned away. He paced, rubbing the back of his neck, thinking.

"If we do . . ." he began, but he stopped as Honor's face brightened. He held up a hand to check her enthusiasm. "*If* we do, Honor, we'll do it my way. No getting involved with wild-eyed rebels. We'll just wait and watch. Do you hear me?"

She smiled slyly. "Do you imagine me tearing into Grenville Hall, brandishing a sword and shrieking battle cries? Of *course* I'll be prudent. You worry too much."

"Someone has to," he grumbled.

She laughed. Then she said with quiet hopefulness, "But we *will* stay?"

"If I agree to that, you must agree to something for me. If no rebellion happens after all, if it turns out that there is no hope of change in England, then you will come away."

Her brow furrowed as she thought about this. "How long will you give me?"

He thought quickly. "Until the Queen's marriage. They say the Prince is on his way, but Lent is coming. The Queen won't be married in Lent. So that leaves three weeks. If there's no rebellion by then, we go. Agreed?"

He saw the struggle going on inside her. But finally she nodded.

Thornleigh felt as though a chain had uncoiled from around his heart. There would be no rebellion; it would be suicide for anyone to try. In three weeks he could take her to safety.

"Good," he said, pulling her into his arms. He brushed his cheek over her hair. Definitely lavender. "Isabel's out for a while, the boy said?"

Honor drew back, but only far enough to smile up at him with understanding. "Apparently for the afternoon."

"Even better." He began to untie the ribbon lacing at her cuff. Dinner could wait. He had not felt so happy in months.

CHAPTER FOUR

>─►◄─◦─►◄─◄

First Loyalties

Isabel stood under the lightly falling snow at Martin St. Leger's front door on Bucklersbury Street. The door swung open and Martin stood before her. His cheeks were flushed.

"Everything has changed, Isabel. We're leaving for Kent this afternoon!" He yanked her inside and slammed the door.

"Martin, what's happened?" In his eagerness, Martin was pulling her by the wrist, almost dragging her into the great hall, and she dropped the linen pouch of sweetmeats she was holding. She had just bought it at the apothecary's to forestall her parents' suspicion when she returned to the Crane. "Martin, stop!" He let her go, apologizing, and snatched up the sweets for her. Isabel had never seen him so excited. He was like a boy about to gallop off on his first hunt. They were alone in the great hall, but Isabel could hear men's agitated voices in the parlor at the far end where the door stood open. "*What's* changed?" she asked. "Won't Sir Thomas see me after all?"

"I don't know," Martin confessed, plowing a hand through his hair. "Everything's different now." He shot a glance toward the parlor. A man was pacing by the open door, talking loudly, though his words were indistinct at this distance. His doublet had been thrown off, and he paced in his shirt. A fit man, Isabel noted, perhaps in his early thirties, with a short brown beard and short straight hair. Was it Sir Thomas Wyatt? Someone inside kicked the door shut. "Oh, Martin, tell me!" Isabel said. "What is going on?"

Martin took a deep breath and again raked at his hair. "It was supposed to happen in several places at once, in about six weeks," he began. "Sir Peter Carew was going to collect a force in Devon, and Sir James Crofts was going to do the same in Wales. The Duke of Suffolk was set to raise up the Midlands. And Sir Thomas," he said, jerking his head to-

ward the parlor, "would raise up Kent. But this afternoon"—
his hands flew up in the wild gesture of an explosion—"we
heard that Carew has bolted! Sold his cattle and grabbed the
cash and fled in a fishing boat to France. And the foul
weather has cut us off from Wales—made the roads impassable for our couriers to bring news. And the Duke of Suffolk, he's gone, but no one knows where. He *was* here in
London. But this morning the Queen's council sent for him.
He told the messenger that he was booted and spurred, all
set to come to them, but then he tore off northward out of
London, his servants say. And no one knows where to. So
Sir Thomas says we must begin the uprising ourselves!
Now!"

"But why? What went wrong?"

"Courtenay, the Earl of Devon." Martin's look was murderous. "The Chancellor pressed him about the rumors, and
Courtenay blabbed. At least, that's Ambassador de Noailles's opinion." In mentioning the French Ambassador,
Martin again jerked his head toward the door.

"But why would Lord Courtenay do such a thing?" Isabel
was shocked by the betrayal. "I thought he was to be the fig-
urehead for the uprising. That his royal blood would make
the country rally."

"De Noailles says—"

"St. Leger!" a voice called, and the parlor door flew open
again. The man who had been pacing took a step out into the
hall. "There you are. We need wine in here. I'm parched
from all this jabbering." He frowned, noticing Isabel, and reduced the belligerence in his voice. "Wine, Martin, if you
please." He stepped back inside and closed the door.

"Damn, there's only a scullery maid back there," Martin
grumbled, already running off toward the kitchen. Isabel
heard his muffled call to the maid for wine. She looked
around the hall, so eloquent with the evidence of family life:
a mound of half-worked embroidery, a child's shoes on the
floor, a wooden horse with painted bells, a chess game left
unfinished. She knew that Martin's large family—his long-
widowed mother, his three sisters and their husbands and
children, his uncles and aunts here for Christmas—all had
gone off to the bear garden with the rest of the servants.
Martin was back in the hall in a moment. Isabel glanced at
the parlor door. "Was that him? Wyatt?"

"Yes. Look, Isabel, I've got to go back in. I'll try to get

him to see you. But the way things are . . ." He shrugged to indicate the unlikelihood. "But sit here and I'll do my very best." He took her hand and led her to a chair, shoving off a straw doll that lay on it. He pressed her hand ardently against his chest. "Oh, Isabel, if we leave now God only knows when I'll see you again!"

She leaned close to him and said, "When you've beaten the Queen and saved the realm. Then, come back to me."

He smiled, and his eyes spoke his feeling. He kissed her hand, then hurried inside. The door closed after him.

Isabel sat still, straining to hear the drone of the men's talk behind the door. Her eyes fell on the straw doll on the floor. Its head was twisted askew. A memory flashed in Isabel's mind of a night in Seville, lurid with flames, and a young Spanish woman, a Jew, slumping in her bonds at the stake as the fire was lit around her. She had been garroted—an act of mercy at the final moment in return for her denouncing her religion. Isabel, six at the time, had caught the sight only fleetingly before her parents had whisked her away from the horrifying spectacle, and she had not understood until she was older that it had been part of an *auto da fé,* the huge public executions staged by the Spanish Inquisition in their quest to exterminate all infidels and heretics. Soon after, the Thornleighs had left Seville and returned to Antwerp. But to Isabel, the sight of the woman, as limp and lifeless as this doll, forever symbolized the continuing horrors of Spanish authority. Its memory jolted her now.

She sprang from the chair, ran to the door, and pressed her ear against it to hear the men's stormy talk. There were several voices, edgy, conflicting, interrupting one another:

"This afternoon's impossible, Thomas! My sons are at Basingstoke and—"

"It's fine by me, Thomas, but I've got to have a day or two in Canterbury to round up the men I—"

"My brother and I can go right away," Martin put in.

"Go this afternoon?" a lost voice moaned. "Good Christ, I haven't even got a decent mount!"

"It's *got* to be this afternoon!" Isabel recognized this voice as the one that had earlier called for wine—Wyatt. "Look, the royal council doesn't know about us. Thank God we hadn't yet taken Courtenay into our confidence. But he's obviously blabbed enough to hand them the Duke of Suffolk's scent. All right, that gives us a little time. While they're chasing north after Suffolk, we can get down to Kent. But it's got to be *now*."

"Fine," the Canterbury man said resolutely. "My son and I are on our way. The moment word comes from you, Thomas, the men of Canterbury will march."

"Thank you, Walter! Ned, you, too. Godspeed you both!"

There was a brusque chorus of "Godspeed," and Isabel lurched out of the way just as the door swung open. The two men came out, father and son. Fastening their cloaks, tugging on their gloves, they did not notice Isabel. They strode through the hall, turned the corner into the screened passage, and slammed out the front door.

In the parlor a man was saying, "Thomas, it's not that I can't go this afternoon, but—"

"This afternoon, tomorrow, what's the difference?" This voice was gruff, older sounding. "Real question is, how in the name of Christ do we *pay* for this? Body of God, an army? Thomas, George—think of the expense, will you? You haven't the cash! Neither has Norton there—have you? Or you, Culpepper? None of us has. And that's all our men will want to know if we're asking them to soldier! You won't get—"

"Qu'est-ce qu'il dit?" This querulous voice, Isabel thought, must belong to the French Ambassador, de Noailles; Martin had told her that de Noailles spoke no English. His presence in this gathering did not surprise Isabel. The King of France was a notorious foe of Prince Philip's father, the Emperor Charles. The two monarchs had been warring for decades over pieces of the Italian peninsula. The Emperor, as King of Spain and ruler of the Holy Roman Empire, was lord of half of Europe and of the limitless New World as well, and France was his only real adversary; each was always angling for England's allegiance, or to set England against the other. The prospect of the Emperor's son virtually controlling the English throne through marrying the Queen had enraged the French. The marriage was an event they would do their best to prevent.

"L'argent, monsieur," Wyatt translated testily. *"Il dit que nous n'avons pas assez d'argent."* Isabel translated it in her mind: we have no money.

Noailles was saying that his king guaranteed them money. Money and troops. Isabel was glad now that her mother had taught her French.

Again Wyatt translated de Noailles's words for the others, but his impatience with this apparently ongoing chore was evident in his voice. "So never *mind* about money, Sir Henry," Wyatt concluded. "The Ambassador here has promised money, men, ships. In fact, the French are going to land a force in Scotland. The Ambassador has already outlined the plan to me, and he'll keep us posted about these developments. So—"

"Money, Isley?" a cross voice dug in. "We are setting about God's business here, to keep England free from popery! Money cannot be our thought. We—"

"I tell you," the lost voice groaned, "my best horse is lame!"

Listening, Isabel realized that there was no way Martin could suggest her participation to Wyatt. Not among all these chaotic concerns. She had to act now. If the men were leaving immediately, there would not be another chance.

She ran through the hall toward the kitchen and found the lone scullery maid ambling past the crockery-laden kitchen table carrying a tray with a pitcher and goblets. Isabel almost collided with her. "I'll take that," she said, and lifted the tray from the wondering girl's hands. She hurried with it back through the hall and stopped at the parlor door. She took a deep breath, turned the handle, and pushed open the door with her foot.

Fourteen faces turned to her. Fourteen impatient men. Their leftover bread and cold beef and empty pots of ale littered the round table. Their bulky winter clothing permeated the room with the smells of leather, damp wool, and horses.

"Wine, Sir Thomas," Isabel said, as steadily as she could.

Eleven faces looked away, accepting the intrusion of a servant, and resumed their discussion. But Martin came to her side. And his brother—she was surprised to see Father Robert here—smiled his support from across the room. Wyatt, however, eyed her warily. He approached. Martin introduced Isabel to him, adding proudly, "My betrothed, sir."

"I want her out of here," Wyatt said.

Martin bristled. "Sir, I would trust this lady with my life."

"Ours, too, apparently," Wyatt growled. "Out."

Isabel swallowed. "Sir Thomas, I speak French. I can translate your discussion for the Ambassador."

Wyatt looked startled.

"You can trust me, sir," Isabel urged. "I only want to help."

Wyatt hesitated. But he appeared to be considering.

"Sir Thomas," Martin said, "Isabel already knows the worst about us. Give her a chance."

Wyatt appraised Isabel. "Good French?"

"Le meilleur. Ma mère est une instructrice excellente." The best. My mother is an excellent teacher.

Wyatt thought for a moment. "All right." He jerked his head toward a finely dressed older man at the fireplace—Ambassador de Noailles, Isabel gathered. "Come on," Martin whispered in her ear. She felt his hand squeeze her arm in encouragement as he guided her toward the Ambassador.

"Norton, we haven't heard from you," Wyatt called across the room. "Will your tenants come out on such short notice?" He shot a glance at Isabel. She immediately translated for de Noailles. The Ambassador nodded, clearly pleased at this solution to his ignorance. Wyatt looked satisfied and turned his attention back to Norton.

Norton was gnawing his lower lip. "Look, my house is practically next to Lord Abergavenny's, and he's one of the Queen's most ferocious supporters. I wish you'd consider my position!"

"Your position is going to be prone on a French battlefield, dead," a young man poking the fire said over his shoulder, "as fodder in the Emperor's wars—and all the fighting men of your tenantry with you—if you don't rally with us against the Spaniards."

"With you?" Norton cried. "Christ, Brooke, your own father won't budge from his castle!"

Brooke threw down the poker. "He's sent George and me!"

"But kept well clear himself!"

"How dare you—"

"All right, all right," Wyatt said, placing a restraining hand on Norton's arm. "Let's fight the Queen's men, not each other." The two men looked away, mollified.

A burly gentleman said, "I want to know what arms are available." Several men answered about the stock of their armories. Isabel listened, then gave de Noailles the gist of the talk of swords, longbows, arquebuses, and breastplates.

"You know, Norton's right about Abergavenny." This was the gruff-sounding man who had been concerned about money, Sir Henry Isley. "He's a problem. But he's rich. I say we capture him. Hit him hard, first thing, and squeeze him for treasure. Then hand it out to our men-at-arms."

"No." Wyatt was emphatic. "Listen"—he addressed the whole group—"our declared aim is to keep out grasping foreigners. If we begin by robbing our own countrymen, they'll surely turn against us. And who could blame them? No, I'll not condone sack and plunder."

There was murmured agreement throughout the room at this. Even Isley nodded grudgingly and downed his wine.

For a while Wyatt fielded questions and Isabel kept up a constant murmur of translation into de Noailles's ear:

"Is there any word of support from Princess Elizabeth?" someone asked.

"I've sent a message to her country house. She hasn't replied yet."

"What of the Duke of Suffolk?" Martin asked.

"Lost contact. But he'll be somewhere in Leicestershire mustering a force to join us."

"Will our London friends stand firm?" Isley asked.

"Aye." Wyatt grinned. "You saw the welcome Londoners gave the Spanish envoys yesterday." There was a murmur of laughter. "And," Wyatt said, clapping a friendly hand on Isley's shoulder, "there'll be plenty of gold once the Tower is in our army's hands."

"God will not suffer us to lack for anything," another agreed jubilantly. "Our cause is holy!"

Isabel regarded the last speaker, a fiery young man. The look in his eyes reminded her of the Anabaptists in the Netherlands, the fanatical Protestants so hated by the Emperor—and massacred by him. As a child, Isabel had seen their heads on poles by the river, their eyes staring out with righteous wrath, even in death.

"Our cause at the moment, Master Vane, is to get ourselves down to Kent," Wyatt said coolly.

"Oh, I stand ready, Thomas! And all the fighting men on my estates. Our sacred duty is to put down the papist idolaters."

"Aye," another man agreed, "let's get the bloody Mass stamped out again. I'll bash the head of any man who tells me I'm eating a piece of Our Lord when I mouth a morsel of communion bread."

"Well said, Master Harper!" the fiery young man cried.

"We'll lead the whole kingdom against the whoreson papists among us!"

"That would be a mistake," Isabel said.

The room quieted. Isabel felt all their eyes on her. Her heart pumped in her throat. She hardly knew where her voice—her thought—had come from. But once the declaration was out she felt its perfect rationality. And a surge of power at having said it. She knew she must go on. "Spaniards are the enemy, not Catholic Englishmen," she said. "Tell the country that. Englishmen will fight to keep out Spaniards."

A log in the fire crackled in a small explosion, cascading sparks onto the hearth. In the silence, de Noailles, looking confused, whispered to Isabel, *"Qu'avez-vous dites?"* She whispered back to him in French. No one else moved.

Wyatt was staring at her. "The lady is a strategist," he said quietly. He turned to address the whole group. "She's right. We must not make this a quarrel to divide Englishmen, but one to unite them against a common foe. Vane, Harper, all of you—leave your fulminations against the Mass at home. Bring only your sense of England's rights against the foreigners. Bring that, and your courage, and we shall not fail."

"Bring your weapons, too," Isley added gruffly.

Wyatt laughed. "Aye, Sir Henry!" The others laughed as well, gladly shaking loose the tension of their hours of worry and indecision. "And bring every mother's son you find idly toasting his toes at the fire! Let's rouse 'em up! Let's go now, and be about it!"

The room was suddenly alive with the bustle of departure. Men gulped down the dregs of their wine, flung on cloaks, clapped on hats. They left the room in twos and threes, their voices echoing through the great hall, their boots clomping across its floor. When only a handful of men was left, Isabel stood looking at Martin. He had thrown on his cloak but was standing still, looking at her, too, his desire to get on with the fight warring with his reluctance to leave her. But Isabel knew he must go now with the others. And she would be playing no more part in this great endeavor.

"Martin, wait a moment!" she said. She hurried over to Wyatt who was standing near Isley, giving hurried last-minute instructions as he wrestled into his doublet.

"Sir Thomas," Isabel interrupted, "you will be down in Kent, but Monsieur de Noailles must remain in London, where I presume he must maintain an appearance of neutrality. You will need a go-between. Let it be me."

Wyatt barely looked at her as he fastened his doublet. "The Ambassador has plenty of spies on his French staff, mistress."

"But they will be watched now that the royal council has been alerted."

He turned from her to grab some papers on the table. "He has English informers, too."

"Who will probably slip away," she said, "now that the stakes are life and death. And of the ones who remain, can they be trusted not to mangle the Ambassador's meaning?"

Wyatt was stuffing the papers into a leather saddlebag.

"Sir Thomas!" She grabbed his sleeve to stop him. "Let me help!"

Wyatt looked at her with cold appraisal. "Mistress, do you know what the French say about the women here?" He removed her hand from his elbow and shrugged his arm like a cock settling its ruffled feathers. "They say English women are comely, but appallingly forward."

"The really appalling thing, sir," she replied, "would be to fail because you had refused a helping hand!"

CHAPTER FIVE

The Visit

"**O**h, bother!" Honor Thornleigh dumped her armload of shirts and books into the trunk she was packing at the Crane and answered the knock at her door. A well-dressed gentleman stood before her. He said nothing. He simply looked at her. "Yes?" she asked, somewhat testily. She wanted to finish packing. Richard would be back any moment from the wool market and he'd want to start the trip home. She glanced past the gentleman's shoulder to Isabel's door across the hall. Poor Bel; returning from the apothecary's yesterday she had been distraught at hearing they were sending her to Antwerp next week, and had suffered a sleepless night. Honor had taken one look at the girl's bleary eyes this morning and told her to go back to bed for an hour or two. But she must wake her soon.

"Honor?" the man asked hesitantly.

Honor turned her attention back to him. There was something familiar about him. The smooth red hair, gray at the temples. Yet she couldn't . . . Her heart missed a beat. Edward Sydenham? It did not seem possible! "Edward?" she said. Her hands flew to her cheeks. She had not seen his face in over twenty years.

Sydenham nodded acknowledgment, then stilled abruptly as if he were belatedly struck off balance just as she had been.

For a long moment they only stared.

"I heard you were in London," Sydenham said finally. "So I took the liberty . . ." His words trailed.

"Yes, of course," she said, recovering. "It's just that . . . it's . . ." She, too, fell silent, caught up in the wonder of looking.

"Yes," he said. "It's . . . odd."

The nonsense of the stilted exchange seemed to rush over

them both at once and they laughed. But Honor thought his laughter sounded uneasy. She knew hers was.

"Well, come in, come in!" she said. He stepped into the room. "Good heavens, Edward," she said, trying to keep the blame from her voice, stifling the impulse to slap him—ridiculous, after all this time! "I really thought—"

"You thought I was dead, I daresay."

"Well, I heard nothing from you. I mean . . . after."

"No. I thought perhaps you wouldn't want to. I did hear about *you,* though. Later. That you were all right. So I just stayed where I was."

"Amsterdam?"

He nodded, then said wistfully, "Far from home. For too many years." He gave her a tentative smile. "But I always wondered how you'd got on, how life had treated you. How have you been, Honor?" He glanced around the luxurious room and smiled. "Though I hardly need ask. I've heard, and I can see, that you've done well. And also," he added quietly to her, "that you are looking well. Lovely, in fact."

A facile compliment, Honor thought. With her sleeves rolled up and strands of hair straying from her *touret,* she knew she must appear like a washerwoman next to Edward's finery. "It seems you've managed things quite well, yourself," she said. She was appraising the blue velvet doublet, exquisitely embroidered with gold, under the cloak he had thrown back over one shoulder. The doublet's sleeves alone—blue satin fashionably slashed to reveal dollops of gold silk lining, like rows of golden teardrops—would have cost a journeyman tailor's yearly salary. Such an elegant transformation from the scruffy young man she had known! She was suddenly, burningly, curious. "Tell me everything, Edward. Where have you been all these years? What have you been doing?"

He laughed. "Everything?"

"Everything repeatable." She smiled, gesturing for him to take a chair at a small round table. But he did not sit. "Shall I call for some wine?" she asked. She felt awkward. Why was he here? Why now, after so long? "And . . . something to eat? The Crane makes a superb custard tart."

"No, nothing. Honor, I . . . I only want to talk to you." The earnestness, the gentleness, in his voice and face placated Honor in spite of herself. The old urge to shake him had already faded. Edward Sydenham. She had to admit that she was pleased, after all, to see him—if only to satisfy curiosity.

But pleased, as well, that Richard was out. Richard, she feared, would not be so forgiving.

"I was sorry to hear of your mother's death," she said.

He shrugged. "It was years ago," he said coldly.

"But my affection for that formidable woman has never abated. She helped save my life, you know."

"I heard."

"Your parents were both extraordinary people."

"They were deluded."

Honor knew when she was being told to drop a subject.

Edward gave a quick smile, as if willing its brightness to banish the cloud that had passed between them. "However, Honor, we both have made new lives since then. For me, it's . . . ah, where shall I begin!" he said with a mild look of exasperation. Clearly ready now to talk, he graciously held the chair for her. Even in that gesture, Honor thought, there was a world of difference from the high-strung, selfish Edward of old. And once she was seated, and he was settling himself in the chair opposite, she marveled at his movements, polished yet casual, like a courtier. What had happened to the frantic youth who had clawed at her to get out of the hold of Richard's ship?

"You think I've changed," he said, as if reading her thoughts.

She retreated into bland politeness. "We all have, I'm sure."

"Not you. But then, you did not have to. There was nothing in your character to be ashamed of. The brave and lovely fawn," he said with a smile, "can only become a brave and lovely doe."

She laughed, nodding at his gorgeous apparel. "And you have turned into a butterfly!"

His mouth smiled, his eyes did not. "But, before the metamorphosis," he said, "who can tell what the caterpillar, locked inside its dark chrysalis, must force itself to endure?"

Honor remembered how he hated the dark and small spaces. She did not want to edge too close to that topic. "Well, tell me about the *light,* Edward. For clearly it has been shining rather generously on you."

Finally, he laughed. "Quite true! And I have no right in

the world to complain. I am a lawyer, you know, and the law does not treat kindly those who complain without grounds."

"A lawyer?" She was surprised. "Where did you study?"

"Louvain. I've remained in Europe, you see, ever since I saw you last. Germany, for the first few years. Then Brussels. Brussels has been my base. I've done rather well there."

"In the law?"

"Yes. I've specialized in finance."

"How fascinating."

"It is. The people one meets, you know. I've arranged a loan or two for the Emperor through the banking House of Fugger."

His modest tone belied the importance of the statement. Honor knew from Richard's business contacts in Antwerp that the Emperor Charles had been taking out vast loans for years to conduct his ruinous but never-ending wars; his armies of mercenaries were cripplingly expensive. The transactions had made the family of Fugger the richest banking house in Europe, and any lawyer who arranged business between these two behemoths of power would be well rewarded for his labor. But why was he *here*? Why had he turned up, all of a sudden, at her door?

"And now?" Honor asked.

"Now, I've come home. To England." His face grew earnest. "Honor, I can't tell you the longing one feels, after years of exile, to return to the soil of home."

His candor quite disarmed her. "Yes. I know. I spent twelve years in exile myself."

"Of course. I'd forgotten. Where did you settle?"

"Antwerp. We tried a year in Seville. There's a large English community there, doing very well with the trade of English cloth to Spanish America. But there was such appalling persecution in Spain." She added with a small laugh, "I think Richard was afraid I might take on the whole Spanish Inquisition if we stayed. So, back we went to Antwerp. Oh, it was a good life. Richard—you never did meet Richard, did you?—he was very successful. Our daughter, Isabel, grew up there. And we still keep a house in Antwerp. But, well, I began to long for the old familiar sights. We came home seven years ago, when the Protestant regime here seemed secure. But, of course, in the last few months, all that has changed." She shook her head. "Dear old England—addle-brained, unstable nation that it is!"

"At the moment, it would seem so . . . yes."

Honor heard something in the hesitation in his voice. A testing? A probing? She felt a flicker of excitement. Could it be . . . ? She decided to probe a little herself. "In fact, there are rumors of great unrest," she said cautiously.

"There are," he agreed.

He was looking at her oddly. She decided to edge out a little further. "Some are saying it may lead to rebellion."

He continued to watch her face. "I have heard as much myself."

Had he, indeed? Was that what this was all about? Was he involved in plotting a violent change in England's government? This made-over man with the extraordinary connections? Was that the reason for his unaccountable visit—to sound her out? It would make sense, given the sensibilities they had once shared. Should she say something? No, Richard would call that reckless. He would say she should not show her hand. And he'd be right. After all, even to *speak* of rebellion was, technically, treason. Yet she had to know! But how could she find out without giving herself away?

The silence between them lengthened.

Suddenly he said, "Honor, do you know if any of our . . . former friends . . . are still in England?"

Had she guessed right, then? Had he come to her because she would know the people from the old days it was safe to approach? The ones whose loyalty could be trusted? But Honor knew there was little hope of help from that quarter. The only one left was Leonard Legge, the Crane's landlord. But she recalled that Edward had never met him, either. And she was reluctant to name Legge. She and Richard had helped set him up in business, lending him money to buy the Crane, and he had been an upstanding citizen for years; she felt instinctively that Legge would want no part in rebellion. She shook her head sadly. "There are none left, Edward. Some were caught. Some have died recently. Of the ones who got away back then, most settled in Europe, like us. Amsterdam, Bruges, Antwerp. I've lost contact, but I'm quite sure none ever came home." She paused. She knew she must be careful here. He had not actually *said* that he was looking for supporters. "I'm afraid you'll find none of the old faces except mine."

"That may be enough," he said quietly. He seemed to be struggling with himself about whether to go on. He stood abruptly and took a few steps away from her. His back was to her. He appeared to be fidgeting with a ring. "Honor," he said, "I am going to be married."

This was a surprise. "How wonderful," she said politely. "Do I know the lady?"

"Yes. I am going to marry Frances Grenville."

Honor was more shocked than she could say. The Grenvilles were practically her neighbors. Shocked, and something more. Honor knew that Frances Grenville was a lady-in-waiting to the Queen—the zealously Catholic Queen. A warning whisper shivered through her.

Edward turned to her with a knowing look. "I understand. You're thinking: Frances's father, Lord Grenville, is renowned for his rigid Catholic piety, while Edward is . . . not. But that was the old Edward, Honor. I've changed. I've discovered what's important to me."

Grenville's titled status? she wanted to ask. But she did not.

"And I further realize," Edward went on, "that there's not much love between Frances's family and you. Certainly, Lord Grenville can be a trifle overbearing. I hope to smooth over some of his rougher edges. I know, for example, that he has made some distressing public statements about you and your husband having no clear title to Bradford Abbey."

Honor stifled an annoyed retort. Last summer, after seven years of building a successful wool-trade business near Great Yarmouth, she and Richard had bought the old Bradford Abbey near Colchester to house their burgeoning clothworks and had built a new home beside it. Lord Grenville had harassed this enterprise from the very beginning. "The purchase was perfectly legal," she said, "but he is obsessive about it."

"It's his sister, you see. The poor old lady was once the abbess there and she suffered terribly at the time of the monasteries' dissolution. She refused to relinquish the abbey to the King's men, I'm told. They dragged her up to the abbey tower and . . . they raped her. She hasn't uttered a word since."

"So I've heard, and I am truly sorry for the lady," Honor said sincerely. "But—"

"I know," he broke in. "Lord Grenville seems to believe

that every non-Catholic who crosses his path is personally responsible for his sister's tragedy."

She shrugged. "Or perhaps he just covets our property for himself."

For a moment Edward did not answer. Then he said, "Honor, I've come to you to ask . . . a favor. You see, if Lord Grenville ever found out about my past . . ." He hesitated, flustered. "Oh, God, I know—who better?—that you have every reason to hate me. But, Honor—" He stepped close and caught up her hand. His touch was strangely cold. "I want to make a new life, here in England, with Frances. I want to come home. I hope that you, of all people, can understand that."

She did. Home. It was all she wanted, too.

He was pressing her hand, waiting for an answer, his eyes full of gentle entreaty. Honor was ashamed. He had not come with news of rebellion; only her overwrought fancy had made her believe so. Nor had he come to threaten her with his knowledge of her. It seemed, instead, that they must hold each other's secrets safe. No, he had come simply to plead for peace. *And,* she asked herself, *why should he not have it?* Who was she to stand in the way of his happiness? "Of course, Edward," she answered. "We're all civilized creatures, aren't we?"

Edward appeared extraordinarily relieved. And happy. Even his eyes were smiling now. Honor felt the pleasure of having bestowed a gift. "We really must share a glass of wine to mark this reunion," she said. "And Richard will be along in a moment. And I'll wake Isabel. You should meet them both."

"No, no, I must go," he said. "I'm to meet Frances for dinner at Whitehall Palace. The Queen gives her ladies so little time to themselves. But Frances and I have this afternoon together."

"Ah, then you must not keep her waiting."

Honor saw him to the door. "I wish you every happiness," she said. "And if you find me one day barging into Grenville Hall," she added with a smile that was only a trifle malicious, "and beating your future father-in-law about the ears, don't mind me. I'll just be smoothing Lord Grenville's rough edges in my own way."

Edward looked quite shocked. Honor had to stifle a laugh.

And she could not resist this tiny chance to needle him after all. "Don't worry, Edward, I shall be very gentle."

Across the corridor Isabel was pacing in her room. Her parents' decree of last night clanged inside her head like the bells of St. Paul's reverberating across London's rooftops. Antwerp! How infuriating it was—how unfair!—that they who lived so quietly, so annoyingly unstirred by the great events going on around them, should suddenly declare that the rumors of rebellion were too alarming, and that she and Adam must run to Antwerp. Did they think she was a child? Did they not understand that she would never desert Martin? Had they been *deaf* when they witnessed her betrothal vows to him? Their blindness to the central oath of her life had made her irate to the point of speechlessness.

But even while in their presence she had quickly realized that keeping her mouth shut was actually the best course; essential, in fact, if she was to leave home unobtrusively. Because Martin was not the only one to whom Isabel had made a commitment. Sir Thomas Wyatt was now relying on her, too.

Before they parted, Wyatt's condescension had vanished. But he remained skeptical.

"A woman go-between would be less likely to attract suspicion," Isabel had argued.

Wyatt looked at her hard. "The roads are rough, the weather foul. The going could be treacherous."

It was Martin who had assured him that Isabel was an excellent horsewoman. "I've seen her jump a hedge that many a man would have gone 'round, sir!"

And Wyatt had finally agreed. There had been a quick exchange between him and Ambassador de Noailles, who readily confirmed that he could work with Isabel. Then, Wyatt had simply said to her, "All right," and headed for the door.

Only then had Isabel felt a stab of uncertainty. The men were about to ride down to Kent, full of purpose, but what exactly was expected of her? "What shall I do, Sir Thomas?" she said, following them through Martin's great hall.

"Nothing. Not until we've raised the standard."

"But how will I know that?"

"Oh, you'll hear! You and all of England! Go then to Monsieur de Noailles. He'll tell you what to do. After that, mistress," he added pointedly, "we shall be counting on you." He started to go. Brushing past Martin, he said, "Bid her good-bye, my friend," and left.

Martin and Isabel stood looking at each other, both too full of feeling to speak. He took her face between his hands and kissed her forehead. Impulsively she lifted her face and kissed his mouth. He gazed at her as if in awe and whispered, "You're wonderful!"

And then he, too, had gone.

No, Isabel thought as she paced in her room while the church bells clanged outside, she would not desert. Martin, Wyatt, Wyatt's army—perhaps the whole bold venture—all might be hanging on her steadfastness. She would not be on her father's ship to Antwerp.

Lord Anthony Grenville reached the dim top step of a winding stone staircase in his house near Colchester and paused. An unpleasant odor had snaked into his nostrils. He looked at the wand of candlelight glowing beneath the closed door before him and shook his head. He knew that odor too well. The sweet stench of rotting fruit. Again.

He tapped softly at the door. There was no answer. He had not expected one. He opened the door. Inside the windowless chamber the smell was worse: a rank blend of decomposing vegetable matter, ancient dust, and urine.

But wafting above the stench was the faint, fresh scent of new silk thread. Grenville took heart from that, as always. He closed the door behind him, creating a small gust that made the flames on several white wax candles flare in their wall sconces. He smiled at his sister, seated in her chair and swathed in the soft white wool habit of a Carmelite nun. "Ah, that's a lovely piece you're doing there, dear heart," he said encouragingly.

Eleanor Grenville made no response. She was bent in concentration over her lace-making table, her long, white fingers winding the white silk thread around the maze of silver pins. Eleanor was fifty-seven and her hands did not move quickly, but they did move expertly—winding, tying tiny knots, snipping the silk with a pair of silver scissors. The fabric taking shape among the pins looked like a fantastic dry snowflake, a variation of the hundreds of soft white creations around her. Eleanor's handiwork filled the room.

Lace drooped from her worktable. Lace hung from the

four posts of her bed in the corner. Lace lay scattered on the floor like drifts of snow. Lace hung from hooks in the rafters, and the candlelight shining through its myriad holes made spangled patterns on the walls, themselves covered with folds of lace. Lace had been worked into swatches and frills; into caps, gloves, collars, and stockings; into shawls, chemises, christening gowns, petticoats, and capes—garments that seemed created for a race of ethereal spirits, for they certainly would not withstand the rigors of wear in human life. The room was a fairy cobweb of lace.

Grenville stooped over his sister and kissed her forehead. Her skin felt as soft as chalk powder on his lips. "There's news, dear heart," he said, rubbing his hands together with satisfaction. "That Spanish upstart I told you about is finally out of the way for good. Edward routed him in court yesterday. Quite a victory it was—a stirring show from Edward, I can tell you. I wish you'd been there to see him. I was proud."

As if he were not in the room, his sister lifted her head and examined the handiwork before her with the craftsman's frown of scrutiny. Drifting in thought, she lifted one finger, as tapered and white as an ivory crucifix, and laid it against her pale, pursed lips. Then she set to work again, carefully winding her thread among the pins.

Grenville unbuttoned his doublet and took it off, already uncomfortable in the eye-drying heat produced by three silver braziers in the room. With no windows, the space remained constantly hot. But that was the way Eleanor liked it, Grenville thought with a sigh. When she had first been brought to the house, he had given her one of the finest bedchambers with a large oriel window, hoping its charm would speed her recovery. But the view was of the neighboring Bradford Abbey's stone tower, and seeing it, Eleanor had mewed out a strangled scream, then shrunk into a catatonic stupor that had lasted for weeks. After that, Grenville had brought her to this closed chamber where she would not be tormented by glimpses of the world.

"Yes," he went on expansively, "Edward Sydenham is going to make a fine son-in-law. Frances has done well for herself."

He chatted on, moving about the room and performing tasks that had not been seen to in several days, for no one entered Eleanor's room but him or, in his absences from home, a quiet little maid; for two days the maid had been lying ill with a flux. Grenville collected decayed apples from under a heaped lace tablecloth, making a note to tell the boy who left the food trays on the outside step to substitute preserved apricots for the apples. He added scoops of coal to the red embers in the braziers. He ladled fresh water from a barrel into a basin, which he set on a trivet over one of the braziers. He swished water into the garderobe shute, washing its slime of excrement down the outside of the tower. He swept some moldy crusts dotted with mouse droppings into the coal scoop and scattered them onto one of the braziers where they hissed and shriveled.

"I do hope you'll feel up to coming to Frances's wedding, dear heart," he said as he worked at these tasks. "The Queen is showing us great favor, you know, allowing Frances and Edward's marriage to take place the very morning of the royal wedding. We are all just waiting now to hear what date that will be. But whenever it is, it will be a fine day for the house of Grenville. And Frances will want you to attend her, I know she will." He did not expect a response. He knew his sister would not come to the wedding. She went nowhere. She had not been outside this chamber since the day she had come into it from the abbey, fifteen years before.

Grenville picked up a silver-backed brush from a chest, and the warmed basin of water, and came up behind his sister and set the basin on the floor. Still at her work, she ignored him. He unfastened the white wimple that covered her head except for her face and gently removed it. He began to brush her long hair. It was gray and dry, but in Grenville's mind it would forever be the same lustrous, honey-colored mane that had been her glory when she was sixteen. That was the year their father had declared he was sending her to Bradford Abbey to take novice's vows. She had run to her brother's room in tears at the thought of leaving home, and he had comforted her in his bed and told her that she was privileged to become a bride of Christ, and her beautiful hair had fallen across his chest and he had stroked her in his arms until her tears had stopped.

She had entered the abbey and discovered her vocation. Twenty years later she had become the abbess and was supremely happy in her work for God. Until that day came when old King Henry decided to snatch up all the monastic lands for himself. The King had sent out his soldiers to do his unholy work. And that day, in the abbey, under the soldiers' knives, Eleanor Grenville had discovered hell.

As Grenville brushed her hair, still chatting of family events and the household, Eleanor slowly leaned back in her chair and closed her eyes, drifting in a dream of her own. Grenville came around in front of her and went down on his knees. He unfastened her habit. Gently he undressed her. Candlelight glinted off the white folds of skin at the base of her throat, soft with age, and off the harder, whiter ridges of scar tissue forming the huge obscene X carved between her sagging breasts. Grenville dipped a dry sponge into the basin of water. He lifted it dripping and squeezed it. Gently he smoothed the damp sponge over his sister's throat, her shoulders, her arms. She would be safe here, forever, in his home.

CHAPTER SIX

><+>-0-<+><

News

T he chained bear in the center of the crowded banquet
hall bellowed and swiped wildly at the smoky air. One
young lady screamed. Most of the gentlemen laughed.
Frances Grenville joined the laughter and glanced along the
head table to Queen Mary sitting under her golden cloth of
state. The Queen was beaming. Frances laughed again, this
time from sheer joy. Never had she seen her mistress so
happy.

The banquet at Whitehall Palace was in honor of the Emperor's envoys, who had stayed on after finalizing the wedding treaty, and the Queen had ordered everything to
perfection. The great hall was ablaze with torchlight and
twinkling candelabra. Gold and silver platters of food covered the three long tables, two abutting the Queen's to form
a squared horseshoe. There were creations of sailing swans,
baked and re-plumed; child-sized haunches of roasted,
clove-starred venison; platters of mounded, succulent rabbits
and quail. There were pyramids of Seville oranges, and
sprays of sugared violet comfits, and castles of quivering
rainbow jellies. Boys ran the lengths of the tables hoisting
jugs of the finest French Bordeaux, German Rhenish wine,
and malmsey from Candia. The musicians in the raised gallery were sweating, producing melodies, trills, and fanfares
that had taken the banqueters through dancing, then a
masque, and were now providing a thrilling martial accom-
paniment for the mimed drama with the bear. The tables
were packed shoulder to shoulder with lords and ladies, gentlemen and dames, all agog at the spectacle.

And no wonder, Frances thought. What a brilliant entertainment the Master of Revels was providing: a troop of
actors costumed as ancient warrior Britons in ox hides and
woad-blue faces, bravely defending the Queen from the rav-
aging monster, the chained bear. The lordly Spanish guests

of honor were entranced, their humiliation at the hands of
the London mob a week ago now forgotten. Even the rival
ambassadors were smiling—the Frenchman, Monsieur de
Noailles, with his goblet halfway to his thick lips, the wine
ignored in the moment of delight; and wily Renard, the aptly
named fox of an Imperial Ambassador, staring at the bear
like a child.

But, Frances noted, the chair of the Lord Chancellor,
Bishop Gardiner, was still vacant. Just before the mime began, Gardiner had hurried from the hall, called out by a
mud-spattered messenger. What business could be so urgent?
Frances wondered.

The mime concluded to loud applause. The actors left the
hall. The bear was led out by its handlers. Frances turned to
follow a twitter of excitement from some ladies near the
Queen. Lord William Howard, a plain-talking old gentleman
with a claret-colored face and heavy jowls, had leaned over
to the lady and gentleman next to him and was asking very
loudly and with a broad grin, "Would you like to hear what
I told Her Majesty just now?"

"Hush, my lord!" the Queen said, smiling.

"Well, if you want to know," Lord Howard blustered on,
"I noticed Her Majesty lost in thought. And so I said to her
that I wished His Highness Prince Philip was seated there,
right where you sit, my lord"—he pointed to where the visiting Count of Feria sat beside the Queen—"so that the
Prince might banish thought and care!"

Mary blushed to match her crimson gown, but she scoffed
mildly, "Fie, my lord, why should you say such a foolish
thing?"

"Now, now, dear lady," Lord Howard said saucily, his
jowls quivering, "you know very well you are not angry
with me. Are you, eh?"

At that, Queen Mary laughed with great good humor, and
so did all around her.

Yes, Frances thought, watching her friend the Queen, happiness brought out a lady's *real* beauty. The surface sheen of
prettiness so admired by the young courtiers could not hold
a candle to such radiance from within. Frances shivered, recalling a comment she had overheard at a crowded dinner
the day before in honor of the Queen's betrothal. An insolent
young puppy among the French Ambassador's entourage
had been jesting with his friends in a corner over goblets of

wine. They had been discussing the arrival of the Prince and his retinue of lusty Spaniards eager to taste the pleasures of England. "Wait till they see this churchlike court with the pasty-faced Queen and her scarecrow lady-in-waiting," the Frenchman had smirked. "The Spaniards will need stronger drink than this."

But, Frances thought, it was the Queen who was laughing now, displaying the beauty of nobility, showing the whole world how God rewards the faithful, the resolute, the loyal. Frances closed her eyes for a moment, warmed inside. If only Edward could be sharing this moment with her! For she, too, had been resolute; her devotion to the Queen, though an act of love she in no way regretted, had kept her single all these years. Until now. Anticipating her own approaching wedding, Frances's joy mirrored the Queen's.

Edward Sydenham was pleased. His legal experience had taught him that for every apparent impasse there was an expedient, a settlement, an avenue, an instrument, if one only took the pains to search for it.

Edward stood looking out the oriel window of the comfortable solar in Grenville Hall. The sunset view over the Grenvilles' ancestral demesne lands filled him with a deep sense of peace. Only the aristocracy, he told himself, could produce such order, such stability, such beauty. The snow-plumped fields and meadows, fringed with the tidy cottages of Lord Grenville's tenants and the neighboring tower of the old abbey, were bathed in a golden, rosy light, and protecting the fields, the still, timeless forest was drawing birds home to settle for the night. Home. Edward had become wealthy in Brussels and had sat at the tables of the highest and mightiest. But all of that, he now knew, had been no more than a labor toward acceptance here at home. The hell into which his Protestant parents had once plunged him, and all the lonely years of exile that had followed, could finally be eradicated. He could never completely forget the suffering—especially that day, over twenty years ago, when he had reached his impoverished mother's house after escaping the Bishop's lockup, only to see his mother's face harden at the sight of him; his "duty" in her eyes had been to die for the greater glory of Christ, as his father had, not to live and prosper. But *this* would be a vindication. In marrying Frances Grenville he would be setting roots deep down into the richest, the most permanent, the most traditional English soil. It would make up for everything.

He turned from the window and strolled back to a rosewood table by the fire. On it lay an ebony box, a gift from Lord Grenville to Edward in recognition of his success in court last week against the Spaniard. Edward lifted the box's hinged lid. Resting in two red velvet, upholstered wells lay twin wheel-lock pistols. They were finely crafted, their barrels scrolled with leafy engraving, their butts rounded into carved balls of ivory. Pistols were still rare in England; only wealthy aficionados owned them, using them sometimes for hunting, but mostly for show. Edward grimaced slightly as he studied them. He appreciated the mastery of the German craftsmanship, but blood sports were not to his taste. Still, Lord Grenville's gesture was a decent one; Edward knew the gift had been made in thanks for more than just his victory in court. Lord Grenville, though rich in land, had found himself strapped for cash in recent months, and Edward had advanced his future father-in-law a substantial personal loan. Edward closed the box thoughtfully, fingering its smooth black lid. It bothered him not at all that his wealth was the factor that had won him his suit for Frances. It seemed, in fact, a very comfortable bargain: his money for the Grenville name.

"Ah, there you are," Lord Grenville said.

Edward looked up and smiled. Anthony Grenville, holding open the door for his wife who drifted in after him, had carried his goblet of wine up with him from supper in the hall. Both of them had come to the solar at Edward's request. "Well, what's this about?" Lord Grenville asked, closing the door.

"Yes, why all the mystery, Edward?" Maud Grenville asked, picking up her embroidery hoop from her chair by the fire. An elegant, trim woman of sixty-eight whose smooth face belied her status as a great-grandmother, Lady Grenville sat and began plying her needle and silk as though unconcerned by Edward's summons. But her shrewd eyes darted up at him, betraying her keen curiosity.

"No mystery, my lady," Edward said pleasantly. "Rather, a remedy. A tool, as it were, to pluck a thorn from Lord Grenville's side."

"Which thorn is that?" Grenville asked, and added gruffly,

"Seems were tramping through a whole thicket of 'em these days, what with all these rumors of unrest. I need a scythe."

"Anthony, don't be ungrateful. Look how he got Prittlewell manor back for you. That *was* clever, Edward." Lady Grenville bestowed a smile of approval that had been perfected on eager children and grandchildren.

Edward made a small, gallant bow. "But Frances must be commended, too, my lady," he said. "Her friendship with the Queen secured the royal writ of mandamus, an essential piece of the strategy."

"But the cleverness was all yours," Maud said magnanimously.

"Ha! So it was!" Grenville said with relish. "That Spanish lout never knew what hit him. And now he'll hang before he can figure it out! Ha!" He had moved toward the rosewood table and was eyeing one of the objects beside the pistol box, gifts that Edward had earlier presented to the family: an exquisite Florentine gold salt cellar in the shape of Apollo pursuing Daphne and a rare, illuminated manuscript of Erasmus's *Praise of Folly*. It was the salt cellar that had caught Grenville's eye, and he idly bumped his thick finger over the faintly erotic piece. The irony was not lost on Edward—he was, in fact, amused at the realization—that each man had given gifts he would like to have received himself.

Grenville suddenly gulped his wine, thumped down the goblet, and clapped his hands together, an impatient host. "Come now, let's hear what's on your mind, Edward. Family prayers in a quarter hour, you know. I won't have Father Roland waiting on us in chapel."

Edward knew. The family chapel, the household chaplain—they were all part of Lord Grenville's rigid standard of piety. That was Edward's problem. Any other father-in-law, were he to discover Edward's past, might forgive and forget. But not Lord Anthony Grenville. He would burn down his own house with his daughter in it before he would allow a once-hunted heretic Protestant to befoul his family.

"I understand, my lord," Edward agreed deferentially. "This won't take but a moment." He glanced a last time at the soul-enriching view: the forest . . . the abbey tower. He was taking a gamble, but it must be done.

He smiled at the couple. "The thorn I was referring to is the family of Thornleigh, your neighbors."

"Blackguards," Lord Grenville growled. "You'll be doing a good deed if you can clear *them* off." His wife, too, sniffed her disgust.

"Precisely what I have in mind, my lord," Edward said.

"Oh?" Grenville was interested now.

"I believe, my lord, you are unaware of their past crimes."

"I'm aware of their *present* crimes, damn their eyes! Setting up their weavers with their infernal looms in the very heart of the abbey! The very choir! Where my sister once devoted her life to God! May He strike them down for their blasphemy!"

"Indeed, my lord," Edward muttered. The Thornleighs' commercial use of the abbey, Edward knew, was perfectly legal. Grenville knew it, too. Throughout England, seventeen years ago, the monasteries had been sold by King Henry to the land-hungry gentry. They, in turn, had resold the buildings or knocked them down or converted them into homes and workshops. It was a common practice, but Lord Grenville would always see it as a crime. "However," Edward went on, "I was referring to the Thornleighs' crimes of twenty years ago. Believe me they have done far more wicked things than those you are witnessing at the abbey. Particularly Honor Thornleigh."

Lord Grenville waited, his brow furrowed in anticipation. Lady Grenville had laid down her embroidery, her curiosity now frankly displayed. Edward knew he had them both. Yet he suffered a pang of misgiving. He could not relish this task. If only Honor had settled anywhere but here! Her openness at their meeting in London the week before had touched him. She had so trustingly told him exactly what he needed to know: that none of the old faces were left in England. None but the Thornleighs. And they lived too nearby. Neighbors. The risk was too great.

He began. "In the time of the late King Henry . . ."

He told the story. Birds darted across the meadows to the safety of the forest. The sun's slanting violet rays deepened into a red wash that engulfed the fields and gleamed in a bloodred square of window at Edward's back as he related the facts, dispassionately, thoroughly. The only fact he was careful to omit was his own involvement in the work of those dangerous days. That, the Grenvilles must never find out.

* * *

"Rebellion, Your Majesty! Worse than ever we feared!" Bishop Gardiner's voice sounded bleak in the withdrawing room above the noisy banqueting hall. The dimly lit room was empty but for the Bishop and the Queen and Frances Grenville. Gardiner was a toughened, seventy-year-old veteran of three chaotic reigns, but Frances distinctly heard the quaver of fear in his voice as he repeated, "Rebellion! Full-blown and foul!"

"Treason, my lord," the Queen said as if correcting him, "punishable by death." She sounded calm, but her face had gone white. "Tell me all. Who is their leader?"

"Sir Thomas Wyatt, but there are—"

"Wyatt? The son of the late poet?"

"Yes. His seat is Alington, in Kent, but the alarm comes from Maidstone market where—"

"How many are with him?"

"God knows, madam!" Gardiner burst out, close to fury at her interruptions. A wave of laughter crested from the banqueters below in the hall, as if in mockery of Gardiner's dreadful lapse from courtesy. He tried to compose himself. Sweat sheened his forehead. "However, it appears that Wyatt has most of the gentlemen of Kent behind him. My messenger reported Sir Henry Isley and William Knevett and Lord Cobham's two sons, all standing with him. And there are more, Your Majesty, many more. I said it would be so!"

"And what of their host?"

"At least two thousand men!" Gardiner's voice rose despite his effort to remain calm. "And that is just from Maidstone market!"

"The market?" The Queen blinked as if confused. Frances, too, was unnerved. She wished the Bishop would stop shouting.

"Great heavens, madam, did you not hear what I said? Wyatt raised his standard today in the marketplace at Maidstone!"

"I heard, my lord. You said—"

"He made a proclamation that Englishmen should rally with him to keep out the Spaniards! And two thousand men joined him on the spot!" Again the Bishop paused to collect himself. But when he spoke, desperation blazed from his eyes. "Your Majesty, this is most dire. You *must* reconsider."

"Reconsider, my lord? Reconsider what?"

"The marriage, the marriage! It is offense to the marriage

that has sparked this revolt! I warned you it would be so, madam! And now, look what—"

The door swung open. Three men of the royal council hurried in: Lord Paulet, the Earl of Pembroke, and the old Duke of Norfolk. A single candle on the side table—the only light in the room when Frances and the Queen had followed the Bishop here—cast a stark light over their strained faces. They had heard the news, Frances realized. The Bishop's muddy messenger at the door would have told them. She stepped back to a sideboard in the shadows to search for more candles.

"Is it true?" Pembroke shouted to Gardiner. Pembroke was a big, bony man, a seasoned soldier. Frances caught the Queen's slight flinch at his addressing the Bishop, not her. Pembroke had been a leader in the previous Protestant regime, and the Queen barely trusted him. But he was powerful in the west, so she could not afford to alienate him.

"It is," the Bishop acknowledged grimly.

"And the marriage is their grievance?" Pembroke asked. The Bishop nodded.

"Her Majesty," Pembroke said severely, "should have taken notice of the Commons' petition."

"I have just been telling Her Majesty that."

The Queen said nothing. Under the men's angry gaze she lowered her eyes like a scolded child.

"The Commons made it plain," Pembroke went on. "Before Christmas even, they—"

"Blast the Commons!" the Duke of Norfolk huffed. "And blast your eyes, Herbert, for speaking to Her Majesty in this craven way!" Frances inwardly blessed the old man.

"Your Grace," the Bishop said, his deference to the Duke strained, "the question is not what we should have done at Christmas but what we can do now."

"Trounce 'em!" the Duke said. "Crush 'em!" He lifted an age-spotted hand, snapped it into a fist, and twisted as if he were God wrenching off Wyatt's head. "I tell you—"

But no one heard what he wished to tell them, for they were watching four more men of the council barge in, all feverishly asking questions. Frances had by this time found several more candles and was placing them around the room, and from the mantelpiece she looked over her shoulder at the newcomers. There was the Earl of Arundel, Lord Clinton, Sir Richard Riche, and Lord William Howard, who was the Duke of Norfolk's brother. They all clustered around Lord Paulet who hurriedly explained the crisis to them.

"Wyatt," the Duke chimed in, "is a filthy traitor! And all his scurvy friends! Only one way to deal with traitors. Smash 'em!"

"But how, Your Grace?" Lord Clinton asked with scorn.

"Why, with arms, man!" the Duke sputtered. "With soldiers in the field!"

"And can you raise such troops immediately, Your Grace, from your tenants and retainers? Overnight?" Clinton's contempt almost made his lip curl as he added, with unnecessary blatancy, "Unlike the French, remember, we have no standing army."

"Well, I can raise a good showing, yes!" the Duke said stoutly.

"How many men?"

"Five hundred, perhaps six."

"You can be sure of their loyalty? In *this* fight?"

The Duke's brow furrowed. "Perhaps four hundred," he conceded.

"Perhaps three hundred, Your Grace," Clinton said flatly. "And, for each of us, far less."

No one spoke up to dispute Clinton's statement.

Frances was shocked. Would not even one of these lords boldly declare himself the Queen's champion? She wished the Queen would rage at them. But the Queen was silent, standing slightly apart from the men, her hands clasped together so tightly they were as white as her face. Still looking like a terrified child, she seemed unable to speak.

"And how in God's name can we pay such soldiers?" Sir Richard Riche asked pointedly of Paulet, the Lord Treasurer.

"The Crown's credit in Antwerp is excellent," Paulet snapped back. "The Emperor's sponsorship of Her Majesty ensures that."

"Credit, aye!" Riche scoffed. "At fourteen percent! If that's what you call the Emperor's favor—"

"Please," Bishop Gardiner cried, "the Emperor is not our concern here! Nor the money markets of Antwerp!"

Paulet and Riche scowled but said no more.

"My lords," the Bishop said, summoning his most authoritative voice. "I have advised Her Majesty that I believe the worst danger may be averted if the marriage is called off immediately. Her Majesty would be free, then, to make new marriage plans. If we—"

"Surely you're not proposing Courtenay again," Lord Howard said incredulously. "We hashed through all that months ago!"

The Bishop pounded his fist on the mantel. "I tell you, Lord Courtenay is the right choice! He has royal blood, and the country wants him! And it is not too late for Her Majesty to change her mind. If she does not, and Princess Elizabeth . . ." He stopped himself, but the words hung ominously in the air.

"If Princess Elizabeth what?" the Duke of Norfolk asked, clearly confused by the allusion. "Speak up, man!"

Lord Paulet calmly ventured to explain the Bishop's insinuation. "If Princess Elizabeth marries Courtenay herself, and if the French back the Princess—"

"Body of God, Gardiner," Pembroke interrupted, shaking his head in disgust at the Bishop, "you've been itching to shut the Princess in the Tower for months. Once you get hold of a thing, you're like a dog with a bone."

"My lords," Lord Paulet said anxiously, "we must never send the Princess to the Tower. Think! If the Queen were to die without children, the Princess is next in the line of succession. She must remain so if the country is to be spared the claims that Spain would undoubtedly make on behalf of Prince Philip."

Frances shot a glance at the Queen. This talk of the Queen dying, dying childless, her half sister Elizabeth taking the throne—Frances could hardly bear it! She marveled that the Queen could.

"Forget the Princess!" the Bishop shouted. "Forget everything except the marriage!"

There was a commotion at the door. Four or five more councilors were pushing in. Before any of the newest arrivals could speak, Gardiner turned suddenly to the Queen. "Your Majesty, I entreat you. Before all these lords—before God!—consider the safety of your realm!" He wiped his damp forehead with his sleeve. "Abandon the marriage!"

The room fell silent. It was the first time since the councilors had arrived after Gardiner that anyone had spoken directly to the Queen.

"Before God, my lord Bishop?" the Queen asked quietly, as if struck by his words.

A memory gripped Frances. And she was certain, from the Queen's rapt expression, that they were both recalling the same memory: the vow the Queen had sworn that cold night in St. George's Chapel almost a month ago while the grave-digger's pick raked out faithless King Henry's bones.

The Queen addressed the waiting men, the look of child-ish fear gone from her face. "My lords," she said, "I am sworn before God and country to uphold this marriage. I will wed the Prince."

There was a low groan throughout the room.

"And if my councilors will not stand by me," the Queen concluded bitterly, "God will!"

CHAPTER SEVEN

><←+→-o-←+→-<

God's Sentence

When Edward Sydenham finished his story, Lord Grenville and his wife looked at him in astonishment. Grenville felt for a chair and slowly sat down.

"But, Edward," Lady Grenville cried, her face suddenly bright with revelation, "this is just what Anthony needs! With this information he *can* clear the Thornleighs out."

Edward had expected that Lady Grenville would be the first to see it. Now, she would lead her husband. "Why, the Queen herself would lend a hand to be rid of such vile people if Frances tells her about them," Lady Grenville went on eagerly. "That's it, Edward. You can do your wonders in court to discredit them, and then, once Frances secures the Queen's help, Anthony shall have the abbey lands!"

Edward clamped down a flutter of panic. Here was the danger: the case brought to public court. In a court of law, *anything* might come to light. But he had anticipated Lady Grenville's suggestion and had planned for it.

"Actually, my lady," he said, pleased with the steadiness of his voice, "it might be wiser in this instance not to resort to litigation. It would be tedious and time consuming, what with the conflicting jurisdiction of the church courts in these matters."

"Oh? I should have thought the church court would deal with such a case rather quickly. After all, hasn't the Queen brought back the heresy laws?"

"Not yet, my lady. Parliament is in something of a quagmire over it. The legislation could drag on for several sessions. Years, perhaps. Therefore, it might be best to keep this a . . . not strictly legal matter. Keep it between the Thornleighs and ourselves. What I advise is this. A letter, directly from Lord Grenville to the Thornleighs, outlining the situation that he is now in possession of the damaging facts about their past. Put that in a letter, and I warrant your neighbors will be sailing on the next tide, gone for good."

"Blackmail," Lady Grenville said smoothly. Edward understood her smile. She was not gloating, merely aware of the sweetness of power, and its efficiency.

"Most likely they would move back to Antwerp," Edward said. "I understand they keep a house there."

"Then let them return to it!" Lady Grenville crowed as if already victorious. She turned to her husband. "Anthony, you must write the letter immediately."

Edward silently thanked her. It must, indeed, be done immediately. Honor's parting comment in London that she might barge into Grenville Hall had been more jest than threat, he knew, but he dared not risk her acting on it.

"Anthony?" Lady Grenville prompted pointedly.

Grenville had not said a word since hearing the story. His face was inert. Strangely so, Edward thought, for a man who usually could not sit still.

"Well, Anthony?" Lady Grenville prodded. "Isn't Edward's idea clever?"

Lord Grenville said, very quietly, "God requires more."

"More, my lord?" Edward asked.

"Justice, Edward. Don't you see? This now goes far beyond my personal hatred of these people. If they slip away, they will only infect other parts of Christendom. That would be an offense to God Himself. No, punishment in a situation this grave must be left to God's direction."

Edward felt a chill. Had he miscalculated? Was Lord Grenville so befuddled by religion that he was going to rely on some absurd hope of divine intervention? Was he not going to act? That would be worse than before! The thing half done exposed Edward to uncertainty. And uncertainty could lead to disaster. "But, my lord—"

Before Edward could finish, the door flew open. John, the Grenvilles' eldest son, rushed in. His bony face was distraught. His sparse blond hair was disarrayed like windblown straw. "It's happened, Father! Just as we feared! An uprising!"

Lord Grenville jumped up. "Where?"

"In Kent."

"Who?"

"Sir Thomas Wyatt. And a slew of others. In one day

they've raised over two thousand men from Maidstone alone!"

"Does the Queen know?" Grenville asked. "Should we send word?"

John shook his head grimly. "She will know by now."

A memory flashed in Edward's mind of Honor's words at their meeting. *There's talk of an uprising,* she had said. Later, he had wondered about her insistence on that topic. No, not insistence exactly; it had not even been her words, as such. More like hints, clues that she wanted to speak about rebellion.

Lord Grenville went to the table and snatched one of the pistols from the ebony box. He strode to the door. "Come, John, Edward! We have work to do!"

Edward froze. His mind was groping for some way, any way, to hold Lord Grenville to the course. Grenville *must* force the Thornleighs to leave! "My lord!" he called.

Grenville stopped at the door, clearly annoyed at the delay.

"There's more!" Edward blurted. "I have reason to believe that Honor and Richard Thornleigh have conspired in this rebellion. Our neighbors, my lord, are traitors!"

Honor Thornleigh sat at her desk and stared at the tip of her quill. It was sharp enough; she had just shaved it with the penknife for the second time. And the paper lay before her, neatly lined up, ready to take the ink. But the right words continued to elude her. *Dear Edward* . . . But then what?

She sat back with a sigh and gazed out the mullioned window that looked over her herb garden. When she and Richard had built the house in the summer, finding the abbey impossible to renovate for comfortable family life, Richard had suggested including this small second-story chamber overlooking her garden for her to read in and write. Honor loved the garden. Even now, in winter, when the barren stalks of rosemary and marjoram poked out bravely, if forlornly, above the smothering snow. Even now, because the violet winter light at this twilight hour held mysteries of clarity she never observed in the hazy gold of summer, so companionably thick with pollen and chaff dust and tiny living things. The winter light had a candid, forthright character that showed the world without flattery, with clarity;

which, paradoxically, unlocked mysteries. Objects that seemed blithely familiar in the daze of summer were made remarkable and mysterious under this exposing light. That was the gift of clarity.

She had to smile. She might have been describing Richard, she realized, instead of winter light.

Straightening, she asked herself what, clearly and candidly, did she want to say to Edward? Oh, yes, she had given him a quick assurance at their brief meeting in London. But she now regretted the flippancy with which she had bestowed it. She had been almost cruel.

She had every reason to hate him for the past. He had said so himself. After all, she had risked her life to save him from his own cowardice. But she did not hate him. Life, she thought, was too short to squander on hating. And she was now ashamed of her moment of malice as he was leaving the Crane, when she had succumbed to the pleasure of ruffling him, if only a little, about Lord Grenville. She had been petty. And blind, caught up as she was in her fancy that Edward was bringing news of rebellion. Not that she wasn't still hoping for an uprising that would effect real change in England. But her absorption with that was no reason to deny Edward the peace of mind he craved. What right had she to do so when she craved it, too?

Ah, well, she would make up for those faults of pettiness now. She would forgive herself. And, more importantly, forgive Edward. Odd, she thought, that forgiveness was considered a Christian duty. She had seen few Christians forgive one another. Neither did she feel this was a duty. It was something she wanted to do. It closed an unhealed wound from the past. Edward had come to her with an open heart and she had been too preoccupied to see his need. But now she could make things right.

She dipped her quill. *Dear Edward . . .*

And the words of charity flowed.

Down the corridor, Isabel Thornleigh was pacing in her room. Leaving London a week ago she had hardly been able to think straight, so great was her shock at her parents' announcement that she was being sent to Antwerp. But days of racking her brain had failed to produce a plan to subvert their decree.

Her first instinct had been to ride to her half brother Adam's house and beg his support. But that would be idiotic, she realized. Adam was their father's business partner as well as son; he would most likely *want* to go to Antwerp until stability returned here. Besides, Isabel thought, Adam always did what Father wanted.

She had considered simply riding off to London on her own. But she could not stay with any friends of the family there; they would surely return her to her parents. And the paltry amount of cash she had—her small allowance—would not be nearly enough to pay the expenses of food, lodging, and stabling.

She had thought of riding to the neighboring village to beg help from her best friend, Lucy, the daughter of the Thornleighs' foreman at the abbey clothworks. Lucy was a levelheaded girl and Isabel was sure she could be trusted. But a little more thought dissolved that hope. Lucy's house would be the first place Isabel's parents would look for her. And even if Lucy did have some money to help her get to London, what reason could Isabel give for asking? How could she expect Lucy's friendship to stretch to aiding and abetting an insurrection?

No plan. And no time. The *Curlew* was going to sail in three days!

Back and forth by her window, in and out of the violet shaft of twilight, Isabel paced.

Dusk had deepened by the time Honor finished writing and went downstairs.

"I have a favor to ask," she said, coming into the parlor where Thornleigh stood looking at the fire in the hearth. "A mark of esteem actually, my love, for I'll trust none but you with this task."

She came beside him at the fire. He did not look up. She wondered if he had heard her. "It's a letter to Edward Sydenham," she said. "Would you deliver it to Grenville Hall?" She held it out to him with a playful smile, and added, "I'd take it myself, but the world frowns on married ladies passing secret letters to gentlemen." She was surprised at his continuing silence. Though she had told him of Edward's visit in London, she had expected this letter to elicit some questions from him.

Thornleigh turned his head and stared at her as though,

still, none of her words had registered. He said, "It's happened, Honor."

She saw that something had shaken him deeply. "What has?"

"Rebellion. Calthrop rode nonstop from London to tell me. I've just sent him on to Adam's house. The report is that Sir Thomas Wyatt and two thousand men have risen up at Maidstone." He looked down at Honor's letter that she, arrested by the news, still held out. He took it from her and absently turned it in his hands, his mind on the crisis. "It's come about," he said bleakly, "just as you predicted."

Honor hardly knew what to feel most. Gratification that a revolt had really begun. Disappointment that Richard felt so differently. Curiosity about the leaders, their objectives. Then, suddenly, one thought overwhelmed the others. "I want Isabel sent to safety at once," she said. "Isabel, and Adam and his family. Richard, is there a way?"

"The *Curlew* could sail from Harwich day after tomorrow."

"No. I want them away from the danger *now*."

Thornleigh thought for a moment. "Adam could take them all to Maldon Harbor tonight. It's only five miles. Grover has a small carrack loading there for Bruges. Adam can have it carry them on to Antwerp if I send Grover the money."

"Perfect."

"And you?" Thornleigh hesitated. "Honor, I know I agreed—"

"Yes, you agreed that we'd stay if a rebellion broke within three weeks. And it's happened in less than that."

"I know. But ... damn it, who are these people? Who's this Wyatt? He might be some madman for all we know. Have you any idea what his demands are? Or if he has the slightest hope of success?"

Honor felt her elation at the news evaporate. Who were these rebels, indeed? She knew nothing of Sir Thomas Wyatt. And nothing of who else was involved.

"Wyatt's band might be crushed in a day," Thornleigh went on severely, "and then the Queen will be vicious in exacting vengeance on her enemies, real or perceived. She'll be hunting traitors in every corner of the realm, and to her, heretics are the same thing. Someone will remember you from the past, and talk. And then, how long before the Queen's men come for you?"

Honor realized it was all too possible. "But, Richard, should I really be thinking only of myself?"

"For once, yes!"

"But it's wrong. We shouldn't let other men fight our battles."

"They've *chosen* to fight."

"They're standing up to the Queen! That takes bravery. That's why we should support them."

"All right!" he cried in exasperation. "I'll support them with money! I'll do whatever you want! But, please, Honor, go with Isabel and Adam to Maldon tonight. I'll join you in Antwerp as soon as I can get things cleared away here. Please do this. *Please.*"

The anxiety in his face tore at her. "Let's settle Isabel and Adam first," she said. "Get them packing. And then—"

"No, Honor. No more procrastinating. Go. If you do that for me, I promise I'll stay long enough to arrange some aid for Wyatt."

She nodded. It was settled.

Thornleigh's smile was full of relief. He stuffed Honor's letter inside his tunic as he strode to the door and called to a servant boy, "Jamie, ask Mistress Isabel to come down. Then go to Master Adam's house and fetch him here. Now!"

Darkness had fallen over Grenville Hall. The courtyard echoed with the clack of horses' hooves on icy cobbles, and their nervous whinnying at the violent upheaval of the stable's evening routine. Around the knot of seven horsemen, just mounting, grooms were making final tugs at stirrups and saddles. Other servants hoisting torches stood shivering, having been dragged from the drowsy warmth of their hearths.

Lord Anthony Grenville kicked his spurred boots into his stirrups and impatiently yanked the reins, pulling away from his groom. "There's no time to waste!" he told his companions. He had personally checked his armory and set the men there to organizing the estate's longbows, lances, and armor, but there was still much work to be done farther afield. "John," he commanded as his son settled in his saddle, "call out the archers and get them to London on the double!" Lord Grenville jerked his head in a silent order to two servants standing by. They instantly ran forward to throw open the main gates. "And, John, send word to Her Majesty that you and the Grenville Archers are at her disposal!"

John Grenville nodded. He wheeled his mount away from the other horsemen just as the servants pushed open the gates. Followed by his squire, he bolted out into the night.

Lord Grenville turned to the horsemen nearest him, his younger son and his steward. "Christopher and Master Harris," he said, "off with you to the sheriff for his instructions. Then rouse up the tenantry." The steward and Christopher pulled away and rode off.

"Edward!" Lord Grenville called as his horse tossed its mane, snorting steam. "Ride to Sir Arthur Mildmay's and to Master Crowell's to spread the word. A meeting here, tell them, as soon as they can saddle up."

"My lord, if you could just first write—"

"Enough! There'll be no blasted letter-writing, and no more blasted *talk*! Go now, and do your duty!"

Grenville watched Edward ride slowly away, then turned to his own body servant, saying, "Matthew, you're with me." As the young man adjusted his reins, Lord Grenville looked up at the bright moon. It was as though God were shining a beacon down to watch that His will be done. *And so it shall be,* Lord Grenville thought. *Heretics and traitors must not be allowed to destroy the realm.* Was it a coincidence, he wondered, that Edward had made his extraordinary disclosure on the very night that this calamity had broken upon England? No. God left nothing to chance. This was His sign, Grenville was sure. And now God was relying on him and all the good men of England to wrench the devil's grip from their poor country's neck. A night for justice, indeed. He gave his excited mount its head and rode off through the gates.

The shivering servants in the courtyard waited until the shuddering hoofbeats of Lord Grenville's horse thudded into softness, then silence. Then they hurried back into the warmth.

"I can't go now! You can't ask me to!"

"I'm not *asking*." Thornleigh glared at his daughter. "I'm ordering! Pack your things. Adam will be here in a couple of hours. Then, you're off."

Isabel froze. This could not be happening. In one breath her father had declared the thrilling news that Sir Thomas

Wyatt had raised his standard in Kent. In the next, he had
said she was being sent away. *Now.*

"No!" she cried. "I won't go!"

Honor Thornleigh's reasonable voice broke in. "Bel, this
is a crisis. There may be great danger. Your father and I are
doing what's best for—"

"You're doing what's cowardly! We should be helping
these people, not running away!"

Thornleigh threw up his hands. "Two of you! Was ever a
man so plagued by obstinate women!"

"Isabel," her mother said sternly, "you don't know what
you're saying. If it's Martin you're thinking of—"

"Of course it's Martin! My place is with him!" This was
close to a deception, and Isabel hated stooping to it. She
longed to tell her parents outright about her commitment to
Wyatt's cause. Could she? Would they understand? She was
on the brink of speaking, but she checked herself. They
would *never* understand.

"We've been through this, Isabel," Thornleigh said. "Until
you're Martin's wife, your place is with us. You *will* leave
tonight."

Isabel heard the finality in her father's voice, like an enemy's door closing in her face. She saw that he would not
shrink from binding her and hauling her away. But her
mother? Surely, her mother would not suffer her to be
dragged off against her will! "Mother, listen to me, please!
I've heard some things about . . . the men following Sir
Thomas Wyatt. I believe they have worthy goals at heart.
They want to rescue the Queen from her own folly. And rescue the country from it! We should be giving them our support. If we—"

"That's enough!" Isabel was shocked by the anger in her
mother's voice. "You're a child, Isabel. You're babbling
about things you cannot understand. You have no compre-
hension of the dangers."

The insult stung like a slap. "But I know this cause is
right, Mother!"

"You will not say such things! You will not *think* such
things."

Never had she heard her mother so irrational! She looked
to her father, but he turned his back on her and walked to the
window. Never had she seen him so cruel! They were closed
doors, both of them. She felt hemmed in by their intransi-

gence, trapped. She had to get out. "It's *you* who don't understand," she shouted. "You know *nothing!*"

She turned and ran to the door. But as she reached for the handle the door opened, swinging in, forcing her back on her heels. A man stood there like a wall. An old man, white-maned but solid, bulky in his winter capes. Isabel had seen him pointed out to her in town. Lord Anthony Grenville.

Lord Grenville only glanced at Isabel, then looked past her. The open door obscured Thornleigh at the window, but Honor stood before the hearth, directly in Lord Grenville's line of vision. Lord Grenville walked toward her. As he passed Isabel, she saw the gleam of a metal tube jutting down below his cape near his right knee.

"Lord Grenville," Honor exclaimed as he stopped in front of her. "What an unexpected—"

"I come to execute God's sentence," Grenville declared. Isabel, behind him, saw him raise his right arm and stretch it out straight. She saw the metal tube at the end of his hand gleam in the firelight and, beyond it, her mother's face, her mouth an O of wonder.

"No!" It was her father, shouting.

There was a rapid clicking of metallic teeth, a monstrous blast from the tube, sparks and black powder spewing back around Grenville's head. Isabel saw her mother's head and shoulders jerk back like a yanked puppet, then slip down beyond Grenville's bulk just as he, flinching at the shower of sparks, dropped the pistol.

"*No!*" Thornleigh threw himself toward his wife. Lord Grenville stepped back sideways, startled by Thornleigh's sudden appearance. Isabel saw her mother's inert body on the hearth, her dead eyes open to the ceiling. Her left arm, flung back, was lying in the fire. Thornleigh snatched it out.

Lord Grenville, his eyes fixed on Thornleigh's back, was reaching for his sword hilt. Thornleigh suddenly twisted around, grabbed the fallen pistol by the barrel, lunged upward, and smashed the ivory butt against the side of Grenville's head. Grenville lurched like a beast gored by dogs at the bear garden. He groped again for his sword, but Thornleigh swung the pistol again and the butt smashed Grenville's other temple. Grenville staggered backward, clutching his head. Isabel, frozen, watched as her father smashed Grenville's face, over and over, the ivory butt thumping into flesh, cracking against bone. Grenville thud-

ded to his knees. His torso swayed with his arms hanging
useless, his face a mass of red ruin. Thornleigh stood over
him and smashed until Grenville crashed backward to the
floor and was still.

Isabel looked past the men at her mother. A black hole
gaped in her mother's forehead. Crimson blood drooled from
it down her temple and into her hair. Isabel heard a scream.
It sounded strangely like her own voice ... but it was a
child's ... a screaming child ... alone in the universe ...
lost.

CHAPTER EIGHT

><-+<>-<+<

Colchester Jail

F ather Gilbert, the elderly parish priest, stood before the
Thornleighs' open front door mangling his hat in his
hands. His palms were sweating despite the morning cold.
He had delivered the awful injunction here, as he had been
ordered, and now he wished he were a hundred miles away.
Or even just over the hill, back in his own snug parlor in the
rectory, as long as the doors were bolted. Anywhere that he
could avoid the two haggard, young faces staring at him
from the doorway.

Adam Thornleigh was the first to speak. Tall and sturdy
like his father, the young man seemed slightly less distraught
than his sister, Father Gilbert thought. For the few minutes
that Father Gilbert had been talking to them, arriving at their
entrance just as they were going out, the girl had not said a
word.

"Unconsecrated ground?" Adam asked, hollowly repeating the priest's last words. "I don't understand."

Father Gilbert shrugged, not from indifference, but from
shame at his impotence in this appalling family feud. "I
have been instructed," he said, and added lamely, "by messenger."

"A messenger? From whom?"

The priest twisted his hat, remembering his own dismay
when the breathless courier from Whitehall had banged on
his door at dawn. He mumbled now to Adam, "From Her
Majesty, Queen Mary."

He heard a gasp from the young man. He clutched his hat.
He was God's servant, but oh! the difficult tasks God sometimes expected of him!

The big sorrel mare rocked Isabel as it plodded along the
ice-rutted Great Essex road toward Colchester. Her cheek
against her brother's back chafed against his wool cloak.

She had insisted on coming with him, but he had thought her too unwell to ride her own horse. She held on to him as the horse slowly picked its way toward town.

The priest's shocking pronouncement still echoed in her numbed brain. Unconsecrated ground. Her mother's body was to suffer the ultimate disgrace of burial in the waste field beyond the churchyard. Isabel tried to focus her thoughts. Why had the Queen made such a dreadful decree? Why had Lord Grenville burst in last night to take her mother's life? Why was this nightmare happening? But she found it difficult to think at all. It was as though the workings inside her head were clogged, jammed like the paddles in her father's fulling ponds weighted down with too much soggy cloth. She longed to have Martin by her side—to hold her, to keep her from sinking, to make some sense of what was happening. But she had no idea where he was; somewhere in the county of Kent. It was impossible even to send him a message. She tried to imagine him, marching—somewhere—with Wyatt's rebel army. But all of that—Wyatt's stand, her own pledge to act as his go-between with the French Ambassador, Martin's eager commitment to the cause—all of it now seemed utterly unreal. It was as though Martin existed in some other time and place, some bright plane of happy, hopeful excitement where her mother still moved and smiled.

The last ten hours had been hell itself. Her own voice screaming, the servants shouting and running, her father wildly refusing to let go of her mother's body. The obscene black mouth in her mother's forehead . . . the slick red pool under her mother's head . . . the slime of gore around Lord Grenville's body . . . spattered on Isabel's shoes . . .

The parish constable had barged in, fetched by Lord Grenville's panicked servant. The constable and his men had dragged her father out of the room. The two bodies had been taken to the church. And, finally, the servants had stopped running. It was almost dawn when Adam came. Adam's fingers had dug into her shoulders as he shook her . . . shouted at her . . . *Where have they taken Father?* Her mouth had answered—though she had barely heard her own words, drowned out by the voice still screaming inside her head— *Colchester Castle jail.*

The county jail had been located in Colchester Castle since the thirteenth century and was in sorry disrepair. When the mare plodded under the archway into the precincts, it had to pick its way around a scatter of rubble that had crumbled from the dilapidated walls.

As Adam and Isabel walked into the jailer's musty-smelling front room, two men looked up from their breakfast of bread and beer. One of them quickly abandoned his meal, his eyes darting from Adam's fine cloak and boots to Isabel's furred hood as he rose to meet them.

"William Mosse, keeper, at your service," he said, smoothing back his greasy, graying hair. His spindly frame supported the paunch of the heavy ale drinker. "And how may I serve you this morning, sir?" He smiled. Half-chewed bread foamed around his yellow teeth.

Adam gave him their father's name and held out a silver crown. The second man rose eagerly from the table at the sight of the money. Mosse snatched the coin, glared at the second man, then smiled at Adam. "I'll take you down my own self, sir," Mosse said with a solicitous bow. "And we'll leave my turnkey to break his fast, shall we?"

Mosse led Adam and Isabel down a stone stairway to a short corridor that ran off to their right and left. Here Mosse stopped. The corridor was cold and smelled of damp masonry and urine. Directly ahead, the staircase continued down. To the dungeon, Isabel imagined with a shudder. On either side the corridor ended at a closed door with a grilled square in the top. From the left grill Isabel could faintly hear low voices, shuffling, and coughing. The stench that rolled through it made her suspect that it led to a crowded ward, probably the commons' ward. Mosse started toward that door, lifting his heavy ring of keys.

"No, Jailer," Adam said, and pointed to the right. "My father will be in the gentlemen's ward."

"Commons and gentlemen's, it's all one now, sir. The rains at All Hallow's Eve washed clear through the gentlemen's, ruining all. Standing up to their knees in it, the gentlemen was. Five of 'em perished. That was money down the drain for me, sir, and never a truer word. How's a man to live, I ask you, when half the paying customers is floating belly-up in muck?" He started to unlock the grilled door to the commons' ward. "Now, if it'd been *this* side you'd not hear Will Mosse moaning of it. Nary a farthing do I get from these curs, above what's owing for their victuals, and even then not what a man can count on. Yet my lord sheriff wants

the chambers in the gentlemen's ward yonder made good
again by Lent—and all to be wrought from me turning out
my own pockets. I ask you, sir, is this any kind of a fair
world? No, it ain't, indeed. In a fair world the good Lord
would've sent the rains to wash out this tupenny ward and
not left me to bury five paying gentlemen."

Isabel listened dully to Mosse's complaints. She knew that
jail keepers bought their posts from the sheriff at public auc-
tion, and that they received no salary. To recoup the cash
outlay of a successful bid, jailers were officially allowed to
charge fees from the prisoners for every item of their suste-
nance. That was the way throughout England.

Mosse had unlocked the door but stood blocking the way.
"Now, sir," he said pleasantly to Adam, "a word of business,
if I may. When your good father was brought in last night he
had nary a coin about him to keep the shackles off. I felt
sure he would be good for the fee later—that is, his family
would, if I may be so bold to say so, sir. But what was I to
do? Rules is rules, sir. Where would we be without 'em?
And the rule is: no payment, no easement of irons. But if
you've the wherewithal, sir—"

"Yes, yes," Adam said impatiently. "How much?"

"Two and six, sir, and I thank you kindly. I wouldn't ask
a farthing more, though some I know of would. No, two
shillings sixpence is the rule here, and Will Mosse abides by
rules. We'd be no better than the beasts without 'em, would
we, sir?"

He pocketed the coins from Adam and swung open the
door. Bowing, he extended his arm to indicate that Adam
and Isabel should lead the way. Isabel saw that, past the
door, the corridor continued on, and the ward, dimly lit, lay
at the end. The corridor was narrow, and the three of them
walked in single file, Isabel following her brother, Mosse in
the rear.

As they walked, Isabel heard Mosse whisper by her cheek,
"Your cloak's a mite wet from the snow, mistress." His
breath smelled of beer. "Uncomfortable, that is. I'd be
pleased to carry it off for a quick dry-out by my fire." His
hands touched her shoulders, then slid down her front to feel
for the edge of her cloak. One hand squeezed her breast. Isabel gasped and jumped aside. Adam twisted around. Mosse
grinned innocently at him. "Offering to take the lady's cloak
for a dry-out, sir. No charge."

Adam scowled at Mosse and jerked Isabel forward by the wrist, out of the jailer's reach. "I'll report you to the sheriff, Mosse, if I find—"

"Ah! There's your good father, sir," Mosse interrupted brightly, pointing. "There in the far corner. I'll just run on ahead and unlock his irons." He pushed forward past Adam and slipped into the ward.

It was very crowded. Isabel looked in the direction the jailer had indicated, but she could not see her father. There were too many obstacles, and the light was dim. The ward was a long, narrow stone room whose length was divided by three thick stone pillars. Ragged blankets and clothing were strung between the pillars and the walls to form crude partitions. Isabel guessed that one such section was meant to separate the commons from the gentlemen in this forced cohabitation. Many of the prisoners lounged on thin pallets of straw on the floor and stared blank-eyed at the ceiling. Others were hunkered in circles, tossing dice amid noisy wagering. Others lay in rag-nested corners, curled in restless sleep. Rancid tallow candles in wall sconces gave off a dingy light. There was one small high window, without glass, level with the ground of the outside courtyard. Ice crusted the window's pitted bars.

"Stay close," Adam said to Isabel as they moved into the room. She had to press her sleeve over her nose to block out the stench of human waste, mousy straw, and unwashed bodies. Her eyes watered as she passed a smoky cooking fire. Incongruously, one far corner had been made magnificent by a gentleman's feather bed, and by the liveried servant who stood guard with folded arms while his master slept. The prisoners were almost all men, although Isabel stumbled over the bare foot of a boy shivering against one of the flaking pillars. She also caught a glimpse, behind a curtain of thin burlap, of two skinny women sleeping on the stone floor, as still as corpses.

And then she saw him. Her father sat with his back against a wall, his knees drawn up, his attention concentrated on something he held in his hands. Isabel saw that this posture was necessary because of the short chains that connected his ankle shackles to his wrist cuffs—the irons that the jailer had spoken of. As she and Adam hurried toward their father, Mosse was sorting through keys for the one to unlock these manacles, thanks to Adam's payment.

"I'll just slip these off, sir," Mosse said to Adam, "and you can have a pleasant visit with your father. And I'll send my turnkey down to the taproom to fetch some refreshment for you, shall I? Finest ale in all Colchester town, ask any gentleman here. Brewed by the tender hand of my own dear wife. And only two shillings a pot for the two of you."

He selected a key and fitted it into one lock after another on Thornleigh's irons, still talking to Adam. "My apologies for the crowd here, sir. Sheriff tossed in a baker's dozen last night, what with this rebellion fright. They say the Spaniards are coming to murder us all in our beds, but I don't pay much mind to it. Still, it's got folks worked up. The two over there"—he nodded toward a couple of grimy men crouched over a card game—"they were thrown in last night after butchering a priest, so I'd watch out for them. But the rest of these loafers won't bother you. Debtors, mostly." He finished and straightened, gathering in the chains. "So you just stay as long as you please, sir. Good day, sir." The chains rattled as he swung them over his shoulder and ambled away.

Isabel was staring down at her father. He had made no effort to stand once his chains had been removed, though he did slowly stretch his legs, bent all night from the irons. He glanced up at her and Adam. Almost immediately he looked back down at the object in his hands, a foot-sized, smooth block of wood. He reached inside his boot and drew out a small knife—stuffed away, apparently, while Mosse was present—and began to whittle the wood. He had evidently been interrupted in this work, for Isabel now discerned in the block the rudimentary shape of a boat. A wire tightened around her heart. Her father had always loved ships. Was he carving one now to carry away his grief?

"Father," she whispered. She went down on her knees and laid her arms around his neck. He did not move. Isabel stiffened. Had this vile place overnight driven off his wits? But when she pulled back to see his face she found him gazing into hers with a look of tenderness that cleared away that fear at least. She felt she should be wailing to him about her mother, but no words would come. He looked down again at his block of wood.

Adam knelt on the other side of their father. "Sir, I've . . ." He cleared his throat. "I've brought you this." He held up a purse of coins. Thornleigh glanced at it in silence.

Adam awkwardly tucked the purse into his father's tunic, then sat back on his heels, as adrift as his father and sister. Thornleigh continued to stare at the wood. None of them seemed able to speak.

Suddenly Thornleigh looked up and frowned. "You two should be on your way to Antwerp," he said sternly, as if his children had disobeyed him.

"Antwerp?" Adam said, incredulous. "Good heavens, Father, not while you're—"

"No discussion. I want you gone. Next tide. Understand?"

"But . . . Father, what *happened*? If we're to help you, we must know what this is all about. Why would Lord Grenville do—"

"No discussion!" Thornleigh shouted. A knot of prisoners gambling nearby turned to look. Thornleigh's blast of anger had silenced Adam. The gamblers went back to their dice.

Isabel was staring at her father's hands. They were streaked with dark red stains. And on his cuffs and sleeve and the neck of his shirt were dried brown speckles. Blood. She was aware of a queerly obsessive thought: *We should have brought him clean clothes.* Her brain would proceed no further.

Thornleigh suddenly slumped back against the wall, his surge of anger spent. "Listen to me, both of you," he said flatly. "I'm a murderer. No, save your breath, Adam—that's what they'll charge me with. Grenville's widow will see to that."

Adam blanched. "But you'll have a trial! What you did was an act of self-defense. I saw Grenville's pistol myself. If you hadn't . . . I mean, if he'd managed to reload he would have killed you, too. He was insane."

Thornleigh shook his head grimly. "I think he acted in shock at the news of rebellion. Leapt to the conclusion we were traitors. So he came to . . . remove us." He looked at his son. "A fair trial?" Again, he shook his head. "The Grenvilles have half the county judges in their pocket. And Grenville was one of the Queen's staunchest supporters. His daughter is her closest friend. The Queen will stand by the Grenville family. I haven't a hope of a fair trial."

"My God," Adam said as if something had just dawned on him, "Frances Grenville. They got a message to her and she told the Queen. That's why the priest—" He stopped himself.

"The priest?" Thornleigh asked.

Adam lowered his head. "Mother . . . she's to be buried in unconsecrated ground. By order of the Queen."

"Christ," Thornleigh whispered, aghast. Isabel saw an unidentifiable look pass between the two men, but she was not sure what it meant. She was not sure of anything. She was not sure she would not yet wake up from this nightmare.

"Then you two must get away immediately," Thornleigh said. He held up his hand to stop his son's objection. "No, Adam. I'm a dead man." He spoke without intensity, almost without feeling, as if it were another man's life he was talking about, a stranger's. Isabel realized that she was wrong about his grief; grief had not yet overcome him. She knew it, because she recognized his listlessness as her own. She had once seen a man in an alehouse fight who was punched so hard that the consciousness had drained from his face, but he kept standing for several moments. That was how her father appeared. Struck, but not yet toppled.

"These are my instructions, Adam," he was saying. "You will leave orders with my agent, Calthrop, to sell my property here and send you the proceeds. You will clear out all the cash from my strongbox at home, and you will take Isabel and your family to Maldon immediately and embark for Antwerp. You will settle in Antwerp—you know our friends there to rely on. And you will forget me. Now go."

Thornleigh turned back to his knife, done with talking.

"But, Father," Adam protested, "that's madness! We can't leave you!"

"You have no choice. Don't you see? Everything will come out now. *Everything.*" Again, Isabel saw the strange look pass between her father and brother.

"And when I'm condemned," Thornleigh went on, "all my property will be forfeited to the Crown. Adam, I will not leave my family destitute. That's why you've got to do this. You've got to save my family, just as you would tell your own son to save yours."

"But . . . dear God . . . surely there's some way—"

"There isn't." Thornleigh looked at Isabel. He lifted the hand that held the knife and slowly, lovingly, ran the back of his finger down her cheek. "Poor Bel. No wedding . . . I'm sorry . . . I'd hoped—" He stopped, his words choked off. He quickly looked down at his wood and tightened his grasp on the knife. "Do as I tell you, Adam," he said harshly. "I *command* it. Now go." He began whittling. Gradually he channeled his energy into the wood.

"Father, don't," Isabel begged. "Please, talk to us. Please!"

But his face registered indifference to everything but the mindless task of shaving wood chips. Nothing else seemed to matter to him. Not the vile surroundings. Not his children's pleas. Not his fate.

Disconsolately Adam leaned over and kissed his father's cheek. "Good-bye," he whispered. Thornleigh kept whittling. But Isabel saw that his knife was now gouging ugly bites of wood at random, disfiguring the boat's surface.

Adam closed his eyes for a moment, almost as if in prayer. He stood. "Come, Bel," he said softly, looking down at her. "Let's go home."

CHAPTER NINE

>━◆━◌━◆━◂

Chaos Unleashed

Late that afternoon Isabel stood alone at the edge of her mother's grave beyond the churchyard. In the slight breeze, grains of the freshly mounded earth migrated aimlessly across the grave's surface, sometimes in spasmodic jerks, sometimes at rest as though too weary to go on. Isabel had placed a sprig of holly on the grave, and she watched the dirt and granules of snow drift over it, making a dry, sandy sound that seemed to scrape her heart like a claw.

She shivered. Earlier, the strong afternoon sun had forced the two gravediggers to shed their thick jerkins for their task. But heavy clouds now crowded the darkening sky, and the gravediggers were long gone. The few mourners, too. Adam, though shaken, had declared that the journey to Antwerp must begin tomorrow morning, and Isabel grieved that there had been no time to send word to the many friends who would have attended her mother's burial under normal circumstances.

But nothing was normal. Nothing was right. Incomprehensible things had happened—were happening—too fast. Her mother murdered. Her father cut off and in despair. Her brother as adrift as she. Adam had said a choked prayer over the grave hacked out of this half-frozen field, then hurried off to his house to organize his wife and young children for the trip. But Isabel had insisted on staying by the grave a little longer. The short walk home across the hill was nothing, she had told him. Or so she had considered it in her life before last night. Now, she sensed that every step she would take away from this silent mound, every footfall that would separate her forever from her mother, would feel as wide as a world.

But she could not stand here any longer. Evening was creeping closer. A storm was coming. Already, noisy rooks were alighting on the sanctuary of the church belfry, and other birds were gliding silently over the steeple on their way home to the safety of the forest. The Grenvilles' forest. Isabel shivered again.

Hugging herself, she forced her legs to take the first steps—the first steps to leave England. Underfoot, the snow squealed merciless accusations at her that she was deserting her parents, deserting Martin, deserting Wyatt's great cause. But what was she to do? She was so alone! She walked on. She did not look back until she reached the wicket gate in the walled churchyard. As she closed the gate it screeched at her. She had to fight back the urge to cling to it and never move again. Or worse, to stumble back in panic to her mother.

She heard voices and turned. Three people, two men and a woman, were slowly walking up the churchyard path from the road. The men flanked the woman, and were supporting her as if she would sink if they let her go.

The woman looked up, saw Isabel, and stopped, holding back the men. Isabel recognized her. Lady Maud Grenville. The two women stared at each other, separated by the short path that skirted the snow-shrouded tombstones.

There was no way out of the churchyard to the road except past Lady Grenville. Isabel forced her feet to move forward. The old woman's face came into focus—gaunt, tight, bitter as the face of a witch. Isabel felt its hatred stop her like a wall. She halted an arm's length away.

"Devil's spawn!" Lady Grenville hissed.

Isabel mustered what dignity she could. "Madam, I have just buried my mother. If you—"

"Your mother? A she-devil!" Lady Grenville screwed up her face and spat. Spittle, hot with hate, scalded the corner of Isabel's mouth.

"Mother!" the younger man said, pulling her back.

"Lady Grenville!" the other cried in horror.

With a trembling hand Isabel wiped the spittle off.

But Lady Grenville was not done. "Your mother was a God-cursed heretic!" she screamed. "A demon! When God's servants chained her to the stake, Satan himself came to stamp out the fire beneath her! Satan, saving his own!"

Isabel's mouth fell open. "Madam, you rave."

"Rave?" the witch screeched. "Your family's abominations have destroyed my husband!" She wrenched free of the men and stretched up her arms, her fingers rigid as talons.

She flew at Isabel. The talons struck, tearing back the hood that sheltered Isabel's face and ripping off the *touret* that held back her hair. The fingers stiffened afresh, the nails poised to rake Isabel's cheeks.

"Mother, stop!" The younger man pulled down her arms, and he and the other man restrained her.

Isabel staggered back a step, fumbling at her disarrayed hair, stunned.

Lady Grenville squirmed in the men's grasp. "You gape," she sneered at Isabel. "What, did you not *know*? Idiot! You are the whelp of a she-devil. She carried heretics away on ships, a fiend at work for Satan, her master! Oh, merciful Lord Jesus," she moaned, rolling her head, "if only they *had* burned her all those years ago, burned her to a cinder! If only—"

"No more!" the older man beside her cried. "Christopher, take your mother into the church."

But Lady Grenville shrugged free again. Isabel stiffened, ready to defend herself from the talons. But the woman merely stepped closer and shoved her face close to Isabel's. "Hear this, fool! Your father murdered my husband, a servant of God, and he will roast in hellfire for all eternity. But before he goes to his punishment I promise you I will make him pay on earth!"

"Christopher! You must take her—"

"I know! Mother, come away." The young man again pulled her back. "Come!" He held her tightly and dragged her toward the church.

"He'll pay with his life!" the woman cried back over her shoulder, stumbling away against her will. "As God is my witness, I'll make him pay!"

Isabel tried to stand firm, but her legs felt suddenly weak, and she saw blackness edge her vision in the witch's wake.

"I am so very sorry, Mistress Thornleigh." It was the older man coming beside her, his voice full of sympathy. "Please," he said gently, "accept my apologies on behalf of the family. Lady Grenville is unwell. This dreadful tragedy . . ." He stopped and cried suddenly, "Mistress!" He snatched Isabel's elbow just as she began to fall. He held her up. Isabel felt the rush of blackness recede. She straightened. She stepped back, ashamed, unwilling to let one of *them* see how deeply Lady Grenville's venom had stung.

"Dear heaven, this appalling situation . . ." the man murmured with feeling. "Believe me, mistress, I know you are just as aggrieved as Lady Grenville. I am more sorry for all of this than I can say. My name is Edward Sydenham. If there is anything I can do, please—"

"I thank you, sir," Isabel said, moving away from him. "There is nothing."

Edward watched Isabel Thornleigh as she walked out of the churchyard looking neither left nor right. Under the glowering sky threatening a storm, she moved stiffly as though she were summoning every ounce of effort to remain upright and follow the path. Edward felt sorry for her. But his anxiety soon returned inward. What chaos his disclosure had unleashed! Yet, who could have foreseen it? Who could have imagined that his words about Honor Thornleigh would inflame Lord Grenville to such an act of madness? If only Grenville had stuck to the plan that Edward had so carefully devised! An orderly separation of the families was all he had intended. All he had wanted was peace, security. But now ... Honor Thornleigh killed, Lord Grenville killed, both families aggrieved ... chaos!

He caught up with Lady Grenville and Christopher in the doorless church porch. Christopher was consoling his mother before going in to arrange the requiem Mass with Father Gilbert.

Christopher took hold of Edward's arm. "Edward," he said tightly, glancing out at Isabel's retreating figure, "John is in London with the archers, but I know he would agree with me. I have decided what we will do. I want Thornleigh brought to trial without delay. I want my brother-in-law, Rutland, to preside as judge. And I want Frances to alert the Queen about the urgency of the case." He paused to control his rising emotion, but without success. "I want that murderer's head on a pike by Lent! Arrange it, Edward. For my father's sake!"

Lady Grenville pulled open the church door. "Trial?" she said, staring with hollow eyes down the nave where the altar cross glimmered in candlelight. Her fury had subsided to a quiet, fierce intensity. Her voice was steel. "There are other ways to skin a rat." She started forward, and Christopher lurched to her side to guide her. Together, they went inside.

Edward was left alone. Blood pounded in his temples. A trial? Thornleigh giving public testimony? Thornleigh cross-

examined about his heretic wife's past and her former associates? It was the very catastrophe Edward had been trying
to avoid.

In Kent, Martin St. Leger threw back his head and
laughed with joy. He drained the goblet—his third—and
tossed it down to a foot soldier, then had to tighten his knees
on either side of his mount, for the wine was already heating
his brain. He drew his sword, held it high, and crowed,
"Wyatt and England!"

He kicked his horse's flanks and bounded forward, crossing the muddy expanse of the lower ward of Rochester Castle at a gallop. He reached the swinging straw effigy of the
Emperor Charles and slashed his sword at it, loping off an
arm already tattered by the swipes of the officers who had
struck at it before him. The mutilated effigy twisted in the
air, scattering bits of straw. The banner across its chest, the
black eagle, proud symbol of the Holy Roman Empire, was
cut to shreds.

The crowd of foot soldiers cheered Martin's attack and
shouted, "Wyatt and England!" Caps and gauntlets flew into
the air. Under the glowering sky, the walled castle ward,
packed with soldiers, rang with jubilant voices.

Martin grinned as he reached the line of his fellow
mounted officers on the far side of the ward and wheeled his
horse around to a halt. Wyatt's captains nodded happily back
at him: William Knevett, George Brooke, Thomas Culpepper, Vane, Harper, Norton, Vaughan, and the others. Culpepper handed Martin another goblet. "Spoils to the victor, St.
Leger," he said. Martin laughed, sheathed his sword, and
quaffed down the wine.

Another cheer erupted and Martin turned to look at the
castle steps. Sir Thomas Wyatt had mounted the steps with
a phalanx of anxiously smiling magistrates behind him and
had turned to speak to the massed soldiers. Wyatt held up his
arms in a gesture of victory. "Rochester is ours!" he cried.

His soldiers cheered wildly.

Wyatt laughed and brought down his arms to ask for
quiet. "This is a great beginning! We shall show the world
that England is her own master! Never shall Englishmen suffer overlords from Spain!"

"No, nor from Rome neither!" a soldier called out. Others
murmured agreement.

Wyatt smiled, letting these grumbles against the Catholic Church pass. "Every man among you, take rest now. Your lieutenants will assign you billets. Accept the food and drink that the good people of Rochester are offering. And take heart! When we march out from these walls, we march out to liberate our country!"

There was loud cheering and whistling. "Wyatt and England!"

Martin was cheering the loudest. He threw his own cap high in the air and watched it with slightly unfocused eyes. It was falling down toward his horse's rump, and as he leaned backward to catch it, he lost hold of his reins, sprawled over the horse's rear, and started to slip sideways.

"Whoa!" his brother said, running up to Martin's horse just in time to break his fall. Martin laughed and rolled with suppleness off the saddle and into Robert's arms, then quickly onto his own somewhat unsteady feet. "You have the timing of the angels, Father Robert!" he said gaily, swaying slightly.

Robert smiled. "That's enough wine, Martin, or you'll be suffering the devil's own headache. Come into the great hall now and sup with the others." Already, soldiers were streaming past them into the castle, hungry after the cold march from Maidstone, while others pushed out of the ward toward their billets in the town.

"I need no nursemaid to tell me when to eat," Martin scoffed. He pivoted out of his brother's clasp and started on soft legs toward the remains of the effigy. "Besides, the Emperor is merely wounded," he declared, pulling out his sword again. "Wounded, but not taken." He punched a fist into the air and lifted his face to the heavens and declared with a mock cry of chivalry, "Knights' honor is at stake! It is my duty—" The first drops of icy rain stung his face. He stopped abruptly.

"It's the duty of every sensible man to come in out of the rain," Robert said, reaching him.

Martin grinned sheepishly and fumbled to resheath his sword. Robert threw an arm around his shoulder, and Martin let himself be led toward the castle. Their progress was slowed by the crush of soldiers going in the same direction and by those heading out to the town.

"You knights may feel fresh after those ten frozen miles," Robert said, "but I'm worn out. Especially my feet."

"You could have ridden, too," Martin pointed out.

"I like marching with the men. It gives them a chance to talk to me, to tell me of their troubles."

Martin shook his head in pretended bafflement. But he stole a glance of admiration at his brother. "You're the real knight," he murmured, then added with piping-voiced gusto, mimicking the bravado of a boy, "you could slice the Emperor in *two!*"

They both laughed. Robert shook his head indulgently. But Martin knew he had not been far off the mark. As boys, when they had both been taught the martial skills of longbow and sword, as all youths of their class were, Robert had consistently outshone Martin and all their friends. Robert had the natural adeptness of a fighter, yet he had chosen the church. It was a choice Martin respected, though he did not understand it. But he had no trouble understanding the frustration that had driven Robert to join this army. Married during the previous Protestant regime that had encouraged priests to take wives—hundreds of them had done so—Robert and Meg now had two small boys. But four months ago Queen Mary had declared that priests must give up their wives and children and return to the celibate life, or else give up their vocations and their livings. Scores of married priests had already left England with their families rather than submit. Robert, not willing to stomach the ultimatum, had joined the fighters.

"I'll tell you a truth, brother," Robert said quietly, as if he had guessed Martin's thoughts. "I fear I may not be of any use at all in this endeavor."

"What are you talking about?"

Robert hesitated. "I could not kill a man."

Martin gave his brother's head an affectionate cuff. "You probably won't even get a chance to."

"What do you mean?"

"Well, look what's happened here. The people of Rochester threw open their gates to us as if we were conquering heroes. It'll be like this all the way, I warrant." He looked around. The crowd was finally thinning. "At the rate we're gathering men to us, the Queen will capitulate the moment she sees our host descend on London."

"Think you so?" Robert asked hopefully.

"The Queen would be mad to take us on. You watch. It'll all be over before a single arrow is loosed."

"You sound disappointed," Robert said.

Martin grinned. "I wanted to have Isabel here, away from her family, all to myself. But if I'm right, if everything's over in a trice, she won't even get the chance to come." He tilted up his face to feel the cold rain, still just a drizzle. "By the way, Sir Thomas told me that if we're to get news now about our French support it *must* come from Isabel. The French Ambassador's other spies have all deserted him, the spineless toads. Isabel was right in predicting that."

"Isabel is a clever girl."

"That she is," Martin said with pride. "And loyal and brave." He slowed his pace, lost in thoughts of Isabel.

"Aye, and loyal and brave," Robert agreed with a smile, tugging Martin to get him to move again.

But Martin shrugged clear of him and threw up his arms in a gesture of sheer joy. "And *beautiful*!" he shouted into the cleared yard.

"Yes, yes," Robert said, squinting up at the storm clouds, "the most beautiful maiden on earth. Now, come on in!" Suddenly the icy rain began to thunder down in heavy sheets. Robert ran ahead toward the doors. "*Now,* Martin!" he called over his shoulder.

Martin laughed and ducked his head and hurried in after his brother.

Night fell, and the storm that had broken on Rochester also broke over Colchester. Ice pellets lashed the ancient castle. Wind howled past the high, barred window of the county jail. Snow swirled through the rusty bars and fell in granular showers onto the shivering inmates below, dying upon contact with the warmth of their huddled bodies.

Swinging his lantern, Mosse headed for the far corner of the crowded ward. He stopped and called out, "Hoy! Spaniard! Get over here!"

Carlos Valverde looked around, still crouching at his dice game with four other prisoners on the floor, two of them in chains. Carlos was not chained. He had bought this measure of freedom on his second day here, a week ago, getting his irons struck off by selling Mosse his fine cloak. He frowned up now at the jailer. "Me?"

Mosse glared at him. "How many Spaniards am I hosting?" he asked witheringly. "Follow me."

Carlos tensed, his fingers tightening around his large handful of coins, his winnings. "Why?"

"Because," Mosse answered with a macabre grin, "you've got an appointment."

"With the hangman," one of the gamblers muttered.

"Upstairs," Mosse ordered Carlos. "On the double!"

Carlos stood, his heart thudding. Were they going to hang him inside the jail? At night? That wasn't usual, was it? And wasn't there supposed to be a trial first? That's what the men in here had told him. And he'd hoped that given another week or so before the trial he could make enough money at dice to bribe the turnkey and maybe ... He stanched the desperate flow of thoughts, knowing he was trapped. He had no weapons. His only hope was to fight with bare hands.

But Mosse caught the tightening of Carlos's body as if he had been waiting for it. In one motion he set down his lantern and whipped out his dagger, while yelling, "Rogers! Griffith!" Three turnkeys appeared from nowhere, joining Mosse to form a circle around Carlos. Two had unsheathed their daggers. The third held a truncheon menacingly. Mosse wiggled a beckoning finger at Carlos, challenging him. "Come on, Spaniard. Try it."

The gamblers were watching Carlos. Mosse waited, grinning wolfishly. Other prisoners, too, had turned to look, and a silence like the hush before an execution stole over the ward. Carlos saw it was hopeless. He clamped down his fury and his fear. If this was the end, this was the end. But first he would wipe the sneer off that *bastardo* jailer's face. He sprang at Mosse and stopped only inches from him, and with a roar of rage hurled his handful of winnings up at the ceiling. The coins clattered against the stone, then showered down on Mosse, the turnkeys, the prisoners. There was a frantic, noisy scramble for the money, with men shouting and diving, grabbing and gouging.

At Carlos's bellow Mosse had flinched and his grin had vanished, and his turnkeys were now hopping helplessly out of the way of the madly scavenging prisoners. Carlos pushed past Mosse and strode toward the corridor to the stairs, leading the way. Mosse glowered, snatched the lantern, and hurried after him.

Upstairs, they stopped in the jail's dingy front chamber, part of Mosse's rooms. Wind was rattling the window's wooden shutters like a robber trying to break in. Mosse set his lantern on the table beside his half-eaten supper, a gray leg of rabbit in a pool of congealed grease on a wooden trencher.

"In there." Mosse jerked his chin toward an open door at the side. Carlos stared at it. Was that where he was going to die?

"Move!" Mosse barked.

Carlos walked into the room. It was a small storeroom. Except for a few ale kegs on the floor and a dusty shelf holding some chains, it appeared empty.

"Valverde?"

Carlos spun around. A man stood between him and the door. A stranger. Dressed like a well-heeled servant, this was no hangman, nor even a bailiff's lackey.

The man closed the door, then turned back to Carlos. "Valverde, I have a proposition for you."

CHAPTER TEN

> ⊷⊶◆⊷⊶

Speedwell Blue

Isabel stood with her back to the hearth in the great hall of her parents' home, hugging herself. No matter how close to the fire she stood, she could not seem to get warm. The parlor would be warmer, but she would not set foot in that room of death.

"And she vowed to make Father pay with his life," Isabel said, finishing. "You should have seen her. She was like a witch. Deranged."

Her words seemed to die in the space between herself and her half brother across the hall. He stood at the window, rubbing his forehead with one hand and gazing out at the black void of night. Outside, the storm howled.

"Adam, didn't you hear me?"

"I heard."

"Well, what are we going to do?"

"What Father wants."

"But . . . you can't mean that. Not now. The Grenvilles will have him hanged!"

"I know!" he snapped.

Upstairs a crying baby's voice shrilled, echoing down the empty corridors. The tired murmuring of Kate, Adam's wife, sounded a useless counterpoint of reassurance as the child continued to wail.

Adam repeated quietly, desolately, "I know."

Isabel stared at her brother. In the maelstrom of events he seemed to be drifting away from her, unresisting, like some helpless beggar fallen into the river and carried off by the current. She stiffly rubbed her arms. "I don't understand any of this," she said. "Why Lord Grenville came . . . why the Queen should defile Mother's burial . . . how Lady Grenville can make such threats. But I know it means Father is in terrible danger. And I know we must do something."

Adam turned, though he did not look at her. His face was

haggard. "I need to see to Kate and the children," he said distractedly. "I bundled them over here so quickly. And they've all got to be ready at dawn for the voyage. You, too." He looked at her. "Don't think about the rest, Bel." He started to go.

"No!" Isabel rushed forward and blocked his way. "Adam, how can you?" She grasped his arm. "Don't you even care what's happening?"

He shook her off. "That's enough, Isabel." Again, he started to go.

"You *can't* run away and leave him to die! It's worse than cowardly! It's inhuman!"

Adam spun around. "You have no right!"

"No right? My mother has been murdered before my eyes! She wasn't your mother, so maybe it means nothing to you! But are you so heartless you'll let them kill Father, too?"

He stared at her, his chin trembling. Isabel's hands flew to her cheeks at the cruel thing she had just said. "Oh, God!"

Adam nodded mechanically, turning his face away from her. "It's all right."

"No, no, it's not! Adam, I'm so sorry!"

"I understand. I loved her, too."

"Of course you did." She held out her hand and he took it and they both held on tightly. "Adam," she said through a mist of tears, "why has this happened?"

He gave her a strange look. "You really know nothing about it? You've never even guessed?"

Isabel shook her head. "Tell me." She flicked away the tears before they could spill. She wanted to be strong to hear what was coming.

Adam looked into the fire. He spoke quietly. "Mother and Father didn't want you to know."

Isabel felt a tremor shiver up her backbone. Perhaps she already did know. "Lady Grenville was raving that Mother carried heretics away on ships," she said tentatively. "And that she had been chained to the stake to be burned, but Satan saved her."

Adam went white. "So," he whispered, "she's found out."

Isabel's heart missed a beat. "You mean it's true?"

"It's true."

Isabel felt for a chair and sank into it, slightly dizzy.

"At least," Adam said with a mirthless smile, "true except

for the part about Satan." He came to the chair opposite Isabel, in front of the hearth. "It happened twenty years ago," he said, sitting. "We lived near Norwich then. On a pretty manor called Great Ashwold." Isabel looked at him. Wind-whipped snow lashed the windows.

"You know how things were here in those days," Adam went on. "I mean, before old King Henry made his changes in religion. The Church burned people at the stake for heresy. What you don't know is that Mother fought the Church over it. Oh, quite secretly. She organized a kind of smuggling operation for hunted English Protestants. They came to her, the ones who were in danger of being condemned and burned. She got them onto Father's ships and sent them to safety in the Netherlands." He paused. Upstairs, the baby continued to wail. "But the Bishop's men caught her. They tried her for heresy and condemned her."

"And they were really going to burn her?"

Adam nodded. "At Smithfield fairground."

"What? You mean, Bartholomew Fair?" Isabel found the image eerily incongruous. She and her whole family had spent many happy August afternoons at Smithfield during the annual fairs, laughing at the clowns and jugglers, strolling among the stalls of tinkers' wares, eating hot mince pies and honey cakes.

"They chained her to the stake," Adam went on. "There was a large crowd." He paused and almost smiled. " 'Satan' was Father. I was thirteen at the time. My job was to hold ready the boat on the Thames quay, so I didn't see what happened at Smithfield, but they told me all about it after. When the executioner was about to plunge the torch into the straw beneath Mother, Father appeared on the roof of St. Bartholomew's church and made a bloodcurdling show as the devil. He threw down burning pitch onto a wagon of straw. The onlookers panicked, and everyone began running to escape the fireballs he was throwing, and in the confusion Mother's friends rescued her."

"And then you all sailed to Antwerp," Isabel whispered in wonder.

"That's right. Where you grew up."

"In ignorance." She felt a stab of anger. "Why was I never told?"

"They thought it was safer for you. But now ..." He stood. "Come. There's something you should see."

He picked up a candle in a holder, took Isabel by the hand, and led her up the stairs to her mother's study. It lay in darkness except for the pale light from Adam's candle. He set the candle on the mantel over the cold hearth and turned to a shelf of books beside it—volumes of philosophy by classical authors, and of history, astronomy, poetry. He reached up beside a large, ornately tooled Latin Bible. Leaning against it was a small book bound in blue leather. He took the small book down and handed it to Isabel. "I believe this was her most treasured possession. She said it had changed her life. I think you should have it now."

Isabel lifted the book's two small brass clasps, letting the vellum pages flutter open. Their edges were slightly charred.

"I understand it went through some adventures," Adam said. "She had it rebound, but the book's the same."

Isabel moved closer to the candlelight. The fluttering leaves had settled at the title page on which were printed the Latin words *"de Immortalitate."* On Immortality. Isabel's gaze was drawn to a painting below the title, an exquisite rendering of a flower on a winding green stem, its four-petaled blossom a bold, bright blue. She recognized the wildflower, a speedwell. Her throat tightened. "Speedwell blue," she whispered.

"That's right."

The phrase instantly struck an echo in Isabel's mind of her mother's voice telling the bewitching tale of how Isabel's father had lost his eye. It had been a sort of family fable. Her mother would say that when she was carrying Isabel she had wanted the baby to be born with its father's eyes, speedwell blue. But, she said, she had sensed that the blue fire of Thornleigh's eyes was so rich that it could not be diluted, so she had given him no hint of her longing. Nevertheless, he had guessed her wish. And so, she said, in order to give Isabel the color in his eyes, he had given up one of his own.

"I remember her rocking you on her knee," Adam said, "and cooing those words to you. But, Bel, the phrase had quite a life even before that." He reached behind the row of volumes and drew out from that hidden place a grimy notebook. "This was her journal of the smuggling voyages. It's written in code, and the people involved live far away or are dead, so it's quite harmless now. But the work Mother and Father were doing in those days was very dangerous and they had to be careful whom they trusted. So they used that

phrase—"Speedwell blue"—as a password. The right response was "Speedwell true." If they heard that, they knew
they were dealing with friends."

He came to Isabel's side and looked down at the Latin
book in her hands. "It's an argument against man's belief in
immortality of the soul," he said. "Or so Mother once explained to me after I'd had a go at reading it. Immortality of
the soul is a fairy tale, Mother said. 'That people want a
thing to be true doesn't make it true,' is how she put it."
Adam gave a self-deprecating shrug. "I confess I didn't get
the whole gist of the argument." He looked around the room,
at the desk littered with Honor's notes, at the piles of books
in corners. "She didn't believe in any church's teachings,
Catholic or Protestant," he said, then added in quiet puzzlement, "not even, I think, in God."

Isabel looked at Adam and shook her head in wonder.
"Though she wasn't your mother," she said softly, "you
knew her far better than I."

He nodded with a bleak smile.

"And now," Isabel said, as understanding chilled her,
"Lady Grenville knows, too, doesn't she? Knows everything."

"Apparently she has found out. I presume Grenville did as
well, and that's why he ... committed his mad act."

"And when Frances Grenville got word," Isabel went on,
"she told the Queen. And the Queen hates heretics above all
else."

"Exactly. For Father, there will be no mercy. And now he
fears the Queen's wrath will be directed against us, too.
That's why we must go."

"Go?" Isabel swallowed. Behind her the wind moaned in
the chimney like a creature demented by captivity. "Oh,
Adam, we can't."

"We can, and we must. It's all there is left to do."

"But it's wrong! You must think of some—"

"Don't tell me what I must do, Isabel! You've lived in
blissful ignorance of this knowledge all your life. Frankly,
I'm amazed you never suspected, never even had the curiosity to ask about what drove us out of England years ago.
You've been allowed to live completely selfishly, engrossed
in your own concerns. Cosseted by Father. Praised at your
lessons by Mother. Thinking lately of nothing but Martin.
Well, you know everything now, thanks to that Grenville

woman. And it's about time. But don't think it gives you the right to decree what I must do. I have *always* known," he said, holding up the journal. He tossed it back onto the shelf. "And I know what must be done now. I am responsible for the safety of this family—you, and Kate, and my children. And I have Father's unequivocal orders. I *will* carry out those orders. Do you understand?"

Isabel felt shame sting her cheeks at the rebuke. She looked into Adam's troubled eyes. She saw determination there. And she saw fear. She looked down at her mother's book in her hands, and she realized something else. She knew, with a sudden calm clarity, that she must not—*could* not—abandon the people who were relying on her. Martin. Wyatt. Her father. But a stab of panic followed. How was she to proceed? She looked back up into her brother's eyes, seeking direction. And she saw that she was utterly alone.

"Yes, Adam," she said. "I understand."

Carlos Valverde prowled the jail ward, searching. He was disconcerted to realize, now that he was looking, how many graybeards the place held.

His first attempt to make contact had been a failure. He had come up to an old man shivering cross-legged in a corner and mouthing a crust of bread and had asked him if his name was Thornleigh. When the man looked up and blinked, Carlos had crouched down and whispered the words as he had been instructed hours ago by the visitor. The man had blinked again—then wildly spat at him a mouthful of blood-tinged bread.

The next attempt had begun more promisingly. In the dripping cave that served as the jail's taproom, where Mosse's lackeys sold Mosse's swill-like ale to those who could afford it, Carlos had sat on the bench beside a well-dressed gray-haired gentleman who was slightly drunk and asked if his name was Richard Thornleigh. The man had smiled in a friendly way and replied, "What if it is, sir?" But when Carlos tried the words on him, the man had misinterpreted them as the opening to a ballad and launched into a ribald song about a large-breasted girl lying among the daisies.

Carlos had tried four more prospects, with no success.

Outside, the wind moaned past the high barred window in the four-foot-thick wall. Snow gusted through it, sifting down onto the weakest and sickest, who could not hold on to the better places. After eight days in the jail Carlos was used to the cold; in any case, his quilted leather jerkin and thick boots had always kept him warm enough, even through winter campaigns. The only thing he felt really naked without was his sword. He walked on through the ward as the prisoners began to settle down for sleep. A few had money to buy candles from Mosse, and interspersed among the sprawled bodies and ragged curtains a half-dozen flames flickered in the cold drafts.

"Well, if it isn't the poxy Spaniard."

"Probably looking for a boy to hump. That's what Spaniards like."

The taunts had come from the base of a pillar where two men sat watching Carlos go by. Carlos glanced at them: a potbellied, bearded man and a younger, wiry one. Priest killers; so Carlos had heard. He continued on, used to the insults of Englishmen. Especially *cobardes* like those two who hadn't the courage to face him. If one of them ever did, the garrote tucked inside his jerkin would do for them as well as for Richard Thornleigh.

If he ever found Thornleigh.

He passed the turnkey making his evening rounds with a lantern, and he realized he hadn't much time left. Not if he wanted to get the job done tonight. And he did, very much; he could be hauled out to the hangman at any time, tomorrow morning even. He *had* to accomplish this tonight. He felt a jolt of hope that was almost painful. The visitor's terms had been clear and concise: an immediate, full pardon once the job was done—the visitor swore that his employer had the highest connections—then a hundred pounds to be paid Carlos at a rendezvous at London's Blue Boar Tavern in a week, on Candlemas night. All Carlos had to do was bring proof of Thornleigh's death. He still could hardly believe the immensity of the offer. A hundred pounds! With that he could get out of this God-cursed country and back to the Continent and live indefinitely until some soldiering work turned up. Suddenly aware of what he had been reduced to, bitterness rose in his throat. Eight days ago he had owned three hundred thirty acres of land, a manor house, and lordship over twenty-one farming tenants!

He clamped down the galling recollection. *First things first*, he told himself. And that meant earning his freedom from the gallows.

The only description the visitor had been able to give was that the man marked for death was in his fifties, and there weren't many old men left that Carlos hadn't already approached.

Then he saw another one. He was sitting on the floor against a wall in the shadows, whittling a lump of wood.

Carlos approached and stood over him. "Richard Thornleigh?" he asked.

The man neither glanced up nor gave any word of assent. He simply continued his whittling.

Carlos sat down beside him in the shadows. He reached into his jerkin and held his hand there for a moment. Then he drew out a chunk of dried apple he had been saving. He tore it in two and offered one half to the man. The man ignored him.

Carlos shoved both halves of apple into his mouth. He looked down at the wood in the man's hands. It looked something like a boat. Carlos inclined his head toward the man and said, "I bring a message." There was no response.

Carlos watched the turnkey amble past a pillar, coming closer, and he felt a pang of anxiety. Once the turnkey left for the night and the candles were out it would be difficult to distinguish faces, almost impossible to search any further. This man *had* to be the one. He tried again. "Speedwell blue," he whispered.

The man's hand slipped and his knife gouged the wood, marring the boat. He lifted his head and looked at Carlos. Carlos saw that he had only one good eye. But he felt the strength of its beam bore into him. He almost hoped this was not the man he sought after all. He'd prefer one of the weaker ones.

"What did you say?"

Carlos repeated it: "Speedwell blue."

Surprise trembled over the man's features. For a long moment he said nothing. Then he murmured in wondering disbelief, "Speedwell true."

Carlos relaxed. He had found his man.

"Who are you?" Thornleigh asked.

"A friend."

"But I've never seen you before. Why do you come to me with this?"

"I am here for murder, like you. No hope of escaping the hangman. Until tonight. A man visited me. Told me to use those words to find you. Said only you would give the right answer." The man had also assured him that the words would lure Thornleigh into trusting him. But Thornleigh looked intelligent and wary. More explanation was necessary. "The visitor promised to come back with money for me," Carlos lied, "so I can buy off Mosse and get out of here."

"I see. But ... what does this mean? The password. Is help coming?"

Carlos hesitated, but only for a moment. "That is right."

"But who? There's no one left. Unless ..." He paused. "Is it my old friend Legge? Leonard Legge?"

Carlos shrugged his ignorance. "I am only the messenger. I was told to find you and get you to the taproom. The rest, I know nothing about."

"The taproom?"

Carlos nodded. The taproom was situated between the far end of the commons' ward and the now unused gentlemen's ward, both of which had free access to it. It was off-limits at night; Mosse wanted no one sleeping near his precious kegs of ale. So Carlos knew it would be empty. True, he could do the job out here, but Thornleigh looked strong; there was no guarantee he would die without a scuffle, drawing the attention of some prisoners, and that could lead to complications. Carlos saw no need to take that risk.

Thornleigh looked lost. "But I don't see—"

Carlos held up a warning hand to silence him and nodded toward the approaching turnkey. He and Thornleigh watched the turnkey as he slowly passed by them, swinging his lantern. The turnkey met with a prisoner under the window where the two talked in low voices. "When he leaves," Carlos whispered, "follow me."

Thornleigh said nothing. Carlos looked at him, suddenly anxious again. He had seen resignation like that on the faces of broken men on the battlefield when they knew their wounds were too bad to heal. Was Thornleigh that kind? Had he given up? Would he not even go to the taproom? Carlos had not anticipated that. Well, he thought, hope might get him to move. "I think your friends are coming to the taproom for you, through the other ward," he said. When Thornleigh still said nothing, Carlos added pointedly, making it clear he meant it as a threat, "You may not want to live, *amigo,* but I do."

Thornleigh went back to his whittling. But Carlos noticed that his hands were not quite steady. He also noticed that Thornleigh wore a ring on his forefinger, a signet seal of some kind of tree. *Good,* he thought. *That's the proof to take to the Blue Boar. The finger with the ring.*

They waited. The turnkey finally left the ward. Carlos heard the echoing slam of the grilled door in the corridor that led to the stairs. Then, except for some prisoners' coughing, there was silence.

Carlos turned to Thornleigh. "Come."

They started through the darkened ward. All but two candles had been extinguished. They felt their way slowly past the sprawled bodies and hanging obstacles. Carlos, in front, saw ahead the mouth of the narrow corridor that sloped down to the taproom cave. The corridor was completely dark.

"Go on," Carlos said to Thornleigh as they approached the entrance. "I will watch our rear."

Thornleigh started toward the blackness. Carlos reached into his jerkin for the garrote. One moment's work, and then he could be free. He began to follow Thornleigh.

A blow like a horse's hoof smashed the back of Carlos's neck. He toppled. He lay sprawled facedown, blind, paralyzed, unable to gasp breath. A cannonball knee rammed down on his back, grinding his hip bones into the stone floor, forcing out what air was left in him. "God-rotting Spaniard!" a voice growled. Hands wrenched back Carlos's head, then smashed his forehead down on the floor. His eyebrow split. Fire exploded in his skull. His brain was boiling tar. "No, use this!" another voice hissed. The cannonball lifted from Carlos's back. His body, like a stretched bellows, helplessly sucked in air and the floor's dirt.

He heard a loud thud above him and an "Oof!" Boots scuffled by his face. He spat out dirt, found he could move and see, and rolled over on his back. His brain cleared. To his left he saw that Thornleigh had plowed a bearded man against the corridor wall. To his right another man was on his knees, scrabbling in the dark for something on the floor. Carlos saw what the man was searching for—a length of woolen hose bulging with a rock. He understood. The other man had landed him with this bludgeon and had been about to bash his skull with it, but had dropped it under

Thornleigh's attack. And Carlos recognized both men now. The priest-killers.

Carlos sprang to his feet. Seeing him, the man on his knees gasped, found the bludgeon, and snatched it up. Carlos kicked it from his hands. Defenseless, the man glanced up in panic. Carlos kicked his face, cracking bone. The man reeled backward with blood spurting from his nose.

There was shouting all around as prisoners nearby, jolted from sleep, scampered to their feet and gathered close to watch the fight.

"Who's the big one?"

"The Spaniard."

"Kill him!"

The kicked man, on his back, was trying to get up while still clutching his bloody, broken nose. Carlos kicked him savagely in the side of the head. There was a snap from his neck. The man's arms and legs flopped out. Then he lay still. He was dead.

The prisoners booed Carlos. They wanted the fight to continue.

Carlos ignored them. He swiped away the blood trickling from the gash in his eyebrow and swung around to locate Thornleigh. Thornleigh was still grappling with the bearded man at the wall. The two of them staggered out a few steps into the ward, clutching one another as if in a grim parody of an embrace. They stumbled against a tattered curtain, ripping it down. The bearded man finally pulled away and jabbed a fist into Thornleigh's belly. Thornleigh doubled over and stumbled backward. The bearded man twisted around, ready to attack Carlos.

But Carlos had snatched up the bludgeon. He swung it around over his head as he moved in on the bearded man, then smashed it against the man's temple. The force of it knocked the man sideways. He collapsed and lay groaning on the ground. The prisoners booed and shouted and stamped. Carlos and Thornleigh now stood in the center of a hostile ring.

"Get the poxy Spaniard!" someone yelled. Three or four men lifted their fists, readying to advance on him. Carlos swung the bludgeon in threatening circles overhead. The prisoners crept back.

A bell clanged at the far end of the ward. It was the turnkey's alarm bell. The prisoners' voices rose to an excited pitch. Several scurried away. The clump of remaining ones parted, and Mosse himself came stomping through, followed by the turnkey swinging his bell, and by four other turnkeys with chains slung over their shoulders. All of them carried daggers or truncheons or both. Mosse scowled at the man moaning on the ground, then at the dead man. He glared at Carlos and Thornleigh. "Troublemakers," he growled. "Clap the irons on 'em and throw 'em in the Hole."

CHAPTER ELEVEN

The Hole

Sitting against the wall, Carlos watched the shape of a rat sniff its way down the stone stairs of the Hole. It slipped onto the final dripping step and stopped, nose twitching, as if uncertain whether it was worth proceeding. *Madre de Dios,* Carlos thought, the stench down here was too bad even for a rat.

He eased forward, away from the icy stone at his back. His head throbbed from the blows of the night before. After the fight, he and Thornleigh and the surviving priest-killer had been chained to the walls here. They were the only inmates. *Now,* he thought, *it must be dawn.*

He lowered his head to stretch his neck. Every muscle was stiff. His buttocks felt frozen on the damp earth floor. His toes and fingers were nearly numb. His bladder was uncomfortably full. There was no window, no warmth, no light except what seeped through the grilled trapdoor at the top of the stairs, the residue from a feeble rushlight in the corridor up there; the rat was a mere shadow among shadows. Carlos extended one arm and then the other to stretch his back, and the arm's-length chains connecting his wrist irons to the wall rattled. Thornleigh, who was hunkered beside him, groaned in his sleep.

The rat scurried across to the opposite wall where the priest-killer lay. He was dead. Mosse had chained him up unconscious and he had died in the night. Carlos knew it because he hadn't heard the sound of the man's breathing in hours. He peered at the corpse through the gloom. He could barely make out the shape of the rat near the dead man's outstretched hand. Then he caught the sound of it nibbling a finger. He shivered. He hated rats. That was why he had stayed awake.

And to think of a way out.

He glanced at Thornleigh's slumped form. Strange, he

thought—the man he'd been hired to kill had saved his life; the priest-killers would certainly have finished him if Thornleigh hadn't intervened. But in the few words the two of them had exchanged here before Thornleigh had fallen into his fitful sleep, Carlos had not expressed any thanks. He had nothing to be grateful for, he thought grimly, flinching at the stab of pain as he eased his bad knee. No pardon. No hundred pounds. No freedom. And with Mosse holding him responsible for the murder in the fight—make that two murders, including the corpse across the cell—his next encounter would surely be with the hangman.

He punched the air in fury and winced as the chain snapped taut; he had succeeded only in gouging skin off his wrist with the cuff's sharp iron edge. But there had to be *some* way out! Last night, after agreeing to the visitor's offer, he had tasted hope, and now he would scrape off every shred of skin before he'd let them haul him to the gallows.

He heaved a sigh of disgust at his own internal bravado. Some way out? He knew it was next to impossible.

He forced that thought—too close to panic—to the back of his mind. He fumbled to unfasten his codpiece, then urinated, sending the stream as far as possible, steaming in the air. But a rivulet snaked back around his left boot. He clenched his teeth at the indignity.

There was a clang above. Then footsteps. The trapdoor creaked open. Torchlight pooled over the stairs. Carlos fumbled to retie his codpiece. Someone was coming down.

"Careful. Steps're a mite slippery."

It was Mosse, sounding uncharacteristically helpful, Carlos thought. And someone was following him down. A woman. She flinched at the smell. Her clothes were rich. A lady. What was a lady doing here?

Mosse reached the bottom step and stopped. "There he is," he said, holding out his torch toward Thornleigh who groaned in his sleep, oblivious, and tried to curl up more tightly on the cold floor. The woman shoved back her hood for a better look. Catching sight of Thornleigh, her hand flew to her mouth. Carlos saw that she was young, dark-haired. Pretty.

"A rough sight, I grant you," Mosse said of Thornleigh. "But rules is rules, mistress. And the Hole for brawling's one of 'em. But I'll wake him for you. Give you your money's worth at least." He started forward.

The girl snatched his sleeve. "No," she said, keeping her voice very low. "Not yet."

Mosse shrugged. "Suit yourself."

Standing on the stair, they were separated from Carlos and Thornleigh by a large patch of ice-crusted mud, and their voices had been kept low; Thornleigh slept on, though he squirmed in restlessness. Mosse and the girl ignored Carlos completely.

"Jailer," the girl said in a sudden, fierce whisper, "I want him set free."

Mosse laughed lightly.

"No, listen!" she said. "I've brought more money. Plenty of money." She pulled out a purse, tugged open its drawstring, and held it up to him. "It's all yours."

A lady sure enough, with all that cash, Carlos thought. *And green as a willow sapling. Who else would trust this* bastardo *jailer?*

Mosse took the purse. He was not laughing now. "Let's see," he said. He moved to a dusty table in the opposite corner, not far from the dead priest-killer, whom he did not even glance at. Some chains were spread on the table, and Mosse shoved them to one side and dumped the purse's coins out to count them. Again, Thornleigh shifted miserably in the confines of his chains.

"Jewels, too," the girl whispered eagerly, following Mosse to the table. She loosened her cloak at the throat and showed him a sparkling necklace, then held up her hands to display several rings. "You can have anything. Just let him go. Please."

Mosse was admiring the girl's throat. And her shape. So was Carlos. *Imagine having a girl like that begging for your life,* he thought. What was she to Thornleigh, anyway? Awfully young to be his wife.

"Please!" she said again.

Mosse looked up the stairs as if making a calculation, then back at the girl. "I'd need something more besides."

"More? But this is all I—" She stopped herself. "Yes, of course. I could get you more. I'll bring it later. All right?"

"Not more coin," Mosse said, very quietly. He tossed the empty purse down on the scattered money. "Something softer." He fingered the fur at the edge of her hood. "You."

The girl froze.

"Wha'?" Thornleigh mumbled. His head jerked restlessly on the floor, though his eyes were closed.

Mosse glanced back up the stairs again. "And then," he said, smiling at the girl, "I'll let him go, free as you and me. Now that's an offer more than fair, considering my position, and considering your father's crime."

So, Carlos thought, *Thornleigh's daughter.*

"Is it a bargain?" Mosse asked.

The girl only stared at him, aghast.

Mosse's eyes narrowed in anger at the insult of her response. "All right, then, visit's over," he snapped, grabbing her elbow. "Come on, it's back home with you." He started to hustle her to the steps. But his angry voice had woken Thornleigh. He lifted his head slightly, blinking as if disoriented. The girl looked over her shoulder at her father and stopped. "No, please!" she said to Mosse. "Wait!"

Mosse eyed her with a small smile and brought his torch closer to her face. "Reconsidering, are we?"

The girl gnawed her lower lip.

Thornleigh was struggling to sit up. With his back against the wall he stared at the girl. "Isabel," he said, blinking in confusion. "What are you doing here?"

"Oh, God," she breathed in misery.

"Well?" Mosse said.

She closed her eyes. "Yes," she said, the word a whisper. She made a move toward the steps.

Mosse laid his hand on her shoulder. "Not upstairs. Here."

She turned to him in horror. "No!" she cried.

He set his face sternly, adamant.

The girl groaned. "Not here," she pleaded. "Haven't you a room of your own?"

"That I have, mistress," Mosse said, then added with a withering look, "and in it my wife lies snoring a-bed."

"But . . . I can't!"

Thornleigh jolted up straight. "Isabel!" Forgetting his chains, he lurched halfway to standing. But the chains jerked him back and he slipped on the slimy earth and sprawled on his back, his fettered arms splayed apart like a crucified man.

The girl looked frantically between her father and Mosse. "I can't!" she said to Mosse. "Not here! Not—"

"Then he stays," Mosse said firmly. He waited a moment. "Look," he said, tugging a ring full of keys from his belt and holding it up. "Here's your father's freedom." He shook the keys enticingly. "Take it or leave it."

At the sight of the keys, Carlos felt every nerve tighten. Was there some way . . . ?

Thornleigh had struggled halfway up again and sat against the wall. "Go away!" he cried to the girl. He flailed his hands. "Get out of here!"

Mosse took no notice of him. "Make up your mind," he said to the girl with another glance up the stairs. "I haven't got all day."

She gave a sort of whimper. Her face contorted and she twisted away from Thornleigh, her back to him and Carlos. But she made no move to leave.

Mosse lifted the keys to her ear and rattled them. "I'll even let you unlock his irons yourself, after," he said. "Well?"

Carlos tore his eyes from the keys to catch the almost imperceptible nod of the girl's head.

Victorious, Mosse tossed the keys on the table. He shoved his torch into the wall bracket above the table. He came close to the girl and tugged off her cloak. It fell in the mud. He grasped her shoulders and turned her to him and buried his face in her neck.

Thornleigh gasped. "No!" he cried.

The girl stood rigid, unmoving. Mosse ripped loose the lacing of her bodice. He tugged down the velvet fabric, and the thin chemise beneath, uncovering her breasts. Carlos swallowed. She had beautiful full breasts. Mosse grabbed them.

"I'll kill you, Mosse!" Thornleigh screamed. "I'll kill you!"

Mosse kneaded the girl's breasts, then bent and sucked noisily at her nipple. He ignored Thornleigh's continuing bellows of rage. But they were all the girl appeared aware of. Her eyes were tightly closed, and she held up a hand between her face and Thornleigh as if to hide behind it. All her concentration seemed focused on trying to block out her father's ranting voice.

Mosse fumbled under her skirts and shoved his hand up between her legs. She winced. He wrenched her around to make her face the table, then pushed her over it so that she bent forward at the waist and her head hit the table. She let out a groan as if she had been punched. Mosse hiked up her skirts and threw them up over her back, baring her buttocks. Her body was in profile to Carlos, her ear on the table, her face turned away, but the torchlight above her gleamed golden on the skin of her buttocks and thighs. Carlos felt himself swell and harden.

Mosse prodded the girl's legs apart, making her stumble for balance. He yanked his codpiece to one side, exposing his erect penis. He took hold of her hips and plowed into her. She gasped, and her head jerked up. Thornleigh roared, "Merciful Jesus, no!" The girl's head thudded back down, her other cheek on the table this time, her face toward Carlos. Her eyes were wide-open now. Blazing blue eyes, all-seeing as a stark and cloudless sky.

Mosse pulled out of her and grunted in disgust, "Cunt's dry as a nun." He spat on his hand, then smeared the spittle between the girl's thighs. The girl's hand clenched the edge of the table by her face. Thornleigh howled.

Suddenly the girl twisted around and faced Mosse, her skirts tumbling down. White-faced, with her chin trembling, she stood rigid. Then, stiffly, she lifted her skirts again, uncovering herself to Mosse. Her eyes shot pure hatred at him, but her gaze did not waver from his face. Carlos held his breath. She was forcing Mosse to look her in the eye.

Anger flickered across Mosse's face at her defiance. He pushed her back against the table edge and prodded her legs apart, making her tilt backward on her elbows. Still, her eyes fixed him. He shoved himself at her with a leer that said he was waiting for her to break. But she did not turn. And Mosse's lust was stronger than his will to outface her. Finally, about to enter her, under her unflinching gaze, he closed his eyes.

He rammed into her. Her hands shot out along the table, knocking coins to the ground and the keys, too. Thornleigh strained at his chains until his wrists were bloody.

Mosse pumped and grunted. Thornleigh raged like a madman. Mosse squealed at his climax. The girl made no sound.

Then, Mosse was finished. Still inside the girl, he stood panting, wiping sweat from his forehead. Thornleigh slumped against the wall. He rolled his head back and forth along it, moaning.

Carlos's eyes slid between the keys on the floor and the girl. He wanted the keys, but the girl had amazed him. He thought he had seen every kind of sexual contract that women dealt in, from the tears of raped virgins, sobbing at the theft, to the lewd invitations of camp whores, aggressive in a buyer's market. And he had had women who negotiated every arrangement between those extremes in the give-and-take of lust. But the carnal bargain this girl had made was something he had never seen: she had done it for her father's sake. And, in a bizarre way, by forcing Mosse to avoid her eyes, she had beaten him.

Mosse pulled out of her. Carlos saw a trickle of blood darken the inside of her thigh. *She's a virgin,* he thought. *Or was.*

The girl straightened up from the table, forcing down her skirts. She tugged up the fabric of her bodice to cover her breasts. She bent and picked up her cloak from the mud and drew it tightly around her. She turned and faced Mosse, summoning up what dignity she could. But Carlos saw that she was shaking. And when she lifted a hand to push her hair back from her face, her hand merely skimmed near her hair, the action of someone not quite in control. "Now," she said, "unlock his chains." Despite the quaver in her voice, the command was firm.

Mosse was refastening his codpiece. He glanced up the stairs and smiled. Carlos thought he heard footsteps beyond the open trapdoor. "Like I said, unlock him yourself," Mosse said, and nodded at the keys on the ground.

Carlos was astonished. The *bastardo* wasn't really keeping his bargain, was he?

The girl snatched up the keys and stumbled forward between Carlos and Thornleigh. The hem of her skirt swished over Carlos's boot. He drew up his knees. She knelt down and reached out for Thornleigh's wrist cuff. She fumbled through the keys. "It's the small one, with the string on it," Mosse said helpfully. He was busy shoving the coins on the table back inside the purse.

As Mosse spoke, the footsteps above became the heavy clomp of boots. They reached the top of the stairs. A torch flared at the open trapdoor. The girl was just unlocking Thornleigh's cuffs when three men marched down the steps—a turnkey and two guards. The girl looked around in surprise and stood. Carlos saw that she had abandoned the keys.

"Ah," Mosse said with great satisfaction, "right on time. I do insist that my men stick to the rules, mistress." Looking at the turnkey, he jerked his head toward Thornleigh. "Take him." The turnkey motioned to the two guards. The guards approached Thornleigh and finished unlocking his chains.

"No!" the girl cried. But the guards were pulling her father up from the floor. They shoved him through the room. Thornleigh lurched from their grasp and lunged murderously at Mosse. Mosse jumped back. The guards seized Thornleigh again and manhandled him toward the steps.

The girl ran after them. "No!" The guards ignored her and pushed Thornleigh on. The girl screamed at Mosse, "You promised I could set him free!"

Mosse was picking up the coins that had fallen under the table. "And so you *did*," he said. "And now he's free to visit London town. He's been transferred there by order of the sheriff. That's what he gets for bashing in the brains of a lord." He tugged tight the drawstrings of the purse and called up to Thornleigh, who was struggling between the guards on the middle of the stairs, "And you won't find any London prison a bed of roses like my jail."

As the guards pushed Thornleigh up the final step, Thornleigh wrenched back his head. "Get away, Isabel!" he cried. "Get out of England! You—"

A guard kicked his leg, and the turnkey ordered, "Shut your gob." They forced Thornleigh out of the Hole.

"Go, Isabel!" Thornleigh's muffled voice called down one last time. Their boots scuffled along the corridor. Then there was silence.

Carlos's eyes darted back to the keys. They were still attached to Thornleigh's chains left on the ground. They lay so near him. He knew he could reach them. But any movement would draw Mosse's attention. He forced himself to sit still.

The girl whirled around on Mosse. "You knew!" she said with quiet fury. "You knew it all along!"

Mosse smirked. Of course he had known.

"Where are they taking him in London?" she demanded. "Which prison?"

Mosse shrugged. "Don't know that. But I could find out." He stuffed the full purse inside his grease-stained doublet and sauntered closer to her. She backed away toward the table. Mosse smiled. "And I *would* find out," he said, "if you'll come again tomorrow." He reached out and touched her breast.

She jerked back and banged against the table. She reached

behind her and grasped a chain that lay on it. She swung it wildly at Mosse. But Mosse saw it coming and stepped back and she missed him. He laughed. She moved toward him, the aggressor now. He stepped back farther, closer to Carlos. His grin had faded. "Set that down, hussy," he commanded, "or you'll find yourself tossed in up above with all the other whores."

The girl swung the chain at him again, aiming at his face. Again, Mosse lurched back and she missed him. But Mosse had taken one step too many. His heel touched Thornleigh's discarded chains. Feeling the obstacle, he twisted, and when his other foot came down it became tangled in the chain. He lost his balance. With arms windmilling in an effort to keep upright, he turned and fell onto his backside. The back of his head banged against Carlos's raised knee.

In a sudden, savage motion, Carlos lifted his arm and whipped his own chain around Mosse's neck. Mosse gasped and clutched at the stranglehold. His heels slid in the mud. He swiped behind his head at Carlos's arm, and his nails clawed channels in the back of Carlos's hand, drawing blood. Carlos wrenched the chain in a vicious twist. Mosse's neck snapped. In a final convulsion his foot jerked out, kicking the keys away. Then he lay still.

Carlos looked up at the girl. She was gaping at the dead jailer's head twisted askew. She looked at Carlos in shock and backed away to the table. Her legs seemed to give way. She slipped down to the ground and sat there, panting. She and Carlos stared at each other across the murky room.

Carlos uncoiled his chain from Mosse's neck and let him slump to the floor, then lunged for the key ring. But Mosse, in his death throe, had kicked it beyond his reach. Carlos tried to stretch for it with his foot. But it was still too far away. He looked back at the girl. "Get me the keys," he said.

She flinched at his harsh voice. She was struggling to her feet. Once up, she held herself steady by the edge of the table, eyeing both Carlos and the dead jailer with revulsion. Carlos saw that he had terrified her with his act, his wild appearance—the gash scabbing his eyebrow, the ten days beard and dirt, the blood dripping from the back of his hand—and with his desperate need. "Unlock me," he said. "You are the only one who can."

She hesitated. Then she shook her head as if to herself.

She began stiffly walking toward the stairs. As she passed Carlos, she pulled her cloak tightly around her as if to avoid contamination. In a moment, he saw, she would be gone—his last chance to escape the gallows. "Stop!" he said. She flinched in fright and hurried on. She started up the stairs.

"You owe me!" he called. "I saved your father's life!"

She stopped.

"Last night," Carlos went on quickly, "someone tried to murder him. *Asesinato*. I saw."

She turned. "What?"

"I was near. The assassin, he used special words to get your father's trust. I heard. Then, later, I saw him attack. I called to your father to warn him. There was a fight. Your father was knocked down. I . . . I fought off the assassin. Others fought, too. When it was over, the jailer put your father and me here."

The girl blinked. "An assassin?" she asked skeptically. She looked around. "Where is he now?"

"Gone. I think . . . let out by his . . . *patrón* . . . leader?"

"You mean, his employer?"

"Yes. Set free. That is what I think."

The girl appeared to consider the story. She looked hard at Carlos. "What were the words he used?"

"What?"

"You said the assassin used special words. What were they?"

Carlos hesitated. But he had come this far. And the girl was his last chance. "Speedwell blue," he said.

Her mouth fell open. Carlos knew he had struck cleanly.

"Did my father make an answer?" she asked.

"He said, 'Speedwell true.' "

The girl felt for the stair under her and sat as if stunned.

Carlos wondered if he had miscalculated after all. But the only course now was to plow on. "So your father is in much danger. Someone wants him dead. I do not know who."

"I do," the girl whispered in dismay. "The Grenvilles." Then, even more quietly, "My God, if they know those passwords, then Father is right . . . they know *everything*." She stood. There was determination in her face. "I must save him," she said. Carlos cursed himself. He had inadvertently prodded her to action. She was going to leave. But in the next moment her expression dissolved into the look of a frightened child. "But what . . ." she said in desperation, "what am I to do?"

Carlos saw her helplessness. And, suddenly, he saw his way out. A way to stay alive, to get back his freedom, and more—London and the Blue Boar Tavern at Candlemas. He saw it all clearly. Find Thornleigh. Kill him. Collect the reward. Get out of England.

"Listen to me," he said. "The sheriff will soon be after you—"

"The sheriff? Good God, why?"

"To question you about this," he said, jerking his chin toward the dead jailer. "People saw you come in. People will see you go. If I am left chained here, who will they think did this? And you cannot go on the main road to follow your father. If you do, the sheriff will come after you and stop you. You must take other roads. That will be slow. The guards will have Thornleigh in prison in London before you reach the city. But you do not know which one. And what will you do when you get there—a lady, all alone, with no *protección*?"

He waited, allowing the hopelessness of her situation to sink in. Her stricken face told him she understood. Then he said, "You want to find your father and rescue him, yes?"

"Yes," she said, her voice a whisper.

"Then you need help." With his foot he prodded Mosse's body and added pointedly, "Expert help." He leveled his gaze on the girl. "I am a soldier."

He reached inside Mosse's jerkin and pulled out the purse. By its feel he judged it held no more than ten pounds. He tossed it to the girl, a show of his trustworthiness, then kicked Mosse's body so that it rolled once and lay facedown in the mud. "And you are lucky," he said with a half smile. He rested one boot on the dead man's shoulder as if on a trophy. "Because today, I am for hire."

CHAPTER TWELVE

><><-O-<><

The Road to London

Martin St. Leger ran through the snow-trampled precincts of Rochester Castle and on toward the town's busy western gate. A horse-drawn wagon clattered across his way where it suddenly halted, forcing Martin to such an abrupt stop in the slushy mud that he almost slipped. A cart following the wagon rattled to a halt, too, the carter jerking his horse sideways to avoid a collision.

"Let me by!" Martin called up to the wagoner. "I bring a message for Sir Thomas Wyatt!" He had to shout above the din of voices all around, the loudest of which came from a lieutenant barking drill orders at a company of soldiers.

The wagoner called down to Martin, "Can't budge, sir. Not till the farrier's dray ahead moves on."

Martin panted steam into the cold morning air and impatiently surveyed the commotion in the shadow of the castle's towers. The inside approach to the gate swarmed with wagons, horses, mule-drawn carts, and men-at-arms. Lieutenants called orders at men on ladders propped against the town wall and at men laboring on top of the wall, where hammers clanged and saws rasped. Martin found the sight of Wyatt's army at work richly satisfying despite the delay the obstruction was causing him—despite, even his puzzlement over Wyatt's orders for such extensive strengthening of Rochester's fortifications. Why bother, he wondered, when any hour now they'd be marching out to join the Duke of Suffolk's army coming down from the north, and then on together to London? Yet what a fine start they had made here! Their army of close to three thousand had marched into Rochester two days ago to cheering citizens, gushing wine casks, and hearty fare laid on at the castle, which had quickly become their headquarters. True, the Mayor had fled to London. But the rest of the townspeople had welcomed them as if they were liberators. *And so we are*, Martin thought with a surge of energy as he squeezed past the wagon. *As Wyatt promised, we shall liberate all of England!*

He pushed past a knot of men hauling lumber and bumped shoulders with a tall old soldier. The man's weather-cured face reminded Martin of Isabel's father, who spent so much time on his ships. Martin chuckled as he hurried on. Cautious old Master Thornleigh, he thought; he wouldn't dream of taking action against the Queen, but he, and Isabel's mother, too, would be the first to thank those who were doing so. The thought of the gratitude of Isabel's parents—and of Isabel's pride in him—warmed Martin and spurred him on.

He spotted Wyatt. He was standing on top of the wall by the gate, directing the placement of a wide-mouthed mortar to overlook the Strood bridge. Martin jogged toward the wall.

"Sir Thomas!" he shouted up.

Wyatt turned, wiping gun oil from his hands on a rag.

Martin grinned and called, "News!"

A hundred miles to the northeast the Duke of Suffolk was shivering uncontrollably, though the sun was rising almost in his face. He had just spent his second night huddled in the huge hollow tree near Astley church. His feet were numb. His teeth chattered. The strengthening sun exposed his hiding place as mercilessly as a bailiff's torch. And the yapping dogs were getting closer.

How had everything gone so sickeningly wrong? Only days before he and his sons and the men of his household had ridden into Bradgate, the very heart of his lands. They had roused up the town, and it seemed that every man there had jubilantly agreed to march south to join Wyatt and fight the coming Spaniards. But when the Duke and his sons rode out to alert more of the countryside, few were riding with them.

The Duke had ridden to the gates of Leicester—Protestant Leicester—where all within should have been his friends. But though the Duke had ridden around its walls, Leicester's gates were shut to him.

Word came that Coventry would welcome him. He galloped on to Coventry. But Coventry was shut. And its Mayor proclaimed the Duke a traitor.

The Duke had ridden back with his entourage to his own house at Astley. No help came from Bradgate. No help came from anywhere. And when a messenger galloped in with news that Bishop Gardiner in London had sent forty horsemen to arrest the Duke, the only thought at Astley became flight. The Duke's sons ran through the house snatching the servants' clothes as disguises. They divided up the cash, horses, weapons. And then they scattered.

The Duke had thrown himself on the mercy of his gamekeeper, who had hidden him in this eastward-facing hollow tree a long bow shot from the church. The Duke had waited, shivering under the naked boughs, eating snow, wondering what had gone wrong.

The dogs' barking became louder. He grasped his trembling knees to his chest and squirmed back into the band of shadow against the tree's wall. He held his breath to stop its telltale steam. His gamekeeper had betrayed him. The dogs were closing in.

Martin hurried up a ladder against Rochester's wall and came beside Sir Thomas Wyatt.

"*Good* news, I hope, St. Leger," Wyatt said, tossing aside his oily rag. "I could use it today."

Martin grinned. "Sir Henry Isley's messenger from Sevenoaks just rode in. The fellow was famished, so I set him at table and came across myself. Sir, the word is that Lord Abergavenny and Sheriff Southwell cannot raise above four hundred men between them for the Queen in this county. And the ones they do raise desert as soon as they have the chance!"

"That's good," Wyatt said quietly. "Is that all?"

"No, sir." Martin beamed. "The messenger also reports that Sir Henry Isley has mustered over six hundred men for us! They'll be marching today to join us here. It's just as we said, sir. Englishmen will flock to us to keep the Spaniards at bay."

Wyatt frowned. "Only six hundred?"

"Only? Why, that's just from around Sevenoaks! Sir Henry's brother in Tonbridge will be bringing more. With them, and the thousands Sir James Crofts is bringing from Wales, plus the Duke of Suffolk's army coming from the north—why, we'll be unstoppable!"

Wyatt said nothing. Frowning, he looked out over the snow-rutted stone bridge beyond Rochester's town wall. Be-

hind them, men continued to pull up ropes hoisting baskets
of shot.

Martin looked out at the bridge, too, to hide his disappointment. He had hoped that the good news would jolt Sir
Thomas into action. They must march! Why was he delay-
ing? It was not that Martin doubted the commander's exper-
tise. Wyatt, he knew, had spent seven years fighting in
France for King Henry and then for young King Edward,
serving with distinction at the siege of Landrecies and in the
capture of Boulogne as lieutenant of a strategic harbor fortress. Martin acknowledged that he himself had none of
Wyatt's military experience. But he wished Wyatt had more
zeal. Could it be that he had lost the stomach for this fight?

Wyatt suddenly turned to him. "Where's that blasted girl
of yours?" he asked irritably. "She should have come by
now with news from Ambassador de Noailles."

Martin did not appreciate Wyatt's tone. "Isabel will come,
sir," he said stiffly.

"She'd better. And soon. I *must* know the details of our
French support."

"You can count on Isabel."

Wyatt looked at him skeptically, and then, again, stared
out over the sluggish river and the snowy bridge. From the
bridge, the road led up Spitell Hill to the Thames port of
Gravesend five miles to the north, then on to London thirty
miles westward.

Martin could hold back no longer. "Sir, why do we not
march on London?"

"With only this?" Wyatt said, jerking his chin toward the
men laboring below the wall.

"These men are ready and eager! We should head out now
and have Isley come after us. Then we can converge on London with the others. Hit the city before the Queen can even
muster."

"Good God, St. Leger," Wyatt flared, "are you blind?
Converge on London with what?"

"Why, with the Duke's army coming from Leicestershire.
And Croft's coming from Wales."

"And where are these phantom armies? Tell me that!" He
stared belligerently at Martin's blank face. "That's right,
man. You've got it now. *No one* is coming from the north or
from Wales."

"But—"

"Yes, yes, those men were with us in the planning. But Courtenay's blabbing forced us to begin this enterprise too soon, and now . . ." He threw up his hands. "Croft seems to have vanished. And as for the Duke of Suffolk . . ." He shrugged. "Your guess is as good as mine what's happened to the Duke."

Martin felt panic knife his bowels. "And our support in London?"

"That, thank God, is sure. London is for us."

Martin's panic subsided. The other news was a terrible blow, but not fatal. London was what mattered. If London opened to them as Rochester had, and if they could take the Tower and stand firm, then the Queen was lost. Martin was no commander, but he knew this to be true. Because this fight was a contest of wills—the will of all patriotic Englishmen against the will of a half-Spanish Queen. Turning, he caught sight, at the inside base of the gate, of his brother Robert holding communion services for about two dozen men standing in the dirty snow. Martin had forgotten it was Sunday. He had a sudden thrilling vision of himself and Isabel standing before Robert in a church, pledging their marriage vows while her mother and father looked on, all smiles. He remembered standing as witness when Robert and his Meg had taken their vows. Martin felt a rush of happiness. Robert had the will. Isabel had the will. And the three thousand men who had rushed to follow Wyatt here had the will. "Sir Thomas," he said with feeling, "if London is ours, we cannot lose."

Wyatt looked at him. "You really believe we can do it? With just this force?"

"Isley is coming. And men keep joining us. And, damn it, our cause is right!"

Wyatt looked out at the bridge for several moments in silence. "St. Leger," he said with the sudden, brusque voice of command, "I'm sending you to stop Isley." He beckoned to a young clerk farther along the wall, and the clerk hurried toward him, opening his portable escritoire on the run.

Martin had blanched. "*Stop* him, sir?"

"From marching immediately to join us. There are several manors around Sevenoaks with good armories. Sidney's at Penshurst, for one. Tell Isley we need all the weapons he can get—bows, swords, pikes, pistols—anything." Wyatt was scribbling the order on the escritoire. "No destruction of

property and no looting of anything else. Tell Isley I forbid
it. But we must have more arms before we head for London.
Stay with Isley and help him."

Martin nodded eagerly. Though this meant more delay, at
least Wyatt was preparing for action.

Wyatt handed Martin the order. "Go now. And hurry."

Martin was hurrying back toward the castle's lower ward
for his horse when he heard his brother's voice, breathless,
at his back. "Slow down, Martin! I'm not the sportsman you
are these days!"

"Can't stop, Robert," Martin said, striding on. "I'm off to
Sevenoaks with urgent orders from Sir Thomas."

"I'll come and help you."

"I don't need you."

"I'll come anyway." Robert reached Martin's side and af-
fectionately cuffed the back of Martin's head. "Without me,"
he said, "you might get lost."

A hand was jostling her shoulder roughly. Jerking awake
from a troubled sleep, Isabel was unable to grasp what was
happening or even to remember where she was. She knew
only that she was lying on a hard, cold floor and that every
muscle ached. She turned her head in the gloom and saw
four scabbed welts on the back of the large hand that was
shaking her. Yesterday's horrors came swarming back to her
mind. This was the Spanish mercenary. He was crouching
beside her. The welts were the wounds Mosse had clawed as
he thrashed in the savage stranglehold of these very hands.

Isabel blinked up at the mercenary's shadowed face; his
bulk blocked the source of what little light there was. His
square chin was dark with over a week's growth of beard. A
livid purple scab gashed through one eyebrow. The scab
etched up his forehead and faded into dun-brown hair like
the bristles of a wild boar. The eyes looking down at her
were the color of gunmetal. An instinctive shiver of fear rip-
pled through her. She tried to stifle it, acutely aware that fear
of him was a response she could no longer indulge. This
killer was now her accomplice and partner.

"Get up," he said in a rough whisper. "You must eat. Then
we leave." He stood and moved away.

Leave? Isabel still could not recall where they were. There
was a heavy smell of wood smoke and cow dung and unwashed bodies. A scuffling sound by her ear made her turn

her head the other way, and she felt a jab of pain, for her neck was very stiff. The sound came from a smelly mongrel hound energetically scratching its chin with its hind foot. Bits of debris from its matted fur showered Isabel's face and she quickly sat up, picking specks of the filth from her eye. Beside the dog, four huddled forms lay on the packed earth floor: three children nestled together and a gaunt old man in the corner, his toothless jaws gaping open in sleep. At the far wall, dawn light seeped around the solid shutters that covered the room's only window. Finally Isabel remembered. Driving snow had forced her and the mercenary to stop overnight at this alehouse in a hamlet on the road to London. In the frigid two-room cottage, the family was accustomed to huddling around the hearth to sleep. Isabel and the mercenary had crowded in with them.

She rubbed her neck and looked around. The low-beamed room was murky with smoke. The mercenary, seated at the plank table, had dug a spoon into a wooden bowl and was lifting a mound of porridge to his mouth. The woman of the house, shapeless beneath layers of threadbare wrappings, was bent before the sooty hearth, poking brushwood into a smoking fire. A cow stomped in the adjacent byre, and its steamy breaths gushed in through the lath wall that separated the byre from the family's quarters. Or it might have been her own mare stomping, Isabel thought. She and the mercenary had ridden the mare together away from Colchester jail.

Her stomach growled. She was very hungry.

She got up. With fingers stiff from the cold, she pulled her fur-lined cloak tightly around her and moved to the table. Across it, the mercenary ignored her and went on eating. There was a stool by Isabel's leg, but she remained uneasily standing, unwilling to sit so near him despite her resolution not to be afraid of him. The woman left the fire and fetched two mugs of ale and brought them to the table. She also tossed down another wooden spoon for Isabel. Isabel realized that she was expected to eat from the same bowl as the mercenary.

"Thank you," she said, trying to sound sincere. Expressionless, the woman shuffled back to the hearth. The children on the floor began to stir. One, a mouse-eyed little boy with freckles, sat up and stared intently at Isabel. The woman scowled back over her shoulder as if expecting to witness Isabel's rude refusal of the breakfast.

Uncomfortable under their scrutiny, Isabel pulled the stool to her and sat. She winced, still sore from the defilement she had suffered from Mosse. At the memory her stomach lurched. Her cheeks burned with humiliation and anger. She caught the mercenary glancing up at her, and the recollection that he had seen it all, had watched everything Mosse had done to her, sent a jolt of mortification through her that was as sharp as the soreness. She quickly looked down and pretended her boot required some adjustment. The woman turned back to tend the fire.

When Isabel stole another look at the mercenary he was again busily devouring the gruel between gulps of ale. It was as though none of the awful events of their escape yesterday had disquieted him. They had terrified her. She shivered, remembering. As soon as she had unlocked his chains he had unleashed chaos in the jail. Moving through the ward with purpose and precision he had set several fires, then unlocked the prisoners to run amok through the corridors and up the stairs. She saw the mob trample a boy, and when a turnkey attacked the mercenary with a dagger she saw the mercenary smash the turnkey's head against a wall. But despite the frenzy all around them the mercenary had remained astonishingly cool-headed. He had waited—and restrained *her*—until the other prisoners were swarming through the castle yard and drawing all the jailer's men after them. Only then had he quietly retrieved his sword and dagger from the jailer's empty chamber and led Isabel out through a side door. Avoiding the guards rushing for the stable, he had untethered her mare by the jailer's door, mounted, and pulled Isabel up behind him—for she had come on a man's saddle, expecting to ride out with her father—then had taken the horse out of the castle precincts at a walk, unnoticed in the melee.

They had ridden for mile after mile over iron-hard tracks that jarred her backbone, through ice-rattling woods, past frost-killed hop fields over which the wind swept so mercilessly Isabel had to squint, even behind the mercenary's broad back. Her mind, recoiling from the last days brutal events, and her body, aching from the jailer's violence, had eventually felt numb. When they finally stopped at this alehouse, she had sunk into the oblivion of sleep almost as soon as her shoulders had touched the floor.

She watched the mercenary as he ate his breakfast. He was intensely purposeful even in that. She did not know what crime had brought him to be held in chains at Colchester jail, and she did not want to know. Nor could she pretend any regret over Mosse's death at his hands. Yet his cold-bloodedness chilled her. Still, she had to admit that he was capable and ruthlessly efficient. If anyone could find her father and rescue him, it would be this man.

"Eat," he said. He was halfway through the porridge. Isabel noticed that he had strong, even white teeth.

She looked down. "I'm not hungry," she lied. She had had nothing since leaving Colchester except a slab of wheaten bread and some flat ale when they'd arrived here, but the gray gruel looked revolting.

"Eat anyway," he said. "You will need the strength."

It sounded like a command. Obeying, she picked up her spoon. But her gaze drifted to the window. Had the weather let up enough to carry on? she wondered. The closed shutters made it impossible to tell, but she had noticed that the moaning wind of the night had quieted. She swallowed, gathering the courage to speak; on the road she and the mercenary had not exchanged more than ten words. In a voice lowered to prevent the others from hearing, she asked, "Do you think . . . will we be able to reach London today?"

He did not look up, then he answered between spoonfuls, "Yes."

"Do you have any idea which prison they have taken him to?"

"No."

"Then we must search them all."

"Yes."

Isabel had no more questions. Struck by the enormity of the task ahead, she distractedly dipped her spoon into the bowl. The porridge was cold lumps of gluey pease. It tasted of rancid pork fat. She forced it down. The two of them ate in silence.

The cottage door clattered open. The brewer, a burly, bearded man, came in carrying two buckets of water. His shoulders were hunched from the cold even under his hooded sheepskin coat, and he stomped snow off his boots before carrying the water to his wife at the hearth. On the way he kicked the freckled child's leg. "Look lively, boy," he said gruffly. "Lord of the manor's on his way. He's stopped at Widow Dowd's door for a word, but soon's he gets here he'll want his brew ready in the skins." The boy jumped up to attend to his chores. The two smaller children scuttled out of their father's way. The old man in the corner snored on.

The brewer nodded to Isabel and said, "I've watered your horse, m'lady."

"Thank you, Master Brewer," she said. Her eyes were drawn back to the mercenary. She had seen a scowl flit over his face at the mention of the approaching visitor. She understood. The lord of the manor could well be the local magistrate, and the mercenary was a fugitive from justice.

He stood. "I will saddle the mare," he said quietly to Isabel. "Finish here. Quickly." He quaffed down the last of his ale, wiped his mouth with the back of his hand, and went out the door to the byre.

Isabel nervously paid the brewer for the food and the night's shelter and thanked the silent woman for the breakfast. She made a quick visit to the privy behind the cottage. The air was bitterly cold, but she was glad to see that the day promised to be bright and calm. A dog ran barking down the hamlet's narrow main street. Isabel hurried to the three-sided byre. A cow noisily munched hay by the wall. The mare was saddled—but the mercenary was nowhere to be seen. Suspicion shot through Isabel.

Her first thought was to check her saddlebags. She had left no money in them—it was safe in the purse at her waist—but her other belongings were here. She opened one saddlebag, then rushed around the horse to check the other. Everything was as she had left it.

Glancing across the mare's back, she caught sight of the mercenary moving out from behind the cow with the horse's bridle in his hands; she remembered he had hung it on that wall last night. He was looking at her with a small, grim smile as though he knew she had suspected him. And it was true. After all, the ten pounds she had promised to pay him—though all she could afford with the inevitable expenses of London ahead—was hardly a fortune. Besides, she was asking him to incur great risk in the venture. How could she help wondering if, now that he was free, he might have second thoughts about assisting her? She could not possibly stop him from stealing her belongings and decamping if he wanted to, even now. Or even going on to London with her and then stealing the horse and leaving her stranded. But as she watched him fit the bridle and tug tight the cinch under the horse's belly, ready to carry on, she felt a pang of remorse at her suspicions. How could they work together if she thought such things of him? She *must* trust him.

She rearranged her belongings—paltry though they were—and refastened the saddlebag. She had come away with little more than her mother's book, a change of clothes, and a fresh shirt and tunic for her father. She had not expected to need much else; had expected, in fact, that her bribe of money to the jailer would free her father and send him to safety in Antwerp, while she would carry on to London and help the rebellion. Then Martin, victorious with Wyatt, would come for her. She felt bitterly ashamed now at her naiveté.

The glimpse of her mother's book made her think of Adam. Where was her brother now? she wondered. She imagined him standing on a ship halfway across the Channel and looking back at England, her note in his hand. She had left it in her room before quietly stealing from the house yesterday at dawn and going to the jail. *Adam,* she had written, *I am not coming with you. There are people here I cannot desert. I have taken some of Father's money. Forgive me.*

"Peter Brewer!" a man's voice called. Isabel moved toward the byre's entrance. The shout had come from a man on horseback approaching at a trot along the road. A compact middle-aged squire, he halted his horse not far from the byre and called again toward the cottage door, "Peter, I'm in haste this morning. Can't stop in."

The brewer was already hustling out the cottage door with a bulging leather flask of ale in his hands. "Here's one, m'lord," he said pleasantly as he hoisted the drink up to the horseman. "My boy's filling t'other. Won't take but a moment."

"A moment's all I've got," the man grumbled as he yanked a glove off with his teeth. He tied the flask onto his saddle.

"Why the rush, m'lord?"

"Got to finish my business in Chelmsford by noon," the man said, clearly annoyed. "Sheriff's in a lather over some felon escaped from Colchester. Wants me back to help in the search."

Isabel noticed that the mercenary had moved into the shadows behind a post near her. The post screened him from the horseman's view.

The brewer looked up at the squire and scratched his chin. "Colchester's a long way off to be stirring up folks hereabouts, m'lord."

"Aye. But it seems the blackguard murdered the jailer. Let loose the rest of the prisoners, too. Some foreign blighter, they say. Spaniard or something." He shook his head. "God deliver us from foreigners, eh, Peter?"

"Right enough, m'lord," the brewer agreed. He scowled back toward his front door. "Where's that boy got to? I'll just go hurry him along, m'lord." He stumped back into the cottage.

Isabel watched the squire as he idly looked around the hamlet's dirty street, waiting for his ale. "My lord!" she called out suddenly. "I would speak with—"

Faster than she had said the words, the mercenary yanked her into the shadows, twisted her to face him by wrenching her arm back, pinned her to him, and raised his dagger to her throat. Isabel froze.

"Yes?" the horseman called toward the byre, peering toward its apparent emptiness. "Who's there?"

The mercenary wrenched Isabel's arm higher up her back. She gasped at the pain. The dagger glinted by the side of her jaw. He was crushing her so tightly against him she could feel the thudding of his heart against her breast. Her own heart pounded in terror. His face loomed over hers, a furious intensity tightening his features.

"Is someone in there?" the horseman called toward the byre. He led his horse a few steps closer and stopped, waiting.

The mercenary's steel-gray eyes flashed a warning to Isabel not to make a sound. His dagger point touched her jaw. She could not even swallow. She was frightened, but as she struggled just to catch her breath in his viselike grip she felt anger also swell inside her. His hold was painful and humiliating. And she had had enough of men mauling her. Suddenly her anger boiled over her fear. She jutted her jaw above the dagger in reckless defiance of him. "My lord!" she called out loudly.

The mercenary blinked in surprise. Isabel saw the realization flicker in his eyes: he could not harm her now, or the man outside would find him. His grip on her slackened. She instantly pulled away. Once free, the sunlight at the byre's entrance protected her even more, for he did not dare leave the shadows.

"Good day to you, sir," she called, stepping out boldly toward the horseman. "I would ask a question of you. Do you hear any news of the uprising?"

"Indeed, yes, mistress," the man answered, slightly taken aback by her sudden appearance. "Forgive me, I did not at first see you." He frowned back at the byre. "Are you stopping here?"

"Yes, sir," she said, trying to calm her breathing. "I am on my way to visit my sister, but the bad weather forced us to take shelter for the night, me and ... my manservant. The brewer has been most hospitable. I am just leaving." She waited for the information she craved. Even her anxiety at the thought of the mercenary and his blade not far from her back could not quell her hunger for news of the uprising, and she had sensed by the horseman's words to the brewer that he would be in sympathy with the rebels, or at least with their aim of halting Spanish domination. If only he would stop looking her up and down and tell her. "Pray, sir," she prompted him, "what *is* the news?"

"Ah, yes. Well, mistress, the talk is that Sir Thomas Wyatt's army has taken Rochester. And all without a single man loosing a single arrow."

"You mean ... Rochester opened to him?"

"I do. *There's* news for you, eh?" Isabel realized that he would not dare speak with open approval of Wyatt's treasonous action—not to a stranger. But his admiration for it was plain enough in his twinkling eyes.

The brewer came out and handed the squire another flask. The squire paid him. The brewer, after nodding to them both, went back in.

"Does your sister live in Chelmsford, mistress?" the squire asked, fitting the flask into a saddlebag. "If so, I am going there, and it would be my pleasure to escort you."

"Thank you, sir, but my journey takes me another way."

"Well," he said, adjusting his reins, "you've got a fair day for it. Godspeed to you."

"And to you, sir."

He trotted off down the road.

Isabel looked up at the brightening sun in the clear sky and almost smiled. Wyatt was going to be victorious. Martin was going to be a hero. The news brought the first flush of warmth to her heart she had felt since her mother's murder. But as she watched a rook alight heavily on an oak tree branch, sending a row of tiny icicles crashing to the ground, she shivered again. To succeed, Wyatt needed her information from Ambassador de Noailles. That meant she must get to London, and then to Rochester. But there was her father's life to save, too. And that meant dealing with the mercenary. She turned and went back to the byre.

The mercenary was watching her intently. Isabel hoped he felt ashamed at his misjudgment of her, but though there was some lingering surprise in his expression there was not a trace of contrition.

He untethered the mare. "We go now," he said.

"No, wait." Isabel opened one saddlebag and pulled out her father's tunic. It was of heavy green broadcloth, quilted for warmth. "The authorities know you are a Spaniard," she said, "so they probably have a description of you as well. You can't go dressed as you are. Wait here."

She went into the cottage and quickly bargained with the brewer for his coat. As she expected, he was content to exchange it for the tunic; he only required a warm garment as a replacement. And when she added a few coins for good measure she left him smiling. He had asked no questions and she had told him only that she feared her servant was coming down with a chill. She was glad the mercenary had spoken so few words during their stay; nothing marked him as anything other than English, and her hireling. She returned to the byre and held out to him the brewer's hooded sheepskin coat. "Take it," she said. "It will make you look more like my manservant."

He looked at her with a frown, hesitating. Isabel recalled the heavy thudding of his heart when he had held her in the shadows, and she suddenly realized that he, too, had been afraid. No, it was not exactly fear; he seemed quite hardened to fear. It was more like a desperate will to survive. *And why not?* she asked herself. *It's what we are all fighting for.* The realization touched her. She felt a need to let him know she understood.

"Look," she said, "I know you were afraid I was going to turn you over to that gentleman. But you really must trust me. You were quite right in what you told me at the jail." She looked down, embarrassed again to recall what he had witnessed of her with Mosse. But she was determined to finish. "As you said, I do need you." She looked up again. "And after all," she said, "what possible reason could I have to betray you?" She lifted the sheepskin, offering it. "We must trust each other if we are to succeed in this."

She waited. He said nothing. He was looking hard at her, his gray eyes unreadable as fog.

"Besides," she said, attempting a smile, "you'll be warmer this way."

He took the coat, tugged it on over his leather jerkin, and quickly turned away. He mounted the horse in silence and pulled her up behind him.

They set off toward London as the sun crested above the barren treetops, reflecting prisms from a thousand icy branches.

CHAPTER THIRTEEN

The Clink

Edward Sydenham settled comfortably in the chair before the fire, glad of a few peaceful moments alone before his important audience with the Queen. He adjusted the pearl-encrusted collar of his yellow satin doublet embroidered with black silk tracery and stretched his legs out to the hearth's gentle warmth. He looked around. Frances Grenville's chamber at Whitehall Palace was somewhat drab, given her pious eschewing of the decorative arts as frivolous. His own elegant parlor was far more to his taste. But the room had status—its hearth was evidence of Frances's high standing with the Queen; the other ladies-in-waiting rated only corner chambers with braziers—and it was snug and cozy. At the moment Edward's happy state of mind required nothing more.

He was pleased with the way he had managed things. After the initial shock of Lord Grenville's moment of madness three days ago, and the consequent appalling fright that Richard Thornleigh might be brought to trial to divulge all, Edward was satisfied that he had controlled the damage rather well. At first, the idea of hiring the Spaniard at Colchester jail had seemed—after the admitted thrill of the inspiration—an action grotesque and distasteful. But it had also appeared the only solution to his crisis, so he had ordered the assassination. He had come to London immediately after, but he had left his steward behind in Colchester to make the arrangements with the Spaniard. Edward rubbed his eyes before the fire's glow, remembering how he had suffered two nights troubled sleep over that decision; he had never meant to harm *anyone*. However, the crisis was past. The Spaniard had had ample time to execute his commission; the deed must by now have been done. And now that it was, Edward was forced to admit that he felt no excessive remorse. Sentimentality, after all, was for fools. The main thing was that both Honor and Richard Thornleigh were dead and no longer able to implicate him in any crimes of the past that could mar his plans. The future looked rosy again.

And so did his farrier's daughter, Edward thought with an inward smile. He had noticed her this morning for the first time, bringing breakfast out to her father in the farrier's shed. Plump, cow-eyed, and surely not yet fifteen. He shifted in his chair, his blood quickening already at the image of that certain type of young girl that always aroused him: such a heady combination of docility and fear. Yes, he would have his chamberlain arrange it. The fellow, brought from Brussels, was a prodigy of discretion. It could not be tonight, unfortunately. Tonight he must dine at the Venetian Ambassador's house with the Fugger banking representatives. The Queens' financial business must come first. But tomorrow night the girl could be brought.

The Queen's business, he thought with a flush of contentment. How quickly the rewards of his alliance with Frances were flowing to him!

"Edward."

He turned. Frances stood in the doorway. She was out of breath and her cheeks bore high splotches of color. Strands of her straw-colored hair had escaped her *touret*.

"I came as fast as I could the moment I heard you were here," she said, wringing her hands. She gazed at him with that mixture of adoration and deference he had become accustomed to in their two-month acquaintance. Her nervousness in his presence never varied. She seemed perpetually torn between an impulse to rush to him and an apprehension of being rejected. The plain woman's dilemma, Edward surmised. And her face today, he thought, was plainer than ever. She looked quite distraught.

He stood to greet her, smiling. "My dear," he said, holding out his hands. "Whatever is the matter?"

She rushed toward him, her shoulders slightly hunched in the way of a woman who feels herself too tall. He took her hands and she stood awkwardly while he lightly kissed her cheek. She seemed to be trembling. Tears welled in her eyes. At the corners, Edward noticed, tiny crow's-feet were beginning.

"Oh, Edward," Frances said, her voice breaking, "I still cannot believe it."

He was on the verge of asking what she meant when he
recalled, just in time, that she was in grief over her father's
death. "Oh, my poor dear girl," he said gently. He folded her
in his arms and patted her back. She smelled unpleasantly of
something camphorous. Probably one of her own mixtures,
he thought, concocted to calm her nerves. She did have a tal-
ent at mixing herbal remedies. "There now," he said soothingly. "We must try to put this awful tragedy behind us. You
especially, Frances, hard as it may seem. Because Her Majesty relies on you. You know she does. You must not fail her
now by showing her a grieving face. She needs your
strength."

His words had an immediate effect on Frances. She
straightened bravely and nodded and even managed a wobbly smile. "Yes, you are right, Edward," she said, wiping her
cheek where a tear had made a track down to her mouth.
"And it is so noble of you to think of Her Majesty even in
the midst of our sorrow." But as she spoke, her grief surged
again and her mouth twisted into a grimace as she fought to
master it.

"That's right, my dear," he said encouragingly. "Be
strong." He glanced at the door. "Speaking of Her Majesty,"
he went on, "isn't it time we went? We must not be late for
my audience."

She nodded quickly, immediately contrite. "No, no, of
course not. Come, I will take you." She stopped, looking at
his rich clothes. She flushed and smiled. "Oh, Edward, you
do look splendid!"

He bowed graciously. Following her to the door he
thought how *un*splendid was her own apparel and how mis-
matched. She wore a drab skirt of olive silk topped by a
bodice of ornate turquoise-and-crimson brocade. The brocade was from a bolt made in Persia that he had given her
himself, but it should have been paired with a skirt matching
its jewellike hues; this discord of color, especially on her an-
gular body, was jarring. He recalled something the Emper-
or's Chancellor had told him once at a dinner in Brussels. It
was a phrase the Imperial Ambassador, Renard, had used in
a dispatch to the Chancellor, reporting his first meeting with
Queen Mary: "She is a perfect saint," Renard wrote, "and
dresses badly." The Queen and Frances were two peas in a
pod.

He held the door for his betrothed and they walked together down the corridor toward the Queen's audience chamber. A brachet hound nervously trotted by them, whining and sniffing at doorways as if in search of its master.

Edward and Frances passed several knots of people—courtiers, merchants, priests, ladies—but there was an unnatural quiet. Edward had noticed it as soon as he had arrived at the palace. They passed four of the Queen's ladies standing at an alcove window, deep in a hushed conversation from which Edward caught the words "Wyatt" and "France," and heard one of the ladies' slight gasp. From the far end of the corridor came a man's muffled, angry shout. Edward wondered if it arose from a meeting of the Queen's council behind closed doors; the crisis had reportedly set the unwieldy council to constant bickering.

"Is John here today?" he asked Frances as they walked.

"I wish he were," she said of her brother. "But he is busy arranging billets for his archers in the city." Her brow furrowed with worry. "Such a dreadful to-do over this traitor. Do you know, Edward, two churches have been sacked in Kent? And yesterday, right here in St. Giles, the vicar was shot at while saying Mass!"

Edward nodded distractedly. He was thinking of Frances's brother becoming the new head of the Grenville family. John and he got along well enough, and Edward felt sure John would make no trouble about the agreed dowry; Frances would still be bringing impressive land holdings to Edward at their marriage.

"There are such terrible rumors, Edward," Frances went on as they turned a corner. "Some say an army of six thousand rebels is marching from Wales to join Wyatt. And a courier arrived from Cornwall last night saying hundreds of gentlemen there, too, are up in arms against the Queen."

Edward nodded a greeting to the Imperial Ambassador who was coming up a staircase deep in conversation with Sir Richard Riche. But Renard, ferociously whispering some rebuke to Riche, seemed not to notice him.

"I've even heard that the Scots are massing an army on the border," Frances said, "and that the King of France has sent ten thousand soldiers to join them. Can it be true?"

Edward shook his head. "Rumors, Frances. Do not heed them. The Queen will soon put down this rabble of troublemakers. God is on her side."

She smiled at him, her eyes full of faith. "Yes. And I am

so proud you are helping her, Edward. But do you really
think you can arrange this loan for Her Majesty on such
short notice?"

"I'll know tonight when I meet with the Fuggers' representatives. But," he added with a smile, "I feel confident.
And I mean to assure Her Majesty of it today."

A scream startled them. It had come from the direction of
the Queen's apartments, just ahead. Men and women were
rushing out of the audience chamber into the corridor, running to investigate. Edward and Frances exchanged glances
and hurried forward. Four of the Queen's guards pounded
past them with halberds raised, making people lurch out of
their way. Edward and Frances reached the open door of the
Queen's apartments and entered the dark-paneled antechamber.

The crowded room was in a commotion. A lady had fallen
to the floor still whimpering, and several gentlemen were on
their knees assisting her. Another lady was sobbing in a corner. Lord Paulet was pointing and shouting at a young guard,
"Fetch the palace marshal!" People edged aside.

"Look!" Frances whispered in horror to Edward.

He turned toward the middle of the room where the crowd
had parted. A dead spaniel lay stretched out on the floor, its
tongue lolling. It wore a noose around its neck. Its head had
been shaved in the fashion of a priest's tonsure. A note was
scrawled beside it: *No Spanish papists.*

Edward looked around at the frightened faces. He felt a
slight thrill. There was a great opportunity here. Someone
with an outsider's understanding, like himself, could see
that. He was glad the distraction about Thornleigh was out
of the way. Now, he could concentrate solely on taking the
initiative and forging an indestructible rapport with the
Queen.

The people suddenly hushed. Queen Mary had come from
the audience chamber. She stood in the doorway and stared
tight-lipped at the atrocity on her floor.

The people bowed nervously and Edward bowed with
them. But he was smiling. The upstart rebels held no real
threat, he was sure. The Queen only needed soldiers to destroy Wyatt. Time and again Edward had seen the Emperor's
hired armies smash peasants' revolts and greedy princes' up-
risings throughout the Imperial domains. Money was all that

was needed. Money bought soldiers. And money was what Edward was about to arrange for the Queen.

The Clink. There had been a prison in the palace of the bishops of Winchester on the south bank of London since the twelfth century, and its evocative name had come to stand for all prisons in England.

Isabel and Carlos arrived at the gate of the stone palace on the river after a morning's ride from Essex made tortuous by the necessity of taking secondary roads and tracks to avoid possible search parties and by a piercing wind that had arisen around noon. They tethered the mare and walked in among the visitors and the traders in food and fuel—farmers on donkeys, vintners and firewood vendors in ox carts, water carriers and market women on foot. Although the inner quadrangle of the palace was alive with commerce, Isabel found its orderly bustle a respite after the struggle she and the mercenary had just made through Southwark where the noisome, narrow streets were crowded with the squabbling customers of the brothels, crude inns, and bear gardens for which the south bank was famous. Even so, the savagery of the bear gardens still seemed near, she thought, as the bear-baiting mastiffs' incessant barking from the kennels catapulted over the lead roofs of the palace in the still air.

Isabel looked up. If her father was in this prison, could she somehow manage to get him scrambling over those same roofs, and thus escape to safety? Was it a mad hope? She feared that it was. In fact, her very quest to find him in the teeming city of London with this grim-faced, silent mercenary at her side seemed slightly mad. So be it, she told herself. She could accept the madness—had she any choice?—if only the quest was not hopeless.

The Clink was in the palace cellar, beneath the Bishop's great hall. Inside the prison's iron-studded door, an elderly porter got up from his desk and asked Isabel for four pence, the fee charged any member of the public seeking entrance. Isabel gave it to him, along with her father's name.

"Debtor or felon?" the porter asked, opening an admissions book to a grubby page.

Isabel swallowed. "Felon," she said. "Is he here?"

The porter studied her with sudden sharp scrutiny and looked askance at the mercenary. "Can't say," the porter replied.

"But your ledger—"

"Ledger's for visitors' fees," he sniffed. Abruptly he called out, "Cellarman!"

A man with bushy black hair rose yawning from a stool and ambled toward them.

"Felons' ward," the porter instructed him.

The man nodded. "Tuppence," he said, holding out his grimy hand to Isabel.

"But I just paid the porter," she protested.

The porter sighed. He explained in the tone of a recitation: "No one goes among the felons unescorted. The fee for the escort is tuppence. Pay the cellarman or leave."

Isabel paid. The porter turned back to enter the transaction in his ledger. As the cellarman pocketed the coins he eyed Isabel in a way so similar to Mosse's leering that it made her skin crawl. He said quietly to her, "You can leave your man here."

"I go with her," the mercenary said.

The cellarman looked startled by this unequivocal statement from a servant, but he shrugged. "Suit yourself," he said, and turned to lead the way. Isabel stole a glance at the mercenary, truly glad of his presence for the first time.

The cellarman led them through the porter's lodge, then down a flight of dimly lit stone steps. He unlocked a door and took them into a low, stone-vaulted corridor where male prisoners were strolling. There were many other visitors, too. Isabel was not surprised. All prisons were open to anyone who wanted to conduct business with the inmates, or to drink and sport with them, or merely to gape. Prisoners lounged against the walls, eyeing the new arrivals as they passed.

The mercenary came up close behind Isabel and said in her ear, "Hide your money."

Isabel quickly untied her purse and shoved it deep inside her wide sleeve. Yet she did not feel afraid of the prisoners; though most looked sullen and shabby, they did not appear vicious.

"Debtors," the cellarman said, as if responding to her thoughts. He sidestepped a mound of dog feces.

They turned a corner. The passage became darker; the only light came from the odd, sputtering cresset lamp. Mildew streaked the stone walls. They passed into a dank-smelling room. Isabel drew in a sudden shocked breath. Men were pinned inside wooden stocks in lines along both sides of the room. Their hands and naked feet protruded from holes in the stocks. Several of them lay slumped over the top, asleep or unconscious. One, sitting bolt upright, was weeping. A well-dressed young couple stood staring at him in morbid fascination. A sad-faced woman knelt beside a prisoner at the far end and washed his feet with a rag.

"Heretics," the cellarman said, not looking right or left as he led the way through the room. They came out into a wider space, a dining hall. At long tables visitors sat with prisoners—male and female—eating, drinking, playing cards, tossing dice.

Isabel could not help a fleeting thought of how odd it was that while rebellion was being loosed on the land, the people here seemed untouched by the news. Her thoughts were interrupted by loud voices farther down another corridor— unmistakably female voices. The cellarman led them that way, and the sounds became louder: chatter, sporadic laughter, jeers. Finally they came to its source: a women's ward, though several men were lounging there as well. The room was packed and very noisy. Straw pallets lay scattered around the floor strewn with food scraps. A baby bawled in a corner. A chicken flapped frantically as three women tried to catch it. A bare-bottomed little boy waddled past Isabel. Almost all the women prisoners wore gaudy, threadbare gowns on their wasted bodies, and garish paint on their lips and cheeks. Two of them whistled at the mercenary. One called out to him a suggestion so lewd that Isabel could not help glancing at him in astonishment. He stared ahead, ignoring the catcalls.

"Winchester geese," the cellarman said over his shoulder to Isabel.

"Pardon?"

"Whores."

Isabel blushed. "Oh."

They passed out of the women's ward, though no barrier separated it from the corridor to keep the different wards' inmates from mingling. "What'd you say the felon's name was?" the cellarman asked Isabel as they walked on.

"Richard Thornleigh," Isabel said.

The man looked around at her, brightening. "I know him. Brought in yesterday, he was. Older bloke, right? Kind of quiet?"

Isabel's eyes widened in amazement. She could hardly believe this stroke of luck. There were several prisons in London. Three lay in Southwark, so that had seemed a good place to start, and this was the first one across London Bridge. "That's right," she said eagerly. "Can you take me to him?"

"Aye."

Isabel clamped down her excitement.

They arrived at a barred door. The cellarman unhooked a wooden truncheon that hung at his waist. "Thieves and murderers," he said darkly, and knocked on the door. It was opened by his counterpart. Isabel stepped into a large, dim ward. She immediately began rationing breaths in the foul air. The cellarman slapped the end of his truncheon against the flat of his hand as if preparing himself.

Some of the prisoners sat on the packed earth floor, their wrists chained to the walls. Others, unfettered, lay on matted mounds of filthy straw. A few were walking aimlessly, a few were sleeping. A cluster of them squatted on the floor by a pillar, gambling. There were several women as well—apparently, by their dress, prostitutes from the women's ward. Male and female faces looked around with malevolent stares at the visitors. Another cellarman idly patrolled the ward, truncheon in hand. Isabel saw that the door she had come through was the only exit.

She felt a sudden wave of panic: it would be impossible to get her father out of here! She looked at the mercenary. He was scanning the ward with his usual intense, determined look. His resolution calmed Isabel somewhat; the mercenary knew what he was doing.

"Where is he?" she whispered to the cellarman.

"Over there." He nodded toward a tall, gray-haired man among the gamblers, whose back was turned their way. The mercenary immediately started across the ward to him. Isabel followed, her heart quickening with every step. The cellarman came, too. When they reached the cluster of gamblers the cellarman clapped a hand on the gray-haired man's shoulder and said, "Thornleigh. Visitor for you."

The man playing cards cackled. Isabel felt a stone sink to the pit of her stomach. She knew, even before he turned—a wild-eyed stranger—that it had been too good to be true.

They were halfway across London Bridge.

"Stop!" Isabel said from the mare's back. The mercenary

looked around with a frown. He was walking, leading the horse.

"Stop, I say!" Isabel kicked her foot out of the stirrup and jumped off the mare, but foot and horse traffic flowed around them. She felt trapped. With a feeling of panic she pushed her way through to the side of the bridge.

She reached a gap between the three-storied shops and looked out westward over the gray, wind-whipped Thames. She took several deep breaths of the cold air, but it did nothing to ease her anxiety. They had just left the Clink, and the mercenary had declared it was too late in the day to search another prison: all prisons turned out the public before dusk in preparation for locking up for the night. They must go to an inn, he said, and wait for morning. But Isabel found the decision a torture. To have come all the way to London only to find such heartbreak at the Clink ... and now, to have to wait ... when an assassin hired by the Grenvilles might be stalking her father in some verminous ward at this very moment. It was unbearable ...

She looked out at the water. The river was crowded with barges and ferries from which the watermen's whistles shrilled above prospective passengers' shouts, from various wharf stairs, of "Oars!" and "Westward, ho!" A drayman near the German merchants' wharf was dumping a cartload of refuse into the water. Isabel watched a goat carcass float toward the bridge. In summer, she thought, there would be swans here. Scores of swans forming downy white clouds on the water. The memory pierced her—the summer sweetness of it—like a shard of a poignant dream impossible to hold on to.

She hardly knew which sorrow weighed her down most heavily. The image of her mother's mutilated face had become too horrifying to recall and had retreated to the back of her mind like a wounded beast to its cave. But the other bonds that held her life together were equally threatened, and their claims to her loyalty warred inside her. She was pledged to take Wyatt information about the French Ambassador's support, information that might be essential to the cause—to Martin's very life. Yet the search for her father was keeping her from doing so. But could she leave her father to his fate? Impossible! She glanced toward the city, where Ambassador de Noailles was, then looked anxiously back toward Southwark. The Marshalsea prison was there, and King's Bench prison, too. Was her father chained in one of them?

The mercenary came beside her, the horse's reins in his hand. She turned to him. "Could we not at least manage a look into the Marshalsea?" she entreated.

He shook his head, then nodded toward the horizon. She looked out at the sun dipping toward the Westminster reach of the river. Of course, it was too late. She must wait till to-morrow.

Behind her, a nasal-voiced girl was loudly hawking eels and spiced meat pies to passersby. A group of horsemen trotted down the bridge's center. An ox cart joggled past.

"I despair of finding my father at all," Isabel said bleakly.

The mercenary turned, putting the river scene behind him. He reached out to adjust the horse's bit. "We will find him," he said.

"How can you be sure of that?"

"The turnkey back there said there are seven prisons," he explained, easing the bridle over the horse's nose. "Your father is in one of them. If we keep looking we will find him."

"And then? Will you really be able to rescue him?"

He did not look at her. He *never* looked at her. "There are ways," he said.

His coolness was a goad to her grief. "I have recently watched my mother die, Master Valverde. I will not let them kill my father, too. Surely," she lashed out, "even *you* can sympathize with that! Or perhaps you did not know who your father was!"

His gray eyes suddenly fixed her with what felt like contempt. "No. My mother was a camp whore."

Isabel was shocked. Not so much by the fact as by his indifferent acceptance of it, his total lack of shame. And she felt instantly contrite; for her unprovoked insult, *she* was the one who should feel shame.

He glanced toward the bridge's gateway that led to the city. He moved to the horse's side and jerked the stirrup toward Isabel. "Get up," he said roughly.

Isabel held her tongue. She mounted the horse.

The Anchor Inn, where Isabel decided they would stay, was a small hostelry on cobbled Thames Street. It was snugly tucked away, with its stable and tiny courtyard, between a dilapidated brewery warehouse on the corner up from Dowgate Dock and the walled, fortresslike enclave of the Hanse merchants, called the Steelyard. Isabel had decided against going to the Crane Inn where the owner, Master Legge, was a family friend; she was not certain that Master Legge's friendship would stretch to sympathy at her father being imprisoned for murder, nor to her being accompanied by an escaped felon. She could not trust that *any* of her parents' London acquaintances could be tested that far. Not even Martin's family. *Especially* not Martin's family; she had no wish to endanger the St. Legers.

The Anchor was a scene of blithe family chaos. Isabel and Carlos, the inn's only guests so far, sat at a table in the common room. Isabel was halfway through a much-appreciated mug of ale and a saffron bun. The mercenary, who had downed two mugs already, was busy cleaning his sword. Meanwhile, three of the innkeeper's young children ran about noisily playing hide-and-seek, chased by a yapping black-and-tan terrier, the resident rat-catcher. Two older children, a boy and a girl, neither more than ten, sat in a window seat arguing over a basket of kittens whose mother, indulging the small invading human hands, watched them through eyes narrowed in vigilance. The innkeeper's wife, a woman with rolls of flesh at her waist and under her floured chin, stood at a table pummeling a lump of dough into submission, while the innkeeper himself sat in state in a nook with several of his cronies, earnestly examining a gorgeously combed fighting cock. The room was chilly, for the hearth fires, here and in the kitchen, had been dowsed for the ministrations of the chimney sweep who had just been and gone. The chambermaid, after serving the newcomers their ale, was now busy on her knees at the cold hearth, her head invisible halfway up the chimney and her voice reverberating through it as she invoked curses on the sweep for having left a mess of soot and cinders.

"He's going to drownd," a high voice beside Isabel declared somberly.

She turned to see a small face, a buck-toothed little girl with wild, golden curls. The child was squatting beside the dog's pudding bowl of water on the floor. A finger-sized piece of dough, crudely formed into the shape of a man, had sunk to the bottom. The child was looking up at Isabel with an expression of sad resignation.

"He needs a boat," Isabel said. She reached across the ta-

ble toward a bowl of walnuts and carefully cracked one
open, splitting it into perfect halves. She picked the meat out
of one half and held up the shell. "Fetch him out," she told
the child, nodding toward the water. The child obeyed with
a wide-eyed look of anticipation and held up the soggy pastry man between her pudgy fingers.

Isabel took it, then bent and whispered another suggestion
in the child's ear. The child scampered across the room to
the side of the hearth where a bough of Christmas holly still
lay and brought it back to Isabel. Isabel set to work. She
tugged off a holly leaf and propped it inside the walnut shell
to act as a sail. She shook water from the pastry man and,
turning her back to hide the operation from the child, nipped
off half his body and refashioned him much smaller, then
turned back and placed him inside the shell. She bent over
the bowl and set the tiny craft afloat.

The child beamed. She crouched and was immediately engrossed in prodding the little boat on an erratic voyage
around the small ocean's surface.

Isabel glanced up, smiling, and caught the mercenary
looking at her. He quickly went back to wiping his sword.
Always, he avoided her eyes. But his aloofness did not
bother her now. She had accepted the delay in continuing the
search, and she had made a stirring decision. She was going
to go to Ambassador de Noailles for his instructions—now.
De Noailles was lodged at the Charterhouse just outside
Aldersgate; she could easily get there and back well before
the nine o'clock curfew when the city gates closed. She felt
energized, full of renewed purpose. She would leave as soon
as she finished her ale ... and as soon as she gathered the
courage to say what she wanted to say to the mercenary; his
words on London Bridge had sprouted a doubt in her mind.

The little girl, still beaming, lifted her boat from the water, clearly intent on showing it off. She cried to the mercenary, "Look!" and lurched straight toward his deadly blade.
He jerked the sword up above her head in a movement so
swift the air hissed. The child's mother at the table gasped.
Isabel was astonished at how quickly he had reacted.

The woman crossed herself. "Lizzy, come away from
there!" she called. "Come and help Mama!"

The child had frozen in fear—not of the blade but of the
mercenary's fierce scowl at her. Isabel reached out and

gently drew the child back into her arms. "Go to your mama," she whispered. "She needs you."

The child shot a smile up at Isabel and toddled off toward her mother, giving the mercenary a wide berth.

"Lord, I'll skin that sweep alive!" This came from the chambermaid, emerging from the chimney. Backing out on hands and knees, she cursed the sweep with several imaginative oaths for leaving the hearth in such a state. "Just wait till I get my hands on the wastrel. He'll wish his mother had birthed him in China!"

Her litany of invective had brought her to her feet and out into the room, slapping her hands of charcoal dust. She stopped and gave the mercenary a frankly appraising look while wiping her hands on the top of her dirty apron, leaving thick black streaks down her bosom. Isabel noticed that the young woman, apparently about her own age, was not unattractive under the smudges of soot on cheek and chin. "What won't I do to that little bugger?" the maid finished with a suggestive grin to the mercenary. With her eyes still fixed on him she unwrapped her apron, displaying a low-cut bodice that barely concealed heavy breasts. The mercenary did not look away.

Isabel stood. "I'd like a word with you," she said tersely to him. She moved to the door, out of earshot of the family. He sheathed his sword in its scabbard hanging on the chair and followed her.

"I'm concerned," she said to him in low tones.

He frowned.

"I mean, you seem to know very little about London prisons. We had to be told that the Clink doesn't take prisoners from outside London." The cellarman had explained that fact following the abortive meeting with the other prisoner named Thornleigh. "Well?" Isabel waited for some response. The mercenary only looked away in that habit he had of avoiding her eyes. Exasperated, she asked, "Do you have any plan at *all* for freeing my father?"

He finally looked at her. "No use to talk tactics before you know where the battlefield is."

She considered this. "I see," she conceded.

There was a frantic flapping of wings. In the nook the cock had made a leap for freedom into the air. The men laughed and one of them caught its leg and forced it to the ground.

Isabel felt awkward standing in silence next to the mercenary. "I am going out," she said suddenly. "I have business to attend to alone. I will take the mare. I may be some time, so have supper yourself. The landlady says there's a cookhouse round the corner where she is taking her pies to be baked. I'll see you in the morning. Please be ready early."

She turned to go back to the table for her cloak.

"Wait," he said, catching her elbow. As soon as he touched her he let go of her as if he had been burned. "I do not—" He looked down, angry-faced, unsettled. He spoke through tight jaws. "For food, I . . . have no money."

"Oh," Isabel said. "I'm sorry." She took out her purse and dug inside. As she dropped three shilling coins into his palm she noticed a tough, white rib of scar tissue running the length of his thumb.

She looked up and caught him staring at the ring on her forefinger. "It's just like one my father wears," she murmured. "He uses it to stamp the lead tags that mark his wool bales. See? It's a thornbush. Our family seal." His attention was fixed on the ring with open-eyed interest, and Isabel could not resist a small smile, though a sad one. Perhaps, she thought, under this man's armor of remoteness he was capable of some feeling after all.

He looked at her with a sudden scowl and turned away abruptly, snatched up his sword and coat, headed for the door, and left without a word.

Isabel blinked after him. *What an unaccountable man,* she thought. But she could not waste time fretting over his quixotic moods. She had work to do. And an ambassador to meet.

Carlos stomped up the snow-dusted south steps of St. Paul's Cathedral. *Damn the girl,* he thought. *Damn her soft eyes. Damn her sympathy.* He had not asked for any of it!

He stalked inside the cathedral and halted. The stone-vaulted nave was crowded—London's only covered, public meeting place—and he was not sure where to find what he was looking for. The late-afternoon light glowed duskily through the rose stained-glass window at the east end, making the movements of the people bustling around him look furtive. Porters, maids, and water carriers with tankards strapped to their backs trudged by, taking the shortcut from Paul's Wharf Hill through the nave and on out to Newgate

Street. Moneylenders and their customers stood bargaining at the font. At one pillar servingmen loitered, hoping for work. At other pillars lawyers murmured with their clients. A dog sniffed Carlos's boot. A whore sidled by.

There was a shout. Carlos turned. A woman was chasing a young pickpocket up the north aisle, past groups of gossiping churchmen. Carlos felt his shoulder banged. He whipped back to see a foppish gentleman brushing his red satin sleeve, his face in a grimace as if this contact with a peasant's dirty sheepskin coat had soiled him. The man strode on. Carlos's lip curled. *A week ago I owned a manor house,* he thought. *A week ago I was the lord of tenants and three hundred acres.* His fist clenched around the paltry coins the girl had given him. He grabbed a passing choirboy by the shoulder. "Clerks," Carlos demanded. "To write a letter. Where are they?"

The boy pointed to the cathedral's west end. Carlos saw them—scribes seated at tables writing letters and legal documents for customers. He started across.

He stood for a moment beside other customers at one of the tables and watched a spectacled clerk formulate the mysterious scrawl. Farther along the bank of scribblers a young clerk sat sharpening his quill with a knife, obviously idle. Carlos moved to him. "You can write a message?" he asked.

The young scribe looked up. "Certainly, sir." He took a fresh sheet of paper and dipped his quill. "To whom shall I direct it?"

Carlos hesitated. He did not know the man's real name. But since leaving Colchester the worry had been gnawing at him that the employer who had sent the man to the jail to commission him would have heard of Thornleigh's transfer and the riot and would assume the assassination had been thwarted. Carlos wanted to reassure him, but the only information the man had given him had been: "Bring proof to the Blue Boar Tavern on Cornhill on Candlemas night. If you must contact me before then, ask for Master Colchester at the Blue Boar. They know me there." Carlos had decided against showing his face in person at the tavern. Too risky. There had been search parties out for him in Essex; it was possible they would be looking in London, too.

"To Master Colchester," he instructed the scribe. "Tell him this. 'The work was delayed but I am out and it will be done. Come to the meeting with payment.' Write that."

He watched the indecipherable pen strokes. When the clerk finished with a flourish, Carlos ordered, "Read it back."

The clerk did so. Carlos was satisfied.

"Is that all, sir?" the clerk asked.

Carlos nodded. "How much?"

The clerk smiled and asked for a shilling.

Carlos looked down at the coins in his hand. *Her* coins. *"Madre de Dios,"* he cursed under his breath. He would be glad when this was over and he'd seen the last of her. The last of her dangerous passion to rescue her father. The last of her sympathetic eyes. He tossed a coin on the table.

The young man had looked up sharply at hearing the foreign oath. "You're Spanish?" he inquired.

Carlos only glared at him. "See the message is delivered to the Blue Boar Tavern on Cornhill," he said, tossing down another coin. "Enough?"

"Ample, sir."

Carlos turned on his heel and left.

CHAPTER FOURTEEN

>-+-◦-+-<

Friends

"Can you remember all that, mademoiselle?" Ambassador de Noailles whispered. His broad face was almost totally in shadow in this dim corner of his scullery at the Charterhouse. Though none of his English servants would have been able to understand his French conversation with Isabel even if they could hear it, the furtive location was necessary to keep his none-too-trustworthy French staff, too, from knowing of the meeting.

Isabel managed a smile and assured him that she could remember, though her head felt jammed with the facts and figures of French fleets and infantry companies. De Noailles had declared the situation too dangerous for her to carry the information to Wyatt on paper.

"I wish I could offer you some refreshment before you go," de Noailles said. "But . . ." He gave a fatalistic Gallic shrug.

Isabel understood. The very fact that he had steered her to this deserted scullery off the Charterhouse's washhouse court was evidence enough that her visit was dangerous. She herself had taken the precaution of entering the building through his back garden, her face hidden by her hood. "You are kind, monsieur," she said. "But in any case I must return to the inn. I hear that the citizens' watches at the gates are showing little leniency with the curfew. And it is already dark."

"True," he agreed. His brow furrowed. "I do not like to send a young lady alone out into the evening. The streets are full of ruffians."

"I'll be all right," she assured him. He accompanied her to the back door.

"Wait," he said as if struck by an inspiration. "There is someone else visiting me who is also going back into town. He can escort you." He smiled apologetically. "These days,

I'm afraid I think too much of secrecy. But, in fact, you two should meet."

De Noailles fetched the other visitor and brought him to the back door. He was a lanky man of about thirty with quick eyes and a trim beard that did not quite mask his receding chin. De Noailles made the introductions. The man's name was Henry Peckham. His French was halting, but Isabel could see that he and de Noailles were in accord. "Peckham is organizing the London citizens who are supporting Wyatt," de Noailles explained to her, smiling. He added with obvious relish, "There are a great many of them. Aldermen, even. Ah, yes, the Queen is in for a great surprise!"

There was a burst of maids' laughter from somewhere at the front of the house. Isabel and Peckham took a hurried, whispered leave of the Ambassador and stepped out into the washhouse court where a single hanging lantern on the court wall barely lit their way out into the dark garden. The evening wind made the boughs of the barren fruit trees creak and groan. They reached the postern gate in the garden wall and, in almost total darkness, made their way up a lane to Aldersgate Street where Peckham's horse was tethered. Isabel had left her horse at a hostelry farther down the street; like Peckham, she had sensed that de Noailles's lodging would be watched by the Queen's officers.

Once in the street Isabel felt a rush of exhilaration at this small success with de Noailles. Amid the welter of her difficulties she had accomplished what she had set out to do here for Wyatt's cause. It felt wonderfully satisfying.

On the way to the hostelry, with Peckham's horse plodding behind them and snorting steam into the air, Peckham told Isabel of his clandestine group's activities. They were quietly organizing citizens and arms, he explained.

"Sir," Isabel said cautiously, "may I ask if you are any relation of Sir Edmund Peckham?"

"My father," he answered with a mischievous smile. "He dare not declare himself yet, but he is behind us."

Isabel was impressed. Sir Edmund Peckham was Master of the Mint and a member of the Queen's council. It was thrilling to think that support for Wyatt's cause had reached so high.

And thrilling, too, to realize that as soon as she took the Ambassador's information to Wyatt at Rochester she would see Martin. She could unburden her heart to him of the appalling things that had happened to her family. She could find solace in his embrace.

The young clerk at St. Paul's Cathedral packed the last of his quills and parchment and ink into his portable escritoire. Other scribes filed past him, heading for home. He rolled his head to ease a kink in his shoulder after the long day of writing in the drafty nave. The usual assortment of boring legal documents and banal love letters had been supplemented by a flurry of anxious missives from servingmen to their families in the country, warning of the approaching danger; whether it came from a Spanish invasion or from lawless rebels, the country people would feel hardships either way. All the scribes had been busy until well after dark.

He was about to close the escritoire when his eye was caught by the folded message he had written for the tall Spaniard. He had tucked it away among his papers, reluctant to send it to the Blue Boar Tavern as the man had instructed, yet equally reluctant to act on his suspicions.

He took out the paper and stared at it. What was the right thing to do? He had taken the client's money; professionally, he owed it to him to deliver his message. But what did it mean? *The work has been delayed but I am out and it will be done. Come to the meeting with payment.* What *could* it mean but a veiled message to activate some mischief against England? What could the man *himself* be but a Spanish spy set among unsuspecting Londoners to further the aims of the Emperor?

The Jesus bells above him clanged, startling him. Seven o'clock. The west door opened as a scribe went out, and a gust of wind eddied up the nave, making the pillar torches tremble. It seemed a kind of sign.

He quickly ripped the paper into shreds and scattered them among the clumps of slushy muck on the stone flags. He would not be responsible for abetting a Spanish spy.

"The Queen's men'll trounce these whoreson brigands of Wyatt's, never you fear," a red-faced man declared loftily to his fellows in the Thames Street cookhouse. His ale-slurred speech was slow with deliberation.

"Aye," a man leaning on the counter grumbled, "and then the Spaniards'll be trouncing you and me."

The mustached woman working behind the counter scoffed. "Oh, shut your gob, Jock, what do you know of Spaniards?" With a muscular arm she expertly jerked out the bung in a fresh keg of ale and slid a pewter mug under it to catch the foaming brew. "I say, better to let the Queen have her way than see an English rabble rampaging through the city. For that's what it'll be if Wyatt reaches London, sure as there's a twinkle in a widow's eye."

"What do I know of Spaniards?" the man named Jock belligerently protested. "I know enough that I'll be locking up me daughters if any of those bastard sons of Satan land on English soil!" Pleased with the dramatic power of his retort, he hiked up his breeches sagging below his belly and added, with a sidelong wink at his mates, "But never you fear 'em bothering *you,* Tess. They only go for virgins."

There was laughter along the counter and from the nearest tables.

The barwoman's eyes narrowed on Jock with malicious delight. "Then there'll not be much use in locking up your daughters," she said. "Like the stable door, it's too late once the horse has bolted."

The other drinkers roared. Jock snarled and stared into his mug. Tess, the barwoman, turned back with a grin to filling mugs.

Carlos, listening with half an ear to the inane conversation at the counter, lifted his mug and drained it. He sat by himself at a small table by the cookhouse wall. He set the mug down amid the four others he had emptied. The ale had done little to alter his mood. He had half wished he could get drunk and stay drunk until the job was finished and he had enough money to get out of this godforsaken country, but he was still very sober.

The door opened and a cold gust reached him. He glanced around. It was the girl. With an inward groan he turned his back again, hoping she would not notice him. But within moments she was standing by his side.

"I'll join you if I may," she said. She was still hugging herself from the cold, and her cheeks were red.

He said nothing. She took the chair opposite him and looked across his shoulder to catch the barwoman's attention, then shrugged off her cloak and vigorously rubbed her hands. "At least it's warm in here," she said. She seemed full of energy. Her eyes were sparkling.

A boy of twelve or thirteen shuffled up to the table, wiping his nose on his sleeve. "Ale, mistress?"

"Small beer, please. And," she added, with a glance behind her toward the hearth at the opposite end of the room, "what have you to eat that's hot? I'm famished."

"Rabbit pastry and eel stew. Mayhap a bite of roast capon left, though this crowd's done their worst on it."

"Rabbit pastry would be lovely," she said.

The boy looked at Carlos.

"Ale," Carlos ordered.

The boy left and they sat in silence. The room was stuffy, heated by the huge hearth where two sweaty men worked at thumping bread out of pans, shifting hot pies onto trivets, and stirring stews. The customers, sitting and standing, babbled on, laughing sporadically. There were porters and lightermen from nearby Dowgate Dock, and housewives and servant girls waiting for meat pies and beer to take home.

"Have you eaten?" the girl asked cautiously. She was looking at the litter of mugs Carlos had emptied. "Perhaps I didn't give you enough money," she murmured. "Let me order you some food."

"Not hungry," Carlos said. It was a lie. He had spent her third and last shilling on the drink and eaten nothing. But he wanted none of her charity. It was bad enough he needed to stick with her so she could pay for the inn ... and provide the perfect cover to lead him to Thornleigh.

The server brought the food and drink. The girl paid him. "And another order of the rabbit, please," she said.

Carlos scowled, grabbed the fresh mug, and drank down his ale.

"I hope we can get an early start tomorrow morning," she said, cutting into the pastry. She lifted a bite on the tip of her knife to her mouth. Her lips parted. Full lips. And red, as if roughed from kissing, he thought. But of course it was only from the cold. He looked away.

He heard the door open again as some new patrons stomped into the warmth.

"I think we should try the Fleet prison next," the girl said after a few more bites. Carlos looked back at her. "Do you agree?" she asked. She had leaned toward him to whisper this talk of prisons. He noticed a freckle at the base of her throat, just above the swell of her breasts. It struck him forcefully, and oddly, that such a little thing as a freckle should have such allure after he'd seen her practically naked when Mosse had had her. He wished he hadn't remembered that now. He'd been finding it hard enough to forget. It was easier if he didn't look at her at all.

"Why not," he said, grabbing his empty mug and standing. She looked up at him inquiringly. "The boy is too slow," he said, and started for the counter to get more ale.

"Wait." A warning in her voice caught him. He turned back. She was looking past him toward the counter. She had stiffened and her face had gone pale. "Don't look around," she whispered. "Sit down."

He sensed danger. He frowned at her, his eyes questioning.

"Two guards from Colchester jail are standing at the counter," she whispered, her lips barely moving.

Slowly Carlos sat. His back was to the counter so he had to rely on her face for information. He sat very still, but his hand slipped under the table and across his body to the hilt of his sword. He cursed himself for having succumbed to the room's warmth and hung up the sheepskin coat on a peg. Its hood would have at least masked his face, but it was too far away to fetch without drawing the guards' attention. Mentally, he scanned the room. He knew of no way to get to the door except past the counter. No way out.

"It *is* them," the girl whispered in amazement. "The two who took Father away." A fevered look flashed in her eyes. "They can tell me where he is!" She suddenly stood.

He couldn't stop her. If he grabbed her and she struggled he would only draw attention to himself. She moved past him. She was going toward them.

Carlos clenched his teeth. Attack now, he wondered, before they saw him? No, there were two of them and they'd be well armed. And the way to the door was clogged with people; no quick escape. His only hope was to pretend to be dead drunk. When they came for him he could at least lull them off guard for a moment with this ruse, then lunge at them. He slowly leaned over the table, dropped his cheek on it, and lowered his eyelids almost shut. But under the table his hand tightened around his sword hilt.

He heard every word at the counter.

"I know you from Colchester," she said to them abruptly. Her voice was slightly unsteady.

"You do?" a deep voice asked. There was a pause. "Hold

on, aren't you the girl . . . ? Hoy, Simon, look here. It's that lady what was in the Hole!"

"What?" a second male voice asked. "Christ on the Cross, so it is."

The chatter throughout the rest of the room continued unchanged. Above it, Carlos's ears strained to focus on the girl's words.

"The man you took from the jail yesterday morning was my father," she said. "You brought him to London, didn't you?"

"Aye," the deep voice said. "That we did."

"Where?" There was desperation in her voice. "Oh, please tell me. Where did you take him?"

The second guard said, "Why he's in—"

"Enough, Simon!" the deep-voiced guard cut in. He went on smoothly, amiably, "You're well met, mistress. I warrant you can help me and Simon."

"Help you?" she asked. "How?"

"We was about to head home yesterday when word came with new instructions. So now we're looking for the cur what was chained in the Hole beside your father. A murdering Spaniard. Escaped, he has. But then"—his voice dropped menacingly—"you know all about that, don't you?"

"What are you talking about?"

"About you and the Spaniard scampering off together, clean out of Colchester. Don't deny it. A farrier by the stable saw you run out of the jail together thick as thieves."

"Sir, I hurried from the jail during a terrifying riot soon after you left. I was running for my life. I cannot be held responsible for whatever criminals came out the door behind me."

"Had a falling out with him, have you?" the guard taunted, clearly unconvinced. He tried a different tack. "So, you're looking for your father here in London town, is that it? Maybe we can do business together."

"Business?"

"Look here, mistress," he said placatingly. "Simon and me, we've no mind to be bothering a pretty lady like yourself about your affairs. Our commission is to find the Spaniard and take him back to hang. If you parted company with him, well and good. Just tell us when and where you last saw him, and where you think he might be holed up now.

It'll help us track him, see? You tell us that much, and we'll tell you where your father's at."

Carlos's heart banged against his ribs. Nothing mattered to her but her father—he had learned that much about her. His hand slowly slid out the sword blade an inch, two inches. He was going to have to fight his way out.

"My information in exchange for yours?" the girl asked. Her voice was very thin. Carlos could barely hear her.

"That's it, mistress," the guard confirmed. "A fair bargain, wouldn't you say?"

She said nothing for a moment. A woman in the far corner roared with laughter at some private joke. Carlos felt sweat crawl down his ribs from his armpits. The waiting—the stillness—was torture. Then the girl said, "You tell me first. Where is my father?"

The guard laughed mirthlessly. "Now, now, mistress, that wouldn't be fair. *Ladies* first is what I always say." His voice suddenly hardened. "Where's the bloody Spaniard?"

Carlos decided to strike. He took a sharp breath, tensed his muscles, was about to jump up . . . when the girl said, "I wish I could help you, sir. Truly, I do. But unfortunately I have no information to give you. I know nothing about this Spaniard you speak of. I left the jail in a panic, alone, and came to London alone. I am looking for my father. That is all."

There was a pause. "Maybe she *don't* know," the guard named Simon said.

"Maybe she don't," the deep-voiced guard conceded. "No business here after all."

"Perhaps there is," she said eagerly. "If you will tell me where I can find my father I will gladly pay you."

"All right, mistress. Let's start with paying for this here ale. Simon and me's had a pot each."

"Yes," she quickly agreed. "Here." Carlos heard the faint jingle of her purse.

"And we've got another two or three taverns to check before curfew." There was more clinking of coins. "And beds to pay for before we search again on the morrow." Again, she handed over money.

"Much obliged, mistress. Come on now, Simon, finish up and let's move on."

"But wait, you haven't told me!" the girl protested.

The deep-voiced guard laughed. "Oh, I thought you was

paying us for our *trouble*," he said derisively, "since you've given nothing else. No information from you, no information from us. Now *that's* fair."

The girl said no more.

The guard called over the barwoman. He asked if she had seen a big Spaniard come into the cookhouse today or the day before. She testily told him she had not. He asked if she was sure. "Lord," she said indignantly, "do you think me so daft that Spaniards can come tromping through, and me not know it?"

The guard grumbled an oath. After a moment Carlos heard the door clatter open. Footsteps came toward him. He caught a glimpse of the girl's blue skirt. He looked up. He could tell by the slumping of her shoulders in relief that the guards had gone. She looked at him and nodded.

He felt he was suffocating. He craved air. He stood and snatched the sheepskin from its peg. He headed for the door, pulling on the coat and its hood. He pushed his way out to the street and quickly glanced in both directions. He could just make out the shadowed forms of the guards trudging into the darkness down the slight slope of the street. Taking no chances, Carlos hurried around the corner to an alley. He stopped under a high window where a candle flickered and slapped his hands flat on the cold brick wall. He sucked in deep breaths, forcing the icy air down into his lungs until it stung like knives.

She caught up with him. He straightened. Under the candle's aura her eyes looking up at him were deep pools of trust. He stared at her in wonder. "You could have found your father," he said.

"We'll find him yet, together."

"But it means everything to you."

"Yes," she said softly.

"Then why . . . ?"

She gave an unconvincing shrug. "What good would it do me to find him without you there to get him out?"

"You could hire someone else."

"I cannot hire a friend."

"Friend?"

"You saved my father's life in jail. Against the assassin. I'd call that a friend."

He swallowed.

She shivered, already cold. In hurrying after him she had

left off her hood, and the night wind played with her hair like a lover. "Master Valverde," she said with a sad smile, "like it or not, in this you are my only friend."

He stepped back, away from the pull of her eyes, her voice, her softness. "No. I am only a soldier," he said roughly. "To choose a friend takes ... *cuidado* ... care."

She blinked, clearly hurt. "I'll remember that in the future," she said. "But now, if you please, I'd like to go back to the Anchor. I've missed most of my supper over you. I don't want to miss a decent night's sleep as well. We have a search to continue in the morning."

She turned and started out of the alley. He followed her. He had no choice.

"Transferred?" Edward Sydenham stared at his steward, appalled. "What in God's name are you saying, Palmer? Didn't you reach that Spaniard?"

The steward, a sallow-faced man of forty whose sunken eyes spoke of chronic ill health, shivered on the windy doorstep of Edward's London house. Leaving Colchester, he had ridden through knifing winds all day and reached his master's door in the dark just as Edward was coming out to attend the Venetian Ambassador's dinner. "That I did, sir," Palmer replied. "Night before last, in the jail. And he agreed."

"Don't tell me you paid him before the act, you fool?"

"Course not, sir. I told him he'd get the money after the job and after his pardon. We arranged to meet next week at the Blue Boar."

"Then, damn it, what went wrong?"

Palmer sighed heavily. "Hard to say, sir, because there was havoc at the jail yesterday. All the turnkey could tell me about Thornleigh was there'd been a brawl and Thornleigh and the Spaniard were chained up, and then"—he lifted his hands in a gesture of helplessness—"yesterday morning Thornleigh was transferred to prison here."

"The turnkey told you this?"

"No, sir, the sheriff. He was in a mighty fume over the mess in the jail. Seems the jailer was murdered just after Thornleigh was taken out. There was some sort of riot, and most of the prisoners escaped, including the Spaniard. In fact, the sheriff believes the Spaniard was behind it." Palmer shook his head malevolently. "You can't trust a mercenary, sir. I almost wish he *would* come to the Blue Boar next week sniffing for his fee, because then I'd—"

"All right," Edward snapped. He was trying to think. And cursing himself for not anticipating this transfer. It was a common enough procedure in Essex homicide cases of any importance. But it had happened so swiftly!

"One more thing, sir," Palmer was saying. "It seems Thornleigh's family has deserted him. I got a report that his son and wife and children embarked from Maldon harbor, also yesterday morning. They sailed on a carrack belonging to one Master Grover. The ship was bound for Bruges."

Edward only nodded, almost too distracted to listen. Hiring the assassin had been repugnant to him, but it had presented the ideal solution. But now, he thought with a pang of anxiety, even that vile expedient had failed—and his peril was worse than before. Thornleigh would come before a judge after all, only now it would be a London judge, in a packed London courtroom, with a score of influential people hearing Thornleigh cross-examined about his past ... his wife's past ... Edward's past ...

"Strange thing, though, sir," Palmer said, breaking in on Edward's thoughts. "The daughter didn't leave with the rest of the family."

"What?" Edward asked testily.

"Thornleigh's daughter. She didn't sail. And she's gone from their house."

Edward did not like the sound of this. It was a loose end that could prove troublesome. Given the unstable circumstances, even *one* Thornleigh was one Thornleigh too many. Besides, he recalled that the girl had shown spirit under Lady Grenville's abusive attack in the graveyard. There was something in the girl that was too much like her mother; it pricked Edward's concern. "Find her, Palmer," he ordered. "Have her watched."

An icy wind swept by, riffling the furred edges of Edward's cape like a pickpocket. He hunched his shoulders in the cold. "Oh, Lord," he groaned, "I'll be late at the Ambassador's." There was no time to deal with the problem of Richard Thornleigh now. The Fuggers' representatives must not be insulted; the royal loan was at stake. Edward's credibility with the Queen was at stake. "We'll talk further of this later, Palmer," he ordered. He lowered his head into the wind and hurried on.

* * *

At the Anchor Inn Isabel could not sleep. Her body craved it, but her tangle of worries would not release her mind. The muffled clanging of the bells of St. Mary-le-Bow had sounded hours ago, marking curfew, but she tossed in her bed, plucking at the covers. Was there really any hope that she and the mercenary could rescue her father? And when could she possibly get away to Rochester to deliver her report to Wyatt? And how was she to break the news to Martin that her family had been shattered?

A scuffling in the passage caught her attention. Some late arrival at the inn, she decided. But the sound did not stop. It became a faint banging, intrusive, insistent. She tried to block it out with a pillow and will herself to sleep. God knew she needed rest. But the longer the noise continued—a dull, rhythmic thudding now—the more annoying it became.

She got up to investigate. She opened the door very quietly. The dim passage appeared deserted. There was only a faint red glow from the embers in the hearth downstairs, casting long shadows on the landing ahead of her. But the thudding was coming from the opposite end of the passage. She stepped out and looked that way.

And froze.

The mercenary was standing face-to-face with the chambermaid. But she was not standing. Her naked legs were wrapped around his thighs, her skirts rucked up around her waist, her arms around his neck. He had pushed her against the wall, his hands under her buttocks. One side of her loose bodice was pulled down exposing one large breast that wobbled as she and the mercenary moved together, thudding softly against the wall. He suddenly stood still and looked toward Isabel. Their eyes locked. The maid, oblivious, kept shoving her hips forward and moaning softly.

Isabel ducked back inside her room and shut the door.

She lay on her bed, unmoving, her eyes wide and dry with fatigue. Sleep eluded her like a punishment. Her mind tried to hide in other thoughts, even in her worries. But the picture of his body bent over the willing maid, thrusting into her, overpowered all else. When sleep finally relented and drew her in, she saw his image still.

Carlos lay on his back on the straw mattress, one arm folded under his head, his eyes on the ceiling. The maid, sitting on the edge of the bed, was tugging her clothes back into place, about to leave—"Else that dragon landlady'll skin me alive," she had said. After the interruption in the passage they had staggered into Carlos's room to finish. It had not taken long.

The maid stood and bent over Carlos and placed a wet kiss on his mouth. "Wish I could stay, lover," she sighed.

She went out. He lay still. His eyes remained fixed on the ceiling. But all he saw was the girl's face staring from the doorway. He closed his eyes and saw her still. Was there no escape from her?

No. Not until the job was done and he was gone. Then he would be free.

CHAPTER FIFTEEN

>⊶⊷⊙⊷⊶<

Traitors and Trust

Edward strode into Frances's chamber at Whitehall with a smile. "I have great news for the Queen, my dear. The loan—"

He stopped as Frances and her brother John turned to him from the hearth, their faces wan and strained. Still grieving for their father, Edward realized. He would have to hold his enthusiasm in check.

Seeing Edward, Frances's mourning face lifted into a tentative smile. Her brother nodded a sober greeting. "Edward."

"John."

Edward came solemnly to Frances, his arms outstretched in sympathy. "Gracious, how chilly," she said, taking hold of his hands. "Have you just come in?"

Edward nodded. He did not bother to explain that he had spent the night at the Venetian Ambassador's house following last night's lavish supper with the Fuggers' banking representatives. He was eager now only to report his success to Queen Mary. But the Queen was busy in yet another endless meeting with her councilors. On his way here, Edward had passed gentlemen hurrying toward the royal chamber in twos and threes, with sheaves of papers in their hands and anxious frowns upon their brows. The palace stairways and galleries and corridors fairly buzzed with anxious rumors about the strength of the uprising. But Frances, Edward hoped, could get him admitted to the royal presence.

"Come, warm yourself," Frances said, drawing him nearer the fire. "Although," she added, as grief stole back over her features, "I fear that John and I are cold company."

Edward mustered a suitably mournful smile, though his thoughts were far from unhappy as he anticipated the Queen's gratitude for his efforts.

A couple of men loudly arguing about Wyatt hurried past

the chamber's open door. A wolfhound trotted after them, its eyes wide with worry as though in imitation.

Frances glanced at the doorway. "Her Majesty is beset with problems today, Edward," she said. "Everyone is clamoring at her."

"But I bring *good* news," Edward said.

"The loan? Have you arranged it?"

Edward smiled. "On rather decent terms, too."

Frances beamed. "Oh, Edward, you *are* clever! Don't worry, I'll get you in."

Edward's smile broadened. Frances—his reliable conduit to the Queen. He took her hand and patted it, then turned to John. "Have you heard how your mother fares?" he asked solicitously.

John barked a bitter laugh. "Colder, even, than us. Christopher sent us word. Mother rocks on a stool by day and night, he says. Will not speak. Barely eats. Christopher daren't leave her side. And, what's worse—"

"What's worse, Edward," Frances broke in, "is that in Colchester some are whispering the slander that our father committed murder. Imagine, *murder!*" Her voice was tight with indignation. "When he was only exterminating a heretic once condemned to death!"

Edward shot her a glance.

"Yes," she said. "Mother told us all about the Thornleighs' wickedness."

John slammed his fist on the mantel. "Dear God in heaven!" he said through clenched teeth. "If I had that villain's neck in my hands I'd—" He bit off his words and let out a kind of sob and lowered his forehead to the mantel in a surrender to grief. Frances threw her arms around his neck and gently rocked with him.

Watching, Edward could not help feeling pity.

John swung around, his face controlled with determination. "By heaven, Edward, you're the man to set things right. You'll make Thornleigh pay!"

Edward stiffened, on his guard. He decided it would not be wise to withhold his steward's report about the transfer. After all, there was still time to dispatch Thornleigh in private. "There's a development you may not be aware of, John," he said. "Thornleigh has been transferred to prison in London."

"You mean he'll stand trial here?" John asked.

Edward nodded.

John practically pounced on the news. "Why, that's perfect!" he said. "Now, all the world will learn the facts. No one will dare to whisper against Father's memory again!"

The facts. Edward smiled weakly. He was aware of the fire crackling and of sweat chilling his upper lip. He tried to recall when the next delivery dates for the major prisons would come up, when the pending cases in each would go to trial. He would only have until then to think of some way to deal with Thornleigh.

"And we couldn't hope for a better lieutenant than you, Edward," John was saying.

"Oh?" Edward asked. He was not quite sure what John meant.

"To marshal Thornleigh's trial for treason."

Edward felt his heart thud to a stop. "Trial for treason?"

"We're going to see justice done," Frances said warmly, "and all thanks to you, Edward. John told me. About Thornleigh conspiring with Wyatt."

"Conspiring?" Edward asked, his mouth dry. "Who said so?"

"Why, you did, man," John said. "Have you forgotten?" He gave a bitter, self-deprecating laugh. "I don't wonder. I only just remembered it myself, what with all the evil that's happened. But I was just telling Frances what you said to Father and Mother that night, about how the Thornleighs were implicated with Wyatt. And Frances said—"

"I said, thank God for Edward," Frances finished for him, smiling. "And I'm going to tell Her Majesty all about it. Then we'll see *true* justice done."

"And once Thornleigh's drawn and quartered," John said with grim satisfaction, "maybe Mother can live again."

Edward blinked at them both, unable to speak. Thornleigh, giving evidence in a national trial for treason!

A young woman came in wearily rubbing her forehead. "She wants *you,* Frances," she said testily as she reached the hearth. "Or rather wants that concoction of yours."

"Which one, Amy? Be specific."

"You know. The one she raves about. For her headaches." The young woman flopped down onto a stool by the fire. "Lord," she sighed, "what a day!"

"Excuse me, Edward," Frances said. She went to a corner

where a small cupboard under a crucifix held various jars, carafes, and vials.

The young woman looked up, apparently just noticing Edward. She gave him a glittering smile. "I'm Amy Hawtry."

"Forgive me," John said with cool civility. "Edward, Mistress Hawtry has just joined the Queen's ladies. She shares Frances's chamber. Mistress, this is Edward Sydenham."

Edward made a perfunctory bow. His mind registered that the young woman was blond and pink-cheeked, but his thoughts were unfocused, and his distraction had nothing to do with her beauty, though it was considerable.

"Ah, so this is Frances's betrothed," Amy said, studying Edward with a quizzical smile. "The confidant of princes and emperors."

"Well," John cut in brusquely, "I must go. Edward, I'd ask you to ride with me to Finsbury Field—my archers are drilling there, preparing for the Queen's summons. But I know you are anxious to see Her Majesty."

Edward nodded distractedly. "Quite."

John said good-bye to Frances, nodded to Amy, and went out.

Amy babbled on to Edward, asking questions about the great personages at the Emperor's court. Edward muttered answers, hardly hearing her or himself. Frances came back to the hearth carrying a purple vial.

"That's the one," Amy said, blithely waving Frances on. "Go on. Take it on down to her."

Frances's eyes darted between Edward and Amy, and she gave the young woman a frosty look. But she started for the door. Edward rushed to her side, stopping her.

"Frances, you know that I yearn as much as you to see justice done for your family," he said. "But, really, it hardly seems right to trouble Her Majesty with our personal sorrows when she has so many of her own. You won't mention it, will you? About Thornleigh?"

Frances tenderly touched his arm. "Oh, Edward, you are good to consider Her Majesty's feelings. But think how relieved she will be at this news. To know that one of the traitors who has brought on this calamity is already under lock and key here in her capital! And," she added with a proud smile, "I'll be sure to tell her that the one who can testify to Thornleigh's crimes of treason is you. She'll be so grateful."

Her eyes misted with emotion, and she added, "And so am I. Now, let me take this balm in to her and I'll whisper to her that you are waiting to see her." She went out.

Edward wiped sweat from his upper lip. The room seemed unbearably hot. Amy was speaking to him, but Edward was trying to think. He had to stay to see the Queen and report his success with the loan. But immediately after, he told himself, he could rush home and instruct his steward. He *must* reach Thornleigh before the Queen's officers did.

He hurried out after Frances, rudely leaving Amy blinking after him.

Frances Grenville stood behind Queen Mary, ready to offer the vial of balm, but the Queen, speaking to four of her councilors, was too distraught to notice her.

"Do you mean, my lords," the Queen asked incredulously, "that I have no more personal protection than the two hundred men of my palace guard?"

"That is why you must flee to Windsor!" Bishop Gardiner cried.

"Naturally, we shall keep trying to raise troops," Lord Paulet said quietly, looking at the floor. "But . . ." He shrugged. Frances saw the dark skin like bruises below his eyes, testimony to four sleepless nights since Wyatt had proclaimed rebellion. "Even in Kent, the sheriff and Lord Abergavenny can count on less than one thousand men, and—"

"And the cowards desert an hour after they're mustered," The Earl of Pembroke broke in.

"However," Paulet went on, ignoring the gruff soldier's remark, "my entreaty to the corporation of London for men-at-arms has brought some success." He lifted a parchment scroll and extended it to the Queen. Bishop Gardiner stepped forward and intercepted it. He unfurled it and scanned the writing. As he did so, Paulet said to the Queen, "The order requires your signature, Your Majesty."

"Oh, curse this paperwork, Paulet!" the Duke of Norfolk protested. He was pacing. "Let's go round up these London soldiers. My own lieutenants stand ready to march 'em! Let's throw 'em at Wyatt. Now!"

Paulet explained with a tactful, if strained, precision aimed not only at the old Duke but also, obliquely, at the Queen, "A royal order is necessary, Your Grace. Since the freemen of London are exempt from impressment in the armed forces of the Crown, the city can refuse us these troops. The only exception is if London itself lies in immediate danger of attack. Clearly, that is the case. The difficulty . . ." Paulet hesitated like a messenger with bad news. He steeled himself. "We fear that the city may not be firmly loyal to the Crown."

There was an anxious hush. "Your Majesty," Paulet concluded quietly, "you must sign the order."

Gardiner grunted over the scroll. "Why, this muster is no more than the guilds' quotas, Paulet." He read out with derision, "The Merchant Tailors, thirty. The Mercers, twenty-five. The Drapers, twenty-one. The Bakers, eight." He snorted. "The Poulterers, three."

Frances hoped the Bishop saw the contempt on her face for his belittling of Lord Paulet's efforts. She knew—everyone knew—that in his Southwark palace, Bishop Gardiner went to sleep only after posting his own personal guard of a hundred men; none of these had he offered to the Queen.

"With sixty guilds in all," Paulet replied with some heat, "the total equals approximately six hundred men, well trained and well equipped." He suddenly snapped, "Can you do better, my lord Bishop?"

"None of us can!" Gardiner exploded. "That's the point! It's hopeless! Good God, six hundred against Wyatt's thousands? Plus the French on their way to him with a hundred ships and God knows how many troops, if the rumors are true. None of us can match that! Your Majesty, you *must* retreat to Windsor!"

"The Emperor can match it."

Frances turned to the man who had said this, the Imperial Ambassador, Simon Renard. Until he spoke, she had not noticed him in the room. Renard stood by the window, apart from the Queen's councilors. A handsome young man with watchful eyes, he wore a trim, spade-shaped beard and was richly dressed in black. He stepped forward. Moving between the Queen and her councilors, he turned his back on them. "Madame," he said. "You know that the Emperor is your steadfast kinsman and friend. Only say the word and his ships and armies will be sailing here to defend you."

"The Emperor's armies?" Bishop Gardiner gasped. "On

English soil? Your Majesty, you would make an enemy of every Englishman!"

"And have you joined them already, my lord Bishop?" Renard flared. "Madame," he urged the Queen, "allow the Emperor's might to crush your foes. They are the foes of God!"

"Do not, Your Majesty," Gardiner said, composed for the first time, grimly calm now with certainty. "To enforce the marriage in that way would be nothing less than Imperial rape."

Every other man in the room winced at the crudeness of this image used before the maiden Queen.

Mary herself blushed, but the stain on her cheeks spoke more of indignation than of tender sensibility. Her eyes darted between the men. Finally, she moved to Gardiner and snatched the parchment scroll. She went to the desk and sat. Frances hurried over and readied the ink and quill. Mary dipped the quill and moved her hand to the bottom where her list of official titles led to the place where she would sign, but her hand hovered over the spot. "Supreme Head of the Church in England," she said with disgust, reading aloud the final title.

Frances understood the Queen's revulsion. This was the title that King Henry had wrenched to himself from the Pope in order to divorce his Spanish queen, Mary's mother. It had made Henry an excommunicate and severed England from the Church of Rome. Mary loathed the title as the root of all apostasy. But it was attached to the sovereign. Only Parliament could expunge it, and Parliament, hedging its bets, had not yet done so.

Queen Mary looked up at Renard as though to her only friend. "You see, my lord Ambassador, how every paper I sign in the governance of my own realm fouls me with this abhorred heresy. A queen's titles should wreathe her like garlands, but 'Supreme Head of the Church' hangs on me like a bloodied butcher's apron. I pray for the day that I may call His Holiness the Pope once again the spiritual head of this realm and sign such trash no more." She glared down at the writing. Her councilors waited. Frances felt their silent antagonism strain toward the Queen like a pack of chained dogs.

"However," Mary said with great bitterness, "it appears I have no choice but to wait. I will not break barbarous civil war upon my subjects." Renard looked away to hide his frustration.

Still, Mary hesitated, as if unable to move. Then she said with sudden, high-voiced anger, "But neither will I abide this traitor longer!" She scribbled her signature. Paulet sighed his relief. Mary tossed down the quill. "My lord Duke," Mary said, addressing Norfolk and picking up the scroll, "deliver this order to Guildhall."

The old Duke stepped forward and took the scroll.

"I command you to lead the trained London bands to Kent immediately," the Queen said to him, "and to join with the troops there under my lord Abergavenny. I command you to advance on Rochester with your combined forces and smash this villain Wyatt once and for all."

The Duke bowed deeply and left.

The Queen sat back. She rubbed her temples with her fingertips. Frances proffered the purple vial. Mary took it with a wan, distracted smile of thanks. "My lords," she said, standing, "I am going to Mass, and from thence to confession."

"But, Your Majesty," Gardiner broke in desperately, "will you go then to Windsor?"

"And after confession," the Queen went on as if her Chancellor had not spoken, "I shall spend the day in solitary prayer. I do not wish to be disturbed. I shall entreat God's guidance. I suggest you all do the same." She walked out through a door to her private chapel. For a moment the councilors were too stunned to speak.

"Why in God's name would she send Norfolk?" Pembroke finally sputtered. "The old goat's in his dotage! He hasn't commanded men in over forty years!"

"But, sir," Paulet reminded Pembroke, who was an ally of the previous Protestant regime, "the Queen considers his loyalty unimpeachable. And his religion."

"And my loyalty isn't?" Pembroke shouted, red-faced.

"I only meant—"

"Your damned meddling will cost us dear!" Gardiner was snipping at Ambassador Renard. "It is liable to sink this island!"

"This island is well on the way to sinking itself!" the Ambassador retorted.

The bickering went on, long and loud.

And Frances Grenville had found no moment to speak to the Queen.

On Farringdon Street a hand touched Isabel's ankle. She gasped and backed into the mercenary, away from the stone wall of the Fleet prison. The hand was reaching out through a prisoner's grill, level with the street. "Alms," a weak voice begged.

Isabel stepped away stiffly from the mercenary. Since leaving the Anchor on foot after a silent breakfast a half hour ago they had barely exchanged five words. And on the way neither had looked at the other.

She bent and placed a penny on the prisoner's dirty palm. Below, behind the grill, she saw a shadowy face. "God bless you, lady," the voice said, and the hand was pulled in.

Isabel and Carlos entered the long, four-storied prison building after being checked through the gates by turnkeys. As they made their way into the porter's lodge, passing pockets of visitors coming and going, Isabel sensed that some sort of celebration was in progress; the sounds of festivity beyond the porter's lodge, though muffled, were very plain. She paid the porter and asked if her father was being held within. The porter got up from his stool and offered to take her to the jailer's chamber across the inner yard. As he opened the door for Isabel he nodded toward the crowd ahead. "It's a wedding," he said in explanation.

The small yard was thronged with reveling men and women, but it was unlike any wedding party Isabel had ever seen—a dirty, tattered affair, for the guests were mostly prisoners, and the yard's snow was a soup of slushy mud under the strengthening sun. But the merrymakers, along with several turnkeys, stood laughing and eating at tables laden with roasted meats, bread, and ale. They danced, solo and in couples, to the lively jig of an intent musician sawing on his rebeck. And more than one ale-besotted fellow was lurching through the melee and the muck with a glazed grin on his face.

One of them bumped flat into Carlos. In an effort to keep from falling, the drunkard grappled at the mercenary's sheepskin, wrenching it askew. In the tug of war between them, something fell out of the mercenary's jerkin. Isabel saw it drop into the mud—a coil of thin, tightly braided leather. The mercenary flung the drunkard aside and quickly stooped to retrieve the coil. Isabel suddenly realized what it was—a garrote. She felt a pang of uncertainty. What brutality was he planning to accomplish her father's escape? Could she really rely on his savage ways to see them through? But then, did she have any choice? "You know," she said to him in a tense whisper, "it may not be necessary to strangle *every* person who crosses your path."

He shot her a dark look. He stuffed the garrote back inside his jerkin.

"Come, my lady," the porter called to Isabel. He was standing at the door of the jailer's chamber across the yard. Isabel hurried over. There, she was met by a sight more surprising even than that of the dancing prisoners. The jailer who crossed the room to greet her was her own height, her own shape—in short, her own sex.

"Dorothy Leveland, at your service," the woman said as her porter shuffled back outside. "Will you rest yourself, mistress?" The jailer—trim, tidy, and taut with the authority of middle age—gestured to a chair. "Tipton has my order to bring me any lady or gentleman asking assistance," she said. "And if you don't mind my saying so, mistress, you do look rather fagged."

Isabel thanked her and sat. Carlos remained standing close to the door.

Mistress Leveland nodded behind Isabel toward the merrymaking. "Quite a day, isn't it? Did Tipton tell you about it?"

Isabel shook her head.

"The groom was a prisoner here as a lad. Locked up for debt, he was." Mistress Leveland took her seat behind her orderly desk. "The lad was begging at the grate on Farringdon Street one day when a wealthy draper's widow was walking past. I suppose he caught her fancy. She inquired about him and I explained to her that ten pounds would pay his debt. Well, the widow not only paid, she took the lad into her service as an apprentice. That was seven years ago. And today," she said, smiling like a satisfied matchmaker, "they've come back to celebrate their marriage in my yard where they met. God bless them both, I say." She lifted a goblet from her desk to toast the couple and swallowed a sip. "Will you take some refreshment, mistress? The widow—or, I should say, the bride—has been generous with the feast."

Isabel declined. She explained her visit. Mistress Leveland shook her head.

"You mean, you're sure he's not here?" Isabel asked.

"I am sure of no such thing, mistress." The jailer thumped her palm down angrily on a large open book. "There's no way to decipher who's come or who's gone from my idiot clerk's scrawl here. Drunk again. I've just sacked him." She rose and said with a worldly sigh, "But these are my worries, mistress, not yours. Come. I'll help you in your search myself."

This did not at all fit Isabel's plans. She wanted no one of authority about when she found her father. "Oh, no," she said, "there's no need for you to trouble your—"

"No trouble at all," the woman said officiously as she opened the door. "This way, mistress."

Out they went again to the yard and pushed their way through the merrymakers. Isabel caught sight of the plump, middle-aged bride and her boyish groom, both grinning as they chatted with their guests. Isabel saw that among the dirty inmate guests there was also a sprinkling of well-heeled London citizens. It was an odd social stew. The merchant-class bride was pouring ale for a ragged but pretty, golden-haired prisoner girl of no more than fifteen who was slapping away the roving hands of a jowled gentleman in jewel-studded green velvet. The girl caught Isabel's eye and made a long-suffering face, as if instinctively recognizing a sister, a fellow martyr to the lecher's ways.

"This way, mistress," the jailer said, claiming back Isabel's attention.

They turned into a covered walk between two low prison outbuildings and emerged into another yard, one far different from that which held the wedding party. This was spacious and cobbled. Two of the walls were painted in an elaborately colored pastoral mural, and there were trees, winter-bare but lofty. Under the trees, comfortably dressed men and women, along with the ever-present turnkeys, were strolling and enjoying the pale sunshine.

"Are these your charges, too?" Isabel asked, uncertain.

"They are. Mr. Leveland, my late husband, made certain that the Painted Ground—that's what we call this yard—was a pleasant place for the gentlemen to take exercise in. He told me on his deathbed, Mr. Leveland did, 'Do well unto your gentlemen, Dorothy, and your gentlemen will do well unto you.' " She was leading them through the yard toward the far wing of the building. "That was ten years ago, mistress, and I'm happy to say I've stuck to my husband's advice. If your father is with us, I warrant you'll not hear a complaining word from him about his stay."

Isabel could not help being intrigued. "Your husband bequeathed you the keepership?"

"Aye, he did. It's been in his family for, oh, nigh on five hundred years, and never once out of a Leveland's hands." She added proudly, "My son will have it once he's grown."

She opened the door to the Masters wing. The turnkey posted there bowed to her. Isabel and Carlos followed her inside. The wing, the jailer explained, was divided into two wards, one for gentlemen debtors and one for gentlemen felons. They went to the latter.

The ward was spacious, more like a hall, well lit by windows and cozy with cushioned chairs and tables. Around its perimeter were well-appointed private chambers. As they passed some of these where the doors stood open, Isabel glanced inside hoping to catch a glimpse of her father. In one, she saw a child tossing a skein of wool for a kitten. In another, a bright fire crackled in the hearth before which a man and a woman sat at a table, eating. It was clear that some prisoners had their families living with them.

Several vendors, too, were carrying on trade in the ward room itself. A cobbler was fitting a gentleman for a pair of shoes. A stout lady was purchasing firewood from a stooped old man with a basket of faggots. Men stood talking in twos and threes, and as Isabel passed them she caught snippets of conversation that was undeniably businesslike in nature. One prisoner discussed a house sale with his agent, anxious about the rebellion. Another asked questions of his visiting partner about the fate of an overdue ship's cargo of alum. Another, apparently a tailor, was perusing his apprentice's display of worsted samples and giving instructions on the fabric's sale. Isabel had not known that prisoners were allowed such freedom to conduct their business affairs, and said as much to Mistress Leveland.

"They must, in order to pay *me*," the jailer pointed out reasonably. She walked purposefully on. Isabel followed, snatching looks into this room and that. A big-bellied gentleman bowed gallantly to her. The woman buying firewood gave her a long, appraising look. They had almost come to the end of the ward when the mercenary said, "Stop."

Isabel and the jailer looked back at him in surprise.

The mercenary lowered his head to speak in Isabel's ear. "She is useless," he said. "She does not know if he is here. But some of these hagglers might. They come and go. We should ask them."

The jailer's face hardened. "May I suggest, mistress, that you send your manservant to the taproom while we continue our tour?"

"I will stay," the mercenary said.

"Thank you," Isabel said quickly to the jailer, "but I'll keep him by me." She glowered at him. "He'll stay quiet."

The jailer shrugged. "As you wish. Now, if you'll just come along to the Tower Chambers—"

"Mistress Leveland!" an out-of-breath boy cried, running up behind them. "Master Tipton says you're to come quick!"

"Why, what's amiss?"

"It's that clerk you sacked. He's weeping and wailing, and he's barged into your chamber and smashed a stool! And he's crying out that he hopes Wyatt comes to London and burns down the Fleet! And now he's tearing pages from your ledgers! Master Tipton cannot get him to stop!"

"Run and fetch the bailiff, lad. I'm on my way." The boy dashed on. "Mistress Thornleigh," the jailer said, "forgive me if I leave you for a bit. An emergency, as you see. But do take your time with your search. We'll settle accounts later in my chamber." She hurried off the way the boy had come.

The mercenary, unconcerned by the jailer's crisis, was watching the stooped firewood vendor across the ward. He started toward him.

"No," Isabel said, stopping him. "I'll do it." She walked over to the old man. "Pardon me, sir," she said, "I am looking for a gentleman prisoner. His name is Richard Thornleigh. Do you know him?"

The man's gnarled hands were gathering up the basket handles of his surplus firewood. He glanced at Isabel.

"And if I do?"

"Perhaps if I describe—"

"Gray hair and one blind eye," the mercenary broke in threateningly. "Tell what you know of him, and I will not tell your last customer that you stole back half her wood."

The old man blanched. "One eye? I've seen no such person," he mumbled, and hurried away.

"That was stupid," Isabel said. "You only frightened him off."

"He knows nothing."

"How can you be so sure?"

"If he did he would bargain. He saw your purse."

Isabel grudgingly accepted this. She looked around the room. "I'm going to ask some of the prisoners. There's one over there who—" She stopped, seeing a man approach her. He was short and slight and wore yellow hose on skinny legs that showed under a once-fine russet doublet. A broad yellow feather arched out of his stained yellow cap. Hope fluttered in Isabel's breast. Had this man overheard her inquiry and was he coming forward with information? Just then the mercenary stepped between her and the man, to speak to her. The man raised his arm and tapped the mercenary's back.

The mercenary spun around in a motion of pure instinct, grabbed two fistfuls of the man's doublet at his throat, and almost lifted him off the floor. On tiptoes, the man stared in helpless terror, the feather atop his head quivering. The mercenary's action had been very swift, and in the next moment he seemed to realize his error. He set down his victim. "What do you want?" he asked.

"Nothing, sir!" the man stuttered in fear, backing away. "I want nothing!" He turned, scurried through the ward, and disappeared. The buzzing conversations in the room had quieted. Several people were looking with suspicion at the mercenary.

"He might have known something," Isabel groaned through clenched teeth. "He might have seen my father!"

The mercenary shrugged, an apparent apology.

"Well, go after him!" she whispered.

When the mercenary hesitated she said, "I'll do better alone than with you terrorizing everyone into keeping quiet! Now, go after him! Let me manage these inquiries in a civilized way!"

The mercenary's frown was deep. But he strode away.

Isabel turned. The big-bellied man in the corner caught her eye. He made his courtly bow again and beckoned her over. Isabel smiled with hope. Definitely, she would do better here without the mercenary.

But the man only wanted to invite her to his room to share his dinner. He knew nothing about her father. Neither did anyone else in the ward to whom she spoke. She walked back out to the Painted Ground where gentlemen were strolling under the bare trees and questioned a dozen people there, including two of the turnkeys. But no one had seen nor heard of Richard Thornleigh.

She was turning disconsolately toward another prospect, a man leaning against a wall reading, when she felt fingers brush her wrist. The hand that took hers was small and soft. Isabel turned in surprise to see the dirty, golden-haired girl from the wedding.

"I can help you," the girl whispered to her. She was shorter than Isabel and stood on tiptoes to speak in her ear. Isabel saw that her cloth shoes were torn and soaked with mud. "I can take you to him," the girl said.

Isabel's breath caught in her throat. "To my father?"

"Yes. To Master Thornleigh. Such a nice gentleman." The girl smiled sympathetically. She had small white teeth. Her eyes were soft with understanding. "I know how it feels to be torn away from loved ones," she said. "Come with me."

CHAPTER SIXTEEN

Bartholomew Fair

The golden-haired girl led Isabel by the hand out of the Painted Ground. They went through the walkway to the other side of the yard where the wedding party was still going on, though the bride and groom appeared to have left. The wedding table was now a litter of crumbs, bones, and spilled ale, but jugs were still being passed around, and the number of ragged celebrants had increased rather than diminished. The music had become more raucous and the dancing more abandoned.

The girl led Isabel to a small door in the prison wall. They had to step over a man slumped drunk in the mud. The girl knocked softly at the door. It was opened by a flat-nosed man holding a mug of ale. The girl nodded to him, then led Isabel past him and into the room—a storeroom crammed with sacks and barrels.

"A turnkey?" Isabel whispered, looking back at the man who had let them in. She was beginning to recognize the beefy, bored-looking officials.

"Aye, my lady," the girl said with a smile as she beckoned Isabel to an open door across the storeroom. She winked. "He does a favor for me every now and then."

"I shall reward you well for this," Isabel said. "I am very grateful."

The girl beamed. "That is good of you, my lady."

They were going down a narrow stone staircase. It was dimly lit and cold, and the rank smell brought back to Isabel all the foulness of the Hole at Colchester jail. "Have they put my father in the commons?" she asked anxiously as they descended.

"Aye, my lady, in the Tupenny Ward. A bad mix-up. But you can set it straight with the jailer now, can't you?"

"But how is he? Is he all right?"

"He's fine, my lady. A little sad. He speaks of you. He misses you."

The staircase ended in a narrow, dank corridor. They moved along it. As they approached a ward Isabel had to hold her sleeve to her nose against the overwhelming stench. And the sight when she stepped into the ward made her stop and almost gag. The room was crammed with emaciated men. There was no window, and only one flickering rushlight on the wall, and Isabel saw that all the prisoners lay on the bare stone floor. Some were curled up like worms, shivering. Some lay flat on their backs, too exhausted from the coughs that racked them to even curl up for warmth. Not all were manacled, but of those that were, some wore iron cuffs connected to chains that were bolted to the floor, while others wore iron collars, similarly chained. The chains were less than an arm's length long, and the wrists and necks of the fettered men were black with scabbed blood where the iron had scraped their flesh raw. A foot-wide open sewer ran in under one wall. It cut a channel through the room and gurgled toward a drain beneath the opposite wall. Isabel stood still. Never had she seen such a cesspit of misery.

"Not here, my lady," the girl said, tugging Isabel's sleeve. "This is Bartholomew Fair."

Isabel blinked. "What?"

"It's what we call the Beggars Ward." The girl pointed to a murky far entrance. "We're going down there. By the taproom."

Isabel lurched forward, following the girl, shamelessly relieved that this was not their destination. As she stepped around bodies, several hands reached out and thin voices implored pennies and bread. One hand grabbed the hem of her skirt, but with a grip too weak to hold on. "Aren't they fed?" Isabel asked in horror.

"Only what you'd throw to a dog," the girl replied. "They pay nothing, so they get nothing. Except what friends bring in. Friends outside is important in jail, my lady."

They reached the far entrance, and Isabel let out her pent-up breath. They walked down a corridor lined with pillars. It seemed empty. "Are there no turnkeys down here?"

The girl gave a philosophical shrug. "No need in Bartholomew Fair. The prisoners back there can hardly get up, let alone get out. Oh, some go wandering out in the yard or begging at the grate, but at night the turnkeys lock them back in again. Like the rest of us."

As they walked, Isabel saw a shadow scuttle by behind a pillar. The shadow formed an odd shape, like a fat man with two heads, one head crested like a bird. At the corridor's far end she could see a room with benches and kegs—the taproom, presumably. The spill of its candlelight was the only light in the corridor. The taproom appeared deserted.

The girl smiled, nodding in that direction. "No trade in the jailer's ale today," she said, taking Isabel's hand again. "Not with free drink and vittles up above, eh, my lady?"

They had come to a junction with another corridor. "Tupenny Ward's this way," the girl said, pointing around the corner. But as they turned, the two-headed shadow emerged in front of them from between two pillars, halting them. It turned out to be a short man flanked by a pale youth. The man wore a yellow-feathered cap. Isabel recognized him—the man in the Masters Ward who had run in fear from the mercenary. He stood before Isabel, the youth pressing near him. The girl let go of Isabel's hand and stepped back. The man scowled at the girl. "Where's the fellow?" he asked.

"What fellow?" The girl sounded annoyed.

"Dolt! I told you there was a big brute with her." The man was anxiously peering up the corridor.

"Well, he's not with her now, is he?" the girl said huffily. "Dolt yourself."

"Mind your tongue, hussy!"

"Bastard! If that's all the thanks I get, I'll just take her right on back!"

"Now, now, easy does it, Nan," the man said placatingly.

"Where's my father?" Isabel asked, fear welling in her throat.

"In hell," the man growled.

"You've killed him?" she gasped.

"Not I. Never saw the codger in my life." He spoke casually, busily eyeing her from head to foot.

"But . . . this girl knows his name, and—"

"Well, you're babbling it everywhere, aren't you?" the girl said, a sneer replacing her former friendliness.

Isabel tasted the bitterness of self-disgust alongside her fear. She had been so easily gulled. With a pang of panic she glanced up and down the corridor. It was utterly empty. Everyone who could walk was at the wedding feast.

The man turned his head and said, "Albert."

A huge, filthy man with a curly black beard stepped out of the shadows. The man with the feather jerked his head toward Isabel in a silent command to this giant. Isabel hesitated for a heartbeat, then spun around to run. The giant, Albert, easily snatched her arm. Pain shot through her shoulder. She screamed for help. His grimy hand clamped over her mouth. She sucked desperate breaths through her nose.

"I won't be spoke to like that," the girl sniffed at the other man, still peeved. "Not when I brung her. Not when I do the job while *he* does nothing and still gets half," she said with a jerk of her chin toward the silent youth.

The man with the feather smiled ingratiatingly at her. "Now, now, there's no need to fuss, Nan. You know he only shares what's mine. And you've done good, you have. You're a good girl."

The girl folded her arms across her chest and belligerently declared, "I want her boots."

"And you shall have them, Nan," the man with the feather said soothingly. Then his tone became steely. "But the purse and the finery's for me. Albert," he commanded.

Albert's grip on Isabel tightened. The man with the feather—clearly the leader—yanked off her cloak, balled it up, and lay it aside. He pulled a long knife from a sheath in his sleeve, sliced off the strings that held her purse at her waist, and stuffed the purse into his breeches. Then he reached for her necklace.

"The boots!" the girl insisted.

"All right!" the leader snapped. He nodded to Albert. Albert pushed Isabel to the floor on her back. She kicked and struggled and again she screamed for help. He stomped a muddy boot on her chest to silence her. She gasped at the pain. Albert rested more of his weight on his foot, grinding her down. Her ribs seemed to crack. Every feeble breath was torture. She could utter no sound.

The girl tugged off Isabel's ankle boots, then yanked down her stockings. The leader was at work trying to unfasten Isabel's necklace, cursing its stubborn clasp. He tried to pry it away with the tip of his knife, but it was an unwieldy tool for such small work and he nicked Isabel's skin several times. Finally, he prised the clasp free. He stood, smiling, and turned to the silent youth. Passing the knife to him to free his hands, he lovingly draped the necklace around the youth's throat.

The girl was shoving her foot into the boots and squealing with delight at the fit. The leader bent again and began to twist the ring off Isabel's finger. Albert's foot still incapacitated her, but she was able to wrench back her hand, and she squirmed. Annoyed, the leader sat back on his heels. "You'll lie still," he told her simply, "or you'll lie dead. Choice is yours."

Isabel lay still.

Once the ring was off, the leader fingered Isabel's skirt thoughtfully. "You know, Nan, this is fine stuff," he said. "No call to waste it." He looked up at the youth and said, "Fetch the satchel for all this gear, there's a good lad." The young man turned and left. The leader said, "Albert, move aside."

The giant's foot lifted. The leader began to unlace Isabel's bodice. But now she was free to fight him. She clawed at his face. He recoiled. He touched the red welts rising on his cheek and looked at her as if offended. Then, stiffening his hand, he struck her face. The force of the blow knocked her head to one side. She blinked at the stinging pain. Again, he started to unlace her. She grabbed his wrist and dug her teeth into his hand. He yowled. He struck her again, more viciously. Isabel's head lolled. She tasted blood and saw purple fire behind her eyes. But her hands still flailed at him, though blindly. "Enough larking about," the leader growled. "Albert, turn her off."

Isabel felt the giant's huge hands clamp around her throat. The thick thumbs pressed on her windpipe. She choked with pain, with terror. Her vision darkened. She was going to die. She kicked wildly and clawed at the massive forearms, but she knew she was going to die.

She heard a scrape of metal. "Stand away," a man's voice said.

The choking grip lifted from Isabel's throat. She gasped in air. Tears of pain still blurred her vision but she knew that the man's form standing behind her tormentors was the mercenary. And the glinting metal in his hand was his sword. "Let her up," he said.

Albert and the leader and the girl shuffled back a few steps, their hands raised defensively before the sword. Isabel stumbled to her feet, her bruised chest still heaving. She lifted her head just in time to see the youth come up behind the mercenary, the long knife between his raised hands. The knife plunged. Isabel cried, "Behind you!"

The mercenary spun around. The plunging knife, meant for his back, slashed across his left shoulder, gashing through his coat. But the wound did not stop his turn—one fluid motion that ended in a lunge. His sword rammed into the youth's chest with a dull crunching sound. The mercenary yanked back the blade. The youth clutched his chest, his eyes wide. Blood seeped through his fingers. He collapsed.

The leader screamed. He dashed toward the youth, all fear blocked out, his feathered cap slipping sideways with his sudden movement. The mercenary swung up his bloody sword, ready to strike again, but the leader stumbled past him and dropped to his knees to cradle the youth's head. The mercenary backed up toward Isabel. He felt behind him and grabbed her wrist, his outstretched sword still threatening the giant, Albert. But Albert stood still, apparently unable to move without a command, which the leader was too lost in grief to give. The girl only stared. The mercenary yanked Isabel in the direction of the taproom.

"No," she said. She pointed in the opposite direction. "That way! The door I came in by!"

"It is near?"

"Yes!"

He let go of her wrist and nodded. At his shoulder she saw blood weeping through the gash in his coat.

She ran back toward the Beggars Ward, pain still searing her chest as though knives had been inserted between her ribs. But she dashed on, and the mercenary pounded after her, looking back now and then, his sword at the ready. But no one was pursuing them. They reached the ward and scrambled over the prostrate bodies. Isabel, barefoot, stumbled over a man's chain, and in regaining her balance she splashed into the sewer. Its icy sludge reached to her ankle. Its bottom was furred with slime. She groaned with disgust and ran on, the mercenary behind her. They hurried up the narrow stairs and reached the door to the storeroom. It was closed. Isabel wrenched at its handle. It was locked. The mercenary tried to force the handle. It would not budge. Isabel stood aside, catching painful breaths, as the mercenary threw his sword shoulder against the door with all his weight. But it was barred fast. He swung around, abandoning the door. "Go back," he said.

Down the stairs they went again to the Beggars Ward. And stopped. The leader was there with the girl. But they were on the far side, looking among the prisoners, craning into nooks, poking around bodies. They must have known the storeroom door would be locked, Isabel realized, and they assumed that she and the mercenary must be hiding in the ward. The thought had no sooner formed in her mind than the leader turned and saw them. His face was hard with hatred. And he had retrieved his long knife. Isabel and the mercenary ran toward the far corridor again. But the girl, Nan, was nimbly hopping around the sprawled bodies, and the leader was making his own way forward, viciously kicking prisoners' arms, legs, and heads to clear a path. He was moving fast, but Isabel and the mercenary had almost reached the corridor when the leader cried out, "A crown for anyone who catches them!"

The bodies at Isabel's feet sprang to life. A prisoner grappled her waist with both arms. The mercenary's sword slashed his back. The prisoner yelped and clawed behind him like someone scratching, setting Isabel free. She and the mercenary bolted out into the corridor.

They ran toward the taproom so fast that Isabel hardly felt the rough stone floor scraping her bare feet. They reached the intersection where the young man lay dead, Isabel's necklace glinting on his throat. The mercenary quickly dragged the body out as an obstacle in their wake. Isabel only had time to snatch up her balled cloak before they ran on. By the time they reached the taproom she was panting, but the pain in her chest had cleared.

The taproom was a dirty L-shaped room, cluttered with small tables, benches, stools, and kegs, and cut up with cobwebbed nooks and crannies. They had to stop to get their bearings. Five or six candles guttered on tables. Though the place appeared deserted, Isabel heard dull scuffling and low groans from a nook. She and the mercenary swung around together toward the sound. He stood closer to it, his sword extended. Isabel hurried to his side. Was some drunkard flopped down beside a way out, perhaps? But she saw only a dark, narrow space lined with kegs and the shadowy forms of a half-dozen couples on the floor. They were copulating, lying in varying states of undress, oblivious in their rutting. Isabel caught sight of the green-velveted back of the man she had seen at the wedding, his buttocks bare below his fine doublet. She turned away. The nook led nowhere and she was desperate to find a way out.

She saw one across the room—an open doorway leading into a brick-lined passage. She heard the pounding feet and the shouts of their pursuers coming from the Beggars Ward. It sounded as though enough beggars had been recruited to form a small mob. The prospect terrified Isabel. She lurched toward the bricked passage, but the mercenary stopped her. He pointed farther down the L-shaped room and said, "That way. It is how I came in." They started around the corner and Isabel saw the corridor that he was heading for. The way out! Together they ran toward it.

And stopped. Down the corridor Albert the giant stood. He had somehow circumvented the taproom and he was now flanked by two other men. One held a loop of heavy chain. And Albert had found a cudgel. Catching sight of his prey, he hoisted his weapon with a menacing smile. He started toward the taproom slowly, stalking. His two recruits moved with him.

Isabel and the mercenary backed up around the corner. They stood still in the middle of the taproom. They knew there were only three ways out. In the one to their left, the small mob from the Beggars Ward was closing in. In the one around the corner to their right, Albert and his helpers were approaching. That left the third, the brick-lined passage in the middle. But neither Isabel nor the mercenary knew where it led. It looked very dark, as if unused. It might take them only to another bolted door. And then their pursuers would fall on them. And there was little doubt that the feather-hatted leader, mad for vengeance, would butcher them. They glanced at each other as if acknowledging that they were trapped.

Even the mercenary stood still. Isabel looked at her hands holding her balled cloak and saw that they were shaking.

She heard a crash. The mercenary had exploded into action. He was kicking over benches, smashing crockery, rolling barrels, apparently trying to put as many obstacles as possible between them and their pursuers. Above all the noise he called to Isabel to do as he was doing. Hopeless though the attempt seemed to her, it was better than standing and waiting for death. Dropping her cloak, she threw over a stool, swept mugs off tables, overturned a large crock of ale. The room was darkening. Isabel looked around and saw why: the mercenary was slashing at candles with his sword, lopping off the tops to extinguish the flames. In the diminishing light she saw the leader with the feather bolt in from the corridor . . . she saw a bare-chested man emerge from the lovers' nook with a startled face . . . she saw Albert and his helpers turn the corner . . . then, the room went black. Isabel stood still. But her muscles continued to tremble as she listened to the pursuers at both ends crashing into the overturned litter and shouting:

"Where are they?"

"Can't see!"

"Albert, fetch a torch!"

"Where from?"

"The Tupenny Ward!"

"Right!"

"And hurry!"

A deep male voice at the nook's entrance said, "What in hell is going on?"

"Only a brawl, lover," a woman said in a drunken slur. "They won't bother us. C'm on back."

Someone grabbed Isabel tightly around the waist. Before she could even gasp, a large hand clamped over her mouth. She was half lifted, half pulled several yards backward. A bristly chin brushed her ear and the mercenary's voice whispered harshly, "Lie on your back, spread your legs, and do not make a sound!"

Isabel understood. With muscles still quivering with fear, she did as she was told, even hiking up her skirt to her knees. Near her, the couples on the floor were rustling around in the dark. The deep-voiced man muttered an indignant oath, but the other couples only snuffled drunken laughter and carelessly resumed their lovemaking as the thudding and cursing continued beyond the nook.

Isabel lay motionless on the stone floor. One stubborn candle far across the room sparked maddeningly back to life, destroying the shield of darkness. Its light made it just possible for Isabel to see the dusky form of the mercenary's head and shoulders looming over her above the kegs. He was unbuckling his sword. He knelt by her, merging into the floor's darkness, and she heard a faint scrape as he set down his weapon by her head. Then he quietly wrenched his arms out of the sheepskin coat. She smelled its pungent leather waft over her as he dropped it to hide his sword. His weight came down on top of her. His breath, quickened like a lover's, was warm on her cheek. They lay together, still and silent, their heartbeats thudding as one.

"Forget the torch!" a man in the room cried. "Grab that candle!"

"But which way did they go?"

"Not past us!"

"Not our way either!"

"They must have bolted down the passage to the kitchens," the girl, Nan, said.

The kitchens! Isabel ground her teeth at the agony of knowing she and the mercenary had rejected that chance to flee.

"Should we run after them?" a man asked.

"Let's have a look round here first." Isabel recognized the leader's voice.

She held her breath. The mercenary had hunched his back over her, and his right arm was crooked around her head, supporting some of his weight, so that his shoulder shielded her face. She could see nothing. But she could hear. The footsteps were coming into the nook!

"Mind your own business," one of the lovers on the floor grumbled.

"Shut up," the leader said.

Isabel heard the shuffling footsteps come closer. The mercenary's left hand ripped down one side of her bodice, exposing her breast. She stifled a gasp of surprise. His hand moved down and roughly shoved up her skirt, baring one leg to her thigh, then he caught the crook of her knee and hitched her leg up over the back of his thigh. She heard the men poking around the kegs at the other side of the nook—so near! And someone had apparently used the candle to ignite a rushlight on the wall, for the nook lightened a little. Isabel tightly shut her eyes, willing, like a child, that her own blindness would make her enemies blind.

"What's he look like?" a man's voice asked.

"He's a big bugger."

"And he got stuck with a knife in the shoulder," the girl piped up.

"That's right, Nan!" the leader agreed with eager fierceness. "He's got to be bleeding!"

Isabel saw the dark patch of blood soaking his jerkin right before her face. To mask it, she threw her wide-sleeved arm over his shoulder in a simulation of passion. At this pressure on his wound he made a small groan of pain. His forehead involuntarily dropped to her breast. With another groan his mouth opened around her nipple. Her own mouth opened in shock at the sensation. His hand plowed into her hair, making it tumble over her face.

Through her hair she saw a moving candlelight brighten directly above her. It glowed around the mercenary as he lifted his head. His hand slid up her naked thigh almost to her hip. She buried her face under his right shoulder. His rough-bearded chin brushed her cheek. The men's feet crunched right beside them. *They must see it was him!*

"Bugger off," one of the sprawled lovers growled.

"Aye," a woman on the floor said. "Whoever you're looking for, the bastard's not here."

"This is a waste of time," Nan said. "I tell you they've scarpered down to the kitchens."

Feet pounded into the far side of the room and there was a flare of light as a breathless voice called out, "Here's a torch!"

"Right," the leader said commandingly. "Off down the kitchen passage, all of you! Look for a man with a bloody arm!"

The searchers hurried away. The torchlight faded. The taproom was quiet. The single rushlight flickered. A woman on the floor in the corner giggled.

Isabel stirred beneath the mercenary. He was still half propped up on his good right arm but he did not move. But surely, she thought, it was safe now to leave. She started to draw back her leg wrapped on top of his. The motion brought his hand sliding down her bare thigh. She shivered involuntarily. His hand pressed her thigh. Was this a signal? Was he warning her that the danger was not yet past? She lay still.

She was aware—as she had not been during the terror moments ago—of his palm's callused roughness and its warmth. Aware of her taut nipple tingling, chafed by his jerkin. Aware, too, of the indisputable evidence of his arousal, even through her skirt stretched tight between them above her knees. And what trick was her own body playing on her, responding with such shameful pulses of heat? What wantonness was this in her, to feel such things? Only two days ago she had been virtually raped, yet now ... Suddenly more ashamed than afraid, she started to push him off. But he remained heavy on top of her, unmoving. "Master Valverde," she whispered severely, "they've gone!"

He did not budge. A new fear flared in her: was he too weak from his wound? "Master Valverde!"

He raised his head. He looked down languidly at her candlelit skin.

She snatched up the fabric to cover her breast. She shoved him off. She saw that his right hand on the floor by her head still held his sword. He had never let go of it.

In the prison yard, Isabel stomped through the muddy slush toward Mistress Leveland's chamber, wrenching her cloak around her. She flinched at the cold on her bare, scraped feet, but it only made her more incensed. The mercenary was behind her. At the jailer's door he caught her arm. "Do not do this," he said. "We should go. Now."

"After what we've been through?" she cried. She barged through the door. The jailer and the porter turned in surprise. They were standing over a young clerk who was kneeling on the floor, held down by a burly bailiff.

Isabel burst out to the jailer an indignant account of the outrage she had suffered. "... a *gang* of them, led by a vicious little man with a yellow feather in his cap!" she finished, catching her breath.

Mistress Leveland came forward with a frown and pursed lips. She eyed Isabel's mucky feet, her filth-stained skirt, her disheveled hair. "Everything taken?" she asked. "No jewelry, even, to make good the fee?"

"What are you talking about? What fee?"

"For my time in escorting you, of course. And my patience, mistress, which is running thin. Have you not even a ring?"

"Madam, have you not heard me? I have just been assaulted! And this man has been wounded in my defense! He needs bandages and—" She looked around. The mercenary had not come in. She saw him hanging back outside the door. She suddenly realized the folly of her impetuous action; she was putting him in jeopardy. He had killed the youth down in the commons' passage, and he was already a hunted felon. She saw her terrible error at barging in here.

"No one *forced* you to go wandering below," the jailer said darkly, "and without a proper escort." She crossed her arms over her small bosom. "You have created havoc in my prison, mistress. I had no such trouble before you came. I suggest you leave. But first, how do you propose to pay me what you owe?"

"I tell you I have been robbed! I have nothing to give!"

The jailer gave a disgusted snort of resignation. "I'm the one who's robbed," she huffed. She strode back toward the whimpering clerk, saying over her shoulder to Isabel, "You are lucky this happens to be a very busy day for me." Looking at her porter she jerked her chin toward Isabel. "Tipton, throw this riffraff out."

CHAPTER SEVENTEEN

Disclosures

"The landlord told me I'd find you here," Isabel said. She was standing in the open stable door at the Anchor Inn, a loose bundle in her hands. "You needn't tend Woodbine yourself, you know. Don't you trust the landlord's groom?"

The mercenary looked at her across the mare's broad back but kept brushing the glossy flank as the horse munched hay. "Better if I do it," he said.

Isabel heard the erratic evening wind behind her, eddying snow in the courtyard. The snow had begun to fall soon after she and the mercenary had been thrown out of the Fleet. She had shivered under the drifting flakes as she sat on the tanner's stinking ox cart that the mercenary had hailed to bring them back. Her feet had been cut and almost numb by the time they had reached the inn, and she had had to spend more of her small store of cash on new boots from a cobbler around the corner.

"Shut the door," he said.

Isabel did so and came into the lantern-lit stable. A black gelding and a dappled pony—the only other horses besides Woodbine, her bay mare—swung their heads up from the hay they were munching to glance around at her. She held out the bundle to the mercenary. It was his jerkin and coat, tied up by the chambermaid with a wide, clean rag. The maid had been on her way out of the inn to take it to the stable, but Isabel had stopped her and taken the bundle. "She's stitched up the shoulders in both," Isabel told him. She blushed as the image flared in her mind of him last night with the maid. "But I'm afraid the bloodstains won't come out," she added.

He put down the brush and took the bundle from her and unwrapped it. He tossed the coat onto an upended barrel, but he kept hold of the jerkin and thrust his hand inside it, apparently searching for something.

"What is it?" she asked.

"Papers." He drew out a grimy wad of paper, only far enough to satisfy himself that all was well, then shoved it back inside. He slung the jerkin over the low wall of the stall and picked up the horse brush again.

"Do you make it a policy not to trust *anyone*?" Isabel asked.

"Trust is . . . *un lujo*"—he searched for the English word—"a luxury." He turned back to his work.

Isabel sat on the barrel, taking the coat into her lap. There was much she wanted to say to him, but she did not know how to begin. She watched him. He was working in breeches and shirt—the clean linen shirt from her saddlebag that she had brought for her father. Earlier, she had told the maid to take it up to his room to replace his blood-soaked one, and she saw now, at its open neck, the edge of a bandage over his shoulder wound. The maid had probably stayed in his room to help him wind it on, she thought. She looked away.

Her eyes ranged over the feeding horses, an empty swallow's nest on a rafter above the lantern, the small stable boy curled asleep in the corner straw . . . and again the mercenary. She abstractedly picked bits of dirt off the sleeve of his coat on her lap.

He glanced over at her as he brushed. "Better now?"

"Oh, quite," she said quickly. "The bath was wonderful. And the hot pigeon pie." Arriving back at the inn she had lost no time in stripping off her filthy clothes and bathing— the child, Lizzy, had brought her a cake of lilac-scented soap to wash her hair—and she had changed into the fresh clothes she had brought from home, a rose-colored wool skirt and bodice. She now noticed that he had washed, too. And he was cleanly shaven. It was the first time she had seen his face so clearly. "Does your wound pain you?" she finally asked.

He shook his head. "Just a lot of blood." He looked at her and added stiffly, "*Gracias*. For the shirt."

"It is I who must thank *you*," she said. "If you hadn't made me leave most of my money here before we went to the Fleet, we'd be huddling tonight in some church porch. Or worse." She added quietly, "Thank you, in fact, for saving my life." She smiled tentatively. "A shirt is small recompense."

He said nothing.

"Of course," she added quickly, "it will not be your *only* recompense. Though my money is running low, my father will pay what I promised you, once we find him." During her bath she had thought about this. And about the risks the mercenary was enduring to help her. It was true that he did owe it to her, since she had unlocked his chains in Colchester jail. Yet the dangers he had already suffered for her sake were extreme, and she was grateful. And something else. She was curious. Clearly, he was not the barbarian she had at first taken him for. It took integrity to honor his pledge to her. And today he had showed not only courage, but quickness and cleverness, too, in hiding her and himself among the lovers. She felt a furious blush, remembering his weight on her, his hands on her, his mouth . . . She looked down.

She picked again at the coat sleeve. "That's actually what I came to talk to you about," she said. "My father. I'm not at all sure I'm doing the right thing."

He stopped brushing. "You are not giving up?"

"No, of course not. It's just that I'm . . . not much good at this. And you are. I mean, it's obvious you know what you're doing. You understand those places. Those people."

"Criminals?" he asked with a small smile.

She realized her unintentional insult. "I mean," she said, flustered, "well, I only succeeded in getting myself almost killed. And you, too."

"You warned me of the knife. You hid my wound. You stayed calm. That was good."

She felt an unexpected flutter of pleasure at his praise. "There's something else," she went on. "Tomorrow I have . . . other business to attend to. Urgent business, outside the city." Urgent indeed, she thought; she must report de Noailles's news to Wyatt in Rochester. "So, in the morning," she said, "I'd like you to carry on the search for my father on your own. There's still the Marshalsea prison and Newgate prison and Ludgate jail. I suggest you try the Marshalsea first and—" She stopped, all too aware of her own incompetence at dictating the agenda. She added softly, "Do whatever you feel is necessary. All right?"

He looked at her, resting his arm on the mare's back. "I will need money," he said. "Entry fees. Bribes."

"Yes, of course. I'll leave you some."

"Will you be back tomorrow? After your business?"

"Yes. Probably quite late. If you do find my father—and I pray you will—come right back here. Then we can discuss how to get him free." She paused, unsure. "Is that a reasonable plan?"

He nodded.

"Good," she said.

He tossed down the brush and took up a hoof pick. "Will you take the mare in the morning?" he asked.

"Yes."

"Then I will tell the boy to give her grain."

"Thank you."

He came behind the horse, turned his back to its rear, lifted its hoof between his legs, and began to clean it with the pick. The horse, tethered by a long rope, lazily shifted its weight to allow his ministrations and continued to feed. Isabel, directly across from him, watched him work. She was surprised at how lightened she felt by this quick agreement they had struck. It was a relief to have someone to rely on. It was good to have a friend.

But a friend should have a name. *The mercenary* was how she had thought of him till now. That did not seem right anymore. "What is your Christian name?" she asked.

He looked up, surprised. "Carlos."

"May I call you that?"

He shrugged.

"I take it that signifies consent," she said with a wry smile; his curtness was so familiar to her now. "And I am—"

"Isabel."

"Yes." She wondered how he knew, then suddenly remembered. Her father had called her name when he'd seen her with the jailer. She felt a twisting inside her stomach at the recollection of Mosse, like nausea threatening—and, again, the mortification that Carlos had seen it all. She could speak of anything but *that*! "You know a lot about horses, don't you?" she asked, quickly changing the subject.

He jerked his chin toward the corner straw where the stable boy lay sleeping. "Since I was his age."

"That little waif? He can't be more than five. Didn't your

parents—" She stopped, recalling the stupid insult about his parentage she had made yesterday on London Bridge. "Sorry," she mumbled, "I forgot."

He seemed undisturbed. "My mother had an old horse," he said as he picked the hoof. "She followed the soldiers around Castile. I threw our bundles onto the nag before I could talk. And when I was his age"—he glanced again at the stable boy—"one of my mother's men was a German *reiter* captain, a cuirassier. I tended his warhorses."

"What's a cuirassier?"

"Light cavalryman. A cuirass is armor, here." Still holding up the hoof in one hand, he gestured with the other hand to illustrate a coupled breastplate and backpiece. "A *reiter* is—you know German?"

"Yes. A rider, isn't it?"

He nodded. "Cavalry. A cuirassier is a special *reiter.* Fights with lance and pistol. When the captain took me on, my mother left."

"She abandoned you?"

He pried a stone out of the hoof. "Best thing for me. The captain's squire died of plague soon after and the captain gave me the job."

"So you lived with this captain?"

"A few years. He was killed. Then I got work with a Spanish knight. Sailed with him across the ocean sea. *Conquistadores.*"

Isabel's eyes widened. "You mean . . . to the New World? Peru?"

Carlos nodded. "With Francisco Pizarro."

"But you must have still been a child!"

"Eight, I think. Old enough to blow a bugle and groom a horse." He set down the hoof and straightened, and the curtness in his voice changed, warmed by a satisfying memory. "Cajamarca. That is where I saw the power of cavalry. One hundred and seventy Spaniards on horseback. Five *thousand* Indian soldiers on foot." His flattened hand made a swift leveling gesture. He smiled. "The horsemen won."

Isabel was amazed. She had read the accounts of the near-mythological conquest of the Incan empire, twenty-two years before. The Spaniard Pizarro had captured the Inca leader, Atahualpa, at Cajamarca with a mere handful of *conquistadores,* and with them had then taken control of a land of millions, a strange civilization that had never seen a wheel—or a horse. And Carlos had been part of that legendary campaign as a boy. As a bugler! "Remarkable," she said, "against such odds."

"There is always a way," Carlos said. He added, in the tone of someone instilling a lesson, "Surprise. And attack without mercy."

Fascinated, she asked, "What was it like—the New World?"

"Beautiful," he said with feeling. "The *altiplano*—the mountain plateaus—they are so high, the air so thin, you can see the strong wind bend the grasses, but you hear no sound."

She thought it sounded beautiful indeed. "Did you stay long?"

He shook his head, and moved to pick up the mare's other rear hoof to clean it. "Left with Trujillo, the *conquistador* I came with. He sailed home to Spain with his *parte* . . . his share of the Inca silver. He was rich with that silver. Did not need his warhorses anymore. Or me."

"What did you do? You were so young."

"Joined an Italian captain with a troop of light horse. We worked through the Emperor's lands for years. The captain died of a chest wound in Maintz when I was"—he thought for a moment—"*diecisiete* . . . seventeen. He left me his horse. A Clevelander, big and brave. She could smash a fallen man in armor with her hooves. Fearless."

Isabel had to smile at his sudden talkativeness. Perhaps, she thought with amusement, it was only when he spoke of horses. "What happened to her?" she asked.

"Shot out under me at a battle near Maastricht. A mortar hidden in a ridge of pines. It blew off her foreleg."

"Maastricht? I spent a summer in the country near Maastricht as a child. My mother and I. We were visiting friends, and we picked meadow flowers and ate wild strawberries." This memory of her mother was bittersweet. "And, as I recall," she added, struck by the coincidence, "there was a ridge of pines there. Do you think," she asked in wonder at the contrast in their lives, "it might have been the same meadow?"

Their eyes met, sharing the wonder. He was the first to look away. "Hand me that file," he said, pointing as he kept holding up the hoof. "On the ledge."

She stood and passed it to him, then sat again. "So you've been a soldier all your life," she mused.

He nodded, filing smooth an abrasion on the mare's hoof.

"But how do you come to be in England?" she asked.

"A paymaster in Cologne was hiring for the English King. He needed cavalry to go against the Scots. That was six years ago. I had just fought with the Emperor's troops at Mühlberg. But I had spent all my dead pay on new gear. I needed work."

"Dead pay?" she asked with raised eyebrows. "Don't you have to be dead to draw that?"

He smiled—for the second time, she noted. A lopsided smile that somehow suited his rugged face. "No," he said. "It means double pay. Recruiting officers promise it to attract soldiers who are"—again he searched for the word—"*experimentado . . .*"

"Experienced?"

"*Sí.*" He shrugged. "But my pay was gone. And we had destroyed the Emperor's enemies at Mühlberg, so things were quiet."

"So you sailed to Scotland?"

He nodded. "Brought over a company of light horse."

"*You* brought them? You mean, as a captain?" Here was an even more surprising image of him.

He nodded. "After Scotland most of them went home. I stayed on with the Duke of Northumberland's troops on patrol in East Anglia."

"Things were quiet," she said thoughtfully, repeating his phrase. "How odd. Most people pray for peace. You search for war."

He let down the mare's hoof and straightened, easing his sore shoulder. "I am ready for some peace now."

"You mean you've giving up fighting?"

He snorted. "Giving up work is another luxury. Only a man with a full purse can do that. Or with land." His face darkened. He kicked away a hard clump of dung and said quietly, bitterly, "A few months ago I was given both." He seemed about to say more, then decided against it. He came around to the mare's foreleg and lifted it. He began to scrape the hoof.

But Isabel's curiosity had been sharpened. "Given land? How? What happened?"

He glanced up at her. "Northumberland's reward to me. A

manor by the sea. I moved in, ready to grow a rich man's paunch. I was going to breed horses." Isabel heard the bitterness creep back into his voice. "But somebody took the land away."

"Somebody? You do enjoy being secretive, don't you? Who?"

He shrugged. "Not important." He set down the hoof. "I tried to stop him though."

"I see." She offered a small, sly smile. "I've watched how you 'stop' people."

He gave a short laugh. She laughed, too. It was absurd—laughing about killing. But it felt good, like a burden being lifted. Their eyes met. He was still smiling. Isabel had a vision of Martin looking at her that way. It unsettled her, as though in some indefinable way she was betraying Martin. She stood abruptly, setting the coat down, and moved toward a jumble of leather harness hanging on a post near the mare's side. She began fidgeting at untangling the harness. "I am going to be married," she said suddenly. "As soon as this madness is over."

There was no reply. When she looked up, Carlos, near her, had begun brushing the mare's mane. His smile had vanished. She watched his hands, how as one hand brushed, the other smoothed the mare's glossy neck. She noticed the horse's muscles quiver under his touch. She thought of his hands on her own body on the taproom floor and felt a shiver. Of course, it was cold out here, she told herself; she had come without her cloak. She wondered how he could be comfortable in just a shirt. But then, he was working. And once again he was silent, expressionless. There were aspects of him that were foreign, unknowable. "Have you always fought for pay?" she asked.

He did not look at her. "What else?" His voice had reverted to its usual terseness.

"What else? Why, for justice. Like Wyatt and my . . . like the rebels here are doing. For a cause."

"There is no such thing."

"Of course there is! Do you mean you fought for the Emperor all those years without believing that his cause was right?"

"War is for land. Or for power, the same thing."

"So . . . you fight whoever you are *told* to fight, just for the money?"

"That is how I live."

"But that's *wrong*."

Her accusation hung in the chilly air. The mare stomped its hoof. Carlos looked at Isabel. She saw scorn on his face. "You do the same," he said.

"What do you mean?"

"You do as you are told. You live off your father, yes? He feeds you and clothes you and in return you obey him."

She smiled sardonically. "As it happens, I've just *disobeyed* his order to go with my brother to Antwerp."

"Your father may not like that."

She glared at him.

"And when you marry," he went on, "you will live the same way. Your husband will feed you and clothe you and protect you, yes?"

"Of course."

"And in return you will share his bed and keep his house and bear his children."

"But I *want* to. I *choose* that."

"As long as you choose what the one in power wants. But what if you married against your father's will? He could throw you out. And when you are married, what if you go into another man's bed? Your husband would throw you out. The rules are the same for you as for me. People do what they must. To live."

Isabel blinked, incredulous. "By these standards, if you call yourself a mercenary, then you are calling me a harlot."

"I *am* a mercenary."

The inference was too plain. Her hand flew up to slap him. He caught her wrist and held it. "Words," he said calmly. "They mean nothing. It is what people *do* that counts."

She tugged free her arm. Her elbow struck the harness and knocked it from its nail, sending it clattering to the floor. The noise startled the mare. Its huge head swung around and violently banged Carlos's wounded shoulder. He winced at the pain.

Isabel gasped. "You're bleeding again."

He looked at the red stain widening on the clean shirt. "A little. It will stop."

"More than a little. You need a fresh bandage. Come inside."

"I will finish with the mare first," he said.

"That's nonsense. I'll tell the groom to finish." She touched his elbow. He stiffened. She said sternly, "Come inside. You're no good to me if you bleed to death."

He stood by the bed in his room, waiting restlessly as she used scissors to start a cut in a linen sheet for a bandage. She set down the scissors on the table and began to tear the cloth. He watched her profile in the light of the single candle that guttered near her on the table. He wanted to get away from her, away from her overtures of friendship that had seduced him in the stable—most of all away from the memory of that first time he had seen her, when Mosse had had her. That vision of her practically naked was impossible to forget. And then, this afternoon in the Fleet, the feel of her beneath him, the budlike hardness of her nipple in his mouth. Remembering, his body instantly responded.

He looked away, willing his thoughts elsewhere. "You leave at first light of the morning?" he asked, forcing himself to concentrate on the thread of smoke from the candle as it curled toward the ceiling.

"Yes." She sighed deeply. "My problem is that I need to be in two places at the same time." She looked at him. "Have you ever made promises to two different people that conflicted?"

Yes, he thought. *I promised the visitor in Colchester jail that I would kill your father, and I have promised you that I will save him.* But the visitor offered a hundred pounds. And *that,* he told himself, was what he must concentrate on.

"Well," she continued, tearing the strip, "there is a promise I must honor. But a more fundamental promise, to rescue my father, is keeping me from it."

"Promises cannot always be kept."

She looked at him. "Promises are all we have," she said simply. "They're all that make us different from the beasts." She went back to tearing the bandage.

Carlos watched her with a frown. When she said things like that—so assured despite her worries—he felt confounded, mystified. She had had the same effect on him in the jail when she had forced Mosse, even as he grunted over her, to look her in the eye. In fact, her very reason for agreeing to satisfy Mosse had amazed him: to save her father. Watching her, he could not help wondering about Thornleigh. What kind of man produced such a passionately loyal daughter? "Your father," he said. "How did he land in jail?"

It seemed to Carlos that she tore at the linen with extra fierceness. "I told you I watched my mother die," she said, "but it was not at her bedside that I did so. She was murdered. My father killed the man who murdered her. His name was Anthony Grenville."

Carlos was surprised. "*Lord* Grenville?"

She glanced up. "You knew him?"

"He was the one who took my land."

Her eyes widened with astonishment. "He was the one you tried to stop?"

"Not him. His lawyer."

"Oh, if only it had been Grenville and you *had* killed him! Then, all my family would still be biding peacefully at home!" He heard the tightness in her voice, as if she were trying not to cry. She closed her eyes for a moment. "The Grenvilles," she said, controlled now. "Lady Maud and her sons. I'm sure they hired that assassin in Colchester jail to kill my father."

Carlos said nothing. For all he knew she was right; the visitor who'd hired him had been some gentleman's servant.

"They won't give up," she went on. "And they have great power behind them. Their daughter is the Queen's best friend. That's why we must find him before they do. Do you understand?" Without waiting for his reply, she tore the strip free and said flatly, "Now let's get this done. Your shoulder must hurt."

He pulled his shirt over his head and tossed it on the bed. The wound actually was not painful. The knife had only grazed him. The fresh bleeding had already stopped. He was unwrapping the bloodstained bandage as she came to him. He caught her staring at his bare chest. He had seen that look before in other women's eyes. He knew what it meant. Maybe that was the answer, he thought. Maybe if he took her, now, he could get her out of his blood for good. He allowed desire to surge back.

In one sudden motion he grabbed the back of her head with one hand, grabbed her buttock with the other, and yanked her to him. He pressed her hard against his groin. His top hand slid down to her breast.

She jerked violently out of his grasp. "How dare you!" she cried.

"What? I thought—"

"Thought what? That I'd swoon at your feet? My God, I've seen more finesse in coupling dogs!"

He flushed with anger. "*Mira!* I thought—"

"Well, *don't* think! You're a hired brute! I am not paying you to think!"

He resisted the urge to strike her. The other urge, inflamed by the softness of her body against his, was not so easy to subdue. And its very power in the face of her insults made him feel ridiculous—and more angry.

"I am betrothed!" she was saying. She had moved halfway across the room. Did she think he was going to rape her, for God's sake? For a moment the raw appeal of the thought held him. He could do it. Force her, here and now. Make her insults whimper to a stop. It would be easy. But it would also be stupid. He was dependent on her. Until he found Thornleigh.

"I am betrothed," she repeated, like a catechism to keep her from harm.

"I heard you," he said, snatching up his shirt. "But I see you are searching the rat holes of London alone, so maybe your man changed his mind."

"He was called away. He doesn't know what has happened."

"Lucky for him." He was wrestling with the shirt, trying to find the neck opening, but he only succeeded in making a stubborn ball of twisted material. And a thin line of blood was trickling from the scab on his shoulder.

"Stop," she said more gently. "Don't. You cannot leave your wound like that."

"I have had worse," he growled.

"But this you suffered for my sake. What happened was my fault. In the Fleet, I mean. Let me tend it. I owe you that much. Please," she urged. "Stop."

He did, and stood motionless, as much in anger as in compliance. She approached him warily, the way he himself would approach a half-wild horse that he knew had only paused in its fight. She extended the bandage like a peace offering. He lifted his arm and let her wrap the bandage over his shoulder and under his arm. She wrapped it several times. Her eyes were fastened on the bandage as she worked, but her breathing was still agitated. He stared across the room, trying not to notice the rise and fall of her breasts. Trying not to breathe in the scent of her hair, of her skin.

"There," she said, tying off the bandage. But she did not move away from him. She looked at the floor. She spoke very softly. "I am betrothed. It is a vow I hold more dear than my life." She looked up. His eyes met hers. He suddenly saw in their troubled depths what she was really saying—that she would be faithful despite the temptation. Faithfulness. It was a quality he had never encountered in a woman. Once again she had astonished him.

Her lips parted slightly as she took a breath as though to say more, and he felt desire for her course through him again. He *would* take her. *Have* her. The impulse jolted through him. But he did not move. He could not move. Because even more strongly, and far more strangely—for never in his experience had such a sensation competed with carnal desire—he wanted her to look at him and smile.

He twisted away from her, unnerved. *Madre de Dios,* there was only one way to get her out of his blood. Kill her father, take the money, and get clear of this country. Today was the twenty-eighth. The rendezvous was for Candlemas. Still a few days left. He would find Thornleigh tomorrow and do it, while she was away.

He heard her behind him as she walked out of his room.

Night torches flared in a Whitehall courtyard as a troop of men-at-arms on patrol marched past below Queen Mary's window. The noise made the Queen look up from the devotional Book of Hours she was reading. She set the book in her lap and gazed up at her betrothed. Philip of Spain was hanging in glory on her wall, a huge, full-length portrait by the master painter Titian.

Frances Grenville relaxed the needle she had been plying over the embroidery frame standing before her, and followed the Queen's gaze up to the portrait of the Prince. The painting had been brought by the Emperor's special envoys after New Year's, a part of formalizing the betrothal arrangements. Frances knew how much its arrival had meant to the Queen. Mary had never set eyes on the man she was going to marry, at least not in the flesh. She and her council had been embroiled for months in haggling over the terms of the marriage treaty with the Imperial Ambassador—articles spelling out Philip's precise titles in England; the quota of

Spanish grandees to receive positions in the royal household; inheritance rights of any children of the marriage so as not to be in conflict with the rights of Don Carlos, Philip's son from his first marriage; agreement that the English treasury would be wholly under English control—terms that Mary's council felt would be acceptable to touchy Englishmen. The process, Frances knew, had left the Queen feeling like a commodity in a commercial transaction; it was this portrait that had given her betrothal a human face, had made the man real.

And the Prince did look splendid. Tall, young—at twenty-seven he was a decade younger than Mary—and displaying an air of grave responsibility that perfectly matched Mary's ideal of a pious ruler.

"It is clearest in the eyes, don't you agree, Frances?" the Queen asked, still gazing. "A noble soul shines through the eyes."

"True, my lady." Frances pushed to the back of her mind the nasty rumors that had reached her. The Prince, they said, had kept a lady, Doña Ana de Osorio, as his mistress since he was eighteen. And Frances could not help thinking that the look in the royal Spaniard's eyes seemed more arrogant than noble. But then, she told herself with an inward smile, her own concepts of such things were so colored by Edward. Edward—so truly aristocratic in carriage, and his character so generously, so familiarly, English. But she would never utter a word that might mar the Queen's devotion to the Prince.

"Master Titian is too expert an artist to invent character, my lady," Frances said with a smile. "He can only paint a noble soul where a noble soul exists."

Mary nodded with satisfaction and sighed. The women exchanged a contented glance and went back to their sewing and reading as the troop of men-at-arms marched through the courtyard below.

From his chair Edward Sydenham stared at the naked girl across his parlor. She was on her hands and knees in front of his fire, terrified, awaiting his pleasure. But though Edward's eyes were fixed on her pink flesh, he regarded her almost without seeing her. He was listening for sounds on the stairs outside the door, hoping to hear his steward returning from the prison. Until Palmer reported that Richard

Thornleigh had been dispatched, Edward could concentrate
on nothing else. Nothing except how Thornleigh's testimony,
if he lived, would blight Edward's life forever.

He picked up an ivory letter opener on the desk before
him and toyed with it, distractedly scraping its point over his
thumbtip. The tall clock in the corner ticked, eking out the
moments in a rhythm out of harmony with the crackling of
the fir logs in the grate. Damn it, where was Palmer?

There was a whimper from the girl. Edward blinked, fo-
cusing on her almost for the first time. She was shaking
slightly. He studied her. She was perhaps fourteen, plump,
and very frightened. Her farrier father had been paid generously to deliver her, and Edward's chamberlain had instructed her in what to do, and in the consequences to her
family if she refused. The chamberlain managed such negotiations deftly. Edward had not been pleased with the man's
predecessor; the fellow had once brought him a girl with her
nose bloodied. It had revolted Edward. Violence was the response of peasants.

The girl glanced at him, then quickly looked down. But
Edward had caught the fear in her eyes. It was usually suf-
ficient to arouse him. But tonight it was not good enough.
He could do nothing until Palmer arrived and set his mind at
rest.

The girl was sniffling. A tear dropped onto the Turkish
carpet beneath her. Edward noticed that her dirty hair was a
mousy brown, not glossily dark as he had remembered it after first spotting her the other day. Another disappointment.
He looked away.

At least, he thought, there was beauty in this room. He
had meticulously organized the decor after buying the house
in the summer, and he was proud of the result. Here in the
parlor, illuminated by the pure glow from fine wax tapers
burning in the Florentine silver candlesticks, the beauty was
almost palpable. Lapis lazuli spirals inlaid among tiles
around the hearth glistened like the sunlit waters of the Ae-
gean Sea. Firelight glinted off the million threads of gold,
ruby, and emerald hues in the costly Flemish tapestries on
the wall, and off the painted stars and half-moons artfully
spangled across the ceiling. A silver chalice that slowly
burned coals laced with fragrant herbs perfumed the room.
A shelf displayed three rare books, all exquisitely bound,
their leather covers glinting with gilt letters. These books

were his most precious objects, gifts from the Emperor Charles himself.

Surveying these surroundings Edward felt a moment of peace. He loved beautiful things. Not just to amass them and hoard them, as so many oafish rich men did. He loved beauty for what it represented: a plane of sensibility far above the mire of ordinary life.

He looked back at the girl. She was crying outright now, but was still so terrified that she was trying, quite ineptly, to control it. Edward felt a spark in his loins.

"Come here," he said.

She stiffened at his command.

"Come," he repeated.

She started to rise, shaking miserably.

"Stop. Not like this. Crawl."

She crawled across the carpet.

Edward instructed her. She closed her eyes in revulsion, but she obeyed and shuffled closer between his legs. He sat still as she fumbled at unfastening the red silk ribbons of his codpiece.

A door downstairs creaked open. Edward snatched the girl's hands to still them and strained to listen. There were muffled footsteps below. Then an imperious female voice. Edward slumped with disappointment. It was only his housekeeper berating the boy bringing in firewood.

Edgily he sat back, trying to relax. He motioned for the girl to continue. She closed her eyes more tightly, her tears spilling. Her cold hand reached inside his breeches. Her clumsy, trembling fingers should have been enough. But Edward's worries would not release him.

Where in God's name is Palmer?

CHAPTER EIGHTEEN

><*><>*><

Whit's Palace

A satanic clanging of bells assaulted Richard Thornleigh in his sleep. He thrashed his arm at the nightmare—a giant bell that swung up over Honor and fired a monstrous cannon, exploding in smoke and flame around her face—and he felt pain like a red-hot brand sear his shoulder as his arm recoiled back.

"Forgot the chain, did you?" a deep, sonorous voice asked.

Thornleigh blinked awake in a sweat. He *had* forgotten. In fact, he had forgotten where he was. Groggily he sat up from the bunched cloak that he had been using as a pillow. He turned his stiff neck toward the voice and squinted in the sunlight that shafted through a high window. A silver-haired man sat beside him on a wooden platform that was like a long, narrow bed. One of the man's wrists, like Thornleigh's, was cuffed to a chain attached to a ring bolt in the stone wall. Thornleigh glanced around. The small stone room was bare except for this platform running down the length of one wall. Directly across stood a closed, arched door. To his right, past where the man sat, there was the one high slit of a window. To his left a boy of about fifteen—an apprentice, by the look of his blue smock—sat huddled in the corner of the platform, shivering in his sleep.

Then Thornleigh remembered. He had been brought to this prison room last night after the long cold ride with the guards; driving snow had kept them a day and night on the road after leaving Colchester jail. It had been late and dark when they arrived, and the porter's torch had only briefly illuminated these two prisoners asleep on the platform as the porter chained Thornleigh between them, pending the jailer's instructions in the morning. After the porter had gone, Thornleigh had sat in the dark listening to the man's snoring and the boy's unconscious whimpering, until Thornleigh, too, had fallen into a tortured sleep.

The clanging erupted again, startling him.

"Bells of St. Sepulcher's," the man beside him said ominously.

If Thornleigh had been unsure before of where he was, he was certain now. Everyone who knew London knew what those bells portended. Hard by Newgate prison, St. Sepulcher's tolling iron voice was the first solemn clamor on a Newgate hanging day.

"Time to make peace with the deity," the silver-haired man beside him said. He spoke calmly, resting against the wall. He was using a wooden splinter to clean his fingernails, performing a slow and meticulous job.

"They're hanging us?" Thornleigh asked.

"Aye, sir. We who are condemned will be carted to Tyburn this morning and hanged." The man studied his cleaned fingernails as though unperturbed.

Thornleigh digested the information. He felt no fear. He felt little of anything.

The man glanced over at him. "An objectionable word, is it not—'hanged'?" he asked. "Puts one in mind of hams curing. Personally, I have always preferred that striking phrase of the commonfolk: 'turned off.' No-nonsense, crisp, and concise. As I hope the hangman's skills will prove once we reach the fatal tree."

"Condemned? I wasn't even tried," Thornleigh muttered. Not that he cared.

"I was, if you can call that farce of blind prejudice a trial," the man snorted. "The judge was an oaf of the first order. Show me a legal purist who cannot understand the passions of a man in love, sir, and I'll show you an oaf." He looked hard at Thornleigh, his eyes narrowing under bushy silver eyebrows. "Not been tried, did you say?"

Impassively Thornleigh shook his head.

"Ah, a new recruit. In that case, your stay at Whit's Palace will commence in earnest once you have expressed to Master Alexander your preference regarding accommodation."

Thornleigh did not follow this.

The man's fleshy lips curved into a sardonic smile. "Put simply, sir, *I* am being hanged, *you* are not."

Thornleigh slumped against the wall. He had hoped it was

all going to be over today at the gallows. He felt dead already. But apparently he was not to be so mercifully dispatched. There would be a trial. He could only hope it would come quickly.

The man held up his splinter like a pedagogue with a pointer. "At least—let me be precise here, sir—you are not to be hanged *today,*" he clarified. "This condemned hold does double duty, you see, as first resting place and last resting place. But in both instances it is merely an antechamber to the whipping post or the gallows, after a short stop inside. And the anguish I read in your face—pardon my liberty, sir—but the anguish I see there tells me that it is an act of a felonious nature that has brought you to Whit's Palace, and no mere misdemeanor for which society would be satisfied you could make amends with a mere whipping. Am I correct?"

Thornleigh nodded bleakly.

"Thank you, sir. I do dislike being proved wrong in my judgment of a man's character. And, I am proud to say, I make such errors rarely." He whisked a trace of dirt off the shoulder of his threadbare and faded red doublet. "*Ergo,* the gallows await you, too. But not today."

Thornleigh rubbed the back of his stiff neck.

"You may well ask why I make a habit of studying character," the man went on, evidently wishing that Thornleigh *had* asked. "Well, sir, I will tell you. It is my business. I am an actor. Jack Ives is my name." He proudly lifted his craggy profile. "Some in my position might demure at this pregnant juncture and say, 'I *was* an actor.' But the audience at the Tyburn gallows is always a substantial one, and a discriminating one, and as I find myself at this penultimate hour sound of wind and strong of voice, I see no reason to deprive them of a final, notable performance. *Ergo,* sir, I repeat, I *am* an actor."

Thornleigh almost smiled. If this was bravado in the face of doom it was a fine display. But the anchor of sorrow dragged at him again, and he wished more than ever that he could accompany Jack Ives to the gallows. Then a thought struck. He knew Newgate's reputation as the most vicious of London's prisons; perhaps he would meet death quickly here, after all. Good. The quicker the better. Yet something jarred: was he really in Newgate prison? What had Ives said? "What's Whit's Palace?" he asked.

"Our affectionate name for Newgate jail, sir, after a famous former Mayor of London, one Richard Whittington. He left money in his will for a new prison to be built, like a triumphal arch, in Newgate. Now, was that not a fine gesture? After all, he could have left his money to the widows and orphans or to the destitute. But not our Dick. No, he knew that what the people really wanted was a prison!" Ives flicked the wood splinter to the floor as if it were Dick Whittington's reputation. "May the bugger rot in hell till all Newgate's inmates join him to plague him with petitions of their innocence! Prison, indeed!" he growled—a formidable, prolonged rumble of disgust. Thornleigh did not doubt that anyone who had dropped a penny in the hat at an inn yard to hear Ives wail out King Priam's woes had got their money's worth.

A muffled sound from the boy made Thornleigh turn. The boy was waking up and he blinked, disoriented, as Thornleigh had done. His face was very flushed. He looked at Thornleigh and Ives. He seemed suddenly to recall where he was. "Oh, God," he moaned. His head dropped between his legs. He vomited onto the platform.

Ives snorted. "The Earl of Devon reacted in that way to a new play I once presented. An apt response, in truth. The piece was foul."

Thornleigh watched the boy. "He's in bad shape."

"He's being hanged today, too," Ives explained. "Just as well. He wouldn't last much longer. Jail fever."

Thornleigh noticed that the boy's flushed face was, indeed, damp with sweat. And tiny black spots speckled his hands, his nose, and his ears. The boy hunched back into the corner and sat dazed, shivering in terror in his own mess. Thornleigh looked away. There was nothing he could do for the lad.

He thought of his own children and grandchildren, of how far across the Channel—how far away from all of this—they would be by now, on their way to Antwerp and safety. He had thought of little else on the ride to London with the guards. He had not dared think of Honor—had steered away from her image as he would steer a ship from a reef in a storm; thoughts of her would capsize him into madness. So he'd forced his thoughts onto his children. But it had taken an immense effort of will to suppress his fury at Isabel's violation by Mosse. He had done so only by reassuring himself over and over that Adam would have come after her and comforted her and got her out of the country by now. But the effort had exhausted him. He was drained, by rage and by misery of heart. Only death would put an end to it. Death would stop it all.

"I will tell you something, sir," the actor said with sudden vigor. "I see death as a blessed end."

Thornleigh looked at him. Had the man been reading his thoughts?

Ives chuckled humorlessly. "On that point at least, the cretinous judge agreed with me. 'Retribution for a monstrous homicide,' is how he put it. Oaf. I ask you, sir, what red-blooded man would not be driven to kill, coming home to find his wife in the arms of a villain?"

"You killed your wife?"

Ives looked horrified. "Never, sir! My Joan is the light of my life. Not a moment's wrangling did we have before that seducing villain made his entrance. A loathsome haberdasher, he was. Joan is young, you see, and has a taste for fripperies. I never minded that. A pretty woman must preen and primp as the nightingale must sing. But these things do cost a pretty penny. And, sadly, an actor's riches are mostly the laughter and tears his audiences bestow. His purse is usually a sad, shriveled thing. I have a partner whose skill does help alleviate this chronic problem somewhat, however . . . well, 'Heaven 'tis, the actor's life / But hell on earth for the actor's wife.' "

Thornleigh understood. "You killed the man you found her with."

"I drove a pitchfork through his throat, sir. And a moment of supreme satisfaction it was." He sighed heavily. "But, apparently, only for me. Joan shrieked and locked herself in the dovecote and would not come out for two days. Would not eat. Would not speak. When I could bear it no longer I broke down the door. I was aghast to see the husk she had become. Joan was always a fiery one, but there was no fire left in her. I begged her to come down, to live with me again in sweet harmony. But she screamed that she had never loved me, never *would* forgive me. She scrambled to the dovecote roof and promised to dash herself to death below if I did not leave her. That's when the constable came. A puny fellow. I could have knocked the fool down and been halfway to France by the time he had my scent. But I let him lead me away. I knew that if the fire had gone out of Joan, it was I who'd put it out."

He looked up toward the shaft of sunlight. "I'll leave behind a trunk of costumes, a fine brass horn, and a little bay gelding, and all of it shall be Joan's. She will sell the lot, of course, and find another man. And I pray she will be happy. As for me, I have no wish to cheat the hangman. For, truly, I have not the heart to live without my Joan." He cast an uncertain glance at Thornleigh and asked in a surprisingly timid voice. "Can you understand?"

Thornleigh could. "Yes," he said.

Ives closed his eyes and murmured, "I thank you, sir, for that."

The door swung open and an official stepped inside—a bulky, disheveled man. He beckoned to people in the corridor. "Come in, ladies," he said, "and do not be afeared. The villains are securely chained. They'll not be harming you." He stood at the door, wiping his runny nose on his sleeve, while people filed in past him. There were about twenty men and women, and they shuffled into a tight semicircle in front of the prisoners.

"Oh, Lord, not again," Ives groaned in a whisper to Thornleigh above the scuffling feet. "Our inquisitive public. And that turd there," he said, nodding at the runny-nosed official who was collecting coins from each person as they entered, "is Master Andrew Alexander, our jailer. These ladies and gentlemen are paying him for a gawp at us before we die. A different batch came to the chapel yesterday to watch the boy and me stand by our coffins and be preached at. The boy puked then, too. On the priest's boots."

"Look your fill, ladies and gentlemen," Alexander was declaring in the bored tone of one repeating a set speech. "The depraved faces before you belong to the wickedest blackguards as ever stalked the God-fearing streets of London. Notice, if you will—"

"Bless my soul, if it isn't Rob!" Ives said in an astonished whisper as the jailer loudly carried on. Ives nudged Thornleigh, with a twinkle in his eye. "Rob's my partner, sir. That young scamp in the blue cap." Thornleigh followed Ives's gaze and spotted the young man, a pin-eyed fellow with a stringy mustache.

"Now, this young 'prentice here," Alexander intoned, pointing out the miserable boy chained in the corner, "he robbed his master's strongbox while the trusting gentleman sat at supper."

The spectators murmured their disapproval of such a gross violation of the natural order. One man, to impress the girl he was with, leaned close to the condemned boy and mimed a noose jerking his head to one side while his tongue lolled grotesquely. The boy blanched and urinated in his breeches. Some of the spectators laughed; some made faces of revulsion. Alexander claimed back their attention by launching into a detailed description of the procedure of the imminent hangings. The spectators stared, or crossed themselves, or chattered. Alexander's lecture droned on.

"Oh, Rob's coming here is a treat!" Ives whispered with a wicked grin. "Come, let's have some sport!"

In a sudden, explosive movement Ives jumped to a crouched stand on the platform and let out a bellow like a wounded ox. "Woe to Rome!" he cried. With his chained wrist he banged his temple like a man in despair. He wailed:

> "Oh, woe betide th'assassin's bloody hand,
> That ever dared take up the traitor's stand!
> And Brutus will not live to see the day
> That Rome will blink this faithlessness away!"

The spectators stood in amazement at Ives's outburst. Thornleigh, too, stared up at the actor. Ives carried on declaiming, and it soon became clear that he had transformed himself into the Roman, Brutus, overcome with guilt after murdering Caesar, and about to take his own life with his imaginary sword. As Ives moaned and ranted his way through a suicide soliloquy, the spectators watched, rapt. Thornleigh caught sight of the blue-capped young man, Rob, slipping beside a gentleman wearing a voluminous robe. Just then, Ives thudded to his knees to deliver a booming plea to the Roman gods and raised high his invisible sword, ready to plunge it into his breast. His hands quivered. Tears streamed from his eyes. The people craned their necks and shuffled closer to catch the extraordinary performance. Thornleigh saw Rob's hand flash from the gentleman's robe and back inside his own doublet. *An enterprising partnership, indeed,* Thornleigh thought with a flicker of amusement: *The actor draws the crowd, and the pickpocket collects the price of admission.*

Ives, now wavering on his knees in Brutus's death throes, swung up his tear-stained face to cry out a last request of the gods that all his worldly goods be divided between his wife and Rome. Then he looked straight out at his young partner, fixing him with a menacing glare, and wailed with all the intensity of the foregoing lament:

> "Yes, half of all these riches shall be Joan's,
> Or God will see that Satan fries your bones!"

There were a few puzzled looks at these odd words, but Ives concluded with a resounding quatrain of such wrenching pathos that every eye was again riveted on Brutus's desperate last gasp. Ives pitched over on his back, lifted his head with a final guilt-choked "Caesar!" froze wide-eyed as if he had seen the face of God, and then collapsed.

There was silence. Finally, the jailer himself murmured appreciatively, "Bravely done, old Jack." The spectators burst into a warm chatter of praise. Ives rose and smiled with studied humility. Some of the people came forward to compliment him. Others, more interested in the actual deaths about to be enacted, sneaked in for a closer look at the pitiful young apprentice.

The jailer, Alexander, came and stood over Thornleigh. "You're the felon just in from Essex? Thornleigh, is it?"

Thornleigh, reclaimed to reality, said nothing.

"It's two and six for easement of the chain," Alexander said. "Can you pay?"

Thornleigh dug inside his tunic, brought out the purse Adam had given him in Colchester, and opened it. Alexander peered down at the abundant contents. Listlessly Thornleigh counted out the coins.

Alexander dropped his brusque manner and smiled as he pocketed the fee. He took up his keys to unlock Thornleigh's chain. "You will be wanting to bide on the Masters side, I warrant, Master Thornleigh?" he asked.

Thornleigh shrugged. He didn't care where he was put.

"The Masters side it is, then," Alexander confirmed with a smile. "Tell me, sir, do you play an instrument?"

Thornleigh looked up in mild surprise.

"I take it you do not," Alexander said. "Well, it's no matter, sir." He let the chain swing loose and pocketed his keys. "I hope you'll do me the honor of joining me and my good wife at dinner, sir?" he asked. "We'd be glad of your company, so we would."

Thornleigh said nothing.

"Then it's settled," Alexander said. "Come along now. We'll get you comfortably settled and then we'll dine." He picked up Thornleigh's cloak for him, took him solicitously by the elbow, and led him through the group of spectators. "Viewing's over, ladies and gentlemen," he called out brusquely. "Everybody out. The hangings commence in an hour."

Thornleigh turned at the door to look back at Ives. The actor was sitting again, his legs casually crossed, and was watching his audience depart. His second to last audience, Thornleigh thought. He saw, behind the actor's studied pose of detachment, deep inside the care-webbed eyes, an unmistakable glint of fear. Thornleigh knew there was nothing he could say in farewell that would not be mere vacuous words. Instead, he lifted his hands and applauded. Ives's face snapped toward him. His lower lip trembled for a moment. Then he stood, gathering his dignity, and bowed his head low to Thornleigh in gracious acknowledgment.

Andrew Alexander was a man who loved the musical arts. Every day at noon he and his wife dined with a handful of like-minded gentlemen prisoners while one of them skilled on the lute or the rebeck played for the company's enjoyment. Alexander was explaining all this to Thornleigh as he contentedly watched his wife pour Thornleigh a goblet of malmsey wine.

They and five other paying gentlemen prisoners were sitting at the carved oak dining table in a goldsmith inmate's private chamber and were listening to a lute duet. The two players—one, as Alexander explained, a merchant tanner already three years in Newgate for debt, the other a master baker awaiting trial for beating his apprentice to death—stood by the crackling log fire in the grate and plucked out a lively tune. The paneled chamber was cozy, the fire bright, the dinner succulent-smelling, the company convivial. Alexander's ministrations to his chronically dripping nose did nothing to lessen his enjoyment. He wiped the drips on a rag intermittently and beamed at his newest guest.

Thornleigh took the goblet from Mistress Alexander's pudgy hand. Her cold rings scraped his wrist. She smiled through the dusty white paint on her sagging cheeks and batted her eyes at him. Alexander nudged Thornleigh's other elbow. "Eat up, sir!" he heartily enjoined. Thornleigh looked down at his plate. Alexander had piled it with steaming food.

Thornleigh took a mouthful of bread. He had no appetite despite the poor food on the journey here; since some grisled beef and watered beer at an alehouse halfway to London yesterday with the guards, he had eaten nothing. He stared at the dishes of stewed partridge, smoked eels, and pickled quinces spread before him. The food looked as rich as the fare at London's finest inn, the Crane. The Crane . . . it was there, not quite two weeks ago, that he had begged Honor to leave England. But in the end it was he who had succumbed to her entreaties to wait. And because of his decision, she was dead. The bread in his mouth suddenly tasted like sand.

Alexander, captivated by the gay music, was tapping a dirty fingernail on the table in time with the rhythm. "This tune's a treat, eh, Master Thornleigh? What is it, Rivers?" he asked the goldsmith across the table. "I've never heard it before."

The goldsmith—in Newgate for selling adulterated gold plate—was pushing a quince into his mouth already stuffed with partridge, and he answered with some pride while he chewed, "A new composition by the Queen's choirmaster. My journeyman brought me the prick sheet yesterday."

"From the *court,* my, my!" Mistress Alexander said with great satisfaction, licking her wine-stained lips. "There, Master Thornleigh," she cooed, toasting him, "you won't find better entertainment than this anywhere, lest you pop up in Whitehall Palace itself!"

Thornleigh ignored her. The gathering seemed a mockery of the hollowness in his heart. He gulped down the full goblet of malmsey, then poured himself another, seeking oblivion. But he found none. Trying to hide from the image of Honor's face, he was only assaulted by other guilts.

The Spaniard in Colchester jail, for one. The fellow had tried to help him escape, apparently as part of a strategy to get out himself. But the plan—whatever it had been—had been scuppered by the brawl, and the Spaniard would surely be hanged; perhaps he already had been. Thornleigh felt bad about that.

And then there was the escape plan itself. Who had been

behind it? Who had hired the Spaniard to make contact with him? Someone was coming to the taproom to get him away, the Spaniard had said . . . but who? Who would have known the old password, to pass it along to the Spaniard? Who from the old days was left? Leonard Legge from the Crane? Legge seemed the only possible candidate. And if it *was* Legge, and he had come to Colchester to get Thornleigh out, what had he done when he heard the plan had miscarried? Had he made it back to London and the Crane without bringing suspicion on himself?

Thornleigh shook his head. These things were unknowable, beyond his control. And—a worse guilt—even beyond his interest. Let the world shift as it would. He longed only to die. He looked around and snorted with self-disgust. Die? Here? Only through a surfeit of luxurious living, apparently. Death was merely mocking him, toying with his desire.

Even the musicians seemed to conspire toward his misery. Their lively tune had ended and had slid into a solemn air, a strain both sweet and plaintive, melancholy enough to make even the stoutest heart vibrate with nameless regret. And Thornleigh could name his regret only too well. He knocked back another goblet of wine.

Alexander's eyes had misted over at the melancholy music. But he was smiling down the table at a large man who stood in the doorway. Thornleigh saw that it was a prisoner whom Alexander had introduced to him in the Masters Ward. The prisoner had pointed out to Thornleigh the bed assigned him, had given him some candles and soap, and explained Newgate's daily procedures. Thornleigh had barely listened.

"He's right here, Connors," Alexander pleasantly called out to the prisoner, placing a friendly arm around Thornleigh's shoulder. Thornleigh pulled back and began to pour himself another goblet. He wanted only to be left alone to drink.

The prisoner came to Thornleigh's side. "That'll be four shillings and three pence, sir."

Thornleigh blinked up at him, beginning to feel the effects of the wine. "What?"

"Garnish, sir," Alexander explained amiably. "For the services this cellarman supplied you. It is the custom here."

Thornleigh shrugged. Fees for everything. He dug into his tunic for his money. He could not feel the purse. He rummaged in the other side of his tunic. The purse was not there. He stood and tried a methodical search of every place in his clothing the purse could be. By this time, most of the company at the table were watching him. Thornleigh poked and patted everywhere. "It's gone," he said finally. "My money."

Alexander scowled.

Thornleigh said, "I must have dropped it some—" He stopped. "The pickpocket."

"How's that?" the prisoner asked angrily, as if Thornleigh were accusing him of the crime.

"In the condemned hold," Thornleigh explained, "that actor's partner was fleecing the spectators. He must have fleeced me, too."

"Pay up!" the prisoner said fiercely. He grabbed Thornleigh's throat with one hand. Thornleigh instantly chopped at the man's arm to break his hold and took a step back. But Alexander stood and said, "That's right, Connors, get him and hold him!"

Alexander's surprising command caught Thornleigh off guard, and the prisoner threw an arm around his neck and grappled Thornleigh to him. Thornleigh considered putting up a fight. But the wine on his empty stomach was making him unsteady. Besides, he could not summon the will. He slumped. Let them do what they wanted.

Alexander drew himself up like a judge. "You owe the cellarman his garnish and you owe me for this food and wine," he pronounced. "If you cannot pay in coin, we'll have something in kind. That," he said, pointing to Thornleigh's furred cloak heaped beside him on the floor.

Thornleigh kicked the cloak over to Alexander. Let them take it and leave him alone. Let everyone just leave him alone to die!

"The cloak for the cellarman," Alexander went on, "and your tunic for me."

The prisoner immediately began to unbutton Thornleigh's tunic. Thornleigh offered no resistance. But as the prisoner wrenched his arms from the tunic, something fell to the floor. Thornleigh looked down at it. It was Honor's letter, the one she had give him to deliver to Edward Sydenham the night that Grenville murdered her. He had forgotten he had it. He pounced on the letter to retrieve it.

"What's that?" Alexander asked. "His purse? Get it!"

"No, just a paper," the prisoner said.

On his knees, Thornleigh stuffed the letter into his shirt. He quickly got to his feet and whirled on the prisoner, ready now to fight. To hold on to this letter—this scrap of remembrance of Honor—he was ready to fight anyone.

But Alexander had no use for the letter. Nor, anymore, for Thornleigh.

The cellarman shoved him into the Beggars Ward. The place matched Thornleigh's vision of hell. The gloom seemed phosphorescent. It hung thickly throughout a labyrinth of cracked pillars, cobwebbed arches, and disfigured stone walls, the latter flaking with a chalky dust in some places, slimed with green mold in others. In the many nooks and crannies, shadowy bodies—fifty or more, it seemed—lay prostrate in misery. The stench of excrement made Thornleigh's wine-sodden stomach lurch. From some corner came a dull, scraping sound, like a knife slowly being sharpened. And all around him hummed the faint clang of chains and the low, bestial moans of despair.

The cellarman left him. As the sound of his footsteps faded, the iron door to the ward slammed shut, Thornleigh stood, uncertain where to go. He noticed two men hunkered beside a tiny cooking fire, watching him. One was holding a stick with a morsel of meat over the fire, and the other smiled at Thornleigh through the thin curtain of smoke. Grease from the meat dripped with a hiss into the fire. Thornleigh approached them. The man with the stick quickly set it down, picked up a slingshot, fitted a stone, and fired it at Thornleigh. The sharp missile struck his neck. The other man kept smiling inanely. Thornleigh backed away.

He went under an arch and into a section of the ward that was even darker. It seemed to hold fewer people, too, though there were shadowy humps everywhere that moved. He passed a scrawny woman squatting and scratching at the earthen floor. A scab-crusted old man sat watching her.

Thornleigh made his way toward a dark, empty nook and sat down against a pillar. The spot reeked of mildewed straw. The stone pillar was icy cold on his back, as was the dank floor. He shivered in his shirt and breeches. Panic suddenly flooded his brain: could he survive this cold? But the panic rolled away in an equally sudden wash of supreme indifference. Freezing would be a painless, quiet death. Good. He welcomed it.

His eyes were becoming accustomed to the gloom. He could now make out a group of people crouched in a quiet circle in the middle of the fetid space. There were about a half dozen of them. For a moment he wondered if the cold, combined with the wine, was fogging his brain already, because all the people in the group looked like dwarfs. Then he realized they were children, perhaps five or six years old. He knew that women giving birth in prison kept their babies with them, often for years. Still, the sight was disconcerting. What kind of children did such surroundings breed?

He glanced at a prone form asleep on the floor nearby, an emaciated man. Shock knifed through Thornleigh as he realized the man was a corpse. Its hands and nose and ears were speckled with black. Thornleigh twisted his head to another prisoner a few feet away who was sitting, like him, propped against a pillar. Sitting, but dead. And spotted, as the other dead man was, like a decayed piece of fruit. Thornleigh felt revulsion, like vermin, crawl over his skin. He was in a ward half full of corpses claimed by jail fever.

One of the children coughed softly. Thornleigh turned back to the silent little group. What were the children playing at so earnestly? What kind of game could have such appeal in this den of death? Suddenly, as if a strict parent had come and declared the playtime over, the group broke apart and the children scurried away, scuttling behind pillars, around corners. And Thornleigh saw what had kept them so engrossed at the center of their circle.

It was no game. A man lay sprawled on his back on the floor. His hands and nose and ears were spotted black, but his living eyes stared up in terror at the ceiling. He rasped out one long, tortured breath. And then he breathed no more. Thornleigh saw that his stilled ribs poked up from his narrow chest, which, like his abdomen and thighs, were splotched with a livid purple rash. Thornleigh saw all of this clearly. The children had stripped the fevered man, still living, of all his clothes.

CHAPTER NINETEEN

><+<>+0+<>+<

Grateful Leaders

Isabel's heart lightened as soon as she saw the banners. She was sitting her horse on the hill above the Strood Bridge and gazing across the river at Rochester castle on whose towers Wyatt's bright banners snapped in the wind. They blazoned his daring and success. And somehow their splendid defiance eased the last five days torture over her warring loyalties, to Wyatt and to her father. Finally she was here to help the cause she had pledged herself to. On this hill, thirty miles beyond the stench of London's crooked streets, she took in a deep breath of the clean, cold air tinged with the salt of the sea and felt hope surge through her. Wyatt stood for right, and Wyatt was going to win.

She bent and stroked her tired mare's neck. The horse's muscles quivered in response—just as it had quivered under Carlos's touch last night, Isabel remembered. Last night. What was she to make of his coarse advances? He had shocked her, stunned her. By his outrageous action, yes, but by something else, too. His presumption of dominance. His expectation of mastery.

She knew she was ignorant of the ways of men, Mosse's violence to her notwithstanding. Her slight experience with lovemaking, before she had met Martin, had been limited to nervous schoolgirl hand-holding with her friend Lucy's brother during the May Day rites in the neighboring village. Hardly a worldly past. With Martin there had been a tantalizing taste of more. Despite the constant and annoying presence of family, his and hers, they had managed to steal some time alone that had led to long, enticing kisses and even some breathless tumbling in the late-summer grass by her father's millrace. But Martin's experience, she sensed, was not much broader than her own. They were equals in that respect: both eager to rush into the sweet, heady mystery, but both ignorant of where to tread first. But in that moment last night when Carlos had pulled her to him she understood that for him it was a well-worn path. Carlos was a man accustomed to getting what he wanted from women, and to it being freely given—for she was well aware that what Mosse had done to her was a world apart from what had drawn the chambermaid to Carlos in the shadows of the passage. Carlos was used to mastery. And despite her shock when he had touched her, something inside her had leapt . . .

She sat up straight in the saddle, forcing away such thoughts. She looked ahead at Rochester Castle. Martin was there. She longed to see him. *Needed* to see him. She kicked her heels against the mare's flanks and they began to trot down the hill.

A hawk glided overhead in free and unencumbered flight. Isabel smiled. It was wonderful to be moving forward, to be acting, to feel her impotence since the nightmarish murder of her mother melting away like the ice melting on the rocks beside her and trickling down to the river. At the foot of the hill she approached the bridge manned by a small troop of Wyatt's confident-looking soldiers, and suddenly all things seemed possible: Carlos would find her father today and together they would rescue him; Wyatt would win; she and Martin would be married. Order was going to be restored—to the country and to the chaos of her life. The way lay right before her.

The mare stepped onto the bridge, its hooves clopping hollowly over the wooden timbers. Isabel noticed that the soldiers were eating as they stood duty halfway across the bridge, some munching hunks of bread and cheese, some slurping at fowl legs. They idly watched her approach, and she overheard their brief, bawdy exchange of jests.

A bandy-legged guard with a grizzled, salt-and-pepper beard stepped out in front of the others in a mock-heroic stance of defending the bridge against this attack from a lone female. His mates laughed. The grizzled guard tossed his chicken bone over the side of the bridge and ambled toward Isabel, his thumbs hooked into his belt. He halted in her path, blocking her way, and suddenly spread his arms dramatically wide as if in defiance of a terrible foe. "Who goes there?" he asked in a deep, dread voice consistent with his pantomime.

Isabel smiled at the foolery. "Prince Philip in disguise," she said.

There were guffaws from the other soldiers. "She's got you there, Tom!" one called out with a laugh. The grizzled guard frowned, apparently not appreciating Isabel's bettering him in the jest.

The fellow was no doubt the leader of the guard detail, Isabel thought. She decided she had better not antagonize him further if she wanted entry. She dismounted, stepped up to him with a look of earnest deference, and said, *"Dieu et mon droit."* This was the password Ambassador de Noailles had instructed her to give. She had been careful to deliver it loudly enough for the other soldiers to hear.

The grizzled guard's face immediately cleared. He glanced back at his friends. They were watching in silence now, aware that something significant was happening. When the guard looked back at Isabel his face radiated pride that he was part of this secretive, official exchange. He drew himself up to his not very considerable height and, with a grand gesture with his chicken-greasy hand, welcomed her to cross the bridge.

They walked across side by side, Isabel leading her horse. "Is Sir Thomas Wyatt available to see me, sir?"

The guard looked flustered. "What's that? The commander? Aye, m'lady. Instructed me to bring the lady with the password straight on up, no dithering about. He's yonder, up at the castle." He continued to frown uncertainly, as though distressed.

Inside the town, Wyatt's strength of numbers amazed Isabel. Evidence of it was everywhere. Not only in the large companies of soldiers trooping the streets and drilling at the archery butts, but also in the cohorts of carters handling supply wagons, the blacksmiths clanging at anvils, the esquires hefting saddles, the cooks stirring massive steaming pots over fires. The calm confidence of everyone in their preparations warmed Isabel like sunshine.

She and the guard entered the castle precincts and threaded their way through milling groups of men. The guard told her that the soldiers were waiting to head into the great hall to eat. She looked among them for Martin but could not see him. The guard led her through the castle's main doors and, almost immediately past the doors, to a stone staircase. As they went up, the succulent aroma of roasting pork wafted up from the hall, and Isabel's stomach grumbled. She had eaten nothing since a snatched bite of breakfast before dawn at the Anchor.

Once up the stairs the guard nodded toward a closed door. "Commander's inside, m'lady. Time I was on my way back to the bridge."

"Thank you, sir. Good day."

He frowned and cleared his throat.

"Yes?" Isabel asked. She thought he looked very uncomfortable. He seemed almost to squirm. "What is it?"

"That's twice you've called me *sir*," he said. "Sir's for dandies, them that're cowering now under the Queen's Spanish skirts. This army is for the plain, honest workingmen of England, m'lady. Excepting the commander, of course, for he be the brains behind us. But I be a yeoman and proud of it. If you please, m'lady, you must call me Tom."

Isabel grinned. "England is safe in your hands, Tom."

"Thirty French ships?" Wyatt's eyes widened in astonished delight.

"Under the command of Admiral Villegaignon," Isabel confirmed. She and Wyatt were standing alone in the sunlit solar above the great hall. She could hear the muffled noise of men tramping into the hall to eat. "At the moment," she went on, "the Admiral's fleet is lying off the Normandy coast. Monsieur de Noailles says the ships will bring you twelve companies of infantry."

"Ah!" Wyatt raised his hands and eyes to heaven as if in thanks for deliverance.

"He also says that Admiral Villegaignon can move his fleet among our southern harbors, if you wish. He asks what landing places would suit you best."

"Portsmouth, Hastings, Dover. Tell de Noailles that. Lord, this is great news! And what of the French force bound for Scotland?"

"The King of France promises that troops will soon be landing just north of Newcastle."

"Soon? How soon?"

"Monsieur de Noailles did not say."

Wyatt frowned.

"But regarding the south," Isabel went on, "he has received a coded message from the Mayor and aldermen of Plymouth expressing a willingness to receive a French garrison."

"That's good. Very good. And what news of the Queen's preparations in London?"

"The Tower has been revictualed and its artillery overhauled. The Queen has placed Lord William Howard in command of the city's defenses. Guns are being placed at every gate."

Wyatt scowled at this but said, "That was expected. What size are the Queen's forces?"

"Surprisingly small, sir. The Ambassador believes that at this point she has little more than her palace guard."

"Why, that can't be more than two hundred. Are her councilors too busy bickering to gather their own musters?"

"I do not know, sir. However, the Ambassador suspects that she may be sending the trained bands of the city out against you. Though their force, he feels, cannot be large."

Wyatt said nothing, but Isabel thought he looked worried. However, there was no more she could tell him. She had reported everything the French Ambassador had told her the day before yesterday in his pantry at the Charterhouse. Her duty here was done. Still, she felt an urge to say more.

"Believe me, sir, there is wondrous support for you throughout the city," she ventured. "One hears it everywhere. And Ambassador de Noailles introduced me to Master Henry Peckham who is organizing a great, secret body of support for you. They will be ready to strike with you when you come. London is yours! I feel it!" She looked down, aware that she had overstepped some martial convention with her enthusiasm.

Wyatt gave her a small, grim smile. "I am counting on it," he said. He moved to a table littered with maps, picked up a jug of wine, and poured two goblets full. "Well done, Mistress Thornleigh," he said, handing her one. "I confess that I had almost given up on you. But this news of the French makes up for all." He raised his goblet in a toast to her. "Congratulations," he said, and drank.

Isabel felt a thrill of exhilaration at her successful mission. She drank with him, deeply and gratefully, for she was very thirsty after the long ride. The wine almost instantly swirled to her head and she felt emboldened to say, "It is *you* who must be congratulated, Sir Thomas. Such a great army you have drawn together! You will hardly even need the help from France!"

Wyatt fixed her with a stern look. "Don't meddle in strategy, mistress. Stick to reporting about the French fleet." He turned away, but she heard him murmur, "It just might save us."

She was taken aback. She realized that her understanding of these things—of troop strength and readiness—was imperfect. But anyone could see that the army of English followers camped outside was formidable. "But, sir—"

"You must be famished," Wyatt said, as though to change the subject. He smiled. "Any other messenger, I'd tell him to help himself in the hall. But I'll not toss in a pretty young woman alone among that pack. However, I have a meeting with my lieutenants at the armory and I must leave you. So I'll have some food sent up to you here. All right?"

She thanked him. But there was still more she needed to say. And his mention of his lieutenants gave her the opening. "Sir Thomas, might I speak with Martin?"

Wyatt was downing his wine, about to go. "Who?" he said, wiping his mouth with the back of his hand.

"Martin St. Leger."

"Oh. No. Sorry, you can't."

She bit her lip. "It would mean a great deal to me, sir. Would it upset military discipline so dreadfully to allow Martin a few moments with me?"

"No, I meant you can't because he's not here. He's in Sevenoaks helping Sir Henry Isley march troops to us. He left the day before yesterday. They should arrive soon. I hope so. I can't go on until I have them."

"Oh," she said. Sevenoaks was only fifteen miles away. Could she ask to stay at the castle until Martin returned? She longed for the reassurance that seeing him would bring. But she also knew she must return to London for her father's sake. Even if Carlos did find him it might take days to plan and execute the escape. A wave of resentment swelled inside her. If it were not for her father she could see Martin and be part of these exciting events. She could *stay* here with Martin, and be safe from . . . everything.

"Eat up, have a rest, then get back to London on the double," Wyatt said brusquely.

Isabel nodded bleakly.

Wyatt started for the door. "I'll expect you with another report from Noailles as soon as possible."

"Come back?" she gasped. "But . . . I cannot! At least, not right away."

Wyatt turned. "What's that?"

"I have . . . urgent business in London. Personal business that will keep me from—"

"You *asked* for this job, woman!" he said fiercely. "And against my better judgment, I agreed. I've waited four days for you to show up. And now, when our country's very life could depend on the information that only you can bring, you want to bow out?" He had come toward her and stood glowering in her face. "For some God-cursed social engagement?"

Her anger flared again. It was hardly that she *wanted* to risk her life skulking around London's prisons, for God's sake. "No, sir," she said tightly. "But something has happened which—"

"You're damned right something's happened! While you've been dawdling in London a war's begun! And like it or not, you're part of it!"

She bit her lip and looked down.

Wyatt let out a small sigh of exasperation. "Look," he said, clearly trying for patience, "I know my troops out there must seem like a mighty lot to you, but . . ." He paused, clearly unwilling to divulge military information, but then plunged ahead. "I already have Lord Abergavenny and Sheriff Southwell on my tail. They're near Sevenoaks, too, you see, collecting a royalist army. And the trained London bands you said the Queen might send against me? She already has. Yesterday. The Duke of Norfolk is in command. They arrived in Gravesend this morning, my scout tells me." He frowned at her. "Do you understand what all this means?"

"That Norfolk will attack you here?"

He nodded. "So I should get out and march for London, right? But if I do, Norfolk and Abergavenny will combine and strike my rear. So I should stay and fight from this fortified position, right? Right. I'm staying. But as soon as I have Isley's troops from Sevenoaks, I'll march. And when I do I'll need every scrap of information from de Noailles about what French support and what London support I can count on. I'm relying on *you* for that. Understand? I am depending on you."

There was a cheer outside. Wyatt glanced at the window, then hurried out the door to investigate. Isabel ran to the window. Below in the cobbled bailey stood a ragged circle of Wyatt's soldiers inside which stood two lines of men, a half dozen in each line, all wearing the baggy breeches of sailors. Resting upon their shoulders was a large black demi-cannon. Their leader, a stout man with a face the color of cured oak, stepped forward as Wyatt emerged from the castle. Isabel pushed open the window shutter to hear.

"Sir Thomas Wyatt?" the weather-beaten leader asked. "My name is Winter. Captain Winter. Commander of the Queen's ships moored in the estuary. I was awaiting orders to sail to Bruges and escort Prince Philip to the Queen when we heard what you were doing." He glanced back at his men. "And, well, now someone else will have to ferry the Spanish Prince across if they want him here to lord it over Englishmen. We've come to join you. And"—he smiled—"to make sure of our welcome, we've brought you one of the Queen's guns." He gestured toward the demi-cannon glistening in the sun. He grinned broadly and added, "There's four more beauties just like her on board. And the rest of my men, too."

Wyatt threw his arms around the captain in a joyous embrace. Wyatt's men cheered and swarmed the new arrivals. Tom, the bridge guard, cheered the loudest and danced like a heathen around the muzzle of the demi-cannon, staring it in the mouth in a parody of fearlessness that made the surrounding men laugh.

Isabel laughed, too, as she closed the window again. She moved to the table and poured herself another goblet of wine. *Sir Thomas is too cautious,* she thought, still smiling as she sank into a chair to rest her saddle-sore muscles. *We shall win!*

In Whitehall Palace people were almost crushing Queen Mary. The scene on the staircase was total confusion. Frances Grenville anxiously took the Queen's elbow, making her body a barrier between the Queen and the men clamoring on that side of the broad staircase. The Queen, Frances, and Amy Hawtry had been on their way up to chapel when they had been stopped by a breathless messenger calling up to the Queen. Almost immediately people had come running from everywhere as rumors shot down the corridors, and now the women were surrounded on the stairs by lords and courtiers pushing closer to hear. The muddy messenger on the step below them gulped to catch his breath after delivering the news.

"What's that?" Lord William Howard sputtered over Frances's shoulder. "*All* of Captain Winter's men?"

The messenger nodded, confirming the disaster. "All gone over to the traitor, my lord."

"That means the ship's guns, too," Lord Pembroke growled.

There were gasps, murmurs of outrage, a barrage of questions. Frances tightened her grip on the Queen in reassurance and looked out at the alarmed faces. Bishop Gardiner was snapping at a man tugging his sleeve. Lord Paulet was shaking his head gloomily. Sir Richard Riche was pushing a priest out of the way to get closer to hear. The Earl of Arundel stood scowling at the foot of the stairs flanked by several of his armed retainers. Everyone else was talking at once.

"I ask my councilors present to meet with me in the gallery," the Queen declared. She tried to step down but the way was solidly blocked. "Let me pass," she said quietly.

But the commotion persisted. Frances looked imploringly at the men in front. "Please, my lords!"

"Let the Queen through!" Riche bellowed.

Others took up the cry. "Let the Queen pass!"

The crowd shuffled back to the banisters. Mary moved down the stairs and beckoned the Earl of Arundel to walk with her. Men crowded behind in their wake, their anxious voices almost as loud as before. Less than a quarter of those present were members of the royal council, but no one left; everyone followed the Queen. Frances and Amy did, too, for they had not been dismissed. The whole entourage moved swiftly down the corridor.

Frances saw Edward approaching with her brother, both wearing expressions of wonder at the noisy disturbance. Edward and John fell in and walked beside Frances and Amy. Gratefully Frances felt for Edward's hand.

Amy shook her head. "Lord, such a to-do over a few cowardly sailors!" she said derisively.

"Is it true?" John anxiously asked his sister above the hubbub.

"The messenger is a retainer of Lord Paulet's," she answered. "He is reliable."

"But surely Mistress Hawtry has a point," Edward said.

Frances shot him a look of surprise. But far from showing Amy's blithe nonchalance, Edward appeared unnerved, Frances thought. In fact, quite shaken.

"After all, why such panic over a handful of ships?" Edward went on. "The Emperor will have a *hundred* ships on their way by now, an armada. The Queen is his kinswoman. And he will never let this rabble of Wyatt's destroy the marriage he has planned for his son."

"Thank you, Master Sydenham," Amy said with a smile. "I am glad to see that not everyone at court has lost his wits."

The Queen has reached the doors of the gallery, but the crowd surged around her again and around her councilors trying to get through. The whole mass jammed the way to the doors, still jabbering. No one could move. Frances caught sight of the Queen pressing her fingers to her temples.

"It is not the handful of ships that matters so much," John said grimly.

Edward looked at him. "Then what?"

"It is—how shall I put it?—the symbolism," John said. "The treachery. Every Englishman who is turned by Wyatt cleaves wider the rift between the Queen and her people." He added quietly, "It is a rift that could cost her her crown."

Edward seemed to blanch. Frances suddenly felt anxious about him. "Edward, you look quite unwell," she said.

"Do I?" He waved a hand dismissively. "It's only these negotiations with the Fuggers for the loan. They dragged out so the other night."

"But you must not ruin your health with this work," Frances admonished him.

Amy laughed. "The negotiations were at the Venetian Ambassador's supper, Frances. Did you consider that it might have been *pleasure* that kept him up? Not *everyone* fusses and frets all the time. Do they, Master Sydenham?" She gave Edward a sly look that infuriated Frances.

"Edward is working tirelessly in the service of Her Majesty, Amy," she snapped. "If you think—"

"It's all right, Frances," Edward whispered, his eyes fixed on the Queen across the jostling crowd. "It's not just the work. I'm rather worried about my steward. I sent him on an errand to Newgate last night and he has not yet reported back."

Frances smiled. "Dear Edward, always so concerned for others." She felt so proud of him. A girl like Amy would never understand the worth of such a man. A happy thought struck her: she knew the way to cheer him. She decided to do it immediately. She started to push toward the Queen, but could make little headway through the crush.

"Enough, my lords!" It was the Queen's voice, strident with anger at the crowd. There was instant silence, as though everyone were suddenly ashamed.

"Enough," Mary repeated, controlling herself. "I will hear no more words of fear! God and right are on our side."

"Yes, but are the soldiers?" a voice in the back muttered morosely.

Everyone heard it. The Queen's face went pale. "Do any of you doubt that God will stand by me?" she asked.

The silence hung heavily.

"Perhaps," the Queen went on tightly, "instead of importuning *me*, you could be stirring yourselves to help our cause. *Some* of my loyal servants are doing so. My Lord of Arundel has just told me that he is bringing me four hundred fighting men from his estates. That is heartening news indeed! And Master Edward Sydenham has just negotiated a great loan through the Lombard bankers of London to secure us many more troops. These two gentlemen are busy in the defense of the realm. I thank God for their loyalty and steadfastness. And I suggest that it be an example to you all."

In the silence the Queen turned toward the gallery doors.

"Your Majesty!" Frances called. The Queen stopped and looked back. Frances eagerly pushed through to her. "My lady, Master Sydenham is indeed your faithful servant. He had done more than you know. He has uncovered one of the plotters of the rebellion!"

There was an interested rumble of murmurs in the crowd.

"And the man is at this moment in London!" Frances declared.

"Who is it, Frances?" Queen Mary asked.

"Richard Thornleigh. My father's murderer."

"What? That family of heretics?"

"The same, my lady." Since yesterday, the crisis over Wyatt had so claimed the Queen's time that Frances had not had the opportunity to speak to her of this. It all poured out of her now. "For the murder, Thornleigh has been locked in Newgate prison. But Master Sydenham has discovered that compounded to Thornleigh's crimes of heresy and murder, he has also committed treason. Interrogate Thornleigh, Your Majesty, and I warrant you will learn with what strategems and devices the traitors plan to come against you."

The Queen looked through the crowd in Edward's direction. "Master Sydenham, is it true you ferreted out this man's treason?"

Edward stood openmouthed. His face was as white as paper. It must be his awe at being called by the Queen, Frances thought. She beamed at him and answered for him. "He did, my lady."

The Queen beckoned Edward to her. He stepped forward, stumbling over someone's foot on the way. Frances's pride swelled in her breast as he came before the Queen. Blinking, he bowed.

"I am most grateful to you for marking this traitor," Queen Mary said. She scanned the faces around her. "Is the Sergeant of the Guard present?" she asked.

A guard answered that the sergeant was in the city, busy with martial preparations.

"Send him this command," the Queen said. "He shall take his men to Newgate prison in the morning and bring forth Richard Thornleigh. He shall transport Thornleigh to my prison of the Tower to await his trial for treason—and my displeasure."

Frances closed her eyes, savoring this vindication for her father.

"And to you, dear sir," the Queen said, turning back to Edward, "I wish to give an earnest of my gratitude. It has long been a privilege of the monarch at a battle to bestow thanks to valiant warriors by knighting them at the scene of glory. The efforts you are making to secure the safety of this realm are no less valiant for being fought on a different battlefield. Today I make you a knight. And I appoint you as one of my lieutenants in the defense of the city of London. In this you shall work alongside Lord John Grenville and under the command of my Lord Howard. Kneel, sir."

Shakily Edward went to his knees. The Earl of Arundel passed the Queen his sword.

"This evil is God's test of us, sir," the Queen said to Edward. "Drive back the traitors and you shall have His thanks, as well as an even greater show of mine."

Frances felt tears of pride sting her eyes. *Sir* Edward Sydenham. She caught the Queen glancing at her. The Queen said to Edward, in a warm voice clearly meant for all to hear, "Loyalty is a wondrous virtue, sir. Glad I am that my dear friend Frances will be blessed with such a husband."

CHAPTER TWENTY

><♦><○><♦><

Change of Plan

Thornleigh coughed. It felt like claws ripping inside his gullet. *Throat's swollen,* he thought. *Must be coming down with something ... so cold here.* He saw the irony of his discomfort; after all, he was here to die.

He sat watching a work party across the ward room. A cellarman was overseeing two prisoners as they tossed bodies onto the charnel-house cart. "The corpse cart," the prisoners called it; though he had been down here for only a day and night, Thornleigh had learned that much. The prisoners who weren't chained up had scuffled aside when the cart came, superstitious about being near it.

The cellarman had brought a torch, illuminating this patch of the ward, and Thornleigh could now see the filth that in the gloom he had only smelled: the clumps of urine-spongy straw; the verminous nests of rags inhabited by equally verminous humans; the corpses. He watched the work party's silent movements under the twitching torchlight, thinking the scene looked like some macabre pantomime of Satan's minions tidying up in hell.

He hugged himself more tightly, but nothing stopped the shivering. Late last night he had found this spot, an alcove matted with black straw and shreds of a disintegrated shawl, and he had huddled here, with a couple of red-eyed rats watching him from the corner. The spot offered a little warmth, but nothing stopped the shivering. All night he had drifted in and out of sleep, exhaustion dulling his brain into slumber until nightmare visions jolted him awake again. Cold as he was, his eyelids burned as though sand were grating behind them. And his throat was as parched as a ship's deck becalmed under a baking summer sun. A pail of water had been brought to the door around noon and Thornleigh had gulped down several ladles full, but that was hours ago. Now, he dreamed of water even when he was awake.

Two prisoners near him—new arrivals who were energetically arranging their meager belongings—had been quietly arguing in the corner. Now one of them raised his voice querulously. "I tell you, it's war! There's a hundred thousand Spaniards let loose on our shores, and this fellow Wyatt's out to stop 'em!"

"What's Spaniards to me?" the other groused. "Will Wyatt come to London town is all I want to know."

"Good Christ, what care the likes of you if he come to London or if he battle the bastards on the beaches?"

"If he come to London mayhap he'll burst down Newgate's doors and set us free."

"And why in Christ's name would he be doing that with a hundred thousand Spaniards on his arse!"

Wyatt, Thornleigh thought, shaking his head. The rebels had taken their stand against the Queen five days ago, and yet, to him, what did it matter now if Wyatt won or lost? What did anything matter anymore? Everything was pointless idiocy. Everything was misery.

Yet Honor had been for the rebels; he could not forget that. Honor, always so quick to bristle against tyranny, always ready to assist anyone suffering under that tyranny. So generous. So brave. Even her writings—the anonymously published pamphlets that absorbed her—even those words on paper, pleading for tolerance from Catholics and Protestants alike, glowed with her generosity of spirit.

He suddenly remembered her letter. He had not been able to look at it before because the ward lay in perpetual gloom. But the cellarman's torch now shed enough light to read. A sharp longing shafted through him, a hunger for this contact with her, if only through words she had written to someone else. As the work party heaved another corpse onto the cart, and the two new prisoners continued to bicker, Thornleigh pulled out the letter. He steadied his shaky elbows on his drawn-up knees and read:

Dear Edward,
    Forgive my obtuseness when you visited me in London. You asked a serious favor and I gave you a frivolous reply. Let me now set your heart at rest. Of course I will keep your secret. How could I not, when I trust that you will do the same for me? After all, we heretics must stick together.

Pardon the lapse into levity. The gravity of the matter makes me jest, lacking proper words. For I confess that, for some years, I harbored anger for you, and though it is spent, its shadow continues to make the language of forgiveness elusive.

But I do forgive. I know what hell you have suffered, fleeing England as an outcast, plagued by guilt that others might have died because of you, fearful every day since your return that your criminal past would be uncovered. I suffered that same hell.

But, Edward, love brings peace. You tell me that you yearn for home, a family. And I tell you that, whatever your former errors, your longing for these genuine riches now absolves you.

Be good to Frances Grenville when she becomes your wife. Believe me, as one whose life was saved by love, there is no greater gift.

Your secret is safe with me.

Honor Thornleigh

Thornleigh lowered the letter. The backs of his eyelids burned with threatening tears. He dropped his forehead to his arms bridged between his knees. But he instantly jerked his head back up. He must not weep. That way madness lay.

He looked around the miserable ward. Bodies, living and dead, lay in the shadowy spaces where the floor met the walls, like refuse swept into a gutter. Some who could walk shuffled aimlessly. Most—alive and dead alike—were emaciated. All were beyond hope.

Thornleigh thought: *I am going to die here.*

Like them.

A flame of rage kindled inside him. Death held no terror; he had been welcoming death. But to die like this? Impotent and unresisting? Something in him revolted at the indignity, the affront to Honor. Yes, he thought, to Honor. Had his furious vengeance of her murder led him here only to succumb like these whimpering wretches dazed into passivity and despair? Passivity. That was a debility Honor had never suffered from. On that very evening of her death, she had been active, engaged, writing this letter to reassure Edward Sydenham. Looking at the letter now, he crushed it to his chest and fancied that he could actually feel her strength, her love, emanating from it. He felt it empower him. He suddenly longed to throw off his fetters of inaction, for her sake. Honor deserved that much.

That much, and more. She deserved to have the promise he had made to her redeemed. He had made it that evening, just before Grenville had come. In exasperation at her reluctance to flee England, he had promised that if she would go, he would help the rebels—help this Sir Thomas Wyatt to keep at bay the Spanish Inquisition. He had been thinking then only of giving money to the cause, and neither he nor Honor knew that Grenville was at that very moment riding through their gates to kill her. But the fact that burned in his memory was this: at the penultimate moment of alarm, just as through twenty-two years together they had always somehow forged consensus out of crisis, they had done so again that night. She had agreed to go, and he had promised to help her cause.

He wanted to do it now. To act. For her. To die acting for her. *That* would be a fitting end. That would be a death he could proudly march out to embrace.

If only he could get out of this dungeon of misery ...

He watched the corpse-cart party drag a woman's body, previously stripped half naked by the child scavengers, and heave her on top of the heaped cart.

If only ...

"Idiot!" Edward cried. He raised his hand to strike his steward. Palmer cringed. Edward regained control and lowered his arm. Still livid, he turned his back on Palmer and glared into the fire that whispered in his sumptuous parlor's hearth. The steward bowed his head and anxiously turned his hat in his hands.

Edward watched the restless flames and tried to digest the galling failure Palmer had reported. He had entered Newgate prison yesterday and had remained inside all night in search for a felon willing to dispatch Thornleigh; even the exorbitant fee Edward had authorized Palmer to offer held little inducement for condemned men waiting to be hanged. Finally, this morning, Palmer had found a man eager for drinking money, and they had struck a bargain. But the prisoner demanded to be paid in advance for the job. Knowing his master's need for haste, Palmer had paid. The felon had immediately decamped to the prison taproom where he had spent the money on a spree of drink and whores, had insulted another prisoner, and had been killed in the ensuing brawl.

"Idiot," Edward repeated under his breath in disgust. What could be salvaged of this catastrophe?

He began to pace before the fire, thinking it through. Tomorrow morning, by the Queen's order, Thornleigh was to be moved to the Tower by the Sergeant of the Guard, to await his treason trial. Once Thornleigh was under lock and key in that impregnable fortress, Edward would have no further chance to reach him. So, he thought, he had until morning.

"There's something more, sir," the steward put in hesitantly. "We've found the girl, like you asked."

"What girl?" Edward asked testily.

"Thornleigh's daughter. She's here in London, staying at the Anchor Inn on Thames Street. Seems she doesn't know her father's been put in Newgate, and she's searching the prisons for him. What's worse, she's got that Spaniard working for her."

"What? The one you hired in Colchester? The murderer?" The steward nodded.

Edward frowned. This was an odd wrinkle. How had such an unlikely alliance come about, the daughter and the mercenary? And why? But he could not bother with such questions now. He must deal with the main point, that he had only the few hours until morning to deal with Thornleigh.

At the hearth he stared into the sharp arrows of fire. And there he found his answer.

"Palmer," he said, abruptly turning, "the Grenville Archers are close at hand, are they not?"

"Master John's troop? Aye, sir. They're billeted at the Queen's revels pavilion hard by the palace."

"Good. Who's the best among them? Sturridge isn't it?"

"Aye, sir. He's their captain."

"And I," Edward said with a small smile, aware of the irony, "have been named one of the Queen's lieutenants. Bring Sturridge to me. *Now.*"

An hour later the young captain of the Grenville Archers was standing on the Turkish carpet before the fire, nodding as Edward outlined his orders.

"You understand?" Edward asked.

"Aye, sir. But how will I know this Richard Thornleigh?"

Edward realized the difficulty. And he had no answer; he had never laid eyes on Thornleigh himself. That had been the very reason it had been necessary to give the Spaniard the old password to make the identification in Colchester jail. But the problem was not insurmountable. "You know the Sergeant of the Guard, don't you?"

"Aye, sir. Master Willingham."

"Good. The sergeant will be escorting a prisoner out of Newgate first thing in the morning. That prisoner is your target."

Shivering, Thornleigh folded his wife's letter. He was replacing it inside his shirt when he noticed the black spots on the back of his right hand. Only a few. In the light of the corpse-cart party's torch they looked like gnats. Irrationally, he brushed at them with his other hand as if to flick them away.

And that was when he saw the first child arrive. A girl, perhaps eight years old. She squatted about ten feet from him in front of the alcove, her elbows on her knees, her hands cupped under her chin. She was very thin and dirty. She did not move, but simply stared at him. She had just squatted down when another child, a boy much younger, crept up beside her and squatted, too, watching Thornleigh. And then the rest came, singly or in pairs, until there were nine of them, all hunkered in a ragged semicircle, watching him.

Thornleigh tried to hide his shivering. He knew that the children were waiting for him to fall asleep or die, whichever should come first. But he no longer wanted to die. Not here. Not yet.

He glanced around the crowded ward. There was nowhere to go to escape the children. He must stay where he was and weather this. He picked the girl, the eldest—the leader—and he stared back at her. Her eyes, dark and lifeless, were two huge smudges overpowering her thin white face.

The corpse-cart work party left, taking away the dead and taking away the light. The children in front of Thornleigh became shadowy mounds. The other prisoners settled down into the hushed and feeble motions of night. And Thornleigh sat shivering and staring into the girl's eyes—eyes so deep, empty, and merciless.

Carlos shouldered his way through the pedestrians and carts clogging the market on Newgate Street. His eyes were fixed ahead on Newgate prison. He was walking quickly, alarmed to realize that the afternoon light was fading. He had spent the whole day searching for Thornleigh. Working alone, unencumbered by the girl, he had moved methodically through the Marshalsea prison and King's Bench jail in Southwark, all with no luck. Newgate was the only prison left. Thornleigh *had* to be there. But Carlos realized he must hurry if he was to get inside before they locked visitors out for the evening.

He skirted the stalls of the Shambles, the flesh market set up in the middle of Newgate Street. Housewives and servants were hastening to finish their purchases, even as the butchers and tripe-sellers were packing away for the day. Paupers picked at the refuse on the ground. Beyond the sheds, the bleating of sheep and the bellowing of steers rose from the slaughterhouses and cattle pens.

A flock of children swarmed into the street, boys and girls alike wearing identical yellow kerseys and red hats; Carlos judged they were from the foundlings hospital next door. He had to halt as the orphans dashed around him, screeching with laughter in some private game. He hated stopping like this in the open; the guards from Colchester must still be out looking for him. But the children pinned him inside the swirl of their bodies and he had to wait. He looked up at the prison that lay a few house-lengths dead ahead.

It rose up from London wall, built over the arch of the gate, its flat roof notched with battlements. Carlos made out four upper stories, and grates at street level indicated at least one lower ward. The stench from the grates reached him even with the competing smells from the Shambles. The open gate itself was wide enough to admit four horsemen riding abreast under the arch, and the traffic of farmers, housewives, gentlemen, and priests flowed both ways, on foot, donkey, wagon, and horseback. Several people had congregated around a whipping post just inside the gate where a boy of about twelve, stripped to the waist, was being flogged. As the orphan children zigzagged around Carlos he looked for the prison porter's door. Approaching it was a small gang of shackled prisoners being herded back inside by a turnkey; probably they had been farmed out for their labor for the day by the jailer.

He glanced southward. Less than a quarter mile that way lay Ludgate jail, also built over a gateway arch in London wall, but Carlos knew Thornleigh would not be in there. He had learned from a talkative prisoner at the Marshalsea—

where the inmate population had been mostly debtors, and its compound had looked not too difficult to escape from—that Ludgate jail was reserved for wealthy London citizens accused of larceny, fraud, and the like: gentlemen's crimes. But Newgate was for the harder cases: the murderers, rapists, and violent thieves from all of Middlesex County.

If the Marshalsea had appeared slack on security, Newgate, with its grim barred windows and battlemented roof, looked impossible to escape from. Carlos thought of Isabel, of her naive dream to get her father out. And then he wished he hadn't thought of her. He saw the sun hanging low, just above the roof, and he knew he had no more time. The guards were hunting for him here in London, and there were search parties after him to the north, and he had no means of getting away. No money, no time, and no choice. He had to do this thing, get paid, and get out. He clenched his jaw and shoved aside the last of the children.

He strode toward the door of the porter's lodge. He was reaching for the latch when the door opened. Carlos's jaw dropped. A stack of corpses was moving toward him. He suddenly realized what it was: a cart loaded with the prison dead.

"Mind where you tread!" a sweating man pushing the cart growled.

Carlos lurched back. The cart joggled out, its cargo of dangling arms and legs jerking as if in some death throe. Another man followed pushing out another cart, then a third came after. Carlos took several broad steps away to distance himself. The black-speckled corpses, he had seen, were diseased. He felt nausea worming inside his gut.

The carts with the bodies crunched out into the street where people skittered out of their path. Carlos watched the corpse carts as they were swallowed by the crowd.

The porter's door was still open. Carlos took a deep breath and strode back toward it. A white-haired man inside was shuffling across the room, sorting through a huge ring of keys—the porter about to lock up, Carlos decided. Determination welled inside him. This was his last chance. He *would not* be locked out. His foot stomped down on the threshold. The porter looked up—old, rheumy-eyed, and weak. The two of them were alone in the room.

Carlos only had to get inside.

CHAPTER TWENTY-ONE

><><><>•<><><

Nightmares

"**L**ord, it's the Spaniard's night, to be sure!" the Anchor's chambermaid gaily crowed across the table of cardplayers. "Pay up, you lot!" She cocked a greedy eye at the losers as though she herself had earned the victory.

The card game, with varying participants, had been going on for most of the evening since Carlos's return from Newgate. The common room was packed with royalist soldiers noisily eating and drinking around the blazing hearth. The landlord's children scurried about serving food fetched from their mother in the kitchen and ale fetched from their father in the cellar. The communal tables were sticky with spilled beer and gluts that had dripped from the sheep-fat candles. The soldiers had left a litter of half-empty tankards, ragged hunks of bread, and wooden trenchers that were scraped clean except for streaks of gravy.

The disgruntled losers at the card table reluctantly began to shove coins across to Carlos, to the loud delight of the maid. She was standing at Carlos's back. After every round that he had won during the last hour her hands had squeezed his shoulders a little more tightly, and her breasts had nudged the back of his head a trifle more insistently. He found the pillow pleasant enough, though her squeals of delight were beginning to grate.

Still, nothing could dull his vast feeling of well-being. He grabbed his tankard and downed his ale, then crossed his arms and watched with satisfaction as the coins began to pile up before him. Everything was coming to him now. And more would come soon. Money, freedom, land—everything he needed. Yet it had happened so suddenly, and so unaccountably. He still could hardly believe how, in one stroke, his crisis had been ... not solved, exactly, but ... transformed.

A gold coin winked up at him, reflecting firelight. He had

to smile. For a moment, back at Newgate, he had thought he was lost.

"Locking up time," the old porter had grunted irritably. "Out with you."

Carlos had stood still, feeling strangely impotent. The old man had whisked him out of the lodge like a housewife shooing a child from her clean floor. Carlos had backed out, stumbling, and the porter had shut the door in his face and bolted it.

He had been trudging down Thames Street besieged by thoughts of his failure, when, approaching the Anchor, he saw a flurry of activity in front of the inn's gate. Horses, soldiers, baggage mules, all jostling to enter the inn's small courtyard—even a fletcher's cart stacked with bundles of arrows.

Taking no chances, Carlos tugged up the hood of his sheepskin coat to partially hide his face and pushed through the crowd.

"Valverde!"

Carlos whipped around to the voice.

"Good Lord, it really *is* you!" The speaker was a lean-faced man of about forty with bright, amused eyes. "Don't you remember me? Norwich, back in '49? That unrest the Duke sent us to settle?"

Carlos remembered him. A lieutenant in those days when they had both been working for the Duke of Northumberland. Not particularly capable, but well liked by his men. Gentry-bred but not a first son, so he'd been forced to seek his fortune as a soldier. "Andrews?"

"That's right." Andrews grinned. "Good Lord, Valverde, what the devil are you still doing in England?"

They sat down over tankards of ale as the soldiers continued to tromp through the Anchor and up and down the stairs, settling in. Andrews explained. They were a troop of the Earl of Arundel's men—his yeomen tenants and retainers—just mustered for the Queen and billeted at the Anchor for the time being. Equipped at the Earl's expense, most of them were archers, but many had brought swords and pikes as well as their longbows.

"So the Queen is fighting," Carlos said quietly, watching the activity. He had been aware of Wyatt's revolt, naturally. But in the maelstrom of his efforts to stay alive the insurrec-

tion had held little interest for him. Now, its significance
was dawning. And a bold idea took hold of him.

"She is," Andrews replied. "It took Her Majesty a few
days to rally. After all, it's rather shocking news for a monarch, isn't it?—rebellion just before her wedding. But we'll
trounce these upstarts. No fear of that."

"Who is your captain?"

"Ross. A Lancashire man. Over there." Andrews nodded
toward a squat but burly man parsimoniously doling out
coins to the landlady for the billet. His scuffed leather brigandine was so worn that the iron plates sewn onto its canvas
lining made impressions right through on the leather surface.
His face was red and badly pocked above a thick ginger
beard. Carlos did not know him. Andrews leaned toward
Carlos and lowered his voice conspiratorially. "Bit of an oaf,
Ross is, but a bulldog on the field. He'll do."

Carlos looked around at the familiar signs of martial encampment. The soldiers' longbows and pikes, plus their litter of bedrolls and light armor, were being strewn around the
common room as the company settled down. The inn's
smells of stale ale and musty floor rushes were already overpowered by those of horses and leather, and the bite of metallic smells—swords and harness and armor. The idea that
had sprung up in Carlos's mind began to glow like a polished breastplate in the sun. He felt liberation beckoning—
the liberation of action. No more of this skulking around, of
hiding and sneaking and lying. No more waiting to kill or be
captured. The new idea warmed him like a delivery from the
gallows, like a pardon.

He tested the notion on Andrews. Andrews thought it a
fine idea. Carlos had relaxed for the first time in weeks, and
the evening at the Anchor had stretched out, warmed with
flowing ale, easygoing gambling, and comradeship.

Now, Andrews counted out the coins he owed Carlos at
the card table and grumbled good-naturedly to the maid,
"Aye, lass, it's the Spaniard's night, to be sure."

Carlos began to rake in his winnings and laughed. It felt
good to laugh again, too. The chambermaid whipped out a
kerchief for him to dump the money into.

Andrews glanced at his superior. "Well, Captain?" he
said.

Captain Ross, who had lost heavily in the game, sat
hunched over his own meager pile of coins and stared sul-

lenly at Carlos. He said nothing and made no move to hand over the money he owed.

Andrews laughed lightly. "Here you go, Valverde," he said, shoving the last of his own debt across the table. "Once we've put this trouble down, so the Prince of the Spaniards can have *his* night—with the Queen, that is—I'll try you for some of that back."

"Anytime," Carlos said, scooping the coins into the maid's kerchief. She rushed around and settled on his knee to finish the task of collecting. He let her.

"Another game?" Andrews suggested, drawing out another small purse from his doublet.

Carlos smiled. "Why not."

"Captain?" Andrews asked. "Are you in?"

Captain Ross's eyes, fixed on Carlos, flickered to the chambermaid who was helpfully testing one of Carlos's newly won coins between her teeth. Carlos caught the glimmer of longing in Ross's eyes. He had noticed Ross stealing looks at the girl all evening, his pocked face growing darker whenever she smiled at Carlos or touched him. He had also noticed the fine Damascene blade of Ross's sword, and the way his hand fidgeted on its hilt every time the girl snuggled closer. That combination of honed weapon and honed resentment, Carlos knew, could lead to something he would just as soon avoid. Besides, for his plan to work, he needed the captain's friendship.

"Different stakes, Captain?" he asked suddenly. "You wager a crown, I will wager the girl."

The captain blinked, startled.

The chambermaid's mouth fell open. She stared at Carlos. "What's that?" she cried. She jumped up off his lap, her face flushed with fury. "Bastard!" Her hand flew out and smacked his cheek.

There was a moment of silence at the table.

Carlos bounded up from his chair. His hand grappled the girl's throat. She staggered back a step, choking.

Ross leapt up and his sword scraped from its scabbard. "Let her go!" he boomed.

Carlos's head snapped around. He blinked at the captain's bright blade and allowed worry to crease his face. All the soldiers in the room were watching now. Ross glowered malevolently at Carlos, his sword raised, his lip curled back, breaths snorting from his nose.

Carlos let go of the girl's neck. For a moment his hand hovered over his own sword hilt. Then, suddenly, he dropped to his knees before the captain and threw his arms wide in a gesture of total surrender to the captain's superior prowess.

The maid rushed over to Ross, clutching her reddened throat, gasping in relief. She threw her arms around Ross's neck, looking at Carlos with furious contempt. "Who do you think you are, Master High-and-Mighty Spaniard, offering to trade me like some filly at the fair! I'll be friends with who I want, so I will!" She glared around the room at the men who had sat and watched her almost be murdered, then turned back and gazed at Ross, her rescuer. She hooked her arm in his and nestled close. "And I can see you're the nearest thing to a gentleman among this sorry lot, Captain."

Ross reddened with pleasure. He looked down at Carlos. Carlos returned the look with a small smile.

Ross frowned at him as if uncertain of what he had just seen. But Carlos noted the grudging gleam of thanks steal into Ross's eyes: Ross understood what Carlos had done. "Get up, Spaniard," he said gruffly. "Let's play. Same stakes as before, three shillings." They sat, and the maid stood close behind Ross, still sniffing in wounded indignation.

Music fluted through the air. A young soldier at one of the eating tables had begun tweedling a tune on his wooden pipe. Another man jumped up and began dancing an energetic jig. Others slapped the table in time. They laughed as the children's terrier yapped at the dancer's heels, making him cavort in increasingly wild antics.

"Valverde!" Andrews called above the noise. "Show us that Cossack caper! The way you did in Norwich!" He looked around at his mates. "A Tartar taught him this, watch! Go on, Valverde! Get up!"

Amid the calls of Andrews and the others, Carlos stood to oblige. He quaffed down the last of his ale with exaggerated gusto, as if needing it for fortitude—which brought a wave of laughter—then stepped out into the center of the room. The piper improvised an exotic, almost oriental tune reminiscent of snow-swept steppes. The soldiers gathered around Carlos. The landlord's children peeped between the men's legs to watch. Carlos held his arms straight out at his sides. He began with slow, controlled steps on the spot, alternately crouching and standing, and then, when in the crouch, his feet shot out in the straight-legged kicks of the Cossacks. The soldiers whooped in approval. Gradually the piper stepped up the pace. Carlos's steps matched it, his arms now folded over his chest. Soon, the music was as furious as galloping Mongols, and Carlos, locked now in a crouch and grinning, was kicking frenetically in time. The soldiers in the circle whistled and stomped and clapped. The ones still sitting banged their tankards on the tables in time with the wild rhythm. The children gaped and giggled.

The front door swung open. Isabel stepped in. Cold wind whistled into the room. The soldiers turned to her. Carlos stopped dancing.

"Iss-bel!" the landlord's little girl cried, running to her. Isabel stared in astonishment at the crowd of soldiers. "Issbel, there's dancing!" the child squealed. She pulled Isabel forward into the circle and pushed her in front of Carlos. Many of the soldiers had kept on clapping despite the interruption, and when the piper saw the lady he maneuvered his tune into a genteel but lively galliard. The clapping picked up the new tempo, and the soldiers loudly egged on the couple to dance.

Carlos and Isabel stood awkwardly face-to-face. He did not know how to dance with a lady. And she, he saw, looked almost too exhausted to stand.

Inside the watching circle she fixed him with an intense, private question in her eyes: *Did you find him?* Carlos shook his head: *No.* Her shoulders slumped. She turned away.

The clapping dwindled. The laughter and chatter quieted. The circle drifted apart. The soldiers went back to their tables, to eating and playing dice and calling the children to fetch more ale. Andrews, at the card table, pulled out a silver toothpick to clean his teeth. Captain Ross picked up his tankard and followed the maid to a far corner where the two of them stood talking quietly. The other pair of losing cardplayers had gone to another table where there was food.

Isabel sat on a stool by the fire that a soldier had vacated for her and unfastened her snow-speckled cloak. The little, buck-toothed girl stuck by her side. She always did, Carlos had noted; followed Isabel like a puppy. He sat again at the card table, not far from Isabel, and watched her. Where had she been all day? What had she been doing?

"Lizzy, who are all these men?" Isabel quietly asked the child.

"Sojers. They're going to live with us, Mama says. They're upstairs, too. Even in the stable!"

Isabel looked around and murmured, "The Queen's soldiers."

"Mama has made a *big* pot of stew," the child said, throwing out her hands to indicate a cauldron twice her size. "Do you want some?"

Isabel smiled and nodded.

"*I'll* get it for you! Mama told me I must help serve tonight, too." She added proudly, "Mama needs me."

"I'm sure she does."

Smiling, the child skipped off to the kitchen.

Isabel shivered and rubbed her hands before the fire, eyeing the soldiers anxiously. She met Carlos's gaze. He looked down to scoop up the kerchief, bulging with coins, that he had left on the table.

"I see your day has been a profitable one," she said to him, and added with more weariness than rancor, "if not in the way I had hoped."

Carlos said nothing. He tucked his winnings into his jerkin.

The child skipped back with a trencher of thick, steaming stew. Isabel accepted it with thanks. She dug her spoon into the bowl, then glanced at Carlos. "I hope," she said with a slight smile of scorn, "you will not be tempted to leave my employ now that such great wealth is yours." She ate the spoonful of stew.

"He can't do that, mistress," Andrews said amiably across the table, turning in his chair to stretch out his legs. He politely introduced himself to her, then explained, "A mercenary doesn't change sides in the middle of a campaign."

"Really, sir?" she said. "I did not know that." She looked at Carlos as if for corroboration of the statement. "What's to stop them?" she asked.

"Would not be hired again," Carlos confirmed.

"I see," Isabel said between bites. "Still," she went on to the lieutenant, "his working for me can hardly be called a campaign."

"Technically, it is. He is pledged to his employer until his commission is fulfilled."

She frowned. "I see he has told you all about me, sir."

"Not at all, dear lady," Andrews said gallantly. "But since

he is interested in joining our company, and since the job with you apparently will not last—"

"Joining you?" she said in astonishment.

"Aye, to smash these poxy rebels."

Isabel's face flared, then hardened. She said no more. She ate her food in stony silence. Carlos grabbed a fresh tankard of ale from the landlord's boy going past. There was a burst of private laughter from the farthest table.

"Well," the lieutenant said expansively, stretching as he rose, "I'm done in." He bowed to Isabel. "A pleasure, mistress. Let me know if any of my men here disturb you. Night, Valverde." He glanced at Captain Ross, still talking in the corner with the chambermaid. Andrews smiled and went upstairs.

Tight-lipped, Isabel put down her trencher and came over to Carlos at the table where he now sat alone. The drone of the soldiers went on around them. She glared down at Carlos. "Is it true?" she asked in an angry whisper. "Are you joining the Queen's forces?"

"When my job with you is done, yes."

"That's disgusting," she said with a vehemence that surprised him.

"That is my work," he said evenly.

"Your work today was to find my father! But you didn't!"

"I looked," he said roughly, though keeping his voice low. "The Marshalsea prison and King's Bench. It took all day. He was not in either of them. When I got to Newgate prison they were locking up for the night. They turned me away. But I will go back in the morning. Your father must be there. I will finish this." He had thought it out. In the morning he would convince her that it was too dangerous for her to accompany him into Newgate, the dumping place for the most violent criminals. He would go alone, then come back and tell her that her father had died inside. It wouldn't be much of a lie; Thornleigh was bound to be hanged, and despite her fantasies there was no way anybody could get him out of Newgate. She would have to give up. She would have to leave England and join her brother in Antwerp, just as her father had told her to do. That was best.

And it left Carlos some options. The rendezvous at the Blue Boar was still four days away. Tomorrow, if he did find Thornleigh, he could kill him or even bide his time and go back later and do it. He could collect that money and still join the royalists in the hope of more. His prospects were looking better all the time.

Or he could simply forget about Thornleigh. The point was, now he had a choice.

"*We* will go in the morning," she corrected him emphatically. She added coldly, "There'll be less chance of a card game luring you away if I'm along."

He shrugged. He would deal with her in the morning. But she did not leave his side. She fixed him with burning eyes. "Why will you join the tyrant's side?"

"What?"

"Why not help the liberators?"

"Because they will lose." He drank his ale.

She stared at him openmouthed. "How can you know that?"

"They have no experience as an army. No stronghold in the country. No war chest to hire outside troops. No backup from other powers." He thought he caught in her eye a glimmer of defiance at this last statement.

"Those things can be overcome if they have the will," she insisted. "All of England will join them if they have the will. And they *have,* because they are in the right! They are protecting England from the onslaught of Spain, from the terrors of the Inquisition. My God, you must have seen how they torture and burn people there!"

"I have not been in Spain since I was a boy."

"Well, it's barbaric. And the rebels here have risen up to prevent such appalling injustices from coming here. How can you fight for injustice?"

Carlos almost smiled. She was so green. "Injustice does not end, whoever wins. Soldiers on both sides will pay with their blood, and people like you will live to see that nothing changes."

She lifted her head high. "Thank you for the military lesson, sir. Obviously, you may fight for whomever you wish. I cannot stop you. Now, if you will excuse me, it has been a tiring day and I am going to bed. I ask only that before you rush off to help the Queen, you remember your duty in the morning. As the lieutenant pointed out, you are pledged to me." She turned to go.

He grabbed her wrist. "Isabel," he said.

She blinked down at him in surprise. He had never called her by her name. The intimacy it engendered caught them both off guard. Carlos hesitated. What could he say? That it was easy for her to talk of choosing sides because her class always stayed on top, whoever won, but if he chose wrong he died?

He kept hold of her, not willing to let her go before he made her understand. But how was he to put it? That he had nothing, and that was how most mercenaries died—with nothing, died before they were forty, on some muddy battlefield, forgotten? He began haltingly. "This is my chance. I have seen revolts like this before. They are broken fast. The rebels are hanged and the ruler is very thankful to all who have helped win the victory. I could get ... *un indulto*"—he frowned, searching for the word—"a pardon. Do you see? Even more. I could get a reward. Land. The Queen will be giving out the lands of dead traitors. I could ..." He did not finish. There was no way to explain that this was his chance to *be* something. To be the equal of her class. The equal, even, of the man she planned to marry.

And certainly there was no way to tell her of the relief creeping into his heart the longer he held her. For how could he possibly explain that now, with this way out, he did not *have* to kill her father?

So he said again inadequately, almost beseechingly, "Isabel."

But she had gone very pale. "Dead traitors' lands?" she whispered. She jerked back her hand and took a step away from him. Without another word she turned and fled upstairs.

Thornleigh's head slumped back against the alcove wall, jolting him awake. The ward was plunged in desolate sleep, but for hours Thornleigh had been weaving in and out of consciousness, alternating between sweating with fever and shivering with chills. He licked his swollen lips and tasted salt and longed for water. He knew none would be brought until the morning.

He blinked in the gloom, trying to see. His eyes burned so much that it was hard, almost painful, to focus. Were the children still there? He rubbed his eyes roughly. *Focus!* he commanded himself. *Concentrate!* Yes, they were still there, hunkered in their half ring like so many shadowy goblins. The oldest one, the hollow-eyed girl who was their leader, sat on her haunches idly picking at a scab on her cheek, watching him. Watching and waiting. Thornleigh felt like a cornered rat, but at least with his back braced against the wall he could see all of them. They could not sneak up on his rear. He shook his head hard. *Must not fall asleep!*

But the shivering claimed him again. It took him like a kind of paroxysm, shaking him, and when it was over he slumped against the wall again, exhausted. Then, through the slits of his swollen eyes, he saw one of the shadowy little figures creep closer. And another. Christ, they were moving in on him!

He sat bolt upright with a loud threatening growl. The children stilled. Thornleigh slumped again, panting. He had stopped them with this brief show of defiance but he knew it was just a standoff. He needed to stay vigilant, needed to concentrate. He looked around for something, anything, to focus his mind, to keep his head above the tide of delirium.

He noticed a fist-sized chunk of firewood. It was wedged next to the wall, between him and the child at the edge of the semicircle. He went forward on all fours and snatched it up, then retreated to the alcove and sat again, dizzy from the burst of exertion. With shaky hands he felt inside his boot and drew out his knife. He began to whittle the wood.

It was hard work. His hands were unsteady, his palms were slippery with sweat, and his focus wavered as the fever enervated him. But every glance up at the hollowed-eye girl, implacably waiting, reinforced his perseverance. *He must not fall asleep!*

He was stalking through the room, the barrel of his pistol glinting. He lifted it and pointed it at her mother's open mouth and laughed. There was a detonation . . . he exploded into smoke and blood . . . waves of blood . . . smoke and sulfur choked Isabel's throat . . . she could not breathe . . .

Isabel bolted up in her bed, screaming.

Choking, she tore off the blanket and threw her legs over the side of the bed and lunged toward her mother to catch her from falling . . . but her mother was so far away! And Isabel was slipping on the blood . . . falling, herself. On all fours she crawled across the floor toward her mother . . . *too slow!* . . . slipping in the gore . . . *if she could only reach her mother!*

Someone grabbed her. Someone was stopping her . . . holding her back. She yanked her arms free and beat him with her fists. "Let go, Adam!" she cried. "I've got to catch her! Let me go!"

But Adam did not let go. He clamped her wrists to stop her blows, and forced her arms down. And though she squirmed and tried with all her might to fight him, he pinned her arms tightly to her sides. The pain of the struggle punctured the nightmare, fracturing the images ... pistol, smoke, blood, her mother's mouth, her mother falling! ... Everything suddenly splintered and re-formed into a pattern of shards that made no sense ... Adam slipping in blood and falling to his knees before her ... her father grabbing her wrists to keep her from the mob while the Spanish lords fell from their horses ... the Spaniard lowering himself on top of her in the prison ... protecting her with his body ... blood from his shoulder dripping onto her ...

"It is me!" he said ... and she realized he had been saying it over and over ... "It is me—Carlos!" He said it insistently, as if trying to wake her.

The splintered nightmare vanished.

She was on her knees in the middle of the room. He was on his knees before her, his hands clamped on her wrists. They knelt face-to-face in the shadows. A shaft of moonlight silvered the room. "You screamed," he said.

The pain of his grip brought stinging tears to her eyes. He saw that he was hurting her and let go. "Better?" he asked more quietly.

Better? How could it be! She had not reached her mother in time! Had not stopped her mother from falling! Had not been able to ... *would never be able to* ...

She felt dizzy, as if she were falling herself. She clutched fistfuls of his shirt and held on tightly. Then something in her gave way. She fell against him. And the tears that had sprung in pain now flowed in grief. She would *never* be able to catch her mother ... her mother would fall in her dreams forever, beyond her reach ... forever just beyond her outstretched arms ...

In desolation she threw her arms around his neck and wept. It had been five days since the pistol shot, the sulfurous smoke, the blood, the chaos ... and finally she wept.

He said nothing. He held her with her face against his neck, and she wept.

And then her tears were spent. But she did not leave his embrace. She could find no will to do so. His arms held her so firmly, even though her body shuddered with breaths that came in gulps. The heat of his body and arms enveloped her. It was like a haven.

It was more. It was a surging, living heat, and the pressure of his arms was a pulsing strength. She was aware of the hardness of his body ... of the leather scent that permeated his shirt ... of the smell of his skin. Aware of her lips, wet with tears, against his warm neck. She was wearing only a thin chemise, and the sensation of being nearly naked in his embrace made her almost dizzy again. She felt buffeted by the quickened pulse thrumming through her veins. She drew back a fraction from him, and her tightened nipples grazed his chest. A jolt of heat flashed from her nipples down to her belly and through her legs.

Dazzled by the sensation, she pulled back shakily. His hold slackened but his arms did not release her. He was looking straight into her eyes but his breathing was ragged; it was as if he were forcing his eyes to remain on hers, though his mind ranged all over her body.

The wetness of one of her tears glistened on his chin. It looked so odd—a tear on that rough skin—and she started to wipe it away. He sucked a sharp breath through his mouth in surprise. Her hand strayed toward his open mouth ... her fingertips brushed his lips.

He snatched her hand to stop her. "I am only human!" he said, his voice a rough plea.

Hot blood swept her face. What was she doing! Ashamed, she jerked away from him. She half turned, still on her knees. But the overwhelming power of his presence snared her, as if his arms still held her fast. She could not imagine breaking away from him ... could only imagine sinking back, yielding to his strength ...

Suddenly he was close behind her. He did not touch her, but she felt the heat of his body over every inch of her back. She heard his breathing, harsh with want. But he was utterly still, as though he were waiting to gauge her response. She made no move to reject him. A faint voice in her head whispered that she *must,* but the roar of her blood deafened her to it.

And then his hands were on her. Grabbing her shoulders. Sliding up her neck, his fingers raking her hair. Plunging down to her hips, around to her belly, rumpling the chemise, ranging up over her breasts. Her nipples were hard against his palms. His mouth was hot on the back of her neck. He pressed her against his body and she felt the swell of his erection rock-hard against her buttock. Her head lolled on his shoulder.

He groaned and pulled her backward. She sank, unresisting. She was on the floor on her back and he was over her. They lay in darkness below the shaft of moonlight, and now there was nothing but the sound of his breathing and the feel of him and the yearning of her body. He rested his weight on one arm bent by her head. His mouth covered hers. His hand urgently roamed over her breasts and belly as if he could not get enough of her. Her mouth opened under his. He shoved her chemise up above her breasts, baring her. She clutched his shoulders, the muscles hard. His hand slid between her legs, parting them—so easily—moving to the place of her heat, slick with her desire. At the insistent motions of his fingers she gasped, for it seemed that if he continued, something inside her would explode, but she arched to meet his hand for it seemed that if she stopped, she would die.

He groaned and groped to unfasten the ties of his codpiece.

A fist banged the door. "Mistress Thornleigh?" It was the landlady's anxious voice. "All right in there? I thought I heard you cry out a few moments ago."

Isabel could not catch her breath. His tongue was on her neck, her breast ...

"Mistress? Shall I come in?"

"No! No, I'm ... fine. Just a ... bad dream. It's nothing!"

"Oh. A dream. Well, I won't bother you then." The landlady padded away. "Good night."

His weight was coming down on her, the furnace of his body pressing ...

"No!" This she whispered fiercely to him. He froze. But she felt his heart throughout his body pounding with his need. She tried to push him off. It was like pushing at a boulder.

He lifted his head. The dull glint in his eyes spoke of how far want had overpowered thought. All his strength was channeled into claiming her, and she knew she was asking almost the impossible in asking him to stop. But the landlady's interruption had brought the real world crashing in on her. Martin. Her betrothal vows to Martin. Her promises.

Promises are all we have . . . She *must* not allow this to happen!

"Please, oh, please let me go," she whispered.

He rolled onto his back with a thud, breathing hard. He stared at the ceiling. She quickly covered herself. He lurched up stiffly, sitting, and retied his codpiece. He said nothing, only cast her a glance as he got to his feet. But the glance was eloquent with anger, desire, and bewilderment.

He left her room.

Thornleigh knew he was hallucinating. Ahead of him a small shape was quivering like a ship becalmed on a summer horizon, a ship that was blurred in front of the blazing sun and shimmering in a far-off haze of heat.

Thornleigh swallowed, parched with thirst. The whittling knife slipped in his sweaty palm and he almost dropped it. His whole body was soaked in sweat. He stared at the small, shimmering shape ahead and fought to bring reason to surface through the miasma of his fever. It was no ship, he told himself, it was the boy. Some time ago—was it hours or days?—his attention had been caught by the shadowy mound of this child hunkered nearest the girl leader, because this one—a boy no more than five, the smallest in the death watch—had begun to shiver uncontrollably. *Fevered, just like me,* Thornleigh had realized. An odd affinity with the child had grown in him as he continued to whittle. And the little boy and he had gone on shivering together, both afflicted—the hunter and the prey.

Thornleigh forced himself to look away from the hallucination, forced himself back to the whittling. The boat carving was almost finished. But he felt his strength ebbing.

He knew he was going to die. So wrong, he thought, to die now when he longed to act . . . for Honor's sake . . . longed to meet death on *his* terms, fighting. Longed . . .

A wave of fever swamped him. His knife clattered to the floor. He had not been concentrating. The sound startled him, rattled him. He hunched over on his knees and groped in the dank straw, trying to find the knife. The blade sliced the skin between his fingers and he pitched forward onto his elbow at the pain, but his other hand still held up the carved boat as if to keep it safe. He had not strength enough to hold his weight on one arm, and he thudded down onto the floor.

Lying on his side, he gaped at the children. He saw the girl, the leader, lift her hand. Thornleigh knew it was a signal.

The children started to creep in. Thornleigh tried to stagger up, but the fever was making the room blur and his muscles quiver beyond his control. One thought surfaced: *This is the end.* He could only watch as the hazy images of the children advanced. But the small boy was not moving with them. He was too weak, Thornleigh thought. It was the end for him, too. And then ... Thornleigh did not know what made him do it ... a perversion of the fever? Pity? The need to make some final, desperate act of will? Whatever it was, as the other children crept closer he rolled onto his stomach, lifted the carving up high, stretched out his hand, and offered the boat to the boy.

But even as he looked at the boy the air around that small, still shape seemed to quiver with heat again—a blurred ship on the horizon, lit by a glow from behind like some fiery equatorial sunset. Then, with a sudden bursting clarity of mind, Thornleigh saw that the fire haloing the child was no sun-hazed horizon. It was guttering torchlight across the ward.

The cellarman had brought down the corpse cart to collect the night's dead.

CHAPTER TWENTY-TWO

> ►═◄═◊═►═◄

Robin's Boat

It was not yet dawn and the wind was biting cold when Palmer, Edward Sydenham's steward, trudged over the ice-crusted cobbles toward London wall and stopped before Newgate. The city gate was closed, and above the gateway arch the prison rose up black against the gloomy sky. Beside Palmer was Giles Sturridge of the Grenville Archers.

"Well," Palmer asked in a gruff whisper as he hugged himself against the cold, "where's the best spot?"

"For range?"

"For accuracy, man. I need hardly point out that Sir Edward will no longer require the services of either of us should this mission fail."

The young man took no offense at the warning. Though Sturridge had found Sir Edward's order irregular—some would call it murder—Sydenham was now one of the Queen's lieutenants, and an order from him was an order Sturridge could not disobey. At seventeen, Sturridge's life in a squalid country hamlet had been changed forever when he had won a coveted place in the elite corps of the Grenville Archers; four years after joining he was their captain. He saw the world and his place in it plainly: he took pride in his skill with the longbow, and he left it to the lords and gentlemen to decide where that skill could best be used.

"So?" Palmer urged, glancing about at the houses and shops muffled under a layer of new snow. "Can you accomplish it from here?"

Sturridge studied the dark, quiet street that led out from the prison and into the city. On the far side, a link-boy was lighting the way home for an inebriated gentleman, and the shadows cast by the boy's lantern loomed up on the walls of the shuttered shops. Sturridge's eye roamed over the flat second-story roof above a haberdasher's shop and stopped at a spot nestled between the tops of two dormer windows. He glanced back and forth between that point and the porter's door in the arch of the gate—where the target would emerge from the prison—as if he were gauging the range. But he was only taking time to assure himself that the rooftop position would afford him safe cover come morning when the street would be busy; he would do his duty, he told himself, but that did not mean he must act like a fool. So he already knew, even when the link-boy's light had passed and the haberdasher's shopfront lay again in darkness, that once dawn streaked the sky, the spot between the dormers would ensure his arrow deadly accuracy.

He and Palmer set about finding a way to reach the roof.

Isabel was afraid she might retch at the smell. "But he *has* to be here! You said so yourself!" Though on the edge of desperation she could not bring herself to look up into Carlos's face. Not after last night.

"Here, yes," he said. "But probably dead."

The brutality of his statement made her glance up despite herself. It was a mistake. All her shame at what had happened between them last night flooded back. They stood so close, forced together by the crush of the public noisily milling through Newgate's Common Felons Ward. Worse, his face was grim with the certainty of what he had just said. Even before they had left the inn he had tried to get her to stay behind while he searched Newgate alone, and even after she had refused and they had prowled together through the upper stories here, he had still tried to get her to leave. Now she understood why. He did not expect to find her father alive.

She quickly looked away.

A portly man pushed past them, banging Carlos's still-tender shoulder. Carlos gritted his teeth and muttered a curse. Isabel rubbed her temple. Her head was throbbing. She had found Newgate—overcrowded, vicious, verminous—a more dreadful place than she could have imagined. And the smell was something even fouler than the usual reek of confinement in the other prisons. And she had so little time left . . .

The crowd parted with an ominous hush. A trio of carts piled with bodies rattled through. Isabel saw that the corpses' white faces were speckled with black. Carlos jerked her by the elbow out of the way. But the smell still hit her like a blow: the stench of decomposition. Her hand flew to her mouth as a wave of nausea threatened.

"Jail fever," Carlos said. She caught the trace of fear in his voice. His face was pale.

The carts clattered out. The crowd surged back to life. Isabel took a deep breath to steady herself. She stared at the grilled door ahead, being closed by a turnkey. The carts had come from there. The door led down to the Beggars Ward. It was all that was left.

She had not consulted Newgate's keeper; she would never again trust a jailer, so she had no proof that her father had been admitted here. But they had searched all through the comfortable Masters level and now through the noisome Commons wards, both for felons and debtors, and they had found no trace of him. They had even glimpsed the terrible Press Room where felons who refused to plead were crushed under massive stone weights to extract a plea, without which, under law, the Crown could not seize their property. The only place they had not searched was the Beggars Ward.

"We've got to go down there," she said.

Carlos shook his head vehemently. "He had money. If he was not with the gentlemen, not even in the Commons, he is not anywhere here. We have made a mistake."

"A mistake?" She frowned, trying to concentrate. Above the disorderly din of voices the sweet music of a lute—incongruous and distracting—drifted down from the Masters ward above.

"We should try Ludgate jail," Carlos insisted.

Isabel knew he was catching at straws. "You know Ludgate's only for citizens of London," she said. "It doesn't take prisoners from outside."

"But the turnkey said it is so full here, they have sent some prisoners to other jails."

"Only debtors."

"The jailers can make mistakes. We should try Ludgate."

"No." She started to move to the grilled door.

"Do not," he said. "The fever. It is too dangerous. We must go."

"Carlos, he is down there. You know it."

He looked at her like a man trying to unravel a puzzle. Under his scrutiny, Isabel felt warm blood stain her cheeks. But she held her head high. She told herself that what had passed between them last night was only another aberration of this deranged time they were living through. If she could just fulfill her promises—if she could save her father and help the rebellion and be reunited with Martin—then order would be restored, to the world and to her heart.

She turned toward the door to the Beggars Ward. Carlos groaned and followed.

Sitting on the roof beside Sturridge, Palmer frowned up at the pale sun. It stood high in the sky. "Something's gone wrong," he said.

The archer eased his stiff back against the dormer window and flexed his nearly numb fingers gripping his bow. Both men were wet and cold after hours of waiting on the snowy roof. "Maybe the transfer's been canceled," Sturridge said.

"Something," Palmer growled. "Christ, the master'll have my balls for breakfast." He was getting to his feet. Once up, he crouched to keep a low profile above the people milling in the street. He lowered his head to speak quietly to the archer. "I'm going into Newgate and find out from that poxy jailer what's gone wrong. Stay here. There's still a chance Thornleigh will be brought out. If so, you know your orders."

Sturridge nodded. He watched Palmer pick his way across the roof, his feet sliding on the slippery tiles, then disappear down the ladder.

Underground, Isabel paid the cellarman for admittance. Another demanded money for a candle. She hesitated at this purchase, for her cash had been horribly depleted by the expenses of London. But the candle was necessary, so she bought it. She made no inquiries of either cellarman, having learned to deal as little as possible with these quasi-official prisoners who policed their fellow inmates. Upstairs, she had seen one of them beating a debtor who had snatched a cup of water before paying for it.

Shielding the candle flame with her hand, she entered the ward with Carlos.

There were no visitors down here. There was only filth and misery. The air was so putrid—even worse than above—Isabel could hardly take a breath without gagging, and even with her cloak she had to hug herself against the dank cold. Despite the gloom, she could see that the ward was full. Some prisoners shuffled about, their talk a low drone. Some huddled in corners, one group tending a puny fire, another gambling with stones and crusts of bread. But most lay on the floor, quiet and inert. It became clear to Isabel, with a slow swell of dread as she passed among them, that some were corpses.

Eyes furtively watched from the shadows as she and Carlos moved through the ward. Clumped black straw stuck to Isabel's foot. She kicked it off and moved ahead of Carlos, passing around a stone pillar to reach a prisoner who looked approachable to question. A man sidled into her path, watching her. She stopped. Out of the corner of her eye she saw another man circle behind her. They began to move in on her. Then Carlos appeared around the pillar and moved toward her and the men slunk away.

Isabel questioned prisoner after prisoner. No one knew Richard Thornleigh. No one cared. Some had no strength even to answer.

Shivering, she searched on. A rat scurried by. Isabel heard Carlos kick at it, miss it, and mutter a curse in Spanish. They passed under a crumbling arch and entered the most dismal section of the ward. Here, farthest from the doors where the daily ration of bread and water was doled out, lay the sickest. Isabel and Carlos picked their way over a score of men and a few women, all sprawled on the floor at the mercy of the fever and of the rats. Their gaunt faces and wasted limbs were speckled black. A man touched Carlos's ankle with a palsied hand and whispered an unintelligible plea. Carlos whipped out his sword. The man jerked back his hand, but Carlos still held the blade threateningly above him as if over a viper, his breathing harsh and shallow.

Isabel was surprised by Carlos's extreme reaction; taking a step away from these weak wretches was all that was necessary. But she saw the revulsion on his face. He loathed disease, she realized. He feared it, even. It seemed extraordinary: here was a man who faced danger as a way of life, yet was frightened by sickness.

He grabbed her elbow. "This is useless," he hissed. "We must get out of here!" Sweat glinted on his forehead even in the cold.

Useless? Was it? She was afraid to answer her own question. She had a foreboding that if she did not find her father here she would never find him at all. Never free him. Never catch him from falling. Just like her mother. *Never* . . .

The notion was not bearable. She pushed on.

"Enough!" Carlos said.

The finality in his voice made her turn. "Pardon?"

"This is madness. I am going."

"Then go."

He did not move. "And you?"

"Not until I find him."

"*Mujer loca!* You cannot stay down here alone!"

"It's the money, isn't it?" she lashed out.

"What?"

"Your fee! You're worried that I haven't enough left to pay you. Well, you needn't be. My father has property in Antwerp. He will pay what we owe you as soon—"

"What are you talking about?"

"Or are you just itching to get away to fight for the Queen?" she went on frantically, knowing she was ranting, knowing she dared not face what was unfaceable. "That's it, isn't it! You want—"

"Stop this!" He grabbed her arms. "You must come. This place—"

A laugh made them both turn. The laugh, more like a cackle, had come from a withered woman sitting propped against a wall. Even in the dim light Isabel noticed her mad eyes. "Enough of that, now!" the woman scolded them. Her toothless mouth was locked in a lascivious smile as though she were peeping on two lovers. She sat among a knot of huddled prisoners. Something about the other forms caught Isabel's attention. They were small. They were children. What were children doing in this dungeon?

She looked at Carlos and said as steadily as she could, "Go if you want. I cannot." She pushed out of his grip and approached the children.

Most of them immediately scuttled away, leaving only the hag and one other slight form lying on the floor. Isabel came near. The hag continued staring into space, cackling softly. Isabel knew there was no hope of information from her. She looked down at the other form. It was completely covered with a red blanket. She dreaded that under it was another cadaver. But the form stirred under its covering, which Isabel now saw under her candlelight was not a blanket but a fine crimson brocade cloak. She bent down. "I am looking for someone," she said.

There was no answer from the mound. And no further movement. Hesitantly Isabel reached out to lower the cloak enough to see who lay beneath it and was surprised to feel its lining of luxurious fur. Marveling at this, she brought her candle closer and a small face emerged from under the sumptuous covering. It was the face of a boy. Isabel thought he could not be more than four years old. He lay still and looked up at her with sunken eyes. His hair was as matted as a bird's nest. His face, streaked with grime, glistened with sweat. Black spots mottled his nose and ears.

Isabel felt the tug of pity. "Are you all alone?" she asked. The boy said nothing.

"Where is your mother?"

He only stared at her. Fever clouded his eyes. His breathing was labored. Isabel wished there were some way she could help. If this child's mother had died, what chance had he of surviving, sick and alone in this worst of hell holes where every drop of water had its price? She fumbled with one hand at the purse at her belt, but still holding the candle, she could not loosen the strings. Suddenly a hand relieved her of the candle. She looked up. It was Carlos. He was scowling down at her. But he had stayed.

She drew open the purse and dug into the meager store of coins and withdrew a shilling, then reached down under the cloak and lifted out the boy's hot, listless hand. She put the coin on the sweaty palm and closed the small fingers over it.

"Get away from him!" a high voice demanded.

Isabel rose in surprise and found a girl standing before her, glaring at her. Barefoot, ragged, filthy, the child appeared to be no more than seven or eight; the top of her head came only to Carlos's waist. With a ferocity that belied her size, she forced her way between Carlos and Isabel and dropped to her knees beside the boy. "What she done to you, Robin?" she asked anxiously. "Did she . . ." She stopped as she caught sight of the coin, for the boy had opened his hand to show her. The girl's mouth fell open in amazement. She looked up at Isabel with an expression of wonder, but the wonder was tinged with wariness.

"I only wanted to help," Isabel said. "He looks so sick."

"He'll get better," the girl replied stoutly. She tucked the furred cloak up under the boy's chin. He was shivering horribly. "He's me brother," the girl added, as if this fact made his survival inevitable, a result of her will. And although it was a formidable will, Isabel realized, it would not save the boy. She looked down at the wasted boy, then back at the girl, and knew that she was not alone in refusing to face an unbearable reality.

But how did these children come to be in prison? she wondered. "Are you and your brother alone?" she asked.

The girl glanced up with suspicion.

Carlos groaned his impatience.

Isabel ignored him. It seemed important to acknowledge this tenacious child's efforts. Important—crucial—not to give up. "Where is your mother?" she asked.

"Taproom," the girl said.

"She has some money then?"

"Money?" the girl asked, incredulous. "Nah. The men poke her, then buy her some ale. She's there all day." She explained this unemotionally while eyeing Isabel's purse, as though she believed that answering the lady's questions might, miraculously, bring another coin.

"I see," Isabel murmured. "So you and your brother are on your own."

The girl seemed to take this as a criticism of her abilities. "I got that cloak for him from the cellarman, didn't I?" she asked belligerently. The boy, Isabel saw, was now shivering so violently that the cloak was inching down his quaking body. "Traded everything I had for it," the girl went on proudly. "It'll do the trick, too, you'll see. Robin'll be as right as rain."

But Isabel was no longer listening. She was staring at the boy, at an object uncovered by his shivering. Wedged between his arm and his slight body was a wooden carving. It was a boat. Isabel recognized the workmanship. She would know it anywhere. She had owned just such a toy when she had been this boy's age.

She dropped to her knees to touch the boat. "Where did you get this?"

But the boy was shivering uncontrollably now. "He don't talk," the girl said.

Isabel whirled around to her. "Who gave him the boat?"

"A man."

"In here? A prisoner?"

The girl nodded.

Isabel bit back her joy. "Can you take me to him?"

The girl only snorted in derision, a harsh, cynical sound incongruous with her age. Carlos, examining the boat himself, whispered in amazement, "*Madre de Dios,* he was carving one like this when I met him." Isabel was fumbling in her purse for another shilling. She pressed it into the girl's grimy hand. "Please, please take me to him!"

The girl bit the coin to satisfy herself of its authenticity. She eyed Isabel with a look very much like regret. "Can't," she said.

Carlos took hold of the girl's shoulders, clearly set on shaking her for information. The girl's body tensed like a caught animal, and she emitted a low snarl.

"Let her alone!" Isabel said. She tugged Carlos's sleeve to break his grip. On her knees, she took the girl's hand gently in hers. "The man who made the boat is my father," she said quietly. "I must find him. Please, won't you tell me where he is?"

Isabel felt the girl's dark, somber eyes lock on hers. "Father?" the girl asked, as though she had never thought of grown people having parents. But there was another note in her voice as well, something almost wistful; few children in here knew their fathers. "We was watching him," she said, then added, as if in explanation, "He were ailing bad. But he give Robin the boat. So I told the others not to do him."

"Do him?" Isabel asked. "I don't understand. Please, can't you just tell me where he is?" She heard the desperation in her own voice.

The girl's eyes remained fixed on Isabel's, their gaze older than her years; now, she was the one giving help. "I brung him over here. It's a mite warmer, see?" she said, pointing to the ceiling, " 'cause the gents' hearth is right above. I give him some water, too, what I'd traded for some boots. But it didn't do no good. He was babbling something awful. All about how he was getting out, getting out for *her* sake, he said. Raving, he was." She paused and shook her head, dissatisfied with the result of her ministrations to the man. "He should've had a good warm cover, see? Like this'n I got for Robin." She shrugged, the matter now beyond her control. "If he'd got a cover, he'd have been a'right."

Isabel's grip inadvertently tightened on the girl's hand. "Would have been? Do you mean . . . ?"

The girl nodded. "Corpse cart took him out. But his boots and britches was still on him. I didn't let the others do him, even then, see?" she said proudly, then added, as a statement of simple justice, "I mean, he give Robin the boat, didn't he?"

Isabel was running. Stumbling over bodies in the Beggars Ward, pushing past the idle cellarman, tearing up the stairs. She ran on, merging into the crowded corridor of the Commons Ward. *Dead . . . dead . . .*

She wrenched her way through the crowd and ran on to the main door. She ran without stopping, the squalid surroundings only a blur. But sounds pursued her . . . the scream of a man in the Press Room . . . the mockingly sweet lilt of a lute duet from a window in the Gentlemen's hall . . .

She bolted out of the prison and ran down Newgate Street. Her breath sawed painfully in her chest. Her feet slipped on the icy cobbles. Her hips and shoulders banged other pedestrians, who eyed her with annoyance. She ran on.

But her skirts were heavy, and the burst of energy that had sent her tearing from the Beggars Ward in panic was now spent. She staggered on among the stalls and customers of the Shambles of Newgate Market, hardly knowing where she was. As she felt her legs begin to weaken, a hand caught her arm from behind and yanked her to a stop. It was Carlos, panting steam.

"Let me go!" she cried, and fought to get free.

"Listen to me—" He stopped as a wagon rumbled dangerously near them. He took hold of her shoulders and pressed her back against a tavern doorway, out of the wagon's way.

"Oh, God, let me go!" she wailed again. "He's dead!"

"Listen. Your father—"

"Don't!" She shook her head, eyes closed. "It's over! He's dead!"

"Maybe not."

"You heard the girl! She *saw* him! Saw his body carted out!"

"She saw them take him, yes. That does not mean he is dead."

"What are you talking about? The girl—"

"I was with your father in jail. He was strong. A tough fighter. And no fool. If he said to that girl that he was getting out, I think he may have done it."

Isabel stared at him. It wasn't possible. Or was it? "Got out? But . . . how?"

"The corpse cart."

She blinked at him. Understanding flooded in. "You mean . . . pretended to be dead?"

"Yes."

Hope struck her like a blow. Her knees threatened to buckle. She clutched Carlos's arm. He caught her.

"Where do they take the bodies?" he asked.

She tried to think. Think past the blaze of hope. "The charnel house. At St. Paul's Cathedral."

"We must check there. It is the only way to be sure."

"You're sure?" Edward cried, not yet trusting the rush of joyful relief. "Dead?"

"Dead, sir," Palmer confirmed with a smile. "Of jail fever. Carried out this morning. When the Sergeant of the Guard came for him, it was too late. You see, sir, Sturridge and I had waited on the roof for so long, I knew something had gone awry. So I went in to inquire of the jailer, Master Alexander, about the transfer. I told him that you were anxious to see the Queen's order carried out. And I got the report straight from his own mouth. Jail fever killed Thornleigh, he said. In fact, he was in the middle of explaining the circumstance to the sergeant when I came in. I left the two of them talking and hurried back here to report to you."

Edward paced by his hearth, still hardly daring to believe his good fortune. That sickness should have succeeded in removing Thornleigh when two botched attempts to hire assassins had failed! He was slightly unnerved by the haphazard quality of such an end to his troubles: he had had no control in the ordering of it. But he was mightily pleased, nevertheless, for it *was* an end.

Or was it? He must not allow this triumph to cloud his vision, he told himself. Thornleigh was gone, and that was fine. But there were still two loose ends in this business. One was Thornleigh's daughter, too close for comfort. How much did she know? The other was that Spaniard, roaming free in London. If the Spaniard should chance to spot Edward in the company of Palmer, who had hired him in Colchester jail, he would definitely know too much.

"Palmer, where did you say the Thornleigh girl was lodging?"

"The Anchor."

"Thames Street?"

"Aye, sir."

"Thank you. That will be all. Go and send Sturridge back to his troop."

Alone, Edward stared into the fire, organizing his thoughts. Yes, it could all be arranged quite simply, he thought, and with no risk to himself that he could foresee. Not if he managed the girl properly. He would do it right away.

He was emerging from his front door, adjusting his cape, head down in thought, when a woman's voice from the street reached him. "Sir Edward!" the voice sang out.

It was Amy Hawtry, Frances's fellow lady-in-waiting. She was hurrying up to him, all smiles. "I was just coming to claim you!" she crooned.

Standing on his doorstep beside him she babbled on, congratulating him on his knighthood. She was slightly rocky on her feet, and Edward realized she was drunk. He wished he could shake her off and leave.

"Now, you must come and join us, sir," she said gaily, waving a gloved hand to indicate a small waiting group of friends on horseback—another young lady and two older gentlemen and a couple of servants. They were on their way out for an afternoon of hawking, Amy said, and she had insisted they stop to invite Edward. She hooked her arm in his. "The palace is like a tomb," she pouted, "with all the gallants off playing soldier. Do come, Sir Edward, and entertain me."

"Forgive me, mistress, but I cannot join you in your sport now. Urgent business calls me away."

"Oh, dear," Amy sighed. "And I did so want to hear all about the Emperor's magnificent and naughty court. What secrets you must have been party to there!" She pressed her body against his and lifted her face to whisper in his ear, "Is it true the Emperor keeps a dusky Moorish wench?"

"I am afraid this pleasure must be postponed for another time, mistress," Edward said graciously but firmly, turning her toward the street. "Please carry my regrets to your friends. Good hunting."

She pouted still, but sidled back to the waiting group with only one sultry glance back at him, then mounted her horse and trotted off with her friends.

Edward felt a ripple of disgust. He mistrusted sexually aggressive females as a blot on the proper order of things. The moment had unsettled him. But, as he looked up at the pale sun struggling past a heap of cloud, he felt confidence surge back. His troubles were almost over. The girl and the Spaniard were mere details; he would clear them up easily himself. The main point—Thornleigh's removal—was won. Striding off in the direction of Thames Street, he allowed himself after all to savor the moment of triumph.

CHAPTER TWENTY-THREE

><><><>

The Charnel House

St. Paul's Cathedral, resplendent with rare stained glass and the tallest spire in Europe, rose in the center of St. Paul's walled churchyard, while close by in the northwest corner stood the magnificent palace of the Bishop of London. Around these two great edifices flowed foot traffic and noisy trade. But between them lay a valley of shadow, withdrawn from the bustle, in which were crammed a cloister, a dilapidated chapel, a burying ground, and the charnel house.

Isabel, with Carlos behind her, stood before the charnel house—a long, low shed—and rapped on the wooden door. She waited, still catching her breath, for they had hurried all the way from Newgate. Around her the winter sun glittered off the cathedral's jewel-colored glass and off the palace's tall windows, and, high above, the spire's copper-gilt weathercock jerked in the wind. She could hear the faint hum of haggling voices at the bookstalls between the cathedral's buttresses. She recalled with a sharp clarity the day her father had teased her at those bookstalls, playing at delay to rile her because she was so anxious to make their meeting with Martin, the same day the mob had attacked the Spanish lords at Ludgate. Now, distanced from the lively chatter at the bookstalls, standing in the cold shade where the charnel house hulked so miserably, she waited to be admitted, dreading, with every heightened thud of her heart, what she might discover inside. What if Carlos was wrong, and her father's body was here, among the dead?

No one answered her knock.

Carlos stepped forward and tried the latch. It lifted. He pushed the door open. There was gloom inside, for the shed was lit only by one small, unglazed window. And there was utter silence.

"There's no one here," Isabel whispered.

"No one alive," Carlos corrected grimly. He moved inside.

As her eyes adjusted to the dim light, Isabel saw that he was right. Before her were sprawled dozens of corpses. They lay partially naked on a rough wooden tier that lined three walls. They lay on the earthen floor in table-high mounds, bristling with lifeless elbows and knees and feet, male and female jumbled together indiscriminately, giving an odd impression of lewdness. They lay in open coffins—children, these —ranged on a worktable, as if obediently waiting for their lids. There were baskets of discarded clothing. And there were bones. Cemetery space in crowded London was limited, and the bones of common folk were not allowed to enjoy eternal rest. A heap of them, dug up from the burying ground to make room for the newly dead, lay in a wooden bin beside a far door.

Isabel stepped inside. The stench was overwhelming.

"Stay out," Carlos said. "I will do this."

"No. I need to be sure."

She came beside him and they stood still for a moment gazing uneasily at the dead surrounding them, unsure how to begin. Then Isabel noticed that the skin of the corpses laid out on the shelves was unspotted, while the bodies heaped on the floor were speckled black, and many bore livid purple splotches on their abdomens as well—all were the marks of jail fever. She swallowed her revulsion. "These are from the prison," she said, nodding at the heaps.

They began the search. It was gruesome. They had to push corpses aside to check the identity of others buried beneath, and more than once, as Isabel handled the cold flesh, her stomach lurched. More than once, when bulging eyes stared up at her, or when, as she jarred a head, a black tongue flicked out of a gaping mouth, she had to stand back, dizzy, to recover her breath. And every moment she dreaded that the next black-spotted face that lolled toward her would be her father's. But Carlos, though implacably silent, did not flinch. She noted with a kind of grateful respect how he went doggedly about the business, despite his aversion, grappling the diseased bodies and dragging them out into the feeble light for her to investigate, not stopping until they had gone through each pile.

Finally, Isabel straightened from the grisly work. She felt very shaky. "He's not here." She said it quietly, tentatively, almost afraid to acknowledge the remarkable conclusion: her father had escaped.

A creaking of the back door near her made her whirl around. Carlos was bent beyond the pile of corpses, pushing the last few bodies apart to check them, and he did not notice the sound.

A rotund man stood wheezing in the open doorway, a steaming Cheapside meat pie in his hand. He was frowning at Isabel. "Here, what's going on!"

Carlos suddenly straightened behind the waist-high mound of dead. Scowling in the shadows as he loomed up above the corpses, he looked like one of their grim number sprung to life. The man gasped, dropped his meat pie, and crossed himself in horror.

Isabel sought to calm him, though her nerves were almost as jangled as his. "Sir, we are looking for someone." The man continued to gape at Carlos. "Can you help us?" Isabel asked, trying to claim back his attention. "Are you the caretaker?"

Carlos stepped out of the shadows. His mortal reality and Isabel's explanation seemed to converge on the man's consciousness at once and he slumped in relief. "Pardon me, mistress," he said, pulling out a kerchief and patting at the sweat that sheened his round face. He added with a quick but unconvincing attempt at bluffness, "Now and then, you see, we do get a lousel in here rifling through the deceased's clothing." He looked down dejectedly at the splattered remains of his meat pie in the dirt.

Isabel pressed on for the answer she needed. "You *are* the caretaker then?" She handed him a coin.

"Aye, mistress," he said, brightening at her payment, then pocketing it with a tactful disregard. "And how may I be of service to you?"

"Sir, I am looking for my father."

"Passed on has the gentleman?" he asked solicitously.

She nodded, uncomfortable with this playacting that her father was dead. "But I was not able to view his body," she went on. "It is most distressing, as you can imagine, for I long to pay my last respects. And, of course, to furnish a proper burial through your services." She lowered her eyes to give an impression of sorrow; it was not difficult to simulate, since half her heart feared that this man might produce her father's body after all.

"Quite right, quite right," the caretaker murmured, sensing profit. "Well, now, let me see what I can do. Your name, mistress?"

"I am—"

"No," Carlos broke in. "We should go."

Isabel raised a hand to silence him. She had to be sure! "My name is Isabel Thornleigh," she told the caretaker. "My father's body was removed from Newgate jail this morning. Was a Richard Thornleigh brought to you? He is a tall man, gray-haired, with one blind eye."

Her declaration wrought an immediate change on the caretaker's face. His eager smile vanished. His eyes narrowed with suspicion. "A jailbird? From which ward?"

"The Beggars Ward."

"And he perished of the fever? This morning, you say?"

"So I was told."

The caretaker drew himself to his full height. "Out!" he ordered brusquely, pointing to the door. "Out with you!"

"What? But—"

"Out!" He bustled toward Carlos, waving his pudgy hands at him and Isabel as if to disperse a flock of crows. "Get out, or I'll have the sheriff on you both!"

Carlos took Isabel's arm and pulled her out the door. They were a little way along the graveyard path when Isabel glanced back and saw the caretaker rush out and close the door behind him. He looked ahead and saw her, then quickly waddled away down a divergent path. His abrupt change of temper pricked her concern.

Carlos was right, she shouldn't have given her name. If the Newgate authorities found out her father was missing, not dead, they'd be looking for him, too.

She glanced at Carlos. She had to hurry to keep up with him through the cemetery; he seemed to want to get past the graves as quickly as he could. As they walked, he was looking at his hands with consternation. She understood. She, too, felt as though the diseased bodies had left some invisible but vile residue on her hands. They were almost at the churchyard wall. As they passed through Little Gate and out into the busy thoroughfare of Cheapside, Isabel saw a blue-smocked apprentice hefting a keg out of the back of a loaded ale wagon for a tavern. A thought struck. "Boy!" she called. He turned. Isabel reached the wagon and quickly bargained with the lad, paying him a crown for the keg. Carlos frowned at her, baffled. Isabel told the apprentice to pour out the ale.

He blinked. "Pour it out, mistress?"

"Yes."

"Here?"

"Right here."

The young man shrugged with a look that said he was not responsible for the lunacy of a paying customer. He jerked out the bung, upended the keg, and held it up, letting the frothy contents gush onto the cobbles.

The moment Isabel thrust her hands into the stream of ale, Carlos was in doubt no longer. He plunged his hands in beside hers. They stood side by side, letting the cold foam wash the charnel-house horrors away.

Isabel felt a bubble of happiness rise inside her. She felt quite light-headed—from the joy at not finding her father dead, from the icy zing of the ale sloshing over her hands, from the whole dangerous, macabre search she and Carlos had just been through. She could not hold it in. "The caretaker," she said, laughter bubbling up. "He thought you were one of his charges rising from the dead! He thought you were a ghost!" Her laughter burst out.

Carlos snorted. He threw back his head and laughed aloud with her.

The apprentice shook his head at the folly taking place before him.

The ale flowed to a trickle. The apprentice tossed the empty keg into the wagon, hefted out another, and, still shaking his head, trudged off to deliver his order to the tavern where sane people congregated.

Isabel dried her hands on her skirt. As people on the street pushed past, she wiped tears of laughter from her eyes. She beamed at Carlos, heady with the euphoria of their success. "We did it, Carlos! We searched every inch of that charnel house and he wasn't there. He's escaped," she said definitively, "hasn't he?"

Carlos nodded. "I think so."

They stood smiling at each other, warmed by the accomplishment.

Isabel felt a shadow fall over her face as a horseman rode by. The cold wind tugged her skirt. Her smile faded. "The question now is," she murmured, "where has he gone?"

"Home?"

"To Colchester?" She shook her head. "There's no one left. Even if he wanted to, he has no horse, no money. He's obviously lost the money he had, because he was thrown in with Newgate's beggars."

Carlos nodded, agreeing. "So where?"

The question gnawed at Isabel. Her father might be free, but in what pitiful condition? "Penniless," she said, thinking aloud. "And sick, too. Very sick if the girl was right about his delirious talk. How long can he last, out on his own in such a state, in this cold?"

"He has friends?"

She brightened. "Yes, of course! He would go to a friend's house! He would have to!"

Several horsemen clattered into the crowd not far up the street. Carlos glanced in that direction.

Isabel watched him. She thought of how doggedly he had done what was required in the charnel house, how he had manhandled the corrupted bodies, the tainted flesh that he loathed and feared. Just for his payment? she wondered. Surely more than that. He knew how little money she had left; *she* knew how paltry was the reward she had promised him. Was it for her, then? She forced away the dangerously exciting remembrance of last night, of her actions—his actions—in her moonlit room. That had been a frenzied half dream, a moment of delirium to be obliterated from her memory—never, *never* to be thought of again. But this was something else; he had done things for her that could not be ignored.

"Carlos," she said. He turned back to her. "You've done so much," she said. "Saved my life in the Fleet. Stuck by my side. And you thought of this, too—that my father feigned death to escape. Back in Newgate, when the girl said she saw him taken out, I really believed that was the end. If you hadn't suggested we try the charnel house I would have given up then and there."

"Not you," he said quietly. "You *don't* give up." His mouth curved into his crooked smile. "In a siege I would hate to find you fighting on the other side."

At this image of her in combat against him—so absurd—she had to grin again. She looked up into his eyes, knowing her gratitude shone on her face. "Thank you," she said softly. "For all you have done."

He took her face between his hands tentatively, gently.

She was ashamed, appalled, at her body's instant response to his touch—her breath quickening, her knees softening. He seemed to be studying her. "What is it?" she managed to say.

"You are smiling." He said it as if it were something he had been waiting for, hoping for.

She knew she should pull away. But his touch was so light, a caress. This was not mastery, she thought, this was sheer tenderness. It seemed to startle him as much as her, for he stared at her with a look of wonder.

The blast of a trumpet made them both turn. It had come from the knot of horsemen up the street. The horsemen had stopped beside the Great Cross and the crowd had thickened around them. Four of the horsemen, three dressed in rich fur-trimmed velvets, were mounting the steps of the Cross. Isabel recognized one: the Lord Mayor, Thomas White.

The Mayor held up his hands for silence from the milling crowd. He quickly introduced the men beside him: Lord William Howard, Sheriff Hewett, and the common crier. White beckoned the crier, who came forward, took a broad stance, and began to declare a proclamation.

Isabel could not hear all of it. People were pushing past her and Carlos to get nearer the Cross, and the commotion of shuffling feet and whinnying horses and chattering people drowned out half the crier's words. But she caught the gist of it, a denunciation as traitors of all those who gave Wyatt succor. The crowd hushed and she clearly heard the last of the proclamation. ". . . and any man who delivers up to Her Majesty the traitorous Wyatt, his body living or dead, shall receive from the Queen's Majesty a gift of lands carrying an income of one hundred pounds per year, to be the property of him and his heirs forever!"

Isabel felt suddenly cold. She saw that Carlos, too, was listening intently.

The burgeoning crowd erupted in questions and babble. Three merchants threading their way by Isabel were deep in a harangue. "Not a hope!" one said with vehemence. "Lord Howard has the guns to defend the Queen!"

"But Wyatt has the soldiers!" one of his companions hotly insisted.

"Guns, soldiers, bah!" the third put in angrily. "Neither of you understands the point! Where will the *Londoners* stand? Whither goes their allegiance, eh? That's what everything hinges on! And all of us with property in the city must consider . . ." His voice trailed as the trio pushed on.

But Isabel had heard enough. The proclamation had jolted her like the earlier trumpet blast, blaring out her duty to Wyatt and to Martin. Carlos's jest of a moment before about meeting on opposing sides in a siege suddenly soured, like a compliment one realizes too late is mockery. She had already pulled stiffly away from him. "Well," she said, "we are on opposite sides already. Aren't we?"

"Are we?"

"If you're going to sell yourself to the Queen, we are."

His face darkened. "It is because your man has gone with the rebels, yes?"

She was taken aback. How did he know this about Martin? She had taken great care to give no hint of Martin's whereabouts.

As though in answer, Carlos muttered, "Not hard to figure out."

They stood in silence, avoiding each other's eyes. *There is no time for this,* Isabel thought. She must act. Wyatt was waiting for her. Martin was waiting for her. But what about her father? Could she leave him stumbling penniless and ill through London, his life still endangered by the Grenvilles' vendetta? Once again, her warring loyalties were tearing at her.

"Back to the Anchor, then track your father," Carlos said suddenly, as though he were deciding for her.

Isabel balked. "Why the Anchor? So you can join the Queen's troop there?"

"To get your horse," he said. He added steadily, "Yes, I will join the Queen's soldiers. But I will finish the job with you first. Come. If we hurry, maybe we will find your father by nightfall."

Isabel knew immediately that this was the right course. If she could quickly get her father on board a ship to safety, she could then hurry back to do her duty for the cause. The way was suddenly clear.

Far more murky was her tangle of emotions—both gratitude and trepidation—knowing that Carlos was going to stay by her side.

Newgate's jailer, Andrew Alexander, was pouring a goblet of wine for his honored guest, the Sergeant of the Guard from Whitehall Palace, and pointing out to him the excellent skill of the rebeck player about to perform a composition of Alexander's own hand, when the caretaker of the charnel house bustled in, out of breath.

"I've found your sixteenth man!" the caretaker wheezed.

Alexander looked up, vexed. "What's that?" He hated interruptions in the midday meal music, especially when he was entertaining so important a guest. The sergeant had agreed to stay only for a goblet of wine, but Alexander was hoping that would give him enough time to finesse a post at the palace armory for his son. But this blockhead from the bone-yard had no understanding of where and when to make his pestering reports.

The caretaker stood noisily catching his breath and mopping his glistening face. "I sent you a complaint this morning that I'd only been delivered fifteen of your dead when the tally was for sixteen. Remember? Well, now I've found the sixteenth."

"Fine," Alexander said, waving a hand of dismissal. "Then go bury him, man. Can't you see I'm busy?"

"Bury a corpse that's walked away? That's a rare one, Master Alexander! You tell me how I can bury a corpse that's toddled off, and I'll bury your family for free!" With great satisfaction, the caretaker stuffed away his limp kerchief and gazed at the jailer in triumph.

"How's that?" the Sergeant of the Guard asked, sitting up straighter in his chair. "Walked away? Which dead man? Who?"

The caretaker blinked at the authority of so mighty a personage, resplendent in his armor breastplate. He bowed and told the sergeant unctuously, "His name is Thornleigh, Your Worship. Richard Thornleigh."

The sergeant's mouth fell open. He glared at the jailer. "Alexander," he boomed, "what's the meaning of this?"

Alexander felt his son's hopes for preferment dwindle away like piss down a drain. He smiled halfheartedly. "Now, now, let's not lose our heads, sir," he said, trying to shore up the ground beneath him. He must not have the sergeant think he was not in control of his prison. He had just finished explaining to him that Thornleigh had died of jail fever and was carted out only an hour before the sergeant had arrived to transfer him to the Tower. He turned to the caretaker and scoffed, "What is this nonsense you're telling us, man? Corpses don't walk!"

"This one did," the caretaker replied smugly.

"Oh, really? Did you see him?"

"As good as. I was scratching my head over the puzzle of how I only got fifteen when I was supposed to get sixteen, when this young lady comes in looking for her father's body, just deceased. Lost, it seems he is. In fact, she says, she never actually *saw* his body. Then she tells me his name is Richard Thornleigh. And curse me if that isn't one of the names on my tally. So then I know my sixteenth has scarpered. Skedaddled. I have the answer to my puzzle. And you, Master Jailer, have an escapee."

The sergeant almost bounded up from his chair. "Good God, Alexander, Thornleigh is a traitor wanted by the Queen!" He turned to the caretaker. "Is she still at the charnel house? The daughter?"

"Oh, no, Your Worship. I shooed her out so as I could come here to—"

"Damn! She could have led us to the traitor!" Adjusting his sword, the sergeant started to cross the room. As he passed the caretaker, he commanded, "You, come with me back to St. Paul's. Maybe someone saw the woman, saw which way she went." At the door he looked back at Alexander. "And you, Jailer, had better unleash your dogs and organize a search party for Thornleigh if you value your neck!"

CHAPTER TWENTY-FOUR

~>+<0>+<~

Betrayed

Isabel made her way through the Anchor's crowded common room toward the stairs. The place smelled sourly of ale dregs and stale sweat from the soldiers' encampment, though most of them were out at this noon hour. In the morning, when she and Carlos had gone to Newgate, the rank and file had left under the direction of Lieutenant Andrews to drill in Finsbury Fields, preparing for the rebels. But now, in their place, a noisy bunch of the innkeeper's gaming cronies had taken over the room to watch a cockfight. Isabel could not see the birds behind the screen of the men's bodies, but she heard frantic crowing and scrabbling above the men's loud haggling. As for soldiers, only a handful of officers were left, sitting quietly at a far table and finishing a dinner of cold meat and ale. As Isabel passed them she caught the eye of the soldiers' captain, whose heavy ginger beard could not hide his badly pocked skin. She also noticed three men standing apart from all the activity—dull-eyed, rough-faced men; one, completely bald—who seemed to have no connection with either the gamesters or the soldiers. Isabel shivered. She had seen enough faces like that in prisons lately.

She started up the stairs, suddenly buoyant at the thought that she would soon find her father at some friend's house, and the knot of her problems would finally unravel. Her mind busily sorted the likely possibilities: her parents' acquaintances, her father's business associates. Carlos was already in the stable saddling the mare. *This* search would yield success quickly; she felt it.

She opened the door of her room and was surprised to see a man in rich apparel standing at the window with his back to her. He turned at the sound of the door. But even before he faced her, Isabel recognized him from the red hair smoothly combed below his jewel-studded hat. It was the man who had spoken to her in the graveyard at home six days ago—the day she had buried her mother and Lady Grenville had spat at her. He was some relation of the Grenvilles. A warning prickled her.

"Mistress Thornleigh," he greeted her in a low tone of sympathy, moving toward her with outstretched hands. "I have just learned of your father's tragic death. Please accept my profound condolences."

Isabel stood stiffly, wondering how he had heard, and determined to give no hint of her conviction that her father was still alive.

"Of course you do not remember me," he said with a humble smile. "Edward Sydenham. We met at—"

"I remember you, sir," Isabel said. "You are a Grenville. Are those three henchmen below yours? Have you come to plague me, since the Grenvilles can no longer plague my father?"

He almost winced. "You are bitter, mistress," he said softly. He lowered his head as though in shame. "And with good cause, I warrant. But I entreat you," he said, raising his chin with a swift return of pride that seemed so native it was more like grace, "see me for what I am. Though I will soon have the privilege of making Frances Grenville my wife, my name is my own, as is my honor, and so both will remain."

"Forgive me," Isabel said, somewhat mollified. "I do recall that you spoke kindly to me when we met." What could this man possibly want with her? she wondered. And how could she get rid of him? For her task here was simply to collect her small remnant of money and then be off with Carlos. "How can I help you, sir?" she asked. "I confess I am in some haste to keep an appointment."

He smiled gently. "It is I who hope to help you. And thereby help myself." He motioned to a chair. "Will you allow me to explain?"

She resisted his suggestion to sit.

"Please," he said. "It will take but a moment."

She saw that she must listen before he would go. She sat. He closed the door on the noisy cockfight below, then came before her.

"I have been following the troubles of your unfortunate father," Sydenham said, "first in Colchester jail and then in Newgate prison. It has been my desire to alleviate his plight in whatever way I could. Now, sadly, that chance has been forever removed." He paused. "By the look in your eyes I see that you wonder why I come to you now, when your father has passed on."

She said nothing.

"And, of course, you must wonder why I have concerned myself in this business at all." He looked at her earnestly and declared, "I want to end the evil that hatred has wrought." He sighed heavily, as though uncertain he was capable of explaining the deep significance of his statement. "Mistress, I have traveled a good deal in the German lands. I have seen the extraordinary suffering there—the wars, the civil strife, the hatred that poisons the very air between families who once lived contentedly as neighbors. And all this over religion. Catholics slaughtering Protestants. Protestants butchering Catholics. Now, I fear that the same unspeakable turmoil lies in store for England. I wish with all my heart that I could somehow stop it before it begins."

The last avowal had been uttered with passion, but now he smiled ruefully and nodded his head as if in answer to some silent, inner challenge. "It is true—there may be precious little that one man can do to halt this tide of evil. Be that as it may, I have pledged myself to effect whatever small good I can. And one such act which I feel it is in my power to accomplish is to make peace between our families, Grenvilles and Thornleighs. Religion was the spark that has razed the happiness of both our homes. Both families have suffered appallingly in this tragedy. Both still suffer from the wounds. I want most earnestly to halt these ravages, to begin the healing." He took a step closer to her. "It is most grievous to me that fever took your father before I could do anything to help him. But, mistress, I can still help *you*. Will you allow me?" He paused for an answer. "If not," he added with a self-deprecating smile of great charm, "you consign a man to failure. And I sense you are too tenderhearted a lady to commit so uncharitable an act."

Isabel looked down at her hands in her lap, feeling torn by suspicion; Sydenham seemed all benevolence, but he came from the enemy. She dared not reveal her belief that her father had escaped and was still alive. "You are most kind, sir," she said. "But I do not see in what way you can help me now."

"Mistress, I know that your brother and his family have removed to the Continent. I am certain that you wish to be reunited with them. But I suspect—pardon me, harsh times call for harsh words—I suspect that your resources have run low. And, well ... you are so alone."

"No, sir, I am not alone. I have a good man helping me."

Sydenham let this pass. "There is grave trouble brewing in England," he said, "with Wyatt's rebels rampaging in Kent and threatening to advance on London itself, as you no doubt have heard. I would consider it an honor if you would allow me to cover the expense of sending you away from this scene of personal grief and impending conflict, and of reuniting you with your brother. I have friends among the Flemish captains whose ships are currently moored in the estuary. A word from me, and any one of them will guarantee you a passage complete with every luxury and security. And once across the Channel, you will be furnished with an escort at my expense to ensure your safe arrival at your brother's door. Will you let me arrange this?"

For a moment Isabel was tempted. Not tempted to leave England, of course, but to somehow accept Sydenham's money, a commodity she was sorely in need of. But an inner voice still warned against the man who was betrothed to Frances Grenville. "I thank you for your offer, sir. But—" She broke off at the loud sound of boots tramping outside the door.

The door swung open. A thick-set soldier in a breastplate strode in while two men-at-arms stood in the doorway. Isabel jumped up from her chair. The soldier stopped, looking surprised at Sydenham's presence. "Sir Edward," he said in confused acknowledgment.

"That's her!"

Isabel gasped. It was the charnel-house caretaker. He was leaning in between the men-at-arms, his round face damp with sweat. "That's the daughter!" he cried, pointing at Isabel from behind his shield of the soldiers' bodies.

"Sergeant!" Sydenham said in outrage. "What is the meaning of this?"

"Pardon me, Sir Edward," the sergeant said, recovering from his surprise, "but I must remove this woman for questioning. Her father, as you know, is wanted for treason."

"Her father is dead. Did they not inform you at the prison?"

"He is not dead, sir."

"I tell you, Richard Thornleigh died this morning of jail fever," Sydenham said.

"No, sir, he did not. He only feigned death to give the Newgate turnkeys the slip. He has escaped. In the Queen's name, I am organizing a manhunt to recover him."

Isabel struggled to control her pounding heart. Her enemies had discovered her father's ruse, and they were now after him . . . as a traitor! She glanced at Sydenham. At the sergeant's pronouncement the blood had drained from Sydenham's face. It struck Isabel with some force that he was indeed as sensitive to her father's well-being as he had claimed. Yet what good was his solicitude now? What could he do? What could *she* do? Her father was to be hunted down like a dog . . . she herself was to be taken into custody . . .

The sergeant reached for Isabel, finishing his explanation to Sydenham, "And this woman may know where the traitor is hiding."

"I know nothing, sir!" Isabel protested as he grabbed her arm. "Please!"

"Wait, Sergeant," Sydenham said. The sergeant halted. Isabel turned, still in his grasp. Both of them looked at Sydenham. The motions of his mind seemed to wildly flicker in his eyes, and when he spoke his voice was edged with apprehension though his words were calm and reasonable. "Sergeant, this innocent lady is still distracted at the news of what she took to be her father's death. I believe she has no knowledge whatever of his whereabouts. However, if you require confirmation of that, please do take into account her distraught state." He hooked his arm in a friendly way around the sergeant's arm and leaned his head close to say, very low, "Give me a few moments alone with her, man. I believe I can clear this up in no time. A kind word with ladies, eh? What do you say?"

The sergeant looked doubtful. "I am responsible for the traitor."

"Sergeant," Sydenham said with a new firmness that was tinged with a threat, "you know that the Queen has made me one of her lieutenants in the city's defense, under Lord Howard. Are you questioning my authority?"

Still frowning, but sobered by the admonition, the sergeant gave a brusque nod. "Five minutes, Sir Edward. My men and I will wait outside the door."

The soldiers retreated. The door closed. Sydenham and Isabel were alone.

He flashed her a fierce look. "*Do* you know where he is?"

Isabel hesitated. Apart from his smooth words of conciliation, what reason did she really have to trust Sydenham? Besides, though she suspected her father had sought refuge with some friend, she had no way of knowing *which* friend. "No," she said.

He strode to the window. He stood staring out, utterly motionless, as though he had forgotten Isabel was in the room. Then he twisted around to look at her, but with such intensity she felt he was almost looking through her. She shivered. Suddenly he shook his head like a man waking. He gave a short, helpless laugh. "Forgive me, mistress," he said, throwing up his hands, "I hardly know where I am or who I am! Such extraordinary news! It is most wonderful, is it not?"

"Wonderful, sir?" she asked, incredulous. Wonderful that her father was the object of a national manhunt?

"Why, to learn that your father lives!"

"Ah, yes," she said, remembering her earlier dissembling to him, "that *is* wonderful, most certainly." She rung her hands. There was no more dissembling now. "But the Queen's men will find him! They will bring him in, and then they will . . ." She could not finish. The traitor's death, prescribed by law, was public castration and disembowelment.

"Then we must see that they do *not* find him," Sydenham said evenly. "We must find him first."

"We?"

"Mistress Thornleigh," he said with feeling, moving closer, "I told you I want to help you. I thought, when I came here, that all I had to offer you was passage out of England. But now I can do so much more, for you and for your father. I can help you both to safety."

"Good God, how?"

"I have agents. I will send them out to search. When they find your father, I can get him and you aboard a Flemish galley. You'll both be halfway across the Channel before the Queen's men realize he's gone."

Isabel stared in disbelief. "You would do this? For us?"

"Most willingly. I know Thornleigh presents no real danger to Her Majesty. There are enough *proven* traitors for her to deal with at the moment. However, I cannot mount a private search without your assistance. You know your father better than anyone. You must tell me every place he may have gone, every friend who might give him succor, every hole where he might try to hide. That is the only way we can reach him before the Queen's men do. What do you say?"

"But how can I? The sergeant is taking me into custody!"

Sydenham waved a hand impatiently. "You will not be taken. Leave that to me. Let's you and I just agree to work together and find your father. All right?"

She blinked at him, trying to think. Yes, she could use his help to send her father away, then remain herself to help Wyatt. But—

"*Do* accept my offer!" he said, half pleading.

A loud wave of groans from the gamesters below reached them. There was a scraping at the door. The sergeant, coming back. Sydenham fixed his eyes on Isabel. His tone became implacable. "Mistress, make no mistake, you are in need of my protection."

The door latch lifted. Isabel glanced at it distractedly. There was no time to think!

"Quickly," Sydenham urged. "Will you let me help you?"

The door swung open. Isabel looked back at Sydenham. "Yes!" she said.

The sergeant strode in. "Well, sir?"

Sydenham faced him squarely. "Sergeant, it is just as I told you. This lady has no knowledge whatever of where the traitor may have gone to ground."

"All the same, sir, I must take—"

"Have you any evidence against Mistress Thornleigh to make an arrest, Sergeant?"

"Well, no, sir, but she—"

"Then I suggest you stop harassing her and leave and begin your search. Recover the traitor. That is where the Queen's interest lies."

The sergeant frowned, unsure.

"Meanwhile," Sydenham added evenly, "this lady will be a guest in my home. I will personally vouchsafe her good behavior." Looking the soldier in the eye, he challenged, "If that presents a problem for you, I suggest you take it up with Lord Howard. Good day to you, Sergeant."

The sergeant shrugged, still displeased but apparently unwilling to force the issue. "Very good, Sir Edward," he said, and added with the barest threat in his voice, "I'll know where to find her at any rate." He turned and beckoned to his men. They followed him out. Their boots clomped noisily down the stairs.

Isabel stared at Sydenham, struck by the display of power he had just wielded. She finally found her voice. "Thank you," she said.

He bowed graciously.

"But, sir, as for my coming to your house—"

"I do apologize," he interrupted, "that such an arrangement was necessary to satisfy that beef-headed soldier. But you saw that it *was* necessary." He made it quite clear by his tone, polite but pointed, that Isabel had no choice. "I only hope," he went on amiably, "that the comforts of my home will in some small way make up for the encroachment upon your liberty." He smiled disarmingly. "And after all, mistress, this rough soldier's billet is no place for a lady."

He held out his arm to her. "Shall we go? I'll send a servant to collect your belongings and settle your account."

Gently but firmly, he guided her out and down the stairs. Her mind was in turmoil, grappling with the sudden, alarming change of things. Her mind darted to Carlos, waiting in the stable. She must speak with him, explain all this. And then? Was this the last she would see of him?

She and Sydenham moved through the common room where the cockfight was still in progress. A bird crowed frantically and a jubilant shout went up from the gamesters. In the corner the soldiers, having finished eating, were rising to leave. Sydenham led Isabel past all these men and out the front door. They were in the courtyard, Sydenham steering her toward the open gate, when Isabel stopped and said, "Wait. I must go to the stable." She started across the cobbled yard. She heard a thud in the stable.

Sydenham hurried after her to prevent her. "My house is nearby, mistress. There is no need for your horse. I will send a servant back to fetch it."

"But I must see someone first."

"The Spaniard?"

Her mouth fell open. Did this man know *everything* about her? "Yes. I cannot leave without speaking to him." She turned again.

Sydenham grabbed her arm. "No."

Irritated, she shook him off and started toward the stable door. The door burst open. Carlos was pushed outside so violently he staggered forward for balance, blood trickling

from his lower lip. Isabel froze. The three rough-faced men
stomped after Carlos—Sydenham's men. Steadying himself,
Carlos raised his head and saw Sydenham. Shock swept his
face. "You," he breathed. Then, in a roar, "My land!" He
lunged at Sydenham, his hand instinctively swiping for his
sword. But the sword had been taken away, and Carlos was
immediately grappled from behind by two of the three men
and wrestled to his knees, his arms twisted up behind his
back. The third man, the bald one, whipped out a dagger and
held it to Carlos's throat, then looked back at Sydenham as
though for instructions.

"No!" Isabel cried. She lurched toward Carlos. Sydenham
restrained her. "Tell them to let him go!" she said. "He is
with *me!*"

Sydenham shook his head sadly at her. "I had hoped to
save you the distress of hearing this, but . . ." He fixed his
eyes on her soberly. "It is from this man above all that you
need protection."

She tried to control her anger. "Someone has misinformed
you, sir. This man has shown me nothing but loyalty. Now
tell your—"

"He is a Spanish mercenary, correct? Valverde by name,
correct? Oh, mistress, that he has somehow managed to en-
snare your trust is one of the most abominable crimes ever
perpetrated."

"Que diablos!" Carlos was wildly struggling to get to his
feet. Isabel, still held back by Sydenham, twisted to look at
Carlos. The bald man glanced at Sydenham. Sydenham gave
a nod. The bald man lifted his booted foot and plowed it into
Carlos's belly. Carlos grunted in pain. Isabel gasped and
cried, "No!" Carlos was doubling over, still kept on his
knees by the two helpers as the bald man cracked his knee
up against Carlos's face. Carlos's head snapped back, blood
gushing from his nose.

"Stop!" Isabel screamed.

Sydenham took hold of her more firmly. He almost shook
her. "What do you really know of this brute? Of the murders
he has committed?"

Isabel felt frantic at Carlos's groans of pain, but she struggled to stay calm. She must make Sydenham understand.
Only he could call off the henchmen. "I know he has done
some . . . reckless things," she said. "Sometimes, killing can
be justified."

"Find justification for this if you can, mistress," Sydenham proclaimed. "The Spaniard has been hired to kill your father!"

A cold stone dropped to the pit of Isabel's stomach. The stable door banged in the wind.

Sydenham sighed heavily. His face creased in concern, as though he were loath to bring her such distress. "Five days ago," he explained, "I went to Colchester jail to see what might be done for your father. I arrived too late. Thornleigh had just been transferred to London. And there had been a riot in which most of the prisoners had escaped, including Valverde. But I did speak to the sheriff. He told me that the previous night Valverde had made an attempt on your father's life. The assault was foiled, and in the ensuing disturbance both Valverde and your father were chained in the dungeon. In the morning your father was taken to London, and the riot occurred. There was great disorder in the aftermath. However, the sheriff was able to ascertain, from statements drawn from some recaptured prisoners, that Valverde's assault on Thornleigh had been paid for. That's right, mistress. He is an assassin, hired to murder your father."

Isabel's eyes turned slowly to Carlos. His head had fallen forward and was lolling between the henchmen on either side who held him down on his knees. The snow-dusted cobbles in front of him were speckled red with blood from his nose.

"Iss-bel!" Isabel turned toward the high, singing voice. It was the child, Lizzy. She had romped out the door of the inn, but she stopped suddenly and stared at Carlos, her eyes wide. She glanced at Isabel, seemed to realize that Isabel was not in the mood to play, and ran back inside.

Sydenham sighed again, even more deeply. "Which brings me to the real reason that I feel so personally implicated in this tragedy, mistress. It pains me more than I can say to have to tell you this, but . . ." He took a bracing breath. "I have come to the disturbing conclusion that the order for this assassination comes from Lady Maud Grenville. She sent her servant to the jail to commission Valverde. You see, she is quite unbalanced by the death of her husband. You experienced it yourself that day in the graveyard—the irrational depth of her enmity. And I can think of no other person who would wish your father dead. Can you?"

Isabel was staring at Carlos's blood dripping onto the cobbles.

Sydenham said very quietly, "This man has been using you in the hope of reaching your father, to murder him. This is the man you must fear."

Her voice struggled out feebly. "No. He . . . we . . ."

"Dear lady," Sydenham said, gently taking her hand, "if you are trying to convince yourself that this brute has experienced some miraculous change of heart it will only bring you more grief. He is pledged to murder. For profit. Whatever you have been able to pay him, Lady Grenville will have promised him tenfold that fee. Besides, I know how it is with mercenaries. They never change sides in a confrontation. It is a kind of honor with them. Indeed, it is their only honor."

Isabel's voice failed her. But she shook her head in stiff jerks of denial.

Sydenham said quietly, "I see you are loath to believe the worst of him. Well, perhaps *he* can convince you." He nodded to the bald man, who grappled Carlos's bloody chin and jerked up his head.

Sydenham stepped toward Carlos. "I wish you to disabuse this lady about your character. Explain to her the commission regarding her father that you accepted at Colchester jail."

She watched Carlos. Through his pain his eyes slowly focused on her. "Carlos?" She heard the tremor in her voice. "What he is saying, it's all lies . . . isn't it?"

The bald man shook Carlos's head as if to shake an answer out.

Isabel cried, "Let him speak!" Then quietly, hopefully, "Carlos?"

His eyes flicked from Isabel to Sydenham, then back to Isabel.

She felt his silence like thick hands around her neck, slowly squeezing. *"Tell me it's a lie!"*

"Isabel . . . that was before I—" He winced as the henchmen wrenched his arms higher.

"You don't deny it," she breathed in horror. "Oh, dear God . . ."

Carlos struggled to stand. He made it up. One of the men holding him kicked his foot out from under him. Carlos collapsed to his knees again and the henchmen snapped back his arms. The bald man's fist struck his jaw. Carlos's head rocked back. He groaned, then cried out, "Isabel!"

Sydenham took control. "Take this felon to Newgate prison," he ordered his men. He slid his arm around Isabel's waist. "Come home with me." Supporting her, he led her out the gate.

They yanked him to his feet and twisted him around to face the stable. He wrenched to get free. The bald man rammed an elbow into his back. Carlos gasped at the pain. The other two began to haul him toward the stable. He dug in his heels. They pried him from the spot and dragged him to the stable doorway. He kicked out a leg and slammed it stiff against the doorjamb. The bald man told the other two to step back with Carlos and hold him up. He came around to Carlos's front and plowed a fist into his belly. Carlos buckled and they let him fall to the ground on his back. They grappled his feet and dragged him through the stable doorway. His head banged over the stone threshold.

They slung him into the straw beside Isabel's horse. He lay writhing, clutching his stomach, blood dripping from his lip and nose into the straw. They stood over him. He managed to say faintly, between heaves to catch his breath, his gut on fire, "He told you .. to Newgate . . ."

The bald man sneered. "He told us something else before we come here, mate." He looked at the other two. "Resisting lawful arrest, right, lads?" Then, back at Carlos, "My master says resisting arrest be a capital offense. And if there be one thing my master do know"—he grinned as he reached for a pitchfork—"it's the bleeding law."

He hefted the pitchfork and motioned to the other two. They moved into position on either side of Carlos. Carlos made a lunge for one man's legs, wrapped his arms around him and brought him down. They wrestled on the floor, Carlos on top. The bald man kicked Carlos in the ribs. Carlos recoiled. The other two men grabbed him and rolled him onto his stomach, spread-eagled, and pinned him down by standing on his arms. Carlos groaned, the pain excruciating. From the corner of his eye he saw the bald man raise the pitchfork. He struggled frantically against the impossible weights. The pitchfork stilled for its descent, positioned above his shoulder blades.

"There he is!" a woman's voice cried.

Carlos heard many feet pounding in. The men standing on his arms staggered backward amid scuffling and curses. Carlos rolled over. He stared up in wonder. There was a brawl all around him. Captain Ross had led the attack. Ross had disarmed the bald man of the pitchfork, and seven of his royalist soldiers were tearing into Sydenham's three men. The soldiers quickly prevailed. A woman hung back nervously at the doorway—the chambermaid.

"Now get out, you whoreson dogs!" Ross growled, brandishing the pitchfork. "Or me men'll slice your throats and leave you in the ditch as the first work of the rebels!"

Sydenham's men stumbled toward the door and fled.

Ross ordered his soldiers back inside the inn. They left, but the chambermaid came to Ross's side. Together they watched Carlos struggle to his feet, clutching his bruised stomach. "I don't know what you've done, Spaniard," Ross said gruffly, "and I don't want to know. But I'm telling you, get out of London now. That high and mighty gentleman what set his curs on you is the Queen's man. I won't be seen in company with you."

Carlos spat blood and wiped more of it from his chin. He kicked at the straw, searching for his sword. When Sydenham's men had first come upon him they had tossed it somewhere here. But he could not find it. He turned to Ross. "Give me a weapon," he said weakly.

Ross snorted. "Christ, why don't you just ask for me head on a platter! Get out, I tell you. Now!"

Carlos hobbled toward Isabel's mare. She was already saddled. He untethered her and, wincing, mounted her. He looked down at Ross. "Let me have some money," he said.

Ross rolled his eyes to heaven.

The chambermaid nudged Ross. "Aw, give him a bit, Captain," she said. She nuzzled closer. "Look at him. It's like Lizzy said, they've half killed him."

Ross's eyes narrowed on Carlos. "What happened to the pile you took off me at cards last night?"

"It is inside, in my room. It is yours."

Ross considered this. "Right. Here," he said, tossing up a gold sovereign.

Carlos caught the coin. He nosed the mare around and reined her toward the door.

"Spaniard," Ross said as he wrapped his arm around the chambermaid. "Good luck."

CHAPTER TWENTY-FIVE

><

Havens

At midnight, falling snow eddied fretfully in the wind above the small Kentish town of Malling as though nervous about resting on a spot where the county's royalist troops were camped. It gusted around the towers of the castle and the former Benedictine nunnery and swirled above the market square where campfires flickered, until finally, snared by alley walls between the church and the thatched houses, and by bare trees near sheds and pigsties, it collapsed in ragged drifts. In all these shelters—castle, church, houses, and sheds—the Queen's officers, horsemen, and foot soldiers were settled for the night.

Lord Abergavenny, commander of the Kentish royal forces, tramped over the grainy snow, finishing his tour of the sentries' posts, his pace brisk against the cold. He reached the town's farthest watch fire. The half-frozen sentry, stomping for warmth by his fire, straightened as he saw the commander approach. Abergavenny gave him a curt nod and came beside him.

"All's well?"

"Aye, my lord."

Both men gazed out at the black, silent countryside and the blacker forest beyond. An owl hooted. Near a tent behind them a horse's hoof clopped on hard ground as it changed position. Then, apart from the wind rattling the bare branches of the forest like an army of chattering teeth, all was quiet.

Almost too quiet. Even the snow had stopped falling.

Though far from satisfied, Abergavenny had to acknowledge the proof of silence. He nodded good night to the sentry and started back toward the castle. He had left Southwell, the sheriff, sound asleep there, sated from his supper and mulled wine. Southwell was his relative—had married Abergavenny's niece—but Abergavenny found the man's in-

difference rankling; Southwell seemed incapable of understanding their precarious position. Not ten miles to their
north Wyatt lay snug inside Rochester with his host—over
three thousand men, at latest report, and a French-led army
already marching down from Scotland. Abergavenny expected Wyatt to attack Malling at any moment. And what
fight could the pitiful company here put up? Abergavenny
and Southwell between them had been able to attract a mere
six hundred men. Six hundred—from all of Kent! And desertions increased daily. Abergavenny's sentries at every
point around the town's edge were as much to keep his own
troops in as to keep Wyatt's out.

Up the street Abergavenny could see the three watch fires
in the market square. He passed an alehouse alley where a
skinny dog, snuffling through a rubbish heap, cringed and
watched him until he went by.

Abergavenny strode through the square. A dozen soldiers
were keeping watch. Another fifty or so, the overflow from
the crowded billets, were scattered among the roofed stalls
along the market periphery, curled inside asleep. Abergavenny smelled bacon and heard it sizzling on a stick over one
of the fires. He was aware of the sentries' eyes on him. He
did not have to glance at them to know the expressions on
those faces—the sullen, grudging looks. Most of these men
wanted only to be at home tucked up beside their warm
wives. They were not soldiers. They were yeomen, tenant
farmers, laborers, craftsmen. Abergavenny had promised
them payment by Candlemas. He groaned inwardly. Candlemas was only three days away. God only knew where he
was going to find the money, for he had inherited an estate
much encumbered by his father's debts; loyalty to the
Crown, and to the Queen's largesse, was his only hope for
the future. Yet pay them he must if he was to keep these men
from skulking back to their hearths.

He shook his head glumly. England had no standing army,
not like France. And apart from large ordnance, she had no
modern armaments either; almost a century and a half after
Agincourt, longbows and pikes were still the order of the
day. England was backward, Abergavenny grimly admitted
that. His six hundred raw recruits here could be cut to bits
in moments by a dozen mounted *landsknechts,* the famous
Continental mercenaries. And his clutch of inexperienced
young officers—in their posts through high birth, not

ability—would be able to do no more than helplessly watch the slaughter. It was true that Wyatt's force would be equally ill-trained and ill-equipped, but that was small consolation to a commander of discontented farmers, many of whom, he knew, had no quarrel with Wyatt's declaration to keep Spanish domination at bay.

He trudged on, finally breaking clear of the sullen stares in the marketplace, and headed up toward the castle. He took some comfort in the orders from Whitehall that had been delivered at supper: he was to march to Gravesend tomorrow. Good. The past three days stuck here in Malling had been three days too many. His men were restless. He would be glad to be moving.

A shout broke in on his thoughts. He halted. More shouts arose and Abergavenny heard a cry of "Treason!" He turned. The excited voices were coming from just beyond the market square. He started back down the street on the run.

"We are betrayed!" a voice wailed from a window.

In the square soldiers were scrambling out of stalls, half asleep, frightened, rummaging for weapons. House doors banged open. Partially dressed lieutenants and townsmen spilled out into the square. Dogs were barking. There was confusion everywhere.

The shouting was loudest near the middle watch fire where the words "enemy!" and "spy!" peaked above the edgy voices. Abergavenny pushed his way through the bodies toward the fire. By the flames, two soldiers held a man hostage between them. A serving man, Abergavenny judged by the man's clothing, and one who had been riding long and hard; his hooded sheepskin coat was stiff with frozen snow, and his breeches were hardened mud up to the knees. But he stood grim-faced and composed, warily eyeing the hostile faces surrounding him. He was tall, and looked strong, especially between the two jumpy young men grappling him. Behind him, a boy held the reins of the mount that the captive had apparently ridden in on, a mud-spattered bay mare, its head hanging.

"Who is this?" Abergavenny demanded.

There was a clamor of replies:

"Won't say! Claims he'll talk only to you, my lord!"

"He's Wyatt's spy!"

"Aye! Sneaking in on us in the dark!"

Above the voices, Abergavenny glanced angrily at one of

his lieutenants, a bull-necked man who was still buckling on his sword. The lieutenant took the commander's cue and shouted for silence. The cacophony hushed.

Abergavenny approached the captive. In the twitching firelight the man's gray eyes locked on his own. His lower lip and one nostril, Abergavenny noted, were crusted with dried blood, and there was a livid yellow-purple bruise on his eyebrow. "Who are you?"

"I bring news," the captive said. "An enemy force lies eight miles west."

There were widespread whispers, some of dismay, some of mistrust. "A foreigner," someone grumbled. "Listen to the way he talks!"

"What's your name?" Abergavenny asked.

"Valverde."

There were more murmurs: "What's that, Spanish?" And, "Bloody foreigner, right enough!"

Abergavenny ignored his men's comments. He spoke only to the suspect. "An enemy force? You mean Sir Henry Isley's?"

The man nodded.

"I've already had scouts' reports about Isley," Abergavenny said dismissively. "His wild little band has been raiding around Sevenoaks." He added loudly for the benefit of the more fearful among his men, "Brigands, that's all."

"More than a band," the captive said. "Five hundred strong, at least. I saw from a hill."

Abergavenny was shocked by the number. He regarded the suspect with narrowed eyes. "Have you been sent with this message from one of Her Majesty's commanders?"

The man shook his head. "I come to join you. I am a soldier." Anxious, the young conscripts restraining him tightened their grip.

Abergavenny scowled. "A soldier?" he asked derisively, glancing at the man's empty scabbard and at the winded mare, equally unburdened of arms. "With no weapons?"

The conscript who was holding the suspect's right arm sniggered. "He's come to slay us with his foreigner's garlic breath."

There was nervous laughter.

With a savage snap of his arms, the hostage elbowed one captor in the belly and shot his other elbow upward to the second man's chin, making him bite the tip of his tongue. The two young soldiers doubled over, blinking in pain and shock, the one on the left spitting blood. The suspect remained standing perfectly still between them, attempting no escape. But his very calmness after his burst of violence was frightening. He repeated in a quiet voice, like a threat, "I am a soldier."

Some of the men who had been crowding in shuffled back warily.

Abergavenny was angered. The last thing he needed was a bully eroding his men's shaky confidence. "Lieutenant!" he barked. "Interrogate this clod, then put him under guard at the castle."

"Then I talk with you?" the man said insistently to Abergavenny, even as the lieutenant came for him with sword drawn.

Abergavenny bristled at the man's audacity. He had every intention of sounding him for information after the lieutenant had softened him up, but he was damned if he would let the bastard tell him his job. "You'll do as you're bloody told!" he flared.

He was about to turn on his heel when the captive said, "Wait. I have papers." He reached inside his jerkin, pulled out a folded wad, and handed it over.

Suspicious but curious, Abergavenny unfolded the grubby, dog-eared papers and tilted them toward the firelight. They were letters of recommendation. Eight of them. He glanced over the writing, and his eyebrows lifted as he recognized several of the names as illustrious Continental commanders. He murmured, reading, "Beltran de la Cueva, Duke of Albuquerque. John Dudley, Duke of Northumberland. Jean de Lyere"—he glanced up in admiration—"de Lyere, the Emperor's mustermaster, no less." He handed back the papers, looking at the Spaniard with new interest. "Most impressive," he said. He was itching now to sign up this valuable mercenary, worth ten of his green officers. But he did not want to show his hand. Without taking his eyes from the Spaniard, he motioned to the bull-necked lieutenant. "Disperse these men," he ordered. "Then that will be all, Lieutenant."

As the soldiers shuffled back to their bedrolls, Abergavenny said, "I can use an experienced captain, Valverde. I am delighted that you've come to offer yourself to the Queen."

"What do you pay?"

Abergavenny smiled mirthlessly. "All the cold gruel you can eat."

"My fee—"

"Come, come, Valverde," Abergavenny interrupted with glacial geniality. "Let's not pretend. With your background, and with testimonials like those—especially in this hour of national crisis—you could have marched into the Queen's presence chamber at Whitehall and asked any price. Lord Howard himself would have thrown himself at your feet to get a veteran captain of cavalry like you. But instead you race down to Kent in the middle of the night and skulk into my little camp on a winded ladies' horse, with no armor, no sword, no lance, no arquebus—not even a longbow." He paused. "Just what are you running from?"

The mercenary scowled and looked away.

Abergavenny smiled, pleased to have struck home. "Come up to the castle," he said agreeably. "Tell me more about Isley's force. Then we'll talk terms."

Carlos and Abergavenny sat on stools before the hearth in the great hall, talking in low tones, while Carlos's sheepskin, spread over the firedogs, hissed softly as it dried. Behind them, over a hundred men lay sprawled in sleep on the floor. The tall torches and rushlights were all snuffed, and the high expanse under the carved rafters was dim above the low-burning fire. Carlos's head throbbed and his left ribs still ached from the blows of Sydenham's men, but his muscles, tense from his bone-chilling ride from the Anchor, were finally beginning to relax before the fire's soft waves of heat. The hot wine from the pewter goblet cupped between his hands was gradually warming his insides, too, along with the bread and leftover beef he had just wolfed down. And the martial smells—leather and damp wool, tracked-in horse dung, and the pungency of crushed straw beneath so many soldiers' bodies—were almost comforting in their familiarity. But there was a coldness deep inside him—in his very blood—which would not be thawed; something that had been frozen by the hatred in Isabel's eyes.

"So Isley has looted the armories around Tonbridge, too, eh?" Abergavenny mused bleakly. He and Carlos sat almost knee to knee, their eyes absently searching the low red flames. Carlos had told the commander almost all he had seen and heard on the way about Isley's troop of five hundred.

Carlos nodded in confirmation. "Penshurst was their last raid."

"Ah, Sir Henry Sidney's place. They'll have got a fine haul there." A shaggy deerhound bitch at Abergavenny's feet snuffled in her sleep.

"Tomorrow Isley marches to Rochester," Carlos said.

Abergavenny turned to him. "How do you know?"

"I followed two soldiers into an alehouse. They talked to the barkeep."

Abergavenny groaned. "Good God, five hundred more recruits to swell Wyatt's ranks."

Carlos was aware of a movement in the shadows behind the commander. Abergavenny seemed to sense it, too. He twisted around, his hand ready on his dagger hilt. "Who's there?" he demanded.

A wiry young man stepped forward tentatively. He was in stocking feet. "Pardon, my lord," he apologized, but Abergavenny had relaxed. "I couldn't sleep. I only wanted a closer look at the Spaniard. I think I know him."

Carlos scowled at the lad without recognition. "My nephew," Abergavenny said curtly to Carlos. "One of my lieutenants. Studying to be a lawyer."

Having got closer, the young lawyer was peering at Carlos's face. "By heaven, it *is* him!" He looked triumphantly to the commander. "My lord, did you know? This man is a hero!"

Abergavenny started in surprise. "What?"

"It was in Scotland, six years ago," the lieutenant said eagerly. "The Battle of Pinkie Cleugh. I was only twelve then, serving my lord Clinton as his page. But I saw it all. What a victory! Against such odds! And this is the very man!"

"I don't know what you're talking about, lad," Abergavenny said. "Six years ago I was fighting in France."

"Exactly!" the young man said. "The French!" He lowered his voice to keep from waking the men in the hall, but his excitement continued to shine in his face as he crouched beside his uncle and explained. "The French had entrenched themselves in Scotland all the way up the east coast, my lord. With their help the Scots had amassed a huge army. It was a perilous threat to England, you may recall. So, with some sixteen thousand men under my lord Somerset, we

marched north to meet them. We had a few hundred mercenaries from the Continent. This man was among them. He'd
brought over a company of his *swart reiters*—forty light
horse. But even with these mercenaries our army was less
than two thirds of the Scottish host.

"Well, my lord, they were waiting for us east of Edinburgh. Twenty-four thousand of them! They quickly broke
our ranks. We thought the day was lost. Some of our troops
were running for the beach, hoping for salvation from our
ships. Then"—he looked at Carlos—"this Spaniard turned
everything around. He rallied his light horsemen and they
charged. The Scots froze in amazement. The Spaniard
hauled back our artillery commander and got his guns on the
rising ground behind our line. We tore the Scots apart with
ball and hail shot. They broke and fled. We chased them and
killed them for miles back to Edinburgh. A total rout!"

Abergavenny gave Carlos an appraising smile. "Better
and better," he murmured.

The young man was now gazing at Carlos with unabashed
admiration. He stood up. "Sir," he said sheepishly, "might I
shake your hand?"

They shook. The young man grinned.

"All right, Arthur," Abergavenny said. "Get some sleep
now. Valverde and I have matters to discuss."

When he had gone, Abergavenny poured more warm wine
to refill Carlos's goblet. "So," he said, "you overheard
Isley's men talking of his plans, eh?" He spoke brusquely, as
if their earlier conversation had not been interrupted, but
Carlos heard in Abergavenny's tone a new readiness to trust
him, perhaps even to discuss tactics.

Carlos nodded. "They told the barkeep their commander
will march around you to the west, then go on to Rochester."

"Give us a wide berth, eh? To the west, you say? That
will take them through Wrotham parish." Wearily
Abergavenny rubbed his brow. "Well, I'm moving out in the
morning, too," he said with grim satisfaction. "I've just had
orders from Whitehall to march to Gravesend and rendezvous with the Duke of Norfolk. He's arrived there with a
force of eight hundred. Together, we are to strike Wyatt in
his Rochester lair before he can advance to London." He
knocked back several mouthfuls of wine.

"Eight hundred of what?" Carlos asked. "Farmers?"

Abergavenny smiled with wry understanding. "No. Men of the London bands."

Carlos nodded approval. He knew the trained London bands were the nearest thing to modern soldiers the Queen was likely to raise. "Good."

"Aye," Abergavenny agreed with relish. "Our first real chance to smash Wyatt."

Carlos shook his head. "Your first chance is here."

Abergavenny looked at him. "What?"

"Isley must pass you to get to Rochester."

"You mean . . . attack Isley?"

Carlos nodded. "Stop him."

The commander's eyes brightened with interest. "Lord, I'd like to nab him!" He gnawed his lip and mumbled, "But my orders . . ." He looked like a man torn between duty and desire. Duty won out. "Christ, Valverde, I've got less than six hundred men. They're green and they're dispirited. And more of them desert every day. To tell the truth, I can't even be sure they'd stick to a fight."

Carlos shrugged. "Must fight sometime."

Abergavenny looked tempted. "But can I risk throwing them at Isley and having them break?" He shook his head vehemently. "No. I've got to keep this force together and deliver it to Gravesend. I can't risk a defeat."

"To let the enemy pass you, that is defeat. Your men will know it. And you will let two enemy forces unite. You should stop Isley here. Deliver his head to the Queen."

Abergavenny thudded his goblet down on the stone hearth. The deerhound looked up in alarm. "Christ on the cross, you think you know it all, don't you, Spaniard? Well, this is England, not some God-cursed duchy of that mad Emperor's where you fellows have been hacking and burning and raping your way through field and town for years. We English may be backward, but, damn it, we're civilized!" He stared at Carlos belligerently. "Why the hell are you still in this country, Valverde? Why didn't you go back home with your prize money after that bravura performance in Scotland?"

For a moment Carlos said nothing. He was desperate for a commission from Abergavenny. He was a marked felon, the Essex authorities were hunting him to hang him, Sydenham wanted him dead, he had no money and no means of leaving the country. And behind him he had left a morass of failure and loss utterly foreign to him. Isabel's hatred had struck him so unexpectedly, like a shot fired out of fog. He felt the desolation of it like a ball of cold steel lodged in his chest. But he could not think about that. Surviving was the job now. His only hope was that Abergavenny would take him on. But this commander was tough, Carlos sensed; he would settle for nothing less than the truth.

"After Scotland I stayed on with a garrison in Norfolk," he answered, staring deep into the flames. "Then I worked for the Duke of Northumberland. His bodyguard. The Duke did not like giving money, so he gave me land, a manor. The Queen came on the throne and executed Northumberland, and another man claimed my manor. His lawyer used tricks, legal tricks, to steal my land. I tried to stop him." He paused. "They sent me to jail."

"For trying to hold on to your land?"

"For murder, in the courtroom."

"You killed the lawyer?"

"I should have," Carlos said darkly. He shook his head. "No. A bailiff." He looked at Abergavenny. It was better to get it all over with quickly. "In jail I killed again."

"A prisoner?"

"The jailer."

Abergavenny whistled softly through his teeth. "So you've escaped, and you're a wanted man," he said, piecing it together. "And I can give you protection, is that it?"

Carlos looked the commander steadily in the eye. "This is my offer. I will fight for you, lead your cavalry. No payment. But in return you will arrange for me a ..." The English word stubbornly eluded him. He frowned in annoyance. "From the Queen," he said, looking to Abergavenny for help in finding the word, "a forgiving ..."

"A pardon?" Abergavenny suggested with quiet relish.

"*Sí.* A pardon."

Abergavenny took up his goblet again and thoughtfully swirled the contents. He murmured, "A pardon is not impossible, of course." He smiled. "You also need a decent trained horse and weapons, don't you?" He lifted the goblet in the gesture of a toast and chuckled. "My, you're going to be rather in my debt, aren't you, Valverde?"

Abergavenny knocked back the last of his wine and stood. His voice turned cold. "So let's first see if you're worth it. Tomorrow, we'll ride out to intercept Isley at Wrotham, just as you suggest. Bring me his head, and a few of his officers in chains. Then you'll get your pardon."

"And your father's London associates in the wool trade?" Edward Sydenham asked amiably as his knife sank into a yielding fillet of poached bream. "What names shall I give my steward?" He brought a bite of the fish to his mouth. It was delicious—one of his cook's best dishes—succulent yet flaky, bathed in a satiny sauce that was lemon-yellow with saffron and piquant with wine.

Isabel glanced up from her plate over whose rim she listlessly balanced her knife, its tip prodding the white flesh of the fish. She had barely touched her food, Edward noted. "Calthrop," she answered tonelessly. "Master Calthrop is his London agent. And there are some gentlemen . . . his friends at Blackwell Hall, the wool market . . ." Her voice drifted. Her eyes trailed down again to the undisturbed food. She stared at the knife tip coated with the creamy sauce.

Above them five musicians in the gallery at the end of Edward's great hall discreetly played a gentle medley of ballads.

"A glass of malmsey, perhaps?" Edward suggested hopefully. She had taken no more than a sip of the Rhenish wine before her. "It's a fine one, sent over by the Venetian Ambassador."

She blinked up at him. "Thank you, sir, but no."

Edward waited. It would not do to pressure her.

"At Blackwell Hall," she resumed with sudden vigor, as though to pretend her reverie had not intervened, "you will find a Master Lockhart, a wool merchant. He lives in Bishopsgate Street. I visited him there once with my parents . . ." Her eyes drifted toward a candle flame. Edward was afraid he was again losing her to her melancholy. "But I believe, sir," she said, staring at the flames, "there is another friend my father would seek out first, before these men. He—"

Startled, she looked up at the musicians. They had launched into a galliard, a sprightly dance tune. It had broken the fragile mood of languor with which Edward had hoped to soothe her. He angrily clapped his hands to silence the musicians. A decaying spiral of sound wheezed from their pipes and lutes and rebecks. Annoyed, Edward waved a hand at their leader, dismissing them. The musicians quietly shuffled out.

"Forgive me, mistress. You were saying?"

"The landlord of the Crane Inn. Master Legge. He is my father's friend."

"Ah. And the Crane would be a fine spot to hide in, so busy a place."

"Yes. I'll go there in the morning."

"I shall accompany you."

"No."

"Pardon?"

"It is best if I go alone, sir. Master Legge, as I say, is a friend, and if he knows my father is wanted for treason he will certainly not consider *you,* a lieutenant of the Queen, a friend. If he is hiding my father he may not speak if you are present."

"Very well," Edward conceded. "But if your father is there, send me a message instantly. I have a meeting at Whitehall in the morning, but believe me I can drop everything to come and assist you both out to a ship and to safety."

"I shall. Thank you." She said it with a simple sincerity that Edward found quite moving.

"Now, we should also be checking with the relative you mentioned. Your late aunt's husband is it? I know you said this uncle lives a long way out, in Somerset. Nevertheless, it's worth—" He stopped. Palmer was clearing his throat from the doorway. Edward frowned at the interruption. "Pardon me, Mistress Thornleigh," he said. "My steward requires a word with me."

The exchange with Palmer outside the door was enough to take away Edward's appetite. He returned to the table. "That Spaniard," he said to Isabel, sitting heavily. "After we left the Anchor he . . . escaped custody."

Isabel's knife clattered to her plate. She looked up. Her face was very pale.

"What's more," Edward added, "he has stolen your horse."

She did not bother looking around the bedchamber to examine her new quarters. She had tasks to do; she did not want anything distracting her. First, she sat at the desk and wrote out the list of names and addresses Sir Edward would need of her father's friends and associates. She worked at this, forcing all other thoughts at bay, while the young maid quietly bustled to prepare the chamber. The girl refueled the silver brazier with coals to radiate a soft glow of heat. She untied the gold silk cords that held the bed's crimson damask curtains, and turned down its crimson silk coverlet. She closed the figured shutters on the mullioned window that overlooked Sir Edward's quiet back garden. She left the basket of clean rags that Isabel had requested, for her monthly flow had begun. Its arrival, among her welter of worries, had brought a great relief; the alternative its absence had threatened, since Mosse's penetration, was a dread Isabel had been living with for a week. She finished writing the list and asked the maid to carry it down to Sir Edward. The girl took it, bobbed a curtsy, and left.

Now she was alone. Carefully, meticulously, she laid out on the bed her meager belongings fetched from the Anchor by Sir Edward's servant. Her blue gown, still soiled from the Fleet prison . . . with Carlos. Stiffly she laid the gown aside on a chair. Perhaps Sir Edward's housekeeper could see to its cleaning.

She carried the other few items to the carved cherrywood chest left open for her convenience by the maid. Kneeling at the chest, its lining fragrant with cedarwood, she set in her belongings. Her hairbrush. Her depleted purse. Her mother's book, its two brass clasps securely fastened. These things were all she had left of home. The tunic she had brought for her father was gone, traded for the sheepskin . . . for Carlos. The shirt she had brought for her father was gone. Carlos was wearing it. She shut the chest.

She stood still in the middle of the room, forcing her mind ahead. Was there nothing more to do? No. Yes, she must sleep. That was important. She tugged off her clothes and finished her *toilet*. She needed rest, for tomorrow there was much to do.

Think only of sleep. Blow out the candle. Pull down the sheet. Climb into the bed. Think only of tomorrow: the Crane, to fetch Father, the Flemish ship to send him away, then off to Ambassador de Noailles. Receive his information to take to Sir Thomas Wyatt. Yesterday Wyatt had said, "Come again as soon as possible." Much to do.

The down pillow was plump and soft. The linen sheets were perfumed with the scent of roses. Everything here was elegant and restrained. Like Sir Edward himself, she thought. *Everything the opposite of Carlos.*

Eyes closed. Think only of the challenges tomorrow. Challenges to face alone. She would make use of Sir Edward's kindness and generosity, yes, but she knew she was alone.

Make use? *"This man has used you in the hope of reaching your father, to murder him."*

And now he had escaped custody.

Eyes open, she lay in the shaft of bright moonlight that knifed its way through the crack between the shutters, a beam to spy on her privacy. On her misery. He had escaped. The man she had trusted. The man whose hands had touched all the secret places of her body. She hated him. Every part of her hated him—the man who was pledged to kill her father.

CHAPTER TWENTY-SIX

><•><•○•><•<

The Ambush

Early the next morning Isabel stood on busy Thames Street across from the Crane Inn. The bright paint on its overhanging sign—a depiction of one of the three famous loading cranes on the river—glinted at her through the morning fog. In the alley beside the Crane a tiny fire sparked, tended by a knot of beggars hunkered around it. A young woman hustled past Isabel holding two squirming geese by their bound feet.

Isabel was about to step across the street, but had to wait as a troop of armed London Guildsmen marched by, their new white coats ablaze with the cross of St. George on breast and back; the uniform had given rise to their name, "Whitecoats." She closely watched them, counting them, knowing she must soon report all she saw to Wyatt. A flock of boys zigzagged after the Whitecoats, chanting falsetto war cries and brandishing sticks as swords. Isabel wished the real soldiers readying to attack Wyatt's army could be armed with nothing more than such sticks, but on the contrary, there was much evidence of frantic royalist preparation. The Queen's nobles, finally committing themselves, were drawing more of their men as soldiers into the city every day, and arming them formidably, it seemed to Isabel. Their tramping boots and cries of muster could be heard in all of London's wards and, in the fields beyond the city walls, the blasts of cannon, too, as artillery officers tested their guns. A faint, acrid odor of the burnt gunpowder drifted constantly in the air. Now very pungent, it flashed into Isabel's mind a memory of Lord Grenville's gun flaring in orange sparks and black powder before her mother's face. A hateful memory, but one that jolted her back to her purpose here this morning: to reach her father. She hurried across the street.

Inside, the Crane's common room was humming with

guests and travelers busily eating breakfast despite the rebellion crisis. Isabel gave a servant boy her name and sent him to fetch Master Legge. She hardly had time to shake the snow from her hem before the landlord pushed through the kitchen door wiping his hands on a cloth.

Leonard Legge was a man with the physique of a wrestler gone to fat. Below his bald crown, thick white hair hung to his shoulders, its blanched color in stark contrast to his florid face, livid as a beet, heightened this morning from his exhortations to the scullery boys in the kitchen. Seeing Isabel, he strode toward her and silently folded her in his beefy arms.

She drank in the familiarity of his fleshy warmth and oniony aroma. Though she did not know the origins of his friendship with her father, she had, years ago, always clamored to be included in her parents' visits to London, for Legge's brood of intrepid grandchildren made exciting playmates, and Legge's wife could be counted on to treat the children, including Isabel, with all the honeyed apples and candied apricots they wanted.

"Poor little Isabel." Legge's deep bass voice was a rumble of sympathy.

His tone told her that he knew—knew everything. Hope buoyed her. She pulled out of his embrace. "He's here, isn't he?"

Legge held a thick finger of warning to his lips and jerked his chin toward the chattering guests. Tossing his dirty cloth onto a table, he whispered, "Come," and started toward a door. Isabel followed.

The door led to a staircase, then up to Legge's small counting room. It lay in gloom, with heavy velvet curtains drawn across the window to mask it—and the inn's strongbox—from any curious eyes in neighbors' bedroom windows. Only a crack between the curtains admitted a spill of the morning light. Isabel quickly took in the room with a feeling of frustration: they were alone here. There was nothing but Legge's counting table, his ledgers, and his brass-bound strongbox. She waited for him. With the door half shut, he was craning out to check the stairwell.

She could wait no longer. "Master Legge, please! Take me to my father!"

He shut the door quickly and turned. "He *was* here, Isabel. He's gone now."

The gloom seemed to press in on her chest, a flat hand of disappointment. "When?"

"At first light this morning."

While she was rising from her soft bed at Sydenham's house! If only she had come here immediately yesterday, not sat at his sumptuous table last night, brooding and waiting for morning!

"Child," Legge went on anxiously, "he's weak as a colt. He came here staggering with fever. I tucked him up and ladled some broth into him and he slept a sleep like death the whole long day and night. Finally, in the wee hours this morning, his fever broke. The worst was over. Still, he needed rest, anyone could see that. But, no, soon after dawn . . ." With his hand he made a vague motion of flight toward the door and helplessly shook his head. "I could not stop him."

"But where has he gone?"

Legge shrugged his ignorance. Then anger flared over his face. "Stubborn old bear," he said. "I told him he was in no condition to leave. But he was bound to walk out of here whether I said aye or nay, walk right out into the snow. So"—he threw up his hands with a sigh—"I gave him a horse and warm clothes, and he lit out."

"But where to?"

"Child, I know not."

"Oh, please think, Master Legge! I must reach him! He is in terrible danger. From the Queen's men, no less! Where could he have gone?"

At her mention of danger, Legge's look of exasperation turned to deep concern. "He would tell me nothing, Isabel. Except . . ." His voice trailed off.

"Yes?" she asked eagerly. "Except what?"

"It was strange. He said there was something he had to do . . . for your mother." He paused to swallow the lump in his throat. "Honor Thornleigh," he murmured, clearly shaken. "Yes, your father told me what happened. What a terrible, terrible thing."

Isabel looked away to shield herself from the weight of his sympathy. She could not let self-pity drag her down now. "Do something for my mother?" she asked. "What could he mean?"

"I have no idea."

"Master Legge, I *must* find him. If you hear anything

from him—or anything about him—please let me know immediately. I am staying . . . with a friend." She told him the address.

He nodded. But he was looking at her in a mournful abstracted way. "It's passing strange," he said. "Years ago, your father and I searched across the Low Countries for your mother, searched through the bodies and the rubble of Münster, afraid that she was dead. Bad times, bad times! And now, here you are, searching for *him*." He crooned sadly, "Poor little Isabel."

She stiffened. No one had ever told her that, about searching Münster for her mother. She felt a stab of the same resentment that had struck when Adam had revealed to her their parents' hidden past: no one had ever told her anything. But more of the pieces were falling into place. "You were part of their secret work, weren't you?" she said. "In the old days?"

He nodded. A smile of pride curved his fleshy lips. "It was I who hoisted her up from the burning stake onto my horse. And all the while your father railed from the church tower like Satan, scattering those fools below." He sighed. "The priests had done their worst to your mother that day, but, by God, once up behind me and galloping off on my mount she hung on to me like a burr! That was Honor Thornleigh—unshakable."

They stood for a moment in silence. A cannon boomed from Finsbury Field. "I must go," Isabel said suddenly.

Legge laid a heavy hand on her shoulder. "Be careful, child. This renegade Wyatt is on his way. If he breaches the city walls, no Londoner will be safe in his bed." He glanced uneasily at his strongbox with its heavy lock. "Wyatt's rabble will fall to sack and pillage and"—he gave Isabel a look fraught with anxiety—"and worse. However," he added stoutly, "the Queen's forces gain strength every hour. And we Londoners who have families and property to protect, we too will do our duty."

Isabel felt a chill. How could she tell anymore who were friends and who were foes? People's loyalties seemed to cross and tangle like outstretched hands in a mob groping for help. In the thicket she could no longer see clearly. Only duty was keeping her on course.

And she had hers to perform, to Wyatt and to Martin. Sir Edward, she decided, must continue the search for her fa-

ther; his agents could cover far more territory, and cover it
far more quickly, than she could. Meanwhile, she must go to
Ambassador de Noailles. She moved to the door.

Legge's puzzled voice reached her. "I don't understand
how you come to be in London, child. Your father told me
he ordered you and Adam to sail to Antwerp."

"Adam went. I stayed."

"In this dangerous time? Against your father's express
command?"

"To save his life!" She snapped the words at him in a rush
of anger, but she knew that the anger was better aimed at
herself: wallowing in despondency at Sir Edward's, she had
missed her father by mere hours!

Legge was smiling at her in an odd, mournful way. "Like
your mother," he murmured. "Just like your mother."

"Sir Henry!" Martin St. Leger shouted. He kicked his
horse's flanks as he galloped along the road's edge, passing
the long column of foot soldiers as they trudged through the
morning fog. Martin cantered toward the rear of the column
with his horse's harness jangling. Clots of mud spewed back
from its hooves and spattered the soldiers. One man, wiping
mud from his cheek, grumbled an oath after Martin, then
darted a sheepish look at the priest marching beside him. Father Robert St. Leger let the man's blasphemy pass, but
without breaking his stride he looked over his shoulder to
watch his brother gallop past.

"Sir Henry!" Martin called again. He could just make out
the commander's mist-shrouded figure at one side of the
road near the end of the line, but Martin's voice had not
carried that far above the tromp of marching feet.

Sir Henry Isley, on horseback, was scratching out a dispatch with a quill, using his thigh to support the paper. Beside him a mounted lieutenant who had provided the writing
materials waited, along with a courier who sat astride the
fast pony that would carry him and the commander's dispatch to Rochester ahead of the main body.

Martin reached Isley and reined his mount to an ungainly
halt of thudding hooves. Stilled, the horse heaved bellows
breaths that made its leather cinch creak and crackle. It
snorted steam into the moist air. Martin was panting, too, after his scouting foray. He had ridden hard the whole eight

miles back from Malling. "Sir," he said, "Lord Abergavenny left Malling two hours ago!"

"Good," Isley grunted. Laboriously he scrawled his signature, then shoved the dispatch at the courier. The courier bounded off on his pony. Isley tossed the quill to the lieutenant, who pulled away to shout at a straggle of soldiers who were falling behind.

"St. Leger," Isley said, frowning at an overloaded wagon that lumbered by, "go and organize that munitions detail." The wagon's cargo of arms clattered as its wheels sloshed through a muddy pothole. "They'll capsize it at that rate, the fools."

Martin hesitated. He was watching the courier gallop into the obscurity of the mist. Half of the marching column, too, had disappeared into it. As he looked, his brother's erect body was swallowed by the fog. "Sir Henry," Martin ventured, "may I speak?"

Isley turned to him. "What is it?"

Martin wiped flecks of mud from his lips, salty with his sweat. "I think Abergavenny means to engage us. On the road ahead."

"What? Nonsense. He's on his way to Gravesend to meet the Duke of Norfolk's Whitecoats. He'll be there by dark." Having finished his effort with pen and paper, Isley was stuffing his hand back into his gauntlet.

"I know our man in his camp told us that, sir. But I saw signs of their departure that lead me to believe otherwise."

"Signs? What d'ye mean, boy? What signs?"

"Their food wagons did not leave with them. The wagons were just starting out when I reached the town. Why would they split up unless the fighting force wanted to get away quickly—to meet us?"

Isley considered this. "Did you hear anything from the townspeople?"

Martin shook his head. "No one would say, of course. They've been cowed. Except—and this is another odd thing—a smith told me he'd been wakened before dawn to fix rivets on a slew of breastplates. Why prepare armor with such haste unless they thought a fight was imminent? There are smiths aplenty in Gravesend."

"But you didn't actually see Abergavenny's army, did you? See him in our path?"

"No, sir. But I hurried back on the main road, knowing

you'd want confirmation of his departure. The idea of his intercepting us only occurred to me on the way."

"Well, don't let it excite you, my boy," Isley said complacently. "He doesn't know we're heading through Wrotham Parish. How could he?" He grappled his reins, the matter concluded. "No, he's well on his way to Gravesend by now, depend on it. Now go see to those munitions dolts. They—"

He broke off. Another scout was galloping furiously toward them down the Wrotham road. The scout's face was ashen under its speckling of mud. "Sir Henry!" he cried.

Isley and Martin glanced at each other. The scout's expression could only mean bad news.

No noise came from Abergavenny's motionless army ranged out on either side of Barrow Green, nothing but the faint sounds of waiting: the soft clack of arrows being joggled in a quiver, the jingle of a horse's harness as it shook its head, the occasional cough. The road through Wrotham Parish passed over Barrow Green, and with Carlos's advice Abergavenny had expertly positioned his men just inside the woods that rimmed the field; the cavalry and half the infantry sat on one side of the road, the remainder of infantry on the other. It was a perfect spot for an ambush. Every eye was fixed on the road that led out of the close-packed trees where the rising ground mist lay shredded among the jagged boughs. Abergavenny's scout who had ridden south had reported back that Isley's whole force was moving ahead quickly. Any moment now they would march into the trap.

Carlos sat his horse—a fine, mettlesome roan gelding borrowed from Abergavenny—and stretched his right knee in the stirrup to ease the pain that cold, damp weather like this always inflicted. His bruised side still ached, too. But his eyes were focused on the row of cavalry to his left, ranged just inside the trees. He was mentally checking their gear, their expressions, the nervousness they had imparted to their mounts—calculating which men he could rely on and which would freeze in action. There were forty-two horsemen in all. They were yeomen or gentlemen of Kent, some young, some middle-aged, all freshly recruited into this cobbled-together company, and all, except a mere handful of the older ones who had seen service in France, untried in battle. Carlos had had no more than three hours in a torch-lit predawn field outside Malling to train them.

A sound snapped the silence—a rook flapping up from a tall pine to the south, rattling the branch beneath it. Half the soldiers edging the field stiffened with fright. One of the horses shied and whinnied. Its rider had difficulty keeping it in line. Another horseman nervously crossed himself. Carlos shook his head. Voices beside him commented softly:

"Think the rebels are mustering rooks now?"

"That's all they can attract, I warrant."

These whispered jests had come from the two young men sitting their horses to Carlos's right, his new lieutenants. Wentworth was a calm, flat-nosed farmer. Swift was a lanky, thatch-haired yeoman's son. Though farmers, both of them rode like they were born in the saddle, and both listened well and learned quickly. Carlos had handpicked them, passing over the haughty sons of the gentry. Surprisingly, the even haughtier officer who had been the cavalry captain had stepped aside without protest when Abergavenny had installed Carlos in his place. Carlos suspected that the man, as untried as his recruits, had been secretly relieved.

The company waited for two hours. The mist cleared. The morning became overcast, dull, and still. There was no sign of Isley.

The men became restless. Carlos watched with mounting disgust as the infantry lines began to fray. Some men squatted to rest their legs, weary of standing. In one unit, a few archers had moved over to the fletcher's cart, pretending their arrows or bowstrings needed repair, and were lounging there. On either side of the field, among both infantry and cavalry, men began to chatter quietly.

Exasperated, Abergavenny trotted his high-stepping mount up beside Carlos. "Where the devil is Isley?" he hissed. "Blast his eyes, what would make him stop his march so soon after leaving his camp?"

Carlos said nothing. His gaze had been drawn to a broad hill about two miles to the north, its bare crown just visible above the wooded fringe around Barrow Green. When they had arrived here, Abergavenny had told him that the road to Rochester followed that mound, called Wrotham Hill. Now, Carlos suggested quietly, "Send another scout."

"Why?" Abergavenny snapped. "The last one hasn't even come back yet." His horse lowered its head to cough. Abergavenny tugged back the reins so fiercely that the horse grimaced in pain at the pinching bit.

"Not south," Carlos said. He pointed north toward the hill. "That way."

Martin St. Leger threw back his head and laughed. The relief was exhilarating, just like the light wind that eddied around him on the slope of Wrotham Hill, ruffling his hair as he watched his company of soldiers below him slowly moving up the hill. He had pulled off his steel helmet to let the breeze chill his sweaty scalp. He admitted now that he had been afraid; it had given him no satisfaction back there to find his suspicions about Abergavenny proved right. He only thanked God that the scout had reported the planned ambush in time, and that Isley had instantly recalled the courier bound for Wyatt. Nevertheless, this last hour had been tense.

All during the difficult march in a wide arc around Barrow Green, on a track little used even in summer, and tortuous in winter—half slippery muck, half iron-hard ruts—Martin had been nervously watching the trees that had hemmed in the slow-moving company on either side. He had been afraid every moment that Abergavenny's soldiers would fall upon their rear. But they had reached the foot of Wrotham Hill unhindered, and had flowed smoothly back onto the road to Rochester, and Abergavenny was miles behind them now. Isley's whole company—four hundred sixty foot soldiers, twenty-five horsemen, munitions wagons, and mule carts—was advancing confidently up the long slope. The tramp and jangle of their marching rang with a fresh vigor.

In sheer delight Martin kicked his heels against his horse's flanks and bounded down to join the company. As he trotted past Robert, Martin grinned at him. Robert smiled back and nodded his head in approval.

Martin sought out the commander, for he was longing to get Isley's permission to let fly the company's pennons now that they were in the clear. The breeze, he told himself with a smile, had risen like a victory celebration, bidding them to rejoice in their success. They had given Abergavenny the slip.

Carlos sat his horse at the head of the stilled cavalry ranks, fuming. It had been a good half hour since the scout, sent north at Carlos's urging, had galloped back to report that Isley had evaded the ambush. The scout had seen the churned up track in the woods where Isley's company had passed Barrow Green. But, *madre de Dios,* it was taking longer to kick this mess of farmers into marching order to pursue the enemy than it would to hustle dead-drunk soldiers out of a whorehouse.

Carlos's cavalry was waiting at the northern edge of Barrow Green where the road fed into the woods. Behind them, the field was a scene of confusion. Right where the road funneled into the trees, a rut had snagged the wheel of a fletcher's cart. The cart had toppled, and infantrymen were picking their way around the spilled litter of arrows and longbows. Others were jammed up behind the bottleneck. The cavalry, clear of the mess, was waiting—Carlos's swift commands had resulted in a reasonably orderly falling in of their ranks—but this rabble of infantry, he thought, was hopeless. No one was moving out.

Irritably Carlos scratched his neck above the too-small steel cuirass. This breastplate, too, was on loan from Abergavenny, like the horse, sword, and demilance. And like his freedom, Carlos thought bitterly. Abergavenny had made it clear that any hope of a pardon depended on the success of this engagement against Isley.

Carlos glanced around at the thick trees. From here he could no longer see Wrotham Hill to the north. He pulled away from the cavalry ranks, edged around the chaotically milling infantrymen, and trotted out into the middle of the field again. Nearby, Abergavenny and a young captain were badgering the scout. Carlos looked back toward the hill. No movement there. The enemy must still be somewhere in the woods between this field and the hill. It was not too late to pursue. If only Abergavenny would move.

"How could you possibly lose his trail!" Abergavenny ranted at the scout. "He's got five hundred men trampling the earth!"

"Not lose him exactly, my lord," the scout defended himself. "But there's three or four tracks in the trees yonder. They branch out beyond where I saw he'd passed. He might be on any one of them. His people are from hereabouts. They know these woods."

"My lord," the young captain ventured bleakly, "Isley might even be *over* Wrotham Hill by now. If so, we'll never catch him with a lead like that."

"Christ on the cross," Abergavenny growled, "he'll be halfway to Rochester by the time we can stumble onto his trail!"

"Hoy!" someone cried from the wreckage at the bottleneck. A mule had got loose and was running for the field. Men picking up broken arrows stumbled out of its way.

In exasperation Carlos threw his head back to suck in an angry breath. And then, from the corner of his eye, he caught the wild splashes of color on distant Wrotham Hill. Threads of red that flicked like tiny vipers' tongues. Pennons.

He tugged the reins to bring his horse around for a clear view. There was no mistake. Not yet at the crown of the hill—edging just above the treetop fringe of Barrow Green—were eight or nine pennons, snapping in the breeze above a company of soldiers.

Carlos did not hesitate. He dug his heels into his horse's flanks as he called out to Abergavenny and pointed at the hill, "There!" He bolted past Abergavenny and galloped up to the waiting line of cavalry.

"Don't be daft, Robert," Martin said with a laugh. "Of course we must be married by you."

Martin proudly sat his mount beside his brother who marched at the edge of the company. The forward part of the troop, the great bulk of it, where Martin and Robert were, had reached a broad plateau on the hill, and had settled into an easy stride on the flatter ground. "Isabel wants you to officiate," Martin added. "And so do I." He smiled, his eyes on the fluttering red pennons ahead, his mind on Isabel.

"Believe me, nothing would make me happier," Robert insisted. "But you must face facts, Martin. To the present English Church I am an outcast because I have a wife. If I conduct the ceremony, will your marriage be legal? Will it be sanctioned? This is what you must consider."

"You're one of God's priests," Martin said with confidence, turning his helmet in his free hand. Both it and the brigandine he wore were spoils from their Sevenoaks raids. "You were anointed with holy oil by the hand of the Bishop. No half-Spanish papist can undo that fact, Queen or no."

Robert's admonition was swift and stern. "Parliament can, Martin." He sighed and shook his head sadly. "And I confess, I know not what *God's* word on your union would be."

"Going to marry are you, sir?" the man marching beside Robert asked, looking up at Martin.

Martin grinned. "That's right, Dawes. Just as soon as you and I have swept the Spaniards out."

"Well, sir," the man replied, scratching a chin stubbled with silvery fuzz, "marrying looks good to the man that's roaring to get into it. But marrying can be a trial for the man that's been some time *settled* in it. Now, if there's a chance that the vows you're about to take be not fast in the eyes of the Lord, like the good Father here says, my advice is, jump at that chance." He winked at Martin. "There's many a man who'd dance and sing, waking up of a morning to find his marriage chain's been broke."

Martin laughed. "I'll never be one of those, you can—"

He did not finish. An odd sound was being carried on the breeze. Or rather, it was no sound at all, more like a stopping of all the sounds of the hill. Martin twisted in his saddle. The company behind had halted. Martin stood in his stirrups, still looking over his shoulder. The rump of the column on the slope had halted, too. In the silence of the soldiers' unmoving feet, a low, deep thudding reverberated. Martin felt its vibration tremble up his horse's bones and tingle his backbone. The dull drumming blended with another low sound from the soldiers at the lip of the plateau—a hum of fear. Martin yanked his horse around. As he saw where the thudding was coming from, his helmet slipped from his grip and tumbled to the ground. Enemy cavalry was storming up the hill.

"Archers!" Martin yelled the command. His voice clashed with the shouts of other officers. "Archers!" they cried.

But in the forest of frozen foot soldiers, only scattered handfuls of men were obeying the order. They whipped arrows from their quivers, pulled taut their bowstrings, and let the arrows fly. But the paltry barrage fell like a sprinkle of water on a house afire. The cavalrymen's charge came on unbroken. Their line thundered up the slope, swords high, lances out-thrust—a bristling, monstrous wave rolling implacably uphill. There was a moment more of stunned immobility from Isley's foot soldiers. And then they broke.

They ran sideways across the plateau in both directions. Even Isley's horsemen galloped headlong to escape. Martin tried to hold steady his panicked mount as the tide of stampeding men streamed around him. He could no longer see Robert.

The enemy cavalry burst up over the lip of the plateau. On the flat ground their advance became unstoppable. The man leading the charge shot out his lance to the right in a gesture of command, and half his horsemen swung around in an arc to contain the foot soldiers running toward that eastward side. Cornered, Isley's men turned on their heels and started to tear westward across the plateau. The horsemen stormed after them. They reached the fleeing men. The attackers' swords came hacking down. They were merciless. The victims staggered, toppled, wailed, and bled.

Martin's ears rang with the screams all around him. He held high his sword while trying to tug his horse around. He looked frantically for Robert. If he could just haul Robert up behind him they could gallop out of this massacre. The westward slope led down to forest. The horsemen would not follow into those dense woods.

As Martin finally turned his horse, a foot soldier stumbled toward him, his arm severed at the elbow, and crashed into the horse's chest. Crimson jets spurted from the elbow. Terrified by the smell of the blood, Martin's horse reared. "Martin, look out!" It was Robert's voice.

Martin twisted in the saddle. Robert stood behind him. Unarmed, he was pointing a warning. Martin twisted back to look. A horseman was bearing down on him with a lance outstretched. Its tip glistened with blood. Martin knew he had to move fast, but he could not leave Robert unarmed. He whipped around and tossed Robert his sword. Robert caught it. Martin kicked his horse, making it spring sideways out of the path of the attacker, then swung around to go back for Robert.

But the horseman, too, was now heading for Robert. His ramrod-stiff lance was aimed at Robert's chest. Robert stood erect. He raised the sword—a strong man whose early martial training surfaced automatically. He watched the oncoming horseman, ready for him. Then, he looked down at the blade as if with a sudden horrified realization of what he was about to do. He tossed the sword to the ground. Martin heard the horseman's grunt of surprise. His lance wavered downward. It plunged into Robert's belly. The horseman expertly yanked the lance out from its target of flesh, twisting Robert's body around like a weather vane, then galloped on, engulfed in the morass of flailing cavalry and their falling victims.

"Robert!" Martin bounded toward him. His brother was rocking on the spot, his hands spread over his bleeding abdomen. Martin came alongside him and reached down. "Take my hand! I'll pull you up!"

Robert lifted one bloody hand, but a spasm made him double over, both hands again gripping his belly. Martin snatched a handful of Robert's collar but it was impossible to haul him that way up onto the horse.

Martin swung his leg over the horse's neck and jumped off. Keeping hold of the reins with one hand, he threw his arm around Robert's waist. He was trying to lift Robert's foot into the stirrup when Robert lurched back in pain. The reins slipped out of Martin's hand. The riderless horse reared up, disoriented, and bolted out of the fray.

Holding Robert, Martin looked about wildly. All around them their comrades were falling and writhing and screaming under the cavalry's savage attack. But a good number had broken free, and were running, spilling down the westward hillside. Martin and Robert staggered after them. They made it over the lip of the plateau and started down the slope, stumbling over rocks, slipping in icy gravel, desperately heading toward the sanctuary of the forest at the foot of the hill.

"Wentworth!" Carlos yelled above the clamor of the slaughter. "Halt your men!"

"Impossible, sir!" the young lieutenant called back. "I've tried!"

Carlos had tried, too. He felt almost hoarse from yelling the order to capture, not kill. There was no need any longer to kill. The rout was complete. Abergavenny would soon be along, and if he wanted to execute the prisoners, fine; Carlos's job was to capture them.

But the loyal gentlemen of Kent were out of control. Though less than fifty of Isley's foot soldiers remained standing the killing went on. A pair of horsemen had pinned a helpless soldier between their mounts and were taking turns maiming and blinding him. One horseman slowly chased an exhausted soldier who ran in zigzags like a stunned hare. Another, dismounted, stood over a dying foot soldier and hacked at his legs.

Carlos spat out some grit. He knew there was no way to stop the carnage. He had not had enough time to establish his authority with these inexperienced men. Besides, he had seen this kind of thing before; nothing was more vicious than countryman killing countryman. The frenzy had to run its course.

He cantered to the westward edge of the plateau to investigate. Many of the enemy were escaping down the hill to the woods. As he watched, several more disappeared into the trees. Carlos cantered back to Wentworth and told him to take some men and go after the escapees. "Capture," Carlos ordered. "Kill if they resist." The lieutenant rode off.

Carlos looked back at the butchery with contempt. He was unsettled, too, by an incident during the attack. A foot soldier he had charged had stood firm, sword in hand, but then, at the last moment, had tossed away his sword. Too late, though, for Carlos to break his charge. With only a heartbeat until impact Carlos moved his lance, but only succeeded in deflecting his strike from the man's heart—a quick kill—to his belly. Carlos scowled at the recollection. Inflicting a belly wound was novice's work. He did not like making such mistakes.

He caught sight of the horseman who had been chasing the exhausted soldier in circles. The victim had collapsed on his back over a dead mule, and lay in impotent terror while his tormentor ripped open his breeches with his lance tip and prodded at his genitals. Carlos kicked his horse and charged. Pulling up beside the horseman, he lifted his foot high and kicked him out of the saddle. The man thudded to the ground and thrashed in the mire of muck and blood.

Carlos looked around. The mayhem was finally abating. The battle was over. And despite his disdain for the pointlessly cruel aftermath, he was satisfied with the outcome, an unqualified victory.

Carlos had earned his pardon.

Martin had never known such merciless cold, nor such despairing darkness.

For hours he and Robert had been hiding in the forest, huddling in the V of two huge fallen tree trunks. Hardened snow lay around them, its crust as brittle as glass. Above, dense branches and thick clouds blotted the moon. Only a ghostly sheen of silver limned the bare trees and the woodland undergrowth, like a film of cold, white ash.

Martin's back was pressed against the icy tree trunk and Robert lay sprawled in his arms. Martin's body no longer responded to the commands of his mind. His teeth chattered uncontrollably, and every muscle twitched in ceaseless shivers. But he knew his misery was nothing compared to his brother's. He had pulled Robert between his legs and thrown his arms around his shoulders, hugging him, hoping the heat of his own body might dull the edge of Robert's suffering. It had not.

Robert lay on his back, his head lolling on Martin's chest. His agony was terrifying to watch—a constant shivering punctuated by spasms from his belly that made him buckle and writhe, groping his abdomen. After the spasm he would lie in exhaustion, gasping for breath. But soon the gasping itself brought another spasm, and he would buckle again in agony. And so it had gone for hours, an endless circle of anguish, with no rest, no oblivion, like a torment conceived by Satan himself.

"... and Willy's birthday is next month, isn't it? He'll be two?" Martin voice was hoarse from carrying on his desperate monologue in Robert's ear. For an hour he had babbled on about Robert's children and other family matters praying that such talk would soothe his brother's fevered mind. It had not.

"... and I know Isabel has sewed Willy a lace cap ..." Martin heard the slurring of his own words from the cold. He raged inwardly at this further loss of control. He needed strength to watch over Robert until dawn. In the light, he would surely be able to find some woodsman's hut where he could get help to carry Robert back and tend his wound. But not tonight. In this darkness he would get lost, and then Robert, left alone ... No, tonight Martin dared not move.

His head thudded back in exhaustion against the iron-cold bark. With every breath, cold air stabbed his lungs, needled his skull. Inside his icy leather boot, his right foot felt frozen. Earlier, he had taken off his stocking and used it to plug Robert's wound, trying to stanch the incessant flow, the blood oozing over Martin's hands. Now, the stocking was soaked, Martin's right toes were numb, and his hands were ice-cold with Robert's blood.

Martin looked up at the black branches and tried not to

listen to the frightful sounds among the trees. The woods were full of the groans of wounded, dying men. Martin had passed some of them when he had hauled Robert to this spot: one with a snapped lance shaft jutting from his thigh, one dragging a mangled foot, one covering his blinded eyes as if in some macabre version of a game of hide-and-seek. Now, the wounded all lay hidden, sprawled throughout the snow-deadened forest, but their moans drifted up to the tree-tops that creaked in the wind. Martin closed his eyes and tried to block out the piteous sounds.

But another sound kept tormenting him, this one inside his head, a memory of the slaughter. He heard, over and over again, the voice of the horseman the moment before he had rammed his lance into Robert's belly. The man's fierce, furious grunt had been an unmistakable oath, but the words were not English. Something foreign. Something Spanish. As he recalled the moment, Martin's teeth stopped chattering, so tight was the grinding of his jaw. Before today he had merely felt scorn for the Spanish, for their arrogance and errors in religion. Now, he detested Spaniards above every evil on earth.

". . . at the pond!" Robert wailed. ". . . lost her rosary! Meg . . . catch her!"

Martin jerked upright. His arms wrapped again around Robert. He cradled Robert's head between his hands, and he rocked him to soothe him, to stop his delirious cries. He caressed his brother's face, willing him to endure. But his fingers, slick with cold blood, slid over Robert's clammy cheeks.

Robert's head lolled again, his fit of delirium past. He lay still. Too still. A sweat of panic pricked Martin's upper lip. He swiped the back of his hand over his mouth and tasted blood. His brother's blood. He almost gagged. Then Robert's body shuddered again, convulsing. Martin watched the agony, unable to help. It passed. Robert lay gasping.

In exhausted helplessness, Martin pressed his cheek against his brother's cold hair and listened to the dirge of wounded men's moans around them.

CHAPTER TWENTY-SEVEN

Loyalty Tested

"**B**een straggling in all morning, they have, m'lady. Had a bad time of it yesterday on Wrotham Hill. And an even worse night in the woods." Tom, the grizzled guard, shook his head and repeated with quiet dismay, "A bad time."

Isabel stood with him at the entrance to the great hall of Rochester Castle and stared openmouthed at the scene before her. On their way up from the Strood Bridge Tom had told her the bare facts of the disaster—how Sir Henry Isley's company of five hundred, marching from Sevenoaks to join Wyatt's army here, had been cut down by Lord Abergavenny's cavalry. But nothing Tom said had prepared her for such a scene of hopelessness.

Scores of wounded and frostbitten men lay sprawled around the hall. They lay on the floor, shivering. They sat propped against the walls, staring. They stood, mumbling their stories to knots of quiet soldiers who crowded around to hear and to help. They shuffled forward in a line-up at the hearth where a cook ladled broth into their bowls. Castle soldiers handed out dry clothing. Boys tore fresh bandages and gaped at the survivors' red-black wounds. There was activity everywhere, but it went on in hushed whispers above the moans of the suffering. The very air of the dank hall seemed heavy with despair.

"So many!" Isabel said, shocked by the huge number of broken men. But despite her sympathy for these wretched survivors, Martin was her foremost concern. Tom knew Martin by name but not by sight, and so had not been able to ease her mind.

"And Sir Henry?" Isabel asked him now.

"Hid all night in the forest like most of these men, so I heard, but nobody's seen him come in. Someone said he caught a stray horse and lighted out to Maidstone. Someone said they saw him lying dead in a stream in the woods. But the poor fellow what reported *that* also says he saw Satan in the woods eating a dead man's heart. Daft from the cold, he was." Tom passed a hand helplessly over his forehead. "One thing's for sure, m'lady. 'Twas a night these poor devils will never forget."

Isabel shivered. She was soaked and sore after her ride from London through the sleety rain, and she would have to face hours more of it on the return ride if she was to get back to Sydenham's before nightfall. But it was not her wet discomfort that made her shiver. It was the creeping dread she felt as her eyes raked the crowded hall for Martin's face. She could not see him anywhere.

Two soldiers supporting a hobbling man passed slowly in front of her. She craned around them. There were too many people in the way. Leaving Tom, she moved into the hall. She had to step over a litter of wet boots and bloodied gauntlets and discarded helmets. A soldier on the floor beside her groaned. A doctor shook his head as he examined the man's foot. It had already turned black from frostbite. Isabel turned away. She had almost reached the line of men waiting for soup when someone grabbed her elbow.

"Mistress Thornleigh." It was Wyatt. "Come upstairs to the solar," he said. "I must hear your report."

"In a moment," she said, still searching the survivors' faces. She tried to move forward.

Wyatt held her back. "Now."

"No, I must look for Martin. He—"

"Later. I *need* your report."

"But he might be here. He might be hurt."

"He hasn't come back," Wyatt said flatly. "Come."

"But someone might have seen him. I must ask. Let me go." She strained against his grip. "You don't even care about him! Let me go!"

"Don't care?" Wyatt forcefully twisted her around to him, anger flashing in his eyes. He spoke in a harsh whisper. "You mourn one man. I mourn three hundred and fifty!"

She stared at him in horror. "Three hundred and . . . ?"

"Dead or wounded or lost," he said. Isabel saw how deeply he was shaken. Wrotham Hill, the first armed clash of the uprising, had been a devastating setback.

But Wyatt had no time for despair. "Now come with me." He tugged her toward the stairs. Sobered, she offered no resistance. He had not declared that Martin was dead, only that he had not yet come back. That left room for hope.

"You're soaked," he said with a frown at her wet cloak as they reached the stairs. He stopped a soldier carrying in an armload of dry clothes, and snatched a coarse, gray wool cape from the pile. He handed it to Isabel. Gratefully she whirled off her sodden cloak and gave it to the soldier in exchange. The cape was a man's—too large, patched, and stinking of manure. But it was dry.

"So?" Wyatt said as soon as they were alone upstairs.

"First," she began, "there is a price on your head. The Queen is offering lands worth one hundred pounds a year to anyone who captures you, dead or alive."

Wyatt shrugged. "Tell me of the French troop ships. Have they landed yet in Portsmouth?"

"Monsieur de Noailles believes they have sailed, but foul weather in the Channel is hampering their landing."

Wyatt cursed under his breath.

"But there are other encouraging reports from the south, sir. The Queen's commander there, the Lord Warden of the Cinque Ports, cannot raise more than a handful of men against you."

Wyatt looked far from encouraged. "We'll have enough coming against us, and soon. After Wrotham Hill yesterday, Abergavenny will have made his rendezvous with Norfolk in Gravesend. Their combined force will be on their way here by now. Thirteen hundred of them." He irritably slapped the back of a chair. "Damn it, I need to march! We've been here a bloody week. Where's the blasted French army coming from Scotland? What does de Noailles say?"

"He expects his courier to arrive with news of them at any moment. They must be on the march south already, he says."

"But there's no firm report of them?"

She shook her head.

He walked to the window. "And in London?"

She decided to tell him the good news first. "Master Peckham's clandestine resistance group of citizens is very strong, sir. Nine aldermen have secretly contacted either him or the Ambassador, offering support for you."

"They're good for men and arms?"

"Yes. Peckham represents at least ten score leading householders. They and all the apprentices and journeymen of their establishments will come forth when you require them.

And the Ambassador says they have an extensive cache of weapons."

"Good. That's good."

"However, sir"—now the bad news—"the Constable has installed new guns at the Tower."

"Yes? What have they got?"

Isabel closed her eyes in concentration to summon up the statistics that de Noailles, nervous about committing anything to paper, had hastily drilled into her yesterday. She had gone to his lodging immediately after she had seen Legge at the Crane. "In the Diveling Tower," she said, "a new nine-foot culverin of four thousand pounds with a four-inch bore. On the roof of the Iron Gate Tower, a battery of culverins and demi-cannon, three thousand pounds each. There are fourteen lasts of gunpowder stockpiled at the ordnance depot. Three six-foot falconets have been placed over the Water Gate. They are each five hundred pounds in weight, and of two-inch caliber. And there are other pieces, mostly demi-cannon, mounted on the roofs of the White Tower, the Cradle Tower, and the St. Thomas Tower."

Wyatt frowned. "Powerful," he muttered.

"Also, the royalist defense force in London is growing." She paused, reluctant to cumber him with the news of the lords' burgeoning musters. But he had to be told. "The Queen's councilors," she went on, "press more of their men into arms daily. Sir Edward Sydenham told me that the Earl of Arundel alone has provided the Queen three hundred foot soldiers and fifty horsemen. And Monsieur de Noailles says that, all together, the lords have now brought perhaps a thousand soldiers into the city."

Wyatt was looking at her sharply. "Did you say Sir Edward Sydenham? I understood him to be close to the Queen. One of her lieutenants under Lord Howard. How did you come to be speaking with him?"

She hesitated. But there was no way around the truth. "I am a guest in his house."

Wyatt's eyebrows lifted. "Living with a royalist?"

"He is a kind gentleman, sir. He is helping me with . . . a private matter." She had no desire to blurt out her family's tragedy. There was nothing Wyatt could do; her father's fate lay in her hands. And, she thought thankfully, in Sir Edward's hands, too. This morning, armed with her list of her father's business associates, he had sent his agents out to investigate; it had given her the chance to come here. "But I assure you," she added quickly, "Sir Edward has no suspicion whatever of my involvement with you. I have been very careful."

Wyatt was regarding her with new interest. "This situation is ideal, mistress. You will be able to gather invaluable information in this royalist's house. Maybe even details of the royal commanders' strategies. Stay there. Spy on Sydenham."

"Spy?"

He smiled sardonically. "Don't look so shocked. What do you think you've been doing so far, making these reports?"

"But . . . Sir Edward is a friend. He has shown me much kindness. It would be . . . a betrayal."

Wyatt's wry smile vanished. His voice was mocking. "Ah, so you will report about royalist strangers but not about royalists you know and like. Is that it?"

She flushed with anger.

"Mistress Thornleigh," he said more gently, "war is hard. Sometimes we must betray in order to be loyal."

She swallowed. Of course, he was right. The cause they were all fighting for was more important than one man. "I understand," she said.

"Good. Now, about those Tower guns—"

But her attention was suddenly dragged away. An anxious volley of men's voices had erupted below in the castle courtyard. Perhaps, she thought, it was more survivors of Wrotham Hill returning. "Sir Thomas, I have given you all the information the Ambassador told me. Please, let me go now to look for Martin."

He hesitated, then nodded. "Good luck."

In the courtyard it was just as she had thought. A scatter of Isley's bedraggled men, more dead than alive, had stumbled in, and castle soldiers had run to them with blankets, calling out for news of other survivors. Isabel pushed among them in the misty rain. She questioned half a dozen before a castle guard finally told her, "Aye, I saw St. Leger, mistress. Early this morning he came in. He was heading toward St. Margaret's."

The church of St. Margaret's was dim. Looking down the pewless nave at the lone man kneeling before the altar candles, Isabel could not be sure it was him. Then he raised his head to look up at the gold cross, and his damp brown curls glinted in the candles' glow. Joy coursed through her. He was alive. "Martin!"

He looked over his shoulder. He got to his feet and started toward her. He was limping. Isabel ran forward. She met him halfway down the nave. They threw their arms around each other.

Martin was trembling. Isabel started to draw away, for she longed to look at him, but he held her tightly and would not let her go. She pulled back her head. She was shocked by his face. His eyes were haggard, his lips bloodless, his cheeks cross-hatched with red and black scratches of scabbed blood and grime, as if he had thrashed his way through nettles. "Oh, Martin," she whispered.

He took hold of her shoulders and held on as if to steady himself. "Robert is dead."

The words struck her like a blow.

"I watched . . . watched him die," Martin said. "It took all night. Oh, Isabel . . . he suffered so . . ." His voice cracked. "The ground . . . it was frozen . . . and I had nothing . . . nothing that would dig . . ." His forehead dropped heavily onto her shoulder. His body shuddered with sobs. "Dear God, I couldn't even bury him!"

She took him in her arms, murmuring his name over and over in a helpless bid to comfort him. He held on to her and wept.

"Come," she whispered. She led him to the side aisle and sat him down on the steps of an earl's marble tomb. She sat beside him. They were alone in the vaulted church.

Martin, abashed at weeping, swiped at his tears with the back of his hand, smudging the grime on his cheeks. He gave a mirthless laugh. "I've been asleep here . . . imagine," he muttered, as if wanting to talk of anything but Robert. "I got back . . . this morning . . . and the priest let me in, and . . . I fell asleep." He glanced distractedly at the closed church doors. "He's up at the castle now, with the wounded . . . last rites . . ." He looked back at Isabel and tried to smile. "Lord, it's wonderful to see you! Robert would have . . ." Breaking off, fighting for control, he grabbed hold of her hands. She saw that dried blood streaked his fingers, and his nails were cracked and packed with dirt. Had he tried to dig a grave in the frozen woods with his bare hands?

Pity stabbed her heart. She folded him in her arms again. Martin held on to her tightly.

Isabel stroked his mud-clotted hair and tried to control her own dismay. She was appalled by Robert's death—Robert St. Leger had been a good man, and a friend—yet she could not beat back the relief, the joy, at finding Martin alive. She was almost ashamed; grief for Robert, she knew, would come in time, but thankfulness overwhelmed her now.

Martin straightened, swallowing the last of his tears. "Isabel," he murmured. He touched her cheek gently, looking at her with mild surprise as if for the first time. "You look so pale."

"Oh, Martin," she said, her own calamities surging to her mind. How she longed for his understanding! "You don't know what has happened!"

She told him everything. Her mother's murder. Her father's arrest. Her brother's flight. Her dismal search through London's prisons. Her father's escape from Newgate, with the Queen's officers now on his trail for treason, and her hope that she would find him, with Sir Edward Sydenham's help, before they did. She told him about it all. All except the jailer who had defiled her—that would remain her secret pain—and the mercenary who had betrayed her. That wound was still too fresh.

Martin shook his head, lost in horrified amazement at her story. "Your mother . . . dear God . . ."

Isabel looked away. She dared not dwell on her mother's death. That way lay despair. She would think only of what still could be done for her father.

Martin murmured, as though unable to grasp the awful facts, "Your mother . . . your father . . . Robert . . ."

They sat in silence on the cold marble steps, engulfed by their misery. The rain swelled with a sudden drumming on the roof, rude and insistent. A cold, damp draft swept down the nave. Isabel and Martin huddled closer, holding hands. The bare church, stripped by Wyatt's overzealous Protestant followers of all Catholic ornament, hulked around them like a warehouse. Only the great altar and crucifix that Martin had been praying to, and its flanking candles, remained.

The pounding rain ceased as suddenly as it had begun. The church was silent again.

"And now," Martin said bleakly, "you've come to report to Wyatt from Ambassador de Noailles?"

"Yes."

He shook his head. "It's hopeless, you know. Hopeless."

She could not think what to say. He had never spoken like this before. She knew it was his grief. "It may seem so now, Martin. But the French are on their way. And once our army takes London, everything will change." She clasped his hand between hers. "Robert will not have died in vain."

Martin continued to shake his head as if he had not heard her. "No. Hopeless. I have seen the worst. Seen what war really is. It is barbarity. It is savagery . . ." His voice faltered. He glanced at the altar crucifix. "It is . . . unspeakable waste."

"Martin, don't say such—"

"Isabel," he said suddenly, twisting back to her. "You're all I . . ." His gaunt eyes searched her face. "Oh, Isabel, you're all that's left." He took hold of her shoulders. His hands were trembling. "Marry me?"

"You know I will."

"No, now. Here."

"Now?"

"Oh, *please*. I . . . everything's gone, destroyed. Everything except . . . you. I don't know when I'll see my family again, or even . . ." He blinked and shook his head as if he could not face his own thoughts. His fingers suddenly dug into her shoulders. "But we still have each other," he said urgently. "Isabel, I know . . . death is all around us. But we . . . we can still live! Can't we? Please, Isabel. Please say yes!"

She saw the desperation in his bloodshot eyes. The jolt of strength with which he had taken hold of her shoulders was already weakening. He was so exhausted, so spent.

"Yes," she blurted. "Right now!"

He gave a sigh of extreme relief. He grabbed her hands and bent and kissed them, and whispered, "Oh, thank God." Shakily he got to his feet. "I'll fetch—" He winced at the pain in his foot. "I'll fetch the priest." He froze. "Robert"— an aching regret shot through his voice—"Robert was to have done this office."

"I know," Isabel said, her heart breaking for him. She stood with him. Her own voice was shaky now. "And my mother was to have made my bridal bouquet . . ." She

clutched his hands. He instantly tugged them free to grasp
her hands in sympathy, and raised them to his chest. Isabel
leaned against him. She, too, felt drained, beaten, weakened
by so much death . . . and so grateful for Martin's love, his
hope. She said, "We shall speak the vows . . . in memory of
them both."

His chin trembled. "Yes."

Abruptly they embraced. They held on to each other
tightly. Martin drew back. He forced a smile. And then he
started off. He was limping badly. Isabel could see that he
was in pain. "Martin, are you wounded?"

He was halfway down the nave. He turned. "No, frostbite.
I'll lose a couple of toes, I imagine." He looked down,
averting his eyes from hers. "Not the finest specimen of a
bridegroom, am I?" He glanced up at her, and doubt flooded
his face. He asked timidly, hopefully, "Isabel, are you sure
about this?"

She came to him and kissed his cheek. "I'm sure."

She saw tears spring to his eyes. He stroked her cheek.
"Wait here. I'll come back with the priest," he said. "And
then," he added, lowering his voice as if unwilling to be
overheard, "we'll get ourselves out of this blighted kingdom." He turned to go.

Isabel was not sure she had heard him correctly. She hurried after him. She reached him as he threw open the church
door. A wet gust plastered her skirt to her legs. "Martin, did
you say . . . leave?"

He held up a finger to his lips. "Shhh. Yes," he whispered.
"As soon as the priest has married us we'll board the first
ship bound for France. I have an uncle in Bordeaux." He
grabbed her hand. His smile was feeble, but earnest. "We'll
make a new life, Isabel. Away from all this sorrow." He
kissed her fingers. He hurried out the door.

She ran after him, down the church steps to the street.
"Martin, wait!" The rain had not stopped, only sharpened
again to sleet, and it struck her face in wind-whipped nee-
dles. She had to squint to see Martin. She called to him, "I
cannot leave England!"

He stopped in the street. "What?"

A woman in rags was lugging a basket of firewood between them, struggling through the mud. Hammers from the
armory next door clanged. A mounted soldier approached at
a trot. "My father," Isabel called to Martin above the noise.

"I must find him. And . . . and there's Sir Thomas, too. I cannot run away."

"Run away?" He came toward her. "Isabel, what are you talking about? We have to save ourselves."

She stared at him in disbelief. "You cannot have heard a word I told you. Martin, my father is being hunted as a traitor! If they find him they will execute him!" The soldier trotted by and his horse splashed mud onto Martin's legs. Isabel asked, still dumbfounded, "And what about Sir Thomas? He is relying on me. How can you ask me to betray him?" As soon as the words were out she realized the insult they implied: if anyone was about to betray Sir Thomas, it was Martin.

Martin was blinking at her like someone confused or lost. "I heard everything you said. "You—"

There was a shout. Martin flinched and looked over his shoulder. The shout had come from the city gate, behind him at the foot of the street.

Isabel tried to think. The rain stung her face. She held up her hand as a shield from it. "Martin, if you are bent on leaving Wyatt's army, I accept that . . . if your conscience does. But if so come back with me to London. Help me. Father is in hiding somewhere, sick and weak. Help me find him and get him to safety. We—"

"Isabel, I can *never* go back to London! I'd be arrested and hanged. I can never . . . never see my family again . . ." His voice cracked. "You're all I . . ."

There were more shouts, frantic, again from the city gate.

"What about Robert's family?" Isabel stammered. "How can you leave them? Meg . . . his children."

Martin shook his head distractedly. He let out a shuddering breath of exhaustion. Isabel saw that he had no strength, no will, no reserves, to deal with anything but the moment. All that was keeping him going was his conviction that she was coming with him to France. Now.

"Martin, I will marry you. Gladly. Right now if you want. But I cannot leave."

They stared at each other. Rain dripped from Martin's curls. He was shivering. "Isabel, I'm begging you. Do not desert me. Please!"

She saw the raw loneliness in his eyes, saw a glimmer of the horror he had endured with Robert in the night woods.

He took her hand and pressed it to his chest. He whispered, as though it were the only word he had left, "Please."

Isabel's heart twisted. She thought of the day, four months ago, when she and Martin had made their betrothal vow. How many times since then she had glowed inwardly, feeling the strength of that vow! It had meant everything to her. It was her world. But a week ago her family had been shattered and the world had changed. She looked into his red-rimmed eyes. "Martin, do not ask me to abandon my father."

There was a trumpet blast. Martin twisted around. He blanched as understanding struck. "My God, it's an attack!" The alarm bell in the armory clanged. "It's the Duke of Norfolk!" he cried.

People were running into the street.

"Archers!" a captain galloping on horseback yelled toward the armory. "To your posts!"

A citizen splashed through the mud toward his house and shouted up to his wife at a window, "Bolt the doors!"

A woman in a doorway cried, "They're closing the gates!"

Martin swiped rain from his face, trying to collect himself. He grabbed Isabel's shoulders. "We can get out through the postern gate in the east wall ... get a boat, be married in France. Come, Isabel! I beg you!"

She looked around wildly. Soldiers were pounding out of the armory. A horseman galloped up from the gate, head bent, cape flying. The woman with the firewood staggered to reach the door of her hovel. Shouts of fear ricocheted in the street.

A cannon boomed from the city wall. Martin flinched. "They're coming!"

Her horse thundered over the road. Her breath was tearing in her throat. The driving rain blurred her vision. She made out the line of bare, black trees tossing in the wind near the top of Spitell Hill and she kicked the horse's sides again. The horse, heaving breaths itself, struggled up the slope. Just before they reached the line of trees, Isabel pulled back on the reins. The horse halted, panting steam and tossing its head in the rain. Isabel sat, painfully catching her breath.

She had made it. As the city gates were closing she had bolted through and galloped across the Strood Bridge. She had seen only the terrifying sight of the Duke of Norfolk's cannon ahead of her, his soldiers hurriedly placing the guns. She had swerved and galloped toward a track that wound around the back of the hill. She had been amazed when no one followed her. The Duke's men had seemed too busy with the guns to notice her, or care. She had made it up the hill. Now she sat her horse, looking back the way she had come, her mind cringing with regret over Martin.

She heard a horse cough. She twisted around in the saddle. The sound had come from beyond the line of trees. She eased her mount forward. Stopping under the dripping boughs, she stared at the scene ahead. The mass of Norfolk's troop was ranged on the far side of the hill, looking down on the Strood Bridge. There were hundreds of them, horse and infantry, all wearing the mud-spattered white coats with red crosses of the London bands. Their soggy pennons flapped in the wet wind. Their horses whinnied and pawed the earth. They were waiting on the hill—for what, Isabel did not know.

There was a boom of cannon from Norfolk's guns below. A captain on the hill yelled, "Charge!"

But the soldiers on the hill ignored him. No one moved.

Suddenly a lieutenant drew out his sword. He cantered to the front of the host and waved his sword and cried, "To Wyatt! We are all Englishmen!"

There was silence. Then, harness jangled as ten or twelve horsemen rode forward to join the lieutenant. The jangling grew louder as more horsemen trotted forward. Then foot soldiers moved, too, first at a walk, then at a run, and suddenly the whole host was swarming down the hill in a thunder of feet and hooves. Rising above this din the voiced roar crested, as if from one throat: "All Englishmen! To Wyatt! To Wyatt!"

They reached the bottom of the hill and surged around the Duke and his guns. They threw down their pikes and longbows and sheathed their swords and poured across the bridge. Wyatt's soldiers on the walls cheered. The gate clattered open. The London troops rushed inside the town. The Duke of Norfolk watched, dumbfounded. He rode in a frantic circle around his handful of stunned officers. The Duke stopped, spurred his horse, and bolted off in the direction of London. A few loyal men galloped off behind him. The few who had been left manning the Duke's guns ran across the bridge into Rochester.

Isabel gaped. She had seen the whole extraordinary occurrence. The London Whitecoats had come over to the patriots' side en masse. Whatever set-back the rebel cause had suffered on Wrotham Hill, this was a heady vindication. London, now, would surely be Wyatt's.

She watched the last of the Whitecoats run across the bridge and into the embrace of Wyatt's army. Her borrowed cape billowed around her and its soggy flaps lashed her, and in her mind she heard Martin whisper, pleading, "I'm begging you! Come!"

But Martin was gone. By nightfall he would be on a ship bound for France. The fastness of their vows had been tested, and it had snapped. Martin had been the one to test it, but *she* had been the one to break it. But why, oh, *why* had he demanded her loyalty be built upon betraying her father and Wyatt?

She leaned over and clutched the horse's mane in misery. And under the bare trees' dripping boughs, she wept.

CHAPTER TWENTY-EIGHT

> ━┤━◆━○━◆━├━

Appeals

Bishop Gardiner abruptly halted his pacing. "The Queen *must* come out, Sydenham!" he shouted, red-faced. "She must acknowledge our decision!"

From the open doorway Edward Sydenham held up his hands to the Bishop in a gesture that begged for calm. Inwardly, however, he was as shaken as the Bishop and the seven other royal councilors seated at the long oak table. They had arrived at this early morning emergency meeting at Whitehall still staggering from the report of the defection of the Duke of Norfolk's London Whitecoat troops at the Strood Bridge, only to hear from the Earl of Pembroke the even more alarming news: Wyatt's army had just left Rochester and was marching toward London.

The Queen was still sequestered in her private chamber. She had not yet been told that Wyatt was on the march. Her councilors, apprehensive of feeding palace panic, were waiting until she joined them privately. Nevertheless, rumor had crept through the hushed corridors. Courtiers and ladies-in-waiting whispered about it in chilly gallery corners. Servants fretted to one another under shadowed stairways while the cold morning ashes of the palace hearths remained unswept. Soldiers of the Queen's guard murmured in the armory, nervously eyeing the stores of spears and pikes as if the weapons themselves were the enemy. But outside, where the rain drummed on the cobbles of the empty courtyards, no men-at-arms were massing. The immobilized palace inmates acted as though besieged—by fear, by rumor, and by the pounding rain. Everyone was waiting for some direction from the Queen.

Edward closed the door to keep the conversation from being heard beyond the council chamber. "Her Majesty is preparing to join us, Your Grace," he replied, keeping his voice controlled. "She asks your pardon for the delay, and asks your patience."

Bishop Gardiner groaned. Edward lowered his eyes. His deference to these lords was ingrained, and his acceptance of their authority unshakable. Yet he could not help enjoying a shiver of pleasure that the Queen now trusted him more than any of her councilors; the aura of being her intimate gave him immense status. But his thrill of pleasure was short-lived. It was not consolation enough. There were still great dangers. First, there was the Queen's precarious position. Edward's future depended on the Queen's supremacy, but despite the successful, if belated, efforts of council members to raise a good number of troops to defend the city, the Queen still had no field army.

And then there was Thornleigh. Edward's agents had not yet tracked him down. None of the business associates whose names Thornleigh's daughter had supplied had been found harboring him. And, hard on the heels of the news of the defection of Norfolk's troops, the girl herself had come back to Edward's house late last night reporting her failure, too, to find her father with whatever family friends she had gone to see; she had come back wet, exhausted, and disconsolate.

Edward watched the gray rain sliding down the windows beyond the council table and tried to quell his rising panic. If the Queen's officers found Thornleigh first and brought him to trial, then Edward's victory here, his acceptance into the most powerful chamber in the land—his whole, carefully crafted world—would crumble.

Lord Paulet's whine cut into Edward's thoughts. "But we are agreed, are we not?" Paulet asked, wincing from his chronic headache. He looked at the other men around the table. "We are all firm? About Pembroke's replacing the Duke?"

"Yes, yes," Bishop Gardiner insisted. He came to the corner of the table and thumped it. "And the Queen must accept it!"

Edward glanced at Lord Pembroke who stood at a window with his back to the room. As the new commander of the Queen's forces Pembroke was keeping very quiet, Edward thought.

"The real question, my lords," Sir Richard Riche snapped, "is whether our *troops* will accept it. Or, indeed, accept any authority at all."

"How do you mean, sir!" Lord Howard huffed, taking the remark as a personal attack. Howard was in charge of the city's defenses. Seated next to Riche, his bloodshot eyes fixed Riche belligerently.

"I mean the shameful goings-on at St. Katherine's wharf last night!" Riche said.

"What goings-on?" the Bishop asked irritably.

"Did you not hear, Your Grace?" Riche answered, barely controlling his scorn. "The Imperial envoys departed, and—"

"And good riddance," the Bishop shot back. "Their presence was an intolerable aggravation."

"Whatever their presence *was,* Your Grace, it has now been removed." Riche's lip almost curled as he spoke. "God only knows what they will report to the Emperor, what tales of English barbarity! It was bad enough they felt obliged to slip away in the night, afraid of attack from the populace. They stole aboard an Antwerp merchant sloop that lay in the river about to sail, and left their horses to follow. But, Your Grace, obviously you have not heard the worst. Once the envoys were embarked from the water stairs, their escort of the Queen's guard shouted insults after them!"

"What?" Gardiner asked, shocked despite himself.

"Yes! Hurled insults over the water! Fired their arquebuses into the air in a show of contempt!" Riche looked sideways at Lord Howard with a sneer he made no effort to mask. "I ask you, can such men be relied upon?"

"I warn you, Riche!" Howard sputtered. "I'll not have my authority questioned like this!"

"That's the point!" Riche shouted. "There *is* no authority!"

Howard shoved back his chair with a screech of its legs and stood menacingly over Riche. Riche jumped up and jutted his furious face into Howard's. The Bishop had to physically pull the two men apart.

Lord Paulet was rubbing his brow, ignoring the fracas. He spoke quietly, as if to himself. "Even Ambassador Renard asked me what would happen if the Londoners rise up against the Queen. 'What will become of me?' he asked . . ."

Edward longed to say something. He felt that Paulet had touched on the nub of the crisis: where did the loyalty of the Londoners lie? With a prickle of apprehension at addressing these ruling nobles, he opened his mouth to speak. But Lord

Clinton spoke before he could. "We must send out a fresh army," Clinton insisted. He stood up with sudden energy. "Immediately. Cut off Wyatt before he gets to London."

Bishop Gardiner blanched. "And have them rush over to him like the last bunch?"

"That was a direct result of Norfolk's idiotic, premature attack," Clinton said. "He was supposed to wait for Abergavenny's arrival at Gravesend. If he had, and they had advanced together to Rochester as ordered, this disaster would never have happened. But now look!" He threw up his hands and began to pace as the Bishop had been doing. "Almost eight hundred men gone over to Wyatt, and Abergavenny sitting alone outside Gravesend—unable to trust his own men now, I might add. Yes, his cavalry achieved a stirring victory at Wrotham Hill the other day, but even that is turning against us, because Abergavenny reports that the excesses the cavalry committed there have soured many of his foot soldiers. He's had more desertions. The country people around his camp mistrust him. He is even having difficulty getting food from them." Clinton placed his knuckles on the table and leaned over with straight arms to emphasize his point. "No, we must raise a fresh force in London. Demand that the Guilds provide additional contingents. And none but householders this time, no unreliable substitutes. We must equip them and send them out to stop Wyatt!"

There were groans. The others shook their heads, or looked away, or grimly closed their eyes. Paulet droned on, almost to himself, ". . . and now Renard fears the King of Denmark means to join the French . . ."

There was a chorus of clashing voices:

"The Emperor must send an Imperial fleet to patrol the Channel against the French!"

"The Emperor is in Brussels. It would take a week to get a message to him."

"We haven't got a week!"

Edward's impulse to speak shriveled. The councilors were so embroiled in quarreling and conjuring up enemies they would not deal with the overwhelming problem of London. But what could he do? He was no soldier. He loathed the feeling that events were so beyond his control.

"Sydenham!" The Bishop's voice blasted Edward's thoughts. "The Queen *must* come out!"

* * *

"Enter."

"Pardon, Your Majesty," Edward said, opening the Queen's door, "but your councilors anxiously await your presence, and ..." His final words dwindled. He had expected to find the Queen bustling about, preparing to attend the conference. Instead, she sat in her darkened chamber with a blanket on her lap and a prayer missal in her hands as if she had no intention of stirring. Frances, lighting the votive candles on the Queen's *prie-dieu,* turned to Edward. He felt a ripple of revulsion as the two women looked at him from the gloom of their pious niche, like two spiders spinning in a corner.

"It's Candlemas, Edward," Frances gently reminded him.

"But, Your Majesty, the rebels are—"

"We deal with the things most needful, sir," the Queen said—a quiet reprimand. "Our souls' salvation lies therein. Today we mark the Purification of the Blessed Virgin Mary, in reverence, before we turn to the vile misdeeds of men."

About to protest, Edward caught himself. He bowed his head contritely. "Of course."

Frances beamed at him.

"However, Your Majesty," Edward ventured, "matters of some urgency require your attention."

"Which matters?"

He shrank from blurting out the worst, that Wyatt's army was on its way to London's gates and that the Queen's defenses were in a shambles. Such unwelcome news he would leave to the lords. "Your councilors have thought fit to appoint Lord Pembroke to command Your Majesty's forces," he said. "Your consent is needed, Your Grace."

The Queen's face hardened. "Pembroke is a desperate choice."

Because he is a Protestant, Edward thought uncomfortably. But even the Queen must know that Pembroke was all the council had. Already, a quarter of the members of the greater council had slunk away to their country seats to await an outcome; they would emerge when it was all over, to support the victor, whether rebel or monarch. "He is an able soldier, Your Majesty," Edward suggested. "With much experience."

"Aye," the Queen muttered bitterly, "but will he use it to oppose the traitors or to join them?"

Edward said nothing. His suspicions were not far off the Queen's.

In the silence the arrogant eyes of Philip of Spain stared down on the three of them from the Titian portrait. The votive candle flames twitched. Rain dripped from a corner of the casement.

"My lady," Frances said gently, "you asked me to remind you to thank Sir Edward." Edward smiled. He had sent letters with the departing envoys, directed to his contacts in the banking house of Fugger and other powerful men in the money markets of Antwerp, completing his transactions over the Queen's loan. His efforts would bring her the funds she desperately needed.

The Queen brightened. "So I did, Frances. My heartfelt thanks go to you, sir. The loan arrangement was well done. I shall not forget you."

Edward felt emboldened. "Your Majesty, may I speak?"

The Queen nodded.

"It is too long since your London subjects were graced with your presence," Edward said. "And, sadly, in the past days, many of them have been cowed by the traitors' actions. They crave your guidance. Let the Londoners *see* you, Your Majesty. A few words from their sovereign would do more to inspirit them than all the gold of Antwerp."

The Queen seemed intrigued by the suggestion. "Think you so?"

"I do. Your courage will give *them* courage."

"Thank you, sir, for this kind advice. I shall consider it." Her eyes drifted to the *prie-dieu*'s crucifix gleaming in the candlelight. She put aside her blanket and stood, her eyes on the crucifix. She moved toward the *prie-dieu* and seemed about to kneel, but stopped, lost in thought. "There is a task I would ask of you, good sir," she said.

Edward bowed. "Anything, Your Majesty."

"The Constable of the Tower tells me the prison there is crowded with traitors. I want them moved to my prison of the Marshalsea, to await their trials. I ask you to take charge of this business and oversee its completion. Room must be made in the Tower."

Edward could almost feel the warmth of Frances's smile. He understood; the Queen's request did him great honor. "Room, Your Majesty?" he asked. "For what?"

"Heretics, sir. They breed like vermin. My people apprehend them every hour. They have become bold, seeing Satan arm the traitors against me. But once God brings me my deliverance, the heretics shall be exterminated." She smiled at Edward as though struck by the aptness of her own pronouncement. "Did you know, my mother's mother, Isabella, once performed a similar act of piety in Spain? As Queen, she expelled the Jews from her realm, in gratitude to God for her victory over the infidel. I shall emulate her. I shall cleanse my realm of our particularly English poison. The heretics shall all be burnt, as my thanks to God."

Edward's blood turned cold.

"And now," the Queen concluded, kneeling, "excuse me, sir, for I must pray."

Frances quietly guided Edward to the door. He walked out in a kind of stupor, hearing in his mind the terrifying crackle of flames licking up at him around the stake. He had seen his father burn, had been forced by his mother to watch the horror; "We must bear witness," she had commanded, but Edward had only wanted to run. Now, he was barely aware of Frances's quick kiss on his cheek, and of her smile following him from the doorway as he passed through the antechamber where some of the Queen's ladies sat, hushed and fearful, at the fire. A hand touched Edward's elbow to stop him. Startled, he whipped around. He blinked at the slim, jeweled fingers gripping his arm. They belonged to Amy Hawtry. Her face was pale.

"Oh, sir, is it true?" she asked in a strained whisper. She placed both her hands on his chest and leaned close as if for protection. Her lips came almost to his mouth. Edward was dimly aware of Frances's frigid stare from the doorway. "They say Wyatt is coming!" Amy said to him. "They say we are all to be murdered in our beds! Oh, Sir Edward, tell me it isn't true!"

"You're late, Valverde," Lord Abergavenny said in an angry, wounded tone, glancing up from breakfast in his tent as Carlos walked in. Abergavenny flinched as his teeth hit a hard knob of gristle. He tossed down his eating knife in disgust, and it clattered beside his breakfast trencher. The three young officers standing at the back of the tent looked around, trenchers in their hands. Rain drummed on the tent. Abergavenny glanced again at Carlos. "Well?" he mumbled sourly around his mouthful. "Our company not good enough for you?"

Carlos clenched his jaw in silence. Since the victory at Wrotham Hill the commander had been treating him like some favorite son, always wanting him near, throwing an arm around him to share a jest or to pour out his worries, irritated whenever Carlos went off by himself. Carlos had no taste for such a sycophantic relationship. But neither could he afford an argument with the commander. So he said nothing.

Abergavenny spat out the gristle. "Cavendish, you call this mutton? Tastes like dog's tail."

A lieutenant in the back mumbled, "Best we can do, my lord."

"Take it away! Body of God, I'd rather starve."

The lieutenant cleared away the commander's trencher.

Carlos filled a cup from the ale keg. Before coming to the commander's tent he had wolfed down breakfast outside over the cook's cauldron, watching the rain from under the cook's tarpaulin stretched over poles. Now, although he had thought his stomach was impervious to soldiers' rations, the rancid mutton sat in his gut like a rock. Decent food was proving difficult to forage from the hostile country people. The company, marching from their victory at Wrotham Hill to join Norfolk in Gravesend, had been forced by the foul weather to camp here, a few miles south of the rendezvous. And then word had come that Norfolk had prematurely left Gravesend and advanced alone on Rochester—to disastrous results: all but a handful of his men had rushed over to the enemy. Abergavenny's company had shivered in this camp all yesterday as the commander awaited orders from Whitehall. Orders that still had not come. Meanwhile, their scout had reported that Wyatt was moving out of Rochester toward London. Carlos shook his head. He had fought in many confused campaigns, but none as badly led as this. He downed the ale. Flat, and cold as ice.

There was a squabble of voices beyond the tent. Abergavenny stood, rubbing his stiff back, and walked to the open tent flap. "A brawl," he muttered. "Cavendish, go see to it." He jerked his thumb at the other lieutenants. "You two go as well. It looks ugly."

They shuffled out. Carlos was left with Abergavenny who continued to watch the fight, rubbing his tailbone. The morning camp smells drifted into the tent—wood smoke and horse dung and burning fat. A boy in the corner polishing the commander's breastplate yawned.

Looking out, Abergavenny asked wearily, "What do you suppose it's about this time, Valverde?"

"It is always the same. Money or women."

Abergavenny grunted. "No women following us in this bloody weather." He shook his head. "Candlemas," he muttered, "and still I cannot pay these troops."

Candlemas. The fact struck Carlos like a reproach. Tonight he was to have collected his fee at the Blue Boar Tavern for delivering Thornleigh's finger. A hundred pounds. Enough to get him out of this fog-brained island and get him on his feet again somewhere. A week ago it had seemed so clear-cut a mission. Then, everything had become complicated. *She* had complicated it. He had failed.

And now? Now she despised him, and the lawyer, Sydenham, had her in his house. Carlos felt a cold flame of hate in his belly at the recollection of Sydenham in the inn courtyard, murmuring into Isabel's ear.

Involuntarily his hand balled into a fist. He had earned his pardon, yet what did he have? Nothing. He felt as powerless as if he were still in jail, felt like some cringing courtier hanging about Abergavenny's side, awaiting favor. It rankled. Everything rankled.

If all of his failure was to mean anything, he must make a success now. What he needed was land. Land would make up for everything.

But for him to be rewarded with land, the Queen's forces had to win. And this lame army was doing precious little to ensure that.

He knocked back another cup of ale. He had to think of something that would help force a victory.

"Amy, are you afraid?" Frances asked. She spoke quietly, and the agitated ladies-in-waiting in the Queen's antechamber continued with their halfhearted games of cat's cradle around the hearth.

Amy turned quickly from the window. She had been using its rain-darkened surface as a looking glass, nervously smoothing back a lock of her blond hair with the tip of her finger, and Frances's question had startled her. She shivered and hugged herself. "And you are not?" she asked sullenly.

Frances offered an apologetic smile. "I suppose we all are." She looked around at the other young women and sighed. "But it does seem useless to just sit here and quake. Let's you and I go and cheer ourselves with a game of primero, shall we?"

Amy frowned—uncertain or unwilling. "The Queen may want us," she said.

"The Queen will be deep in her Candlemas devotions for some time, and after that she must meet with the council."

Amy fidgeted with her necklace.

Frances looked down. "I am sorry if I have been short-tempered with you in the past. But now ... well, we are both rather in need of some diversion, and ..." She stopped herself. "Oh, never mind," she sighed. She turned to go.

"No, wait, Frances."

Frances saw the fear in the girl's eyes, the dread of being left prey to her own wild thoughts of the rebels' barbarity. "Yes," Amy said firmly. "Let's play."

"Damn you, Valverde, you nearly made me cut my own throat!" Abergavenny scowled over his shoulder as he stood shaving, his razor poised at his chin. The servant boy stood before him with a basin of cold water. "No," Abergavenny insisted to Carlos, "absolutely not. It's a foolhardy idea."

"You need information about Wyatt," Carlos said.

"I need a good cavalry captain more. No. I can't risk you."

"Can you risk letting the enemy pass?" Moments ago, just before noon, the scout had ridden in to report that Wyatt, marching to London, had stopped at Dartford, only seven miles away. Carlos had known at once that it was his chance, and had gone directly to Abergavenny's tent. He pushed on now: "Do nothing to discover his strength, his arms? Let him take London—while you shave?"

"All right!" the commander snapped, "I agree it would be good to infiltrate his camp. I'll send someone. But not you."

"Who else can you trust to come back?"

Abergavenny whipped around, furious at this reference to the mounting desertions. He held the razor in front of Carlos's nose. "Careful, Valverde," he threatened quietly. "I could just leave you behind, you know, in the clutches of these country folk. They're not at all fond of Spaniards."

Carlos's eyes locked with the commander's. "Or you can

send me into Wyatt's camp. And if I get back out, you can
reward me."

Amy giggled, remembering. ". . . but my sister came upon
us in the dovecote, and when my cousin Simon heard her
shriek—his hands were up under my skirt, the randy cur—he
bolted out the door and I don't think he stopped running until he crossed the bridge to the village. Lord, what a coward!" She giggled again.

Amy and Frances were sitting at the card table in their
chamber while the rain dribbled down the window. Frances
was watching her closely.

Amy bent her elbow on the table and languidly laid her
cheek on her hand. Her fair hair tumbled over her shoulder.
She felt her muscles slacken in the heat from the fire in the
hearth, and from the wine warming her veins—a respite
from the worry about Wyatt's army. "But the next night,"
she went on, smiling, "we did it, Simon and me. My first
time." She winked at Frances. "Lord, what a summer that
was, the summer I turned fourteen. And *he* was all of seventeen." She heaved a sigh of regret. "My, but he was a handsome dog."

"Goodness," Frances said. "Such an energetic childhood.
More wine?"

Amy pushed her goblet across the table for more. Frances
poured. Misty-eyed, Amy watched the red liquid swirl into
the cup. She drank several deep gulps. Her fingers felt pleasantly tingly.

"Ah, but those sweet summer days on the home farm
seem a long, long time ago," she sighed. "Daisy-chain making, and paddling in the pond, and merry tumbles in the
hay." She looked across at Frances who sat ramrod-straight
in her hard-backed chair. Amy wondered if she *ever* relaxed.
She sighed again and drank some more, then idly trailed her
finger through a small puddle of spilled wine on the table,
drawing wet patterns. "I thought it was going to be merry
here at court with the Queen, but it's all just 'fetch my missal,' and 'read me that prayer of St. Thomas Aquinas,' and
'hurry along to Mass now.' Lord, I'll be glad when she finally weds Prince Philip." She winked again at Frances. "If
she gets down on her knees once the Spanish Prince is before her, I warrant it won't be to pray!" She giggled so hard

her elbow slipped off the table, and she lost her balance and almost fell off her chair.

Frances smiled. "Your cup is empty, Amy." She poured another goblet full.

Amy swallowed half of it. "Nice, this wine of yours," she said. Her words were becoming slurred. "Sort of a . . . flowery taste. Did you put one of your funny tinctures in it?"

"Yes. For relaxing. Do you like it?"

Amy nodded. "Tastes like pears," she started to say, but the words that slid out didn't sound much like that. She looked at Frances sheepishly. She had not realized she had drunk quite so much. She opened her mouth to make a jest about it, but her tongue felt lodged in her throat. And when she tried to turn her head away from Frances's relentless scrutiny, she found she could not move at all. Even her jaw would not move. Her mouth remained open in a humiliating gape. Her brain pulsed with sudden fright. All of her muscles were frozen. She heard a ringing in her head. The room was becoming dark around the edges. Only Frances's face before her was clear and stark, the firelight jumping over its bony planes.

Amy's body slumped onto the table, her cheek in the pool of spilled wine. Her eyes stared. Her heart pounded in fear. What was happening to her?

She heard the rustle of Frances's brocade skirt. She felt the shiver of a touch on her neck, like a bird's claw. "Come with me, Amy." The words, strangely deep and booming, ricocheted in Amy's head.

Frances grappled a fistful of Amy's hair. She shoved her other hand under Amy's armpit. "I heard about you accosting Edward on his doorstep the other day. Everyone on the street saw you. Drunk, they said you were. Oh, I know Edward spurned your repulsive advances. But this morning I witnessed for myself another of your wanton ploys with him. I really cannot tolerate this any longer, Amy."

Amy was yanked off her seat by her arm and by her hair. Her paralyzed body was dragged across the room toward the hearth. Frances dropped her on her stomach. Amy's head thudded onto the hearth, a foot away from the fire. Her eyes were open and she stared at the flames. But she could not move.

Frances knelt beside her. "I have only this to say, Amy. Keep away from Edward. I know you are a clever girl so I

feel sure I need only say it once. However, some aid in remembering it may be helpful to you." She fanned out Amy's
hair on the hearth so that it lay only an inch from the fire.
She waited. Amy stared ahead in horror. She could feel
nothing but her heart thudding in terror. And then she
smelled it. Her hair was burning. She heard Frances leave
her side. She saw smoke. Unable to cough, her heart about
to explode, she began to drool.

Frances's reverberating voice boomed over her, "I trust
this warning has doused your amorous instincts." Wine
sloshed over Amy's head. She heard the hiss of the flames,
dying. She smelled the sickly sweet odor of wine mixed with
wet, burned hair. Wine dripped down her cheek and her nose
to the hearth. She was aware of a relief so overwhelming it
engulfed her. And then she fainted.

CHAPTER TWENTY-NINE

Candlemas

An elbow jabbed Isabel's rib. A heavy foot pressed down on her toes, then lifted. She winced, but otherwise tried to ignore the crush of the crowd. Standing on tiptoe, she craned her neck like all the others in the packed entrance of London's Guildhall where people were jostling for a glimpse of Queen Mary. From her dais, the Queen looked out at the assembly as if about to speak. The huge hall—almost as large as Westminster Hall—was crammed with citizens anxiously chattering, but everyone suddenly hushed. Isabel held her breath. Was the Queen going to capitulate to Wyatt's demands? Accept her people's wishes?

"Loving subjects," the Queen began formally, "I am come unto you in mine own person to tell you that which already you do know—that is, how traitorously and seditiously a number of rebels have assembled against both us and you. Their presence, as they said at first, was only to resist a marriage determined between us and the Prince of Spain. But you shall see that the marriage will be found to be the least of their quarrel. They have now betrayed the inward treason of their hearts, and soon we will see them demanding the possession of our person, and the keeping of our Tower, and the placing and displacing of our councilors."

The Queen paused as if expecting some hearty response of solidarity from the crowd. But the citizens remained quiet. And Isabel knew this would be no capitulation. The Queen looked about, as if unsure of how to proceed. The silence seemed to puzzle her; her entry here had been all glorious fanfare.

Isabel had heard it from Sydenham's house on nearby Lombard Street. All morning she had been sunk in sleep, seeking its oblivion like a drug after the painful parting from Martin in Rochester, but the commotion outside had awoken her. Hurrying out Sydenham's front door, she had seen the

Queen's entourage pass by at the end of the street as it moved north from Cheapside. The Queen had ridden from Westminster with her lords and ladies, knights and gentlemen, heralds and bishops and continuously blaring trumpeters. Driven by curiosity, Isabel had fallen in with the crowd and followed the royal entourage to Guildhall.

Now, the Queen stood on the hustings—the platform at the end of the hall where the Lord Mayor's court was held—and looked out at the crowd from under a golden cloth of state. She was almost surrounded by pale-faced aldermen. Thomas White, the Lord Mayor, stood on her right, and Lord William Howard, commander of the city's defenses, stood on her left. Sir Edward Sydenham and John Grenville were crowded up beside Lord Howard, and a dozen prominent citizens were crammed in around the Lord Mayor. Isabel caught a glimpse of Ambassador de Noailles complacently studying his feet on the marble floor. And near a wall where a tapestry had been ripped askew by the jostling crowd stood Master Legge of the Crane, anxiously whispering to a friend. It seemed to Isabel that half of London was here. Bakers, goldsmiths, cordwainers, housewives, glovers, constables, haberdashers, leather-sellers. Some had been drawn by animosity, some by respect, most by curiosity. All were waiting for Queen Mary's words. And none more intently than Isabel.

"Loving subjects," the Queen began afresh, "at my coronation I was wedded to the realm and to the laws of the realm. I wear here on my finger the spousal ring, and it never was, nor ever hereafter shall be, left off." She held up her right hand and displayed the ring. "At that coronation, you promised your allegiance and obedience unto me, and by your oath you may not suffer any rebel to usurp the governance of our person, or to occupy our estate. This traitor Wyatt is just such a rebel, who most certainly intends to subdue the laws to his will, and to make general havoc and spoil of your goods."

At this last statement, a drone of apprehension eddied through the hall, a sound almost palpable in its intensity. Isabel saw Legge scowling and nodding his head. He was not alone. Everywhere, men of property were nodding in nervous agreement at the Queen's warning of pillage.

Queen Mary seemed buoyed by the response. Her voice rang out, "And this I further tell you, as your Queen. I cannot say how a mother loves her children, for I was never mother of any. But certainly a prince and governor may as naturally and as earnestly love subjects as the mother does her child. Then assure yourselves that I, being your sovereign lady and Queen, do as earnestly and as tenderly love and favor you. And I, thus loving you, cannot but think that you as heartily and faithfully love me."

This brought a low murmur of praise. Many of the listeners began to smile.

"And concerning my intended marriage," the Queen went on fervently, "against which the rebels pretend their quarrel, understand that I entered into that treaty with the advice of all our Privy Council, who considered the great advantages that might ensue from it, both for the wealth of our realm and also of our loving subjects. Touching myself, I thank God that I have hitherto lived a virgin, and I doubt not but with God's grace I could live so still. But if it might please God that I might leave some fruit of my body behind me to be your governor, I trust you would not only rejoice thereat, but also I know it would be to your great comfort."

These personal admissions—so intimate, so generous—brought more smiles of warmth. The Queen seemed to take courage from them. "And in the word of a queen," she went on, head high, "I promise you that if it shall not reasonably appear to the nobility and commons of Parliament that this marriage shall be for the benefit and advantage of all the whole country, then I will abstain, not only from this marriage, but also from any other whereof any peril may ensue to this most noble realm of England."

"God bless Your Majesty!" a hoarse voice cried.

The Queen smiled. "Wherefore now, as good and faithful subjects pluck up your hearts! And like true men stand fast with your lawful prince against these rebels, both our enemies and yours. If you do, I am minded to live and die with you, and strain every nerve in your cause, for this time your fortunes, goods, honor, safety, wives, and children are in the balance. Fear not the rebels!" she resolutely concluded. "I assure you I fear them nothing at all!"

There was silence. Then a cheer. Then a chorus of cheers. Caps flew in the air. An old man began to weep.

Beaming, the Lord Mayor led the Queen from the dais, beckoning her out of the hall toward the private council chamber. Aldermen surged after them. Citizens in the hall, buzzing with excitement, began to push back out toward the street, eager to spread the report of the rousing speech. The crowd seemed to be flowing in several directions at once, and Isabel was knocked and shoved, then caught up in one of the moving streams and borne outside to the courtyard. Trying to withstand the current she gradually pushed her way to the edge of the crowd. She was tugging her disheveled clothes back into order when she looked up and froze. A man's body was hanging from a gibbet right before her, his eyes staring in death.

"He was caught approaching the Duke of Suffolk's house," a voice behind her said calmly. "He was bringing a message from Wyatt."

She twisted around. It was Sir Edward Sydenham. "A message?" she asked shakily. "What was it?"

"The writing was in code, too cryptic to understand. The man died before divulging its meaning."

She looked back at the dead man, executed right here at Guildhall as a warning. His thumbs were black. His forehead was one livid bruise around a band of small puncture wounds clotted with dried black blood. He had been tortured. Isabel felt suddenly weak . . . was aware of her vision darkening. Dizziness swept her just as Sydenham's arm slid around her waist. "Come," he said gently, supporting her, "let me take you home."

Carlos halted on the frozen stream that snaked toward the village of Dartford. Beyond the bank that rose to the height of his shoulders he could make out the helmet and face of a soldier who was trudging across the path from the village. Carlos ducked. The bank hid him from the soldier's view, and he was satisfied that his horse, left hobbled behind a church a quarter mile back, was well out of sight, too. The stream had seemed the ideal route to penetrate the enemy's camp undetected, but now Carlos could hear that the soldier was coming toward him, and out here on the barren surface of the ice he was exposed. Wanting to appear like a villager, he had brought no weapon except the dagger under his sheepskin coat, but now his right hand itched for a sword.

He looked over his shoulder. A few paces back a large willow tree grew aslant the stream, its branches draping down the bank. On his knees he slid across the ice toward the tree, grappled the trailing branches, and pulled himself behind their curtain. He noticed that the ice here was bluer, thinner. But noticed it too late. The soldier's boots were already rustling the dead cattails on the bank, right beside the willow. On his knees, Carlos did not move.

Through the willow curtain he saw the soldier's pike tip smash a hole in the thin ice. It cracked and crazed right up to Carlos's knees. Slowly he lowered his upper body onto his forearms to spread his weight. But ice water was seeping across from the hole and spreading under the willow branches. It soaked his gloves and his sleeves up to the elbows, and his breeches below the knees, freezing his hands and shins. But he dared not move on the fragile ice.

He heard another slosh of water and glimpsed, through the willow curtain, a bucket on a rope skimming the water in the hole. The soldier grunted as he heaved the bucket out. His feet rustled again through the cattails as he turned to go. Carlos heard his boots faintly crunching ice film on the rutted path. The sound became fainter and finally died away. Still on elbows and knees, Carlos carefully pushed backward out under the tangle of branches. Slowly he moved along to where the ice was thick and secure.

He stood and peered up over the lip of the bank. The soldier was turning the corner of a cow byre at the farthest edge of the village by the first huddle of cottages. Carlos looked to the left and right along the village's perimeter to locate Wyatt's sentries. It was barely dusk, but small watch fires already blazed in three sentry positions. He was sure more watch fires would be lit as darkness fell. But he would not be waiting until then; a man roving around a sleeping camp would draw suspicion. Instead, he had picked this time, the supper hour. The villagers would be heading home to eat, and Wyatt's company, tired and hungry after their day's march from Rochester, would be concentrating on their food. Besides, he needed enough light to see what he had come to see. Dusk gave him his best opportunity.

As he walked along the frozen stream he peeled off his freezing gloves and stuffed them away. The soggy extremities of his clothing remained plastered to his skin. There was nothing he could do about that. At the village edge, he came to a small fulling mill, deserted. Here he had to stop, for on the mill's far side the ice had been chopped way to give access to the water, leaving only a precarious shelf of ice on either bank. There was no way he could continue walking along the stream. He checked over both banks. A sentry was posted on either side, though neither was close to the stream. The one to the right, a long bow shot away, stood over a small fire at the corner of a farmer's field. He was facing away from the stream, warming his backside by the fire. The sentry to the left, even farther off, sat huddled up in the crook of an apple tree, whittling a stick. Carlos climbed up the bank to the mill. Outside the mill doors he found several buckets and a water carrier's yoke. He set the yoke over his shoulders and slung a bucket on either end. Lowering his head in a menial posture, he started toward the village. The sentry by the fire glanced at him idly, then turned to warm his hands. The one whittling in the tree did not even look up.

None of the town's inhabitants bothered him as he passed, though a dog tethered outside a cooper's shed barked furiously at him. A farmer and his son were pitching hay from a cart into an open barn, going about their work as though unconcerned that an army of rebels had camped in their town. Carlos turned onto the muddy main street, where an old woman mumbling her own private pains shuffled by him, ignoring him. The low din of many men's voices reached him, probably from the market square at the village center, he guessed. The voices and the incessant, dull clatter told him that the company was converging there to eat. Soldiers passed him in twos and threes, hurrying toward the aroma of stewing capon and onions wafting from the cauldrons set up in the square, but no one stopped him.

Getting inside had been easy.

For almost an hour Carlos prowled the village, hands slung over his yoke, taking stock of everything he saw. The munitions wagons and the condition of the mules that would draw them. The hundreds of bundles of arrows stacked in the fletchers' carts. The cache of matchlocks, carefully stored in a tanner's shed to keep their match wicks, presoaked in saltpeter, dry. The forest of newly sharpened pikes ranged in a smithy where the air still held a faintly burned odor from the overworked whetstone. The two small cannon tucked into a byre; these must be the guns the Duke of Norfolk had abandoned at Rochester Bridge after his men rushed over to Wyatt. Carlos counted horses and noted how many were fit mounts for cavalry. Above all, as he edged the market square and the villagers' barns where the billeted men returned to hunker down to eat, he counted soldiers. Despite his concentration, he could not prevent an interloping thought when he caught sight of two young officers talking: either of them could be the man Isabel meant to marry. He forced the thought away.

He reached the town's northern edge where it dwindled down toward the broad River Thames. Here, a wooden footbridge straddled the frozen stream that fed into the river. He stopped on the bridge and looked out. A straggle of huts and a strip of dun-colored field, its furrows patched with snow, gave way to thick clumps of trees growing along the Thames. Through breaks in the treeline Carlos could just make out the slate-colored water. Through one such opening a solitary watch fire flickered at the river's edge. There seemed to be no one beside the fire, though it was difficult to be sure from this distance. But Carlos suspected he was right; that the sentry had probably come into town to get his food instead of waiting to have it brought. No breach of discipline would surprise him among these English farmer-soldiers.

A fitful evening breeze made his skin feel clammy, for the walk through the cold air had done little to dry his clothes. It would be full darkness soon, and he still had to get out of town again and reach his horse. It was time to go. But he had not yet checked the river.

His eyes were drawn to a tithe barn at the far edge of the field, near the path to the riverbank. One of its broad doors stood open, and in the shadows under its slate roof Carlos thought he made out the dull gleam of gunmetal. It might be only a trick of the failing light, he thought. Although the sun had dipped below the treetops on the far Thames bank, the strip of sky above the river still quivered with a feeble pewter iridescence. But if it was not a trick of light, the glimmers betokened trouble. He could not see anyone guarding the barn, nor any sign of encampment around it. Probably Wyatt had considered it too insecure a spot, so far from the center of the town where there was ample shelter for all his men. Carlos decided to investigate on the way to the river.

The path to the tithe barn was lined knee-high with the husks of dead grasses. As he moved through, the husks rustled with one voice, like an old man's death rattle. A gull screeched overhead, swooping in from the Thames. There were no signs of any soldiers.

At the barn, Carlos found he had been right. Inside, five big cannon were resting on five sturdy carriages. And in the straw there were bushels of shot and lasts of gunpowder, sound and dry. He wondered where Wyatt could have got hold of such impressive ordnance. He set down his buckets and slipped off the yoke, and reached out to feel the gunmetal, cold against his wind-raw hands. He recalled Abergavenny talking about a naval captain who had deserted the Queen's ships. Had the captain delivered the ships' guns to Wyatt? As he walked around the carriages, he noted the fresh joinery. Wyatt must have had the carpenters of Rochester sweating for days to build these carriages. But it had clearly been worth the effort. The guns were formidable.

He had to move on. He stepped outside. He looked down the path toward the river but the trees obscured the view. He would have to go right to the riverbank to check what he had come down here to see: whether there was any amassment of boats. If so, it could mean that Wyatt intended to ferry his army to the northern shore, to Essex, for his advance on London. Knowledge of that would tip the royalists to concentrate their defenses at the city's eastern gates and the Tower. The information was essential. Carlos took one last look, appraising the river area. The only sign of life was the solitary watch fire glowing faintly through the trees. But it lay to his right; in his direct path to the river there was no one. And soon the daylight would be completely gone. He started toward the water.

Coming out between the trees he saw a sentry at the fire after all—and far closer than he had judged. The sentry, wrapped in a cloak, was seated on a log before the fire, his back toward Carlos. His head drooped, but his body, far from appearing slumped in drowsiness, seemed alert, as if he were studying something he held before him in his hands.

Apart from the evening breeze sighing through the trees, there was silence. Carlos stood still. Any sudden movement on the twig-strewn path could draw the sentry around. He must leave quietly. He had already taken in the riverfront at a glance. There was only one lone skiff, beached in the grass with a jagged hole in its bow. No flotilla. Wyatt would be remaining on the south shore. That was all Carlos needed to know.

He was about to turn when the sentry abruptly lifted his head and looked sideways. Though it was obvious he had not seen Carlos in the shadows behind him, he gazed at the bend in the river without moving, intent, like a dog sniffing the air. Carlos froze at what he saw. The man's profile was clearly lit by the fire. A leather patch covered his left eye. It was Richard Thornleigh.

Carlos's mind flooded with one thought: a hundred pounds for Thornleigh dead, to be paid at the Blue Boar in London on Candlemas night.

That was tonight. And the Blue Boar was only a two-hour ride away. And a hundred pounds meant freedom.

But why did he suddenly feel her warm breath against his throat, just as if she were here, just like that night when she'd cried out from her nightmare and had come into his arms . . .

A fantasy. Forget her. She remembers you only to curse your name. Don't weaken. Not this time.

But he knew he could not attack: a fight might bring soldiers—there could well be sentries just around the river bend—and then he would never get out.

Think of what is possible. Get his trust first. You did it once before.

He had no sword, but his dagger lay in his belt, under his sheepskin. It could slit a throat. It could sever a finger. He stepped forward.

Sitting on the log and rereading Honor's letter for the hundredth time, Thornleigh heard a crunch of twigs behind him and glanced over his shoulder.

"Richard Thornleigh," a voice whispered from the shadows.

Thornleigh dropped the letter. He grabbed his pike leaning against the log and stood, whirling around. A man was approaching him from the path between the trees. Thornleigh could not see his face clearly, but he noted that the man was not dressed like Wyatt's soldiers. "Stop!" he said, lifting the pike and pointing it. Its sharp steel blade glinted in the firelight. "Who's there?"

The man stopped at the rim of the fire's glow. He raised his hands in a gesture of surrender. "A friend," he said. He smiled. "You do not remember me?"

Thornleigh peered at the shadowed face. Holding the pike outstretched, he had to take a wide stance, for the fever had left him somewhat unsteady on his feet.

"Colchester jail," the man said. "Remember?"

Thornleigh suddenly recognized him. The hard face. The strong fighter's body. And the accent. "The Spaniard?" he asked warily. He was not sure. He had seen so many strange and desperate men in the last few days, the faces had become a jumble in his mind. And this one, made lurid by the dancing firelight, was still indistinct.

"Let me come closer, into the light," the man said. He stepped forward, slowly lowering his hands, and approached the log that lay between them. He stopped a few feet beyond the tip of Thornleigh's pike. "See? You know me. Carlos Valverde." He smiled again. "Call me Carlos."

Thornleigh was amazed. It *was* him—the Spaniard who had tried to arrange his rescue in Colchester jail, the one who had made contact using the old password. "Christ," he said, marveling, "I thought they'd hanged you for sure."

Carlos laughed lightly. "I am not so easy to kill."

Thornleigh did not laugh, nor did he lower the pike. Why had the fellow been skulking around in the shadows? he wondered. "What the devil are you doing here?" he asked.

"Came to join up. I am a soldier."

Thornleigh recalled the few words they had exchanged after they'd been chained together in the Hole. "A mercenary," he said.

Carlos nodded.

"Have you talked to an officer?" Thornleigh asked, jerking his chin back toward the town, its rooftops aglow from the market-square fires.

Carlos shook his head. "Saw you first. Good thing, yes?" He was still smiling.

"I'll take you up myself then," Thornleigh said. "As soon as my relief arrives. You'll have to come under guard, though," he said, holding the pike rigid. "Orders."

"Of course. *Gracias.*"

Thornleigh noticed the bruised scar puckering Carlos's eyebrow and remembered that he had got that gash in the fight in Colchester jail. He couldn't help wondering again who had been behind the rescue attempt. It hadn't been Legge, after all; in their brief talk at the Crane, Legge had disclaimed any knowledge of the plan. Yet who else knew the old password? "You never did know who hired you to approach me, did you?" he asked. "Back in Colchester."

Carlos shook his head. "Some rich man's servant. A stranger. Sorry."

Thornleigh let the matter drop. He didn't really care anymore.

Carlos took a step forward. Thornleigh jerked the pike. "That's close enough."

"But I have news. Let me come and tell you. It is about your daughter. I saw her in London."

Thornleigh's mouth fell open. "What are you talking about? Isabel's in Antwerp."

"No. In London. She has been searching the prisons for you."

"Bel? Searching prisons? Impossible. She wouldn't know the first thing about—"

"She has done it. She is very brave. She unlocked my chains in jail. She hired me to find you, to get you free. We have been looking for you. We are . . . friends."

Thornleigh tried to take in the incredible tale. "Bel . . . unlocked you? But . . . what about the jailer?"

Carlos smiled. "I killed him."

"Good God," Thornleigh whispered. He was glad. No man had deserved to die more than that bastard Mosse. But worry instantly reclaimed him. "Why have you left her? Where's she gone? How will she—"

Carlos held up a hand to stop the questions. "She did not want my help anymore. So I came here." His smile hardened. "I need the work." He stepped closer. He was only a handbreadth away from the pike tip.

Thornleigh was still appalled by the news. Isabel . . . in London. What would become of her? "Why did you dismiss you?" he asked anxiously. "She'll be all alone."

"She knows she must join your son in Antwerp." Carlos's tone was consoling. "That was your order, yes?"

Thornleigh nodded dully. He forced himself to accept this assessment. Of course Isabel would go to Adam. What else could she do? A chill breeze lifted, fingering the inside of his collar and making him shiver. Carlos was slowly moving around the end of the log. Their eyes locked. Carlos stopped. Up in the town a ram's horn blared a jubilant note, and soldiers' laughter and high-spirited voices followed it, faintly rolling down to the riverbank. Carlos suddenly winced and bent to tug at the knee of his breeches. Thornleigh saw that on both of Carlos's legs the cloth was wet and plastered to his shins. His sleeve cuffs were wet, too. Carlos nodded toward the fire. "Let me come and dry out? I thought the ice on the river would be solid." His smile became sheepish. "I was wrong."

Thornleigh nodded distractedly, still fretting over Isabel. Carlos moved in. He thrust out his hands above the low flames and smiled at Thornleigh. A thin screech came from the trees. Some creature—a hare?—had been seized by a predator.

Thornleigh suddenly noticed the letter on the ground where he had dropped it. It lay near the fire. Too near; one edge was beginning to curl and smoke. He snatched it up, then straightened quickly, still holding the pike in his other hand. Carlos watched him, rubbing his hands together over the fire.

Thornleigh felt dizzy from standing up so quickly. The last days events had taken their toll: the fever, the escape out of Newgate on the corpse cart, the furtive dash to the Crane, and the frigid ride here from London. He had left the Crane so weakened, it had taken two days of slow riding and long stops at inns before he'd reached Wyatt's army, finally meeting them on their march. He sat down heavily on the log, facing the fire. He set the pike across his knees and drew a long, steadying breath.

Carlos turned his back to the fire and gestured to the paper in Thornleigh's hand. "A letter?" he asked cheerfully.

Thornleigh stared bleakly at it. "From my wife."

Carlos frowned. "I thought Lord Grenville killed her."

Thornleigh looked at him hard. "You know a lot about my family."

"Your daughter told me." Carlos's hand eased into the opening at the waist of his coat, then lay still. "Very sad."

Thornleigh looked down at the paper with a bitter smile. "Well, it's my wife's letter, yes," he said, "but not written to me. It's to a coward named Sydenham."

Carlos stiffened. "Sydenham?" he said with surprise. "Edward Sydenham? The lawyer?"

Their eyes met. "You know him?" Thornleigh asked.

Carlos's face hardened. "I was in jail because I tried to kill him. I had some land, and he stole it with his lawyer's tricks. When I went for him the bailiff stopped me. The bailiff died instead." His tone was grim, but he said nothing more. Yet Thornleigh sensed there *was* more, and that Carlos's hatred of the lawyer was deep.

Carlos asked sharply, "How do *you* know Sydenham?"

The question brought memories swarming back in Thornleigh's mind. The fire crackled behind Carlos. Thornleigh's gaze was drawn into the core of the flames. "Sydenham was once a heretic, a hunted criminal. My wife took pity on such people."

"Sydenham? Hunted?" Carlos sounded amazed. "Why?"

Thornleigh watched the sparks swirl upward in the cold air and die, snuffed out like fragments of his past, fragments of his life. "It was twenty-some years ago," he said wearily. He rested his forearms on the pike across his lap.

Carlos asked impatiently, "What happened?"

Thornleigh watched the sparks. "Sydenham was on the run after escaping the Bishop's lockup," he began. "My wife, Honor, had arranged to smuggle him out of England in the hold of my ship. I wasn't there. The ship lay in Yarmouth harbor, ready to sail, and Honor was about to go back to shore when the port authorities rowed out to search. They'd been tipped about Sydenham. On deck, he saw them approach and he panicked. Like I said, Sydenham's a coward. He wept and wailed to Honor, and she saw that he was going to endanger the entire crew, and friends of ours on shore as well, if she didn't placate him. So she disguised him in her cloak and let him slip down into a skiff. The officials watched him row for shore, thinking it was her. When they boarded, Honor was tucked in the hiding hole in Sydenham's place."

Thornleigh turned the letter in his hands, watching the fire shadows dance over it like frantic ghosts. "But the officers were sure Sydenham had stowed away somewhere," he went on, "so they bunked down on board to wait him out. Honor suffered in that cramped hellhole in the bowels of the ship for three days. Through hunger and thirst. Through a storm. Through sickness. She almost died. All because of Sydenham." He snorted. "*He* went abroad and got rich."

Thornleigh glanced up. Carlos seemed rapt.

"Oh, no harm was done in the short run," Thornleigh went on, tucking the letter carefully back into his tunic. "I came home, and when I heard Honor was hiding in the hold, I swam out and set fire to the ship, then got aboard in the panic and pulled Honor out. We got away without being seen. Things went back to normal, and all was well for a while. But the coward had left evidence on board—his Protestant Bible. And one of the officials had found it. It incriminated Honor. A priest named Bastwick got hold of it, a man who had always been her enemy. He let some time pass. Then he struck. They arrested Honor. They tried her for heresy and chained her to the stake at Smithfield. And they were going to burn her. Until some friends helped me rescue her. Still, Honor and I had to leave England, leave everything behind." He shook his head. "All that misery. All because of the man who was supposed to have received this," he said, tapping his chest where the letter lay. "Edward Sydenham."

Thornleigh slumped. He didn't know what had prodded him to tell this story to a virtual stranger, but now that he had, Honor's spirit seemed near, almost palpable, and he felt as though an anvil had been set on his shoulders: the awful weight of his failure nine days ago to protect her. He felt something more, as well. An urge to explain; a need to make at least one person understand that he meant to counterbalance this crushing tragedy ... if only by a hair. "I mean to die helping these rebels," he said. "For Honor's sake."

He looked up at Carlos. "She wanted them to succeed, you see?" He felt the threatening sting of tears. He pulled himself up to sit straight and took a deep breath to quell the pang. "Wyatt's army marches to London tomorrow, and I'm going to be marching in the front rank. I'm no soldier, but I know what I can do. I can take the first arrow. It's not much. But it might let some of these younger men get past. Then maybe *they* can make a difference." He fixed his eye on Carlos. He heard the hollowness in his own voice as he said, "I'm already dead. Died the night Grenville murdered my wife. I'm just choosing how to fall down."

A drunken soldier's hoot sounded beyond the trees. Carlos's head whipped up. Thornleigh, too, glanced over his shoulder. In a break in the trees he could make out four soldiers—mere silhouettes in the dusk—ambling across the footbridge up beyond the tithe barn. Their voices were giddy with tipsy laughter. "That'll be my relief," Thornleigh said. "Along with his friends, by the look of it." The soldiers left the footbridge and disappeared into the trees, coming toward the riverbank.

Thornleigh was turning back, readying to stand, when Carlos's boot flashed up and kicked the pike from his hands. Carlos clamped a hand over Thornleigh's mouth and pinned Thornleigh's head against his thigh, and held a dagger at his throat. "No sound!" he whispered fiercely.

Thornleigh's mind thrashed. He had been duped! Yet if he could just call out to the soldiers—warn them—Carlos would be trapped. But the hand pressed his mouth and nose so brutally, he could barely breathe. He clawed at the fingers. If he could just manage *one shout* before the blade sliced . . .

"Do not try it, old man! There is a hundred pounds for me if I kill you. Do not make me do it!"

Thornleigh's body jerked stiff, betraying his shock.

"Now you know," Carlos growled. "I was not hired in jail to save you. I was hired to kill you."

In a flash like the firelight glinting off the dagger, Thornleigh saw the truth. There had been no mysterious friend from the past trying to arrange his rescue, only more enemies.

"But your daughter wants you alive," Carlos said, his voice a mixture of resignation and self-disgust. "And I will tell you something more," he added with deadly precision, as though certain that what he was about to say would stun his victim into passivity. "She is searching London for you still. With the help of Sydenham."

Sydenham? Searching for him? A flare of understanding blazed in Thornleigh's mind. Suddenly he knew. Suddenly *everything* was clear. His splayed hands flew up in a stiff gesture that implored: *I will make no trouble . . . let me speak!*

Carlos's fierce grip slackened. Thornleigh gasped a breath and blurted to him, "Sydenham will kill Isabel! *He* hired you to kill me!"

Carlos twisted him around by the shoulders. "What?"

Thornleigh gulped breath. Words came tumbling out, linking the shards of suspicion that had been lying scattered at the bottom of the dark pool of his despair. At Carlos's statement they had burst to the surface and fused. "Sydenham—he's come home to marry." He spoke quickly, urgently. "Marry Lord Grenville's daughter. She's the Queen's best friend, a staunch Catholic. So Sydenham must cover his heretic tracks. Last week the only people still alive who knew his past were me and my wife. Honor was removed. That left me." He looked at Carlos's wondering face. Words rolled out in a rush. "Sydenham's the only one left who knows the password. Don't you see? He sent his servant to you, giving the password so you could identify me, because he doesn't know what I look like. Sydenham and I never met."

Carlos's jaw dropped. "Sydenham . . . hired me?"

"Yes!" Finally, the last piece of the puzzle rammed into place and twisted the wire that had been gouging Thornleigh's heart. "Sydenham goaded Grenville to murder my wife."

He and Carlos stared at each other. "And now ... my daughter is with him."

Turmoil flickered in Carlos's eyes. "He will kill her?"

"If he suspects that she knows his past, yes." The horrifying image was tempered by another thought. "But my wife and I never told her about the old days, for her own safety. I pray God, her ignorance might just save her." An idea took hold of him. "What does Sydenham look like?"

"A fox," Carlos said. "Red hair, thin face, fine clothes."

"Tomorrow," Thornleigh said with steely relish, "I'll have another reason to march in the front line to London." If he could get inside, he could save Isabel and avenge Honor—both in one stroke. He would kill Edward Sydenham.

Loud voices startled them both. The soldiers, though still not visible in the trees, sounded very near. In a moment they would emerge onto the riverbank.

Carlos's dagger flashed in front of Thornleigh's nose. He said in a threatening whisper, "I am going to warn your daughter. Do not raise an alarm!"

Thornleigh watched Carlos jump over the log and head on the run for the thick trees beside the path. With a knot in his stomach, Thornleigh watched him go, traitorously hoping he would make it. *My enemy's enemy is my friend.*

Carlos disappeared into the trees just as the soldiers emerged onto the riverbank.

Edward Sydenham opened the door to his parlor. Seeing Isabel sitting on a low stool by the fire, reading, he smiled and came in, closing the door. "Do forgive me for leaving you alone so long, mistress. The Queen's business," he said with an apologetic shrug.

"Of course, sir," she said, closing the book on her lap. "Those gentlemen in your hall seemed very agitated. Is it bad news about the rebels?"

"Oh, on the contrary. The meeting was euphoric. The Queen's oration this afternoon has had a tremendous effect on the city. The guilds are now promising to furnish a thousand more men-at-arms. It was all I could do in there to contain everyone's enthusiasm. And I must confess to some personal satisfaction in the matter. It was I who urged the Queen to address the citizens." He smiled at her. "My only regret," he added, "is that the business kept me so long away from your company tonight."

Isabel lowered her eyes.

"And," Edward added triumphantly, "I have brought someone to meet you. He is just coming."

She looked up, pale with hope. "Not ... ?"

"No, not your father. Forgive me for rousing your expectations. Though we *will* find him, do not fear. And that is why tonight I have asked this friend—" He broke off at the sound of a light knock. The door opened.

"Pardon, Sir Edward." It was his steward, Palmer. "A gentleman to see you."

A florid-faced man of about forty, with a luxurious black mustache and trim black beard, appeared at the door. Palmer retreated. The visitor came in. His manner was gruff, at odds with his fine attire: a well-cut doublet of moss-green velvet, a filigreed silver sword hilt, a tear-shaped pearl dangling from his velvet cap.

Edward turned to Isabel. "Mistress, allow me to introduce Nicholas Van Borselen, shipmaster."

The man bowed to Isabel. She stood.

"Van Borselen is no ordinary captain," Edward assured Isabel with a smile. "He is shipmaster to Francisco de los Cobos, the Emperor's secretary for Spain and Flanders. He has just delivered letters to Whitehall for the secretary, and his ship now lies at anchor off Billingsgate, about to embark for Antwerp. I have asked him here to meet you."

He went to his desk and from a drawer took out an oval emerald the size of a robin's egg. "Nicholas," he said, "I want you to postpone your departure. Just until this lady comes out to your ship. It may be a day, it may be longer, but you will wait for her. She will come aboard with an older man." Edward reached out and lifted Van Borselen's hand. He placed the emerald in the shipmaster's palm and closed his fingers around it. "You will set sail the moment this lady and her guest are on board. Do you understand?"

"Yes, Sir Edward," Van Borselen said with a heavy accent. His eyes, though hooded and shrewd-looking, flashed excitement. The emerald was worth a small fortune.

"Thank you," Edward said. "You may go."

The shipmaster bowed to Edward, and again to Isabel, and walked out.

Edward moved to his desk and sat, comfortably stretching out his legs, his eyes on Isabel. She seemed lost for words. He knew his calling in Van Borselen had worked its charm;

Edward had suspected that the girl was holding back some information, some names and places where her father might be hiding; now, she would trust him with it all. Edward smiled at her. "You will recognize Van Borselen's ship by the Emperor's flag, the black eagle, on his forecastle deck."

"Sir," she stammered, "you are so kind. I do not know . . . how to thank you."

"Your sweet smile is thanks enough."

She blushed faintly and looked down. She sat again on the stool before the fire, clasping the book to her.

"What were you reading, mistress?" Edward asked pleasantly. "A book of mine?"

"No," she said distractedly, "this belonged to my mother."

"God rest her soul," he murmured.

But he was not thinking of Honor Thornleigh. He was admiring the swell of Isabel's breasts above her bodice. The gown she wore, a lavender-blue satin, was one he had had his chamberlain procure for her, her own clothes having become so bedraggled. He had found it peculiarly satisfying, this fact of dressing her. She really was quite lovely—the thick, dark hair and creamy skin and trusting blue eyes. And the swell of her breasts promised a voluptuous body. Not as young as he preferred, but there were compensations: this girl had awareness. Given that, her blushes and lowered lashes produced an effect that was uncommonly enticing.

She had said nothing in response to his pious comment about her mother. She looked very forlorn, he thought. Almost lost. And there was a pallor to her face that had not been present when he had first met her. It was this pallor, he realized, that made her blushes, when they came, appear almost fevered. Like one afraid, or in pain. It stirred him.

He stood and came to her. He bent and took up her hand and held it. "You have exhausted yourself in this search for your father, my dear. It distresses me exceedingly. Master Thornleigh will not thank me if I reunite him with a daughter fallen into sickness. Tomorrow you must rest and leave the search completely to me and my agents. You must not leave the house. Nor even leave your bed." He smiled down at her and squeezed her hand. "I command it."

She looked up at him as though unsure.

"Promise me?" he said.

"I promise."

CHAPTER THIRTY

>-►-i-‹›-i-◄-<

London Bridge

Isabel was true to her word. All the next day she did not leave Sydenham's house. Not until darkness was falling.

All day, Sydenham had hosted defense meetings in his hall practically without a break, while his steward managed the private search for Thornleigh. As twilight approached, Sydenham and John Grenville hastened off, Sydenham to more meetings at Whitehall, John to join Lord Howard in armament preparations on London Bridge. As soon as they were gone, Isabel quietly left the house. A hurried walk up to Ambassador de Noailles's lodging at the Charterhouse, an anxious wait for him at the yew-canopied wicket gate in his back garden, a furtive meeting with him, and then she was on her way again. But not back to Sydenham's house. Her route lay through the city streets and riverside lanes down to Coldharbour on the Thames, and the Old Swan water stairs.

Everywhere, people were scurrying home before the nine o'clock curfew should sound. Isabel made it in through Aldersgate just before the citizens' patrol closed the gate. On Cheapside, she passed a constable marching his band of armed men toward Newgate to take over the night watch there. In the growing darkness the fear in the city was almost palpable. Earlier, street traders had hastily dismantled their stalls and hauled their wares to safety. Householders had bolted their doors. No children had played in the twilit lanes. Late that afternoon shouting voices had spread the alarm that the rebels' pennants could be seen through the trees on the south shore of the Thames as their army approached along the Kent Road, and Isabel herself had heard the half-dozen ineffectual cannon shots that had boomed across the river at them from the Tower, more in panic than aggression. Wyatt's army had finally arrived. But in Southwark, just across London Bridge, they had halted.

Isabel reached the river just as the curfew tolled from the

Bow Bells. Now, anyone caught out of doors on any pretext but official business would be hauled off by a constable to one of the city's jails. Isabel had picked this wharf just upstream from London Bridge on the assumption—based on what she had overheard at Sydenham's—that Lord Howard was posting his riverside forces in three main locations: at the Tower to the east, on the bridge in the middle, and on wharves near London wall to the west. That would leave the small area around the Old Swan stairs free. She hoped.

The waterfront felt eerie: normal yet different. The barking of mastiffs from the kennels of the Southwark bear gardens echoed across the water as always, but there were none of the usual bursts of bawdy laughter rippling over from the brothels there. The windows of the multistoried shops and houses crowded on London Bridge glowed, as usual, in a spangle of torches and candles, but the nearby docks of Fish Wharf and the Steelyard were dark, empty of the customary link-boys with their lanterns. Muffled voices, as usual, sounded between the buildings above the river's swirling waters, but rather than the night-mellow talk of peaceable citizens, the voices were those of anxious, armed men on watch against the enemy. But Isabel took heart in seeing that she had been right about one thing: the Old Swan landing area seemed vacant of royalist soldiers. Shivering, she walked down to the broad water stairs.

She had to step gingerly, for the stone stairs were slick with a new sheen of ice, and the only light came from a cowardly half-moon that slunk behind clouds more often than it dared show its face. But she had no trouble finding a boat; the landing was crammed with tethered barges and lighters and skiffs. A mixed blessing, she grimly reminded herself; a proclamation that afternoon had commanded that all river craft be brought to the north shore and left there— on pain of death.

She climbed down into a small skiff whose bow already pointed out toward the river. She slipped the painter, sat at the oars, and grasped the handles. Even through her gloves the wooden handles felt cold as gunmetal. The squashed, tattered cushion beneath her wafted a dank odor of mildew. She looked over her left shoulder straight across to the far bank, her destination, and saw the small, flickering lights of torches on the wharf of Winchester House. They looked impossibly far away. She looked sideways to her right, at the bridge. It seemed close, frighteningly so, for she reckoned that her biggest challenge would be to keep the boat from being drawn downstream by the current toward the bridge. There, the river was compressed by twenty piers into twenty-one small but dangerous rapids. A common saw nattered in her brain: *Wise men go over, fools go under London Bridge.* Going over it was out of the question with Lord Howard's men stationed on it, and going under it was what she must avoid; she must go nowhere near it. She wondered if the beefy build of the lightermen, who ferried people and cargo, was a prerequisite of the job or merely a result. Well, she told herself, taking a deep breath, she would now find out.

She pushed off and rowed out into the river. Her first fear was soon removed: the current was not strong. And she was thankful that the night was calm, for any strong wind from the west might also have swept the little boat toward the bridge. Even so, the smothered din of the water rushing through the canyons of the twenty-one stone arches was a constant reminder of the peril, and she kept well west of the bridge as she plied her way toward Southwark.

The going was hard. Not halfway across she had to rest, panting. Despite the cold air, heat prickled her face and sweat slid down over her ribs. Then, suddenly, she was aware that she was drifting with the current; it had deviously strengthened here in midriver, silently locking her into its fluid vise. It was carrying her closer to the stone arches of the bridge. She had to row with extra vigor just to break its hold. Her muscles strained, her feet ground against the bottom of the boat, seeking purchase. Finally, as she glanced over her left shoulder at her destination, the Winchester House wharf torches that had seemed mere candle flames when she set out hove dead ahead in a lusty blaze. And men were moving on the wharf. Wyatt's men.

Only a few minutes more of hard rowing and she would be there.

"But why must she be your guest?" Frances demanded through tight lips. "It seems perverse to favor her. Her family are heretics and traitors."

"My dear," Edward said, "I have just explained—"

"That you are using her to track down her father. Yes, I see that. It is a fine plan, Edward. But is it necessary to bring her into your house? To clothe her and protect her? To entertain her and pamper her? Is she really so attractive a little strumpet?"

He looked at her in surprise.

Her hand flew to her mouth. "Oh, Edward," she said, instantly contrite, "I did not mean that *you* . . . It is just that a man of your standing is a target for unscrupulous girls, and—"

"The reason for her presence in my house," he interrupted, beginning to lose patience, "is that she can lead me to the man who murdered your father. I would have thought that was your paramount concern. It is certainly mine. The Queen's people cannot mount a proper hunt just now, not with all their energy focused on the rebels, you know that. Thornleigh could easily escape from England unless we work fast. Isabel Thornleigh knows her father's friends, his haunts. She offers us our best hope of finding him in time, and of seeing justice done to your family's name. Surely you can understand that." He had stopped short of saying *even* you, but his terse voice betrayed him.

And Frances caught the tone. "Oh, Edward, forgive me," she said, rushing to him, wringing her hands. "This crisis with the rebels has made me quite distraught. Her Majesty suffers so, you see? They are talking of her behind her back—her councilors. They are saying such dreadful, disloyal things. And now, God forgive me, my worrying has made me strike out at you. When I know you are doing everything you can to bring my father's murderer to justice. It is just that . . ." She hesitated, and lowered her head. "Edward, I could not bear that any woman should—"

"Hush, my dear. Let us have no more of that."

"No, no . . . I'm so sorry . . ."

Edward saw tears of relief brim in her eyes, which were already red and puffy. Imperceptibly he pulled back from her. She clutched his sleeve. He stiffly stroked her hand. He said dutifully, "No other woman will ever come between us."

"Do you mean that, Edward?" she cried, smiling. Her tears spilled. Her smile wobbled. "But of course you do! Oh, was ever a woman so blessed as I am blessed!" The tears rolled down her cheeks to the tiny lines that radiated from the corners of her mouth. Her nose dripped. Edward looked away, thinking of Isabel.

* * *

Southwark was swarming with Wyatt's men. Tom, the guard, was leading Isabel from the Winchester House wharf toward the center of the town, to see the commander. He held his torch high as he guided her through the clusters of soldiers milling in muddy Long Lane. They were sorting out posts and billets and arms placement, all in a kind of disciplined chaos. "Like pigs in a sty," Tom growled, pushing roughly at a mule's rear that blocked his way. "But the big guns are set right enough, m'lady, I'll say that much," he added with pride. "One over yonder to command Bermondsey Street," he said, pointing. "One down there at St. George's. Another back at the Bishop's wharf where you landed, so I warrant you saw that one. The last two are being brought up to the bridge. And I'll have a shilling off Jack Peters if those guns blast the bridge gate open before we sleep tonight."

Looking up at a window above a tavern, Isabel noticed an old couple in nightcaps watching the bustle below. "But has there been no resistance?" she asked Tom. "No fighting?"

"Not a blast nor a blow," he answered, grinning. "Folk hereabouts opened their arms as we marched in. No sign of the Bishop, either. I warrant he hied yonder across the bridge when he heard we were coming. And the scatter of the Queen's men that was here? Why, they've come over to join us! Just like t'other day with the daft old Duke's men! The commander says that's how it'll be all over London."

A gang of soldiers with shovels trudged by. "The commander's ordered a trench dug between us and the bridge," Tom explained. He grimaced as he looked back at the bridge a half mile behind him and Isabel, its jagged rooftops bristling in the night sky. He added in a confiding tone of alarm, "No telling what mischief the Queen's men have set up for us *there*."

They came upon Wyatt in front of St. George's. He was standing on the wide church steps in a huddle with a group of his officers. Two boys stood near, holding torches. Below, in the street, men marched past, wagons rattled by, lieutenants shouted orders, cart horses balked.

Wyatt turned and caught Isabel's eye. Surprise flooded his face. "Mistress Thornleigh!" His captains and lieutenants looked at her, too. Isabel cast a quick glance over their faces, irrationally thinking she might see Martin. But of course he was not there.

Wyatt quickly came down the steps to her. He took her elbow. "Come, let's talk." He drew her to the mouth of a lane to be out of the bustle. "So," he said brusquely. "What news?"

Isabel almost smiled; Sir Thomas never changed. No question about how she had made it here, no inquiry about her well-being. Not even any mention of Martin's desertion, although that was surely why he had been surprised to see her. She looked down the lane, littered, after all the rain, with mere strips of snow like dirty bandages. Martin was gone. Gone from her life, forever. She swallowed and turned back to Wyatt. "Much," she answered evenly.

She started with the worst. "The courier that Ambassador de Noailles sent to Scotland was caught by the Queen's men and taken into custody. The Ambassador dare not send another. However, he says the army from Scotland must be on its way."

Wyatt turned away. He seemed to be watching a detail of soldiers lugging a cannon carriage toward an ox, but Isabel could not see his face. He turned back to her abruptly. "What else?"

She hesitated. More bad news. "The Duke of Suffolk, sir," she began. Suffolk, in whom Wyatt had once placed so much hope of raising the rebellion throughout the Midlands, had finally been brought into London, in chains. "He was arrested in Leicestershire seven days ago," she said. "Apparently they found him hiding in a tree."

Wyatt winced slightly, but it was clear to Isabel that he had long ago given up on Suffolk. Still, she understood the significance of this setback. All hope of any help from the Midlands was now crushed.

"What troops has the Queen raised since I saw you last?"

She explained that the Earl of Pembroke had been named the new commander of the Queen's forces outside London, and that these soldiers—the nobles' tenants and retainers—had been grouping in St. James's Park, while the city men under Lord Howard were gathering in Finsbury Field. From these musters, the Ambassador had made a tally of their strength: almost six thousand. "But they are very fearful, sir," Isabel added eagerly, "for they suspect the French are coming, and they estimate your combined force at nearly ten thousand."

Wyatt said nothing.

She went on to tell him all she had overheard at Sydenham's house of his meetings with the Queen's commanders, of details of armaments and their placement. She also explained that a royal order had gone out to break down all the bridges for fifteen miles upriver from London. She ended with a report of the Queen's rousing speech yesterday at Guildhall. Conscious of the weight of all this heavy news she had laid on Wyatt's shoulders, she was eager to lighten the burden. "There is great dissent throughout the city, sir. Many of the Queen's councilors are going about loudly and angrily disclaiming her statement that they were in favor of the Spanish marriage. The Ambassador told me that such talk has sowed great uncertainty and fear among the wealthy citizens. It is undoing much of the spirit of allegiance the Queen fostered yesterday. Meanwhile, Master Peckham's secret group of your supporters gains strength every hour." She outlined to him Peckham's readiness to place his men to help Wyatt when the time came.

Wyatt nodded, reflecting on the implications of this. "Our help inside the city, that is what we must nurture. We've made a good start here in Southwark. I've given orders that I will brook no despoiling. Every crust of bread and every drop of ale taken shall be paid for. I have broken open no doors at the Marshalsea prison nor the Clink to let the prisoners run wild." He smiled archly. "Polity, mistress. This course had reassured the people of Southwark, and they are now actively helping us. I am hoping their example will inspire the Londoners." He looked at her earnestly. "Can you stay awhile?"

"Here? Now?"

"Yes. I'll have some information within an hour or so that must be taken to de Noailles."

She hesitated. She dared not be away too long. She must be back in Sydenham's house before he returned from Whitehall if she was not to stir his suspicions.

"I see that you must go," Wyatt said with the equanimity of a commander accustomed to making do. "Then let me explain now. You must be my link to our London support. You must explain my strategy to de Noailles and Peckham. It is this. My preference is to attack across the bridge come daylight. But it may be too well fortified. I have not yet been able to determine that, since the gatehouse has been closed and barred from the inside. To open it would require blasting with the guns. We're getting them into position now, and we've sent a man up onto the gatehouse roof to reconnoiter. It is his report I'm waiting for. But here is the point. If it proves that London Bridge is too strongly fortified and cannot be taken, I may have to move to the next bridge upriver."

"That would be at Kingston."

"Yes. From there, we can double back on the city."

"Through Charing Cross village," Isabel said, calculating the quickest route. "Then along the Strand. That would bring you to Ludgate."

"Exactly. So, if this plan becomes necessary, it is imperative that our friends inside London concentrate their forces at Ludgate. Peckham must see to it that Ludgate is opened to us when we arrive. It's essential. Do you understand?"

She nodded.

Abruptly he told her he must return to his officers' meeting, and he beckoned Tom to escort Isabel back to her skiff. Without another word, Wyatt left her side. She pulled tight her hood, preparing for the journey back across the river.

The west wind had risen. The rowing was harder. The many lights winking ahead on the London shore—far more than little Southwark had displayed—confused her. And there were so many dimly lit docks, it was difficult, in short glances over her shoulder, to be sure which murky stairs belonged to the Old Swan and which belonged to other landing places: Fish Wharf nearest the bridge, then the Steelyard, Dowgate Dock, the Three Cranes, Queenhithe, Paul's Wharf, Baynard's Castle ... so many wharves in a half mile! She must not veer as far west as Baynard's Castle. There would certainly be a security contingent there. Baynard's belonged to the Earl of Pembroke, and if they should capture her ...

Enough! she told herself. It was pointless to let such fears unnerve her. Baynard's was a full half mile west of the bridge, and with St. Paul's looming behind it, marking it, it should not be difficult to steer clear.

She reached the midriver current. As she lifted her shoulder to wipe sweat from her upper lip, her right oar skipped

across the top of the water instead of digging in. The instant
lack of resistance threw her off balance. She fell backward.
She held the oars tightly, but her right hand plunged with her
fall, and the gunnel, acting as a fulcrum, wrenched the oar
out of its socket. The wind caught the rising blade and
knocked the handle out of her grasp. The oar splashed over-
board. She flailed over the side for it. The icy water
drenched her sleeve. She caught the oar by the tip of its
blade just before it floated off. But by the time she had
righted herself with both oars again, the boat was pointed toward the bridge and drifting with the current at a dangerous
speed. The sound of the water hissing under the arches became a muffled roar.

Frantically she pulled on her oar to turn the boat to face
the London bank. She rowed with all her might. The bow
lurched left, then right, but she kept hauling at the oars, desperately fighting the wind and the current that would suck
her toward the black arches yawning to her left. Her heaving
breaths steamed the air around her like a fog. Finally, a
sharp glance over her shoulder assured her she was nearing
shore. The steep stone edifice of the five-storied Coldharbour rose directly ahead. The Old Swan stairs, though
still shrouded in darkness, must be very close. She was almost there.

She heard a shout. She glanced up to the bridge. A soldier
stood in a narrow break between two houses near the bridge
entrance. He was pointing down at her. Isabel gasped. She
had been seen! Another shout! Two soldiers ran to join the
first one. Their longbows slung over their backs pointed to
the sky like skeletal fingers. Isabel rowed furiously, her
heartbeats pounding in her ears. She wrenched her head
sideways as she pumped the oars. Out of the corner of her
eye she saw her haven. The Old Swan stairs. Only a few oar
strokes more!

An arrow whirred over her head. Her oars froze in
midstroke. Another arrow whizzed viciously by her shoulder
and thudded into the tip of her right oar. She lurched back
into action. She pumped the oars so hard she thought her
shoulders would be wrenched from their sockets. An arrow
speared into the water by her stern. She felt a prick on the
back of her wrist as another one thumped the gunnel by her
hand, grazing her. But she had made it. Her bow crashed
against a barge tethered to the water stairs. The impact jolted

her backward again. She grappled the gunnel, scrambling to get to her feet. The gunnel was slippery. Not with water, with blood. She saw that her wrist was bleeding. But there was no time to stop. The soldiers on the bridge would be running toward her.

She scrambled out of the skiff and across the wobbly barge and ran up the stone steps. She could hear the soldiers' shouts coming closer, and their feet pounding toward the landing place. She bolted across Thames Street and dashed up a narrow alley, so dark it was almost black. She stopped, her heart pounding. Where to hide? She smelled fresh manure. A stable? She groped for the wall and found a half-rotten wooden door. She pushed it open. In the gloom she could make out a big dray horse and a donkey. The soldiers' voices sounded down the street. She ducked inside the stable and pushed the door closed and leaned against it, trying not to make a sound. But she could not stop her breath sawing in her throat, and she almost feared the soldiers could hear the thudding of her heart. Between breaths she strained to listen for their approach. She slid down to the floor and sat, her back against the door, listening, waiting. Her wrist throbbed. With her teeth she made a tear in the hem of her skirt, then ripped off a strip. She wound it around the wound, using her teeth again to help tie the bandage. She closed her eyes and listened for the soldiers.

Thornleigh stood on the flat gatehouse roof and leaned against the parapet, catching his breath. The climb up from the lower, adjacent toll-house roof had left his calf muscles screaming and his pulse racing. He cursed his body, so weakened from the effects of the fever. And he wished he were thirty years younger. *Could have jumped that parapet like a cat in those days,* he told himself. But he could not afford to dawdle. Information about the bridge was crucial, and since the gatehouse was bolted from the inside, this was the only way to find out. Besides, he had volunteered.

He pushed away from the parapet and looked out toward the bridge. He could hear the muffled hiss of the water swirling beneath the arches, but nothing could be seen from here of the bridge street itself, because directly before him the gabled roofs of houses stretched out on either side. Their overhanging top stories almost touched above the street, and also jutted out over the water. A faint glow of torchlights wavered beyond these rooftops. Thornleigh knew the torches belonged to the royalist troops down on the bridge. But he could see nothing of the troops from here. He would have to go down, past the gatehouse.

He moved to the side of the roof and looked down over its edge at the timbered wall sheer below him. It bore one window. Thornleigh saw that although it had been hell getting up here, the next step was going to be worse. He would have to climb partway down and through the window into the gatehouse. It was the only way to get out to the bridge. In the faint light he saw that the rough horizontal timbers would provide some foothold going down to the window. That was something. He took a deep breath and lowered himself over the roof edge.

The window was unglazed. Once his foot had reached the sill, it was not difficult to swing over it. He kicked in the shutters and dropped inside, banging his hip on the sill. He struggled to his feet, rubbing his bruised hip, and found himself on a dark staircase landing. This must be the porter's lodge. He listened. Nothing. The quarters apparently had been abandoned.

He went down the stairs and through the house until he reached a door at the northern end that he judged must issue out to the street about midway along the width of the bridge. He opened the door and found he was right. He stepped out under the overhanging roofs that had obscured his view from atop the gatehouse. The sound of the swirling water reached him again, louder now. This patch of the street was dark, but not far to the north he could clearly see the Queen's soldiers and their torches. He jumped sideways into the shadows to avoid being seen.

Scores of royalist soldiers were moving about, armed with longbows and arquebuses. Their breastplates and helmets gleamed under the torchlight. Their desultory voices rose above the water's hiss. Their three small cannon, pointed in Thornleigh's direction, glimmered. But there was no obvious barrier between the soldiers and him, nothing except a black expanse of street. What had made them stop there?

Slowly, quietly, he moved forward in the darkness, his eyes fixed on the soldiers. He found the answer as his right foot felt the edge. He stopped just in time. Before him yawned a black chasm. He realized what had happened. The drawbridge at the seventh arch had been cut away. All that was left between the north and south sections of the bridge was this gorge, and the angry river frothing below.

"Suicide, Thomas!" Wyatt's kinsman lieutenant, George Cobham, made his point by slicing an imaginary knife across his own throat. It was the concluding remark to a meeting of Wyatt and his officers, held in Wyatt's chamber in Southwark's dilapidated Tabard Inn. Armed with the information about London Bridge that Thornleigh had just reported to the meeting, they had been discussing the feasibility of attacking. Wyatt had thanked them for their comments and dismissed them, but he had asked Thornleigh to stay behind.

As the officers filed out of Wyatt's room, Thornleigh waited, studying the commander's face. It was the first time he had been in Wyatt's presence; it was Cobham who had asked for a volunteer to scout the bridge.

Cobham's voice had not been the only heated one during the officers' discussion. "A frontal attack is absolutely impossible!" Thomas Culpepper had declared.

"Even if we could carry up enough bridging material," Henry Vane had agreed, "we'd be mowed down by their guns."

"That's right, sir," Anthony Norton had put in. "Guns bombarding us from the Tower, and guns in our faces on the bridge."

"And no possibility of an out-flanking movement," Culpepper had pointed out.

"Suicide, Thomas!"

Now, the anxious officers were gone. Wyatt moved thoughtfully to a table and poured two goblets of ale from an earthenware jug. He handed one to Thornleigh, then sat heavily on the edge of the bed, his face a mask. He stared ahead as if Thornleigh were not there. Thornleigh drank down his ale. In the next room, a baby cried. The sound seemed to effect a softening of Wyatt's features. He gave Thornleigh a wry smile. "I married at seventeen. Five children now, three girls and two boys." He sipped his ale, then said quietly, "My son George is my heir."

Thornleigh gazed into the dregs of his own goblet. Outside in the street, heavy boots clomped by as a group of soldiers made their way to the foot of the bridge to relieve the watch. Once they had passed, there was silence again. A church bell tolled faintly from London.

Wyatt shook his head. "Hacked down the drawbridge, eh?" he said, musing. He sounded bitter with himself for not having anticipated it, but Thornleigh also heard the note of respect for an enemy's clever stroke.

"They must have towed it away," Thornleigh said.

Wyatt snorted. "Must be the first time in sixty years that damned drawbridge has even been budged." He drank deeply.

"More like forty-five years," Thornleigh said. "When I was a boy it used to be raised to let ships pass through to Queenhithe. That was when Queenhithe was as busy as Billingsgate wharf is now. But nothing bigger than barges and wherries has gone through for decades." He felt a need to reassure the younger man. "Most people have forgotten the drawbridge is even there," he added. "Stands to reason you wouldn't have thought of it."

Wyatt stood and picked up the ale jug. "Know about ships, do you?" he asked as he refilled Thornleigh's goblet.

"I own a couple."

Wyatt's look at him betrayed a new esteem. "A man of substance, I see. I'd been wondering about Isabel's family."

Thornleigh was taken aback. "Isabel?"

"Yes, I congratulate you, Thornleigh," Wyatt said, pouring himself more ale. "She's doing fine work for us. You should be proud." He lifted his goblet in a toast and drank.

"What? Look, how do you know Isabel?"

Wyatt blinked, puzzled. "Don't you know?"

"Know what, for God's sake? I haven't seen my daughter in over a week, and it's felt like a year!"

"But even before that . . . Good Lord, you really *don't* know! Why, man, she's been my eyes and ears in London. She's been carrying messages between me and the French Ambassador, de Noailles, and reporting to me about our supporters inside London. Invaluable information, all of it." His gaze traveled to the window. "In fact," he said quietly, "I am relying on her now more than ever. Our London support, it turns out, may be all we have." He walked to the window.

Thornleigh felt slightly dizzy.

Wyatt gazed out at the murky street where his troops and carts had left a soup of mud. Snow was beginning to fall, and the flakes jerked around in the erratic wind like tiny lost souls. When Wyatt spoke, his voice was as bleak as the night. "I can't wait much longer for French help. And I have no more than the three thousand men I began with at Rochester." He took in a long breath as if to gather strength. "But London can still decide the day. If London gives the lead, the country will follow."

Thornleigh had barely been listening. "When did you last see her?"

"What?"

"My daughter."

"Oh, she was just here. Left about an hour ago."

"How?"

"In a boat. She rowed."

"Alone? And you let her go back?"

"Her chances are better alone than if she's caught with soldiers of mine."

"Her *chances*? Good God, she's just a child!" Thornleigh thumped down his goblet and turned to go, adding under his breath, "Bastard!"

"Thornleigh," Wyatt's stern voice commanded, stopping him at the door. "You do not know your own flesh and blood. She's a very brave girl."

Thornleigh was struck by the words. He turned and stared at Wyatt. "You're the second man who's told me that."

CHAPTER THIRTY-ONE

><+>-o-<+><

Threats

"Where have you been, mistress?" Edward Sydenham asked solicitously. He stretched out his hand to Isabel to lead her into the passage that led from his front door to the great hall. "My servants tell me you have been out all morning. I was becoming quite distressed."

"You had left by the time I awoke, sir. I remembered another of my father's friends, an old sea-going man. I've been to see him."

"And? Any news?"

She shook her head and looked down, pretending despair, but in fact fearful that her face would betray her lie. She had not gone to old Pilot Tate's house; he had died at Christmas. She had gone to Ambassador de Noailles to deliver Wyatt's urgent appeal about Ludgate. It had been impossible to do so the night before. She had eluded the soldiers from the bridge by hiding for a terrifying hour in the stable. Then, dodging the citizens' patrols all the way back, she had barely made it into Sydenham's house and hurried up to her room before she had heard him arrive home from Whitehall. They had not met again until this moment.

"And what is this? Why, Mistress Thornleigh, you have hurt yourself!" He was helping her off with her cloak as they approached the great hall, and she had not been quick enough to pull down her wide sleeve to hide the bandage on her wrist.

"Oh, it was nothing, sir. I was too anxious getting the groom to saddle up this morning. I made the horse jumpy, and it nipped me." She forced a light laugh. "Serves me right for rushing so."

He was gently holding her arm and examining the bandage with a look of concern. His fingers brushed up her forearm under her sleeve. She stiffened and pulled back. Sydenham looked hurt. Isabel instantly regretted her response. It had been purely reflexive—a shudder at his long, cool fingers touching her—but it now seemed petty, especially when she considered how much he was doing to find her father, and trying, as best he could under nerve-wracking circumstances, to make her comfortable in his house. All while she was spying on him.

"Thank you for your concern, Sir Edward," she said sincerely, "but really, the hurt is nothing. If I—" She stopped, aware of voices in the hall. She looked at Sydenham. "Another meeting?"

He nodded, and said in a low, confidential tone, "A rather important one. The Queen's commanders are here, plus a good number of others. That is why I wanted to reach you before you came inside. John Grenville is with them, you see. I thought it would be prudent if I escorted you through." He added apologetically, "John and Frances are having difficulty understanding your presence here."

"Oh, sir, you are kind."

He smiled, slipped his arm around her back, and guided her forward. He opened the passage door and they entered the hall together. At least two dozen men, standing in small groups, turned expectantly. Their martial dress looked incongruous in Sydenham's elegant hall, with its walls hung with exquisite Flemish tapestries, its minstrels' gallery fronted with rich paneling, its windows glazed with costly painted glass. Most of the men reacted with disappointment to see it was only Sydenham with a woman.

"Excuse me, gentlemen," Sydenham said. "This lady is my guest. I shall not be a moment." He led her past the stern, impatient looks. Isabel recognized Lord Howard's jowled, claret-colored face from his previous visits here. And the fidgety Lord Mayor, Sir Thomas White, anxiously pacing. And John Grenville, tall and haughty, his pale blue eyes narrowed on her in hatred as she passed. The others, a collection of middle-aged men who, by their hardness or craftiness or both, had safeguarded their lands and authority through three violent reigns, looked equally grim. She judged that the smooth-chinned young man with the long blond locks and dressed in yellow satin—so out of place among these rough, soldierly lords—must be the Earl of Devon, Lord Courtenay; his reputation for foppery was well known. She could only guess at the identity of the others, but she knew that among them must be the Earl of Pembroke, Lord Abergavenny, Lord Clinton, and Sir John

Brydges, the Constable of the Tower—all of them powerful servants of the Queen.

Sydenham bent his head to murmur soothingly in her ear as they walked. "You must forgive their brusqueness. We have been waiting for a captain of Abergavenny's who infiltrated Wyatt's camp and is going to edify us about the strength of Wyatt's men and arms. The fellow is unconscionably late. The commanders are somewhat vexed."

Isabel could see that. She was glad to reach the door at the far end of the hall and leave behind the irritated stares. She was exhausted from her night's terrors on the river and from her morning with de Noailles, and she longed for the peace of a few hours sleep in the soft feather bed upstairs. But rest must wait. Her task now would be to listen in on the commanders' meeting from the squint hole behind the minstrels' gallery.

A shuffle of heavy footsteps sounded at the other end of the hall. The passage door swung open.

"About time!" Abergavenny burst out in anger and relief. "Gentlemen, this is Valverde. He got into Wyatt's camp at Dartford in disguise and he saw a great deal. He'll report, then you can ask him whatever you like."

Isabel twisted around. Carlos had stopped just inside the passage door. Two young lieutenants waited behind him.

Carlos was staring at Isabel. The roomful of men seemed to dissolve into a fog as her eyes locked with his. Sydenham had turned as well, and stiffened at her side. "That Spanish dog again," he said. "I'll—"

"A traitor is here!" Carlos shouted. He lifted his arm and pointed at Sydenham.

There were incredulous looks among the commanders. "What's that?" Lord Howard asked, baffled. "Did he say a traitor?"

Carlos's accusing finger continued to point at Sydenham. "Him! He keeps in his house the daughter of a rebel!"

The stunned gathering suddenly buzzed with voices.

"The woman?" someone asked in bewilderment.

"How dare you!" Sydenham bristled.

"What is the meaning of this?" the Mayor demanded.

"Really, Valverde," Abergavenny said. "You can't—"

Carlos's sword scraped from its scabbard. There was instant silence. "I was in Wyatt's camp and I saw Richard Thornleigh," Carlos declared. "Thornleigh is a traitor." He pointed his sword at Isabel. "And she is his daughter."

Isabel's mouth fell open. Sydenham blinked. John Grenville pushed forward. "You saw Richard Thornleigh?" he demanded. "With Wyatt?"

"More than saw. Thornleigh talked to me." Carlos looked hard at Isabel and spoke loudly and clearly. "Thornleigh told me his wife supported the rebels. Now that she is dead he lives only to help Wyatt attack London. He said he will march in the front line, said he will take the first arrow so that other men can come after him. He is *loco*. And he is a traitor." His sword tip jerked between Isabel and Sydenham. "The woman here is the daughter of that traitor, and this *bastardo* keeps her! He is one of them!"

Isabel's legs felt like thin reeds. Sydenham was staring, dumbfounded. The commanders began shouting questions, and crowding closer, and demanding answers—of Carlos, of Sydenham, of one another.

Carlos did not wait. Glancing at the two young lieutenants behind him, he jerked his chin toward Sydenham. "Take him!" The young men looked surprised and reluctant to act against so illustrious a gentleman, but their acceptance of Carlos's authority was absolute. They advanced on Sydenham.

"The woman, too," Carlos said. "She must be questioned." He strode toward her. Isabel's mind screamed for escape, but to turn and flee would be proof of guilt. Trembling, she stood firm.

"Abergavenny!" Sydenham cried in outrage as Carlos and the two soldiers reached him and Isabel. "This is absurd! This man is an escaped felon!"

Carlos thrust his face an inch from Sydenham's nose. "No longer," he snarled, his teeth bared in a grin of vindication. "I am pardoned!"

Sydenham staggered back a step from Carlos's malevolent energy. Carlos's two men took hold of Sydenham. The commanders watched in astonishment. "Abergavenny!" Sydenham protested again, his outrage now tinged with a plaintive whimper. Carlos ignored him. He was looking at Isabel. He sheathed his sword, preparing to take her. He grabbed her elbow. She tried to pull back, but could not budge out of his iron grip. He beckoned his men. "Come!" They pulled Sydenham. Carlos pulled Isabel.

His accusations, the advance, the arrest—all had happened so fast under Carlos's direction that the commanders stood gaping. Carlos's lieutenants were struggling with Sydenham.

Carlos was in the passage with Isabel before anyone could stop him.

Carlos slammed the passage door behind him and Isabel. He dragged her toward the front door. But to open it he had to let go of her with one hand, and she squirmed out of his grasp. She twisted back toward the hall. He caught her by the arm, wrenched her around to face him, and pushed her up against the wall. "Listen to me!" he said in a harsh whisper. But she was not listening, for she had sensed that he expected her to try to push away, so instead she slumped and dropped to the floor. She was free.

She started to scramble past him on hands and knees, desperate to get to her feet and run back to the hall. But he was quicker. He caught her by the back of her dress between her shoulder blades and dragged her backward along the floor. He pushed her to sit up against the wall. She flopped back, limp as a doll, the breath momentarily forced out of her, but she instantly began struggling to get up. Dropping to his knees, he straddled her legs so that she could not rise. He forced her by the shoulders against the wall, his face inches from hers. They stared at each other, both breathing hard.

From inside the hall they heard Sydenham rage at the lieutenants, "Let me go, you idiots!"

"This is a disgrace!" Pembroke agreed.

"Stop!" Abergavenny bellowed. *"Let Sir Edward go!"*

Carlos's eyes flicked anxiously toward the hall, then back to Isabel. "You must come!" he said. "Sydenham—"

She spat in his face.

His eyes filled with such a strange intensity that for a moment she did not know if he was going to strike her or kiss her. He did neither. With her spittle still on his cheek, he began to haul her up to her feet. She resisted. "You've killed him, haven't you!" she cried.

"No! Get up!"

"Then it's all lies! You didn't see him! If you had, you would have killed him!" She squirmed to break free.

"I did see him. Listen to me! You must not stay with Sydenham! He—"

The passage door flew open. "Valverde!" Abergavenny shouted in horror. "Release the lady! She cannot be held for the crimes of her father! Let her go!"

Men crowded into the passage. Abergavenny and Howard pulled Carlos up off Isabel. Sydenham rushed to Isabel's side and helped her to her feet. Struggling for balance, she threw her arms around Sydenham's neck. He clasped her waist.

Carlos lunged for Sydenham. It took three of them to restrain him.

"The man is insane!" Sydenham cried, tugging Isabel to safety out of Carlos's reach. As he helped her toward the hall, she glanced back at Carlos. He was staring after her, his face a mask of fury.

That evening Edward Sydenham and John Grenville stood at the edge of Thames Street waiting for a troop of soldiers to march by. John watched them, impatient to move on.

"How did the Thornleigh girl get that wound?"

"Hardly a wound, John. A horse bit her."

The troop passed, their torches flaring in the night wind. John strode into the street, leaving Edward to follow. They were on their way to London Bridge. John had insisted that Edward inspect the defenses with him. Edward would rather not have come, but John was, after all, the head of the house of Grenville now.

"A horse?" John asked suspiciously. "Are you sure? Were you there when it happened?"

"No. Why do you ask?"

John grabbed Edward's elbow to halt him. "I was on the bridge last night with my archers. My captain, Giles Sturridge, fired on a boat rowing fast toward the Old Swan stairs. It was dark, but Sturridge thinks he might have hit the rower in the arm."

"Well?"

"It was a woman."

Edward frowned. "What are you saying?"

"That the Thornleigh girl may be a spy for Wyatt."

Edward sighed, concealing his irritation. He spoke lightly. "John, I know you and Frances find the girl an irritant. And the Lord knows we are all under a great deal of strain just now. But do you not think it a trifle farfetched to cast her as a traitor?"

"Her father is. And a murderer."

"Indeed. But she has nothing on her mind except finding him and getting him to safety. She is obsessed with that. Believe me, she is barely able to see the crisis around her let alone involve herself in rebel heroics."

John started to walk again, obviously unconvinced.

Edward followed. The nine o'clock curfew tolled. They were approaching the foot of the bridge when John said, "Now that we know where Thornleigh is, the girl need hardly stay with you any longer. You have no more use for her. Tell her to leave." He glanced at Edward with a disapproving frown and added, "And let Frances know that the girl is going."

Edward smarted at the reproof. Clearly, Frances had been whining to her brother. "Of course," he murmured.

"I will have the Thornleigh girl watched," John went on. "She may incriminate herself before tomorrow is out."

"Why tomorrow?"

"You heard Pembroke, did you not? Ah, no, by then you had left the hall to comfort the girl," he said with a kind of sneer. "Well, while you were gone Pembroke outlined what he feels Wyatt's strategy will be. Wyatt cannot possibly come over the bridge, and to cross downriver, to the Essex shore, he would need a fleet to ferry his army. Also impossible. So Pembroke feels he will march upriver to Kingston and cross there. That will bring him back to London at Newgate or Ludgate. And he will probably start out tomorrow."

Edward felt a tremor of fear. There would be real fighting. He had not thought it would come so soon. He was about to speak when a gunshot blasted from the bridge.

"Come!" John said, hurrying forward to investigate. Edward reluctantly followed.

The bridge was crowded with soldiers. There were perhaps two hundred of them, jostling in the narrow street with longbows, arquebuses, and torches. John pushed his way through with Edward in tow. A heavy-jawed sergeant with a torch met them halfway to the drawbridge gap. "Arquebus shot, sir," he reported. "Ours."

"Why? Has Wyatt attempted some kind of attack?" John asked as he pushed on toward the gap.

"No, sir," the sergeant said, falling into step beside him and Edward. "Seems there's a wild man on Wyatt's side."

They approached the gap. Lord Howard stood behind a row of five royalist arquebusiers who had fanned out along the gap with their guns poised on forked rests. The long wicks, looped over the gunbarrels and soaked with saltpeter, smoldered as the gunners waited for an order to fire.

Lord Howard turned. "Ah, Grenville. Sydenham. What do

you make of it?" He pointed across the gap. "Fellow over there's capering about like a mad monkey!"

John and Edward came up beside Lord Howard. Edward's eyes stung in the residual sulfurous smoke from the discharged arquebus. He squeezed between two cannon, avoiding their cold touch. He was glad so many soldiers stood nearby. He peered across the gap.

There was no light on Wyatt's side of the bridge except for the glow from his troops' torches well beyond the Southwark gatehouse. And there was no sign of life on the bridge in the deserted houses between the gatehouse and the gap. But there was a lone figure standing on a flat roof at the gap. Edward could just make it out, a mere silhouette in the darkness.

Lord Howard snorted. "What an imbecile. He doesn't even look armed."

Grenville smiled in agreement. "What do you think, Sydenham? *Non compos mentis?*"

Across the chasm, the man's silhouette suddenly moved to the edge of the roof. "Sydenham!" his hoarse voice yelled. Yet he was not looking at Edward. It was as if he were challenging the whole dark city. "I'm coming for you! I know what you did to Honor. I know *everything!*"

The Queen's men looked at Edward curiously. Fear, like a cannonball, slammed his stomach.

The featureless silhouette on the roof raised its arms, fists to the sky. "Sydenham!" it shouted wildly. "I'm coming! *I'm going to kill you!*"

It was nearing midnight. Edward was kneeling before the altar of the Virgin Mary in the private chapel of his house. John was on his knees beside him. As they were leaving London Bridge, John had solemnly suggested that before continuing home to the Grenvilles' townhouse on Bishopsgate Street, he and Edward take a moment in Edward's chapel to pray for the Blessed Virgin's help in the coming battle.

The chapel was small and dark. Edward never came in here. He loathed its mawkish Madonna, its gloomy oak slab walls, its wax altar candles as pale as a corpse's skin. Most of all he loathed its airless silence, like a tomb. He stole a glance at John. John's eyes were closed, his hands clasped in supplication, his lips silently mouthing a prayer.

Edward closed his eyes tightly as well, but not in prayer. He was trying to control the tremor of his muscles. But the man's hoarse threat on the bridge still reverberated in his skull, sending a fresh shudder down his backbone. The man had to be Thornleigh *"I know!"* he had cried. Somehow, Thornleigh had traced his wife's death back to Edward. Everything had unraveled. Thornleigh was coming for him. Thornleigh was going to kill him.

What was he to do? Oh, Christ, what was he to do?

He tried to think, but he was too aware of the small chapel pressing in on him. Its sour smells of stale incense and musty brocade made his stomach lurch. Beside him, John's prayer seeped out of his mouth in fervent murmuring, and the words crawled into Edward's ears like insects. He squeezed his eyes shut, but in his mind he saw the slab walls creep slowly toward him, cramming him like boulders. He felt the air sucked out of the tiny space, saw the altar flame gutter in the starved air and die, felt his lungs begin to collapse . . . the place was a coffin!

His eyes sprang open in terror. His heart was banging against his ribs. He made fists and dug his nails into his palms to bring himself back to reality. He forced himself to see and hear what was *real*. The altar candle still burned. The Madonna still looked down with her long-suffering gaze. John's inane prayer droned on. *That's better,* Edward told himself, subduing his pounding heart. *Now, concentrate! Identify the problem. Devise a solution. Think!*

What had John told him on the way back? Edward had been so stunned by Thornleigh's threat, he had barely listened to John. But now he began to recall John's words. Something about Ludgate and Newgate, and posting the Grenville Archers. Yes, that was it. And if the rebels were going to attack at one of these western gates, Edward realized, Thornleigh would be among them. In the front line—that's what the Spaniard had said. At the thought of fighting, Edward's bowels churned—he could almost see Thornleigh raging toward him with a bloody sword—but he forced himself to imagine the scene.

There must be an answer here. There must be some way out.

Isabel sat in the velvet cushioned window seat of her bedchamber and looked out at the skeletal arms of the apricot trees in Sydenham's orchard—black, bony fingers grasping toward the night sky. The costly, scented candles around the room cast a gentle glow, and the brazier radiated soft waves of heat. But Isabel felt cold. Her mind still reeled from Carlos's attack and his astounding declarations. The news that her father was with Wyatt had stunned her.

She looked down at her mother's book on her lap. Could that be true, too? Could her mother really have been sympathetic to Wyatt's stand? Was there no end to the surprises of her parents' characters?

So many mysteries. But no answers. She stared at the book. Would her mother have known what to do now? she wondered. No; she doubted that her mother had ever had to deal with such overwhelming problems. And yet, these glimpses of her mother's hidden identity made her wonder . . .

She ran her finger over the book's leather cover, wishing it could offer some solution, point the way for her. Why had this slim volume meant so much to her mother? She did not pretend that her Latin was as proficient as her mother's had been; it had taken her until now, in snatched readings, to finish the short text. But she understood its message, and why the church authorities would consider it a dangerous heresy: it dared ask whether immortality of the soul was merely a man-made fantasy. Yet why should that concept have held such significance for her mother? The book had changed her life, Adam had said. How?

Isabel felt resentment rise in her again over the secrets her parents had kept from her. Secret voyages, burnings, rescues, mysterious books. She frowned at the volume. What possible good could this dry tome, this philosophical discourse, do for her now with her terrible, *real* problems?

In bitterness, she cast the book across the bay window onto the opposite seat. It tumbled on the cushion, and its cover fell open to reveal the title page. There, the brilliant blue speedwell flower gleamed back at her like a mild rebuke. She suddenly saw the flower afresh; saw it as an expression of the author's message. It was as if, with the flower's beauty, the author meant to quell any terrified question of life seen as meaningless, cut off from the universe at the moment of death; as if he were offering the resounding answer that the earth was bountiful enough in natural splendor and meaning without the fantasy of an afterlife.

But the painted flower said something more to Isabel, something far more personal. Its fragile, veined petals seemed to quiver as if under her mother's breath as she used to whisper the family fable about Isabel's eyes. *So your father gave up one of his own eyes to fill yours with this wondrous blue* . . . Isabel shook her head with a sad smile. Such sweet nonsense. Yet as a child she had believed it—and adored her father for his sacrifice.

Tears pricked her eyes. How was she to save him now? And to think that while she had been talking to Sir Thomas last night in Southwark, her father had been there! At first, coming alone here to this room after Carlos's attack, she had been filled with hope. Wyatt would surely prevail in the coming fight, and then she and her father would be reunited, and all the Queen's power and all the Grenvilles' venom would dissolve, and she could start to put her sorrows—over her mother, over Martin—behind her.

But soon the dark shadows of doubt had crept in. Carlos had also reported that her father planned to march in Wyatt's front line. Isabel was no military strategist, but it was obvious that even if Wyatt was victorious, the first men attacking a fortified city would likely be cut down. If her father was going to be among them, she could not save him. It was a harrowing thought.

And harrowing, too, her mortification over Carlos. Despite every prompting of her mind to despise him, she had felt something far different at that moment when he had exploded into Sydenham's hall and their eyes had met. Something in her had leapt. Now, sitting in the window seat, she shook her head violently to dispel the taint of his image. What degeneracy was it in her that made her body turn toward the man, like some mindless green shoot toward the sun? How could such feelings exist in her for a man who was her enemy in every way, who murdered for money, who had crowed about her father's whereabouts to a hall full of her father's enemies?

And yet, something gnawed. Something was not right. She knew Carlos to be practical, never prone to take a risk unless it was his only chance, in which case he would charge ahead without restraint. And although he had joined the Queen's army, she knew he had no romantic zeal for their cause. Besides, he said he had been granted a pardon by Lord Abergavenny, and therefore enjoyed security again. So what had he hoped to gain by his wild accusations this afternoon? Why would he risk arresting Sir Edward Sydenham in his own hall, among Sydenham's powerful friends—and arrest Isabel, too—on such a paltry pretext? He must have known he had no hope of taking Sydenham away, nor her. Why, then, had he tried? It was almost as though he had blurted out her father's whereabouts and tried to haul her away for questioning all in some fit of madness. Yet even as he had dragged her into the passage, she had known he was not using his full strength against her. He had been in full command, not mad at all, as though, while he had raged and created chaos, he had been bent on one thing: getting her out. Why?

There was a soft knock on her door.

"Come in."

It was Sydenham. He poked his head inside with an apologetic smile, than walked in. He was carrying a goblet. "Nothing can make up for the ordeal you suffered this afternoon at the hands of that barbarian," he said, holding out the goblet like an offering. "But I hope a little spiced wine may soften some of the hardest edges."

Isabel stood and managed a smile. "You are all thoughtfulness, sir." She took the silver goblet. Its warmth made her realize how cold her hands were.

"I thought you might like some company," Sydenham said. He gestured tentatively toward the window seat. "May I?"

"Oh, please," she said. "My own thoughts are such a misery, anything will be better than—" She stopped, realizing the implied insult of her words.

He smiled. "Well, if misery in this case does not exactly *love* company, toleration will be quite acceptable." He laughed lightly, but Isabel saw that his mirth was forced, and that he was far from relaxed. He made a motion inviting her to drink. "Do try it," he said.

She sipped the wine. It was warm. The taste, like the aroma, was exotically spicy.

"Do you like it?"

"Delicious."

"An infusion of claret, nettles, white ginger, and cloves. Or so Frances tells me. She sent me a cask at Christmas. I've enjoyed it myself. This is the last of it." He added in an abstract way, "Frances is clever with such things, you know."

He moved to the window seat. He picked up the book and idly glanced at it, but it was clear his mind was elsewhere. He sat, putting the book aside. When he looked up at Isabel again, his smile was gone. "Mistress Thornleigh," he said. "I have come to apologize. Abjectly." His voice was quiet, heavy with sadness. "I have failed. With your father." He shook his head morosely. "Extraordinary. Who would have thought he would go to the rebels? And according to that appalling Spaniard, he actually means to march in the front rank." He gave her a sudden sharp look. "What do you make of such a statement?"

Isabel had no doubt. "I believe it to be true."

He nodded seriously. "So do I." Isabel thought she saw a tremor go through him.

"However," he went on, "there may still be a way to save him. It is only a chance, mind you. A slight chance."

"Yes?" She moved eagerly to the opposite cushion and sat. Earlier, she had wracked her brain for a plan to get to her father in Southwark, thinking that if she could plead with him she might persuade him to leave Wyatt before the attack on London. After all, how much help could a one-eyed old man be to such an army? But she had been unable to think of any way to reach him. Crossing London Bridge was out of the question; it was bristling with royalist soldiers. And the river was equally impassable; not only was every boat, by royal order, tied to the northern shore, but also, following the incident last night in which the bridge soldiers had fired on her, every wharf was now being watched by sentries. The city was completely cut off from Southwark.

"The situation is bad, I grant you," Sydenham said with a frown, as though reading her thoughts. "However, a plan has occurred to me. It centers on the fact that the Earl of Pembroke is certain Wyatt will attempt an attack of London at Ludgate or Newgate."

Isabel felt a prick of alarm that the royalists should so quickly have deduced Wyatt's strategy. But then, perhaps at this point it was obvious, given Wyatt's lack of alternatives. At least they did not know that he had decided on Ludgate. In any case, it was her father's fate in this that concerned her. Was that wrong, she wondered, when Wyatt, and so many with him, were about to risk their lives? Once again, her warring loyalties were battling inside her. But, she told herself, Wyatt surely had no more need of her. The French would arrive soon—any hour now, de Noailles had said—and Peckham, leading Wyatt's London supporters, would be throwing open Ludgate to welcome Wyatt's army. She was no longer necessary to the cause. But, maybe, she could still save her father.

She waited for Sydenham to tell her how. A coal on the brazier popped in a small shower of sparks. A dog down the street howled like a wolf.

"Accordingly," Sydenham went on, "we will be concentrating our forces at the western gates. John Grenville has already received orders to post the Grenville Archers inside; they can quickly be moved to the gate Wyatt attacks. The archers will be positioned on the rooftops of the buildings immediately inside, and their mission will be to repel any rebels who make it through. I am no military man, but even I can see that, given the narrow passages available through the gates, such a placement of the archers offers an almost unassailable position of strength. And they are the finest in England. No rebel will get past their murderous hail of arrows."

Isabel shivered, thinking of her father, of Wyatt, of Tom . . .

"Now," Sydenham said earnestly, leaning toward her, "this is my suggestion. I shall persuade the Grenville Archers to single out Richard Thornleigh and spare him. Though they fire on every other rebel who breaches the gate, Thornleigh shall walk through it unscathed."

Isabel blinked. "Persuade?"

He gave a small smile. "I am a wealthy man. I can make it well worth their while. No one will know. The archers will be killing rebels, so who will notice that they are sparing one?" His smile evaporated. "This plan offers a small hope, mistress, that is all," he warned. "In no way does it remove all jeopardy from your father. Pembroke's troops will be stationed outside the gates, and I can do nothing about them. But, should Wyatt breach a gate—which is only too likely— then the archers can preserve Thornleigh. If we can reach him, you can both then row out to Van Borselen's ship and sail out of the country."

Isabel realized that she had been holding her breath. When it came out, it came in a rush of astonishment. "You would do all this for us?"

He took her hand. "We have come thus far together in our quest for reconciliation. I do not intend to shirk at the last moment. Do you?"

Isabel felt a shudder threaten at his hand's cool touch, but she suppressed it. What business had she shying from him when he was offering her her father's life! Impulsively she took up his hand and held it to her cheek to prove her friendship. "Sir Edward, there are no words . . . how can I ever repay you!"

He looked at her strangely. "Repay?" he murmured as his gaze slid down to her breasts. "My dear, the war between our families has caused so much suffering. Peace is its own reward."

She nodded. He moved closer to her and touched her cheek. She did not shrink back. Not from such a friend. "There is, however, one service I would request of you," he said softly.

She flinched in spite of herself, so suggestive was the remark and the look in his eye. "Certainly," she said steadily. "What can I do?"

"For our plan, I must give the archers an exact description of your father. But I confess I do not know what he looks like. Would you furnish me with such a description?"

Isabel smiled as her schoolgirl fears of him dissolved. A reprieve of hope for her father washed over her like a tide. "Take me to the archers," she said eagerly. "I shall tell them myself!"

He smiled. "That will not be necessary."

All the next day the city held its breath. Not for over a hundred years had a rebel army come so close to London. But Wyatt made no attack from Southwark. And the Tower cannon were silent, for the Queen's council feared provoking the people of Southwark by firing on them.

London waited.

In Westminster, judges hearing cases wore armor beneath their robes. In Whitehall, the Queen received Mass from a priest wearing armor beneath his vestments. The soldiers of the Queen's personal guard trooped into her private chambers in armor with their pikes and poleaxes, sending her ladies scurrying and whispering in fear. All of London's gates were shut and bolted, and the watch was doubled on every one. The city had become a fortress. The Queen's court was like a garrison.

But still, Wyatt made no move.

CHAPTER THIRTY-TWO

> ⊱━◦━◦━⊰

The Broken Gun

Wyatt's cannon boomed from the Southwark shore, sending frightened gulls screeching and flapping above the rooftops of London Bridge. The cannon shot arced through the dawn drizzle and splashed into the humped, gray water of the Thames. The blast had only been an insolent salute to waken the Queen's soldiers camped on the bridge; a departing sneer. Sir Thomas Wyatt could wait no longer. He was about to march his army out of Southwark and head southwest to Kingston.

Thornleigh stood in the rain among Wyatt's army gathered at the foot of London Bridge. Mules were already harnessed to the rest of the big guns from the Queen's ships, and the few score horsemen steadied their anxious mounts, but the great mass of the soldiers were on foot. They watched as Wyatt jumped down from his horse and strode toward the bolted gatehouse entrance. In a theatrical gesture of defiance, Wyatt lifted his gauntleted fist to the timber doors and banged. He turned to his soldiers. "When we came to Southwark I knocked! Now, twice have I knocked and not been suffered to enter! Next time I knock at a London gate, I will be let in, by God's grace!"

His men cheered. Thornleigh stood silently and stared at the drizzle-shrouded city across the water—where Sydenham was.

The artillery officer at the canopied cannon lit the fuse again. It boomed a second salute. Wyatt mounted his horse and led out his soldiers. Cheering, they followed.

Above them, at their backs, the rising sun was struggling to lighten the pewter sky.

It was noon by the time Carlos cantered through the rain toward St. James's Field a mile west of London wall.

All morning in Westminster he had paced, waiting for or-

ders in a crowded corridor while the commanders and the
council bickered over troop placement. Carlos had finally
left. He had rubbed down his horse, eaten a cold meal of
bread, cheese, and ale, honed his sword, then had come back
and waited again in the corridor, growing ever more disgusted with the leaders' delays and confusion. Finally,
Abergavenny, stomping out of a meeting, had thrust a paper
at him. "You're posted to Courtenay, the Earl of Devon."

"Where do I find him?"

"In St. James's Field, mustering with the others," Abergavenny said, and added vaguely, "Devon could use some
help."

Carlos was about to go. "I will take Lieutenant Wentworth, yes?"

"Take whoever you want," Abergavenny had said, and
strode away.

St. James's Field was churning with men and horses.
Carlos and Wentworth trotted past the ragged groups of
archers, pikemen, and arquebusiers, each company going
through flustered motions of drilling on the soggy grass.
Carlos thought, *The arquebuses will be useless in this rain.*

A lieutenant directed him to Devon's troop across the
field. Carlos took heart as he approached, for he saw at once
that it was a decent-looking squadron of cavalry he had been
posted to. The sergeant pointed out the commander to him.
"The Earl's yonder, under the elm," he said.

Carlos looked toward a dripping tree under which the
young nobleman sat a strong white stallion. Devon's long
yellow hair was straggly in the rain, and the purple plume of
his hat drooped soggily. He was leaning over his horse's
mane, struggling to disentangle the reins that were twisted
over one of the horse's ears. Leaving Wentworth with the
sergeant, Carlos trotted over. He pulled off his gauntlet to
fish out the paper under his breastplate. Handing it over
to the Earl, Carlos explained that it set forth his orders to
join the Earl as his captain.

"Orders?" Devon snapped. "No one told *me*. Blast Pembroke! Lord Commander, ha! I will not suffer many more of
his insolent 'orders,' I can tell you!" As he petulantly flicked
his reins, his hat slipped off and tumbled onto the muddy
grass.

Carlos looked away, letting Devon fidget on with his
horse's harness. Carlos was about to draw on his gauntlet

again when an itch on his cheek made him raise his hand to scratch. He hesitated. It was the spot where Isabel had spat at him yesterday. He half expected that if he touched it he might feel a small crater where her spittle had burned. It had felt like that, like boiling pitch, her hatred on his skin.

He shook off the thought. He scratched, then drew on his gauntlet. He had a job to do here.

He looked around the field. Not far beyond it, toward the river, the towers of Whitehall Palace loomed through the slanting rain. He looked south. Wyatt would come from that direction, from Kingston, heading for the city. He surveyed the field itself, crowded with men and horses and small cannon. Some archers were confusedly following orders to group. Some horsemen's mounts were slipping on the wet foothold. The Queen's forces did not have discipline, Carlos admitted that. But they did have numbers—maybe eight thousand now compared to Wyatt's three. And they did have cavalry.

The rain streamed. Wyatt's soldiers trudged silently along the miry road over Putney Heath, their feet squelching in the mud. The cannon carriages thudded and creaked over the water-filled pits. The mules alone could not pull the cannon over these huge depressions and through the thick mud, so teams of men had to help, straining with ropes over their shoulders, their clothes spattered with muck to the waist. Even so, the cannon constantly bogged down and had to be wrenched, pulled, lifted, and rocked free.

Thornleigh marched beside Wyatt who was mounted on his bay. Wyatt was eager, impatient. "Time is everything now, Thornleigh. Cannot disappoint our London friends, eh? They're ready to welcome us. It'll be just like in Rochester and in Southwark. Think of it, not a jot of resistance, all the way we've come since Maidstone! Yes, England wants our victory, Thornleigh. And though we may not have the French beside us, by God we'll have the Londoners!"

Thornleigh looked up. "Not the French?"

Wyatt shook his head soberly. He lowered his voice, and Thornleigh heard bitterness in it. "Ambassador de Noailles has been building castles in the air. This," he said, gesturing to the trudging army around them, "is all we have." His smile returned. "But these are brave men. And London is awaiting us. And once the capital is ours, the rest of the country will clamor to join us. I feel it!"

Thornleigh watched him. It was clear Wyatt was happy to be marching; the days of inactivity had been hard on him—twelve days since he had first raised his standard for rebellion. He was excited now. Every few minutes he would ride back to check the cannon, dismounting and walking beside the men hauling the ropes, encouraging them. Then he would ride back to the vanguard to urge the company on. Thornleigh forced his aching legs through the sucking mud and said nothing. The men, he thought, needed rest and food and dry clothes more than cheering words.

The company dragged on past Wimbledon Common and the deer park of Richmond Palace, and finally trooped down into the riverside town of Kingston at four o'clock in the afternoon. The rain had not abated. It had taken them ten hours to cover twelve miles.

Kingston Bridge was a narrow wooden causeway resting on piles. About thirty feet of it had been broken down to prevent Wyatt's crossing, though the piles still stood. A guard of some two hundred royalist soldiers were posted on the remainder of the bridge and on the far bank.

Wyatt did not hesitate. "Bring up the guns!" he commanded. The great naval guns were jostled forward, loaded, and aimed at the far bank. Wyatt gave the signal to fire. The cannon boomed and roared. The Queen's soldiers on the bridge and on the far bank turned and ran in terror. Wyatt's men cheered wildly. Thornleigh smiled to himself. Perhaps a little encouragement was what the men had needed after all.

Wyatt ordered the repair of the bridge. He had his sappers bring up ladders, planks, and beams that they roped together. While the work was going on he gave the rest of his men leave to snatch a few hours sleep in the town. With fingers numb after hammering at bridge planks, Thornleigh wolfed a bowl of gruel in a widow's cottage while his cloak steamed beside her small peat fire to dry. He hunched on a stool by the hearth, bone-weary, and stared into the peat's red glow, remembering Carlos's description of Sydenham's red hair. Thornleigh did not sleep.

By nine o'clock in the evening the bridge was repaired. By ten o'clock the entire company had trooped across the bridge. In the darkness, lashed by the icy February rain, they started back toward London.

* * *

Frances Grenville shook Queen Mary's shoulder as the Queen lay in bed. "My lady, wake up!"

Frances had tried to be gentle, but the Queen's eyes sprang open as if a cannon had blasted over her head. She jerked the bedcover to her chin and cringed. "Blessed Mother of God, are the rebels upon us?"

Frances squeezed the Queen's hand comfortingly. "Not yet, my lady," she said, careful to keep her voice calm, "but here are my lord Bishop and divers gentlemen come urgently to speak with you. You must rise and dress."

"Bishop Gardiner? Here? Now?" Queen Mary lifted her head from the pillows and peered past Frances toward the door. Frances's trembling maidservant, who stood by with a candle, stepped nervously aside to allow the Queen to see. Three gentlemen stood in the doorway anxiously looking in, their faces mottled with shadows from the orange glow of the antechamber hearth. Soldiers with pole-axes crowded in behind them. The shortsighted Queen blinked, confused by the muzziness of sleep. She glanced across the room at the brass clock, a gift from the Emperor. Frances looked, too. It was three in the morning.

"Your Majesty, all is lost!" Bishop Gardiner cried. Abandoning decorum, he pushed into the Queen's bedchamber. "Wyatt has taken Kingston Bridge and crossed! You must flee!" The two other gentlemen, Paulet and Riche, rushed in after him.

"Flee?" The Queen propped herself up, staring. Her face was white above her white linen chemise. "Flee where?"

"To Windsor!" Riche cried.

The Queen fumbled with her cover, trying to rise. Frances snatched up a fur-trimmed velvet gown and threw it around the Queen's bare shoulders. The Queen got to her feet, then wavered as if dizzy and groped for Frances's hand. Frances guided her down to sit on the edge of the bed. "Windsor?" the Queen asked faintly. "Now?"

"Now!" Gardiner cried. "There is not a moment to lose!"

"A barge awaits, Your Majesty," Paulet urged. "Do, please, rise and come!"

"Yes, yes, of course, my lords, if you think—" The Queen stopped suddenly. She stared at her *prie-dieu* as if struck by a thought. "My lord Ambassador. Is he here?"

"Renard?" the Bishop asked, bewildered.

"Yes, send for him," the Queen said.

A servant was sent running down the corridor to Renard's chamber. The Queen took hold of her prayer missal, then sat immobile on her bed, the furred gown awkwardly askew on her shoulders. Gardiner went to the window, fretfully looking out left and right into the darkness. Paulet, subdued by fatigue, sat on the far corner of the Queen's bed and buried his face in his hands. Riche stared vacant-eyed at the *prie-dieu*, obsessively picking at a scab on his neck. Some of the Queen's ladies could be heard whispering in fear in the antechamber. The maidservant sobbed quietly in a corner. Frances alone seemed able to function. Quietly, efficiently, she laid out clothes for the Queen.

Simon Renard arrived slightly out of breath. Paulet jumped up. Gardiner twisted around. "You have heard the news, Renard!" he cried, wringing his hands. "Tell Her Majesty that she must leave for Windsor now! From there we can get her to the coast and across the Channel. Tell her!"

Renard's eyes widened in surprise. But he quickly recovered. He rested his keen gaze on the Queen. He spoke calmly. "If you leave England, Your Majesty, rest assured that you will be safe under the Emperor's protection, and that you will live in ease and luxury in whatever part of the Emperor's domain you wish to make your home. But be aware also that by running you throw away your crown. Your flight will be known and the city will rise up. They will seize the Tower and release the prisoners. The heretics will massacre the priests. Your half sister Elizabeth will be crowned Queen—a Protestant Queen. Holy Mother Church in England will perish."

Gardiner gaped. Paulet thudded back onto the bed.

"And," Queen Mary whispered, "I will have eternally desecrated my mother's memory." She looked at her English councilors with suddenly hard eyes. "Thank you for your advice, my lords," she said with a bitterness Frances had never heard from her. "But I will stay."

Thornleigh hugged himself against the wet and cold as Wyatt's army marched on through the low, marshy land between Kingston and Brentford. March? Thornleigh thought, wincing. More like stagger. The whole force was staggering, shivering, sopping—silent in their misery. There was only the incessant sound of boots and hooves and carriage wheels, all sucking through mud. Thornleigh glanced at the grim faces around him. Some of the ones who had started out beside him were gone; hunkered down in Kingston when the trumpet blew to march out, they had stayed put. But the ones still here, Thornleigh judged, would stay until the end. What choice did they have? Only victory now could save them from the noose. Thornleigh did not fear hanging, and he had his own reasons for carrying on.

Wyatt plodded on his horse beside Thornleigh, as wet as any of his men. At one point, when a young soldier collapsed on his feet, George Cobham asked Wyatt why they needed to push on so punishingly. "It must be near three in the morning," Cobham said. "Why not find shelter in a village and let the men rest?"

"Cannot do it," Wyatt said. "Got to be there before daybreak."

Thornleigh understood. If success now depended solely on Wyatt's friends inside London, then it was essential to attack before dawn. In the sleepy, small hours Londoners could find courage to risk opening the gates for the rebels, but their courage might fail them once their neighbors were about and the Queen's soldiers amassed. *Dawn,* Thornleigh thought. *It will be Ash Wednesday.*

As they squelched through the virtual swamp that was the road at Turnham Green, someone behind shouted, "Look out!" There was a crash. A man screamed. Thornleigh looked back. Two of the cannon carriages had collided in a pothole with a crunch of their heavy wheels. A man had been trapped between them, and one of the great guns had crashed down, smashing his leg. Voices rose in a clamor. In the darkness, the men milling at the scene were mere shapes to Thornleigh, but the whimpers of the injured man and the shouting around him were proof of great confusion.

The cannon barrel was wrenched up and the man was pulled free. But the gun was hopelessly mired in the mud, and a wheel on each carriage was shattered.

Wyatt looked at the ruin, aghast. "Wheelwrights!" he shouted. "Torches! Lieutenant, get this mess repaired!"

A team of steaming men worked, their tools hasping in the rain, their curses flying as the splintered wood and slippery metal refused to reshape themselves in the men's numb, raw hands. An hour slid by. Then another. Thornleigh went to Wyatt. "You said we must get to London. Why not leave the guns behind?"

"Impossible."

"Why? You have three more cannon."

"Good God, Thornleigh, ordnance like that could make or break the day!"

"But wasting time here can only break *us*."

"I will not leave the guns!" Wyatt insisted. "Guns kept me from crossing London Bridge. Guns won me Kingston Bridge. Guns can win me London!" He lowered his head and collected himself. He spoke wearily. "Look, Thornleigh, the enemy is strong. I dare not abandon any advantage that might help even the odds. Understand? We will not leave the guns."

But Thornleigh understood what Wyatt had forgotten: the enemy now was time.

It was four in the morning of Ash Wednesday, and in the palace chapel Father Weston was wearing a breastplate beneath his robes as he said a private Mass for Queen Mary and Frances Grenville. Weston dipped his thumb into a saucer of ashes and drew a black cross on each woman's forehead.

The Queen and Frances returned to the Queen's bedchamber. While soldiers ran shouting down the corridors, and the Queen's ladies sobbed in the antechamber, Mary and Frances knelt before the *prie-dieu.* They prayed for over an hour.

But Frances's thoughts strayed to Edward. She had memorized the words of the note he had sent her the day before. Such a loving note! In it, Edward had assured her that the Thornleigh girl would be leaving his house the next morning. *This* morning, Frances thought, glancing at the nightblack window. Ash Wednesday. She wished she could hurry the dawn.

Frances looked back at the Queen's drawn face beside her. Although the Queen still hugged her missal and stared at the jeweled cross before them as if in a trance, her lips were now still, and Frances judged it safe to interrupt her devotions. Frances herself felt satisfied that God had heard her own concise prayers.

"My lady," she ventured, "might I ask a small favor?"

"Of course, Frances. What is it?"

"There is talk of looting if the traitors breach the city gates. I am worried about some valuables in my family's townhouse, things my father entrusted to me. There is a silver rosary that belonged to my great-grandmother and was blessed by the Pope. And there is a locket with a relic that my father gave me, and—"

"The locket with the hair of St. Theresa?"

"Yes."

"A sacred treasure, Frances."

"Yes, my lady. And a sacred trust. But I fear for its safety. Might I go and bring these valuables back to the palace for safekeeping? Could you spare me?"

The Queen looked anxious. "You will hurry back?"

"I would not leave you long, I promise."

The Queen smiled wanly. "Take my carriage. And a guard. I shall send with you my personal order for the night watch."

Within an hour Frances was approaching Ludgate. The guard at the gate passed the Queen's written order to the watch, and the heavy timber double doors shuddered open to let the carriage through, then clattered shut behind it. But Frances did not go to her family's house on Bishopsgate Street. She went to Lombard Street, to Edward's house. She stopped on the opposite side from the house and sat back in the carriage to watch the front door, waiting to see the Thornleigh girl leave, waiting for the dawn.

At four in the morning, Isabel heard drums beating in the street and heralds calling all fighting men to wake and arm themselves. Isabel was sitting in the window seat—sleep had been impossible—and she let her mother's book slip from her lap as she jumped up to look out. She pressed her cheek against the cold glass, trying to see past the corner of the orchard to the street, but all she could make out was the moving glow of torches, their wavering light making the bare limbs of the fruit trees seem to twitch in ghostly gyrations.

The drums rumbled again. People ran by shouting. This was the moment, Isabel thought. Wyatt was coming. She stepped back, telling herself to be calm, reminding herself there was nothing more she could do for now. She could imagine three possible outcomes. Wyatt would be victorious, and then she would go out and find her father and all would be well. Or Wyatt would fail but her father would make it through Ludgate thanks to Sydenham's instructions to the archers. In that case, she would still have to reach him—she could run to Ludgate in ten minutes—then get him out to Van Borselen's ship. The third possibility, that Wyatt would fail and her father would be killed, Isabel did not allow herself to consider. In any case, all she could do now was wait.

Her door swung open. Isabel whirled around. It was Sydenham. He had not knocked, and now he stood in the doorway looking lost. His face was very pale. "I see you cannot sleep either," he said. "No one can, of course. The servants have all run out. I must go soon, too. I am just waiting for John Grenville's summons. I wonder . . ." He hesitated. Isabel realized that he was very frightened. "I wonder if you would join me downstairs?" He added quietly, "This time, it is I who need company."

"Of course, sir," she said. Waiting alone up here was agony. And he looked so desperate. She picked up the book—she had kept it near her in the last days as a kind of talisman—and walked to the door. Sydenham stood there looking at her intently and did not move to let her pass. She started forward again, thinking he would turn and leave first, but he took hold of her wrist, stopping her halfway through the doorway so that they were standing almost breast to breast. "So steadfast," he murmured. His scrutiny made Isabel uncomfortable, and again she had to chastise herself for such an ungrateful response to him, her benefactor. She managed a smile, then moved past him.

Downstairs, there were no servants in evidence except the steward, Palmer. He stood by the entrance to the hall, fidgeting with his dagger, and he started nervously as Isabel and Sydenham passed him on their way to the parlor. Sydenham opened the parlor door, ushered Isabel in, and closed the door behind them. A fire blazed in the hearth, and candles had been set about the beautiful room as though in expectation of a quiet evening of cards and conversation.

There were shouts outside. Sydenham flinched. Isabel looked out the window beside Sydenham's desk. Men were running down the street in twos and threes. Isabel noticed a carriage—a rare sight—standing across the street in the darkness, the coachman on top huddled in capes against the cold. One of Sydenham's wealthy nobleman neighbors, planning to flee with his family, Isabel decided. Drums sounded faintly farther down the street.

Sydenham hurried to the window and drew the velvet curtains to block out the commotion outside. "That's better," he said, clearly unnerved. He looked around, as if hoping for some diversion. His eyes fell on the chessboard on the desk. It was a beautiful checkerwork of jetwood and inlaid mother-of-pearl. The pieces were exquisite carved creations of ivory and ebony. "A game perhaps?" Sydenham suggested, gesturing to the board.

Isabel accepted and sat. As Sydenham stood beside her to arrange the pieces in their starting positions, Isabel laid the book between them on the desk.

"Ah, yes, your mother's book. I never did get a chance to peruse it," Sydenham said, setting the knights in their places, then the pawns. Isabel sensed that he was talking on to steady his nerves. "And now," he added wistfully, "I never shall."

"True, sir. By tonight I must certainly be gone from here, whatever the coming day holds." The thought of the worst that the day might hold made her shiver. She looked down at the volume. "You will think it odd, but this book gives me courage. It reminds me of my mother." She opened the cover to the title page where the painted blue flower glinted. "This drawing," she explained with a small smile, "was very special. When I was little, my mother used to tell me that my eyes were like my father's, speedwell blue."

"Speedwell blue," Sydenham murmured. He held a white Queen in his hand. "And your lovely eyes match your steadfast character—speedwell true."

He set down the Queen, the final piece on the white side, her side. He began to arrange the black pieces. His hand worked under Isabel's eyes, setting up the pieces as he talked on about the chess set. But Isabel saw nothing. She heard nothing. Nothing but the peculiar phrases he had just spoken. The words careened around inside her head, echoing, colliding with other words, words Carlos had spoken in Colchester jail just before she had unlocked his chains

"You said the assassin used special words," she had said to Carlos. *"What were they?"*

"Speedwell blue."

"Did my father make an answer?"

"He said, 'Speedwell true.' Your father is in much danger. Someone wants him dead. I do not know who."

But Isabel knew. Finally, she knew. Knew why Sydenham had taken her under his wing and urged her to tell him every place her father might have gone to hide. Knew why his touch sent currents of mistrust coursing through her. Knew that she had betrayed her father. Knew it all ... because Sydenham knew the password.

The truth, the facts, came slamming in at her. It was Sydenham who had hired Carlos to assassinate her father. That had failed, so Sydenham had made a friend of Isabel to track his quarry. Then, yesterday, when they both had learned from Carlos that her father was with Wyatt, Sydenham had devised the scheme with the Grenville Archers. Isabel had no idea why he was so bent on her father's death, but she understood one thing with blinding clarity. He had not ordered the archers to spare her father, but to slaughter him. And she had given a description to enable them to do so!

The archers. They would be on their way to the gates at this moment . . .

"Mistress Thornleigh?" Sydenham's voice broke in. "Are you unwell?"

She stared up at him.

"I too am very anxious," Sydenham said shakily. He looked at her. "I confess that your loyalty, your determination through all of this, quite humbles me." He touched her cheek as if he would draw some of that determination. Isabel's stomach lurched at his touch. "However," he said very quietly, "there is nothing we can do until the storm breaks, is there?" He sat down across the desk from her. "Come, let us play," he said.

Isabel looked down at the board. The white pieces were lined up facing the row of black. The game was ready for them to begin.

Edward watched Isabel's hand tremble as she moved the first pawn. He noted her carefully lowered eyes, the tension in her shoulders, the heightened pulse thrumming at her throat. He cursed himself. He had let the password slip out. She knew.

But did it really matter? He had no further use for her. He had only to keep her here until he received his summons. Then, she could be dispatched with little fuss.

She glanced up at him. The clock ticked. The fire hissed. Edward smiled and moved out his knight.

CHAPTER THIRTY-THREE

Ash Wednesday

The rain had stopped. Carlos halted his horse near the royal hunting preserve of Hyde Park and gestured to Lieutenant Wentworth to carry on with the Earl of Devon at the vanguard of the cavalry troop. As they trotted past Carlos, he looked around, shifting his foot in the stirrup to ease his sore knee. Out here, two miles west of the stinking streets of London, the fields smelled fresh after all the rain. The clouds had moved off and the day promised sunshine. It was seven o'clock on the morning of Ash Wednesday.

Carlos looked up at the cleared sky. *As blue as her eyes,* he thought. Where was she now? Safe out of Sydenham's house, he hoped. Certainly, since he'd let her know that her father had gone to Wyatt, she had no need to stay with Sydenham. Yet Carlos couldn't be sure she'd go; she was so full of hatred for him that she might not have believed him. *Madre de Dios,* what a botched job he'd made of warning her. He clenched his teeth in bitterness, thinking of it. A trumpet sounded in the distance, and he kicked his foot back into the stirrup and straightened. He had to concentrate on the battle ahead. He took a deep breath of the bracing, cold air. At least it was a good day to fight.

He cantered forward and caught up with Devon's cavalry moving along the causeway. Devon had been ordered to take up a position at Charing Cross, about a mile west of Ludgate. On the way, they passed the other royalist forces, almost all of them in position now, Carlos noted. Lord Pembroke's ordnance was set at the highest spot on the causeway, the big guns directly facing Wyatt's imminent advance from the southwest. The main body of the Queen's foot soldiers, with arquebuses and pikes and longbows, flanked the causeway. Besides Devon's horsemen, there were two other troops of horse under Lord Clinton, the heavier in a field to the northwest, and the light horse at the eastern edge of

Hyde Park. Also, as Carlos approached the village of Charing Cross with Devon's troop, he could just make out, at nearby Whitehall Palace, Sir John Gage's soldiers standing ready at the palace gateway, their pikes glinting in the strengthening sun. Carlos frowned. He could not understand why Wyatt had not attacked before daylight. It had been twenty-four hours since he'd left Southwark. Why the delay? Whatever had held him up was going to cost him dearly, because Pembroke's forces were all in place now, while inside London wall Lord Howard had organized the citizen-soldiers at the gates. But Carlos doubted Wyatt would get as far as the gates. If he did, Carlos thought grimly, he deserved to.

"My lord!" At the shout Carlos turned in his saddle. A scout galloped past him and came alongside the Earl of Devon, calling, "Wyatt has reached Knightsbridge!"

Carlos turned to Wentworth. "Knightsbridge?"

The young lieutenant pointed across the fields. "Just below Hyde Park, sir."

About a mile south of here, Carlos thought, trotting on. He glanced around at the horsemen behind him, Devon's cavalry. He had found them well trained, though surely not by Devon himself; the fop was riding on ahead like some boy drunk on dreams of glory, his silk-tasseled sword already out and brandished high. And Carlos had discovered that in other ways these men were just as ill-prepared as the rest of the royalist soldiers. Some were frightened, a few seemed recklessly bloodthirsty, many did not believe they should be fighting Wyatt at all. More than once Carlos had overheard grumbled remarks that Englishmen should be helping, not hindering, the man who was out to stop the Spaniards from coming into England. But they did not say such things aloud in Carlos's presence. They regarded him with a kind of respectful fear; his reputation from Wrotham Hill assured that. That was fine with Carlos.

As the troop approached Charing Cross, Carlos studied a slight, bare rise on the northern edge of the village. Wentworth, following Carlos's gaze, said, "St. Martin's Field." A good place to deploy into line, Carlos thought. But Devon seemed not to have noticed the rise; he was leading the troop right down into the narrow village street. Carlos realized that he would have to point out the high spot to Devon. He shook his head. If this was to be his day to make a name for himself, he had his work cut out for him. He cantered forward to Devon.

"Your move," Edward Sydenham said. He licked his dry lips.

Isabel stared at the chessboard. For an hour she had sat with him in the predawn darkness witlessly playing chess, insensibly listening to his increasingly erratic conversation, praying that he would leave. Dawn had come and they had played on, with the curtains beside them still closed and the candles burning. Game after game Sydenham had played with a driven concentration, getting up only to throw logs on the fire. Game after game Isabel had lost. Her mind was numb from trying to think of a way out, and from dissembling, for she could not risk letting him suspect what she had discovered about him. If he did, she did not doubt that he would never let her leave. And she *had* to get to Ludgate. It had been the longest two hours she had ever spent.

Horse's hooves clattered in the street and a voice shouted up, "Sir Edward!" Sydenham tore back the curtain and threw open the shutter. Isabel squinted in the bright morning light. The breathless voice in the street yelled, "Master Grenville bids you come, sir! Every man is needed in the fight! Wyatt is coming to Ludgate!" The messenger pounded away.

Dread fluttered across Sydenham's face at the mention of fighting. He stepped back from the window so abruptly his elbow knocked the white Queen from her black square of sanctuary and she clattered to the floor. Sydenham seemed not to notice. He licked his lips again and swallowed hard. It was as if fear were drying him up from the inside. "I must go . . ."

Isabel slumped in relief. The agony of waiting was over. Once Sydenham left, she could go, too. But another dread instantly took its place. When she got to Ludgate, what could she do?

"I must arm myself . . ." Sydenham was rummaging in his desk drawer. Fear flashed in his eyes. Fear wavered in his voice. Isabel wished his fear would choke him.

He drew out an ebony case and laid it on the desk beside the chess set and opened it. Inside were two red velvet upholstered wells. One was empty. The other held an elegant wheel-lock pistol. With fumbling hands Sydenham lifted out the pistol. Its barrel was scrolled with leafy engraving and its handle curved into an exquisitely carved ball of ivory. Isabel's own mouth went dry. The pistol was identical to the one Lord Grenville had used to murder her mother.

Was he going to kill her now, too?

She pushed back her chair so fast, its legs screeched under her.

With his eyes locked on her, Sydenham inclined his head toward the door. "Palmer!"

Isabel ran for the door.

It swung open. "Stop her!" Sydenham called just as the steward stepped in, blocking Isabel's exit. "Hold her!" Sydenham shouted.

Palmer grabbed Isabel and pushed her into the room. She stumbled toward the hearth. Sydenham and Palmer moved between her and the door, backing her toward the fire. Desperately she eyed the open doorway behind the two men—the only way out.

Sydenham still held the pistol. Isabel saw again that horrifying moment of sparks and smoke and the obscene hole in her mother's forehead. She looked Sydenham in the eye. "The pistol was yours," she said. "You sent Grenville to kill my mother."

He stared at her, his mouth working strangely. "No . . . no, it wasn't like that. Grenville grabbed the pistol. I . . . could not stop him. I never—"

"And now you've sent the archers to kill my father! In God's name, why do you hate us so!"

A bittersweet smile wobbled over Sydenham's mouth as he gazed at her. He took a step closer to her. He was unbuttoning his doublet. Isabel held her breath. "You are quite wrong," he murmured. "None of this was my desire. I do not hate any of your family. Especially you." He shoved the pistol inside his doublet, then grabbed her face between his hands. He kissed her full and hard on the mouth. Isabel shuddered and wrenched her head out of his grasp, wiping her mouth in disgust. As she did, she caught sight of a tall, pale woman standing in the doorway, watching. Isabel's eyes flicked between Sydenham and Palmer. Neither of them was aware of the woman. When Isabel looked back at the doorway, the woman was gone.

A cannon boomed. Sydenham flinched. Distractedly he moved to the desk and fumbled in the drawer for packets of shot and stuffed them into his doublet. "Palmer, I must go.

This woman is a traitor. Hold her here until I return and she can be taken to prison. If she attempts escape, use your weapon."

Palmer drew his dagger. "Aye, sir."

Sydenham refastened his doublet over the pistol. He looked back at Isabel. "I ... am sorry ..." he mumbled. He turned and walked out, closing the door behind him. Isabel stood eye to eye with Palmer. After a few moments she heard the faint slam of the front door. She was alone in the house with the steward. And his dagger.

"Sit down," Palmer said tonelessly, gesturing with the blade toward the stool at the fire. "The wait may be long."

Edward walked the half mile without seeing what was around him. He went west along deserted Cheapside, then along Paternoster Row, with St. Paul's a blur beside him, then down Ave Maria Lane. He turned the corner of Ave Maria and saw Ludgate dead ahead ... and stopped in amazement. The big double wooden doors of the gate stood wide-open. Why had Lord Howard not shut the gate?

Outside it, Fleet Street lay deserted. Inside stood perhaps forty men—but not Howard's soldiers, Edward realized. These looked like the citizens' watch. Some were portly, older men. Some were tugging uncomfortably at their unfamiliar brigandines and awkwardly adjusting swords. But they all looked zealous. A lanky man stood on the steps of the gatehouse door to the left of the gate, and the others had crowded in to hear him above the noise of cannon booming in the distance. Edward recognized the speaker. Henry Peckham, a prominent citizen. He recognized several aldermen, too. Edward was appalled, realizing what had happened. The citizens' watch had betrayed the Queen. Led to treason by Peckham, they had opened Ludgate and were waiting to welcome Wyatt.

With a pang of dread Edward saw that there was no sign, either, of the Grenville Archers. He looked around frantically for them. The three stories of Ludgate jail rose over the gate above the six-foot thickness of London wall, and pale faces peered out from the jail's barred windows, but there were no archers. None stood on the roof of the gatehouse to the left, either, though a ladder was set there.

Edward looked to the right of the gate, to the Belle Sauvage Tavern with its painted, jutting sign of a wild man standing beside a bell. Up on the tavern roof a crude scaffold stood bare; yesterday Edward himself had been part of the deliberations for erecting the scaffolding as a platform for the archers. But where were they? Still at Newgate? With Howard's men? Were none of them aware yet of Wyatt's coming here to Ludgate?

The group of rebel citizens around Peckham broke apart to take up positions around the gate. Edward ducked into the doorway of the Belle Sauvage, but the attention of Peckham's men was firmly on the gate and no one seemed to notice Edward. Crammed into the doorway, he tried to think, but his mind was clogged with fear. Thornleigh was going to come marching through that open gate. Thornleigh was going to hunt him down and kill him.

Where in God's name are the archers?

Rebels' cannon shots whizzed overhead above the Earl of Devon's cavalry on St. Martin's Field. Carlos turned in his saddle and watched a ball plow into the brown grass beyond the rear of the cavalry line. Two more shots whirred over their heads. Wentworth, beside Carlos, cringed slightly. The horses that were lined up on either side of them whinnied and shied. Carlos saw the anxiety in the faces of the men as they tried to calm their mounts.

"Shouldn't we fall back, sir?" Wentworth nervously called to Carlos above the blasts.

Carlos shook his head. He had been carefully watching the cannon shots. Every one had flown high. Either Wyatt's guns were damaged by all the rain, their accuracy fouled, or his artillery officer was not experienced enough to make the instant, necessary adjustments—or else Wyatt was only firing warning shots, unwilling to kill Englishmen. The latter was the most likely, Carlos decided. Such a tactic fit the pattern of the rebel leader's faint-hearted, delayed campaign all the way from Rochester. Nevertheless, the noise alone was frightening Devon's men. And Devon himself sat his horse like a statue, white-faced and rigid. "No," Carlos answered. "The enemy must pass in front of us. Devon will attack." He nodded toward the road. "Look."

They both looked down at the road, no wider than a cart track, leading from Knightsbridge through Charing Cross. Wyatt had turned onto it from the causeway to avoid Pembroke's cannon, and had halted his column just west of

Charing Cross. His whole army—almost all foot soldiers—were stopped near their own smoking cannon. "Army" was too grand a word, Carlos thought, for it looked like Wyatt had even fewer than the three thousand Carlos had counted in their camp at Dartford. Desertions, no doubt; Carlos could see no sign that Wyatt's losses had come from any skirmishing with Pembroke's troops.

"Attack?" Wentworth repeated, glancing uncertainly over at their white-faced commander. Devon had placed himself behind the cavalry line, but every shot of the cannon had made him creep in closer, and his stallion's shoulders were now crowding between the rumps of two other horses. Wentworth looked back at Carlos. "The commander doesn't seem about to do that, sir."

Carlos gritted his teeth. It was true. Devon was no more capable of leading an attack than Carlos's horse was able to fly. They would sit here while Wyatt passed right before them, and do nothing. Carlos looked out beyond the mass of Wyatt's men. He could not see any of Pembroke's troops from here, but it was clear that they, too, had sat immobile on either side of the mile of causeway between Knightsbridge and Charing Cross and had done nothing. They had simply let Wyatt pass. Carlos knew why. Each commander was too uncertain of his men, too afraid of mass desertions, too downright timid. They were going to let Wyatt reach the city walls, and then they would rely on the city forces within to stop him. Carlos fumed in silence. The enemy was so easily within their grasp. It was maddening to watch.

Another cannonball whizzed over the horsemen's heads. Carlos did not watch this ball land. He was looking intently down at Wyatt's company. He was almost certain he could make out Thornleigh standing at the front of the waiting column ready to march in first. *He's as good as his word,* Carlos thought. *And as stubborn as his daughter.* He grimaced, pushing out of his mind the thought of the two of them. He yanked his reins, wanting action. He must try to talk some sense into the idiot nobleman. As he turned his horse's head, he caught a last glimpse of Thornleigh waving his arms toward the city as if anxious to march forward. Carlos shook his head. *Foolish old man.*

* * *

Isabel sat on the stool before Sydenham's fire, a prisoner. Palmer sat at Sydenham's desk guarding her, his dagger in his hand. In the distance, cannon boomed.

Isabel was staring into the low fire, but her mind was on Ludgate. The scene she imagined there ate at her like the small, sharp flames eating the logs. She was sure that Wyatt's inside supporters would have the gate open by now, and her father, advancing at the front of Wyatt's army, would march straight in beneath the Grenville Archers on the roofs. Instructed by Sydenham, they would slaughter him.

She had to get to Ludgate.

Desperately she tried to think. What could she do to get free of Palmer, to get out? It seemed impossible. She was alone ... she had no weapon ... no way ...

No way? Words faintly echoed in her head. Carlos's words, that night they had talked in the stable. *There is always a way. Surprise. And attack without mercy.*

A trumpet blasted outside. Palmer twisted abruptly, knocking over several pieces on the chessboard, and peered out the crack between the closed curtains. Apparently seeing nothing alarming outside, he relaxed. He turned back and noticed the fallen chessmen. He set down his dagger on the desk and meticulously began to rearrange the pieces, frowning in puzzlement as if unsure of their exact placement. He glanced up and caught Isabel watching him and quickly took up the dagger again.

Isabel turned back to the fire. The low-burning logs, the blackened brick interior, the ornate firedogs, the poker ...

Always a way ... Her heart began to beat fast. Palmer's careful handling of the chessmen—his scrupulous concern for his master's possessions—sparked a thought in her. She glanced up at the high shelf behind Palmer where Sydenham's rare books, priceless gifts from the Emperor, lay in state ... but beyond reach.

Her eyes fell on her mother's book beside the chessboard on the desk. Suddenly she stood. Palmer sat up straight, alert, the dagger ready. "May I at least read?" Isabel asked, pointing to her mother's book. "The waiting is tiresome."

Palmer frowned, skeptical.

Isabel walked forward. Palmer got up, glaring at her, the dagger raised threateningly. "Get back," he said.

"Certainly," Isabel said, reaching the desk. "I only want this." She reached out for the volume, adding with a touch of scorn, "It is only one of your master's precious books. See?" She fanned the pages before him. "No pistol hidden inside."

Palmer grunted, displeased but unwilling to make an issue of it. "Sit down," he said gruffly.

Isabel turned with her mother's book and went back to her stool. Though the fire had burned low, there were still enough orange-blue flames, like liquid teeth, rippling along the blackened logs. She placed the book on her lap, lifted the two brass clasps, opened the cover, and glanced through the pages with sightless eyes. Palmer settled back in his chair.

Isabel reached for the top of the page in front of her and ripped it out of the book. Palmer stiffened in his chair. "What are you doing?" he snapped.

Isabel leaned forward and dropped the page into the fire. It curled and shriveled and blackened. Palmer gasped and jumped up. Isabel tore out another page and cast it into the fire.

"Stop! That's the master's property!"

Isabel crumpled several pages together, wrenched them out in a handful, and flung them onto the flames. She flipped back the book to the title page where the beautiful flower's colors glinted in the firelight, and tilted it so that Palmer could see the gorgeous painting. She ripped the page free. She bent over the flame with it.

"Stop!" Palmer ran forward, sheathing his dagger as he came. Isabel jumped up as Palmer lunged for the book. They struggled over it. Isabel suddenly let the book go. Palmer had it. Isabel snatched up the hearth poker. Palmer's eyes flashed with sudden furious understanding. He dropped the book. He whipped out his dagger as the book tumbled toward the fire and Isabel smashed the poker against his head.

Palmer crashed to the hearth on his knees, dropping the dagger. His arms flailed out wildly at Isabel. She raised the poker and brought it down on top of his head again, then again. He toppled and sprawled on the floor on his side.

Isabel froze at the blood gushing from his forehead, at the blood pooling on the floor and snaking toward the painted page that lay between them . . . and at her mother's book being consumed by the fire.

CHAPTER THIRTY-FOUR

><·+·0·+·<

The Battle of Ludgate

"**L**eave the guns!" Thornleigh yelled to Wyatt.

Wyatt looked down from his horse. Grime was embedded in the lines of uncertainty that furrowed his face. He looked quickly across to his battery of smoking cannon. The gunners were firing at will, aiming over the heads of the line of royalist cavalry on the incline of St. Martin's Field, as Wyatt had instructed them. Wyatt looked back to Thornleigh. He was about to speak when one of the cannon boomed again. The cannon carriage recoiled, and the men around Wyatt winced at the noise. Thornleigh watched the cavalry on the slope. They did not break. None of the shots had come near them.

"If you're not going to use the guns to kill, leave them!" Thornleigh shouted at Wyatt. "They only hold us back!" He pointed toward the city. "We've got to move on!"

Wyatt looked around. His men were anxiously awaiting some order for action. He took a deep breath and shook his head sharply as if to clear it of all previous thoughts. "Right!" he said. "Cobham, maintain your troop here at the cannon. Sergeant, keep firing high. The rest of you . . ." He paused and drew his sword and pointed it toward London. He stood in his stirrups and shouted to his men, "Onward! On to our London friends! On to Ludgate!"

The men took up the cry. "To Ludgate!" they cried. "Onward!" They rushed forward to follow Wyatt. "To Ludgate!"

They marched four men abreast. Thornleigh kept in the front rank. He glanced anxiously up at the Queen's cavalry on the slope as he and Wyatt's men moved toward Charing Cross. But the horsemen remained in line, unmoving as Wyatt's company marched into the village. Wyatt's men tromped down the narrow main street, passed the great cross, then marched out of the village again and carried on eastward along the Strand. Thornleigh was amazed that the

Queen's horsemen had not attacked. But he tried not to think of that possibility. He forced his concentration onto the muddy stretch of the Strand before him, glancing around only now and then for royalists, hoping he could continue unmolested along this last mile. He wanted only to make it into London and reach Sydenham.

He could see house-shaped Temple Bar looming ahead, and boundary between London and Westminster. From there it was just a half mile to Ludgate.

A cannon shot screamed overhead above Devon and Carlos. Then another. Devon dropped his reins to block his ears with his hands. His horse reared and Devon pitched backward. Carlos caught him before he toppled. Another shot screeched above them. Devon wriggled away from Carlos's arm. "Let go, you fool!" Devon screamed. His skin seemed tinged with green; his eyes were wild. He scrabbled for the reins at his horse's neck. Jerking and tugging the reins, he yanked his mount around. "We are destroyed!" he cried. "All is lost!" Frantically he dug his spurs into his stallion's sides. The horse bounded into an instant canter. Devon clung to its neck as it galloped southward toward Whitehall. Carlos looked around. Devon's leaderless horsemen were jostling and murmuring in fear. The cannon salvo paused long enough for Devon's faint cries across the field to reach them. "Destroyed! Lost!" A half-dozen horsemen instantly raced off after him. Panic broke out among the men:

"The commander!"

"Sound retreat!"

"Is it surrender?"

"We are lost!"

Horses began jostling, uncertain of their riders' shaky commands. Carlos galloped back to Wentworth. "Keep those men in line!" he yelled, pointing to the right. Circling the lieutenant at the gallop, Carlos headed back to the other end of the line where three more men had just fled and another was urging his confused horse to follow. Carlos drew his sword over the last man's head and brought the blade down, slicing the man's reins in half. The man groped for the remnants by the bit, fumbling for control. As the other horsemen stared in amazement, Carlos galloped in a tight circle in front of them, his sword held high, and shouted, "Next man who deserts will feel my blade across his throat!"

The horsemen fearfully reined in their mounts. There was silence. The salvo from Wyatt's guns on the road started up again. The horsemen winced, afraid to stay, afraid to leave.

The Earl of Devon's red-eyed stallion clattered over the cobbles into the gateway of Whitehall Palace. "All is lost!" Devon shrilled. The men of Sir John Gage's troop at the gate scattered apart to let him in. They had heard the frightful roar of the cannon up by Charing Cross, but no one knew what was happening. Their anxious questions exploded like a hail of shot:

"Has the Earl surrendered?"

"Has Wyatt won?"

"Is it a rout?"

Panic swept the courtyard. Gage's soldiers bolted toward the great hall where the men of the Queen's personal guard were stationed. "Pembroke has gone over to Wyatt!" some of them shouted on the run. Panic took hold of the Queen's guard and they slammed the hall doors on Gage's men, keeping them out. Panic trembled through the knots of the Queen's ladies huddled in the great hall's corners. "God have mercy upon us!" one cried.

Queen Mary walked quietly, stiffly, out the rear of the hall. She mounted the stairs to the empty gallery above the gatehouse. She went to the windows and looked out toward Charing Cross. Beyond the village and the hedged fields and the houses lining the Strand, the walls of the city stood implacable under the bright morning sun.

Mary could hear the commotion all through the palace: women screaming and sobbing; Gage's soldiers, barred from the hall, running through the corridors. She saw soldiers burst out from the kitchens and dash through the wood lot and toward water stairs on the river, deserting. She stood alone, watching. Shakily she made the sign of the cross, touching her forehead and heart, leaving the priest's anointed cross of ash a sooty smudge on her pale brow.

Isabel ran all the way. She turned the corner of Ave Maria Lane and stopped abruptly at what she saw ahead. Peckham had done it. The big doors of Ludgate stood wide-open. There was no sign of royalist soldiers, and fifty or so of Peckham's men stood milling at the gate, ready to defend it. Isabel saw Peckham himself pointing to direct a man into position. He glanced around and saw her and threw her a brief smile that said he had half expected her to join them. Then he strode on to the small door of the walkway that led through London wall beside the gate and opened that door, too. Peckham had done everything possible to help Wyatt into London.

Isabel saw Sydenham, too. But he did not see her. He was cowering in the recessed doorway of the Belle Sauvage Tavern, trying to remain unnoticed, his eyes fixed ahead on the gate. Isabel looked up to the roofs on one side of the street, then the other. There were ladders, and there was scaffolding on the rooftops, but there were no archers. She looked out the open gate to empty Fleet Street and felt a surge of hope—no archers anywhere! She could hear the blasts of cannon not far off. Wyatt was coming! She quickly pictured it all. The French had joined Wyatt's men and helped them cut down the Queen's army on the way. Wyatt and her father were going to march victorious through the gate Peckham held open for them, to be thronged by cheering Londoners streaming from their houses. It all seemed possible. Wonderfully possible!

There was a drumming of horses' hooves. Isabel turned. Rounding the corner of Ave Maria Lane, horsemen were galloping toward her. There were at least twenty of them, all wearing the white coats of the loyal London troops. Lord Howard rode at the head, his jowls waggling in fury. "Shut that gate, by order of the Queen!" Howard cried.

Isabel dashed into an alley by the Belle Sauvage and turned to look back just as the horsemen galloped past her. The last glimpse she had of Sydenham was seeing him cram himself, white-faced, deeper into the tavern's entrance.

"The gate stays open!" Henry Peckham cried. His men had drawn their swords and stood firm in their defensive line. There were at least twice as many of them as Whitecoats.

But as the last of the horsemen thundered past Isabel, a mob of perhaps fifty armed loyalist citizens came running after them. The street shook with the combined thud of feet and hooves. Among the citizens, Isabel caught sight of the broad red face of Master Legge of the Crane, her father's friend. Legge, like the others with him, was out to defend his property from rebel plunder.

These loyalist citizens swarmed up beside Howard's

Whitecoats, ready to fight with them. Howard raised his sword. "Down with the traitors!" he cried.

His loyalist faction set upon Peckham's faction. The two groups raged at one another with swords, pikes, daggers, and fists. Men slashed, kicked, gouged, and rolled in the mud. Isabel peered out from the alley, holding her breath. While the two factions skirmished, the gate remained open.

Another sound of tramping feet made Isabel twist back. John Grenville was riding down Ave Maria Lane toward the fracas and behind him ran a string of men. Isabel ducked back into the alley as Grenville rode past her, but she clearly saw that each of his men running after him wore on his breast the Grenville badge of three green towers, and each had a longbow and a quiver slung on his back. The famed Grenville Archers.

Grenville reined in his mount well back of the continuing skirmish at the gate and motioned to his archers. They raced to either side of the street. Isabel pressed her back against a crude cellar doorjamb in the alley wall, for she dared not look out and be seen by Grenville. But she heard the scuffling of the archers as they climbed the scaffolding up to the roof of the Belle Sauvage. And she could see, across the street, that they were scrambling up the ladder to the flat roof above the gatehouse, too.

"Sturridge!" The frantic voice, just around the tavern corner from Isabel, was Sydenham's. "Giles Sturridge! Stop!"

"Sir Edward?" The man's voice came from partway up the scaffold.

"A hundred pounds, did I say? Make it two hundred. No, five! Five hundred pounds if you kill Thornleigh!"

"Will do, Sir Edward!" the archer said eagerly.

Isabel stiffened against the doorjamb, and a jutting nail dug into her back like an arrow.

"You must not fail me!" Sydenham hissed wildly.

"Sturridge, get on up there!" John Grenville yelled from the middle of the street. "Sydenham, stop holding him back! Let him go!"

A cry from an archer on the gatehouse roof rose above the skirmishing of Howard's and Peckham's followers. "I can see the rebels! They're at Temple Bar! They're almost here!"

Isabel gasped. Heedless of Grenville, she looked out

around the corner. The two fighting factions at the gate suddenly stood still, apparently as dumbfounded as Isabel that the moment was at last upon them. Wyatt was coming. And the gate still stood wide-open.

Isabel's eyes flashed up at the archers, then down at the uncertain faces of Howard's Whitecoats and citizens. Would they all remain loyal at the final moment, or would they defect, rush over to Wyatt just as she had seen Norfolk's army of Whitecoats do at Rochester? She looked straight ahead at the open gate. Her father was about to come marching through it. And Isabel knew she could not entrust her hopes to a mass defection. Even if every Whitecoat went over, even if Legge and his citizen comrades threw down their arms, even if the mass of archers refused to fire on Wyatt's soldiers, the man named Sturridge would surely loose the fatal arrow—for five hundred pounds. No, her father's only hope of survival was for Lord Howard to shut the gate.

Isabel rocked back against the alley wall, appalled at the choice that lay before her. If Ludgate was closed, Wyatt and his cause would be lost. But if the gate stayed open, her father would surely die.

Wyatt's cannon kept pounding the slope at Charing Cross above the Earl of Devon's nervous horsemen.

"They are firing high!" Carlos shouted to the horsemen, slashing his flat hand in a line above his own head in illustration. "See? Always high!"

The cannon roared on, but the horsemen relaxed somewhat, and soon, with Wentworth's help, Carlos brought the troop back to order. They sat their horses, waiting for his command.

Carlos looked down the Strand toward London where Wyatt's small army, having left their troop firing the cannon, could just be seen marching on. Carlos had to strain to see them. Very soon they would be out of sight. And soon after that they would reach Ludgate. Carlos took a long look at his anxious men. If he was going to act, it had to be now.

He lifted his sword and pointed it at the sky. Slowly he lowered the sword tip toward Wyatt. He kicked his horse's flanks. "Charge!" he yelled.

His horse bounded forward into a gallop. Carlos lowered his torso over the horse's neck and tightened his legs against its sides and tore down the slope toward the road. For sev-

eral moments he was riding alone. Then, he heard them, the
pounding hooves of sixty horses racing down the hill behind
him—the familiar, thrilling thunder of a cavalry charge.
Carlos's breathing settled into a quickened but steady
rhythm.

He galloped past Temple Bar and saw them ahead on
Fleet Street: Wyatt's army. They were marching by houses
and laneways, looking lulled at having passed so far unmolested. Then one of them, a young soldier at the rear, heard
the thunder of the hooves. He turned and shouted something.
Several more of them twisted around.

"Lieutenant!" Carlos yelled. Carlos veered at a gallop toward the right of the column while pointing his sword to the
left. Wentworth, following the order, cut to the left. Suddenly acting with the assurance of men well led, half the
cavalry galloped after Carlos and the rest followed
Wentworth. They fanned out along Wyatt's column like the
arms of a nutcracker. Then they set upon Wyatt's stunned
men.

Wyatt's soldiers tried to defend themselves, but they were
no match for quick-maneuvering cavalry who could wield
lethal swords from the height of their mounts. A young soldier screamed as his back was ripped open by a horseman's
slashing blade. Another knelt in the mud in terror with his
arms wrapped over his head. Two horsemen galloped after a
soldier running away. The running man was knocked down
by the first horse's chest, and the horseman following
crushed the fallen man's rib cage under one merciless hoof.

Carlos galloped ahead to the vanguard. A bearded man at
the head of the rebel column sat his horse and shouted orders. It had to be Wyatt. Carlos counted six other mounted
officers, all looking slightly dazed. None of them was near
Wyatt. Carlos galloped forward, his sword out-thrust. He
wanted to take Wyatt alive; the reward would be greater.

Foot soldiers staggered out of Carlos's way. Wyatt saw
Carlos coming. His sword was drawn as well. Carlos tore
on, closing the gap between them. But instead of slashing
his sword at Wyatt as he passed, or reining up alongside him
to fight, Carlos came galloping straight at his side. He
rammed his horse into Wyatt's. Wyatt pitched sideways out
of his saddle.

The two horses whinnied in pain and danced awkwardly
to find their balance. Carlos slapped the flat side of his

sword on Wyatt's horse's rump. The animal bounded away. Carlos wheeled again, then jerked his mount back toward Wyatt who had staggered to his feet. Carlos galloped forward and was almost on him when Wyatt suddenly toppled to the ground. Carlos saw that a man had thrown himself at Wyatt's legs, knocking him down to save him. It was Richard Thornleigh.

Carlos wheeled again, about to try once more to get back to Wyatt, but by now several of Wyatt's officers and men had crowded around their leader and held swords and pikes outstretched, forming a bristling human armor around him. And Carlos saw one of Wyatt's horsemen barreling toward him. He realized he could not reach Wyatt. He was alone without the backup of infantry—he had hoped that Pembroke would have rushed in to cover his attack, but there was no sign of Pembroke. So he veered away and galloped back toward the center of Wyatt's company.

Or what was left of it. Scores of Wyatt's men lay writhing and gasping in the mud. Carlos's horsemen continued to cut them down with ferocity but with little organization. Despite Carlos's earlier yelled order that they flank Wyatt's entire column, most of the horsemen had got no farther than the middle of it before plowing in to attack. The result was that the horsemen were embroiled in a melee with Wyatt's center, while his rear guard was escaping and his vanguard was running forward.

Suddenly six of Wyatt's mounted officers bore down on Carlos's horsemen in a bid to let their vanguard escape. Carlos managed to turn his men to this attack, chiefly by leading it with his own slashing sword. Enmeshed in the fray, Carlos glanced toward Wyatt's vanguard. Wyatt was leading them on toward Ludgate, on the run. Beyond them, Carlos could see London wall a quarter mile in the distance. And he could just make out Ludgate itself. He was shocked at what he saw there. Were the doors really standing wide-open?

A pike seared across his thigh, ripping his breeches and tearing his skin. He twisted back to see the foot soldier beside him readying to strike again. Carlos slashed his sword across the man's throat. As the man toppled, Carlos cursed himself for having looked away. The pain in his thigh was hot as pitch, and blood was already soaking his knee, but the pike had not cut deeply into muscle. He fell back into the fight against Wyatt's officers. When it was done, three of the officers were dead, two had been unhorsed and lay wounded, thrashing in the mud. The last one was fleeing across a waste lot at the gallop behind a veil of churned-up mud.

Hundreds of the men of Wyatt's rear guard were fleeing, too. They headed in every direction. Some were running back the way they had come, a few were staggering aimlessly, many were disappearing behind houses and down the lanes that led to the river.

But Carlos was concerned only with Wyatt. The rebel leader, with about three hundred of his men left, was rushing on, very close to Ludgate.

Inside Ludgate the two factions, Lord Howard's loyalists and Henry Peckham's defenders of the gate, had fallen back to fierce fighting moments after the archer's cry that Wyatt was coming. Howard's men had advanced a little toward the gate, and the archers' arrows from the roofs had taken their toll of Peckham's men. But the archers had to restrain their fire, finding it difficult to separate rebel from royalist in the hand-to-hand fighting below them. Amid this confusion, Peckham's men were stoutly maintaining their defensive line.

Isabel pushed away from the alley wall and moved out around the corner. Bodies lay strewn in the mud like discarded rags. The wounded were crawling or stumbling away toward the sides of the street. Isabel caught a glimpse of Legge near the gate, holding a man in a vicious headlock. She saw Peckham throttling a gasping man on his knees. She saw Grenville, still on horseback, hacking his sword at a man with a pike. She saw Sydenham, still cowering in the tavern doorway.

And Ludgate still stood open.

Isabel clenched her fists at her sides, immobilized by indecision. She looked up at the archers on the roof of the Belle Sauvage. The sun, climbing to its noonday zenith, bleached the colors from the archers' clothes, darkened their faces, and made silhouettes of their bodies. They stood with legs apart, their arrows fitted in their bows and the bowstrings pulled taut to their chests, forming a frieze of deadly potential.

Isabel could hold back no longer.

She raced toward Legge just as he dragged the man he was fighting down to the earth. A tall comrade of Legge's kicked the fallen man.

"Master Legge!" Isabel yelled.

Legge looked up in astonishment. "Isabel! What in God's—"

"Follow me!" she cried. She grabbed the arm of Legge's comrade. "You, too! Help us!" she shouted. Letting go, she ran past them both. Legge and the tall man stared after her, uncomprehending.

Isabel ran straight toward Henry Peckham's ragged line of defenders. Peckham's strangled victim lay at his feet, and Peckham was wiping muddy sweat from his brow when he caught sight of Isabel. He quickly nodded to her, an unthinking acknowledgment of her right to pass. Legge and his friend exchanged quick glances of amazement at her success, then bolted forward to join her. Peckham, believing the men with her were friends, did not blink as they passed him; then he turned and lunged toward a royalist coming at him with a dagger.

Isabel and Legge and the tall man raced toward the open timber doors under Ludgate's high stone arch. Isabel grasped the big iron fitting at the edge of one door. She tried to push the door closed. It was too heavy. "Help me!" she cried to the tall man. "Master Legge, close the other door!"

Legge dashed across the gap to the other door. He had just taken hold of its iron bolt when a man lunged at him from behind, knocking Legge forward and scraping his forehead against the door. Legge turned and swung his fist at the man's jaw, felling him. Isabel saw Legge's bleeding forehead, then whipped around to see a man lurching toward her. It was Edward Sydenham. He was coming at her with his bare hands uplifted like claws.

Thornleigh's leg muscles and lungs were screaming in pain. He had run nonstop after escaping the attack of the Spaniard's cavalry, and he ran on now, ignoring the pain, ignoring the questions that the sight of the Spaniard had unleashed, because now he could see Ludgate's doors standing open not a quarter mile ahead.

Wyatt was running beside him. And Thornleigh thought there must be three hundred of their men running behind them. Most were out of breath, many were bleeding, but all were unquestioningly following Wyatt. And, like Thornleigh, Wyatt's eyes were fixed on their goal, their haven, their reward—the big wide-open doors of Ludgate. They were going to make it in.

Then Thornleigh heard it again—the murderous thunder of a cavalry charge. He twisted around. It was the Spaniard again. His horsemen fell on their rear, again. And tore them to pieces, again.

But again Wyatt stumbled free and carried on with a fraction of his company. Now, there were no more than fifty of them. And Thornleigh stuck by Wyatt's side.

Sydenham's hands were almost at Isabel's throat when Legge butted his bleeding head into Sydenham's side. Sydenham thudded to the ground, the wind knocked out of him. He clawed impotently at the muddy cobbles in a frenzy to get up, but Legge's tall comrade grabbed him by the feet and hauled him to one side to clear the door's path, while Legge ran back to the other door. Isabel stared at Sydenham in amazement: he had tried to prevent her from closing the gate. He seemed obsessed, beyond caring whether he was jeopardizing Queen Mary's throne as long as his own scheme to see the archers kill her father succeeded. A shudder ran through her as she realized that the betrayal she was committing against Wyatt was no less aberrant.

There was no time for such thoughts.

She lunged for the door and grabbed hold of the iron bar and pushed. Her arm muscles quivered with the effort, but the door did not move. The tall man rushed back to help her. Isabel turned and threw her back against the door. Across the gap, Legge was pushing hard at the other door, his shoulder against it, his face red. Grunting with the labor, Isabel finally felt her door budge. It began to move slowly. So did Legge's door.

The huge hinges creaked, the heavy timber doors gained momentum, and Isabel had to hasten her walk into a lope to keep up with the accelerating speed. She and the tall man were almost running with the door when, with Legge's door edge no more than an arm's length from hers, she looked out and saw Wyatt's meager troop not even a quarter mile away, coming down Fleet Street toward her. Through the closing gap of the huge doors she caught sight of Wyatt at the head and of her father at Wyatt's side. Her father's gaze locked onto her face, unbelieving. Wyatt saw her, too. The last glimpse she had, like an arrow piercing her eye, was Wyatt's stunned look as he stared at her.

The doors slammed shut. Legge drove home the long iron bolt.

Edward heard Howard's men cheer. He scrambled to his feet and saw that Isabel and the two men had succeeded in closing the gate.

An archer on the gatehouse rooftop, looking out to Fleet Street, shouted jubilantly, "The Queen's cavalry are routing the rebels!"

Edward looked up to the gatehouse rooftop where the archer was pointing out over London wall. "The rebels are being slaughtered!" he cried.

Howard's men cheered wildly. The suddenly closed gate seemed to infuse new strength into them and simultaneously to drain it from Peckham's men. All around Edward, Howard's loyalists began striking stronger blows and Peckham's men began falling.

Edward felt dizzy with hope and fear. If Wyatt's soldiers were dying outside the gate there was every reason to hope that Thornleigh was dying, too. Maybe he already lay dead. But with the gate shut it was impossible to know. Edward's eyes fell on the small door of the walkway that led under London wall. The door was closed. What if, just beyond the gate, Thornleigh was running toward the walkway, about to burst in here looking for the man he hated.

Edward pulled the pistol from his doublet and ran toward the walkway. His fingers fumbled to load the pistol as he reached the small door. He wrenched up the door's latch. He stepped into the stone walkway, a tunnel through the eight-foot thickness of London wall. The door at the opposite end was shut. The door behind Edward creaked shut, too. There was no light in the tunnel. Edward walked on, his footsteps echoing, the old terror of small places invading him again and tightening every nerve. He could hear the muffled shouts and cries of men as he approached the far door. He reached it and in the darkness clawed over its wooden surface to find the bolt. Slivers gouged his palms, but he finally wrenched the bolt aside. He kicked open the door and ran outside ... and gasped at the scene of battle before him down the street.

* * *

Carlos called it mayhem. Pembroke's infantry had finally arrived, and a troop of Clinton's cavalry, too—all to subdue no more than fifty, the pitiful remnant of Wyatt's army. The rebels were fighting bravely, but their resistance was hopeless. Vastly outnumbered, they were slipping in mud, crawling through puddles, bleeding, and dying. Some had managed to escape the blows of the converging royalists and were dashing in all directions away from closed Ludgate. They were running, sliding around house corners, careening down lanes toward the river.

Carlos saw Wyatt standing still with an expression of disbelief on his mud-flecked face. Carlos galloped toward him.

Isabel was almost knocked down by a rebel soldier running toward a lane. She had hurried after Sydenham through the walkway under London wall. Back inside, after closing the gate, she had caught sight of him, and one look at his white but resolute face as he drew out his pistol had told her the worst. She had come after him, hoping somehow to stop him. But now, in the melee before her of soldiers running and horses rearing and men fighting and shouting and falling, she had lost Sydenham. Nor could she see her father. If she could only reach him, she thought, she could pull him away down a lane. There was a maze of docks and breweries on the riverfront. She could hide him there. If she could just find him before Sydenham did.

A horseman galloped past. Isabel lurched out of his way. His face was turned from her but she recognized him anyway. Carlos.

Edward had forced himself to come toward the fighting, but he cringed on the edge of the fray, terrified of getting closer, yet burning with a need to locate Thornleigh, dead or alive. His pistol trembled in his outstretched hand. And then, through the mass of fighting bodies, he glimpsed a face. A tall man, gray-haired, with a patch over his left eye—just as Isabel had described him. Edward's heart thudded in his chest, then seemed to stop, for Richard Thornleigh was looking straight at him. "Sydenham?" Thornleigh called hoarsely, unsure. Edward blanched—and knew he had betrayed himself. Thornleigh began to advance on him. He moved

through the melee steadily, with an implacable fixedness of
purpose, stalking Edward.

Edward held up the pistol in both hands. But men were
running by in his line of fire. And his hands were trembling
badly. He could not get a clear shot.

Wyatt's face showed that he knew it was over. He looked
up and saw Carlos coming, and his sword drooped at his
side. Carlos reined in alongside him. "Sir Thomas Wyatt?"

Wyatt nodded bleakly. He turned his sword in his hand so
that he was grasping the tip, and the handle was uplifted toward Carlos. Carlos accepted the gesture of surrender. He
took Wyatt's sword and sheathed it in his saddle. He beckoned over a lieutenant to bind the captive's wrists with rope.
Carlos looked the rebel commander in the eye and said, "I
arrest you in the name of the Queen."

Isabel froze. Searching for Sydenham and her father she
had suddenly caught sight of them both. Her father was
walking steadily toward Sydenham. And Sydenham had leveled a pistol at her father. They were only a few arm's
lengths apart.

She twisted around and saw Carlos. She did not stop to
think. She ran to him and grabbed his stirrup. He looked
down at her in amazement. She pointed to Sydenham. "You
hate him, too!" she cried. "Stop him!"

Edward cocked the trigger. He fired. Sparks singed his
face. The ball whizzed by Thornleigh's ear. Thornleigh kept
on coming. He reached Edward and swatted the pistol out of
his grasp. He grabbed Edward's throat. Edward clawed at
Thornleigh's arms, felt Thornleigh's thumbs jamming his
windpipe, felt his throat on fire, saw red flames sheet behind
his eyes. Suddenly Thornleigh let him go. Thornleigh
slumped to the ground on his knees. A royalist soldier behind him had jabbed a broken lance against his ribs, then the
soldier had twisted around to fight another opponent. Thornleigh toppled onto his back and lay in the mud groaning.

Edward saw his chance. Still choking from Thornleigh's
attack he dropped to all fours, crawled through the mud to
the fallen pistol, grabbed it, and scrambled back to Thornleigh, who still lay moaning. Edward steadied himself on his

knees, snatched another ball from inside his doublet, loaded
the pistol. He pressed the barrel end to Thornleigh's temple.
"*Alto!*"

Edward twisted his face up. The sun glared behind the man
on horseback, but Edward knew the voice. The Spaniard.
Edward twisted back to Thornleigh. He cocked the trigger.

The flat of the Spaniard's sword smashed his wrist so violently, it spun Edward around on his knees and the pistol
flew up out of his hand in an arc. Edward screamed as pain
seared up his arm.

"Sydenham," Carlos said, "I arrest you in the name of the
Queen."

"Arrest?" Edward sputtered, still grimacing at the pain.
"On what grounds?"

Carlos bared his teeth in an icy smile of satisfaction. "I
find you with the rebels. I arrest you as a traitor." He called
over a sergeant. "Bind him," Carlos ordered. The sergeant
pulled Edward to his feet, trussed his wrists, and began to
haul him away through the mass of men.

Isabel had rushed to her father. On the ground, he was
wincing at the pain in his side. "My God," he breathed
through clenched teeth, "it *was* you . . . at the gate! Why—"

"Father, come with me!" She struggled to help him up.

But he resisted. "Where's Sydenham?" he said, getting to
his knees and twisting to look.

"Never mind him! Come!"

"No!" Thornleigh pushed her off. "Leave me!"

A trumpet blared. Isabel looked around frantically. There
was still a commotion all about her, a din of voices, but the
nature of it had changed. It was no longer the clash of battle
but the clamor of victory. Through the crush of men, Isabel
glimpsed Carlos watching her from his horse nearby. And
Lord Howard was riding toward them. He was followed by
a pack of his Whitecoat officers, and behind them came a
throng of cheering Londoners on foot—householders, both
men and women. Isabel saw Legge among the crowd. Lord
Howard was calling orders for his officers to arrest the rebels and to round up the ones who had run away.

Isabel grappled her father's arm and tried harder to pull
him to his feet. She could still get him away, get him down
to the river, hide him. It was still possible. If only she could
get him up!

Lord Howard rode right past them and pulled his horse to a halt before Wyatt, not far from Isabel and Thornleigh. Finally, Thornleigh stood. Isabel threw her arm around his neck and tried to drag him away. But still he resisted.

Lord Howard glared down at the rebel commander. "A kingdom you have risked, Wyatt, and nothing have you gained. Except a date with the executioner." He prodded his sword tip at the rope binding Wyatt's wrists. He looked around at the soldiers' sweating faces. "Who is responsible for this arrest?"

"I am," Carlos answered, edging his horse forward.

Howard looked at Carlos with a frown. "Did you also lead the charge from Charing Cross?"

"Yes."

"What is your name?"

"Valverde."

"Ah, yes, Abergavenny's Spaniard." Howard's frown broke into a broad smile. "Well done, Valverde. A fine day's work. Believe me, Her Majesty will show you her gratitude most generously."

"With land?" Carlos asked.

Howard barked a laugh. "With whatever your heart desires, I warrant!" He turned to one of his officers and, with a jerk of his chin toward Wyatt, said with cold authority, "Take the traitor away."

The officer hustled Wyatt off like a common thief.

"My lord!" a voice wailed out. Howard looked to his left. Edward Sydenham was frantically pushing through the crowd to get to the commander.

"Ah, Sydenham," Howard said mildly.

Panting, Sydenham pushed between Howard's horse and Carlos's horse and stuck his bound hands up in the air in front of Howard to demonstrate his grievance. "My lord, I protest! An injustice has been done me!"

Howard frowned at Carlos. "You again?"

Carlos nodded.

"Your first error," Howard said sternly. "Sir Edward Sydenham is a gentleman beloved of the Queen. Lieutenant," he said to a nearby officer, "untie Sir Edward's hands." Howard looked back at Carlos. "As I recall, you tried once before to take Sir Edward into your custody. If this is some kind of personal vendetta—"

"Sydenham is a villain!"

All heads turned to where the hoarse voice had come from.

Isabel winced. It was her father who had cried out. Everyone was looking their way, but no one seemed sure of who had spoken. Isabel tried to think quickly. They were surrounded by people, so Lord Howard could not see them. She lowered her head to mask herself and shouted, "Aye, Sydenham betrayed Her Majesty! I saw him at the gate. As it closed, he tried to open it again to the rebels!"

There was a murmured agreement among Lord Howard's soldiers. "Aye, I saw him, too," one called out.

"So did I," a deep voice said with authority. It was Legge. "Sydenham was trying to keep the gate open, that's sure. I had to bash him out of the way to stop him."

Lord Howard looked at Sydenham anxiously. "Sir Edward, what say you to these charges?"

Everyone's attention was on Sydenham and Howard. Isabel grabbed her father's arm and whispered fiercely, "Father, now is our chance. Come away!"

But Thornleigh stood rooted, his gaze fixed on Sydenham.

Sydenham's eyes had a hunted look. His mouth worked. He seemed to be fighting for words. Isabel caught a glimpse of John Grenville in the crowd, watching Sydenham through eyes narrowed in suspicion.

"Sir Edward," Lord Howard repeated, concerned, "here are divers good citizens claiming to have seen you do treason. You really must answer and—"

"I will answer for him!" Thornleigh shouted. He shrugged off Isabel's restraining arm and stood alone, rocky but defiant. He pushed through the crowd and stopped between Lord Howard's horse and Carlos's. He faced Sydenham.

"My lord," Thornleigh said evenly, looking up at Howard, "my name is Richard Thornleigh. I am a rebel. In fact, my lord, I am a criminal."

There was a hush as Thornleigh's declaration hung in the air. He turned back to look at Sydenham. When he spoke again, his voice was flat and implacable. "My late wife was a criminal, too. And a convicted heretic. She was once sentenced by the church to burn at Smithfield. I thwarted the burning and carried her off. But even before that day, my wife and I and a band of comrades had broken almost every law of this realm, and of Christendom, too. And this man," he said, his gaze never flinching from Sydenham, "was one of our outlaw company."

There were indrawn breaths. Lord Howard blinked in astonishment. Isabel pushed through to her father's side. Sydenham's face had drained to the color of parchment.

Thornleigh thrust a hand inside his muddied tunic and pulled out a paper. Isabel saw that it was tattered and stained and charred at the edge. Thornleigh unfolded it. "This," he declared to Howard, "is proof of what I say. It is a letter my wife wrote to her friend, Edward Sydenham, two weeks ago, on the day she died." He lifted the paper and read aloud:

"Dear Edward,
   Of course I will keep your secret. How could I not, when I trust you will do the same for me? We heretics must stick together ... I know what hell you have suffered, fleeing England as an outcast, plagued by guilt that others might have died because of you, fearful every day since your return that your criminal past would be uncovered. I ..."

"Give me that," Howard interrupted.

Thornleigh handed up the letter. Howard perused it for a moment with an expression of growing alarm. He finished by reading aloud, in a voice of wonder, " 'Your secret is safe with me.' Signed, 'Honor Thornleigh.' "

Howard stared for a long moment at Sydenham. Then he turned to Carlos. "Valverde, take Sir Edward to prison with the rest. These charges must be investigated." He looked at Thornleigh. "And take away this criminal, too."

CHAPTER THIRTY-FIVE

>—►—◄—◙—►—◄—◄

Smithfield

It was almost warm. The morning air held a promise of spring. That was Isabel's first thought as she stepped out of the stable into the courtyard of the Anchor Inn after a sleepless night in the straw.

Blinking with arid eyes, she looked up through the bare chestnut tree limbs that stretched above her head. The pale sun hovered inside a pearly mist. And last night's beads of ice, which, in the moonlight, had been clinging to the underside of the branches like frozen tears, had now melted, and gleamed as if changed by some merciful hand into pearls. A crow flapped noisily into the tree, beating broad black wings, scattering a shower of droplets. Isabel quickly lowered her head, but a drop slithered down the back of her neck like an icy finger. She saw her face reflected in a sludge puddle at the shadowed base of the tree trunk, the puddle rimmed with tiny picks of ice like teeth. This was not spring. And there was no merciful hand anywhere. Today, her father was going to hang.

She left the Anchor and started walking toward the church of St. Michael's Cornhill.

"Prisons can't hold all the buggers," a Guildhall constable had told her of the rebels last night. She had stood on the marble floor of Guildhall with a crowd, waiting through five hours of hasty mass trials. Finally, her father, among a batch of twenty rebels, had come before the judge. The judge had listened to the single witness, a Billingsgate fishmonger—only one witness was required by law—then had sentenced the twenty to hang, and had called in the next batch. "Nigh on six hundred've been nabbed," the constable had told Isabel. "They found 'em cringing in the warehouses like riverfront rats." So many arrests had been made that churches throughout the city were being used to hold the captured men.

The church of St. Michael's Cornhill was only a few blocks away from the Anchor. Its facade was shadowed by tenements built on the crammed churchyard fronting Cornhill. A crowd had already formed, eager to watch the prisoners about to be taken out to execution. Isabel pushed through toward a guard. He saw her coming and yawned.

"May I see my father?" she asked.

The guard shook his head and scratched the morning stubble on his chin. "See him at the gallows."

She had already known the answer. Her plea had become mere rote. Over and over last night, first at Guildhall and then here at St. Michael's until curfew had sounded and she had been forced to leave, she had asked the same question. Over and over she had been told to go home.

Home? Walking away along Cornhill last night she had wondered, *Where is home?* Her family's abandoned house at Colchester, barren now of every sound of life? She could not go there. Martin's house on nearby Bucklersbury Street? It was to have been her home as well, but it, too, would be barren of sound, save the weeping of a mother for two lost sons. She would not go there. The Crane Inn, whose owner, Master Legge, had once been her father's comrade, and who had helped her close the gate on Wyatt's brave men? She could not bear to go there.

So she walked on like some lost child until she found herself outside the Anchor Inn. Her money was gone. She went around to the stable. No one was there. The stable looked the same as on the night she had found Carlos grooming her mare, and he had talked about his life, about *Conquistadores* and the wide New World. The stable's same inhabitants—the dappled pony and the old black gelding—glanced over at her, munching their hay. The stable boy was gone, probably out with the rest of London's waifs, excitedly peering at the prisoners packed into the churches, but he had left behind a hunk of bread and a dried apple. Isabel sat down in the straw and ate a few bites. Here, there was no one to tell her to go home.

She looked up at the stall where Carlos had slung his jerkin that night, and a thought crept up on her. The day that he had burst into Sydenham's hall and made that wild attempt to take her into custody, had he simply been trying to get her out of Sydenham's house? Had he somehow learned that she was in danger from Sydenham? Learned it from her father in Wyatt's camp? The facts fit. And what had she done? Fought him, spat at him, done everything she could to make him hate her.

Yet what did any of that matter anymore? Carlos was now one of the Queen's captains. And Wyatt's rebellion was crushed. And her father was going to hang.

Wearied by misery, she had sunk into a black and heavy sleep in the straw and had woken to the discordant clang of church bells.

"Here they come!"

The doors of St. Michael's opened. The crowd crammed in closer. Isabel stood on tiptoe and craned her neck to see past the heads and shoulders. Filthy, bleary-eyed prisoners were being led by guards out of the church. The prisoners filed out in a silent, shuffling line. There were perhaps forty. Richard Thornleigh was one of them. His face was gray, his expression lifeless, but he walked with his head up. That alone set him apart from the other condemned. Among all the bowed heads—bowed in fear, in remorse, in shame before the crowd—Thornleigh looked straight ahead, not so much defiant as uncaring. Isabel remembered seeing the same look on his face the day after her mother's murder, when she and Adam had visited him in Colchester jail and he had finally turned away from them with a desolate calmness to go back to his whittling.

"God-cursed traitors!" A clump of fresh dung smacked a prisoner's neck. He jumped like a skittish colt, but, disoriented, made no move to wipe away the slimy mess. Some of the crowd laughed.

The guards prodded the prisoners into Cornhill Street and they started walking westward. Isabel did not know where they were being taken. She followed with the crowd. A few boys darted up to the sides of the moving pack of the condemned. The rest of the people kept close behind, like so many waiting scavenger birds. Isabel tried to edge between two guards to reach her father, but was pulled away. "Follow with the rest," the guard said, and shoved her roughly back.

The entourage of the condemned and the crowd moved slowly along Cornhill. At the Weigh House, where merchandise from abroad was weighed on the Great Beam, the carters and porters and packhorses were forced to make way for the execution party, and Isabel heard a carter grumble at the inconvenience. It seemed to her hideous that the gross money-changing business of the city was carrying on.

They reached the tall houses at the foot of Cornhill. Merchants congregating in the passages that ran through to Lombard Street glanced disinterestedly as the prisoners walked by. Butchers and buyers stood watching at the edge of the covered Stocks Market. Women leaned out of windows, pointing as the condemned passed. More people joined the following crowd.

The entourage made its way into Poultry, passing haberdashers and grocers. Isabel tried again to push through to her father, and again was shoved away. Her father walked on without even turning his head.

At the Great Conduit—the lead water cistern in the middle of the street—lounging water carriers with buckets strapped to their backs watched them pass. Here, the street widened out into Cheapside, and the moving execution party had to flow to one side of the market stalls ranged down the street's center. On Goldsmith's Row, beams of sun glinted off the gold platters and goblets displayed in the goldsmiths' windows. Shoppers stood in the doorways, watching.

On they went, past Mercers Hall, past Ironmonger's Lane where the clanging and hasping sound of the foundries on nearby Lothbury reached Isabel above the shuffling of feet around her. Only a block away was Blackwell Hall, the woolcloth market where she had often helped her father check the apprentices' reckoning of cloths and bales. On they went past Bread Street, where the smell of fish cooking at the Mermaid Inn made Isabel's stomach lurch. On past the tenements of St. Martin-le-Grand, where thieves and whores and poor immigrants lived, many of whom now ambled out to join the execution parade.

On into Newgate Street, passing its slaughterhouses and drinking shops, its country women hawking turnips and tallow and winter apples. They came to huge Christchurch, and the guards suddenly halted the party. Isabel heard some commotion ahead and craned to see. More rebel prisoners were being brought out from the church, another hundred at least. Isabel caught sight of Edward Sydenham among them. His once-fine clothes were foul with dried mud, and one satin sleeve was ripped at the shoulder. His face was white as paper. Pushed by a guard, he stumbled in among the swollen ranks of prisoners. He stood blinking as though in disbelief, gnawing a fingernail.

Newgate rose ahead. From its four stories above the open gate, faces peered out from the barred prison windows. The swollen entourage pushed on under the stone arch and passed through. The bells of St. Sepulcher clanged beside them. The entourage turned right, wound its way up Giltspur Street, came to Pye Corner, and went by the Hand and Shears Tavern. Finally, Isabel realized where they were heading. The execution ground at Smithfield.

Walking at the side of the grim parade, her whole concentration had been on her father as he trudged on, his head unmoving, his gaze straight ahead. But now that she knew that Smithfield was so near, a kind of panic overtook her. She pushed once again toward her father, and this time, whether because the guards were too busy keeping prisoners in line or because they simply could not bother with her anymore, she made it through to him. She came beside him. He did not glance at her but kept on walking, his expressionless face set straight ahead.

"Father," she said, keeping in step with him. "Father, please look at me!"

But he would not. She felt his estrangement like a knife to her heart and made a helpless sound. His response was something worse than disdain, it was repugnance. She felt it like a turning of the knife—and knew where it sprang from. It was because of Ludgate. She recalled his look of horrified amazement at seeing her shutting the gate. Shutting Wyatt out. Abandoning his last men to death or capture. But did her father not know she had done it for him? All of it— leaving Martin, betraying Wyatt—all had been to save him.

But she had failed. It had all been for nothing. He did not want to be saved. He did not want to know her. His rejection robbed her legs of their strength, and she reached for his arm. He shrugged her off with a gesture that was part disgust, part apathy. She stumbled along beside him in a kind of daze. Whether he would speak to her or not, she would stay with him to the end.

"Stop him!" The guard's voice came from ahead in the condemned pack. Isabel peered around bodies to see. Edward Sydenham was trying to claw his way out. A woman in the crowd tripped him and he toppled. People stepped back around him, some laughing. A guard hauled

Sydenham up to his feet and shoved him back into line. He staggered on, hemmed in by the crowd and by his fellow prisoners as if by walls. Isabel saw that he was shaking.

"Halt!" the guard barked from the front of the line.

They had arrived.

Isabel looked around. Smithfield was a famous fairground in summer: Bartholomew Fair. On one August visit when she was a child, she had skipped around the stalls, munching a gingerbread cat her father had bought her. She had dashed back to grab her mother's hand and beg for a Bartholomew Baby—one of the painted dolls—until Adam, laughing, had taken her to pick one out. In stall after stall, heads of roast pig had stared out, and their succulent aroma, plus the din all around of fortune-tellers, horse traders, ballad mongers, and performing animals, was intoxicating. That was summer. In spring and autumn Smithfield was used as a market for horses and sheep. But now, on this drear February morning, it was nothing but a large expanse of bare earth pocked with clods of dung.

She looked across to the Augustinian priory church of St. Bartholomew the Great. Here, she thought, in front of this church twenty years ago, her mother had been tied to the stake to burn as a heretic. Here, on the church's lantern tower, her father had leapt about like Satan, terrifying the crowd and rescuing his wife. The tower was gone now, pulled down at the dissolution of the monasteries, and the church was used by Sir Richard Riche as a residence. Isabel looked to the north of the fairground. Not far from the church there were empty sheep pens, a stagnant pond, and the Elms. This last name was the Londoners' grim jest: some time ago a stand of elms had been replaced by gallows.

A large party of officials was quietly waiting at the Elms. Among them were several gentlemen of the Queen's council on horseback and her military commanders. Five open, empty wagons stood by, ready to cart off the dead. On each wagon a guard wearing a tabard of the royal livery in green and white sat on the seat, waiting. There were also two dozen guards standing in a wide, broken half circle, each with a longbow at his back. A fletcher's cart with extra arrows was stationed nearby. The hangman, hooded in black, already stood with his helpers on the gallows scaffold.

And there was one other face that completed this picture

of horror for Isabel. Carlos sat his horse beside the gallows. He was part of the Queen's execution party. He looked impressive in a new gentleman's doublet of some rich material in black. Even his mount was new, a fine gray Arab. Isabel could not be sure from this distance, but she imagined that the silver sword, its handle gleaming in the scabbard against his thigh, was also a gift from the grateful Queen. Had the Queen awarded him lands, too? Maybe even knighted him? Isabel looked away. The mercenary had been well rewarded. He had got everything he had always wanted.

Voices rose. Another long stream of prisoners was being led in from Aldersgate. Trudging up, they joined the halted gang where Isabel stood. The condemned now totaled several hundred.

The execution party at the Elms were all staring at the huge crowd of prisoners. There was a gap the length of a long church aisle between the two groups; a chasm, Isabel thought. She stared at the Elms. Five gallows. Two nooses hanging from each one. Ten men could be hanged at a time.

As if spurred by some primeval impulse, the crowd at the rear surged forward around the halted mass of prisoners. Isabel and Thornleigh were standing at its edge, and as people jostled past them, Isabel was almost knocked over. The people were running forward to claim choice viewing places at the gallows.

Frances Grenville pulled aside the stiff brocade curtain at the window of the Queen's private chamber in Whitehall. As the morning light struck her face she squinted, her eyes accustomed to the dim interior. Since dawn the Queen had been praying, thanking God for her victory and deliverance. She had just finished her orisons, and Lord Paulet had been admitted to the chamber.

"A pardon?" Frances heard the Queen ask, repeating the suggestion that Paulet had just put to her.

"Yes, if there is any among the rebels you would spare, Your Majesty," Paulet explained dryly. "If so, now is the moment to do so. A messenger could deliver your pardon to Smithfield immediately."

"Oh, no," the Queen said, frowning as though at some young person's rash, emotional outburst. "I think not, my lord." She moved to a small mirror on the wall.

"As you wish, Your Majesty," Paulet murmured. He was

fully recovered after the crisis, and had proffered the suggestion of pardons with all his former punctilious care for proper form, but with little concern.

Yes, everything was back to normal, Frances thought, still looking out. Calm had been restored in the city. Rewards had been handed out to the loyal; her brother John had already been made a baron. The rabble traitors were being dispatched today en masse at Smithfield, while Wyatt himself lay in the Tower awaiting a more significant, ceremonial execution. "Good day, Your Majesty," Paulet said placidly from the doorway. He bowed and went out.

The bells of St. Sepulcher's tolled. Frances pulled her gaze from the spire of St. Paul's rising above the thicket of lesser steeples that made up the London skyline. She looked down at the courtyard below. A mongrel dog prowling the cobbles came upon a spaniel bitch. The two animals eyed each other. The bitch stood still while the dog slunk around her and sniffed her rear. Frances shuddered and quickly turned away from the window.

She caught sight of the Queen at the mirror, her head bent as she tried to fasten a necklace at the back of her neck. "Let me help you," Frances offered.

"Thank you, my dear. I cannot seem to manage the clasp," Mary said as she handed over the necklace. It was a circlet of pearls and emeralds with a large pendant cross of gold and pearls and an oblong ruby at the crucifix center. Mary looked at Frances earnestly and added, "This is the first time I have worn it, you know." Her voice was vibrant with a sense of occasion. Frances understood. The necklace was a gift Prince Philip had sent along with his portrait. To the Queen, it was a proxy for the wedding ring she would soon be wearing.

Frances joined the necklace's two golden ends at the back of the Queen's neck, then rested one hand on the Queen's shoulder and looked into the mirror. Mary lifted her head and her eyes met Frances's eyes in the reflection. Mary smiled. The jeweled cross nestled just above the thin gold necklace Mary always wore, the only possession of her mother's she had been allowed by her father to keep, so many years ago.

A thought struck the Queen and she gasped a small breath. "Oh, my, I forgot, Frances. Forgive me. Sir Edward is among the . . . the ones at Smithfield, isn't he? My dear,

shall I call Lord Paulet back? Dictate a pardon? If you wish
it, I will do so instantly." She laid her hand lightly on
Frances's hand that had lingered on the Queen's shoulder.
"When all were deserting around me, Frances, you never
wavered. And when I think of you near that awful battle at
Ludgate, and . . ." She shook her head. Frances had told her
about it, and about its aftermath. Frances had been at the
rear of the crowd when the traitor Thornleigh read out the
damning evidence of Edward's guilt. "Only bid me,
Frances," the Queen said now, "and Sir Edward shall be
spared."

Frances stared into the eyes of her monarch and friend,
the woman she had shared twenty-five years with, through
Mary's childhood joys as a princess before King Henry
turned on her mother, then through the years of hardship and
degradation. During all that time, Frances had never once
seen Mary despair of her religious faith. That the Queen was
now offering to pardon a man who had proved to be guilty
of the one sin she could never stomach—the sin of heresy—
was proof indeed of an unshakable loyalty to their friendship.

Frances looked toward the window. A pardon for Edward?
She saw him in her mind as she had seen him in that shat-
tering moment, standing in his parlor and reaching out for
Isabel Thornleigh. Placing his mouth on hers. Kissing her.
Frances felt the sting of tears at the back of her eyes. But no
tears welled. She was squeezed dry of tears. "No, my lady,"
she said, turning back. "Edward betrayed you. He betrayed
us all. And for that he must pay."

CHAPTER THIRTY-SIX

⊶•⊷⊷•⊶•⊷⊷•⊶

The Fletcher's Cart

"**O**oh, look at that one kick the air!" a woman in the Smithfield crowd exclaimed.

"He'll be kicking at Satan's pitchfork soon!" a man bawled back merrily.

The crowd laughed. Ten condemned rebels were swinging from gibbets. Isabel thought she was going to be sick. One of the hanging men was Tom, the stalwart guard who had guided her through Wyatt's camps.

These ten dead were the fourth batch. Thirty had already been hanged and cut down, their bodies taken away on the wagons in which, moments before, the same men, living, had been carted from the condemned ranks and delivered up to the gibbets. When the first executions had begun, the crowd had watched in a hush of awe. But someone had shouted a ribald jest as the wagon brought the next batch forward, and people had relaxed. Now, the atmosphere was more like that of the summer fair, with people joking and chattering, some women among them hawking pies and ale.

Isabel stood by her father's side watching as if she were in the middle of her own nightmare. A handful of men from the crowd had remained hovering at the edge of the condemned pack, perversely relishing the prisoners' terror close-up in the moments before they were carted to the gallows. One of these men leered at Isabel, mouthing words she could not distinguish above the crowd's noise. Her father, though, had not spoken a word to her, nor even looked her way.

There were now only sixteen prisoners in front of her and Thornleigh. A wagon rattled up. The guard on the seat got down and helped the guard on the ground, the latter a gap-toothed man whose temper was already stretched taut from his job of corraling the front prisoners. Together, the two of them shoved the first ten men into the wagon, thinning the rank in front of Isabel and Thornleigh down to six. The wagon rumbled off toward the Elms with its prisoners. The gap-toothed guard shoved Thornleigh forward—he would be in the next batch to go to the gallows—then grabbed Isabel's shoulder and pulled her out of the line.

"No!" she said, struggling to go back. "Father!"

The guard shoved her aside again so roughly she stumbled. "The woman's brainsick," he muttered to the man still leering at Isabel.

"String her up, too," the leering man suggested. "That'd be a sight. I never did see a wench swing."

Isabel heard the terrifying clatter of another wagon. She whirled around. It had come so soon! The prisoners just taken were not even at the gallows yet. This wagon was smaller than the others, no more than a cart. The guard-driver stilled the cart horse not far from Thornleigh and jumped down from the seat. Isabel clawed at the driver's back, desperate to delay him, to stop the nightmare. He shrugged her off without even turning. He strode forward, reached out for Thornleigh, clamped his hand on the back of his collar, and yanked. He dragged Thornleigh to the side of the cart. Thornleigh twisted around and faced him. The driver's back was to Isabel, but she saw her father's astonishment. "You!" Thornleigh said. "What are you—" The driver's fist smashed Thornleigh's jaw. "No!" Isabel cried. Thornleigh staggered and dropped to his knees. Blood dripped from his lip.

"What'd you do that for?" the gap-toothed guard asked, puzzled. The leering man pushed in closer to see.

"He called the Queen a bitch," the driver replied.

Isabel caught the accent. Her eyes flew to his face. It was Carlos. He wore a tabard of royal livery over his doublet. She reeled at this final blow: Carlos was carting her father to the gallows.

"Bastard," the gap-toothed guard growled in response to the insult to the Queen. He kicked Thornleigh in the stomach. Thornleigh doubled over, still on his knees, moaning.

"Bastard," the leering man eagerly agreed. Joining in, he kicked Thornleigh's forehead with a vicious crack. Thornleigh jerked back and lay on the ground, suddenly still.

"No!" Isabel screamed. She dropped to her knees at his side. Her father was unconscious.

The gap-toothed guard turned back to his other prisoners.

"Keep in line, you lot, or it's your brains kicked out, too, instead of a nice tidy hanging!"

Isabel jumped up and turned on Carlos, her fists raised to strike him. He grabbed her wrists and yanked her close and said quickly in her ear, "Help me get him in!"

She blinked at him. Help him haul her father to his death? To be strung up unconscious like some slaughtered buck? Was he mad? But Carlos was already dragging Thornleigh's inert body to the cart's open rear. He heaved Thornleigh's torso up and flopped him onto the lip of the cart platform, then grabbed his legs and rolled his body in. Thornleigh came to rest on his back, unmoving.

"You *can't*!" Isabel flew at Carlos. She struck several wild blows on his chest and head before he snatched her arm and twisted it around to the small of her back. In pain, she swayed. He picked her up in his arms and threw her into the wagon alongside her father. The floorboards scraped her backbone, and her head struck something sharp. She glanced around to see the tip of a longbow.

"That's right," the leering man said gleefully to Carlos, "hang the wench, too!"

Isabel was scrambling on hands and knees toward the back of the cart to attack Carlos again. He grabbed hold of her hair as she came up to her knees, and he held her head rigid. "Lie down!" he said into her ear. "We will take him away!"

Isabel froze.

"Stop those prisoners!" Carlos yelled with sudden authority, pointing away from the cart. The gap-toothed guard immediately stomped off in the direction Carlos was indicating, looking for the would-be escapees. Carlos quickly strode to the front of the cart, got up on the seat, took the harness reins, and flicked them. The animal moved. The cart lurched forward. Isabel, on her knees, was thrown onto her side, and the longbow's tip scraped her shoulder. Lifting herself onto her elbow, she saw that the bow was one of many, all unstrung, lying in two stacks at the front of the cart. And there were quivers of arrows, too, lashed together with twine to form a bristling bale. Carlos had stolen a fletcher's cart!

Isabel looked out the back. The gap-toothed guard was watching the departing cart with a puzzled look. But another wagon was drawing up beside him and the condemned, and he shrugged in annoyance and went back to his job of shoving prisoners into the wagon. The leering man, however, started to walk after the cart, watching Isabel with a chilling smile of anticipation over her imminent hanging.

Isabel dropped to the floor and lay flat on her back to keep from being seen by anyone else. Her father lay beside her, unmoving but breathing regularly, though shallowly. Blood from his split lip trickled down his jaw. The cart creaked on at what felt like a crawl. On her back, Isabel could see nothing but the rough wooden planks of the cart's sides and the misty sky above, but she heard the crowd's laughter and chatter, first swelling as the cart lumbered past the voices, then growing fainter and fainter. Dare she believe it? Was Carlos gradually steering the cart away from the crowd? Away from the place of execution? She slipped the tips of her fingers through a crack in the cart's side and held on tightly, not for balance, but to keep her body still, to keep from leaping up to see if this miracle was real.

She could bear it no longer. She raised her head just enough to look out the back over her feet. As she did, the Smithfield crowd sent up a roar of approval as another ten bodies kicked and swayed under the gallows. The dying men looked small this far away, twisting under their ropes, but Isabel easily identified the one hanging third from the left. Edward Sydenham.

She caught a glimpse of the leering man who had been following the cart. He had halted at the border of the crowd, but was still watching with a scowl as the distance between him and the cart lengthened.

Isabel dropped her head to the cart floor again, breathing hard. She heard Carlos muttering Spanish to the horse and she felt the cart's motion change slightly. They were turning at the curve in the road, she judged—the one at the edge of Smithfield as it narrowed into Giltspur Street. She tilted her head backward to look at Carlos and saw him upside-down. Above the seat-back, only his shoulders and head were visible, and his neck was a band of sun-weathered skin between his cropped hair and the tabard collar. He was saving her father. *Everything* was upside-down.

"Halt there!" The man's voice had come from the front of the cart—someone on the road. Isabel stiffened. A guard posted at Smithfield's boundary? She pressed closer to her unconscious father, though the high cart sides and seat hid them. "Where're you off to, then?" the voice asked.

"Whitehall, Sergeant," Carlos said. "Orders of Lord Howard."

"The palace? Why?"

"The Queen asked to see these two dead ones."

Isabel heard the sergeant's incredulous snort. "Havers," he said gruffly, "have a look." Isabel realized there must be two of them, maybe more. She flipped onto her stomach and tugged her skirt tight between her legs to make it look less like a skirt. She threw her cloaked arm over her father's stomach to mask his breathing, then buried her head and legs as far as possible under his side. Then, she lay as still as a corpse. She heard a horse plod closer, moving along at the cart's side. Then a voice, presumably the man named Havers, at the cart's rear: "Must be important buggers."

"Not anymore," Carlos said laconically.

Havers chuckled. So did the sergeant. "All right," the sergeant said. "Carry on."

The cart jolted forward again. Isabel did not dare yet come out from under her father's shoulder. The cart creaked on, Carlos keeping its pace at an unsuspicious crawl. Finally, Isabel stole a glance up at the sky. The tavern sign of the Hand and Shears passed overhead. That meant they had passed Pye Corner. They were less than a quarter mile from Newgate, and once they got under that arch and were inside the city, who on crowded Newgate Street would notice another cart? Isabel's heart pounded. They were going to make it!

She lifted her head enough to peer across her father's chest and out a crack in the far side of the cart. Carlos was taking them around another bend in the road. Through the crack Isabel could just make out, in the distance, the leering man walking quickly toward a trio of horsemen stopped at the entrance to Smithfield. The trio, she realized, had to be the sergeant and his guards who had stopped them. The leering man pointed toward the cart.

The horsemen looked. The sergeant angrily gestured forward. The three of them kicked their mounts. In a moment they were cantering toward the cart.

"The guards!" Isabel cried up to Carlos. "They're coming!"

He looked over his shoulder. He whipped the reins. Startled, the cart horse quickened its pace, but only for a moment, then settled down to its previous sedate walk.

Carlos jumped from the cart seat onto the horse's back. It skittered and whinnied in alarm. Carlos kicked its sides hard. It burst into a canter.

Isabel stuck her hand through the crack in the cart side and held on tightly as they careened around the corner and passed under Newgate and clattered into the city, the cart's boards and wheels groaning and squealing. People scattered out of its way. Isabel looked back. A hay wagon was lumbering across their wake, blocking her view of the pursuers, but she heard their horses' hooves thundering hollowly under the stone arch of Newgate. And then she saw the horsemen again, rounding the back of the hay wagon, pounding after the cart.

Carlos drove the horse recklessly eastward along Cheapside, dodging pedestrians, horses, wagons, all at a bone-jarring pace. Isabel was thrown against one side of the cart, then against her father's prostrate form, and she flung her arm over him to hold him as steadily as she could, the pretense of death abandoned. The longbows and bundled arrows clattered against the cart's corners. In one violent swerve, as Isabel fought for balance, she tore her eyes from the pursuers, and by the time she looked out again there was no trace of them. She caught sight of a familiar Candlewick Street cobbler's sign and knew that Carlos had swerved the cart south. People on foot and on horseback filled in the street behind them. Isabel breathed again. She sat up. Carlos had shaken off the guards.

But he hardly slackened the pace. The cart rattled onto New Fish Street. Isabel could see the gate tower of London Bridge rising in the distance ahead. She realized with dismay that Carlos was racing for the bridge—that he had no idea of the escape plan with Van Borselen's Flemish ship. The plan had been so firmly in her mind for so long that no other had occurred to her. But was it folly to depend on it? Could she really expect Van Borselen to still be waiting? With Sydenham dead? She had to risk it. She shouted to Carlos above the din of horse's hooves and cart wheels, "Not the bridge!"

"What?" he called back.

"East, to Billingsgate wharf!"

"No! Southwark, across the bridge! Safer there!"

"No! There is a ship for us! Go to Billingsgate!"

But they sped on southward. Isabel was about to scream

at him again, frantic that he was not following her directions, when he suddenly turned east on Thames Street. She groaned with relief.

The tall merchants' houses that crowded Thames Street obscured the water, but the fishy reek of the river was unmistakable. Isabel craned over the side of the speeding cart. A thicket of masts rose up ahead, bobbing around Billingsgate wharf. She looked out behind the cart—and gasped. The horsemen were back!

"The guards again!" she yelled to Carlos.

He bent over the horse's neck and whipped the animal on. They were nearing the turn to the wharf. But Isabel suddenly had doubts. Billingsgate wharf was a market. It would be congested with people and stalls and mules. To get through it Carlos would have to slow to a crawl, and the horsemen would surely catch up. "Keep going!" Isabel shouted. "To the Customs House!"

"Customs? But—"

"Do it!"

Carlos cursed in Spanish, but he kicked the horse on. The thicket of Billingsgate masts passed by. It was not far to the Customs House. Isabel shouted, "Here! Turn!"

Carlos swerved sharply. Isabel was thrown against the side of the cart. Her father moaned. His eyelid fluttered. He was groggily becoming conscious. The cart lurched to a sudden creaking stop. Isabel got up on her knees to look out. They were on the customs quay. The water downstream was heavy with river fog. Behind them, the narrow street passage onto the quay was empty. Directly ahead, the Customs House looked closed. Isabel realized with a grim relief that she had been right: the day of executions had brought a holiday to the officials. She moved to rouse her father.

Carlos had jumped down and quickly tied the horse to a rail, and was now running back toward the cart, tearing off the cumbersome tabard. "Which ship?"

Isabel looked out at the river. Under the overcast sky, fifteen, maybe twenty large foreign ships lay out at anchor, scattered from Billingsgate near the bridge all the way out to the estuary. Those farthest eastward toward the estuary were obscured in the river fog, with only the odd streak of a mast or a bowsprit visible. Isabel scanned the ships closest to Billingsgate. Was Van Borselen's carrack there? She could not

tell. In the still, damp air, all the ships' flags of identification
were hanging limp.

Horses' hooves clattered in the distance.

"Which one?" Carlos urged again. He hopped up into the
cart and moved past Isabel and Thornleigh toward the jumble
of longbows at the front. He snatched up a bow and
looked back at her. "Hurry!"

Isabel frantically looked out at the ships. They all looked
so similar! She forced herself to look carefully. But still she
could not tell. Then a caravel pivoted at its bow anchor, and
its stern slid a little downstream, revealing, behind it, the
Flemish carrack. The fog was already creeping toward the
caravel's stern, but the Flemish ship was still visible, and on
its foredeck a canopy of sloping material had been erected,
with the Emperor's black eagle proudly displayed. Isabel
pointed. "There!"

Carlos glanced at the ship. "Good. Get out!" Standing on
the cart, he had braced the longbow against his instep and
was forcing the string into the bow's grooved tip. Then he
ripped open a bundle of arrows. "Get a boat!" he said.

Isabel glanced down to the water stairs where three skiffs
nudged the stone wharf, their painters tied to iron rings embedded
in the stone. She looked back and gasped. The horsemen
were barreling through the narrow passage onto the
quay. The sergeant had picked up more guards on the way.
There were at least ten of them.

"Go! Now!" Carlos yelled. He had fitted an arrow into the
bow and stood aiming over the cart horse's head toward the
horsemen. He left the arrow fly. It whirred through the air
and pierced a guard in the chest. The man jerked back in the
saddle as if punched, with his arms flung wide, and he toppled
from his mount. Carlos fitted another arrow and this
one struck a guard's shin, making him scream. The other
horsemen halted in an abrupt clatter of hooves and harness.

Isabel shook Thornleigh. "Father, come! Hurry!"

Thornleigh slowly tried to get up, but Isabel saw that he
was too weak from the beating, too dazed, too exhausted.

An arrow thudded into the back of the cart seat.

Isabel ducked. Carlos dropped to his knee behind the seat
and quickly fitted another arrow. He glanced at Isabel.
"Go!" He straightened up above the seat-back and loosed
the arrow, then ducked. Isabel heard a muffled cry from the
street.

She hopped out the back to the ground and leaned in to grab her father, hoping to drag him to the edge of the cart. But he was too heavy for her.

Carlos saw it. He threw a furious frown at Thornleigh, then glanced back at the horsemen. They were fanning out at the street passage, dismounting, seeking shelter in doorways and alleys from Carlos's fire. Carlos quickly fitted another arrow and loosed it, then slung the bow over his shoulder. He grabbed a quiver and slid it along the cart floor to the back and jumped out to the ground. He hauled Thornleigh out between himself and Isabel. Thornleigh staggered. "He can't walk!" Isabel said. She and Carlos each threw one of Thornleigh's arms around their neck and ran with him, dragging him, toward a skiff at the water stairs. Carlos dumped Thornleigh into the skiff's bow.

An arrow thudded into the side of the skiff. Carlos and Isabel whirled around. Isabel caught the flash of a green tabard behind a chimney on a smithy's low roof. Another arrow splashed into the water. The cart horse was straining at its tether at the rail, its eyes white with fear.

Carlos looked at Isabel. "Get in!" She clambered into the skiff.

"Take the oars!" Carlos said.

Isabel realized Carlos was making no move to get aboard. "But you must come with—"

"Row!" he said. He jerked the painter knot free of the iron ring and tossed it aboard.

Isabel watched dumbfounded as he ran back to the cart, reached for the quiver, grabbed another arrow, and fitted one into his bow. He stepped out into the open, aimed, and let the arrow fly. It clanged off the smithy chimney and rattled on the roof. Carlos ducked back behind the cart just as an arrow whizzed over his head. Another hit the water step, its tip screeching along the stone. Carlos hunkered behind the cart. Another arrow clattered into the cart wheel spokes.

Isabel's hand flew to her mouth. He was so exposed, even behind the cart. And the guards had all found sheltered positions to fire on him. She glanced at her father. He sat slumped against the gunnel but was struggling to get up, as if to help. "Stay here, Father!" She scrambled out of the skiff, looped the painter through the ring, and ran back to the cart. She crouched beside Carlos, panting.

He waved his arm angrily at her. "Get out of here!"

"You can't stay!"

"You need cover to get out into the river! I will hold them off! Go!"

"But they'll kill you!"

Ignoring her, he dumped the quiver of arrows, slewing them out along the lip of the cart's floor. He whipped out his sword and laid it among them, then fitted another arrow, stood out, fired, and ducked back.

Isabel stared incredulously at the sword. "What can you possibly do with that? There are at least eight of them left!"

He glanced at the sword as he snatched another arrow. "Last resort," he said, almost to himself. "Now go!"

"No, I won't leave you! Not after what you've done for me and my father."

"Not for him," he said, fitting the arrow. He looked at her. His voice was low. "I do this for you. Go. *Ve tú con Dios.*"

Isabel felt her heart in her throat, as if it had swelled inside her breast. "But . . . you'll *die* if you stay!"

"That is my work."

"To die?"

He smiled grimly. "It was only a matter of time."

"No! I won't have it!" She grabbed his sword. She was surprised at its heaviness. "I'm sick of everyone asking for death!" she cried. An arrow thudded into the cart floor inches from their backs. Carlos twisted around to gauge its source, and before he could stop her Isabel had stepped back to the wharf edge. She heaved the sword around in a wide arc and let go of it. It splashed into the water and disappeared. Carlos stared after it in appalled disbelief.

"Now come with us!" Isabel cried, rushing back to him.

Two arrows whizzed by. Carlos looked at her, his eyes wide. "No . . . they will fire on you as you go. I must—"

"They won't be able to *see* us! Look!" She pointed out to the river. The fog had rolled in swiftly, and now it shrouded all the ships in the middle of the river. Van Borselen's carrack could no longer be seen. Only a band of water was still visible between the wharf and the bank of fog.

Carlos blinked at the sight.

"Come!" Isabel said. She took hold of his sleeve and pulled. He came forward. Unsure, he turned to look at her. Isabel turned, too, about to push him toward the skiff.

The arrow pierced her thigh from the back. Its force, like

an ice pick, buckled her legs. Lightning jolted up her backbone. Limp, she fell forward.

Carlos caught her. "Isabel!" He lifted her in his arms and
ran. With her face to the sky, Isabel gazed at the pearly vista
yawning overhead.

Carlos reached the skiff. "Thornleigh! Take the oars!"

"My God ... Bel!"

"Move!" Carlos yelled.

"Yes ... yes!"

Isabel was jerked in Carlos's arms as he kicked free the
painter. She heard a clatter, felt the wobble of the skiff, felt
his arms tighten around her to cushion their fall as he thudded with her onto the bow seat. Fire blazed through her leg.
Holding her on his lap, Carlos flung her arm around his neck
for her to cling to. Her head lolled against his chest. An arrow crunched into the skiff's gunnel.

Carlos's voice, loud above her ear: "Row to the Emper-
or's carrack!"

Her father: "But ... where is it?"

Isabel lifted her head. The fog was coming at them like a
white wall. There were no ships. There was nothing. Nothing but the fire raging in her leg and the wall of pearly mois-
ture, about to suck them in.

"Just take us into the fog!" Carlos ordered. "I must get the
arrow out!"

"Oh, God, is she—?"

"Row!"

Splashing oars. The boat rocking wildly. Guards' shouts
from the quay. Arrows hissing overhead. A tearing of cloth
as Carlos's dagger ripped her skirt up from the hem to reach
the protruding arrow. Cold air swept the burning skin of her
thigh.

Then, suddenly, the arrows stopped hissing. The oars
stopped splashing. They were inside the fog. Gasps of exhaustion came from her father and ragged breaths from
Carlos, his chest hot against her cheek. Faint curses came
from the quay. For several moments there was no sound beyond these, except the lapping of low waves against the
skiff.

Carlos gently lifted Isabel's head. "The arrow," he said to
her. "It must come out. If I pull, it will be worse. I must
push it through. You understand?"

She blinked, afraid. The pain was fire. His face stared at her through a sheet of fire, red and orange and gold.

He said, "Hold on to me."

She sat up and placed both trembling hands on his shoulders. He reached over her leg and grasped the arrow at its feathered end and snapped it off. The vibration quivered up through the arrow's shaft into her thigh. He clenched his teeth, preparing to push the arrow through. She closed her eyes tightly, anticipating the pain.

"No," he said quietly. "Look at me."

Their eyes locked. Under her hands on his shoulders she felt his breath drawn in and held. Her eyes did not waver.

He jammed the arrow shaft up. The arrowhead slit through the skin at the top of her thigh. Fire roared down to her calf. Fire raged up to her hip. Her fingernails dug into his shoulders. His eyes never left hers as he wrapped his hand, wet with her blood, around the arrowhead. He wrenched it up. The shaft sucked out of her thigh. The fire became lava boiling through her veins. She gave herself to Carlos's eyes, craving their cool gray depths.

Her neck muscles gave way. Carlos whipped his arm around her back just before she went limp against him. He cradled her head against his chest. Her eyelids trembled, and she saw her blood, bright on his fingers. But the edges of her vision were darkening.

"She must have help!" her father was saying hoarsely. "Where in God's name is the ship?"

Isabel forced her head up. Over Carlos's shoulder, she saw it. The Emperor's black eagle on the awning, wavering dully, blurred by fog, like a spider trapped in ice. "There," she said. But she was not sure her voice had come out beyond her lips. There was no strength to make it more than a whisper. She lifted a hand, as heavy as a hanged man, and pointed to the eagle. "There . . ."

The blackness overtook her.

CHAPTER THIRTY-SEVEN

>━◆━○━◆━◄

New Loyalties

It was a familiar sound, and comforting. The creak of wood on wood of a ship making good way in partnership with the wind. As a child, Isabel had listened to it often enough at night as she drifted into sleep, snug on a berth in her father's caravel.

She opened her eyes to the ceiling, suddenly awake. This was not her father's ship. The cabin was unfamiliar. A desk sat at the foot of the berth she lay in, and on the desk was a buff ledger with a black eagle embossed on its cover. This was Van Borselen's ship. This was his cabin.

They had made it.

Yet she could remember nothing of coming aboard. How long had she been lying here? The cabin's window above the desk was shuttered, but rosy sunlight seeped around its edges. Was it morning? Had she been unconscious, asleep for a day and night? The faint splash of waves against the hull and a soft *whump* as a puff of wind hit a sail told her they must be out in the Channel.

A dull pain throbbed through her left leg. She pulled herself to sit up. She lifted the blanket, and then her skirt, splotched reddish-brown with dried blood, and looked at her leg. A fresh white bandage was wound around her thigh, its ends neatly knotted on top. She saw, in a flash of memory, the bloody arrowhead breaking through her flesh as Carlos had pulled out the shaft. Carlos. She dropped the blanket and leaned back against the wall behind her head and saw him. He was asleep, sitting low in an armchair by the head of her berth, facing her. His legs were stretched out before him, his arms folded over his chest. His head rested on his shoulder in sleep.

Her eyes traveled over him. The familiar, scuffed riding boots. The new breeches, their fine, black wool speckled with dried mud after the frantic ride from Smithfield. The tooled, leather scabbard at his hip, empty of sword. The rich black velvet doublet, its new sheen marred, like the breeches, with the dust of dried mud. She looked at his large hands, one tucked under his folded arm, the other resting in the crook of the opposite elbow. She looked at his face, his chin shadowed with stubble, his right eyebrow puckered with the scar from Colchester jail. She had to admit something she had never before allowed herself to acknowledge. Rugged and strong, he really was a most beautiful man.

And astonishing. He had given up everything. All that the Queen had just rewarded him with. Riches, status—everything he had craved. She remembered lying on her back in the cart as he took them from Smithfield and seeing him upside-down. She thought: *That's how everything has been for two weeks—upside-down.* Her parents' newly revealed characters. Martin deserting her. Sydenham's friendship. Carlos rescuing her father. No one was the person they had *said* they were. Isabel wondered, was she? She recalled Carlos saying, that night in the stable, *"Words. They mean nothing. It is what people do that counts."*

He had done something extraordinary. He had given up all his hard-won rewards just to save her father. And the fact that he had made this sacrifice—had been ready, in the end, to give up even his life—amazed her now with a rush of happiness that seemed to swell her breast and force her breath away. *"I do this for you,"* he had said on the wharf.

His eyes opened and focused on her. He sat up quickly and roughly rubbed a hand over his face. For a long moment they looked at each other. The ship listed gently, creaking.

"How do you feel?" he asked.

She wondered. How did she feel? "Alive," she said quietly. *Unlike Wyatt's men,* she remembered with a stab of guilt. She closed her eyes at the thought.

"Pain?" he asked.

Pain, indeed—the torture of self-awareness. She had done a terrible thing. An unforgivable thing. She had destroyed Wyatt and his cause. Tears pricked her eyes as she thought of his trusting men . . . of Tom. Her chin trembled.

Carlos stood abruptly. "There is a doctor. I will get him, yes?"

"No. No, it's not my leg."

Carlos sat and pulled the chair closer to her, frowning with concern. "What then?"

She bit her lip to hold back the tears. "I was helping Wyatt. Taking him messages. But in the end I betrayed him . . . to save my father. Sydenham had set archers at Ludgate to kill him. I shut the gate." The baseness of her act struck her now with its full impact, like a sentence of death. "Wyatt's men died because of me!" she blurted in wretchedness. She glanced up at Carlos. There was surprise on his face. It made her torment cut deeper. She turned away.

"Not because of you," he said. "They were going to die anyway."

"No, not if the French army had come! And if—"

"There was no French army. They would never invade to help such a revolt—Englishmen were not enough behind it. A French force, alone in hostile territory?" He shook his head. "Suicide."

Isabel stared at him. She realized, with a shock, that it must have been true. That the help coming from France had only been Ambassador de Noailles's wishful thinking. A fantasy. "But . . . Wyatt *did* have a strong following," she insisted. "He and his men could have done it alone. They were so dedicated."

"In war, that is not enough."

"It might have been, if London had been opened to them. You told me Pizarro did it. You said he conquered Peru with less than two hundred men."

"Pizarro struck like lightning. His attacks were ruthless. And once he had stunned the enemy, he had the might of all Spain behind him." He leaned closer to her, his arms resting on his knees. "Wyatt took Rochester, then he waited. The worst mistake. It gave his enemy time. He came to London with almost no support. Then he refused to kill." He shook his head again and said definitively, "Wyatt did not have a chance. From the beginning."

Isabel felt a wave of pity for the man who had led the doomed rebellion. But she felt a release, too, like a dam breaking. This absolution from Carlos broke her heart. Her tears spilled. Her very relief made her weep in shame.

But weeping would change nothing. And she knew, deep in her bones, that there was no solace for her. Even if her closing the gate had had no bearing on the outcome of Wyatt's rebellion, the fact remained that she had betrayed him. Her culpability for that, she knew, was a burden she would have to carry for the rest of her life.

As she wiped the tears from her cheeks she was aware that Carlos was studying her face in wonder. "You really shut the gate?" he asked.

She looked down, far from certain that her mere acceptance of guilt entitled her to any kindness. "Like my father," she said, "you think I am wicked. So disloyal."

"No. I think you are . . ." He hesitated, searching for the word. He did not find it. Instead, he reached out and touched her cheek gently, uncertainly. "I wish . . ."

A spark spiraled through her body, firing her blood. His touch had always had that power over her.

Carlos swallowed, but said no more. He did not have the words. He did not need them. She knew what he wished.

He wiped the trace of a tear from her chin. "Is this for your man?" he asked. A wrangle of emotions played over his face: tenderness, jealousy, hope. "You cry because he was hanged?"

Isabel realized that he meant Martin; that he thought Martin had been executed as part of Wyatt's army.

Carlos added awkwardly, "I understand. It makes you sad." He had tried to force somberness into his voice, but he did not do it well; his satisfaction at Martin's removal was obvious. His hand rested on the bed near her.

"No, Martin didn't hang," she said. "He left England days ago. Like me, he was disloyal." Struck by the irony that she and Martin shared this shameful distinction, she added bitterly, "Like me, he's safe."

Carlos's face darkened. He drew back his hand. Isabel saw that he had misinterpreted her words. He did not know that Martin was gone from her life. How could he? She longed to explain, and was about to speak, when there was a clatter at the door. It opened and her father's pale face peered in. Carlos got up.

Thornleigh's expression was full of relief at seeing Isabel conscious, awake. A sigh shuddered from him. "Thank God," he whispered.

He stepped in and came to the foot of her bed. He glanced at Carlos. Carlos moved to the window and opened the shutter. Thornleigh came hesitantly to the chair and perched tensely on its edge, as if not sure that Isabel would suffer him so near. His shoulders were hunched. "How are you, Bel? Is the leg terribly painful?"

She was struck by how much weight he had lost; during

the crisis, she had not noticed it. But she saw now. Saw, too, that his face was haggard. A scab had formed on his lower lip where Carlos had struck him at Smithfield, and there was a purple-green bruise on his forehead where the leering man had kicked him. She recalled a thought that had taken hold of her when she had seen him in Colchester jail the day after her mother's death. He had seemed like a man who had been punched but had not yet toppled. That same look of dazed uncertainty hung about him still.

"It's not too bad," she answered quietly.

He was plucking at the overhanging edge of the bedcover, avoiding her eyes. "The doctor on board says you're strong. Says the wound will heal in no time."

She nodded.

"Bel, I . . . I want to say—" He stopped and glanced again over at Carlos. Carlos turned and walked out. He closed the door behind him.

"Bel," Thornleigh said. "There's so much to say . . ." He shook his head, despairing of finding a way to begin. He looked down at the floor, distractedly rubbing one hand over the other. "I couldn't forgive you . . . for Ludgate. I wanted to die. Then you saved me, and—"

"It was Carlos who saved you."

He ignored this. He repeated, "I couldn't forgive you, and that was wrong. But you were wrong, too, Bel. Sacrificing Wyatt and his men, just for my sake. That was not justified. Do you see that now? See how wrong it was?"

She watched him. His brow so furrowed, his fingers aimlessly rubbing the back of his hand. Wrong? she wondered. She was only too aware that her act at Ludgate was a weight that would always be with her—but wrong? The judgment seemed somehow simpleminded, childish. She had made a decision at a moment of crisis, nothing more, nothing less. No "right" decision had been available. Faced then with the dilemma that, whatever she decided, she would be responsible for someone's death, she had made a choice. That was all.

She would not apologize. She would live with what she had done, live by her actions. She was a child no longer.

Her father's gaze was on her, waiting for her contrition; a parent. And yet, had *he* not been wrong all these years—and her mother as well—to keep from her the facts of her family's past, facts so at odds with the character of her parents as she had always known them? But, she realized, her father and mother had had to make a decision, too. They had chosen to keep her ignorant, in the hope of keeping her safe. Was that wrong? No. Forced to make a choice, they had made one and stuck by it.

My mother, Isabel thought. Who was she, really? Would she always be a mystery? In Isabel's recurring nightmares during these past two weeks, over and over her mother fell, just beyond her reach. Was understanding of the woman she was mourning going to be beyond her reach forever, too?

Her father held the key.

She reached out for his hand. "Tell me about my mother," she said. "Tell me about the woman you wanted to die for."

His body jerked as if he had been struck. For a moment Isabel thought he was in pain from his beating yesterday, but he was staring at her, utterly still. His mouth pursed tightly as if he feared to let out a demon inside. His chin began to tremble, then his shoulders. His mouth gaped open, beyond his control, and a sob ripped from his throat. Then another. Loud, ugly sobs such as Isabel had never heard come from man nor woman. Dry, desolate howls.

She reached out for him with both arms. He dropped to his knees on the floor by the bed. Isabel caught him. She held him in her arms. He sobbed on her breast, retching out the grief he had pent up for two unendurable weeks. "Honor . . . Honor . . ." His trembling arms closed around Isabel. She held him.

Her own tears spilled. All she had wanted through these harrowing days was to be there, to catch him when he fell. Now, she had.

The ship rocked them, creaking and sighing. From above them came the faint sound of the sails luffing in the wind. From below, the sound of waves splashing against the hull. And finally, Richard Thornleigh told his daughter about the remarkable woman who had been her mother.

When he was done, when the last of Isabel's questions had been answered and her father was resting back in the chair, drained but calm, she reached inside her bodice and took out a crumpled piece of paper. She unfolded it and tried to smooth it out as best she could. In the sunlight that streamed through the window, the beautiful speedwell painting shimmered on the page. She had saved it. She lifted it to her father, offering it.

"Here," she said. "To remember her."

He shook his head. "You keep it. I have her," he said, tapping his heart, "here."

Isabel stepped out on deck into the bright noonday sun. The white sails aloft gleamed against a cloudless, bold blue sky. A crewman jogged past Isabel, heading for the fo'c'sle, and blinked at her bare feet. True, the air was chilly in the salty breeze, but the deck underfoot had been warmed by the steady sun; besides, Isabel's mind was not on such things. She was looking for Carlos.

She had stopped just outside the cabin door below the quarterdeck. Farther forward, past the mainmast, Captain van Borselen stood with a crewman up on the forecastle deck. They were pointing at shrouds, discussing some matter of rigging, and did not notice Isabel. She saw Carlos. He was standing at the port railing, looking out to sea. She moved toward him slowly. The dull throbbing in her thigh had swelled to a drumming, but it was not too terribly painful if she kept her weight off it and favored her good leg. Over the sound of the waves and sails, Carlos did not hear her approach.

"Bel, wait." Thornleigh came after her, a blanket in his hands. Isabel stopped not far behind Carlos. He had heard Thornleigh's voice and glanced at them both over his shoulder. But he did not turn.

Thornleigh reached Isabel. "It's too cold," he said, wrapping the blanket around her shoulders. "What are you doing out here?"

She said nothing. She was looking at Carlos. Thornleigh's gaze followed hers. He inclined his head to her and whispered, "I think he's in love with you, poor fellow."

"Poor fellow?"

"Well, I mean Martin." Thornleigh looked soberly at his daughter, and his tone became earnest. "Bel, there's no reason why your happiness should be denied you. We'll bring Martin to us in Antwerp. He won't want to stay in England now, in any case. He can work for me. Adam and I could use the help. We'll send for him immediately. All right?"

Isabel's eyes did not waver from Carlos. Her father had spoken clearly; Carlos must have heard. "Martin is in France, Father," she said with equal clarity. "He left days ago. And I won't be sending for him. I wish him well. But I never expect to see him again."

Carlos turned around at the railing.

Thornleigh blinked at Isabel. "What? Martin and you aren't . . . ?" He looked quickly at Carlos, then at Isabel, then back and forth between the two of them, his face registering a growing suspicion. But on Carlos's face Isabel saw hope.

Thornleigh took Isabel's elbow and lowered his voice. "This is no man for you. You're grateful to him, of course, I know that. *He* knows that. And I'll reward him for what he's done. But don't let gratitude blind you to reality. He's a rootless mercenary. He has nothing."

Isabel and Carlos continued to look at each other.

"Bel, listen, I . . . I don't feel entitled anymore to dictate to you . . . or to withhold my consent, but this—"

"I'm glad to hear it, Father," she said, glancing at him with a smile. She looked back at Carlos. "The only consent I need is his."

She caught Carlos's response, a wide-eyed stillness of surprise.

"Master Thornleigh!" Van Borselen shouted from the forecastle deck. He stepped forward and called out in his heavily accented English, "I am told you own ships, yes? Would you come and look at this halyard?"

"What's the problem?" Thornleigh called back.

"I had refitting done in London. I want to hoist the spritsail but the rigging is"—Van Borselen shrugged in bafflement—"English-fashioned." His crewman had turned and was watching Thornleigh as well, waiting.

Thornleigh cast a final bewildered look at Isabel, a final frown at Carlos, then reluctantly went to join the captain at the bowsprit.

Carlos moved toward Isabel. They stood together awkwardly, gazing at each other, silent.

Isabel looked around past Carlos's shoulder, westward toward England. "I'll never go back," she said quietly. "There's nothing for me there."

Carlos nodded eastward toward Europe. "And that way there is nothing for me. I want no more soldiering." He added with a crooked smile, "I do not even have a sword, thanks to you."

She blushed, recalling her mad moment on the quay when she had tossed his sword into the river.

The ship jostled over a swell. A jolt of pain shot up Isabel's thigh. She winced. Carlos took her arm and led her back to the steps leading up to the quarterdeck, and eased her down onto a stair. He stood before her and looked across the main deck, southward. He spoke hesitantly. "I have been . . . thinking. The New World. There are not enough horse breeders in New Spain. A man could make a good life there with a *rancho* . . . raising horses." He looked at her hopefully, uncertainly.

She looked southward. Out there, beyond the world of gray water, was a new continent, warm and green and lush. A new world, indeed. A new life. She said, "I'd like to see those mountain plateaus you spoke of, where the wind bends the grasses, but you hear no sound."

She looked up at him and saw the wide-eyed look again on his face. "What is it?" she asked.

"You are smiling," he said.

"So are you."

He grinned. He sat beside her and took up her hand and looked at her. A frown of doubt flitted across his face. "Rootless, your father said. He is right. I have never had . . . a family."

"Is that what you want?"

"I want you. Forever."

"You have me. That's a family."

He grinned again, but still with that look of wonder. He took her face between his hands and kissed her, hesitantly at first, then hungrily. She pulled back her head to catch her breath. She touched his cheek, then shyly smoothed her hand up over his bristled hair. It felt surprisingly soft.

She glanced toward the forecastle deck where her father was leaning out over the bowsprit, explaining the rigging to Van Borselen. It was good to see him taking an interest. *In time,* she told herself, *he'll be drawn back into living.*

Time, she thought, looking back at Carlos. It was what they all needed. Time to see and hear and feel life at the proper pace again. "When we get to Antwerp," she said suddenly, "come and meet my brother and his family. Stay with us." She smiled. "It will give my father time to get used to you. And besides," she added with a slight blush, "before we embark to new worlds, I need to get to know you myself."

He shrugged. "I have a bad knee. Everything else you already know."

She laughed.

"But," he said, smiling, caressing her cheek, "I think I will need a long time to know *you.*"

She went into the haven of his arms. Smiling, she nestled her face against the warmth of his neck. *Take all the time you want, my love. Take forever.*

Author's Notes

The dates and chronology of events of the Wyatt rebellion are accurate in the novel, with the exception of one liberty, fashioned for the dramatic purposes of my story: the mass trials and hangings of the rebels actually began three days after Wyatt's surrender at Ludgate, not the following day, as I have depicted. (The Queen pardoned the last four hundred rebels in a publicly orchestrated display of her clemency in which the prisoners were led to her palace to beg for mercy beneath her window.)

The histories of the prisons of London make riveting stories on their own. Two specific facts may be of interest to the reader. First, the jailer of Newgate prison in 1554 was, indeed, the Andrew Alexander who appears in the novel—an accomplished musician, and a man who later became notorious for his cruelty to Protestants imprisoned in Newgate by Queen Mary. Second, although I have created the character of Dorothy Leveland, the Fleet jailer, the keepership of the Fleet prison was, indeed, in the hands of the Leveland family for several centuries (they held a manorial title in Kent to which the post belonged), and two of the earliest keepers were women—widows of keepers who inherited and ran the family business.

"Jail fever" is now believed to have been a form of typhus.

The author of an historical novel strives to create a seamless blend of fact and fiction. Of the characters who appear in *A Dangerous Devotion,* the ones who actually lived are Queen Mary; her councilors and military commanders; Sir Thomas Wyatt and his circle of supporters, including the Duke of Suffolk; the rival ambassadors, Antoine de Noailles and Simon Renard; and Henry Peckham, the organizer of Wyatt's London support. The rest—the Thornleighs, the Grenvilles, Carlos Valverde, Edward Sydenham, and the St. Legers—are fictional.

In the case of Carlos, his record of employment by the previous English regime and his award of land fit the historical facts of the English Crown's use of foreign mercenaries. Henry VIII hired German, Italian, and Spanish mercenaries to fight the French at Boulogne and to defend the English frontier against Scotland. Henry's son Edward VI used thousands of foreign mercenaries to defeat the Scots at Pinkie Cleugh in 1547, and then kept a large number of these veterans on to quell unrest within England. For this information, and for other sixteenth-century military details, I am indebted to Gilbert John Miller's fascinating book *Tudor Mercenaries and Auxiliaries 1485–1547*.

Some notes about the fate of the various historical figures who appear in the novel follow.

Sir Thomas Wyatt was held prisoner in the Tower for a month, then executed on Tower Green.

The Duke of Suffolk was also beheaded within the month (to be soon followed by his daughter, the nine-day Queen Jane, who had been in the Tower since Mary's accession six months before). Princess Elizabeth was arrested in the flurry of panic after the uprising, and was kept a prisoner in the Tower until Mary released her two months later.

Following the rebellion, Mary began a widespread persecution of Protestants. By the end of 1555, seventy people had been burned at the stake for heresy, and by the end of her reign, three years later, the total of burnings was nearly three hundred. As James A. Williamson states in his book *The Tu-*

dor Age, "The total was small compared with the record of the Netherlands, but it was stupendous for England, which had never seen anything approaching it before." These killings earned the Queen the title "Bloody Mary."

The Queen went ahead and married the Spanish Prince Philip in July 1554, five months after the rebellion. In 1555 Mary persuaded herself she was with child and unwisely announced her hopes to the world. The "pregnancy" turned out to be a tumor. Mary was devastated. The remainder of her short reign was no less full of sorrow. Her husband had stayed in England only long enough to fulfill his conjugal duties, then left to oversee his father's empire of Spain, the Netherlands, and the colonies of the New World. In 1557, for Philip's sake, Mary threw her country into his war with France. Philip returned to his wife to oversee the raising of an English army for this enterprise, then promptly left again, never to return. England suffered a humiliating defeat in the war, resulting in the loss of the port of Calais, the last English toehold in France. The war also bankrupted Mary's treasury.

Defeat in France, desertion by her husband, endless plots against her fomented by English Protestants in league with the French—all these griefs broke Mary's spirit. After months of illness, she died in November 1558 at the age of forty-two. The country's church bells rang joyously at the accession of her half sister Elizabeth, who took the throne at the age of twenty-five. Intelligent, wily, and fiercely dedicated to England, Elizabeth ruled her kingdom with a sure hand and a politic doctrine of religious toleration for the next forty-five years.

My Prologue, in which Mary digs out the entombed remains of her royal father and burns him as a heretic, sprang from a comment in J. J. Scarisbrick's monumental biography of Henry VIII. He reports that, for decades after Mary's reign, there was "whispering" that she had secretly ordered this deed done. So, when you go to St. George's Chapel at Windsor Castle and stand on the spot in the aisle where Henry VIII is said to be buried, it may be true that you are walking on the King's bones . . . but then again, maybe not.